NORA ROBERTS

Birthright

PIATKUS

❧❧ *Visit the Piatkus website!*

Piatkus publishes a wide range of bestselling fiction and
non-fiction, including books on health, mind, body & spirit,
sex, self-help, cookery, biography and the paranormal.

If you want to:
- read descriptions of our popular titles
- buy our books over the internet
- take advantage of our special offers
- enter our monthly competition
- learn more about your favourite Piatkus authors

VISIT OUR WEBSITE AT: **www.piatkus.co.uk**

Copyright © 2003 Nora Roberts

First published in Great Britain in 2003 by
Judy Piatkus (Publishers) Ltd of
5 Windmill Street, London W1T 2JA
email: info@piatkus.co.uk

First published in the United States in 2003
by
G. P. Putnam's Sons

The moral right of the author has been asserted

A catalogue record for this book is available from the British Library

ISBN 0 7499 3449 2

Printed and bound in Great Britain by
Mackays of Chatham Ltd, Chatham, Kent

HELEN FORRESTER

Three Women of Liverpool

Madame Barbara

Grafton

HarperCollins*Publishers*
77–85 Fulham Palace Road,
Hammersmith, London W6 8JB

www.harpercollins.co.uk

This omnibus edition published in 2005
by HarperCollins*Publishers*

Three Women of Liverpool
Copyright © Helen Forrester 1984

Madame Barbara
Copyright © Helen Forrester 1999

The Author asserts the moral right to
be identified as the author of these works

ISBN 0 00 773415 8

Printed in Great Britain by
Clays Ltd, St Ives plc

Three Women of Liverpool

Author's Note

The author would like to thank very much the Institute of Oceanographic Sciences, Bidston Observatory, Birkenhead, the Liverpool Record Office of the Brown, Picton and Hornby Libraries, her brothers and sister, and many friends and acquaintances for supplying her with much useful information on the subject of the great May blitz on Liverpool.

It should be pointed out that this is a novel, and the sailors' canteen, the situations and the characters are imaginary. Whatever similarity there may be of name, no reference is made or intended to any person living or dead.

In the spring of 1941, Admiral Erich Raeder wrote a memo to the Führer of the German Reich, Adolf Hitler. It said:

"An early concentrated attack on Britain is necessary, on Liverpool, for example, so that the whole nation will feel the effect."

THURSDAY 1 MAY 1941

He felt better, more sure of himself, now he was back in Liverpool and had a ship again. He had a new identity card safely tucked into the old wallet his father had found for him; it was surprising how naked you felt without a piece of paper to say who you were. Robert Owen, deckhand and fiancé of Emma Thomas, once more officially existed.

The clothing the Red Cross lady had found for him, to replace his lost kit, fitted well; the brown leather jacket would keep the wind out like nothing else would. He had had his faded blond hair cut in honour of his date with Emmie and he had a present for her in the brown paper carrier he was holding. His legs had stopped shaking.

Panic had, once more, struck him when, earlier that morning, he had entered the crowded Mercantile Marine office in search of a new set of papers and a new ship. At the thought of going to sea again, he had for a moment turned to jelly. He had not really walked to the huge mahogany counter; he had been nearly lifted off his damaged feet and edged towards it by the heaving, shouting mass of drunken seamen, all trying to get attention.

The clerk on the other side of the wide counter, a pimpled youth young enough to be his son, had been unexpectedly understanding of the tall, drained-looking deckhand in front of him.

"Two days on a raft, floating around in the Channel?" he had queried incredulously. "I'd have thought there was enough shipping down there that they would have spotted you in a few minutes."

"It's a lot o' water." Robert had tried to sound nonchalant. "Corvette out of Southampton picked me up." Again, he felt the ghastly fear that his hands would lose their grip on the raft and he would slide off and drown. "I were the only survivor." Try as he would, his voice still held a quiver.

"You were lucky."

"Aye, I suppose. Anyway, t' doctor says me feet'll be all right now. He signed me off yesterday. It were the cold water that effected 'em."

"Cold can do some rotten things to you," agreed the clerk. He chewed the end of his stub of pencil and ran his finger down a list. "There's the *Marakand* loading in No. 2 Huskisson. They're short a deckhand. How about it?"

To a fisherman who, until his last disastrous voyage, had always worked in his father's smack, one ship was as good as another, so he took the clerk's proffered fountain pen and shakily applied his signature where the boy pointed with his finger. A ship was a ship, and if he were going to marry Emmie he needed the money. If he did not go to sea, he would be called up for the army – at fourteen shillings a week. Better the devil you knew than the one that you did not.

Afterwards, until he got a better grip on himself, he stood on the handsome steps of the old Customs House, his hands in his pockets, the brown carrier bag swinging from his wrist. Beside him, legs astride, hands behind his back, stood the huge policeman who kept order amongst the tough clientele of the Mercantile Marine office. The sun lit up the long row of medal ribbons on his chest, but

12

failed to soften a face with an expression that could have quelled an angry regimental sergeant-major. However, he said very cordially to Robert, "Nice mornin'. Ready for off agen?"

As Robert nodded affirmatively, the nervous twitch of his right eye was not lost on the constable and his expression returned to its usual grimness. Poor devil. Sent to sea again before he's fit, I'll bet me life. Just like the last war. He turned again to Robert and added, as if to offer some comfort, "You know, you're sometimes safer at sea than you are in Liverpool, these days, what with the air raids and all."

"Could be," Robert agreed, and then plunged down the steps, head bent to the wind, to make his way towards the gangway of the floating dock from which the ferry boats sailed across the river Mersey. There, he would meet Emmie.

With subs as numerous as cockroaches waiting for you once you'd crossed the bar, any minute could be your last. But this was also true of the hapless civilian. Air raids had been uncomfortably frequent all winter, and it worried him deeply that Emmie lived in Toxteth, within a half a mile of the much pounded dock area.

This was no way of thinking, he told himself crossly. He began to whistle firmly and winked at a very pregnant girl with a small child wrapped in her shawl. She sniffed and turned her face away from him. He grinned. Nothing like a Merseyside woman. As pretty as they come, like his Emmie with her soft voice with its Welsh inflections – and her warm body, surprisingly flexible for a middle-aged woman.

She was waiting, her face turned towards the multitude of shipping on the glittering river. A plain

13

navy skirt flapped against thin legs and she hugged a heavy blue cardigan against her chest, while the breeze whipped at her brown curls.

"It'll ruin me set before he ever comes," she muttered despondently and tried to smooth her ruffled locks. With her long, thin face and straight, determined-looking nose made pink by the fresh air, she appeared to the casual observer to be a nondescript woman approaching middle age. But Robert Owen was certain that she was the best thing that had happened to him in his entire life.

His mother, who wholly approved of her, said that the best thing that had ever happened to Emmie was that both her parents had finally died and had thus set her free.

"Like livin' in a box all her life, poor lass," she had told her son. "Now mind you give her some freedom, share with her, like. Too many women are nought but slaveys."

He had grinned and kissed her plump rosy cheek and had promised.

While Emmie waited, she thought again of the spate of wrath which she had, that morning, suffered from her sister-in-law, Gwen Thomas; and she wondered how much longer she could endure living with her. The moment she was married she would move out and find a room on the other side of the river, a room which she could make into a little home for Robert between voyages, until the war was over and they could hope for a better place.

Gwen had been furious that Patrick, the eldest of the family which lived next door, had shot an arrow through the glass of the Thomases' back bedroom window. Then, instead of being suitably apologetic, he had

14

calmly asked for his arrow back. Emmie had burst into laughter at the sheer nerve of the lad, and this had set Gwen off on one of her lectures about responsibility and morality, which Emmie had endured with gritted teeth. What on earth had her brother, David, ever seen in the woman? A skinny, nagging ferret, she was.

She suddenly caught sight of Robert. Gwen was immediately forgotten and she ran towards him along the gently heaving dock, her whole body aching to hold him and be held by him.

Later, when he broke it to her that he would be sailing again in a day or two, she stroked the side of his face, as if to imprint on her memory every line of it. She touched the heavy blond brows and the tobacco-stained moustache. "Dearest Robbie," she whispered, "come back safe. I can't live without you." She snuggled closer. "You know, I never had a proper sweetheart before – I never had the time or the chance."

His lips curved mischievously under his moustache. "I know," he replied. "It were the biggest shock of me life when I realised it. Did I hurt you?"

Her thin white face was suddenly scarlet. "No – well, not much." She bit her lips, and then asked shyly, "Did you mind? Me not being at all experienced, like?"

"Nay, luv." He stood up suddenly from their seat on the top deck of the ferry and pulled her to her feet. "It were the nicest thing that ever happened to me – as if you'd been waiting for me." He held her closer. "But I can tell you, my girl, you were a real fast learner, you were."

"Well, at least I'm clean – no disease, I mean." She laughed self-consciously, her lower lip between her teeth. Then she looked at him wickedly out of the corner of her eyes, a plain woman suddenly made pretty.

Emmie mechanically handed twopence to the plump, untidy clippie and received her tram ticket. Now Robert was about to sail, she felt deserted, unbelievably alone. At 39, she had never expected to marry; at that age one was on the shelf. She had many times told herself that such things were not for everyone; and she had done her best to ignore her inward longings, which could make nights a sleepless misery. She had had to try to be happy that she had nursed both her parents until they died. Then, when suddenly she was free of them, she had believed that she was too old for anything but more work. Domestic work, at that.

As she sat down on the slatted wooden seat of the tram, she asked herself bewilderedly whether it was really only four months since her father had died of heart failure. He had been a regular soldier, injured in the First World War, during army manoeuvres in 1915, and subsequently confined to a wheelchair for the rest of his life. And then, within a week, her mother who had been bedridden with arthritis for twenty-three years, had followed him, as if her reason for living had gone.

With both of them to nurse, no wonder I hadn't even time to wink at the milkman or gossip with the neighbours, thought Emmie. No time – and no money, to make myself look nice enough to find a husband. She closed her eyes, as she remembered all the lifting of them, the washing for them, the repulsive tasks of caring

16

for people well-nigh helpless. And her father forever filthy-tempered and her mother so fretful and in such dire pain.

Being Mrs Forster-Harrington's daily cleaning lady and cook had been rough, too, though her grand Victorian house had been very conveniently close to Emmie's tiny row house. Every morning, since the age of thirteen, she had run backwards and forwards from it and thus earned a little to augment her father's army pension, worried all the time that while she was away her father might fall out of his chair by the window or her mother might need her chamber pot. For twenty-six years she had stoically polished and scrubbed the house, through wars and Depression, until she knew every niche in the carved newel posts, every crack between the slate kitchen tiles. She did it while kind old Mrs Forster-Harrington, dressed in black silk, sat in her drawing room like Queen Victoria and mourned the death in 1918 of General Sir Alfred Forster-Harrington.

"Gone a bit soft in the head, she had, but proper kind for all that," Emmie had confided to Robert. "When I think on it, I were real lucky to have a job — so many didn't have one. But it were all work, Robbie. I never had a minute for meself. I never been to the pictures till you took me."

"Didn't they have any friends?" asked Robert incredulously. "To visit them, while you went out?"

"Not they. Me mam always said as soldiers often don't make many friends 'cos they move so much. Years ago, one or two serving men come to see me dad for a little while — but, you know, they went away — and some of them was killed in the war." She paused, and then added, "And they was both so short-tempered, they put people off, like."

After her mother's funeral, her brother, David, his wife, Gwen, and their sly, gangling 13-year-old daughter, Mari, all decorously clothed in black, had come back to Emmie's house. They had sat drinking tea in the living room, while Emmie wept out to David her fears for herself. She was panic-stricken that she did not earn enough to pay the rent and keep herself.

Gwen had sat silently sizing up the furniture in the tiny room. It's good, she had reflected. Can't buy that kind of stuff nowadays, particularly since the war began. Me best dishes would look great on the Welsh dresser. Young Mari, who had occasionally visited her grandparents in the front bedroom, had told her that there, also, the furniture was big and shiny and, therefore, probably good; David had said that the dead couple had inherited practically all of it from their parents. Now, David should inherit it, since he was the eldest; but if Emmie continued to live in her father's house, Gwen knew that David would never take the furniture from her.

While he listened to his sister's woes, David Thomas had stirred his tea with slow turns of the tin spoon. He felt tense and tired in his black Sunday suit and stiff white collar, and curiously breathless. He felt little sense of loss at his parents' death. His father had bullied him and his mother had been a nagger, though he felt sorry that she had had so much pain. Their death had, however, reawakened a strong sense of guilt regarding Emmie. He had berated himself that she had carried the whole load of his parents' invalidism, and Gwen, here, had done nothing whatever for them. He ought to have

18

pushed Gwen harder, to take an occasional turn, so that Emmie could have gone out a bit. Emmie wasn't a bad looking woman and she had a real sweet manner with her – maybe got it from that Forster-Harrington woman. Given a chance, she might have married, and then he would not have had her on his hands now – though how any husband of hers would have put up with his parents, he could not imagine. Anyway, on his hands she was, and he knew he had to do something to get her started again.

With a slow ponderous movement, he put his spoon down in the saucer and rubbed the dark jowls of his face, while he looked out of the corner of his eye at his virago of a wife.

"Maybe I could go into service – Mrs Forster-Harrington might be glad to have me live in, now she's so old," Emmie sobbed, her pointed nose red from weeping.

"Nay. You're free now. You can do better'n that," her brother replied heavily. He was not going to see her thrown into the kind of jail that living-in domestic service could be. She'd had enough. She deserved better. "With the war on, there's a lot more work around for women now." He took a large breath and steeled himself, as he turned to Gwen. "She could have our middle bedroom for a while – till she got settled, like," he suggested.

Gwen sucked her teeth and turned a scornful glance at the dishevelled Emmie. Who wanted a plaster saint in the house? Another person to cook for?

But her husband's face reflected a stubbornness which had defeated her many a time in their married life, a woodenness which sometimes reminded her of

19

his father. She stared back at him uneasily.

David added, "She'll get work soon enough and then she can pay her shot, couldn't you, Emmie?"

Emmie gave a long shivering sigh and glanced uncertainly at Gwen. Gwen had, for the moment, put on her chapel expression, as Mari called it, a thoroughly virtuous look. It had suddenly been made clear to her how she could acquire her parents-in-law's furniture with a minimum of infighting.

"Aye," she agreed. "She can have the middle room — and there's space enough in the house, if I move our furniture round a bit, for the furniture from here."

Though very suspicious of Gwen's sudden acquiescence, Emmie said thankfully that, of course, she would pay. "And I could help you in the house," she added, as she wiped her eyes with the backs of her hands. Until she got on her feet, any company would be good company. And there was little Mari — she liked Mari.

Mari stopped munching seed-cake and unexpectedly interjected, "It would be nice if you could live with us, Auntie Emmie."

Emmie smiled waterily at her. From time to time, the child had come on her own, or with David, to see her grandparents, and Emmie had always spoiled her with a bit of cake or a sweet biscuit and a loving hug. To Mari, her aunt was easier to gossip with than her mother was. Mothers had a way of jumping on you, Mari had always thought, if you so much as said a word out of place.

With a satisfied smirk, Gwen rose, to indicate that they should leave. Once the furniture had been moved into her house, she would hold on to it; possession was nine points of the law. And if, in order to do this, she had to put up with a paying sister-in-law in the house for a while, it was cheap at the price; very different from having a couple of invalids wished on you, a fear which had haunted her all of her married life.

She sniffed. Despite the local gossips' accusations of neglect, David *had* visited his acerbic parents occasionally, and had spent good money on winter clothes and coal for them. Only Emmie had said thank you, according to David. And, she recollected bitterly, no one seemed to have ever given *her* any credit for getting by with that much less money.

iii

It proved simple to obtain work. After asking what experience she had, the employment exchange sent her to a sailors' canteen, set up in Paradise Street by a church group.

Stout, beaming Mrs Robinson, a volunteer who managed the place, was delighted to have an applicant willing to do washing up, clean lavatories and scrub floors. Furthermore, she liked the well-mannered, grey-eyed woman with a face as innocent as a nun's, yet old enough to keep young seafarers at bay.

"We have a lot of volunteers on the staff, but occasionally they don't turn up," she explained to Emmie. "Then we have to manage somehow, so we have four full-time paid people, two for each shift."

Emmie smiled and said she could cook, too. Mrs Robinson looked at the marvellous reference from the Honourable Mrs Forster-Harrington – and increased the wage offered by five shillings a week.

21

At seven the next morning Emmie was given a white overall and the prettiest flowered apron she had ever worn, and was sent across a small back yard to scrub two very dirty lavatories.

The yard was cobbled and was obviously much older than the buildings surrounding it; it had been adapted as a light well and was lined overhead with office windows. Little of the spring sunshine penetrated it; only a small square patch of sky far above hinted at the beauty of the day.

With her long, straight nose wrinkled in disgust, Emmie used up four pails of hot water and a whole bottle of pine disinfectant and, to the relief of the other members of the staff who had to use the ancient thrones, as well as the seamen, she had left them cleaner than they had been for half a century.

When she returned to the canteen itself, she saw that the front door was hospitably open, though round the entrance stood a wall of sandbags to protect it from blast. The two big windows facing the street had been pushed up; their panes had been criss-crossed with black tape, to minimise the danger of flying glass, and on either side big, old-fashioned shutters, their hinges well oiled, hung ready to be folded across the windows at night.

Two volunteers were wiping down the tables and chairs. They were both dressed in matching sweaters and cardigans, one in pink, the other in green. Over their tweed skirts they had tied flowered aprons similar to Emmie's. One had a string of pearls round her neck, the other a gold chain with a cross hanging from it. Though they were about the same age as Emmie, Emmie thought she had never seen two more beautiful young ladies. They greeted her cheerfully and asked her name; she did not dare to ask them their names.

Bringing with her a strong smell of sausages grilling, Mrs Robinson rushed in from the kitchen carrying a pile of clean ashtrays. "Put one of these on each table, Emmie," she ordered briskly.

"It's funny-peculiar how small things change your life," Emmie remarked to Mari later on. "All the happiness I've got came because I had to put an ashtray on a certain table. Proper queer, when you think on it."

As Emmie put down the last ashtray, two men, anxious for a late breakfast, swung themselves into chairs at the table. Both wore navy-blue turtleneck sweaters and shabby jackets over them. They grinned up at Emmie.

"Mornin', duck. What you got for brekkie?" The speaker must have been in his sixties, judging by his almost bald head fringed by tightly clipped white hair. Black eyes, like a friendly magpie's, surveyed her.

Emmie blushed slightly. "I don't know. I can smell sausages."

The other man was younger, fair-haired, with a full moustache tinged orange by tobacco smoke. He laughed, and Emmie's blush grew redder, because she felt she had given a stupid answer. Her fingers fidgeted with a corner of her flowered apron. After a second, he said to his companion, "It doesn't matter what it is, Dickie. I'm that hungry, I could eat an elephant. Had to wait hours at the bloody hospital, in spite o' being so early."

"Aye. Bring two plates of whatever's cooking," agreed his companion, taking a well-charred pipe out

23

of his pocket and then opening up an oilskin tobacco pouch from another pocket.

Emmie flashed them a shy smile and fled to the kitchen. She reported anxiously to Mrs Robinson.

Mrs Robinson paused, a half-open packet of dried eggs in her hand. Then she chuckled. "Here, take a pencil and notebook from over there, and ask them whether they want tea or coffee, bread or toast, and would they like porridge to start with."

Flustered, Emmie snatched up the notebook, while Mrs Robinson called after her, "We've got scrambled eggs, sausages and baked beans."

Emmie waited, pencil poised, until the men looked up from their conversation. Behind her, other men rolled in with the typical sailor's gait, each man's head bent slightly forward, chin tucked in, from years of living in boats' confining spaces, where heads could be easily bumped. Coughing, hawking, talking, they scraped chairs back from the tables, while the volunteers advanced purposefully, notebooks in hand.

The man with the moustache watched her curiously, as she took his friend's order; when she turned to him she found herself facing rich blue eyes, narrowed as though used to staring into sunlight. The face was weatherbeaten, lined and filled with strain. He smiled at her and she lowered her eyes modestly, as she wrote the order down. Her mother had been warning her since the First World War about being forward with men. Not that she need have worried, thought Emmie. When you're keeping house you live in a daytime world of women, children and very old men. Even the tiny shops she had patronised had been largely run by women, and her parents had never allowed her to go out at night;

when she had once or twice protested at this, her father had, in a tremendous rage, shouted her down, threatened her with his stick and told her that it was bad enough that they were left alone in the mornings while she was with Mrs Forster-Harrington and went for the groceries. Many of her neighbours were equally tied to their homes, she knew, by a horde of children, the sick or the old, and by sheer lack of a penny of their own. She submitted.

This morning, she was being rapidly surrounded by an ever increasing crowd of lively, talkative men. It felt very strange, nervously exciting.

"Tea or coffee?" she inquired of her younger customer, forcing herself to look at him. He grinned, a slow, friendly smile, which made all the sun wrinkles on his face stand out. Her heart gave an uncomfortable bounce. "Tea," he replied, and then asked, "You new here?"

"Yes," she said shyly, smiled briefly and hurried back to the safety of the kitchen. A whole lot of questions about men tumbled into her mind. Here, this very morning, she was going to meet more men than she believed she had met in the whole of her desperately narrow existence, and she really knew very little about them.

When she was a young girl and her mother was still able to move around the house a little, she had not dreamed of being tied to her parents for the rest of her life. She had hoped for a handsome sweetheart in soldier's uniform, with fine legs bound up in puttees; but her parents had kept her rigidly reined in and, very soon afterwards, the horrible battles of the First World War had taken nearly all the young men of the district, and hardly any of them returned. "Round us, there must have been three girls to every man," she guessed, as through the day she trotted patiently backwards and forwards to the tables; and once she suddenly felt sick, as she realised that the same thing was going to happen to the young girls now hoping for a husband. The young lads were again going out to die. And for what? How many men in this very room would be alive twelve months hence?

The man with the moustache came again the next morning, this time for a cup of coffee and a bun. He sat at the same table. Dickie was not with him.

Emmie snatched her notebook out of her apron pocket and scuttled across the crowded room to take his order, afraid that one of the volunteers would get there first.

"Mornin'," she greeted him shyly, wondering what had brought her to him at a run. He was sitting with his elbows on the small round table, chin resting on clasped hands. At her voice, he glanced up quickly and smiled. Despite the smile, he looked drawn and very tired.

"We got a bit o' bacon," she whispered conspiratorialy. "Would you like some?"

He had already had breakfast with his parents, out at Hoylake, but he was delighted to be specially favoured. "Ah would," he said, the smile broadening into a grin.

When he took his cup of coffee from her instead of allowing her to lay it on the table, she noticed that his hand was not too steady. The cup wobbled in the ill-fitting saucer and then tipped over. He was deluged in coffee.

She whipped a tea towel from the belt of her apron and gave it to him to wipe himself down, while they had

26

a rueful laugh together. "Lucky your trousers is navy blue," she told him. "Stain won't show."

When she brought his bill, he asked her rather diffidently if she would like to go to the cinema with him the following night.

Gwen was scandalized. "At your age!" she exclaimed. "Lettin' yourself be picked up."

Mari had giggled, and said, "It's exciting for her, Mam." Her mother's look was sufficient to freeze her into silence and, with tight lips, the 13-year-old again bent her head over her knitting.

Shaken by a series of emotions she had never expected to be able to give range to, Emmie had turned appealingly to David.

"I'm free now," she said to him, a little break in her voice. "I'm goin' to enjoy meself as much as I can."

David folded his newspaper up carefully. "And so you should," he said, regardless of his wife's grim disapproval. "Be careful who you're with, that's all."

"He's a real nice fella," responded Emmie, looking defiantly at Gwen. Inwardly, she wondered what kind of a man she had drawn out of the pack. He was certainly nothing like her father. She was trembling with nervous anticipation, as, after tea, she washed her face and did her hair. Instead of her usual bun, she rolled her long hair over a shoelace tied round her head and the result was a smooth, neat roll which framed her face; she had got the idea from a women's magazine which Gwen subscribed to. As she tucked in a few precious hairpins to make sure the roll did not slip, she wondered frantically if he were married.

Now, homeward bound on the clanging tram, she reflected fondly on the memory of that first date. There

27

had not been an air raid and they had laughed together as they stumbled round in the blacked out city. He had insisted on bringing her all the way home to her brother's house and he had actually kissed her before leaving her. With joy mixed with fear for his safety, she once more felt under her glove the small garnet-and-pearl ring which a couple of weeks back he had given her.

He had produced it shyly and had confessed when he had slipped it on to her finger, "I never thought much about getting married before – always seemed to be too much to do, fishing with me father. Prices was so bad we never made much – not enough for me to keep a wife as well. Being Methodists, me and me brothers didn't drink and we didn't dance, so we didn't meet too many womenfolk – a few neighbouring girls – but never anyone like you, Emmie. You're beautiful and I want you so bad."

They had lain in the damp April grass, amid the Meols sand-dunes, not too far from his home. Great rolls of barbed wire stretched along the beach, to protect it from possible invasion. The Home Guard, keeping their nightly watch, had left them undisturbed. Rumour had it that both the beach and the dunes were mined, but they forgot everything in their need for each other. While the sound of the waves rolling softly up the shore, and a silent sea mist drifting inland, cut them off for a little while from a world in torment, two gentle, deprived people found an ecstasy granted to few.

They lay for a long time in each other's arms, until Emmie giggled suddenly.

"I was thinkin'. Supposing I have a baby! It *could* happen, even at my age."

Robert had lifted his head and kissed her again. "Not to worry. It'll have a proper father. I wouldn't let you down, luv." He held her tightly, and then said, "If anything should happen to me before we can be married, and you're in trouble, go to me mam and dad. They'll take care of you."

"Oh, Robbie," she whispered with a sigh. "You have to come back safe."

"I'll do me best," he said, with a forced laugh. "But don't you forget. Me dad's earning enough now to keep you for a while."

She lay quiet for a moment, and then she said in a puzzled voice, "It's funny that it's taken a war to give us decent wages, isn't it?" She rolled over him until she was lying on top of him, her head on his shoulder, and then she sighed. "But I'd rather manage on poor wages and know you was safe." She felt him stir under her again and scrambled hastily to her feet. "Enough, luv, enough. I got to go to work on the morning. And you got to have the hospital check your feet again. The cold and wet you suffered on that raft must've been proper awful." She dusted down her skirt and buttoned up her blouse, looking down at him impishly. "But, you know, I wish your feet were still just a bit bad, so as we could have more time together before you have to go to sea again."

He had swung himself to his feet and caught her in his arms and kissed her long and hard. "Aye, luv, I don't want to go either."

Another time, while they sat on a bench underneath a chestnut tree in Sefton Park, she had told him about her life with her parents. He had marvelled at her patience and endurance. She had shrugged her shoulders and said, "I only did what a lot of single daughters have to

29

do – who else will look after people like that? Couldn't let them go into the workhouse. We could just manage if we all three lived together. But there wasn't nothin' left over for going to the pictures or suchlike, even if I'd had the time. We was lucky to have a low rent and something to eat each day. We'd have fair frozen to death some winters, if David hadn't bought some coal."

"It'll be easier from now on, luv," he had promised her. And she had felt indeed that a new life was unfurling for her as surely as the tiny leaves sprouting on the chestnut tree.

"Rialto Cinema," shouted the clippie, and Emmie came sharply back to the present.

iv

Gwen Thomas always averred that her life was never the same again after that young scoundrel, Patrick Donnelly from next door, had at dinnertime on Wednesday shot an arrow through the back bedroom window of their small row house.

"There was broken glass all over our Mari's bedspread. Ruined, it was," she complained angrily to Emmie and to her husband, David.

She was sick to death of her new, Irish next-door neighbours. A pack of sloths, she fumed. She had nearly choked when the 13-year-old boy had calmly knocked at her back door and had asked for his arrow back.

A small bundle of outrage, thin lips drawn back over blackened broken teeth, she had hissed back, "Arrow?

You ain't gettin' no arrow from me, young man. You're goin' to get a bill for seven bob for puttin' t'glass back, and I hope your dad gives you a good beatin'."

Large, calculating blue eyes, fringed with long black eyelashes, looked calmly back at her. "It were an accident, Mrs Thomas – and you could say it were blown out in the last air raid and get it mended easy." He grinned at her beguilingly, a grin that usually worked wonders with middle-aged lady teachers.

It did not work on Gwen Thomas. She wanted to strike him with the broom she was holding; but he was as tall as she was and heavily built for his age. She felt uneasily that he might hit her back. She shook a bony finger at him.

"And what good would that do me, beyond makin' a liar of meself?"

"T' city might do it for free."

She slammed the door in his face.

Bow in hand, he stood staring at the cracked black paint on the back door. All that fuss about a window, when any night the Jerries raided Liverpool hundreds of windows got broken. Old bitch.

On the way out of the tiny brick-lined yard, he gave the cages holding David Thomas's racing pigeons an angry shake. The pigeons fluttered madly round and round their prison in alarm. Next time he shot at a cat, he reckoned crossly, he should take a look at what else was in the line of flight. As his father often said, you live and learn.

"Patrick! Patrick! Coom 'ere. I want yer to go a message, afore you go back to school," he could hear his mother shouting from their kitchen. "Coom 'ere, afore I come after yez. Where are you?"

He dropped his bow into a corner behind the lavatory in the yard and slunk uneasily into the kitchen.

In her living room, Gwen sank on to the sofa, leaned back and flung a skinny arm across her chest. "He's started me palpitations, he has. Mari, luv, pour me another cuppa tea and bring the aspirin bottle."

Mari was just putting on her school blazer, preparatory to returning to school, but she obediently ran upstairs to her mother's bedroom to get the aspirin bottle and, on her return, poured a cup of tea from the aluminium teapot keeping warm on the hob in front of the fire.

"I don't suppose he meant to break the window, Mam," she pleaded, turning a thin, well-scrubbed face towards her mother who was lying back with her eyes closed.

Gwen ignored her plea. She shook a couple of aspirins out of the bottle, popped them into her mouth and swallowed them down with a gulp of tea. "Mind you come straight home," she told her daughter, without opening her eye. The girl slowly buttoned her blazer and, with a sour grimace towards her mother, she left for school. Palpitations! How come every time her mother fell into a fit of rage, it was called palpitations, and when she, Mari, was angry, it was called a sinful paddywack.

As she kicked a stone down the road towards school – her mother hated her to do anything so vulgar – she ruminated on the subject of Patrick. Though she was scared of him, she found him a fascinating subject for thought. Her school friends thought he was the handsomest boy in the neighbourhood and he was so excitingly wild – and a wicked Catholic, too. Only last

32

week, at the end of the street, he had fought off three Protestant boys and left them all with bleeding noses. Cock of the walk, he was, thought Mari a trifle wistfully. But her mother's warnings about men had been drummed into her ever since she could stand, and while the other girls, Protestant and Catholic alike, giggled hopefully whenever they passed him, she held back and passed with eyes cast down, her satchel carried neatly on her back, to cover her long black plait so that boys could not pull it.

v

Emmie descended from the tram and walked briskly down a side street towards her brother's house. The wind sent bits of paper skittering before her, and a red-faced baby, which seemed to have got dust in its eyes, was wailing unhappily in a pram set outside one of the front doors. In a gutter, two small boys in brown woollen jerseys were quarrelling loudly over their coloured glass marbles.

"Evenin', Miss Thomas."

At the sound of the deep Irish voice, Emmie's lips clamped together. She half turned towards the lanky man in blue air raid warden's overalls, who had fallen into step with her. His battered old retriever, Sarge, nosed between them as if anxious not to be ignored, and she bent to stroke his dusty muzzle. "Evening, Mr Donnelly," she replied a little stiffly, uncertain how to treat him.

Patrick's father, with his shrieking wife and bevy of unwashed children, had been, according to Gwen, a

33

no-good out-of-work until he had been made a warden. "Keeps fighting cocks, if you please. Says a bad shoulder keeps him out of the army, ha! For ever shouting at you to 'put that light out'. Never seems to miss the slightest chink in your blackout curtains. Thinks you're signalling to the Jerries if you so much as carry a candle down the yard when you got to go to the lavvie. Work? He lives the life of Riley."

For his part, Conor Donnelly regarded Gwen and David Thomas as worse than a packet of starch, with their highly polished and scrubbed house front, their ritual of Sunday clothes and chapel-going, their disapproval of little boys who sometimes got caught short and piddled on the pavement, and ate conny-onny butties while sitting on their adjacent front doorstep. Ellen Donnelly had expressed the opinion that, "Them holier-than-thou types is the worst. That Mari'll be in trouble with the boys in no time at all, at all."

Conor Donnelly could not imagine how anybody could endure such a regimented life, without even an occasional bout of drinking or fighting to break the monotony. Of course, since he had become an air raid warden he had had to mind himself a bit. He had to stay sober while on duty and be a bit careful when he was carrying stolen goods for a small group of friends who preyed on lorries serving the docks.

When he and his family had been bombed out in the previous autumn, the city had rehoused him in the empty row house next door to Mr High and Mighty David Thomas, plumber. That bombing had been a basketful, that had. Poor little Ruby, his eldest daughter, and old Sarge had been buried for nearly four hours. A bloody miracle that the rest of them had been at the pictures at the time.

Miss Thomas, now she was different. She was polite to his wife and sometimes she made jokes with the kids. On Easter morning she had filled Ruby's hands with toffees — must have given her most of her ration — to share with the other kids. She was a very quiet woman, he mused, but with a bit of encouragement from the right fella she might be more lively than she appeared. His face crinkled up in a grin, as she glanced up at him. He ventured a mild joke and was rewarded by a shy laugh.

Emmie forced herself to attend to what he was saying. With his face a polished mahogany from years of inadequate washing and his long, yellow teeth, he was an oddity to her; yet his sheer bouncing gaiety was infectious and she could understand why he had been chosen as an air raid warden — he would be a real tonic if you were in trouble.

They turned towards their adjoining front doorsteps. Conor pushed open his unlocked door, while she inserted her key into her brother's carefully burnished Yale lock. Before he entered, Conor turned to point up to the sky, where a few clouds were building and a slight haze was dulling the sunshine.

"Bit o' luck and them clouds'll form a nice cover afore midnight. Should mean no raid."

"Aye. It's been over quiet lately, hasn't it? Makes you wonder what's brewing."

Conor nodded agreement. "Well, keep yer fingers crossed."

"I got to work the late shift at the canteen tonight, so I'll be up and about anyways," Emmie confided.

As usual, the slam of the Donnelly's front door caused a slight shudder to pass through the Thomases' house and rattled the wooden signboard nailed to their door. The faded board announced *David Thomas, plumber, est. 1914. Prompt attention.*

The noise immediately brought Gwen Thomas out of the back kitchen. She clucked fussily, as clearly through the dividing wall came the sound of Ellen Donnelly's strident voice above the shriek of a child. Conor's voice rumbled back.

"Really! Slammin' t' door like that! Brings all the dust down. And me just finished cleaning." Red-ringed, faded blue eyes looked impatiently up at Emmie, as Gwen licked her finger and ran it along a ledge to pick up an offending grain of dust.

Emmie hung up her coat, gas mask and handbag on the hall peg. While she nerved herself to deal with Gwen, she picked up the floppy, brown carrier bag given to her by Robert. She was always anxious not to break up her tenuous housing arrangement by letting her bitter, pent-up resentment burst forth at Gwen's never having given her the slightest help with her parents. She was grateful for David's protection and did not want to move until she was married. Though she was now paying very adequately for her lodgings and she also helped Gwen in the house, Gwen never considered it necessary to thank her and was often barely civil.

Nothing annoyed Gwen more than dust and dirt and untidiness, and her shining, neat house indicated how successfully she dealt with them. Almost invariably wrapped in a black cross-over overall dotted with blue forget-me-nots, she was a bundle of muscles. Because she kept running her fingers through her greying red hair with its tight natural curl, it tended to stand up in a wild bush. Tonight it was in particular dissarray, indicating a trying day's battle with her household gods.

"'T' glazier hasn't got no glass for Mari's bedroom window," she grumbled, as she followed Emmie into the living room, where a cheerful fire blazed in an old-fashioned cooking range gleaming with blackleading; at its side, the brass tap of the hot water tank winked in the light of the darting flames.

David Thomas was seated in his armchair beside the fire, and he looked up from his perusal of the *Liverpool Echo*. "'Allo, la," he greeted Emmie, and then he said to his wife. "I'll nail a bit o' plywood over t' window when I've had me tea. It'll be safer for Mari than glass."

"Where *is* Mari?" inquired Emmie, smiling down at her brother.

"She's away out to tea with her friend, Dorothy." Gwen clicked her tongue and reverted to her grievance. "I'll teach that lad, even if his mam won't. He'll not get his arrow back." She continued to grumble, as she went through to the back kitchen. Emmie followed her with the carrier bag.

She interrupted Gwen's tirade, by saying, "Robbie set a line while the tide was out yesterday. He caught ten whiting and he's sent you two. They feel real heavy."

"That's proper kind of him, I'm sure," replied Gwen coldly. She seized a pot of boiled potatoes and deftly drained the water from them into the sink. Through the ensuing steam, she added with a sniff, "Being engaged to

37

a fisherman has its advantages, I suppose. T' fishmonger didn't have so much as a cod's head left today, by the time he got to me. Ever so long, the queue was."

"Well, there's the makin's of a nice dinner here," Emmie soothed.

"Humph," grunted Gwen. "Here, take the potatoes and put them on the table for me." She sighed. Provided Emmie could be prevented from taking her parents' furniture with her, she would be thankful when the woman got married and left. When the pieces had been moved into the house, nothing had been said as to the ownership; but Gwen burnished them determinedly; they were hers, because David was the eldest and should inherit.

What little Emmie said about the furniture indicated that she took it for granted that, since she had lived with it all her life, the furniture belonged to her. Besides, in the middle of a war, where else would she get furniture from for a home?

She had brought Robert home for tea one Sunday and Gwen had made it clear that she strongly disapproved of a woman of sober years suddenly marrying a man she had known less than four months. It did not occur to Emmie that Gwen had been smitten by a lingering envy of her blatant happiness, her obvious contentment.

"I must hurry," said Emmie, as they sat down to their meal. "I got to be in the canteen by seven. Mrs Robinson and the others were ever so kind about me engagement, giving me a bit of time off when Robbie was free."

Gwen responded tartly, "Well, I hope you're doing the right thing." She stirred her tea hard, in the hope of making half a teaspoonful of her sugar ration sweeten it adequately. She made a face when she sipped it. "Picking up a man like that don't seem like a good start to me."

Emmie ached to slap her.

"Now, Gwen," her husband warned. "Emmie got to know him in the canteen. That's not picking up. And he took her home to Hoylake to meet his mum and dad – quite proper. He's given her a nice ring, too."

Gwen shrugged her shoulders slightly and poured another cup of tea. Emmie kept her eyelids down and wondered if Gwen had ever been in love with poor David – or with anything except the shiny aspidistra in the front room or the bronze soldiers looking down at them from the living room mantelpiece.

To distract Gwen, David said, "I'll get me tools and do Mari's window."

That brought Gwen back to her favourite complaint – the Donnellys. "We ought to have moved from here years ago – the whole of Toxteth's gone to pot. The minute Mrs Tasker died next door I knew we'd never get decent neighbours again."

"House were empty for months. T' landlord held out for too high a rent." David gritted his teeth as he pushed away his empty plate.

"Oh, aye. And how does he pay seventeen shillings a week on an air raid warden's wages, I'd like to know. Maybe it's true that he's hand in hand with a gang o' dock thieves."

"Gwen!" David was shocked. "That's just idle gossip. Because he sometimes has lipsticks or silk stockings for sale? He could buy 'em easy from a merchant seaman on the New York run. It don't make 'im a thief."

vii

The sharp wail of the air raid siren made David jump. He had been washing himself in the kitchen sink, in preparation for going to bed, and he stood in his undervest and trousers while he dried the back of his neck. He was numb with fatigue after a long day working on the intricacies of the plumbing of the Royal Infirmary, and he felt again a small, choking pain in the middle of his chest, a pain that had been bothering him occasionally for a couple of weeks.

"Blow them," he muttered, and hastily finished drying himself.

He leaned over the sink to pull back the blackout curtain and look out of the window. There was enough moonlight to cast a shadow of the house across the back yard. Behind the neighbouring chimneys, searchlights suddenly sent seeking fingers across a starry sky. It was much too light for safety. He dropped the curtain into place, making the flame of the candle on the drainboard dance, as Gwen came hurrying from the living room. She carried a steaming kettle in one hand, and the warning had obviously flustered her.

"For goodness' sake, get your dressing-gown on and something on your feet. We'll have tea on the cellar steps. What a nuisance they are."

As she flung two teaspoonsful of tea into the pot, she went on anxiously, "Our Mari's not in yet, from

40

Dorothy's. She's real late. I'll have to have a word with that young lady."

"I could go and fetch her," David offered, without much conviction.

"No. It'd just mean two of you out in the flak. You get out the blankets and cushions and take them on to the cellar steps, while I do the tea tray." She jumped suddenly, as the steady boom-boom of anti-aircraft fire made the windows rattle. Sometimes the guns sounded more menacing than the bombs did.

David would have been thankful to crawl into bed and risk being blown out of it. He did not feel, however, that he could go to bed while Mari was still not home, so he obediently arranged the cushions on the cellar steps, for them to sit on. With the slope of the staircase overhead, this spot offered good protection and the least likelihood of being crushed.

With a sigh, he sat down and arranged a blanket over his knees. While Gwen held the tea tray a little high, he tucked another blanket round her. He took the candle from the tray and set it on a small shelf above their heads. Gwen scolded, "Be careful, stupid. You'll upset the tray." She stirred the pot balanced uncertainly on the tray on her lap, while he listened for the battery to start firing in nearby Princes Park; the sound would indicate to him how close the raiders were. Beyond the rumble of more distant guns, however, all he heard was Donnelly's front door slam. Likely, Donnelly was in for a busy night.

Gwen's lips curled. "That'll be him goin' down to the wardens' post. Bangin' the door, as usual. No manners, that man."

Their own front door slammed. Quick footsteps ran

41

along the narrow, linoleumed passage, then stumbled through the dark living room and into the kitchen.

"That you, Mari? Come on down, quick now."

Mari was panting, as she whipped a cushion off the shelf and almost slithered down the concrete steps, her long bare legs flashing white in the candlelight.

She sat down close to her mother. Like many families seeking refuge in this safest corner of the house, they always sat very tightly together, so that if the building was hit they either died or survived together.

Gwen felt her trembling and lifted down the candle to have a closer look at her. The girl's face was blenched and her eyes stared unblinkingly at her mother from behind the candle flame.

"There, there, luv. No need to be scared. You're safe home now," she told the girl quite gently.

Her father turned towards her and added reassuringly, "It don't sound as if they're interested in the south end of the town tonight."

Above them, a number of aeroplane engines throbbed increasingly loudly.

"They'll be some of ours," David declared authoritatively. "Always know the difference by the sound o' the engines."

His words were immediately belied by a shrieking whistle passing over them. Instinctively, they ducked and flung their hands over their heads for protection. The tea tray on Gwen's lap rocked perilously. There was a moment of silence: then a deafening explosion which shook the whole house above them. They waited, like rabbits hiding in a thorn bush from a fox. A piece of plaster plopped from the ceiling on to the tray, and a cloud of thin dust enveloped them.

Mari buried her face against her mother's bony legs and whimpered in terror. The next bomb in the rack would hit them; she knew it. It would be a judgment on her for what she had allowed Patrick Donnelly to do to her.

He had been bothering her for weeks, touching her when she passed him, holding her against the wall of the alley one day, when she had run down it to visit Dorothy; not hurting her, just making her feel funny when he pressed himself against her. It had been most funny-peculiar, because, despite all her mother's warning about not letting a man come near her, she had wanted him to remain close. Perhaps the warning didn't apply to boys, she argued to herself.

Tonight, he had pushed her into a street air raid shelter, which nobody used except as a urinal. He had held her tightly against the wall and her silent struggles had been of no avail against his considerable weight. When in scared despair, she had stopped wriggling, he had lifted her skirt and gently stroked between her legs. And she knew now that she was on her way to hell. It had felt wonderful, incredible; and he had laughed when, not understanding the driving impulse, she had put her arms round him. He had said it was nothing to what he could do. If that was nothing, she decided without really knowing why, it was a good thing that the air raid warning had begun to shriek and that they had both run for home.

Now the bombs were falling all around her. God must be very angry with her.

"Incendiaries! Incendiaries!" Conor Donnelly could be heard, calling his firewatchers to the street.

Despite his wife's protests, David insisted on going

43

out in his dressing-gown to check his roof, back and front. He came back very soberly and hauled the blanket round himself again. "Looks like the whole town's alight. Hope our Emmie's all right." Then to his crouching daughter, he said, "Don't take on so, Mari. Everything's going to be all right. We're quite safe here on the steps."

You don't know what a wicked daughter you've got, thought Mari, not lifting her head from her mother's knee. God could do anything to us tonight.

viii

As the guns in Princes Park began to roar, Ellen Donnelly finished spreading the washing on her wooden airer in her living room and then heaved the heavy rack up to the ceiling again and tied the rope firmly to hold it there. The clothes began to drip depressingly onto the rag rug below and onto the otherwise bare floor. A few droplets reached baby Michael asleep in a battered easy chair. She edged the chair away from under the rack and flung her black woollen shawl over the sleeping child.

There was a quick patter of bare feet on the stairs, and her eldest daughter, Ruby, still in her clothes, dashed into the room. She was brought up short by the sight of her mother seating herself calmly on a wooden chair in front of the fire.

"Mam, shall I bring Brendy and Nora down? The guns sound awful." Her voice was tightly constricted, as she tried to control her panic. After the dreadful experience of being buried in the ruins of their former home, the sound of the air raid warning always brought her close to a bout of hysterics. Her breath came in tight gasps and, from under a fringe like a Skye terrier's, eyes gleamed with tears.

"Aye, luv. Coom 'ere." Her mother held out a stout red arm to her and thankfully the skinny 12-year-old cuddled close to her heavy breast. "It ain't likely we'll be bombed again."

The guns continued to growl and, after a minute, Ellen said, "Let's have a look-see outside. Then we'll decide if we should bring t' kids down." She rose, and went to the front door, Ruby trotting closely behind her for comfort.

With a strong, red hand on either door-post, she leaned out as far as she could. The wind caught her untidy mop of shoulder-length hair and flapped her long black skirt. Metronomic searchlights flicked back and forth across the sky as if to time the drumming guns, and high in the heavens a bright flare floated gently; it silvered the slate roofs of the close-packed houses, gave a halo to a church spire and outlined the solid mass of a nearby tenement building.

"Reckon they're doin' Wallasey and Birkenhead tonight," she opined comfortingly. "Quite away from us. We'll let the kids rest for a bit. You come and sit by the fire with me and we'll have a drop of your dad's whiskey."

Ruby did not like the taste of whiskey, but since the disastrous raid which had robbed them of their home, her mother had often given her a teaspoonful of it, and it made her feel better. Now, she went to the dying fire to warm her bare feet, while her mother tried to guess where Donnelly's latest hiding-place for the bottle might be. In such an empty home there were not many places to look.

She found it on the windowsill, behind the blackout curtain, and she sat down while she eased out the cork. Ruby came to lean against her. The glow from the fire lit up their faces, as they solemnly took a sip each from the bottle. Then Ellen took a good gulp, and gasped as it caught her throat. She laughed and set down the bottle under her chair and again put her arm round Ruby.

The front door was flung open. Patrick strolled slowly in, determined to show that he was not afraid of air raids. A cool breeze followed him in.

"What you bin up to?" Ellen inquired truculently. "You're lookin' too pleased with yourself by far."

"Haven't bin doin' nothin'." The satisfied grin on his face belied his words, but she knew from experience that she would get no more out of him.

A screaming whistle overhead wiped the grin from Patrick's face, but, hands in pockets, he stood his ground, while Ruby clung shrieking to her mother. Blast swung the front door hard open and shook the old house. The blackout curtains billowed like sails in a sudden gust. A mass of soot descended the chimney, obliterated the fire and covered all of them in black dust. Little Michael, covered by his mother's thick shawl, continued to sleep, but from upstairs came frightened howls.

Ellen wiped the soot off her mouth. "God's curse upon the buggers!" she cried, and bent down to reach for the whiskey bottle.

A piece of debris landed on the roof with a sharp crump; then, for a moment, unearthly quiet.

A nerve-racking clatter in the street and the familiar

sound of her husband's running feet caused Ellen to burst out again, "Incendiaries, blast 'em!"

Patrick went to the door. The darkness was broken all along the street by sparks hissing from the small, vicious fire bombs. Dark shadows carrying sandbags ran to dowse the scary, sizzling devils, and one or two bravely tried to put them out by holding dustbin lids over them. Patrick seized one of the sandbags in the hall and ran gleefully out to help.

Opposite, a furious Bridget Mahoney flung up the empty frames of her bedroom window, sat out on the sill with her back to the street and struck out with a broom at an incendiary which had lodged in the gutter of her home. She managed, after a few wild shots, to hook it out and it fell into the street, where Patrick pounced on it happily and covered it with sand. Bridget eased herself back into her bedroom.

"Ow!" she exclaimed, as she caught her arm on a jagged piece of glass left in the window-frame. The blood gushing out looked black in the moonlight. Hastily she picked up her discarded apron from the bedroom chair and wrapped it tightly round the wound.

Early the next morning, a sympathetic Ellen Donnelly bathed off the apron stuck on the deep, ugly cut and rebandaged it tightly with a bit of an old pillowslip brought by Bridget. Afterwards, they finished the rest of Conor Donnelly's whiskey and, despite the pain, a fulminating Bridget went off to work in a large garage, where she spent her days sewing aeroplane canvas. As usual, her little boys went to school with clean hands and faces, and stomachs full of porridge.

About ten o'clock, an exhausted Conor arrived home. He was covered in dust from working on the results of a

47

direct hit on a dairy three streets away. "Three dead – and twelve cows spattered all over," he informed his sleepy wife. He went straight to the window and flicked back the half-drawn blackout curtains. "Where's me whiskey?"

"Me and Bridget Mahoney drank it," his wife said dully. "She were hurt." She was holding Michael to her breast and he was sucking eagerly. She did not look up.

In two strides her husband reached her. He struck her hard across her plump face. Then he stumbled upstairs to their bed and flung himself on to it.

ix

To alleviate the excruciating boredom of raidless nights, the clerks and shop assistants on fire guard duty in the buildings near the sailors' canteen would take it in turns to nip into the canteen for coffee. Mrs Robinson had once remarked that they complained when nothing happened and then they complained when there was a raid. "Then they're scared stiff, poor souls," she added.

Emmie had looked up at some of the steeply sloping roofs along which a firewatcher might have to clamber to get at a fire, and had been thankful that up to now the regular canteen staff had been excused from fire-watching.

Tonight, she entered the canteen through the narrow side passage which led into the light well at the rear. The light well was already shadowing and she fingered the long hat pin she kept under her coat lapel, until she had slipped through the kitchen door. You never knew who might be lurking at night in such a gloomy place as a light well, she told herself. A hat pin was a girl's best defence.

She greeted Doris, another paid member of the staff, who was shaking up a huge basket of potato chips above a vat of fat. Near her, with a bulging sack between them sat two volunteers patiently peeling and slicing further supplies for her. One lady dropped a handful of irregularly sliced chips into a bucket of water, and moaned, "This must be the most unromantic job in the whole war."

Emmie had lost some of her awe of these well-dressed ladies, and she teased them. "Now what would the boys out there do without chips? They couldn't go on without your chips. Proper miserable they'd be."

The volunteer nodded her head in rueful agreement and picked up another potato between her beautifully manicured nails. Then she chuckled. "You're quite right – they all seem to keep going on chips."

Emmie took her new lipstick from her handbag and clumsily outlined her lips in front of the kitchen mirror. She grimaced at the uncertain result. "Painted women are the devil's children," Gwen had told her. She smiled at herself in the mirror.

After years of having only Mrs Forster-Harrington to talk to, Emmie was happy in the company of the canteen staff. The customers were usually fun, too, she thought, though she did not always understand the jokes they made; and she was sure that to many she was only a pair of chapped hands bringing plates of food.

As she closed the wooden shutters over the big kitchen window looking out at the light well and then slotted the iron bar across them, she thought wistfully of Robert in his new ship. Perhaps after the war, when he could go back to being an inshore fisherman again, he could be at home more often, depending only on the time of the tides for his trips in and out.

She went to attend to a small window on the same wall. Carefully she drew a pair of old grey velvet curtains over it. Then she lifted the telephone off the table nearby and tucked it tightly against them, so that cracks of light would not show at the curtain hem. She had never in her life used a telephone and regarded it with some deference; Mrs Forster-Harrington had felt it unnecessary to have such an intrusion upon her privacy.

Despite the wail of the air raid siren, a steady buzz of conversation came through the thick tobacco smoke. Liverpudlians are not easily stopped in mid-argument, she reflected with a little smile. The men's aplomb lessened her own fear, and she bustled round her tables as if nothing unusual was happening outside.

In the kitchen, Doris stood clutching the edge of the pig bin in which all the kitchen scraps were kept for feeding pigs. She was trembling violently, her lined face as white as the tiles on the walls. She had lost home, husband and children in the Christmas air raids the previous year and the memory was still agonisedly fresh.

Lady Mentmore, a countess, lifted her beringed hands from the washing-up water and went to comfort her. Not by even the flicker of an eyelid did she show her own nervousness.

The gunfire was heavy and the quick thump-thump of bombs hastily discharged was unnervingly close. From a table in the corner near the kitchen door came the piercing sweet sound of a mouth organ. Almost immediately a strong tenor voice joined in with the words, *She'll be comin' round the mountain when she comes*. There was a general roar of voices raised to sing what she would be wearing when she came, and Emmie tut-tutted to herself, as she dried dinner plates at record speed for the countess. What would Lady Mentmore think of such naughty words, worse than anything she had heard since she left school? Proper wicked little boys' words they were. Through the open door, she glimpsed the men's faces, red from exposure or yellow from too much confinement below decks. They glowed with pure mischief as they thought up new verses, each bawdier than the last. Doris gave the countess a watery smile and the countess unexpectedly chuckled.

The canteen closed at midnight, but most people there stayed on until the All Clear sounded about one o'clock. The volunteers murmured that they hoped all the ferry boats had not been sunk. "You can't walk on water," one laughingly remarked. Doris hoped the trams out to Bootle would still be running, and Emmie, who could walk home, hoped fervently that she would not be accosted by thieves, because she had just been paid. She transferred her pay packet from her handbag to her coat pocket and checked that her hat pin was still under her lapel; too many petty thieves, either singly or in small gangs, haunted the ill-lit streets and she was always nervous.

The light of the fires in the city made the shadows of the buildings still standing look even blacker than usual. She glanced at the sky. It was flushed in several directions and the smell of burning tobacco and smouldering rubber was thick in the air. Service vehicles of various kinds, with shaded headlamps, moved like dark ghosts. Except for two drunks helping each other along, there seemed to be no pedestrians. She began to run.

FRIDAY, 2nd MAY 1941

At half-past one on Friday morning, when Emmie let herself into her brother's house, an overwhelming smell of soot greeted her, but when she had lit a candle in the hallway, she was thankful to see that everything looked much as usual. She went straight upstairs, undressed and crept thankfully into bed.

At six o'clock the sound of Gwen's alarm jerked her awake, and she heard Mari next door clamber out of her creaky bed. Yawning, she crawled out herself, poured water from her ewer into a hand-basin on the wash-stand and splashed her face with it.

As she dried herself with a worn white towel, she whipped back the blackout curtains and saw a cheerful sun in a pale blue sky. Behind the houses across the back alley, the sky was flushed, but she argued hopefully to herself that it could be because the sun had not long risen. She hurried into an old cotton frock.

In the living room, the curtains were already drawn back, and David Thomas was kneeling on the hearth rug, clearing the ashes and soot from the hearth. "'allo, la," he greeted her amiably, between small, persistent coughs. "Proper mess, eh? Soon get t' fire goin', though."

Emmie agreed. Every stick of furniture was covered with a fine film of soot. It clung to the bronze Roman soldiers ornamenting each end of the high mantelpiece; it had coated the net curtains at the window and the fancywork runner across the middle of the table; even the four precious oranges in the fruit bowl on the sideboard were black. Gwen was going to be hard to live with today, she thought wryly.

David gave a sudden enormous sneeze and little puffs of soot rose round him.

Emmie clicked her tongue. "I'll get the floor cloth and wipe down the table and chairs, so as we can have brekkie," she said briskly. "Has the milk come?"

"I haven't looked."

Emmie went to the front door and peeped out. No milk bottle sat on the doorstep. "Well, I'm blowed," she exclaimed. "He's never missed before, not even in the Christmas blitz. I'll have to open a tin. Gwen's not going to like that."

Where the dairy once had stood, the milkman and his twelve cows lay neatly shovelled into bags, awaiting transport.

As she worked the tin-opener into a tiny tin of Nestle's milk, Emmie asked, "Did you have any incendiaries up here?"

"Aye. Had to put 'em out with sand. Woman who stores the stirrup-pump wouldn't open her door. Keeping the pump for herself, she was, in case her own house caught fire."

"That's proper awful."

"It was. I hope the warden gives her what for, today."

David, in clean overalls, was dispatched on time to the Royal Infirmary, where he was still repairing the plumbing damaged in the Christmas raids. A dreamy Mari was slapped by Gwen for not getting on with washing herself at the kitchen sink, scolded for not eating her cornflakes and was sent to school comparatively free of soot smudges.

With endless buckets of hot water and small amounts

of the irreplaceable, rationed soap, Emmie spent the morning washing down every nook and cranny of the living room and Gwen's bedroom, which was the only bedroom with a fireplace. The blackout curtains were taken into the back yard, put over the clothes-line and beaten, the net ones were washed and hung out to dry. The fireplaces were blackleaded and the oranges carefully scrubbed with a nail brush. Gwen herself sprinkled tea-leaves over the red, Belgian carpet in the sitting room and solicitously brushed it, remembering sadly the number of weeks it had taken her to pay for it, shilling by shilling. The china ornaments on the mantelpiece were lovingly bathed in the kitchen sink, the various messages printed on them in gilt twinkling *A present from Blackpool* or *Greetings from Llandudno* through the soapsuds. Gwen nearly cried. Lovely holidays those had been. She wondered when they would be able to go to the seaside again.

One of the whiting which Robert had caught made a consolingly large fish pie, some of which Gwen, Emmie and Mari ate at lunchtime. The rest was put away for David's tea.

Gwen reminded Emmie that she was due at Blackler's Store at one o'clock, to help in Dress Materials. She was very proud that she went to work two afternoons a week. Just before lunch, she changed into her best black dress, with its neat white lace collar, and her Sunday black stockings and shoes.

After she had left and Mari had returned to school, Emmie filled the kitchen bowl with hot water dipped from the oven tank beside the living room fire, stripped herself in the back kitchen and washed herself all over, in an effort to remove streaks of soot. Gwen did not encourage such scrubbings in the bedrooms – it made too many splashes on the polished linoleum.

ii

Next door, a sullen, resentful Ellen fried up some boiled potatoes and an egg and shoved them in front of her husband seated at the table. Conor was unusually quiet as he ate the food. When Ellen sat down by the fire, picked up 3-year-old Michael and gave him her breast, he stared past her, as if he were looking at something behind her.

The youngster suckled contentedly and Ellen enjoyed the physical pleasure of it, but finally her husband's oppressive silence became too much for her.

"What's to do with yez?" she asked sulkily.

He poked listlessly at his fried egg and sighed heavily. "It were a bad night, last night. The dairy were a shambles – blood everywhere – from the cows mostly. And them two women in Plum Street – bits of one of 'em hanging from the tree out front."

"Jesus Mary!" exclaimed Ellen. She shuddered, and Michael lost her nipple and complained fretfully. Her anger at Conor's striking her was forgotten in fascinated contemplation of this horror. She pushed her nipple back into Michael's mouth. "Maybe t' Nazis won't come again," she tried to comfort.

"There's nuthin' to stop 'em. 'specially at night. Play ducks and drakes they can." He contemplated a piece of grey potato on the end of his fork. "T' kid at the corner house 'as got a broken arm and bruises all over – part of the roof fell in on 'im. His dumb cluck of a mother left him in bed 'stead of bringing 'im down to the cellar."

"Poor little divil." She hugged her child closer and remembered, with a tremor, how close she had come to losing Ruby. What an evening that had been. The rest of the family had returned from a Christmas visit to the local cinema, to find the rescue men just hauling her out, unscratched, from under the kitchen table, which her grandfather had fashioned from oak fifty years before. She wondered idly if, when he had made it so solidly, he had had an intimation that it would save a life. Bless the sainted man. And God preserve her from another night like that.

iii

When Emmie descended from the tram, at her usual Church Street stop, on her way to work that afternoon, the traffic seemed nearly as busy as usual, though everywhere there was a strong smell of burning, and there was a general haze in the sky.

At the door of the canteen, she bumped into Doris, who promptly complained, "Me pore feet. Had to walk all the way to Bootle last night. Not a tram working. Bloody miles."

When Mrs Robinson and two volunteers arrived, they also looked tired after being up half the night, though all three were immaculately dressed. One of the volunteers, Mrs Starr, said, "I thought I was going to be late. We lost all our windows and I've been hammering old rugs over the downstairs ones ever since daybreak. First time I've ever used a hammer!"

59

Emmie listened to the lament. Did the stupid woman imagine that they had all been able to spend the morning in bed? In her opinion, complaining never did any good. You just took what life threw at you and did the best you could.

When the siren went, Emmie was busy serving a surge of men who had just come in after the closing of the public houses.

"Blow it," she exclaimed irritably, and some of the men made obscene gestures towards the ceiling. They were none of them drunk – publicans spread their meagre consignments of beer and spirits too thinly for anyone to achieve that happy state – but they were loquacious. Some of the language they used, as they consigned all Germans to Kingdom Come, made Emmie wonder innocently to Doris how Robert managed not to pick up such words.

Doris, trying to be brave, laughed shakily. "There never was a sea-going man what couldn't swear – your Robbie knows his manners, that's what it is."

While she doled out fish and chips – a little fish and a lot of chips – Emmie meditated on Doris's remark and realised that there was a side of her beloved which she did not know much about. For a minute or two, the sickening loneliness she had felt when her mother's coffin had been lowered into her grave was revived; and her new world of Robert Owen and the canteen seemed suddenly distant and alien.

As she cleared a table hastily evacuated by the buildings' firewatchers when they had fled back to their posts, there was a high-pitched swish-swish overhead.

Emmie froze. For a second all conversation stopped. The tiny silence was succeeded by a tremendous roar.

The room shook and the electric lights dipped. Everyone looked towards the ceiling.

A tumbling rumble announced the descent of the debris flung up by the explosion. Another roar, another series of rumbles.

Emmie stood terrified, the crockery rattling on her tray, as the guns began to answer the challenge of the planes.

"Put your tray down, luv, or you'll break everything." Deckie Dick, the friend of Robert's who had breakfasted with him on the morning he had first met Emmie, took the tray from her and put it back on the table. "Those two was away over ..." he began.

His voice was drowned by a crash that numbed her ears. His arms went round her and she was clamped against an old navy sweater that reeked of perspiration, as he sought to protect her face and head. In the kitchen, Doris screamed.

"Phew! That was near." Deckie Dick slowly let her go and she giggled nervously. As the guns continued their steady tattoo, a man at the next table chipped Dick, "You never misses a chance with the girls, do you?" Dick gave him a playful punch on the head, and Emmie slipped away to continue her clearing of tables.

Another crash, somewhere at the back of the building, brought Mrs Robinson running from the kitchen. "Gentlemen, there is a shelter downstairs. Take the staircase to the left of the front door. I think it would be a good idea ..." She was cut off by a series of appalling crashes, when again all faces automatically looked up at the ceiling. A crack zipped across it, but it held.

"Come on, lads. Everybody downstairs. Come on."

Deckie Dick began to move amongst the tables, touching men on their shoulders and pointing to the staircase. He turned to Mrs Robinson. "Get your ladies down, missus. It's going to be a bad night."

Without a word, she hastened back to the kitchen, where Doris was trying not to have hysterics in front of a pile of fish which she had been flouring. The fish was now covered with heavy dust.

Outside, fire engines raced pell-mell through the darkness, amid the shrill blare of burglar alarms set going in the shaken buildings opposite. Boots pounded past the front door, as rescue crews and air raid wardens ran by.

The customers no longer felt the need to look brave; the pandemonium outside was bad enough to justify a retreat, and they followed the volunteers down to the basement as fleetly as they would have abandoned a sinking vessel. Mrs Robinson, white-faced captain of her little ship, refused to descend until everyone was safely down. Then she quietly followed her crew.

At the foot of the stairs, she closed a very ancient, heavy door, bound with iron, hung there, presumably, to keep out eighteenth-century thieves and rioters. As she lowered the iron latch, she heard the upstairs front windows and shutters blow in, and the tinkle of slivers of glass sweeping across the canteen, to bury themselves in walls and tables. The blast reversed itself and blew outwards, causing a resounding crash of crockery from the tables. There was a muffled bang, when the shutters hit the empty window-frames again.

"Pooh!" she exclaimed. "Just in time." She sank down thankfully on one of the timeworn school benches which had been provided as seating.

The shelter was a windowless cellar, used for years for the storage of coal to heat the building. Its only entrance, other than the stairs, was a pavement light of heavy glass set in an iron frame. This could be swung upwards to facilitate the delivery of sacks of coal; in the construction of the shelter, it had been left as it was. A simple bolt on the inside held it down and it would form a convenient escape hatch from the basement to the street in the event of fire. Though the walls had been freshly whitewashed and the floor well swept, there was still a smell of coal. As a first line of defence against fire, a stirrup-pump with several buckets of water stood in a corner. In another corner was a small table; on it lay an electric ring and a clutter of much used tea-making apparatus. A single bulb hanging, unshaded, from the centre of the ceiling provided the only light.

Some of the men stood around smoking, while others slouched on the benches. Four of them sat cross-legged on the floor and prepared for a long wait by dealing out a pack of cards. The two volunteers sat primly together, backs straight; two middle-class women determined to be stoical.

A shivering Emmie sat by Doris with her arm round her. The bombed-out woman was sobbing quietly to herself, tears glistening on her rouged cheeks.

"Have a cigarette, me duck. It'll calm you."

A tall, thin seaman, a cigarette wobbling at the corner of his mouth, squatted down in front of Doris and generously proffered a precious packet of Player's. "You like one, luv?" he asked Emmie.

Doris smiled wanly, but made no move to take a cigarette. "Neither of us smoke," Emmie responded for both of them. "Ta, all the same."

The man turned back to Doris. "Well, you start. You're the woman that was bombed out, wasn't yez?"

Doris's eyes clenched shut. She nodded agreement.

"You should smoke. It helps. See, I'll show you how."

Her mind diverted, Doris opened her eyes. He was not a young man and bore all the marks of years of seagoing, of rotten food and working in cramped spaces. He grinned and lit a cigarette for her, drew the first breath on it and handed it to her. "There y'are, luv," he said, his sallow, hollow-cheeked face compassionate.

Emmie watched him wonderingly, captivated by his easy goodwill. Really, she thought, men *can* be kind; and she remembered, for a second, her father's unremitted bad temper. Who else, of the male sex, had she really known, other than him – and stolid, dull David? They had been no particular recommendation for their sex. She had taken Robert purely on trust; and how lucky she had been. The squatting seaman wondered why she suddenly smiled so sweetly.

While Doris cautiously puffed at her first cigarette, the barrage of noise persisted, as in steady waves the Luftwaffe swept over the doomed port. They were guided, at first, by the fires started the previous night and then by huge conflagrations which now began to flare in every direction. Far down the river, the flames' reflection danced on the water, lit up the rooms of suburban homes and warned ships at sea not to cross the bar. Forty miles away, in the Isle of Man, residents peeped between their bedroom curtains, to watch the blaze on the horizon mount higher and higher. "Liverpool's getting it again," they told each other in shocked whispers, so as not to wake the children.

In the shelter, two young deckhands who had drunk a

lot of beer decided that they must go to the lavatory. In a brief lull in the noise outside, they ran up the stairs, across the littered canteen, out through the kitchen door to the cobbled light well, where stood the ancient loos. As they relieved themselves, they look fearfully back over their shoulders through the open doors. What had once been, long ago before the offices had been built round it, the courtyard of a rich merchant's house now seemed to be a deadly funnel, down which bits of debris, shrapnel and occasional sparks travelled with unnerving rapidity. After a quick peek through the empty window facing the street, they were thankful to get back to the shelter.

"Proper shambles out front," one of them reported. "Beams and wires and stones scattered all over. Them last ones must've hit real close."

One of the card players looked up from his seat on the floor, pushed his plug of tobaco into one cheek and said, with a faint sneer, "Don't need a crystal ball to know they're close. Listen to 'em now."

"Ah, shut yer gob," retorted the returned youngster, hitching his braces up under his jacket.

"Now, gentlemen, this is no time to get upset," Mrs Robinson interjected hastily, having no illusions regarding the shortness of tempers amongst her usually overwrought, seagoing customers.

The young man made a wry face at Mrs Robinson and drifted over to the other side of the room, while the man on the floor muttered irritably, "Think they're bloody heroes every time they go to pee."

The second young man had kept his mouth shut, but now he said, with a tinge of wonderment in his voice, "There's a WVS canteen parked at the corner. T' women's doling out tea and sandwiches as if they was in their parlours at home. Feedin' the firemen, I think they are. Ordinary women just like me mam. And the flak flying round 'em like confetti."

A fast salvo of bombs nearly deafened them. Everybody crouched, hands over heads, fully expecting to be buried. When they found they had survived, they ruefully rubbed piercingly painful ears. From the ceiling, whitewash snowed gently.

Suddenly, all heads were raised; all noses sniffed. Smoke. The smell of burning wood was unmistakable. Fear jumped from one face to another. Some people rose quickly to their feet. Doris whimpered, and Emmie felt a rising panic.

"Hold it. No point in getting scared." Deckie Dick got up and put his pipe into his trouser pocket. "I'll nip upstairs and take a dekko for you. If I call, you come up orderly, mind."

The men quickly made a passage for him. Elderly, well-known and with forty years of seagoing experience spanning the First World War, he commanded respect. He ran swiftly up the stairs, the deck of cards which gave him his nickname bulging in his back trouser pocket.

The crowd relaxed slightly as, above the now more distant rumbles from outside, they could hear him working his way through the tumbled furniture of the canteen overhead. The back door slammed, indicating that it was still on its hinges.

Nothing was burning in the light well, though it was smoky. In the flickering light of fire reflected in the remaining windows of the offices across the street, he made his way to the front door with its protective sandbags. He flattened himself against the battered wall of sandbags, as a whistle sounded overheard. A huge explosion from South Castle Street sent shock waves running, and his ears rang. He listened, as intently as his hurt ears allowed. The throb of engines seemed to come from a greater distance, but in the street the smoke was thickening rapidly. Taking a big breath, he ran across the street and looked back up at the roof of the building housing the canteen. There was no sign of its being on fire, though it was outlined against a scarlet sky. The buildings on either side also showed no hint of fire.

He raced back across the road and down the steps again to the shelter. He reported, panting, "T' smoke's nothing, as far as we're concerned," and then paused to get his breath while another series of detonations drowned him out. Emmie felt her courage draining from her and she and Doris clung to each other. He continued, "There's some big fires not far away – and I could hear machine guns for a minute. Bloody Boche going for the firemen." He looked at the anxious faces surrounding him. "If we try to move, like as not we'll walk into more trouble. I'd say stay here." He sat down suddenly on a bench, aware that he was no longer as young as he had been. He looked down at his shabby boots, while men slowly resumed their seats.

When his heart had stopped racing, he said diffidently, "Think I'll walk up Lord Street and see what's to do. T' rescue squads must be hard-pressed at the back there. Anybody want to come?"

The men stopped their subdued gossiping and looked uneasily at Dick, and Dick said, "Them as has wives and kids, maybe you shouldn't. A couple of you is perhaps like me – you can please yourselves."

"My family is killed in Antwerp," said a melancholy Dutch voice from the far end of the room. "Who to rescue? This is shops and offices round here. Nobody here." He got up, a big, handsome blond man towering over most of those present.

"There's firewatchers and caretakers in every building," replied Dick simply. "Young girls, some of them watchers is."

Two men in naval uniform stood up and the four of them, without a further word, eased their way through to the staircase. Not to be outdone by the Royal Navy, two merchant seamen followed them.

Mrs Robinson said brightly, "As soon as the raid is over, we'll see if we can clean the canteen up, ready for business tomorrow."

The women nodded tired agreement. Emmie was stiff with fatigue and the enforced idleness; the worst thing about air raids was, she thought, that you couldn't hit back.

The electric light went out. Emmie gave a frightened squeak and Doris drew in her breath quickly. The glowing ends of lighted cigarettes looked like red eyes staring in the darkness. A man laughed shakily. A voice from the gloom said bitterly, "If that isn't the bottom!"

There was a jingle of keys and change, as Mrs Robinson rummaged in the depths of her shabby crocodile-skin handbag. "I've got a match somewhere. There should be some candles in the drawer of the table."

Someone lit a match and a male voice from near the floor said, "I've got a torch, Missus."

The beam seemed as brilliant as a searchlight.

"Oh, thank you," she cried, stumbling over feet as, guided by the torch, she went to the table. She snapped the drawer open. "Really!" she exclaimed. "This is too bad. Somebody has stolen both the candles and the matches. There's not even a stump here."

There was an angry murmur through the room. Petty theft was a way of life in Liverpool. Now, with everything in short supply, it could cause real problems. The owner of the torch, however, said magnanimously, "Anybody as needs to move, tell me and I put me torch on."

Batteries were harder to obtain than candles, so when a young voice said, "Thanks, friend," it expressed the feelings of everybody.

Listening to the clamour outside, while sitting in total darkness was far worse, thought Emmie. The minutes seemed longer; the noise wrapped one closer. People tended not to talk; instead they huddled together for comfort.

Gwen had told her of a woman in the next street, who had clung to a perfect stranger in the street's unlighted shelter, while they sat out the Christmas Eve raid, the year before. In their terrible fear, they had become sexually aroused, and now she was pregnant by a man she had never seen. Shocking, Gwen called it; but David, with unexpected understanding, had said that it was Mother Nature's way of seeing that people who had died in a disaster were replaced.

Gwen had responded tartly, "More likely they didn't know right from wrong."

As she hugged Doris, Emmie wondered if she herself were pregnant, or whether the change of life was making its presence felt. Though frightened, in her secret heart she hoped that she was still young enough for a bun to be in the oven, Robert's little one.

"I hope Robbie's sailed and out of this rumpus," she whispered to Doris.

"You might get a letter tomorrer," Doris suggested. Her own heart ached at the thought; even the letters her dead husband had written to her when they were courting had been lost, with him, in their burned-out home.

The racket outside seemed to be slackening, the explosions further away. "Sounds like they might be doin' Bootle or Seaforth," suggested a disembodied voice.

"God spare us," exploded Doris. "Haven't we had enough up there?"

iv

The women stood forlornly at the top of the shelter stairs. The All-Clear had sounded; the noise abated. Through the gaping front windows, the whole town seemed to glow, the shattered room lighted up as if a good coal fire was burning in the old-fashioned grate. As they moved forward, glass and china crunched beneath their feet. The counter, which normally held the tea and coffee samovars, flanked by plates of buns and sandwiches, had been swept clear. Both samovars lay on their sides on the floor, silent humps in pools of black liquid, their copper exteriors reflecting the dancing light from outside.

The light from outside did not penetrate the kitchen,

so Mrs Starr struck a match. "Ah, that's better," she cried.

Though very dusty, the kitchen was practically undisturbed. The telephone, which Emmie had put on the sill to hold down the blackout curtains of the small window, had fallen on to the table beneath the window. Emmie lifted the curtain to peer out and was surprised that, at least there, there was still glass to look through.

Mrs Starr, one of the volunteers, asked Mrs Robinson a little diffidently, "Would you mind if I phoned my son to say I am all right?"

Mrs Robinson looked up from her task of setting out candles and lighting them. "Of course not," she replied.

The phone was dead. Mrs Starr sighed, and looked at her watch. It was nearly 3 a.m.

An air raid warden paused by the open front door. "Anybody here?" he shouted. Drawn by the sudden flare of the candles, he clumped towards the kitchen. His face was gaunt, eyes burning with fatigue. A striped pyjama collar stuck out untidily from the neck of his uniform.

"Are we safe from the fires?" Mrs Robinson asked, after greeting him.

"Aye. There's a firewatcher on the roof – young Dolly – she'll tell you if fires out t' back are spreading this side."

"What's burning?" Mrs Starr asked.

"Church House. It'll be gutted. Too far gone to save. And the Corn Exchange and the White Star building – God knows how many others. Bootle's calling for fire-engines out there, but they can't spare none from here." He heaved a sigh. "Must go check next door. Ta-ra." He crunched his way back across the strewn canteen floor and they heard him curse as he caught his boot against one of the recumbent samovars and it clanged like a bell.

v

While Emmie and Gwen cleaned up their home and David laid new waterpipes in the Royal Infirmary, Conor walked round his district to assess the damage of the previous night.

"Rain'll do more damage than t'bombs," he told the already very depressed families, who a few streets away from his own home had lost their roofs. "I'll get you some tarps to lay over the rafters."

He returned to the post and put in a request for tarpaulin. Then he retrieved the front and back doors of the oldest couple affected, and helped the old man hang them again.

From nearby homes still comparatively undamaged, older women, silent, hands clasped over their stomachs, drifted over to watch and then to help their stricken neighbours shovel plaster and soot out of their chaotic little homes. Children, too small for school, found jam butties thrust into their hands by strange, smiling women. Buckets of water and trays of tea were lugged from several streets away, where water was still available. Friendships which were to last a lifetime were made between tearful outbursts from women beginning to quiver from delayed shock. The acute shortage of young, strong men to help was remarked upon and an extra tear was shed for those of them fighting in Greece or on a warship somewhere in the

Mediterranean. And slowly, painfully slowly, some order was restored.

While he munched a very dry sandwich, back at the post, Conor wrote out his reports. After that, seething with rage, he went to see the bitch who had refused to produce the street's stirrup-pump, at a time when the whole road had been littered with incendiaries.

God, how he needed a drink. He seemed to be floating, rather than walking. Lightheaded, that was the word. And what a fool he had been to put at the back of the cellar of the post the half dozen bottles of whiskey he had lifted from a lorry unwise enough to park in the district a couple of days before. Now, the post was as busy as a tram terminus and he could not retrieve them without its being noticed. If he had found a better place for them, he could have had a drink right now and flogged the rest for good money.

He slammed down his fountain pen and went home.

With one side of her face still slightly swollen from the blow he had given her, Ellen was in no mood to be conciliatory. Practically the whole of the family's bacon ration piled on his plate, however, suggested that the storm might be passing. He was too tired, too overwhelmed by other people's troubles laid upon his shoulders, to make an effort to break the silence between them, and as soon as he had mopped up the last bit of grease from his plate with a piece of bread, he announced that he was going to bed.

Within minutes, he was sound asleep, and did not hear Ellen shouting exasperatedly at Patrick's back, as he went out of the front door.

"I'm not going to bed at seven o'clock, no matter how many raids there are," he had said obstinately. "I'm

73

goin' to see a pal." And he had wandered out into the deserted street, with a lazy grin at her over his shoulder.

He slipped through the soft spring evening, to the unfinished, roofless air raid shelter where he had taken Mari and where she had reluctantly promised to meet him again. He hung around outside it for nearly an hour, but Mari did not come.

A thoroughly scared Mari was certain that the previous night's raid had been arranged by God particularly to punish her.

He walked back home, clenched fists in trouser pockets, shoulders hunched, muttering angrily under his breath. Nothing but a stuck-up Judy, that's her. Wait till he caught her again. Yet, beneath his rage, he felt no true desire to harm her; only a craven fear that she would not come again; a young Romeo who had not yet managed to persuade his Juliet to fall in love with him. Wait till he was a Spitfire pilot, he reassured himself, with embroidered wings on his tunic; then she'd come crawling, and he might just condescend to take her to a dance.

At half-past ten, he was sitting despondently on the basement steps, listening to the guns and whistling to himself, while a fearful Ruby crouched close to him, pulling nervously at her thick, black fringe. Their sleepy father had tumbled back into his overalls and gone down to the post.

vi

Dress Materials at Blackler's had, that Friday afternoon, been busy. Women were buying dress

74

lengths, in anticipation of clothes being rationed; Gwen herself had several such lengths stored away in the mahogany chest of drawers brought from Emmie's home. Out of her wages, she was also holding a little money in order to buy two pairs of silk stockings, which a girl from Hosiery had told her, during her tea break, had at last arrived.

She was surprised when her supervisor sent her over to the Dress Department to help out.

"They're rushed off their feet," she explained. "People wanting mourning clothes."

When, homeward bound, she descended from the tram at the corner of her street, her feet ached abominably. She had sold so many black dresses that she felt deeply dispirited. At one point, she had been positively thankful to be faced with a giggling 15-year-old who wanted a pale blue bridesmaid's dress.

"Me sister's boy friend's got a forty-eight-hour pass. Comin 'ome Tuesday night. Me mam's nearly out of her mind tryin' to get everything ready for a wedding on Wednesday mornin'." The girl's flippant elation had made several sad-faced women turn on her with reproving murmurs of "Really! At this time?" Unable to relate to the grief of strangers, she had gone away happy, with a fluff of blue net carefully packed in tissue paper.

"Phew!" Gwen groaned, as she tottered through the twilight. The sky was still an unnaturally bright pink, but she was too tired to care. She thought only of her clean bed, with David, solid and reliable, snoring on his side of it.

"Where's your dad?" she asked Mari, as she took off her Sunday hat, black velveteen with a bunch of feathers

75

held by a *diamanté* brooch, and laid it carefully in its box.

The girl lifted a wan face from gloomy contemplation of her arithmetic book and wiped her pen nib with a piece of blotting paper. "I don't know, Mum. I'm scared. It's late for him."

"Ach, he's probably doin' overtime. What did you do with his bit of fish pie?"

"I kept it hot for a while. Then it got so dried out in the oven, I put it back in the pantry."

"Good girl."

Good girl? Mari chewed the end of her plait nervously, and sighed, and tried to forget the extraordinary sensations within her.

About midnight, David staggered in and thankfully plunked down his heavy tool-box.

"Worked late and then I had to walk home," he told them as, regardless of the guns roaring outside, they scuttled round to get him his supper. "There's a proper raid on down town. The sound of the planes diving, as I come along, give me the willies, they did. Hope our Em's all right."

Gwen had forgotten entirely about Emmie and now she paused, tea caddy in hand, a twinge of conscience striking her.

"Anyway, we can't do anything about her," he went on practically, as he sat down to his fish pie. "We should go to bed. They're not bombing round here – too busy with the town to bother us." He turned to Mari and said with a grin, "Your room's a deal safer with the window being boarded up. Maybe young Patrick did you a good turn."

Mari stared at him for a second, her smile frozen on

her face. Then she said diffidently, "I suppose he did."

Gwen climbed nervously into her bed and pulled the clothes over her head, to shut out the sound of chugging aeroplane engines. Two hours of sitting on the basement steps had made her back ache and to lie down was a blessed relief. David put his head on his pillow and began to snore immediately. Mari lay quietly in the stuffy darkness of her room and wondered what had really happened to her. Could you have a baby if a boy touched you?

None of them heard Emmie's flagging footsteps, when she came in. Groaning sleepily, they got up again at six o'clock in the morning and were astonished to find her sound asleep in David's chair, a cold cup of tea beside her on the bookshelf.

SATURDAY, 3 MAY 1941

Gwen stared unbelievingly at the shattered windows of Blackler's store. She seethed with indignation. An attack on Blackler's was, she felt, an attack on her personally. It was *her* store.

She glanced along its usually immaculate frontage. Little piles of swept-up glass stood waiting to be shovelled away. The gaping holes which had once been windows filled with merchandise labelled with large, cheerful notices of special bargains, had been cleared; only one or two, where the glass, by some fluke, remained intact, still bravely displayed for the benefit of the weekend invasion of shoppers from Wales a collection of special offers.

And the Welsh were coming in in force. Dressed in their best, they came by train and bus not only to buy but to make holiday, joining shoppers from the Liverpool suburbs, in touring the damage wreaked on the city and viewing the roaring fires. People from slum and suburb alike walked into cafés and grocery shops whose fronts had been blown out, and stood around feasting on food not yet salvaged. Rowdy groups, dodging the already harassed police, calmly looted anything they fancied, laughing and joking and getting drunk on wines and spirits they found in the grocery stores. Not a few owners defended their little broken shops with cricket bats, battered symbols of integrity.

As, later on, she snipped lengths of material for a customer who spoke, with disgust, of the behaviour of a group of hooligans she had seen, Gwen said bitterly,

"You'd think we was a circus, the way they gape – and a free-for-all. Rob their own mothers, they would."

"Aye," the customer agreed heavily. "Who'd have believed it?"

ii

David usually finished work at twelve noon on Saturdays, and Gwen had left a dish of stew in the oven for his midday meal. It grew dryer and dryer and finally shrivelled up on the plate, because David had not, that morning, been pursuing the incredible intricacies of the plumbing of the Royal Infirmary. He had, instead, been pounced on by his supervisor, immediately upon his arrival, and had been sent by taxi out to Bootle, together with his mate, Arthur, a grizzled ancient, back in the work force after four years of retirement.

"Bloody chaos out there," the supervisor had told them. "No water. Gas lines flaring up in the streets. Electric's out. Report to the town hall. They'll tell you where to go."

They were joined by two electricians, who had also been impounded, and as they sat in the taxi, tool-boxes rattling in the luggage compartment by the driver, they looked out in astonishment and no little trepidation at increasing turmoil, the further north they proceeded.

The driver had to pick his way through miles of littered streets made muddy by burst water lines and, in places, lacings of fire-hoses temporarily abandoned for lack of water pressure. Timber yards crackled and smoked on both sides of the road, the draught of the flames making it hard for the driver to keep the taxi stable, for a scarifying few minutes. Occasionally, they would be redirected by police or special constables, to detour a mass of masonry spread across a street.

When they finally found the streets they were to work in, after being redirected by a series of city officials, they stood for a moment bewildered, their tools at their feet, wondering where in earth to start. Civil defence workers of every kind toiled amid the havoc, while the homeless scrambled over the debris in an effort to pick out some belongings which might still be usable. In desperate efforts to help families still entombed, some of them got into the way of rescue workers cautiously digging through piles of bricks, mortar and shattered wood, to get at victims for whom there was little hope. Others stood in forlorn groups, an occasional sob indicating some poor soul for whom it was all too much; still others were unnaturally cheerful, thankful to have survived; the true hardship of their situation would hit them later.

A hundred yards up the street, a cracked gas line gave way. A white sheet of flame roared upwards, its deadly heat threatening further damage. Rescuers and inhabitants scrambled over debris to a safer distance.

"Good God!" exclaimed Arthur, and turned to run.

David caught his arm. His breath came in frightened gasps, but he said, "It could blow the whole street up. Better find the valve. See if we can turn it off." He grabbed a tool from his box and followed by a protesting Arthur ran towards the explosion. While wardens shouted to them to come back, they searched likely spots for the valve they needed, and, within a minute or two, found it. A quick twist and the flame subsided. David stood very still for a moment, holding on to Arthur, while the pain in his chest subsided, a shivering unsung hero, like many others that day.

Soon, watched anxiously by housewives, black-shawled against the morning coolness, David and Arthur were set to work by a city hall official to reconnect a major break in a water line. The women were desperate for water to clean their damaged homes and wash the dirt off their children and themselves. The Women's Voluntary Service brought food both to workers and watchers, and they stood around in the street, their children about them, while they thankfully sipped mugs of tea. Their voices were shrill with nervous tension and they wound their shawls tightly round themselves for comfort. To David, it seemed particularly wicked that people so painfully poverty-stricken should have their tiny, crowded homes broken open like eggs. "And the men at sea – or struggling to keep the docks working," David muttered angrily to Arthur.

There was no question of going home that night; the need of them in Bootle was too grave.

As twilight approached, he and Arthur paused to stretch themselves and eat the sandwiches brought to them by the indefatigable WVS canteen staff. They both became aware of a general movement in the neighbourhood. Women, pushing perambulators or pushchairs loaded with children and bedding, were so numerous as to form a long procession in the now partially tidied up street.

"Where do you think they're goin'?" he asked Arthur.

"Walkin' out to Huyton, to sleep in t' fields, I expect. It's a deal safer'n staying here overnight."

David nodded. Except for an occasional shout to a child to mind himself, the procession was strangely quiet. There was a dull acceptance in the passing faces, framed in dusty, tousled hair. Dragging boots made a slow shuffling sound on the gritty street.

"They'll be back in t' mornin', bright and early no doubt," remarked Arthur, "to check on their homes — and sent t' kids to school – if the school's still there."

iii

Mari and her friend, Dorothy, went to the Saturday, children's programme at the cinema that afternoon and then went home to Dorothy's house for tea.

While his mother sat on the front step, nursing Michael and enjoying the sunshine, and Ruby and Nora played skipping on the pavement, Patrick sloped around the alleyways, hoping to find Mari. Unsuccessful, he irritably teased his father's fighting cocks and for his pains got a long scratch on the back of his right hand.

Conor Donnelly's area had been mercifully free from incidents on the previous night, so while he had a comparatively quiet day, he wandered down to the Hercy Dock to see if he could find an American sailor off a tanker, with nylons or lipsticks for sale. Both fetched good prices on the black market.

iv

As Gwen bustled into her home about eight o'clock that evening, she felt more energetic than she had done for some days. A few hours of good sleep, despite the noise of the raid, had restored her, and she had enjoyed at Blackler's the close feeling of unity amongst her companions, engendered by their joint dislike of the large influx of sightseers and ill-intentioned riff-raff into the town.

Mari was sitting alone, by the fire, slowly turning the heel of a sock, one of a pair she was knitting as a contribution to a parcel being made up for the men of the King's Regiment. Two of the girls in the class had fathers serving in it, stationed at Hull. Mari was a good knitter, having been taught by her mother as soon as she could hold a pair of butcher's skewers and a ball of wool.

"Yer dad not in?" Gwen inquired, as she once more returned her best hat to its box.

"No." Mari paused, needle in stitch.

Mari was feeling a little less panic-stricken about Patrick. She had stuck close to Dorothy all day, and after tea they had rearranged Dorothy's doll's house and put up new curtains in it. Mr Hale, Dorothy's father, who had to go to a chapel meeting, had kindly walked her home, since it was on his way. They walked slowly because he limped; Dorothy said he had been wounded in the First World War at a terrible place called Passchendaele, and, as had sometimes happened in her grandfather's house, Mari was reminded that the results of war stayed on and on, long after the battles were finished. Did it mean, she wondered fearfully, that her life would be different after the war? Would she, all her life, drag a foot or, much worse, be jeered at because she had been disfigured? She nearly choked, when she remembered that her grandfather had once told her that he had a friend kept permanently in hospital because he had almost no face.

She had thought about this, as she sat quietly knitting; it was all mixed up with a hodge-podge of ideas about Patrick. To her relief, her figure had not swelled up as she knew a pregnant woman's did, so she had begun to think that being caressed all over by a boy's exploring fingers did not produce a baby, and that was a relief; she had heard of girls who had committed suicide because they were pregnant and did not have a proper husband.

The explosive feelings that Patrick had aroused in her must mean something, though. She longed to ask her mother about it, but dared not. Could such an exciting feeling really be wicked? She wondered if she could ask Aunt Emmie; after all, she was engaged and must know something about it.

As Gwen put the kettle on for tea, she was not particularly worried about David; he had done a lot of overtime recently. Both mother and daughter jumped apprehensively, however, when someone thumped on the front door.

"Your dad? Hurt?" Gwen exclaimed.

As they ran along the passage, getting in each other's way in their sudden sense of urgency, they heard Conor Donnelly outside, shouting, "Mrs Thomas! Mrs Thomas!" Gwen reckoned that if the warden brought the news, it must be bad. She flung the door open, letting out a little light from the candle on the hall table.

"Get in, get in," Conor ordered testily. "Enough light to guide them from Berlin."

He hastened over the doorstep and shut the door behind him.

"What's to do?" Gwen asked anxiously, while Mari's blank little face went whiter than usual.

"Och, it's all right," he answered, seeing their frightened faces. "Yer husband rang the post, from Bootle, to say he mayn't be back till tomorrer night."

"What? Bootle? What's he doin' there?"

"It's terrible out there, missus. They need every man they can get."

"How'll he get his dinner?"

"Same as the firemen and everyone else workin' out there. From the WVS canteen, I 'spect."

"He's too old to be gallivanting round out there. He needs his sleep." Gwen's voice was angry.

Conor's deep blue eyes registered such scorn that Gwen quailed slightly. "So do we all. We're none of us youngsters, Mrs Thomas."

She was disconcerted at the snub, and her irritation at this man and his slovenly family increased. She said tightly, "Well, thank you for bringing the message. I don't know why he didn't phone earlier."

"Phones out of order, like everything else," he replied, fully aware of her distaste of him.

Gwen went slowly back to the living room and sat down on a footstool close to the fire. It was wasteful to have a fire in May, but she justified it by cooking on it, and now, suddenly, she was grateful for its comforting warmth. For the first time in her life, the idea that she might be widowed occurred to her; Conor's description of the dire straits of Bootle had struck home; accidents happened in such awful situations.

While Mari made tea and toast for their supper, the virtues of her patient lumbering husband surfaced in her mind. She remembered, with a pang, the sturdy Welsh youth who had proposed to her, as they walked soberly in Princes Park after chapel. They had had to wait seven

88

years before they could afford to be married, and, sipping tea beside the fire, she wished they had not wasted their youth. Why, she wondered bitterly, had she been so coldly virtuous? And now it could all end in a holocaust in Bootle.

She and Mari had lain in bed a scant hour, when the air raid warning dragged them out again. "We'll get dressed in the living room," Gwen said resignedly. "It'll be safer down there."

"Poor Aunt Emmie," Mari exclaimed. "Stuck down town again."

v

Ellen Donnelly blasted furiously all them Jerries and their ilk, as she, too, that Saturday night shepherded her family down the cellar steps.

During the day, she had hauled a mattress down into the dank basement and on this she persuaded Ruby, Nora and Brendy to lie down to sleep. It was not quite so safe as sitting on the stairs, but as she remarked, "Beggars can't be choosers."

Patrick sat moodily on the top step, watching his mother nurse Michael to sleep again. The candlelight caught the white hairs amongst her brown mop and deepened the lines on her shiny red face. He felt a sudden twinge of pain that his mother was growing older. Though she was always demanding to know where he had been and what he had been doing, he loved her with a passion that frightened him sometimes. He was inordinately jealous of his father, and, when his father struck her, he boiled with inward anger that he was too small and cowardly to defend her. When I'm bigger, I will, he always told himself. He resented the succession of babies that occupied her lap, and only Ruby, eleven months younger than him, escaped being bullied by him whenever he was in a bad temper.

The noise of the anti-aircraft guns began to shake the old house.

vi

Unaware of the frantic clean-up done by candlelight after the previous night's raid, a dozen men were lounging round the tables of the sailors' canteen, gossiping amid the usual cloud of tobacco smoke.

Mrs Robinson arrived at the same time as Emmie. She was carrying two parcels and Emmie took them from her. "These are heavy," she exclaimed.

"Crockery oddments, my dear. After last night, we're dreadfully short. These are a donation from Lewis's – I went in to see them this morning."

In the kitchen, Peggie Evans, another paid member of the staff, was tidying up the last of the muddle from the lunchtime rush. "'T' fish is finished," she told Emmie and Mrs Robinson, "'T' butcher brought plenty of sausage, though, for tonight. And there's still a lot o' dried egg."

As she put on her overall, Emmie told her how the fish had been covered with dust the previous night. "At first we was goin' to throw it out. Then Mrs Robinson said what waste. So we washed it very carefully and put it in the larder. Did you have any complaints?"

"Never a word. Deep fried, there'd be nought the matter with it." She took her coat off a hook and her handbag out of a drawer. "Was I ever glad I wasn't here last night. It must've been awful."

"I were scared out of me wits," admitted Emmie. "I got a proper laugh, though, out of the note you've pinned on the sandbags round the door. 'Open for business – very open.' "

"Aye. I thought t' lads 'd believe we'd given up on 'em, with the shutters closed, like."

"You know we had the till cleaned out, during the raid?"

"No?"

"Somebody took the whole night's takings. Must've done it while we was in the shelter. We didn't stop to lock the front door."

"Stinking buggers," said Peggie forcefully, as she clapped a blue beret on her head. "Tara-well."

Doris did not arrive. She lay dead in the arms of the seaman who had taught her to smoke, under the wreckage of a shop doorway which had suddenly collapsed on them, taking both their lives while they made love.

A white-haired grocer's wife, Mrs Atkins, and the silent, elegant Lady Mentmore were redeployed to cover the work. "Perhaps she'll phone later," suggested Emmie.

"Is the phone working?" Mrs Robinson looked harried. She was bone-tired, her plump, middle-aged body refusing to run at its usual pace.

Emmie went to the table by the window and cautiously lifted the receiver and put it to her ear. "It's still dead," she announced.

"Oh, dear! What a nuisance! The crater down the street must be responsible for that. I saw the Post

Office Telephones van there, as I came in."

Mrs Atkins looked up from her carrot scraping. "It really was an awful night. And it could have been worse. I heard this morning that they were worried about a munition ship called the *Malakand* in Huskisson Dock. It's being loaded for the Middle East. And with the fires and that being so bad up the north end – poor Bootle – they were mortally afraid it would explode."

Emmie froze, the fork with which she was pricking sausages poised to stab. "The *Malakand*?" she exclaimed in horror. "My Robbie's on that." She turned a stricken face towards the carrot scraper. "He never told me it had munitions in it."

Mrs Atkins soothed, "Well, nothing's happened to it yet. Perhaps it will sail today."

Emmie nodded assent and slowly and heavily she pricked the neat pink rows of sausages. She tried not to weep. To sail the Med with ammunition in the hold! Even if he got out of port safely, it could be a death-warrant! She wanted to scream 'No' to God. Was He really almighty? She wanted to faint, to escape the fear which pierced her. But she could not, must not. In a war, she must not give way. Quietly, she went on with her work and missed the pitying glances of Mrs Atkins and the countess. The countess said practically, to Emmie's back, "I think we all need a cup of tea."

As she filled the four cups from the samovar, she herself was not feeling very well. The previous night, an incendiary, apparently a dud, had fallen through the thatched roof of her house, and it had taken the combined efforts of her two elderly maids and herself to lift it out of the water tank into which it had fallen. They had thrown it out of the attic window on to the lawn, where it had unexpectedly exploded. A small incident, not worth mentioning, but it had tired her. She yawned behind a heavily beringed hand, as she added lots of sugar to Emmie's tea; she understood that the lower classes enjoyed plenty of sugar.

vii

Saturday night, when you should be down at the local, sitting by the fire and telling funny stories over a pint of bitter; instead you were stuck in a sandbagged shop labelled A.R.P., listening to the pandemonium in the skies and hoping that nothing fell on you. The strain was telling on Conor Donnelly. He told himself irritably that he had had it up to here. And to add to it all, he had quarrelled with Ellen over a drop of whiskey – and she was still as sour as yesterday's milk. He went to the door and glanced up at the sky.

The brilliance of the flares had put the stars out, and the air smelled as if a million rubber tyres were burning. The shriek of bombs descending on the flaming city centre, about a mile down the hill, could hardly be heard above the concerted roar of their impact, the drone of heavy engines and the scream of night fighters as they dived. Nearer, in the park, the anti-aircraft guns kept up a steady barrage at the bellies of the bombers, which glistened like slugs, in the light of darting flames.

Inside the post, three women wardens were placidly waiting for a tin kettle of water to boil on a primus stove, their imperturbability belied by their ghostly faces. A grey-haired voluntary warden, Montagu Smith, who came in each night there was a raid, was snatching a nap on a camp-bed. In the daytime, he was the manager of the bank round the corner.

Conor had always thought that anyone who had a bank account, never mind worked in a bank, must be hopelessly stuck up. But this pot-bellied man had won his admiration the previous November. He had crawled into the shifting debris of a house, to hold the hand of a dreadfully injured old man until a doctor crawled in, too, to give the victim an injection to ease the pain while they got him out. Then they had worked the remainder of the night together, under enemy machine-gun fire.

The half-washed Irish labourer and the well-shaven polite banker supported each other. Conor never gave himself credit for the friendliness he exuded, the enthusiasm with which he would do a good turn. Montague – our Mont, to all the wardens – had a quick, orderly mind, able to size up the immediate needs in some of the horrid situations which they faced together.

"G' us a cuppa tea, Glynis, luv," Conor asked one of the women. He was hungry. In a day or two, Ellen would get over her sulks and boil up a good stew. Meanwhile, he could whistle for it. A short burst of machine-gun fire directly overhead made everyone duck instinctively. He wished suddenly he had made it up with Ellen. What was a drop of whiskey anyway, in a world where one bullet could finish him? He chewed his thumb uneasily while Glynis made the tea.

Glynis Hughes eased her tin hat further back on her head and grinned up at him. She was a small, brown-skinned woman, suggesting descent from the little people who roamed Britain before the Celts arrived. Her husband was serving in the South Lancashires and she was temporarily living nearby with her mother. She worked in a factory which made aircraft parts and she made many a lewd joke about her production of joysticks. She was used to coping with the appetite of a labourer in a steelworks and she still shamelessly bought any food she could find on the black market. Now she asked, "Like a Spam sandwich?"

"Ah would, if you can spare it."

She took out from a shopping bag a white, confectioner's paper bag and from this she carefully drew out a sandwich two inches thick with a thin slice of Spam in it. "I brought some bikkies for you girls," she told her companions, "Chocky ones."

The other two women's faces lit up. "Mm. Where did you get them from?" They, too, were housewives permanently scrounging through the shops for extra food. To earn the money for it, they worked as labourers, cleaning oil drums at a petrol installation.

Glynis giggled. "Ask no questions, you'll be told no lies."

Conor wolfed the proffered sandwich and a chocolate biscuit. He felt much better and walked outside to take another look at what was happening.

The sky was a brilliant pink, with rolling billows of smoke making rosy cushions above him. There was no one, not even a cat, in the street. He went back into the tiny shop and leaned against the wall by the telephone girl, to gossip.

He was jolted upright by a fast puffing sound, closer than the general roar, then a pause, while everyone held their breath. A heavy crump and everyone breathed out.

"Land-mine," Conor said. "Unexploded."

"Must have fallen in the park," Glynis commented, relief exuding from her.

"Here comes another," squeaked the telephonist, as she laid her head on her table and clasped her arms over her tin hat. The trainlike sound came again and Conor tensed.

An enormous explosion shook the old shop, reverberating round them in swelling waves. The telephone girl was nearly lifted off her chair, and cracks ran up the grubby walls. Mont was on his feet in a split second, clapping his helmet to his head. "My God!" he exclaimed.

A colossal growl, like that of some huge animal, indicated the fall of heavy masonry; it was followed by a rapid tattoo of smaller pieces on to the roof and into the street.

"The tenement?" breathed Glynis through chattering teeth. "The Dwellings?"

"Could be," Mont replied, as he loosened his torch from his belt. All of them dreaded a direct hit on the huge five-storey tenement nearby. It was built in a circle, round a communal yard, and was packed with young families.

Conor had already gone. He ran madly down the pink-lit street and turned left. He was brought up short by an impenetrable cloud of dust. Other than the heavy grumble from the skies, there was a weird silence.

Then, from beyond the dust cloud, came scream after scream of pain and panic. "Oh, Jesus, help us," shrieked a woman's voice.

Doors of the row houses close to the warden banged open, as shaken tenants came rushing out. Mont panted up to Conor, and said, "I'll tell Josie to phone R. and P. We're going to need a lot of help."

Conor cleared his throat and spat. "Better have a

closer look first. Could be only the houses facin', not the tenement itself."

They both took out handkerchiefs to cover their noses from the cloying dust; it was so thick that the beams of their torches were reflected back, as if they faced a wall. They turned the lights down to their feet and picked their way round huge slabs of concrete and piles of bricks, interspersed with threatening electric wires. The dust, now mixed with a strong smell of gas, made Mont cough. He tripped over a broken beam and fell, barking his shins and hands painfully, and got up again. Behind him, Conor could hear other people scrambling over the wreckage; they were shouting to each other, as they converged, and above and beyond the sound of their voices came the screams of the half-crushed.

"'Allo, la," Conor called. "I'm the warden. All men come to me." Dear God, send me some wi' a bit o' savvy, he added to himself. Judging by the curses behind him, he was not going to have to *ask* people to help tonight, which was a welcome change. He hoped Tom Massey was on duty – biggest bloody rozzer in the whole police force. He knew he could use a dozen heavyweights for this job.

A shrieking woman blundered into him. She clutched his arms and shook him. "Me lads – me lads!" she yelled into his face. She was naked, her clothing blown off her, and long, black hair flicked across his mouth, as she half turned to look back at the carnage slowly emerging from the fog.

"Hold on there, luv. Did it hit clean on The Dwellings?"

"Aye, into t' middle yard." She clawed at him. "For Jesus' sake, get me boys out."

Throughout the raid, Conor and Mont, with the Rescue Squad, sweated and cursed their way into the ruins, sickened frequently, occasionally triumphant when they brought out the living, until in the early morning, a filthy, bloodstained Conor went back to the post to write out his report. New orphans, new widows, new cripples and a band of homeless. And what for? What was it in truth all about? God's curse on them all. He rubbed his torn and dirty hands on his overalls and reached for his pencil.

viii

Arms round each other, Gwen and Mari cowered on the cellar steps, certain that each strident screech above their heads would be the last thing they would ever hear.

The petrifying crash which destroyed The Dwellings made both of them scream. Tinkling glass and a rushing draught told them that the windows had blown in.

"Me sitting room! Me aspidistra!" Gwen wailed. Her Holy of Holies would be exposed to the weather – and thieves!

Mari began to cry.

The roar of the attack on the city centre was undiminished, but locally it was as if everything held its breath, as if the explosion of the land-mine had taken everything with it. Gwen and Mari loosed their grip on each other and raised their heads.

The quiet was broken by a frantic banging on the back door. "Missus, missus! Come quick," a boy's voice cried.

Patrick! Mari scrambled to her feet.

98

Her mother caught her by her bare ankle. "You stay here, miss. I'll go."

In the pink light coming from between the flapping remains of the blackout curtains, it was easy to see the familiar terrain of the brick-tiled kitchen. She flung open the back door. Five shadows tumbled in together, wailing like forgotten babies.

Gwen surveyed five shocked faces, in the uncertain light. "For Heaven's sake, what's to do?"

"It's Mam. She's hurt real bad," Patrick gulped. "Coom and help her."

Gwen swallowed. "Where is she?"

"She's lyin' by t' front step. Ah can't move her. Coom quick." The usually bumptious Patrick was beside himself, his face ashen.

Crowded close to him, the other children broke into loud howls. Ruby led the hullabaloo. Her mother, her only defence against the terror of the raids, was lying inert at the door of her home; and Ruby was convinced that all the houses would collapse any minute and she would again be buried.

Despite Gwen's own nervousness and confusion, the sickly smell of the children's unwashed bodies penetrated to her. Repulsed by it, she snapped at them, "Now you be quiet. I'll get a candle and go and have a look at your mam."

As the candle was lit, the howls tailed off into small sobs. The flame showed the small, barefoot crew in more detail. They all had white rivulets down their dirty faces.

For safety's sake, Gwen decided that the children could not return to their home with her; the gunfire was too heavy. She lit another candle and handed it to

Patrick. "Sit on the cellar steps with Mari – all of you. Get a move on, now. It's not safe up here. And mind your feet on the floor – there's glass all over. I'll be back in a minute."

Ruby, dragging a protesting Michael, led the way timidly. Patrick wiped the tears from his face, put on a defiant air and stood on the top step, leaning one shoulder against the wall to stop himself shaking.

Mari half smiled at him as she looked up the steps, but he did not even glance at her. She felt unexpectedly hurt. She turned her attention to Ruby. Gosh, how she smelled.

The clangour of fire-engine bells came clearly through the roar of the blitz, as Gwen, candle in hand, hesitated in her front doorway. What would she find next door?

A string of incendiaries slithered down a short distance away. Vicious pencils of flak suddenly peppered the road in front of her. She bobbed back into the hall. The candle blew out. With it still in her hand, she crept down the two carefully whitened steps of her own front entrance, as if by making no sound she could outwit the German pilots. Then she turned into the immediately adjacent front doorway of the Donnellys and stared into their hall. In dismay, she dropped the dead candle and it rattled away on the pavement.

Just inside, Ellen half lay, half sat, against the weathered door. One hand was flung across her breast. Her eyes, wide with shock, stared at the wall opposite her.

"Oh, my goodness!" Gwen took the two steps in one stride and knelt down by the woman. "Mrs Donnelly? Are you hurt?"

There was no reply. Gwen put out a careful hand and

touched her face. She did not move. The body was surrounded by the effluvium of human excrement, and a primeval fear of death clutched at Gwen's throat. In an agony of indecision, she glanced up at the small piece of sky she could see above the roofs opposite; in the flushed torment there, the battle raged on. Her breath came in short pants and she wanted to run away, out of Liverpool, away from the dirty horde on her cellar steps, away from this scarifying hulk of a woman. But there was nowhere to run to; even the street across the doorstep was a death-trap.

She took a big breath and pulled herself together. How did one make absolutely certain that a person was dead? She might still be alive – in shock – wounded only.

A resonant bang nearby, followed immediately by a shower of bricks and mortar on the doorstep, galvanised Gwen into action. Still kneeling, she leaned forward and tried to heave Ellen further into the hall. Ellen's arms flopped and her whole body reeled towards Gwen's tiny frame. In horror, Gwen let go and scrambled to her feet. Ellen slumped to the floor.

Doing her best not to vomit, and risking the descent of further missiles, she ran a few steps to the nearest street shelter and called hopefully through the doorway, "Anybody there?" But only a faint echo came from its stinking darkness.

She ran back to her own house and scuttled through the length of it. On the cellar steps, the children were sitting as rigidly as images; one little boy was crying heartily. At the sound of her footfall they turned to look up at her, the whites of their eyes gleaming in the candlelight.

"I'm going through the alleyway to Mr Baker's next door but one," she told them quickly. "To get some help for your mum. You all stay close, now. Everything's going to be all right."

She ran through the brick-walled back yard, out of the tall, plank gate and down the alley, which, with its narrowness and high walls, seemed to offer more protection than the front street. She reckoned the Baker family, also, would be in the basement and they would hear her knock more easily if she tried the back door.

"Mr Baker," she shrieked, above the rat-tat-tat of machine-guns. Fearfully she glanced upwards and then renewed her bangs with her fists.

"Wasser marrer?" inquired a richly Liverpool voice, as the door was opened a narrow crack.

"It's Mrs Thomas. Mrs Donnelly's hurt bad and I can't lift her into the house meself. And Mr Donnelly's on duty and me husband's in Bootle." The words poured out, as she wrung her hands helplessly.

The door swung open immediately to reveal, in the light of a kerosene lamp, an elderly man who looked, thought Gwen, a bit like a tortoise wrapped in a dressing-gown.

The wide mouth in the crumpled face opened. "Step in, step in. Let me get me slippers and tell Mother." He padded away, towards the cellar door.

Gwen thankfully entered the kitchen and shut the door behind her. By some fluke of the blast, Mr Baker's kitchen window was still intact. As fear gave way to resentment, she wondered crossly why her windows should always be those to be broken. Why should she get landed with someone wounded? And have to let in five disgusting kids?

102

Mr Baker came panting up the cellar steps again, his dressing-gown now tightly belted, his misshapen feet encased in carpet slippers.

"Where is she?" he inquired.

"By her front door. It's open."

"Coom through then."

Seething with suppressed vexation at the unfairness of fate, she followed him through his front door, round the tiny bay windows of his home and that of the Donnellys, and up the latter's front steps. From behind the closed door of the kitchen, Sarge began to bark.

Mr Baker put the lamp down on the floor. Very gently he lifted Ellen's arm. A piece of shrapnel was deeply embedded in her side. He held her wrist for a moment, but there was no sign of a pulse.

He got laboriously to his feet. "Let's get her in and shut the door."

As a postman, he was used to lifting awkward weights and he soon pulled her along the bare wooden floor, by putting his hands under her arms from the back. Then he quietly shut the front door; it cut off a lot of the noise from outside.

He looked carefully at the wound. It had bled little and he toyed with the idea of pulling out the piece of shrapnel. Better to leave her as she was, he decided. With womanly care, he turned her on one side to look at her back. Another sliver protruded for about an inch from under one shoulder-blade.

"I reckon she were hit first in her chest and she half turned into the house, and the second piece hit her in the back," he said to a shocked Gwen. "She's dead for sure." He laid the body flat on its back and gently closed the staring eyes. Then he glanced round him, puzzled. "Where's all the kids?"

Gwen licked her white lips. "All in my house, with our Mari."

"That's proper kind of you, Mrs Thomas." He took a crumpled handkerchief out of his dressing-gown pocket and, with a grimace of distaste, wiped Ellen's life-blood from his hands. Gwen stood uncertainly before him, her hands clasped tightly together. Her irritation had faded and she felt numb, unable to make herself think.

"It's more'n anybody's life's worth to go up to the post in this," Baker went on heavily. "As soon as the All-Clear sounds, I'll get up there and tell him – and get some help to move her." He rubbed his almost non-existent chin, grey with a day's beard, and then smelled the dried blood still on his hands. Sickened, he dropped them to his sides. "The kids'll do fine with you." He looked down kindly at the small wraith in front of him. "Five of them, isn't there? Poor little buggers – excuse the language."

At the remembrance of the repellent collection sitting on her well-scrubbed steps, Gwen felt nauseated again. But she could not, in all conscience, send them back home, while their dead mother lay where she did. "Donnelly'll have to get a relation to come in and look after them," she said.

"Aye," he agreed. "I'll leave it to you how you tell them."

Gwen stared up at him, aghast. How could *she* tell them? Surely it was not her responsibility? But Mr Baker's mind had gone on to other things, and he said, "I'll let the dog out in the morning, if Donnelly isn't back."

In her own house, she faced the children, as they rose

expectantly from their uncomfortable seats on the steps. Ruby held a sleeping Michael; she looked as if she might faint.

Mari was in the kitchen, calmly making cups of cocoa for their guests, while the early morning breeze fluttered her long white nightgown and made the gas jet dance.

The sounds from outside indicated that the attack had shifted slightly to another part of the town, though the rhythmic beat of engines overhead continued.

Gwen looked resentfully at the little crew and cleared her throat uneasily, while the children waited like marble statues in a cemetery. She said carefully, "Your ma's hurt rather bad. Mr Baker next door but one is looking after her. He'll send her to the hospital." She cleared her throat again, some pity for them seeping into her. "You're not to worry. Everything's goin' to be all right."

Relief dawned on Ruby's face. She said to Nora and Brendy, aged 7 and 6 respectively, "See, I told yer so. We're all goin' to have a nice cup o' cocoa, and when the raid's over, we'll go home to bed." She turned to Gwen. "I could go to Mam now – the kids'll be all right with you and Mari."

"No. No," Gwen responded hastily. "Your mam wants you to stay to comfort them."

When she turned to fuss round the cocoa maker, Patrick followed her and stood squarely in front of her. His face was grim and the fine, blue eyes looked at her fearlessly. "I *know*," he said scornfully.

"Well, don't you say nothin' for the minute," Gwen murmured out of the side of her mouth, like a convict. Then, feeling ashamed, she added, "I'm real sorry, lad." She felt like adding, I'm sorry for me, too.

Mari glanced up from her stirring, surprise and fear

mingled in her expression. Patrick's face crumbled, tears welled up again.

He's only about 13, Gwen thought, for all he's so big. Instinctively she moved towards him and put her hand on his shoulder. She tried to reassure him. "It'll be all right when your dad comes," she said.

Mari bit her lips to restrain her own desire to cry. She put four cups on a brightly printed tray, filled them and took them to the children on the steps. She said with forced cheerfulness, "Here you are, ducks."

When she turned back to pour out cocoa for her mother and Patrick, she saw with a pang of jealousy that her cold, fastidious parent was holding Patrick's head against her skimpy chest and crooning, "Never mind, luv, never mind." And Patrick, tough cruel Patrick, was actually crying as if his heart would break. Her own lips quivered, as she took down some more cups from their hooks.

Gwen herself was in torment. The children must stay with her until their mother's body was removed. That meant they would probably have to sleep the rest of the night in her house; and they probably had nits in their hair – she would have to burn the pillows afterwards, which would make David thoroughly angry because of the cost of new ones. But what else could she do?

She was personally revolted by their dirtiness; even this beautiful boy smelled as if he had never had a bath since he was born. With a sigh, she urged, "Have a cup o' cocoa, luv. Make you feel better." She took a cup from Mari and handed it to him. "What was your mam doin' at the door on a night like this?"

He took a small gulp of the scalding liquid. "There were a terrible bang – and then it were dead quiet, like.

So she run up to see if it were the houses opposite what were hit – 'cos they'd need our help, if they were." He faltered, and then went on, "I heard her cry out and I run up meself – and there she was on the floor – and she never said nothin' – and I knew." His cup rattled against his teeth, as he took another sip.

"God rest her." Gwen put her empty cup down on the drainboard. "We'd better get down the steps. You, too, Mari. We'll wash up tomorrow."

SUNDAY, 4 MAY 1941

Ruby's arms were stiff from holding the dead weight of young Michael. Every so often in his sleep, he would nuzzle into her non-existent breasts, looking for the comfort of his mother's milk. Then, frustrated, he would whimper and sleep again.

Patrick sat with eyes closed and fists clenched. He was tortured by the idea of his mother lying alone in the house next door. He wanted to go to her, look at her, try to wake her from her long sleep. But he was afraid of the demons in the sky, afraid of facing alone the fact of her death. After a while, his head fell forward, his mouth opened and he, too, slept.

Just before five o'clock, they all awoke with a jerk to a profound silence, except for Gwen who continued to snore.

Mari shook her mother's arm. "Ma, it's stopped. They've gone."

"Who? What?" Gwen jerked her head from against the cellar wall and blinked. She had been having a nightmare, a nightmare in which the whole house crawled away as a result of the infestation brought in by the Donnelly children. Through her fogged brain, she heard the long, thin cry of the All Clear.

"Phew!" she exclaimed. Then she gazed blearily down at the appalling weight of responsibility sitting on the inhospitable stone steps below her.

Brendy, aged 5, struggled awake and stood up on wobbling legs. He stared round the alien staircase and then roared tearfully, "Where's me mam?" He started to struggle past the knees of the other children, to get to the top of the steps, howling like a miserable dog. Nora, a year older, turned to follow him. She began to whimper. As she threatened to teeter backwards down the steps, Ruby grabbed her wrist.

"Leave me go," the child yelled savagely. She began to beat her big sister in the face with a small clenched fist.

Patrick got up slowly. With frightened, bloodshot eyes, he glanced down at his hostess and then at the other children. A curling spiral of unvented rage ran through him. "Brendy! You shut up or I'll clobber yez. Mam's been hurt and can't come to yez."

Brendy's howls came down a full octave, and Nora stopped trying to get a hold on Ruby's hair to tear it out; when Patrick decided to hit someone, he often distributed the favour throughout the family. Nora's white-lashed eyes narrowed and she made an obscene gesture at Ruby.

Patrick addressed his snivelling siblings again, his voice suddenly placating. "Mrs Thomas is going to let us stay here, aren't you, Mrs Thomas?" His eyes were on Gwen now, pleading, defeated.

Gwen was dizzy with lack of sleep and could not bring her mind into focus. She rubbed her face and then ran her fingers through her frizzy hair. She nodded. Even if Ellen Donnelly's body had been removed, the children would feel the absence of their mother more keenly in their own home and would ask more questions – and she did not want to have to break the news to them that they would never see her again. Better by far to keep them in her own home and let Donnelly do the job in the morning.

She stood up. Her whole body ached. And where was David in all this? He should be at home taking charge of everything. It was unfair that she should carry the whole burden. She began to simmer with resentment. And Emmie hadn't turned up either, to give her a hand.

"I want to pee," wailed Brendy, clutching at himself.

"For heaven's sake, take him down the yard," she ordered Patrick, as she yawned mightily. "Tut, he hasn't got any shoes on – lift him over the glass in the kitchen – and no socks neither – 'is poor little feet is purple."

It was as if Brendy's sad straits forced her awake. She turned to her drooping, equally sleepy daughter. "Mari, get the dustpan and brush, and get the glass off the kitchen floor, so the little boy – and the little girl – you ain't got no shoes neither, luv? – don't cut their feet."

Nora was not to be wooed by a kindly tone. She stuck her finger in her mouth and looked sulky. Gwen turned to Ruby. "And you, what's your name?"

"Ruby, missus." From beneath her shaggy fringe two sad eyes gleamed dully.

"Well, you got shoes on. You bring the baby upstairs with me, and we'll put him on a potty and then into bed. The little girl can wait in the living room a minute, till Patrick comes back with the little lad." She lifted a stiff, unyielding Nora up the stairs and deposited her on the living room hearthrug, which seemed to be clear of broken glass. The child ignored her and stared around the strange room.

Thankful that someone seemed to know what to do, Ruby trailed upstairs, a fretful, complaining Michael in her arms. She looked with awe at Emmie's bedroom into which she was ushered. Though its pretty, rose-covered curtains, which normally masked the blackout curtains, had been torn by glass, to Ruby it looked like a film star's bedroom. A matching curtain hung from a corner shelf, to make a wardrobe, and Ruby eyed its cascade of printed flowers wonderingly. The window glass had fallen in a rough heap beneath the sill, and Gwen leaned over it to slip the ripped blackout curtains across the casement.

Ruby shivered in the draught. She felt as if she had expended every scrap of energy she had, and she was sick with apprehension about her mother; she was silently counting the minutes until morning, when she could ask her father how she was and whether she could go to the hospital to see her.

Gwen pulled out a rose-wreathed chamber pot from under the bed. Michael objected violently to being held over it, and kicked and screamed. Gwen persisted until he made water – she was not going to have her beds soaked. A puddle was left on the heavily patterned linoleum. With the enraged child under one arm, she pulled back the bedclothes, to expose the whitest sheets Ruby had ever seen, and then shoved the little boy into bed.

"Now you be quiet," she ordered sharply. "Your Ruby's going to come and lie by you and make you warm, aren't you Ruby?" Ruby assented and started to climb into bed, shoes, dress and all, but Gwen looked at her in such a scandalised fashion, that she hastily reversed herself and pulled off her faded cotton dress and hooked it on to the bed knob. Then she kicked her worn lace-up shoes under the bed.

"That's better," Gwen approved.

Emboldened by the approbation, Ruby inquired, "Me mam? Which hospital did they take her to?"

Gwen looked at the whey-faced, skinny child nearly as tall as herself, the bony chest half-covered by a grubby vest. She knew nothing of the silent terror with which Ruby had faced the night; she saw only that the girl was swaying on her feet. She replied carefully, "Mr Baker was going to see about her being taken to hospital. I don't know which one, though. But you don't have to worry. Mr Baker is proper kind, and Mrs Baker will have gone in to comfort her, until the ambulance arrived." The latter statement made her realise what an accomplished liar she could be, but she cringed at telling the brutal truth. "Now you get into bed, and in no time your Dad'll be here and tell you all about it. Mr Baker was going to send a message up to the post as soon as the All Clear went."

Ruby smiled weakly and climbed into the wonderful bed. Two pillows and real white sheets – and blankets. Gwen tucked her and the complaining child into the bed and left them, taking the candle with her. As soon as she had left the room, Ruby got out again and felt around for the chamber pot.

"Our Emmie is going to have to make do on the sitting room sofa, when she comes in," Gwen told Patrick, who was waiting by the cold fireplace in the living room. He was still holding Brendy. Brendy's head had sunk on to his brother's shoulder and he was sound asleep. Patrick had managed to light the gaslight which hung from the middle of the ceiling, and a bright shaft lit up the back yard. Gwen tushed, and ran to the window to close the dusty blackout curtains over the flushed dawn sky. The breeze blew them up into the room, so she hastily picked up her work-basket and balanced it on the sill, to hold them down. A clatter of glass dropped into the kitchen rubbish-bin told her that Mari had done what she had been ordered to do. Gwen sighed, and turned to survey her remaining unwanted guests. "Now, what to do with you?"

"Dunno," responded Patrick mechanically. Round and round inside his head, went the picture of his mother as he had last seen her; nothing else touched him.

"I know. I'll put the girl here ..." She paused, and then asked, "What's your name?"

A malevolent, pinched face was turned up towards her. "I'm Nora," the tight lips spat out.

Gwen recoiled slightly. What a horrid, wizened-faced brat. "I'll put you and the little lad here – Brendy, isn't it? – in our Mari's bed. Mari can sleep with me." Not for all the wealth in China could she bring herself to put any of the children in her own huge double bed; she would never sleep comfortable in it again, she told herself. "And you, Patrick, can kip down on the sofa here. I'll get a blanket out for you. But first bring the kids upstairs."

She preceded him, the candle flame streaming a thin line of smoke behind her. "The whole place smells of smoke," she remarked over her shoulder, "but it's all from outside. Nothin' to worry about."

Patrick did not care what the place smelled of, as long as he could lie down, curl up and try to obliterate the fact that his maddening, bossy, beloved mam was dead.

Nora's stony expression relaxed and she followed Gwen up the carpeted staircase, sidling along like a stray dog in search of something to eat, sniffing, touching everything. She went straight to the dressing

116

table and, standing on tiptoe, reached over to pick up Mari's most prized possession, a china lady in a crinoline.

"You put that down!" Gwen's face was dark with immediate anger. "You don't touch nothin' in this house, young lady."

Nora glanced up at her with pale, expressionless eyes. Slowly she opened her hand and let the china figure drop. It broke into three pieces.

"You naughty little vixen," Gwen shrieked at her. She caught the child by the shoulder and gave her a sound slap on her bottom. "Our Mari'll be broken-hearted, she will, you little devil. Get your frock off and get into bed afore I mairder you."

With a look of complete satisfaction on her face, Nora removed her dress, to show only a pair of tattered knickers.

Gwen pulled a chamber pot from under the bed, this one with a pattern of violets to match the mauve curtains. "You pull them panties down and pay a call," she ordered a bridling Nora. Nora did not seem to hear, so Gwen took her by the shoulder and shoved her down on to it.

Patrick had stood with Brendy in his arms, waiting for Gwen to finish with Nora. He was used to loud voices and slaps and to Nora being a trial to his mother; it was nothing out of the ordinary.

Boiling with rage, Gwen whipped back the bedclothes and he thankfully put Brendy, fully-clothed, into the bed. "And you get in, miss, and let's have no more trouble," she ordered Nora. Nora, knowing the precise breaking point of most adults, felt it was wise to comply.

Outside the bedroom, Gwen and Patrick came face to

face with a bewildered, sulky Mari; she did not like her room being taken over by two dirty kids. "You get into our bed, Mari – on your father's side. I don't know what we do when he comes home. And I don't know what he's going to say."

She opened a drawer of a fine oak chest on the landing, one of the pieces of furniture appropriated from Emmie's home, and took out two thin, but clean, blankets. "You go make yourself comfy on the sofa in the living room," she told Patrick.

She had to repeat her command before Patrick took any notice. As Mari passed, she had caught his hand and squeezed it. "I'm sorry," she had whispered, and he realised with a gleam of comfort that she understood how he felt. He wanted to cry on her shoulder. To Gwen he said, "Yes, missus."

While Gwen lay, rigid and awake, beside Mari, Mari suddenly remarked, "You know, mam, it's over half an hour since the All-Clear went, and Auntie Emmie isn't in yet."

"Your aunt's big enough to take care of herself. She'll be in just now – probably gossiping somewhere." Gwen could not take any more; she had been tried beyond endurance, and the very thought of Emmie and her Robert added to her grumpiness. The sly bitch and her greediness about the furniture.

Though Emmie went through the motions of being a good sister-in-law, her bitter resentment against Gwen's refusal to help with her sick parents was all too apparent. Mari's reminder that Emmie had not yet returned made Gwen feel that she did not care if the woman never came back; yet, underneath it all, her Methodist conscience smote her hard – Emmie had

118

carried a terrible load which Gwen could have eased. Angrily, she turned over in her bed. If Emmie were dead, she would be free of the remainder of her own sins of omission. Savagely, she *wished* her dead, as she lay seething with frustration at her current predicaments.

Suddenly, as a new horror occurred to her, she sat up in bed beside the sleeping Mari. She had never looked to see what had happened to her precious sitting-room – the aspidistra in its big, green pottery bowl, set on a table in the bay window, the settee and two easy chairs which she had recently recovered herself in bright orange-flowered cretonne, and the piano, still not quite paid for, which Mari was learning to play, taught at a shilling a lesson by Mrs Cooper down the road. Was it all ruined by the blast?

She could not bear it, if it were all spoiled. She started to turn back the bedclothes, to go down and look, and then flung them back over herself. She could not endure to know now, and she turned her face into her pillow and quietly wept herself to sleep.

Patrick, too, cried – into the patchwork cushion on the sagging horsehair sofa. The pain was so great that it was as if the shrapnel in his mother's body had pierced him.

A light tread descending the staircase made him lift his head abruptly. Was Mari coming down?

"Pat, where are you?"

"Here, Rube." He let his head fall back on to the cushion.

"I were so scared, Pat." She crept towards him through the darkened room and knelt down by the sofa. He sat up and her seeking arms went round him.

"It were the worst raid." Patrick's voice was more gentle.

"I'm worried about our mam. Mrs Thomas don't say much."

Patrick ran his tongue round his lips. Then he said very softly, "She's dead, Rube. Didn't you realise it?"

"Oh," she gasped, putting her hand against her mouth to control an involuntary shriek. "No, Pat. I thought she'd fainted."

She put her head down on his blanketed lap and he could feel her shivering. Then she began to sob. He sat stiffly under her weight. "Don't, Rube," he muttered. "Don't."

"I can't help it. What are we goin' to do without Mam?"

"Dunno," he replied thickly. But he did know. It happened all the time when mothers died. Ruby would take her mother's place. Like many another motherless girl, she would learn to wash and cook for the family and tend little Michael. He was glad he wasn't a girl. He lived for the day when he would be big enough, hefty enough, to go down to the docks and stand in the pen, to be picked again and again for work, because he was the biggest and best. And he would bring home real wages and take a pretty girl, like Mari, to the pictures. Ruby would slave most of her life for nothing, because her mother was dead.

No wonder Ruby wept.

ii

During this terrifying Saturday night and Sunday

120

morning, while Gwen coped with her unwelcome visitors, five hundred German bombers converged on the already stricken city, with orders to wipe it out, make it unusable by the convoys of ships from the United States.

They were met by Defiant fighter planes darting bravely in and out of the searchlight beams, in an effort to confuse and harass them. But the Defiants were too slow and their guns were wrongly placed, and not all the gallantry and skill of their crews could compensate for the planes' deficiencies.

There were not many seamen in the canteen that night, nor had the firewatchers come in for their accustomed snacks. Deckie Dick was seated in his usual place at the centre table, from which vantage point he could look out of the window to watch the passing scene and also observe all that was going on in the canteen itself. He idly shuffled the deck of cards, from which he derived his nickname, from one hand to the other, as he regaled a bored younger merchant seaman with the story of the rescue work he had participated in the night before.

When the first bombs whistled down, neither staff nor customers sought the shelter of the basement, but when suddenly the attack seemed particularly near and intense, everybody dropped what they were doing and fled for the stairs. As they tumbled down the curving flight, the window shutters flew open with an angry rattle; the front door was blown off its hinges and shot across the canteen, followed by a torrent of sand from burst sandbags. As the blast receded, the door flew out again, to crash against the lamp post on the pavement.

Miss Piggot, one of the volunteers, had tripped on the

bottom step and fallen, taking a swearing, flailing Scot down with her. Now, they both picked themselves up off the stone floor and ruefully rubbed their knees. "My poor stockings," wailed Miss Piggot, lifting her skirts to look at the tears. Mrs Robinson pushed her to one side and quickly closed the stout door which guarded the foot of the staircase. She sat down on one of the benches and smiled at a thin, pimpled Royal Naval rating already perched there. He was rolling himself a cigarette, with trembling fingers. "Soon be over," she told him comfortingly. He replied wryly, "I'd rather be at sea." And her plump face creased with laughter.

"Phew!" exclaimed Emmie, as she sat down by Deckie Dick. "That were close." She shivered and rubbed her bare forearms, as if she were cold.

"Aye. Looks as if we're in for a bad night." He looked tired beneath the grey stubble of two days' beard. As a night watchman, he was not used to heavy physical labour and he had spent the previous night heaving beams and chunks of stone out of the way of rescue squads. As he glanced down at Emmie's anxious face, he was thinking he would be thankful to be back at work on Monday night, when he could, between his rounds, kip down in a warm corner of the warehouse which he watched. He leaned his bald head, with its fringe of white hair, against the whitewashed wall and closed his eyes against the glare of the single electric light bulb hanging from the ceiling. Pity the lodging house in which he lived was so noisy; otherwise he could have slept in a bit longer that morning.

As the raid progressed, the electric light began to flicker, so Mrs Robinson opened her capacious handbag and took out a candle and some matches. She lit it and then glued it down on to the corner table, by drips of its own wax. Then she blew it out.

The uproar outside became intense. "Good thing they're bringing in mining engineers, to help out," remarked Dick, his eyes still closed. "They can advise the heavy-rescue men."

Emmie nodded and leaned forward to rest her face on her hands, to stop herself shaking.

Mrs Robinson turned to the taciturn countess, who was seated stiffly opposite her, her ankles crossed neatly, her skirts precisely arranged around her. "I wish I had shut the canteen at ten o'clock," she remarked. "I had an uneasy feeling this morning that there would be another raid tonight."

The countess looked down her Norman nose and sniffed delicately. "On no account should you have closed. It would show that we are intimidated." Her wonderful diamond rings flashed, as she dismssed the Luftwaffe with an impatient gesture.

The naval rating drew on his cigarette and stared at her. Proper rum old dame, she was. If he were as rich as she looked, he would be thirty miles away from any place like Liverpool.

A gaunt and hunched ship's stoker, sitting cross-legged on the floor playing cards with three others, suddenly looked up. "Can yer smell smoke?" he inquired nervously of the company.

"Be funny if we couldn't, after last night's effort," grunted one of his fellow players. He shuffled his cards secretly, close to his face.

"I mean in here," the stoker responded irritably. Holding his cards to his chest, he got up, went to the door and opened it. Conversation ceased. He crept up a couple of steps and peered around, then bolted down again, as a huge swish followed by a roar and the sound of tumbling masonry indicated a hit nearby.

"Shut the door, you bloody fool," shouted a highly alarmed voice.

"Had to take a look-see," grumbled the equally shaken stoker. "T' canteen might've bin bairnin' over our heads."

Emmie fidgeted unhappily beside Deckie Dick. Why planners never put lavatories in air raid shelters was beyond her. It was certain that they must live far away from air raids; otherwise they would have known that the banshee wail of the warning was like a switch turning on your waterworks. She wondered if some of the fellows felt as she did, and she giggled shakily.

Deckie Dick opened his eyes. "What's ticklin' yer, luv?"

She blushed and whispered into his ear. He laughed, and replied, "I'm in the same boat."

The card players had been murmuring together. Now the owner of the pack knocked them together and put them in his back pocket. They got up and stretched. "Got to get back to the ship," they informed Mrs Robinson, "raid or no raid."

Mrs Robinson, alarmed, half rose from her bench. "You can't go out in this, Mr Petersen. No one would expect you to." But she read the panic in their eyes, and she sank down again. A ship out in the river might seem a safer place than the bedlam surrounding them.

Their opening of the door let in a dull roar, punctuated by occasional shouts and the sound of lorries from the docks being driven in low gear, as drivers tried to get themselves and their loads to safety.

They scurried up the steps, only to throw themselves flat on the littered floor at the top, as another deafening detonation made the old building shudder and sent bits of plaster flying from the ceiling. The subsequent rumble of falling masonry confirmed their opinion that, if they *could* get away, they preferred to be aboard ship. Who wanted to be buried under eight floors of eighteenth-century stone blocks?

As they scrambled over the remains of the sandbag wall, they were shaken to see that the street was as light as day.

"Get under cover," shouted an irate auxiliary policeman, running towards them half sideways, like a crab, to gain the greatest protection from the office walls.

The men took no notice of him and sped past him, bent on reaching the overhead railway which might well still be running and would take them south, away from what appeared to be the raid's main targets. In so doing, they saved their lives.   With her face buried in her lap and her arms clasped over her head for maximum protection, Emmie prayed that Robert was safely out of the port. She jabbed Deckie Dick with her elbow, and shouted above the noise, "Do you think Robbie will've sailed yet?"

Dick paused before answering. He knew that the *Malakand* had not yet left dock and he knew what she was being loaded with. But why add to the girl's worries? He answered her quite cheerfully, "She may have got away this mornin'."

Relieved, Emmir returned to worrying about the need to go to the lavatory.

In No. 2 Huskisson, Robbie heaved the last of a series

125

of spitting incendiaries off the foredeck and into the water.

"Watch it!" shrieked one of his mates, and pointed upwards.

Robbie whipped round.

A barrage balloon, half deflated, loosed from its moorings, was settling into the rigging.

Someone shrieked to Robbie, "Get away. It'll explode."

Robbie scrambled aft and with the rest of the crew watched helplessly as the grey monster was pulled and pushed by the breeze. A particularly strong gust loosened it and it flopped on to the for'ard deck.

Several men started towards it, but they were grabbed and held back by more cautious seamen.

A second later, the grey, silky mass burst into flames, a huge, scarifying ball of fire.

Regardless of the deadly cargo beneath their feet, the officers ordered hoses out and for fifteen agonised minutes the crew deluged the roaring fire with water, while more incendiaries were scattered down on to the hapless freighter.

A Nazi bomber swooped along the nearby dock sheds dropping a further load of incendiaries. Orange flowers of flame burst from the roofs, and in minutes a mighty conflagration stretched from Huskisson to Seaforth, like a brilliant multicoloured curtain. The wind generated by the fire sent huge fingers of flame out to the boat, and the crew found themselves surrounded by fire licking along the ship from stem to stern. Robbie could see the raw terror which struck him, reflected in the eyes of the others; yet they and the auxiliary firemen sent to help them held on to their hoses until, through the noise of the blaze, came the firm voice of the shore relief master, "Abandon ship."

Black, singed and panting, they regrouped on the dockside and were immediately put to work jetting water into the holds, while a special tender was sent for, to bring oxy-acetylene apparatus to the boat.

"Goin' to try scuttlin' her – cut a hole in her side," a fireman said to Robbie, as they sought to hold a wriggling hose towards the ship.

"Aye, they'd better be quick," Robbie gasped, "or we're all for Kingdom Come, and half of Liverpool as well."

iii

There was a fumbling at the door of the canteen shelter. Mrs Robinson hastened to open it, and an air raid warden entered in a puff of smoke. His tin hat was askew and he was swaying with fatigue. "Just checkin' who's here," he assured them, and, pointing to each person, he counted the number present.

"What's happening up there?" asked Mrs Robinson. Her face was wan and her lipstick smudged, giving her a clownlike appearance.

The warden flopped down on the end of a bench and the weary shelterers turned towards him. He took off his tin hat to rub his bald head. Emmie noticed that his trousers were thick with dust and there were holes in the knees.

"Lewis's store is a raging inferno," he said to Mrs Robinson, in answer to her query. "Must've lost most of their firewatchers. T' firemen is stuck for water." His

127

dispirited voice lifted a little, and he grinned, "T' fire brigade has pumped all the water out of the Adelphi's swimming bath into Lewis's. That'll larn that snobs' paradise."

A ripple of laughter at the expense of the city's finest hotel went through the company.

Too bad about the firewatchers, thought Emmie, but if you didn't laugh at what was funny you'd soon go mad.

"Our telephone at the post is out," he went on more soberly. "Bloody havoc without it. Seen a couple of post office engineers just now, slinging lines every which way, to get us connected up again. And there's another two of them sittin' in a crater right in the street here, splicin' telephone lines as calm as if they was havin' afternoon tea at Lyons'." He stood up and stretched. "It's a bloody miracle they're not dead."

"Should we try to move out of here?" asked Mrs Robinson.

"Nay. You're safer here than anywhere. South Castle Street, at the back here, is a shambles, what with fire and direct hits. I'll come back and tell you, if the firemen think you should move."

"Do they need men up there?" inquired a lanky individual in battered beige denim trousers, as he got up clumsily from the floor.

"Not now, they don't. They will when the All Clear goes, though."

"Not tonight, Josephine. Sit down again," cracked a wit.

The warden clapped his helmet back on to his head, grinned in a friendly way and clumped back up the steps.

A collective sigh went through the company and they settled back to wait again.

The light went out. Mrs Robinson quietly lit the candle. Its flame seemed to emphasize the lined faces of the men and women, picking out a drooping eyelid, a blackened tooth, the sole of a shoe with a hole in it, the glitter of a cheap ring on a chapped hand.

From the gloom, a forlorn young voice informed its neighbour, "Me leave's up at eight o'clock tomorrer mornin'. Got to be back in camp by then. I were on me way to the station when this lot started. Ah coom in 'ere, thinkin' it'd all blow over in an hour."

"You got a bleedin' hope, mate. You live around here?" Deckie Dick inquired.

"Aye, wi' me gran. Lives in Pitt Street. She were scared enough last night, without this on top."

Emmie remembered that a heavily built youth in battledress had scuttled into the canteen when the first bomb fell. Poor lad. No more'n eighteen, he must be.

The young voice continued, a little muffled from the owner's face being buried in his lap, his tin hat perched atop the back of his head. "Dunno whether to go back home or go t' station and show up late at camp anyways."

"Report back to camp," rumbled several voices, and Deckie Dick added, "Aye, you'll be in real trouble if you don't – absent without leave, they'll jump you for. There's people as'll look after your gran." He raised his head from his lap, to look at the crouching boy. "I'll go meself, if you like. You give me your address and her address. I'll go and see her tomorrer – and I'll write to you straight away. You'll get it the next day."

The boy glanced up quickly at Dick's ruddy,

129

good-natured visage, faintly lit by the candle. "She'd be proper pleased. She's real lonely," he said somewhat more cheerfully.

With Mrs Robinson's fountain pen, he clumsily printed the addresses on the back of a café receipt and passed the paper to Dick.

Dick folded it up carefully, put it into a shabby wallet and returned the wallet to his back pocket. Above the wallet he pushed in a grubby comb; he always said that a comb was the best defence against pickpockets or even plain losing your wallet. Now he thought that it would not hurt him to go and sit with some old Irish biddy for an hour, to help a youngster. It would be something to do. He had been lonely ever since his wife's death a year earlier.

The noise outside gradually lessened, as if the main target of the raid had been shifted. Ears pricked and heads were cautiously raised.

Emmie thought for a second that she heard women's voices outside. Women's Voluntary Service van, she guessed, feeding the firemen and the wardens. My, she could use a cup of tea herself.

"I'm goin' upstairs," announced Deckie Dick heavily. He winked down at Emmie.

Emmie promptly jumped up. "I'll come, too."

It was evident from a lewd gesture on the part of Deckie Dick where he was going, and Mrs Robinson said apprehensively, "Emmie, you should not go upstairs yet; it's too dangerous."

Emmie was immediately defensive. Nobody was going to tell her any more what she should or should not do; she'd had a bowlful of that from her parents. Besides, if she didn't go soon, she'd wet her knickers.

Emmie smoothed her skirts and tossed her head. "I'll be all right, Mrs Robinson. Dickie'll look after me." She glanced teasingly at Dick, as if single-handedly he could force the Luftwaffe into retreat.

Left to himself, Dickie would have run up the stairs and urinated just outside the front door, and then returned as fast as his tired legs would have carried him. But Emmie would be counting on his going through to the backyard privies.

The man sitting next to Dick yawned and glanced at Emmie. "You lucky bastard," he muttered to Dick.

Dick laughed. He felt that at his age it was a compliment.

In the middle of the wrecked canteen, they paused to look through the gaping hole where the window had been, at the dancing shadows on the wall of the building opposite.

"Good Heavens!" Emmie exclaimed fearfully. "There must be an awful fire behind our building."

"T' warden said as we were OK. Come on now, quick." His words were nearly drowned in the rumble of a series of bomb explosions, as the Luftwaffe took a run at the centre of the fire they had started alongside No.2 Huskisson.

Except for glassless windows, all the buildings round the light well seemed undamaged, though the sky glowed red above them. They ran across the cobbled yard, glass crunching under their feet, and with sighs of relief paid the long-delayed calls.

Close to hand, the tumbling roar of a wall collapsing brought them both out at a run, Emmie still pulling up her knickers. It buried the warden beneath its shattered stone, as he ran along the street. Another bomb

131

exploded in the fire at the back of them, sending a shower of sparks into the air. Emmie screamed.

A further swish and crash made Dick hurl her to the ground, his plump body on top of her.

"Jesus, save us!" she shrieked, as she hit the unfriendly cobblestones. She clung to him.

"Keep yer head down. God, that was ..."

With a deafening crash, the whole of the canteen was blown out.

An agonised blow on the forehead made her yell again, as she and Dick were lifted by the blast. Then, clinging to Dick, she was rolling and falling. She saw the ground beneath them crack and open in a tremendous yawn, as if in some unearthly dream. Dick seemed to slip from her, as she hit sliding rubble and then half fell, half slid, down and down on to a shuddering floorspace, mercilessly bumped and bruised as she went. She was aware, in a split second, of the earth closing over her as if a great door had been slammed, of a dreadful weight on the lower part of her body and of an ear-rending storm of noise. Then silence, except, from nearby, thin horrifying screams like souls crying out in Dante's *Inferno*, as she sank into oblivion.

iv

In smothering dust, Emmie fought for breath. As she coughed and choked and spat, the pain in her head was all-encompassing. She endeavoured to raise a hand to clear her face of rubble, but both hands were pinned against her stomach by a huge, warm solid mass; she shuddered as she realised what it might be.

She tried shaking her head and then moaned when the movement not only added to the pain in her head, but pulled her hair as well; its longer strands appeared to be caught under some unyielding weight.

Suddenly she sneezed enormously, her nose ran and she could breathe a little more easily. Small anonymous pieces of rubble, dislodged by the sneeze, slipped down the sides of her face.

As greater consciousness seeped back into her and she laboured for air amid the cloying dust, the dawning knowledge that she was buried made her tremble violently.

She became aware of stinging pain all over her face, in addition to the throbbing in her head. Cautiously, fearfully, she opened her eyes a slit. She could see nothing.

She was blind! She was sure of it. The trickles she could feel from her eyes must be blood, not tears. She screamed in horror, a howl of pure terror. Dust again entered her throat and the screams became strangled coughs. Then the pain in her head overwhelmed her and she faded into unconsciousness again.

She came round slowly, aware now of being surrounded by reverberating, booming noise. The ground under her, if it were ground and not a floor of some kind, vibrated continuously, adding to her own shuddering. The sagging weight on her body also moved slightly. At first her fogged mind believed the movement was also caused by the noise; then a large breath was exhaled, followed by a series of coughs.

In sudden joy, she croaked, "Is that you, Dick?"

Though she got no reply because of the paroxysm of coughing, she felt a hand run down the side of her and heard a faint rattle of what sounded like pebbles falling as the same hand apparently explored a little further. Then, with a satisfied grunt as the coughs eased, the body carefully rolled over until it was positioned tightly beside her. A series of muffled curses in a man's voice came from close to her ear. Thankfully she took a larger breath, to ease her constricted lungs, only to set off a further desperate coughing which threatened to cause her to vomit, as powdered plaster cloyed her throat again.

Above her, there was a series of ominous creaks, and in the distance the sound of water trickling. The surrounding uproar seemed to have decreased.

"Hold it, luv. Hold it," came a frantic whisper. "Yer noise'll bring the whole issue down on us. Breath shallow, if you can."

She did her best to control the coughing, lifting a hand, tingling with pins and needles, to cover her mouth. Between efforts to clear her throat, she giggled hysterically, "Oh, Dickie, I'm so glad you're here."

"*I'm* not," came the dry response. The body packed tightly beside her fidgeted slightly. "God spare us!"

She began to laugh wildly at this, only to choke again and to have her hair pulled painfully as she moved.

"Hold your hush, luv," he cajoled softly and caught one of her hands as if to comfort her.

She sobered as best she could. "Are you hurt, Dick?" she inquired hoarsely.

"Not much, I don't think. Wind kicked out o' me." His breath came laboriously. "Feel like I did after a fight once, in a bar in New York. Got beat up." He squeezed her hand. "How about you?"

He could feel her trembling increase. Carefully, he lifted an arm round her, as she whimpered, "Dickie, I think I'm blinded. I can't see anything. Me hair is caught under something – and me face is all wet and sticky. I'm afraid to touch it."

He did not reply for a moment and then he assured her, "Well nobody could see in this dark. Are you sure? Open and close yer eyelids. Do they work? You're lying on your back, aren't you?"

"I can move me lids. They're awful sore."

"Humph. Well, try touching round them, very lightly, to see if the eyes is still in their sockets."

Sickened by the implication, she nevertheless moved her fingers cautiously round her cheeks and over her closed lids. She moved her eyes from right to left and then blinked. "They seem all right," she announced with marked relief. "They're running like mad."

"Aye, you probably got dust in them; but it's my bet you'll be all right, when there's light to see by. I were lucky – I had me face against you when we fell. Can you move your legs?"

Diverted, her trembling lessened, and she obediently bent her legs slightly and wiggled her feet. He felt the movement, when she arched her back. "All of me seems to work," she announced with a tremulous laugh. "I can't turn me head, though, 'cos me hair's caught under summat."

They lay quiet for a minute, while the dust thinned. Then she asked pitifully, "How long will it take 'em to get us out, Dickie?"

He sighed – carefully, so that he did not commence to cough again. He had been thinking about this and was privately convinced that it would be a miracle if they were ever found. While Emmie had been unconscious, he had lain over her, dazed by the fall, his mind trying to grapple with the mystery of where they were.

They had been in the light well, lying on the ground, against the wall of the canteen under the little kitchen window. They must, he argued, have fallen straight through a fissure opened up by the bomb explosion. Yet, could they fall though a solid yard? He had definitely fallen through open space – he would remember the sensation until the end of his days.

The answer seemed to be that they lay in some old cellar under the cobbled yard. And who would dream of looking for them there? Only the people in the shelter knew that he and Emmie had gone into the yard, and judging by the fearful groans and shrieks with which his ears had been tortured for a moment or two after the bomb fell, those in the shelter were either dead or dying.

If all the buildings had come down, there could be sixty feet or more of debris above them. This had to be the end. And yet in him, bruised and scared as he was, lay a tremendous passion to live.

"How long, Dickie?"

"Dunno." The dust was settling now and it was much easier to breath, but delayed shock caught up with him and he fainted. Emmie felt the body stuffed in beside her relax and she thought he had died. She poked him with her elbow. He did not respond. "Dick! Oh, Dickie!"

Total fear engulfed her again and she began to scream helplessly, rendered almost insane with fright. She gibbered at him, as she tried to reach his face and finally succeeded in running one hand over it. Then she felt his chest heave slightly. She quietened and it seemed as if he were sleeping, and indeed he did pass into a light slumber.

She lay sobbing softly and between the sobs prayers tumbled from her lips. Promises to lead an immaculate life if only God would get her out of the tomb in which she lay came almost incoherently forth, as she tried to make a pact with the Almighty.

"I'll never hate Gwen no more. I'll help her all I can. She can have the bloody furniture. Oh, Jesus, hear me. What will Robbie do if I die? He's been so lonely for lack of a wife, oh, God. Have pity on him, if not on me. I know I'm as wicked a piece as ever was made, but I'll never miss chapel again, I won't. God have pity on me."

Deckie Dick became gradually aware of this litany, as he awoke and his mind began to clear. He was himself afraid of death, particularly a painful death. How would the Grim Reaper strike? Would the debris shift, to slide down and crush them? Would they die of thirst? Or starve like rats? Or, worse still, be eaten by rats before they had a chance to starve?

There was an increasing smell of escaping gas, faint but distinct. Deckie Dick also addressed his prayers to whatever Gods might be to let the gas thicken and engulf them. It would be a comparatively quick death; he had thought of sticking his head in the gas oven after his wife had died. With one son, Georgie, killed at Dunkirk and the other one, Billie, long since emigrated to the States, there was no one left to care about him. Now he wished, prayed, that this quick death might be granted to him and to the sweet woman lying next to him. Selflessly, he begged that there be at least sufficient concentration of gas to render her unconscious, so that she never knew what hit her, even if it was not sufficient to snuff out a tough old devil like himself.

V

Conor staggered into his crowded post, and Glynis Hughes looked up from tending a stout woman with a knifelike pain in her chest. The woman was nearly purple in the face and Glynis had been trying to keep her from going into hysterics, until one of the First Aid men, who had been called from the Dwellings, arrived with some more nitro-glycerine. The man followed Conor in, pushed him aside and plunged through the crowded room. Glynis snatched a spoon from a used teacup and handed it to him. She held the struggling woman, while he forced the life-saving liquid down her throat. In seconds, the pain abated, and Glynis thankfully left her to the care of the new arrival, while she pushed her way over to Conor, who stood like a zombie amid the crowd, his eyes half closed with fatigue. He was covered with grey-white dust, except across his knees and stomach, where his unform and the dust were stained dark red. Around him, the room hummed with voices, through which cut the sound of the telephonist relaying details of casualties and damage as they were brought to her. The line had been broken during the night and, despite a quick repair, the telephonist was having difficulty, as she laboured in a high-pitched voice to overcome the crackling of the line.

"Got a cup o' tea, Glynis?" his voice grated, as she reached him.

She eased her little buttocks past the back of the

138

telephonist's chair and laid a hand on his arm. "Sure. I'll get you one. But – but first I got to tell you somethin'. Come out in the street a mo'; it's quieter."

How am I going to do it? she worried. He always teased about his old woman, but he was fond of her for certain. And she was a kind woman, me mam always said. Dumbly, Conor allowed himself to be ushered into the street and a little away from the gossips by the door. Glynis turned and looked up at him compassionately. "Conor," she whispered.

"Is it one of the kids?" he asked, suddenly alert.

"No, Conor. It's Ellen." She grasped one of his hands hanging limply by his side. "She's gone, Conor. Mr Baker came earlier. Said she got a piece of shrapnel straight to her heart. 'Twas instant. She didn't suffer. I'm so sorry, Conor." She was trying not to cry, as he stared unbelievingly down at her. "The kids are all right. Your next-door neighbour – Mrs Thomas, isn't it – she's got them all and is taking care of them. The house is OK, too."

Conor licked his dry lips. "Where's Ellen?"

"She's laid out in the church hall – along with the others from The Dwellings. Monty got her picked up from the house real quick, in case your kids went in there. He's still here, if you want to pop over and see her."

His hand clenched hers tightly and the weary eyes closed. "I'm accursed," he said bitterly. "Accursed."

Glynis shivered. "Don't say that."

"First we lose everything we got, and nearly little Rube as well. And now Ellen."

"Go and see her," urged Glynis, a little desperately. "Father O'Dwyer'll be there, no doubt, to talk to."

"And what good will that do, to me or to him? And what good can I do for Ellen – Ellen!" He almost shouted and then his voice broke.

"You have to arrange her funeral – I'm sorry to say it."

He looked round him, like an animal trying to escape when cornered, then back at the tearful woman still holding his hand. "Glynis, down behind the filing cabinet in the post there's some whiskey – there's half a dozen bottles and more in the cellar. But don't say nothin'. Just get one out for me."

She smiled through her tears. So he did indeed smuggle whiskey. "To be sure," she said. "Trust me. We'll have a hot cup of tea with a good swig in it. You come back in, lad, and sit down a minute."

When she returned to him with a steaming cup of tea smelling strongly of whiskey, he was seated on a wooden chair, his face in his hands, and was weeping. Opposite him a middle-aged man, wrapped in a blanket, his bare feet sticking out from under it, sniffed and caught the odour of the spirit. Out of the corner of her eyes, Glynis saw the tired eyes light up. "I'll bring you a cup – exactly the same," she promised. "In a minute."

She put the cup and saucer into Conor's hand and then put an arm over his shoulder. He turned to her and hid his face against her breast. The tea slopped into the saucer. "I'm damned, Glynis," he mumbled. "Why Ellen? She never done anything wicked in her life!"

"I don't know," she replied sadly, and patted and stroked him, as if she were comforting one of her children.

When Gwen heard the knock on the front door, she thought it was David returning and that he had mislaid his key. She flew down the stairs clad only in her long, white nightgown and thankfully swung open the door.

She did not recognise for a moment the anguished man on the door step. Then a familiar Irish voice, with an unaccustomed wheeze in it, greeted her politely. "Mornin', Mrs Thomas. I'm told you kindly took me kids in?"

In the interests of modesty, she wrapped the cotton folds of her nightgown more tightly round her. Then she said, "Yes, indeed, Mr Donnelly. They're here. I think they're still asleep."

Without being invited, he stepped into the highly polished hall. Gwen's lips tightened, when he failed to wipe his feet on the doormat, a new one with the word *Welcome* knotted into it. He brought with him a strong smell of whiskey – and raw meat, was it? She shivered as she shut the door quickly behind him.

He looked uneasily round the hall and then sighed. "Do they know?" he asked her bluntly.

"No. Come in here for a minute." She ushered him into the small sitting room, and nearly cried out at the sight of her biggest aspidistra lying smashed in a pile of earth on her new red, imitation Belgian carpet, a carpet which had only two more payments to be made on it before it was entirely hers. Despite the breeze coming through the glassless windows, the room smelled cold and dank from disuse. Both the cretonne curtains and the blackout were in shreds. Gwen felt, in sudden rage, that she could happily strangle a German with her bare hands.

"What happened?" Conor almost snapped at her, as he turned to her.

A little frightened of the tight, frozen look of the filthy, tear-stained face in front of her, she stuttered an explanation. "Patrick knows," she finished up. "He's asleep on the sofa in the other room."

"I'll have to tell 'em, Mrs Thomas." He looked at her imploringly, hoping she would do it. But she was on the defensive now. There was a limit, she told herself. Enough that she had had these dreadful children thrust upon her. She couldn't.

"What if I get Patrick in here, and you talk to him?" she suggested.

He nodded, and turned to look out of the devastated window, while she gathered her nightgown even more tightly round her and went to get the boy.

"No!" she exclaimed in genuine horror, as she looked down at Ruby and Patrick tightly intertwined under the blankets on the sofa. She bent down and tapped Ruby on the shoulder. The girl woke with a jump. "Your father's here," she announced frigidly. "He wants to see Patrick in the sitting room. You stay here, miss." She would deal with their shocking indecency afterwards. Brother and sister sleeping together! She was scandalized.

Hardly comprehending what she had said, the two children looked up at their outraged hostess. Patrick yawned and then, without a word, he swung himself off the sofa and lurched unsteadily out of the room. Mrs Thomas pursed her lips and stared down at Ruby. Ruby slowly laid her head back down on the cushion she had shared with Patrick. She began to cry helplessly.

Gwen turned towards the fireplace and rolled back the hearthrug, preparatory to making the fire. "I should think so, too," she muttered angrily. "Such behaviour I never did see."

Yesterday, Patrick would have sworn that he hated his father. But now the object of his jealousy was dead and his father suddenly seemed a pillar of strength. He stumbled towards him and Conor held him, while they both wept heartily. Finally, Patrick snuffled, "Rube knows."

In the living room, Gwen put down her poker. She was suddenly cold. without a word to the weeping girl, she ran quickly upstairs to get her dressing-gown.

Immediately she vanished, Ruby sat up, untangled herself from the blankets and ran, barefoot, into the sitting room and flung herself into her father's arms.

With an arm round each of his children and tears smudging his dusty face, Conor asked them not to tell the little ones that their mother was dead. "Tell 'em she's in hospital being mended," he suggested. "Better they know when your gran comes down from Walton. I tried to phone the post there, so as to get hold of her quick — it were dead — so I wrote to her, but with it being Sunday today, she won't get it till tomorrer." Gran was his own mother. Ellen's mother lived in Dublin — and he realised suddenly that he must write to her as well.

"You all stay with Mrs Thomas, till I can get home. And you help her, Rube."

Ruby agreed sulkily that she would help her. "Pat, you feed me cocks — and beg a few scraps from Mrs Thomas for Sarge." The boy sniffed lachrymosely and nodded agreement. He could hear Gwen in the next room raking out the fireplace. Even the sound of the poker seemed angry.

Gwen was just putting a match to the paper of the newly laid fire, when Conor entered, Ruby hanging on to his arm. Patrick followed, his face stony.

Conor loosed himself from his daughter and bent down to seize one of Gwen's coal-blackened hands and shake it hard. His breath stank of whiskey; still kneeling, she recoiled from him.

"It's proper kind of you to take in me kids, Mrs Thomas. I'll not forget it. Mr Baker said you would keep them for a while. By the looks of things, I won't be home until tomorrer – at least. It's terrible up at The Dwellings. You never saw anything like it. Keep the kids away – it's no sight for them. I've written to their gran, but with everything being upset in the town she probably won't get the letter till tomorrer afternoon at earliest." He paused for breath and looked at her anxiously.

"I – but – I ..." she began, a fearful sinking feeling in her stomach.

He burst into speech again. "I tried to get the wardens' post up there on the phone. Can't get through to anybody." He seemed to take it for granted that she would keep the children with her, and went on, "We won't tell the little ones their mam is gone, till their granny comes to comfort 'em." He took a turn about the room, while Gwen watched him, speechless for once. "You can say she's in hospital, doing fine, soon be home, like."

She opened her mouth, to make an excuse for not keeping the children, but he deflected her by asking, "Where's your hubby?"

"Still workin' out at Bootle. And our Emma isn't in yet."

Overwhelmed by his own troubles, Conor failed to realise that Emmie must have been in the thick of the air raid. He said mechanically, as he hugged Ruby again and turned towards the door, "She'll probably be in just now."

While the children saw their father out, Gwen leaned forward and mechanically struck another match to light the fire, which had failed to kindle. She sat on her heels, watching the flames creep through the newspaper and wondered what to do. There was not enough food in the house to feed everybody and little money in her purse to buy more. David would be furious if she exceeded her housekeeping money. Mechanically she gave the fireplace a quick whisk with a brass-handled hearth brush, and then continued to sit listening to the wood crackle, feeling exhausted, defeated.

Ruby watching her, hesitated in the doorway and then advanced diffidently. She put her arm shyly round Gwen and said, "Don't cry, Mrs Thomas. I'll help yez."

Startled, she turned in the curve of the child's arm. A little stiffly, she put her own arm round Ruby. "Well, thank you, Ruby." The girl smelled to high heaven. Hadn't her mother taught her to wash herself? Perhaps she hadn't been taught not to sleep with her brother, either, she meditated grimly. She scrambled to her feet. She *must* do something.

While Mari still slept, Ruby and Patrick were set to work, she to sweep up the remaining glass in the living room and he to tack some pieces of old lino culled from the cellar, over the gaping windows. The table was laid and a small helping of cornflakes put out for each child.

"And after breakfast, if you're going to be here overnight, everybody had better have a bath."

Both Ruby and Patrick were taken aback. They had never had a bath; only an occasional wash all over in the kitchen bowl; they were saved from having to reply by Nora and Brendy rushing down the stairs in a panic, having forgotten where they were. They surveyed the living room with popping eyes, broke into roars of tears and demanded to go home to Mam. Ruby mothered them both and soon they were shovelling cornflakes into their mouths, while they watched very suspiciously the preparation of the tin bath set in front of the fire.

Michael shrieked from upstairs and Ruby ran up to him. He had soaked the bed and was standing on it, holding the brass head rail. In the half darkness of the room, Ruby held him to her and told him Mam would be coming soon to fetch him. No amount of soft talk, however, would persuade him to eat cornflakes or even drink milk from a glass. He wanted his mother's breast.

Gwen surveyed him in harassed silence for a moment, as he sat on Ruby's knee kicking out in a furious paddywack. Finally she said wearily, "He'll eat when he's real hungry. Let him be for now. We might as well bath him first." She moved the dish of cornflakes away from Michael's flailing arms. "Do you have any clean nappies or pants for him at home? And any clean clothes for the other kids?"

"There's some," Ruby answered her doubtfully. "Me mam washed Thursday." She dreaded that Gwen might command her to go to fetch them. Her stomach churned at the idea of finding her mother lying so still in the hall.

Patrick came in from the kitchen, carrying a steaming bucket of water to tip into the tin bath. "I'll go and get

146

'em," he said heavily. "I got to feed the birds – and Sarge. They'll have taken Mam to hospital by now – won't they, Mrs Thomas?"

Gwen had forgotten about Ellen. She hesitated, and then said, "I think so, lad."

Mr Baker had remembered to let the dog out into the tiny back yard, and Sarge greeted Patrick ecstatically. He padded into the house behind the boy.

Patrick went straight to the front hall, almost hoping that his mother would be lying there, made comfortable by nurses, and that she would open her eyes and say she was fine, just waiting for the ambulance. But there was only the quilt from Ruby and Nora's bed piled against the wall. Slowly an all-consuming rage spread through him, that strangers had taken away his mother without his seeing her again. He kicked angrily at the quilt, and Sarge, who had been nosing round it, slunk back, tail between legs. He stamped his feet and then banged his fists against the wall, bent his head and hit that too against the hollow plaster. "Yer pack of sewer rats," he screamed at the anonymous ghosts who had come in the night to carry away his mother. He forgot about the clothing he was supposed to collect and ran through the house, up the stairs and down again, kicking open doors, screaming obscenities which echoed through the house, yelling what he would do to a German if he ever met one. He picked up some used cups from the kitchen table and slammed them on to the floor and crunched the broken pieces under his boots, until the fury of frustration waned and he stood sobbing helplessly in the deserted kitchen.

There an anxious Ruby found him. She put down on the floor an extraordinarily clean Michael, clad only in

147

his jersey. The child was sucking his thumb, tears still wet on his face. He glanced round the kitchen, looking for his mother. Small sobs shook him from time to time and he stared in a dazed fashion at his big brother.

Ruby put her arms round Patrick. "It's no good, Pat. She's gone."

The boy pushed her away and turned his back on her. He mopped his eyes with the end of the woolly tie of his jersey.

"We have to find some clothes for Mrs Thomas."

"Damn her."

"Don't knock her, Pat. She's trying to help. We'd be in a right muddle without her – and no Dad either."

He turned a dark, passionate face on his sister. "I can't stand her. I'm not having no bath. I'm going to see what Dad's doin'."

With a huge sniff, he swung past her, opened the front door and slammed it after him.

Ruby stared after him, her whole body trembling with fear of the responsibility left to her, fear of offending Gwen, fear of not being able to cope with Michael, Nora and Brendy, fear of being terribly alone to face everything – perhaps yet another air raid that night.

vii

"It's quietened," Emmie pointed out. "It must be Sunday morning by now. We've been here ages, Dickie, and I'm so parched. Are you thirsty?" The voice was thin and quivery.

"Aye, I am. 'Could use a pint." He cleared his throat. "Yer know, there's a bit o' water here, somewhere. I can hear it trickling – faint, like."

"I know. It's not very far, but I can't move 'cos of me hair." Emmie's voice quavered and threatened hysterics again.

"There's a straight wall on t' other side of you, isn't there?"

"Yeah." She raised her arm up as far as she could reach, and winced with pain from bruises acquired in her fall. "There's enough space above me – I think – for me to sit up. She ran her fingers along the obstruction above her. "It feels as if there's a very big rough stone over us. It slopes down towards you, till it must touch you. If I could turn on me side, I could give you more room."

"Sardines in a bloody tin," he snorted. "Can you reach over your head to your hair where it's caught?"

"Mm. I've bin tryin' to pull some of it loose."

"I've got a penknife in me pocket. I doubt I can get it out, though. I've hurt me wrists, and me hands is as sore as hell."

"Oh, Dick! You never said you was hurt?"

"It's nought terrible. Could you reach in me right-hand keck pocket?" She felt him wriggle himself slightly upward, so that he was more level with her.

With her long, bony Lancashire fingers, she hunted feverishly down his side, stretching as far as she could. She touched his belt. "Lower," he instructed her. "Look, I'm goin' to ease meself a bit across you." She felt his head move across her shoulder till it lay against hers. He tried to ease the dead weight of his body over her arm. He grunted. "That's it. See if you can reach now."

149

The long fingers ran down his thigh, paused and then scrabbled at the pocket opening. "If you truly can't get it, I'll put me own hand in — but it's that tender, I don't want to."

"Hold still," she advised him. "I'll winch the pocket lining out." She giggled nervously. "You've got all sorts in here. I got your hanky out."

"Well, don't lose it. Put it where you can find it. We'll wipe our faces with it."

She obediently hauled it out and stuffed it down her chest.

Again the long, exploring fingers. He gritted his teeth; not with pain, but to control the sudden arousal which her warm nearness and her gentle fingers was exciting. The tendrils of hair against his cheek were having their effect, too. Many times, when he had seen Robert and Emmie walk out of the canteen with arms around each other, he had been pierced with envy and wondered what she would be like to bed. Now, however, crammed in a hell-hole which was likely to be their coffin, his desire for her was so strong that he longed passionately to roll back on top of her and have her.

She was his best friend's girl, he reminded himself forcefully, and with eyes screwed tight he kept himself rigidly still, until she almost shouted, "I got it. I got it."

"Good," he muttered, and took a large sighing breath and promptly sneezed.

She was panting with the effort she had made and began to cough again. When the paroxysm had passed, she cleared her throat, and said, "Afore I start sawing at me hair, I'm going to wipe your face with the hanky." She paused, and then added with a tremor in her voice, "Me own old dial is too sore. I'm bleeding a bit, I think."

"Ta." Poor kid, he thought. If her face is ruined, how'll she endure life, even if we are rescued?

She could feel his breath on her cheek. "Is *your* face hurtin' at all, afore I touch you?"

"No, Em. I think I were pressed against you when we fell."

His face was carefully wiped. She spat on a corner of the hanky and ran it clumsily around his eyelids. God, how he wanted her. She was surprised, yet pleased, when a kiss was planted on her cheek. She pushed the hanky back down the front of her blouse. "Now," she said almost cheerfully. "I'm goin' to start chopping. Proper sight I'll be when I'm finished." It was comforting to feel the man's warmth against her, especially when a particularly loud crash made the whole structure above them vibrate, and small rushes of debris slithered down on them.

The smell of gas had gone, Dick realised. The firemen must have managed to turn off the main. So much for that. He did not know whether to feel relief or disappointment. Willy-nilly, as shock had receded and been replaced by more mundane yearnings, a faint hope crept into him, that maybe the bomb that hit the canteen was not engraved with his and Emmie's names, that they might, by some miracle, be found.

Whimpers came from the girl next to him, as she tugged and cut hair by hair. She sighed and stopped work, to rest herself for a moment. Then she said without preamble, "We must have fallen into somebody's cellar – right under the yard, 'cos we was still outside – and I fell and slid quite a ways." Her voice was mournful. "I ache all over from it. Who'd build a cellar under a yard?"

151

"Plenty o' people, not too many years ago – about a coupla hundred, maybe. For keeping smuggled goods in – or privateers hiding their loot."

"They would? How'd they bring the stuff in?"

"A hidden door from the cellar under the building – where the shelter was, like."

"There weren't no back door out of that shelter."

"Could've been bricked up when they built the present building."

She sighed, and recommenced the cutting of her hair. If she could get her head free, perhaps she could move enough to find the water that trickled so maddeningly close to her. As they lay at present, Dick could not move much either.

viii

Though the raid was over, and to Emmie, deep in her prison, the din seemed less, the noise outside from the roaring fires was sufficient to make everyone converse in shouts.

With shoulders hunched and bodies bent close to their jetting hoses, firemen had managed to advance a little into the raging inferno of South Castle Street, at the back of Paradise Street. Then the water pressure fell to a trickle and they had to beat a hasty retreat. Petrol in a pump caught fire and it blew apart. Dispirited men watched helplessly as, fanned by a light breeze, the flames began to eat their way towards Paradise Street. Wandering wisps of smoke worked their way through the wreckage. Neither Emmie nor Dick said anything, as they lay rigid with fear in the face of this new menace.

The building in which the canteen had been housed had blown outwards across the street. It effectively blocked the movement of traffic, already in difficulties because of the bomb hole further down, in which Post Office engineers struggled to restore some kind of telephone service for the authorities.

A gang of Army Pioneers, aided by volunteers, both civilians and servicemen, inched their way down the centre of Paradise Street, shovelling smaller rubble into wicker skips; larger pieces were hauled to one side. "For Christ's sake, why don't they bring in some cranes?" groaned a man in blue mechanic's overalls, as he heaved and shoved in company with a German Jewish pioneer. They turned to move a huge metal desk which had lain upside down under the girder they had just shifted. "Jesus!" the mechanic exclaimed, as he stooped to get a grip on it. With all his strength he heaved and rolled it on to its side – and looked down in horror at what had once been little Dolly, the firewatcher.

Her uniform had been blown off her. Terribly crushed, her entrails spread out, only the long gleaming hair indicated that there lay someone who had been soft and pretty.

The Pioneer looked down at her in silent pity, while the less hardened civilian shouted, "Curse them, curse them!" beside himself with horror. He bent down and gathered the frail, sticky remains up as best he could and took them to the pavement. There was nothing to cover her with. Soon, he knew, somebody would come along with a bag to put her in. Weeping, savage with rage, he went back to work.

Help *was* coming. Through moonlit lanes and narrow streets snaked a stream of fire engines and ambulances, water tankers, kitchen lorries, mobile canteens and vans of food. Rescue parties, including miners and demolition experts, spent an uncomfortable night crammed into trains as they converged on Liverpool. Through broken roads, spanking clean American soldiers manoeuvred bulldozers and dump trucks, and great shovels, also mounted on caterpillar tractors, bigger than anything most Britons had seen before. They would eat into the choked thoroughfares and make a path for other vehicles.

The looters came gaily from the suburbs and the countryside, to rob those who had already lost so much.

ix

An unexploded land-mine, sitting quietly at the back of a deserted insurance office, suddenly blew up and the ear-splitting bang shook Emmie's and Dick's tiny refuge. It shook not only the debris above them, but the ground on which they lay, like some huge earthquake. In terror, they clutched each other, their heads buried into each other's shoulders, to avoid the dust which rose once more around them. Bits and pieces rattled and fell above them. The great stone over their heads held, however, though the beam which was holding down Emmie's hair shifted slightly and the remaining strands of her hair were freed.

"My God!" Dickie's teeth were chattering helplessly, as the bang was followed by a series of rumbles, gradually dying away into quiet.

Ears pricked, they waited for the next onslaught, but there was only the creaking and shifting of the ruins and the occasional splash of water. Very dimly, they also could hear what might have been slow traffic and, at times, felt the faint vibration of it.

As the dust settled again, Dickie muttered to a whimpering Emmie, "It *has* to be morning – that bang were too big for a bomb – it were something special. Come on, luv. Now's the time to feel around for a stone and bang on that wall by you, so a rescuer knows where to look."

Emmie stirred and half sat up. Dickie exclaimed at her sudden movement.

"Me hair came free in the last shake-up." She laughed tremulously and felt round for a likely stone.

For nearly half an hour, they banged steadily, to no purpose. During that time they had both, shamefacedly, to urinate and now lay in wet clothes.

As they rested, feeling surprisingly weak, Emmie said, "David – me brother – 'll be out lookin' for me. What about your folks?"

Dickie explained that he had nobody and that this was his weekend off from his duties as night-watchman at a seed warehouse. "They'll wonder where I am come Monday, though, when I don't turn up for work."

"Gwen – that's Dave's wife – she won't bother. She hates my guts. Be glad to see me dead, I truly think. All she cares about is her house. If you breathe out, she'll dust all round you."

Dick laughed. "She can't be that bad."

"She is," insisted Emmie. "Dave's proper patient with her. It'll be him as comes to find us."

"The wardens and the Rescue Squads is good at finding buried victims," Dick replied, to reinforce her hope of help.

155

David was, however, sound asleep on a bunk made of chicken wire in a street shelter in Bootle. He had worked until the siren went, on repairing water pipes in narrow, badly damaged streets, while housewives and children hung round him, waiting for the taps, or at least the fire hydrants, to start gushing again. They also had no gas with which to cook, and often torn chimneys made it impossible to build a fire in a grate. Once water was restored, a good many kettles got boiled in the back yard on a fire made from splintered beams. In most cases their tiny stores of food were ruined, tins laced by slivers of glass, the contents of cupboard blown into pieces and lost in the general mess of broken plaster.

On Sunday morning, fed by a grateful housewife, David and his mate, Arthur, continued to work, laying new water pipes. Two streets away, another gas main sent a scarifying sheet of flame into the sky, threatening to engulf the slums around them in fire.

A little soothed by the thought that David would be seeking her, Emmie said to Dick, "You'd better have your knife back afore I lose it in the dark."

He fumbled round until he found her hand and the knife. As he slipped it into his shirt pocket, he felt her begin to sit up again.

"My God! Me poor back," she groaned, as the stiffened muscles were stretched.

"Now watch it," Dick warned. His voice sounded muffled, the words coming reluctantly from a parched throat. "Move carefully. If you touch something solid, don't push it or we'll have an avalanche down on us."

"OK." If she could stop shivering, she thought, she would be less clumsy. The shivering would not stop, however. As she sat up, it became a wild shaking, her teeth chattering uncontrollably.

Dick heard her wincing, and the shuffle of her skirts against the loosened earth, as she finally got herself seated upright. Instinctively, she turned towards him, to bend forward and touch him. "Ow!" she squeaked, as she hit her head on the sloping stonework over him. When she rubbed her scraped forehead, it hurt much more than she had expected; there was a trickle, which might have been blood, down over one eyelid, and she whimpered slightly as she carefully wiped it away with a shaky finger.

"Steady on, girl."

"Suppose I move too far away and I can't find you again?" she croaked.

"Na," he assured her. "We're like a pair o' mackerels in a tin – waitin' for the tin-opener."

Her shaky laugh was close to being a sob.

She heard Dickie sigh with relief as the pressure of her body on him was eased when she moved. Very carefully she tucked her feet under herself and then kneeled up. She promptly hit her head again and sat back dizzily until the throbbing stopped. In a wild hope that there might be an aperture through which they might creep to greater safety, she rapidly ran her hands up and down and along the wall beside her. Her spirits fell, when she found that the huge rough-hewn stones of the wall met tightly with the sloping slab which roofed them over. There was enough height on the wall side for them to sit up, if they kept their heads bent, and she reported this to Dick.

"That'll be a relief," he replied. "I'll stay put till you've felt right round."

157

She crawled with difficulty a foot or two along the wall, until, where her feet had rested, her exploring fingers found what felt like a metal girder sloping the opposite way to the stone above her. She tried to reach over it, but the way was blocked with rubble; she managed, however, to slip her hand under it and work her fingers through a pile of cobblestones and plaster. As she eased her hand carefully in, there was a loud creak and dust began to rise.

"For God's sake!" Dick's voice held panic.

She snatched her hand back under their sheltering slab. "I'm doing my best," she said crossly, and then sneezed. The sound was answered by another small rattle of debris from the same direction. She stayed frozen until the last small piece seemed to have dropped. Then she voiced the need of both of them. "I wonder where the water's running?"

"Let's listen hard."

The sound indubitably came from somewhere beyond the iron girder.

She burst into tears.

"I'm comin' up beside you, Em. Just sit still. Steady as you go, there's a girl."

He wriggled out of his narrow niche, his shoulders aching sharply, the rest of his bruised body complaining bitterly. Guided by her whimpering, he hauled himself alongside her. He sat, panting and dizzy half leaning against her, and then he straightened up. "Phew, that's better." He listened again, and then said, "There's water there all right. May be from the pipes leading to the canteen taps."

Emmie sniffed. "Doesn't matter where it's from. It's on the other side of a bloody great girder, and the girder's too big to either climb under or over. Even if you could, there's a lot o' smallish bits very loose there." she tried to still her chattering teeth, and then quavered, "I don't know what we did to deserve this. We're not wicked."

Dick gave a rattling laugh. In the pitch-darkness, he tried to visualise the tiny space in which they found themselves. Then he said ruefully, "War's like the weather; it falls on the good and the bad alike. Only them what starts it takes care to be well away from it." Then, with determined cheerfulness, he went on, "Never mind that. First, I'm going to move forward a bit, so you can lie along this big wall. You lie on your stummick, and very, very slowly slip your hand under the girder again and work your fingers into whatever's there. See if you can feel wet. It'll be easier for you to do than me – 'cos o' me weight, like. I'm plain fat."

"Right." Her voice was a little firmer. After a tight squeezing past each other, she managed to do as he had suggested, and she worked her arm further and further under the girder until part of her shoulder lay under the unyielding metal. It was all bone dry.

With her arm still stretched into the rubble, she lay and listened carefully. "It's no more'n a foot beyond, I'm sure," she wailed in despair.

"Not to worry," Dick wheezed. "It might make a puddle in time and we'll be able to reach it. Have you still got me hanky?"

"Yes. Down me chest."

"Good. If it makes a puddle we can reach, we'll get at it by soaking the hanky in it."

She remained prone for a moment, while she mentally savoured the joy of cold water. Then she cautiously withdrew her arm and heaved herself round until she could sit up.

"Eh, I'm that sore, and you must be, too," her tremulous voice came out of the darkness. "Why don't they come? It's been pretty quiet for a while now. It has to be morning. Surely they'll be lookin' for us?"

"As soon as you hear anything that sounds like them coming, we'll shout as hard as we can, so they know we're here. And we'll bang with the stones again."

"T' warden what come to the canteen counted us all. He'll tell the rescue men how many people to look for."

"Aye, he will."

Outside in the street, the Pioneers carefully consigned the warden to the mortuary and, with him, the remains of the police constable, who would at least have known there were people sheltering in the canteen basement.

Further down the street, in a bomb crater, a newly bathed and clean-overalled Post Office Telephones engineer relieved his exhausted colleague. Elsewhere, linesmen continued to string wires from anything they could hang them on, in an effort to re-establish communications within the city.

As less fatigued aid arrived from other towns, a mood of ebullience spread amongst the toilers. This was the end of this run of raids, they told each other. Everybody would be able to go to bed tonight and sleep it off, ready for work on Monday.

Emmie found Dick's hand and held it, as she dozed. Sometimes a very distant rumble shook their tiny lair; it sounded like big lorries moving, a promise of rescue, and they were comforted.

Without warning, there was an enormous roar, a detonation greater than any previous one, and the whole ruin in which they lay shivered and groaned. Loud cracks overhead made Emmie scream. She flung herself against Dick; in equal terror, he turned and clung to her. Again, a tremendous dust enveloped them. Instinctively, they ducked their faces into each other's shoulder, cowering together as they nearly choked.

The pandemonium died away to a rumble, only to be followed immediately by a whole series of explosions which shook their precarious shelter. Almost directly overhead they could hear the fall of masonry followed by the lesser sound of smaller debris slithering like a hundred snakes down through the wreckage. The great piece of stonework above them shuddered.

A terrified rat scuttled across Emmie's lap, sending her into hysterics.

Despite the desperate efforts of its crew and the fire brigade, fire had finally reached the main hold of the *Marakand*. Surrounded by flames, dive bombed all night, firemen and crew had been unable to scuttle her, and now, under whatever cover they could find, they crouched defeated. A four-ton anchor, blasted into the air, fell into the engine-room of a hopper and sank it as well. Acres of dock and warehouse were mowed down by the tremendous blasts and the ever-encroaching fire. Only after seventy-four hours of almost continuous racket did a weird silence descend on the embers of a whole district.

"I never want to see anything like it again," Robbie muttered fervently to his deckhand friend, as their captain checked his sooty, worn-out crew. "I'll be thankful to go to sea again."

Fogged by fear, unable to produce even one more scream, Dick and Emmie lay tightly together, both breathing shallowly. Each time the torn building over them lurched, a fresh poof of dust would surround them and they would cough and splutter.

Outside, the late spring morning was made horrible by a blizzard of burned paper which blew about the city, getting into people's eyes, clinging to clothes and faces like black snowflakes. The burned records of innumerable enterprises flattened during the night had been caught by the wind and whirled out of every broken building. Up and up they went into the smoke haze, to descend again in a supernatural storm. Through the smoke, flames still licked greedily.

By noon the road outside the canteen was passable to a single line of traffic driving very carefully, and further efforts were being made to find the remainder of the firewatchers assumed to have been on duty with Dolly. The air raid warden on day shift and new police, all looking wondrously spruce, had come on duty, and a heated altercation broke out between a demolition squad foreman puttering along the edge of the debris, and the new warden.

"How was I supposed to know there was a canteen there? There weren't no warden around, nor a cop for that matter, on this street. Thought it was all offices – and as for firewatchers, I've only got one unaccounted for now."

"Well, there *was* a canteen here and it'd be open," replied the warden irritably, "and we'd better get weaving on it." By his accent the demolition foreman must be from Manchester, presumably one of the over three thousand men which the warden had heard were being sent to Liverpool. No wonder the man didn't know where anything was.

"How many people, do you reckon?" inquired the foreman resignedly.

"Could be as many as forty."

"Good God! Somebody should've told me." He scratched his crew-cut hair and put his helmet more comfortably on his head. "They didn't say nothin' in the command post."

The warden raised a gloomy face from contemplation of the anonymous piles of wreckage round him. "The command post lost nearly the whole shift."

As he strode towards them, the police constable in charge of the area, looked bleary-eyed, despite a clean and tidy uniform. He had just arrived, to commence his shift, only to find a new command post being assembled and nobody very sure of what the situation was. "Looks as if Constable Wilson got it last night. We can't find him," he was told. Heavy-hearted, he had taken the first telephone call on the re-established line. Now he shouted towards the warden, "There's a phone inquiry about a Miss Piggott – serving in the Sailors' Canteen – do you know if that's bin tackled yet?"

"I only just coom on duty," replied the warden defensively. "And t' command post's only just bin replaced – pack of strangers. There weren't nobody in a fit state to tell nobody nothin'. Joe, here, he just coom from Manchester." He cocked a thumb towards the lugubrious foreman, who looked even more glum.

The constable's face went red with suppressed rage. Bloody fool, why didn't he use his common sense and show the new foreman? Poor Wilson and the command post couldn't help being dead.

"Get a bearing on where the entrance was," he ordered the warden through gritted teeth, "and explain to the foreman how it were laid out. I'll get you more help, and alert ambulance people. The entrance to the shelter underneath the canteen was to the left of the entrance from the street." He ran back to the newly reconstituted command post.

While the warden, like a questing terrier, trotted up and down the partially cleared street, the foreman assembled his squad and checked that they were equipped with shovels and crowbars – and skips to hold the rubbish they would have to remove.

The warmth of the fires, further over, was born towards them, making them sweat. The hiss of water hitting flame and the drum of pumps bewildered the warden. If it were only quiet enough to climb the rubble and listen; then they would stand a chance of hearing survivors tapping. There were other noises to add to the confusion: explosions from No. 2 Huskisson dock; detonations, as Lancashire mining engineers showed another demolition squad how to break a way through mountains of wreckage, without bringing an avalanche down on themselves; the lives of men with demolition experience were to be preserved at all costs – their peculiar skills were all too rare. In a nearby street, a huge bulldozer manned by American soldiers was slowly crunching its way through a blockage, and that also added to the racket.

"I've got it," shouted the warden triumphantly, as he rubbed one eye watering with a mot in it. "Opposite the stump of this lamp-post."

Huge and ponderous as the foreman was, he immediately began to climb the fall opposite the broken lamp standard, walking with surprising lightness, probing gently with his crowbar, before committing his team to the search. When he was satisfied that he understood the lay of the pile, he set his men to work. "Come on, lads. Quick – but careful – mind." His melancholy expression fell still further. "Doubt anybody's alive under that."

A portly gentleman in a business suit and bowler hat accosted the watching warden, "Excuse me. Can you tell me where the Sailors' Canteen is? My wife was on duty there last night, and she has not come home this morning. When I tried to telephone, I could not get through."

The warden looked up sharply and then bit his lip with tobacco-stained teeth. "Aye," he said slowly, with a sigh. "It were here. They're workin' on it now, as you can see."

The gentleman's ruddy complexion went glistening white. His grey, military moustache quivered; words would not come. Finally, he breathed, "I was afraid of that."

The warden caught his arm, concerned that he might collapse. "Sir! They could be safe in the shelter – it were a good stout cellar." The warden had not an iota of hope. But then, he told himself, you never knew what quirk of fate could save the life of someone. "What was – is – her name, sir?"

"Clara Robinson, Mrs Clara Robinson." The man was already out of his black jacket and folding it neatly. He laid it down by the lamp-post stump and placed his bowler hat on top of it. "Thank you," he said fairly steadily, as he got a grip on himself. Then he turned and picked his way over to a labourer clearing a path from the edge of the fall inwards. "Give me a shovel. I'll help you," he said between tight lips.

"Best stay back, sor," a middle-aged Irish navvy, working ahead of the other labourer, advised him. "It's dangerous." He lifted his pick again and swung it down on the obstruction before him.

"I *have* to do something," Alec Robinson said firmly. He undid his gold cufflinks and rolled up his shirt sleeves.

The foreman came carefully down the slope of the pile, placing each foot precisely so that he did not fall into the debris.

The warden shouted up to him, "T' cellar had a pavement light what led right into it."

"That'll save a lot." The foreman's face lifted slightly, as he redirected his men, to facilitate the unearthing of this narrow window of heavy glass framed in iron and set directly into the pavement to give some light to the cellar. If it had not been pounded into the ground, it could give the rescuers immediate access. Then he turned and sized up the blenched business man who was working his way towards him.

"You could clear some space at the edge of the pavement," he told him kindly. "Make a way through to where the road has been cleared. We'll need a bit of space to lay 'em down, maybe, when we bring 'em out." He saw Alec Robinson's eyes widen with horror, and added hastily, "They could be hurt." He turned to the labourer. "Find 'im a shovel."

Alec Robinson thankfully took the proffered shovel and bent to the task, his heart heavy. An ambulance was already nosing its way cautiously along the street, followed closely by a fire pump. A wobbly stream of water was directed at the ruins further back, to damp them down and possibly contain the fire raging behind them, until the rescuers had finished their work. The stream was weak because of fractured mains, and the turbulence in the air caused by the fires themselves blew much of the water back on to the firemen and the rescuers. Still, they persisted.

While the workmen picked their way in with meticulous care, para-medical personnel, black bags in hand, came at a shambling run along the littered pavement opposite.

They were too early, so, with tin hats pushed to the back of their heads, they lit cigarettes and stood gossiping about a new film one of them had seen.

In what seemed to have become their own private bomb crater, the clay-bespattered telephone engineers continued their patient splicing of lines.

When Alec Robinson paused to mop his forehead, he was approached by a tall cadaverous man dressed in the grey uniform of a chauffeur. The man took off his peaked cap, revealing a bald head across which a few wisps of white hair had been carefully plastered. "Sir, I'm looking for the Sailors' Canteen. I'm Higgins, sir. The mistress has not come home, and we – that is, Mrs. Fleming, the housekeeper, and me – thought I should come down on the bus, to see if she's all right – the car being mothballed for the duration, sir." He turned and surveyed the appalling wreckage. "I trust I'm not looking at the canteen?"

Alec Robinson replied gruffly, "You are. Who is your mistress?"

"The Dowager Countess Mentmore. She's a volunteer."

A minute later, a chauffeur's cap and jacket were carefully laid by Mr Robinson's bowler hat and black jacket, and the demolition foreman had to find work for another volunteer.

The rescuers worked like moles, shifting obstructing masonry, splintered woodwork, pieces of filing cabinets and desks, a slippery cascade of law books, a huge Victorian lavatory, all interlaced with electric wires which might still be live, and miles of water pipes and gas pipes. A lot of this was passed back and piled on the pavement. Stout pieces of timber, desk drawers, finely panelled oak doors, all were used by the labouring men as props in the twisting passageway they were making. Every time there was a further explosion from No. 2 Huskisson this perilous little entry was shaken by the blast, but still the men perservered.

x

That dreadful Sunday, as Emmie lay in Dick's arms, her mind wandered. Both of them were drained by fear, thirsty beyond words and very hungry. It seemed to her that she was lying in Robbie's arms on the sandhills, behind the great sea wall at Meols, and they were talking of building a small cottage not too far from there, with a good slate roof and a parlour for best occasions.

She woke suddenly, not sure what had alerted her. Instead of the sunlight on the waving, coarse grasses of the sand hills, she faced a midnight blackness. She touched Dick's face with her hand, and he stirred and muttered hoarsely, "OK, luv?"

"Mm," she replied. She shivered; the wall felt cold against her back.

It felt wet! Her cotton blouse and petticoat were

168

sticking to her back. She must have sweated heavily or wet herself again. But there it was once more – a cold drop, a trickle down a strand of her torn hair and across her neck.

"Dickie," she gasped. "Wake up. There's water running down the wall behind me back. I can feel it."

Water? He swallowed and tried to answer her, but his dried lips would barely move. He felt clammily cold and he shivered.

"Sit up, Dick. I'm goin' to turn meself over."

"Can't sit up, 'cos of the slope over me," he managed to reply thickly. She was right, though. He could smell the odour of water on dust – and he could also smell an increased amount of smoke. His heart leapt with fresh apprehension. He eased himself away from Emmie, to help her turn.

Emmie was as excited as if they had already been rescued. Her mind cleared as, wild with hope, she knelt up and ran her hand along the wall. There *was* a steady dribble down it at one point. She put her sore cheek against it and then turned to lick it. Her tongue was promptly covered with grit, but it was moistened, none the less. She tried again and spat out the grit. "There's only a bit," she announced in a fractionally clearer voice. "I'm going to try and soak your hanky, though."

The water flowed faster, forming a small pool round her knees. The handkerchief was soon quite wet and she passed it to Dick to suck. He thankfully wiped his lips and put a corner in his mouth. He too had to spit out grit, but the relief was tremendous. He managed to move a little out of his niche and curve himself round Emmie as she knelt, to dip the hanky again into the wondrous little pool.

Emmie undid her skirt button and awkwardly hauled off her blouse, cursing roundly when she caught her elbow on the rough wall. She pressed the garment into the tiny stream. As it became wetter, she struggled to get out of her cotton petticoat in order to soak that also. "It'll make a little store of water," she puffed.

"I'm sorry I can't see you."

She blushed, and managed a small giggle. In the dark, she had not considered her nakedness. Thankfully, she pressed the sopping blouse to her throbbing face. She tried to wipe it gently but it hurt too much.

All around the great slab that protected them water began to drip, to a point where, no matter how they lay, they became wet, and they again huddled in each other's arms, to keep warmer, while they speculated on the source.

"Could be a leak from a pool which built up somewhere above us," offered Dick. "And now it's sifting down to us."

Their little lair shuddered, as a quick series of explosions from the *Marakand* shook it; a heavier splatter of droplets fell round them. Dick felt Emmie begin to tremble and he held her closer. Again he was tempted to take her, now that the air felt cleaner and he could breath properly. She wriggled more tightly to him and he knew that she wanted him. She turned on her back and he moved on top of her, so that there was space above them.

Despite the limited space, it was a wild lovemaking, as if both of them were young and filled with the frantic desire of youth. Every terrifying shift of the broken buildings above them; every great blast that numbed their ears as the deadly cargo of the *Marakand* wreaked havoc, though adding to their fear, also intensified their passion, until finally they lay exhausted and almost unbelievably at peace. They continued to caress each other, Emmie with a strange wonder that some one other than Robbie could make her feel so good. As she stroked him, she murmured incoherent endearments and he chuckled. "Not bad for an old man, eh?" he joked, and fell asleep.

He was awakened by her hoarse voice saying, "Dickie, I thought I heard something scrabbling about then."

"Eh, what?"

"Listen? Is that a voice?"

They held their breath; then without a further word felt round for the stones they had used to bang the wall with.

Frantic with hope, they both banged, and shrieked, "Help! Help! Help!"

Emmie's voice was much weaker than she realised, her throat swollen from her earlier screams, and Dick's was not much better; he realised ruefully that he had exhausted himself with Emmie; it was hard to get breath enough into his lungs to yell.

They paused to listen again. They could hear only the groans of the pile above them, as it slowly settled. Emmie began to cry.

xi

Gwen felt, that Sunday, that her life had been broken into, just like burglars broke into houses, that her house was as good as doorless and anybody could plunge in and out of it without so much as a by-your-leave. Never before had she had to extend a hand to anybody; she prided herself on minding her own business, on having the whitest doorstep in the street, the best-dressed daughter and the cleanest-looking husband – and, of course, getting her washing out on the line before any of her neighbours, on a Monday morning. Sunday was a day to meet one's friends at chapel and show off the hat one had retrimmed, and to anticipate with pleasure eating one's meat ration, slowly braised in the oven while one was at service.

And instead, she was surrounded by the most awful bunch of little horrors anybody could have wished on her. She surveyed them grimly, as they sat round the table at midday, eating like starving dogs. It was a pure miracle, she thought, that she had managed to provide a dinner at all; just like the story of the loaves and fishes. The Thomases' meat ration had been extended into a stew with the aid of a bag of potatoes, culled from Mrs Donnelly's kitchen, and three pennyworth of fades – discarded, shrivelled vegetables – from the corner shop. Nora, who had been entrusted with the message to the corner shop, had also brought two loaves of yesterday's bread and some milk – on credit. "The first time in me life I ever arst for anythin' on tick," moaned Gwen.

Patrick had been soundly clouted over the head by his father, for coming to view the ravaged Dwellings, and he now sat sulkily shovelling stew into his mouth, while Gwen slapped a couple of spoonfuls of it on to her own plate. She picked up her knife and fork and began to cut the tiny cube of meat, when suddenly she remembered.

"Emma!" she exclaimed, and put down her fork.

Ruby looked up from her task of feeding an unwilling

172

Michael with bits of bread sopped in a saucer of gravy. Mari who had got up only in time for the meal, asked with a small yawn, "Isn't she in bed?" She smiled across at Patrick, but he dropped his eyes and did not smile back.

"It were such a hectic morning, I clean forgot her. She never come home."

Mari stared at her incredulously, while Ruby stuttered, "Do you think she caught it last night?"

Mari licked her lips. "What about Daddy?"

"He'll be all right." Gwen's reply was automatic. Her husband was always all right, as dependable as the Liverpool one o'clock gun, which, before the war, had marked the time for the city. No one had told her of the carnage in Bootle – or, indeed, in the city itself; the wireless had merely reported a raid on a north-west town.

She sighed, as she looked round the table. Only Ruby and Mari were interested in Emma; the others continued to eat, Brendy happily pushing bits of vegetable into his mouth with his hand. "Really, Brendy," Gwen expostulated. "Use your spoon, you naughty boy." He took no notice and she leaned across the table and gave his hand a small slap; then she stuffed a spoon into it. He tried shovelling.

She turned to Patrick, as being the only older male present, and said agitatedly, "I'll save her some dinner, anyway. And you, when you've finished, run over and tell your dad she's missing. He'll know what to do. He'll ask about her for us."

Patrick nodded agreement. If he had a real message to deliver, surely he would be able to stay to watch the men at work on The Dwellings. He quickly ate the last mouthful on his plate and half rose from the table.

"Have your pudding first," Gwen ordered. "A few more minutes ain't goin' to make no difference."

Pudding as well. For the first time that day, Patrick's spirits rose a little, and he ate eagerly the large helping of bread-and-butter pudding she put in front of him.

"Where did Miss Emmie go?" he inquired.

Gwen explained about her job in the Sailors' Canteen in Paradise Street and that she was on the evening shift. She ran her fingers through her greying red curls. She had been too busy to comb it and had not even washed her face.

"I'll take me dad's bike and tell 'im first; then I'll ride down to Paradise Street and see what's to do there." He looked excited at the prospect and gave Gwen the same beguiling, conspiratorial grin that had mesmerised Mari in the air raid shelter. Mari, seeing it, felt again the extraordinary sensation which his exploring fingers had introduced her to. She flushed and went slowly on with her dinner.

"I hope she's all right," Gwen said mechanically. "She might've gone over to see Robert Owen's mother." In her heart she felt that Emmie was a deliberate nuisance in not turning up for either breakfast or dinner. Serve her right if she'd got killed. Decent girls came straight home. And then there were all those merchant seamen hanging around the canteen – a lot of no-goods with only two ideas in their heads, drink and women.

Patrick could not find his father at The Dwellings because he had taken half an hour off to go to see the local undertaker about his wife's funeral. He reluctantly approached the constable in charge of the incident, who promised to put an inquiry about Emmie in motion immediately, and to let Mrs Thomas know as soon as he had news. The constable refused to allow him to go close to the ruins, so Patrick again mounted his father's rusty bike and sped away to join the sightseers in the town. At the top of Duke Street, he was stopped by a soldier with a rifle on his back, who wanted to know his business and promptly turned him back.

Patrick knew the town like a rabbit knows its warren. He gravely cycled round the corner out of sight, then dived down an alley and proceeded along back ways. He did not return for tea.

xii

Gwen gave the children a tea of bread and margarine and home made gooseberry jam and sent them out to play in the street. It was the first day in her married life that she had given barely a thought to the condition of her little house, except nearly to weep over the bed which Michael had wetted; it was now being dried out with the aid of three hot-water bottles. She sat with eyes closed, wishing passionately that David would return. He would know what to do about the Donnelly children – and Emma and the windows – and the fact that she was going to be over her housekeeping money.

She was sound asleep in the chair, mouth open, gently snoring, when Conor Donnelly, followed by Ruby, walked in through the open front door.

She awoke, startled to see an awful apparition standing before her on her rag rug. It was white with dust from head to foot, the face caked. Two red eyes glared out at her from under a battered tin hat; ominous brown stains marked the front of him. There was a faint smell about him as if of a butcher's shop, mixed with old sweat. A gap in the face was mouthing something about Emma.

Frightened, she jumped to her feet so quickly that she nearly knocked him down.

"It's me dad," explained Ruby simply.

Gwen forced herself into wakefulness. "Did you say Emma?" she asked. Then, without thinking of the effect on her fireside chair, immaculate in faded cretonne, she said, "My, Mr Donnelly, you look dreadful! Sit down. Would you like a cuppa tea? Have you had your tea?"

Conor flopped thankfully into the little chair and tried to smile. "Ta, I could use a drop."

"No trouble." To offer a cup of tea was a strict convention, but she surveyed him with dismay. Never in her life had she seen anyone look so dreadful. Even the chimney sweep at the end of a day's work – or the coalman – never looked as bad as that. For once her Methodist training surfaced, and she asked impetuously, "I got a bit o' dinner left. Why don't you wash your hands and face under the kitchen tap, while I make it hot for you?"

He had eaten nothing hot for forty-eight hours and he accepted eagerly.

It was amazing what a bit of hot food would do for a person, thought Gwen in gratified surprise, as she watched Conor polish off the dinner intended for Emma. Scuttling round to make the food ready, she had forgotten again about Emma, but now as he slurped at a cup of tea, she remembered and inquired if he had news.

He sighed. "Aye, I have, Mrs Thomas. The canteen's flat. They're digging into the shelter under it now."

"And Emma's in it?" Her heart bounced uncomfortably. It was one thing to wish a person dead or gone; quite another to probably have the wish granted so promptly.

"I suppose she's there. They're trying to finish the job afore it's dark – same as we bin doin' at The Dwellings."

"Do you know how things are in Bootle?"

Anxious not to scare her unnecessarily, since her husband was out there, he played down the shocking fate of Bootle.

"Me hubby didn't even come home for his dinner," Gwen remarked quite crossly. "Don't they know men have families to look after?"

Conor ignored the remark and pursued the question of Emmie. "Miss Thomas were engaged, weren't she?"

"Yes." Gwen was surprised that he knew. She had forgotten that the engagement of a woman of mature years would have been an interesting piece of gossip to be mulled over by the fire in the local public house.

"Is he at sea?"

"I doubt it – yet. They were loading at No. 2 Huskisson, according to Emma."

"What?"

Gwen jumped. "At Huskisson. Why?"

Conor told her the news, received over the post telephone, of the fearsome destruction wreaked by the exploding *Marakand*. "Most of the bangs you've been hearing today is from her," he finished up.

"Well, I can't say as I think much of him, to be truthful – but I wouldn't wish that on him." She had a sudden picture in her mind of the tall, well-built man, ruddy-faced and blue-eyed, and knew in her heart that she was deeply jealous of Emmie. Emmie was so

177

content, so satisfied, as if part of the time she was moving in a dream. David had never made her glow like that. She felt a surge of longing go through her thin frame and she examined her nails carefully so that Conor would not read her feelings in her face.

Conor said heavily, as he got up from his chair, "I'll see if we can trace him. Robert Owen, deckhand, on the *Marakand*, wasn't it?"

She nodded absently.

MONDAY, 5 MAY 1941

Neither Emmie nor Dick admitted to each other an increasing hunger; hunger was something which had been with them, on and off, all their lives. At her brother's house, Emmie had for the first time enjoyed adequate meals, though Gwen was by no means generous in the portions she gave her. Now, however, she endured a clemming misery.

As they became wetter, the water which had been such a Godsend became a trial. Dick shivered constantly, teeth chattering, from the cold as well as from nervous strain.

Not only did they lie in puddles of water, but in their own urine and ordure, and the odour vied with the smell of smoke and wet plaster; the wisps of smoke saved them, however, from attacks by rats, the contemplation of which made both of them heave at times; the vermin with which Liverpool was infested retreated as the fires advanced.

At one point they thought they heard the scrape of metal on stone and then a distant shout. In response, they banged the wall with a stone and cried out again and again. The wall was as thick as a castle keep and if there was anyone there, the frantic cries went unheard.

In a sudden burst of fury, Emmie had said venomously, "If I ever get out of this fix, I'll go into munitions. I'll send them something to make *them* smart, I will."

"You can make good money at it," Dickie replied practically. "A lot more'n you could servin' in a cafe."

181

This idea had set her off on a laboured, barely audible description of what she would like to do after the war, if she had some savings. "I'd buy a nice little sweet and tobacconist's," she confided to Dick. "It'd give me some real independence – and summat to do while Robbie's at sea."

"He might like to swallow the anchor and help you."

"Nay," she insisted, with unexpected woodenness. "He can have 'is own job. This is for me. I never ever thought o' planning for meself afore this." She contemplated a hopeful future for a little while. Then she said, her voice cracked and broken, "You know, a lot of women get tired of being bossed all the time, but unless you got money you got to put up with it. I'm tired of it. I want to be free – and Robbie will benefit. We'll have more money for both of us. Go on holidays and suchlike."

Sporadically, they planned holidays and dreamed of sunny beaches, until an ache in Dickie's back became a piercing pain; his temperature started to rise and finally his speech to wander, until he was talking to Emmie as if she were one of his sons.

Emmie, too, began to feel light-headed, and the unbroken darkness robbed her of any knowledge of the passage of time. Unaware of the frantic battle being waged in No. 2 Huskisson, in which her beloved Robbie fought as hard as anyone, she concluded from the intermittent booms which shook the ground beneath her that it was night and a raid was taking place at a little distance from the town centre.

Just before midnight, and continuing well into Monday morning, enemy aircraft swept over the east coast, like a cloud of disturbed hornets, curved round

182

over Liverpool Bay and followed the shining Mersey to their target.

The anti-aircraft guns had been reorganised during the day, to good effect, and a heavy barrage greeted the raiders, making it difficult to bomb accurately. Nevertheless, incendiary bombs deluged the city, and the haphazard scattering of high explosives brought out of bed at a run all those citizens brave enough to retire in the first place. People sleeping on the platforms of the underground railway forgot the hardness of their sleeping place and turned over thankfully, and those in air raid shelters or out in the fields beyond the city congratulated themselves on their forethought, miserable as they might be. The stunned victims of the earlier raids, now herded into schools and church halls, faced this further threat to their safety, and more than one such shelter became a bloody grave before morning.

Though night fighting was a new art, the pilots in their slow Defiants used all their ingenuity to defend the port. "Learnin' on t' job, like us," one auxiliary fireman remarked cynically, as he gazed upwards for a moment at the fireworks in the sky. A thin cheer went up from his battered brigade, when a Nazi airman was spotted bailing out and floating downwards, his parachute spread above him. "Hope he gets lynched," cried several savagely tired Liverpudlians; but he was picked up from the river the next morning, drowned, like so many of Liverpool's own men.

Ignoring the pandemonium and the danger, Rescue Squads still picked their way delicately through great heaps of what had once been a city. With the aid of shaded lamps or, infrequently, a floodlight, they peered and called and probed, with occasional success, while

183

searchlights flicked like mad pendulums back and forth across the sky and malevolent pieces of flak flashed like javelins amid the rescuers.

Panting, trying to keep calm, Emmie held the head of a babbling Dick to her naked breast, clasping her arms tightly over him as she sought to protect him. As the hubbub continued, furious sexual desire engulfed her again. It boiled in her, an urgent, primitive need, and she murmured incoherently to him. Dick himself was aware only of a warm, comforting presence in a world of nightmare, as pneumonia took hold of him. His breath came in harsh rasps.

"Don't let him die, oh, God. Don't let him die," she implored, as she realised there would be no response from him. While the ear-splitting din round her increased, she began to believe that he was indeed dying; her self-control deserted her, her mind gave way and she shrieked like a rabbit in a snare.

ii

As she saw Conor out of the front door, on Sunday evening, Gwen managed to insert into his monologue the suggestion that the children might now return to their own home, since it was fairly certain, from experience in other raids, that the Germans had finished this onslaught. Shocked, Conor had turned back and vehemently begged her to keep them with her for one more night.

"Their nan should be here by tomorrer night," he assured her. "She'll stay a few days, though she's still got me dad to care for at home. Then Rube will have to manage for us — we'll hope the raids'll be finished by then."

When Gwen still demurred, he insisted, "I *can't* stay home with them tonight. They need every man they can get at The Dwellings. What would people say if I stayed home, I ask you?"

Because of what people might also say about her, Gwen reluctantly agreed to keep the youngsters.

She went slowly back indoors. In the yard, Conor's dog started to bark and then to whine. "Blast him," she muttered viciously. The kitchen door to the yard opened, and Patrick entered, the dog sidling after him. He looked white and strained and glanced at her uncertainly before dropping his eyes to the importuning dog and patting it.

He's scared, Gwen sensed. Frightened to death of something.

"What's up, lad?"

"I don't think anybody's alive down there," he burst out, his breath coming quickly, as if he had been running.

"Where?"

"Down Paradise — where your Emma was."

Gwen felt herself go cold. So the worst had happened. She had wished it and she was responsible. She wanted to be sick.

"It's somethin' terrible down there, missus. You should see the fires." His lips trembled. He had seen what he feared even grownups could not cope with and he was frightened, humbled. Dreadful Mrs Thomas looked suddenly like a pillar of strength; her basement steps a safe stronghold.

The gates of hell yawned before Gwen. If you wished

a person dead – and it happened as you wished – it was as good as murder. She gaped at the beaten child whose grubby hands clutched for support at the back of the chair. Then she said very slowly, "What you and I need is a cuppa tea." She tried to pull herself together, and added, "And I'll make you gooseberry jam butties to go with it." She walked unsteadily past him to the kitchen and he and the dog followed her forlornly.

Faintly from the street floated the voices of Ruby and some neighbouring little girls singing a skipping song. The thud of the rope stopped and a quarrel broke out, in which Nora's strident shrieks predominated. A few moment later, a flustered Ruby dragging a recalcitrant small sister interrupted the tea making, and from the staircase another voice chimed in, as Brendy, clad only in his vest, howled, "I want me mam. Where's Mam?" He came pattering into the kitchen, pushing his way past his sisters.

Gwen gulped and half closed her eyes. "Be quiet!" she cried exasperatedly. "Shut up, Nora." She bent down to catch Brendy, who threatened to exit through the back door in search of his mam. "Hey, you're supposed to be in bed, now."

Nora stopped her battle with Ruby and joined in with Brendy. She looked up resentfully at Ruby and cried, "Aye, where's me mam?" She pouted, and rubbed her arm where Ruby had slapped her.

Gwen snatched up Brendy and tried to soothe him. "Your mam'll be back soon," she told him, patting his back gently. "You know she's gone to hospital to be mended."

Though she heard both Patrick and Ruby catch their breath behind her, this was sufficient to reduce Brendy's howl to a sob. "Where's she broken?" he asked with a trace of interest.

Gwen sighed. "She's got a cut – just there." She touched Brendy's protruding ribs. "The doctor'll sew it up – and then she'll get better and come home, I hope."

"Get away," Nora exclaimed in disbelief, her pout wiped off her face. "With a bloody needle?"

"Don't you use language like that round this house, miss," Gwen scolded. "Or I'll wash yer mouth out with soap." Nora bridled, her sly eyes peeping defiantly between the almost white lashes. Gwen went on, "For sure, they stitch cuts up with a needle – and white cotton."

"Well, I'll be buggered!" Nora's eyes opened wide with amazement. "They couldn't?"

Gwen put down Brendy, picked up Nora's hand and smacked it on the back. "I told you to mind your language, you little vixen."

Nora scowled and was silent.

Brendy pulled at Gwen's apron. "When'll she come?" he asked piteously.

"Soon, luvvie, soon. Now you come up to bed. You'll get cold down here."

After Gwen, Ruby and Patrick had shared a pot of tea and he had told them some of the details of the shambles in the town, including the information that the rescue squads were still digging for survivors, Gwen sat white and silent for a moment. Then she said heavily, "You'd better go and feed your dad's cockerels."

He went grudgingly into his own back yard and stood watching the birds in their separate cages pecking at the black market corn, as he sprinkled it in front of them. When he unthinkingly put his fingers on to the chicken wire which held them in, one bird pecked him. He swore at it. The burst of anger brought him out of the lethargy into which he had sunk, and as he sucked his finger, he watched with interest a plane high in the sky. It climbed in the pearly atmosphere until he could hardly hear its engine, and slowly a great ambition rose in him, to fly himself, to be a bomber pilot and give the Germans what for. He looked at the closed back door, where his mother had been fond of leaning, her latest baby in her arms, to catch the sun and wait for him to come back from school. Tears welled up and with them a murderous desire for revenge, a boiling tide of feeling which stayed with him for years. "I'll teach 'em!" he cried, as tears of grief ran down his face.

iii

Gwen crawled into bed beside Mari. In the next bedroom Michael whimpered fretfully.

"I wish Ruby could shut that kid up," she fumed uselessly.

Mari stirred uneasily. "He's hungry, Ruby says. He wants his mam. She used to feed him from her breast. I seen her."

"Good Heavens! That's not decent. He's far too old for that."

"Ruby says that's why he wants his mam so bad."

Gwen cleared her throat, a little embarrassed. "Well, a little girl like you shouldn't be talkin' about such things." She turned over, and buried her head in her big feather pillow. Mari thought she had gone to sleep, but she said abruptly, "I'd better get him a titty-bottle from the chemist tomorrow." She sighed, and then went on, "Till I can teach him how to drink from a cup."

A resounding crash, an hour later, took the corner grocery shop, and the sunken-cheeked woman who kept, it straight into oblivion. Mother and daughter flew out of bed. Nora, Brendy and Michael were howling in unhappy unison with the air raid siren.

Ruby met them on the landing, with a bawling Michael in her arms. She was panting with terror, her big grey eyes nearly popping out of her head. Nora and Brendy crowded behind her.

"Downstairs, quick," ordered Gwen, as she struggled into her dressing-gown. "And you, Mari, take the candle – and don't drop grease on the stair carpet."

Patrick had opened the front door and was watching the Defiants darting in and out amid the searchlight beams. "For goodness' sake, come in," yelped Gwen in nervous concern. "That's how your mother caught it."

He shut the door reluctantly as the other children scampered through the living room to the kitchen and the cellar steps. Inspired, Gwen snatched her sweet ration out of the sideboard drawer as she went past, and what had threatened to be a weary, noisy gathering became suddenly happily quiet when she distributed toffees all round.

At half-past four on Monday morning, they went gratefully back to their beds.

At five o'clock, David was dropped at his door by a car intended to carry the walking wounded.

He staggered into his home and sank thankfully into the familiar depths of his easy chair. He leaned his head back and the pain in his chest surged again. To hunt for the matches and light the gas jet was out of the question;

he concentrated instead on trying to breathe. Finally, the spasm passed and he sat absolutely still, beads of perspiration coating his forehead, until he heard Gwen running down the stairs. She hurried in, tying her plaid dressing-gown round her, as she pattered across the linoleum. Patrick stirred but did not wake.

"Dave!" she exclaimed. "Am I ever glad to see you." She peered at him in the half light. "Golly, you look dirty. Have you had any tea?"

David felt as if he were floating along in a mist, everything distorted, nothing close to him. He breathed with effort, afraid to move much, lest the pain recommence. The staircase up to bed loomed as an impassable barrier. "I'd like a cuppa tea," he managed to reply. He closed his eyes, and the faintest smile broke the exhaustion of his face, as he envisaged the whole of Liverpool afloat on pots of tea.

Gwen quickly folded back the little hearthrug. "Aye, David, what a time I've had. I've got all the kids from next door here. Patrick's there." She gestured towards the sofa, half hidden in the gloom. "Poor Mrs Donnelly – struck down in her prime."

"Dead?"

Gwen was kneeling in front of the fireplace, quickly raking out the ashes and then stuffing balls of newspaper and pieces of firewood into the grate. She paused and turned a pinched, weary face towards him. "Saturday night."

As best he could, David tried to pay attention to the story of the children, the windows, the broken aspidistra bowl, the dog in the back yard and Emmie's absence. Finally, she said, "And last night the gas went off. I put a whole shillin' in the meter and nothin' happened."

David sat with his eyes closed. Emma! "What did you do about Emmie?"

"Told Mr Donnelly and he's inquiring."

He knew he could not go out himself to look for her, so he simply nodded and said, "You can draw a couple of quid from the Post Office Savings. Aye, I hope she's all right." After these garbled instructions, he allowed himself to rest.

He was hazily aware of her feeding a horde of children, correcting them sharply and dispatching them to school. He woke sufficiently to return a hearty kiss and a hug from his daughter, doing his best to appear merely tired. Gwen had handed him a cup of tea, but he sat with it on a little table beside him until it went cold.

When Ruby left him, Michael yelled and had to be held back from following her. As the front door slammed, he threw himself on to the floor and kicked and screamed, arms flailing.

David was thankful when the piercing howls became sobs and then the sobs were separated by silences, as the little boy discovered David staring at him. The blazing blue eyes closed and, thumb in mouth, he went to sleep on the hearthrug at David's feet.

Gwen had run upstairs to put on her clothes, and now she came down and said, "Thank goodness, that's over. He won't eat, 'cos his mother used to feed him herself. I'll get him a titty-bottle from the chemist when I go down the road." She turned to survey David. "Would you like some cornflakes for your brekkie? Or do you want to get washed first?"

"Nay," he replied slowly. "See if you can get the doctor to come. I keep getting a pain in me chest."

"Pain? Why didn't you tell me? You don't look well, that's for sure."

The detail of the cramp in his chest was laboriously explained to her, as she flung her coat over her flowered overall and crammed her beret over her errant curls. She half ran the quarter-mile to the doctor's house.

According to his troubled wife, the doctor had been out all night. She would send him over as soon as he returned.

Breathless, Gwen returned more slowly. She was sick with fear. Was it a heart attack? Or warning of a stroke? She must keep him quiet – and that meant keeping Michael quiet, as well. She'd pick up a bottle and teat from the chemist when she passed his shop, if he were open.

As she went to turn into the chemist's doorway – she could see him inside, though the "Closed" sign still hung on his door – she bumped into Mrs Hanlon, a big, florid woman, the wife of a docker who lived a few doors away. Mrs Hanlon was bubbling with the exciting news of the demise of the corner shop and its owner, which lay in the opposite direction to the doctor's house and had consequently not been seen by Gwen.

"And what you goin' to do, now Blackler's is burned down?" the woman asked, wrapping her black shawl more tightly round her and leaning forward to breath into Gwen's harassed face.

The news was a real shock to Gwen, and Mrs Hanlon seemed to expand and contract, like a balloon in process of being blown up. Blackler's gone – and with it, presumably, her wages. Gwen's heart sank.

"And Lewis's," went on Mrs Hanlon ruthlessly. "T' firewatchers must've been roasted alive."

Gwen felt as if the whole universe was crushing down on her. "I got to go to the chemist," she intervened desperately. "Mr Thomas is sick."

Mrs Hanlon ignored the interjection and prattled on happily about The Dwellings and the pile of bodies there.

Suddenly, with overwhelming passion, Gwen hated her. Was it really a Roman holiday to her? Didn't she realise that every bomb that fell was like a huge stone in a pool; the effect grew and grew, like ripples in a pool. Not only did it destroy homes; it upset completely the lives of everybody near. And for what? For what?

As the remorseless voice went on and she tried unsuccessfully to ease herself behind Mrs Hanlon in order to rattle on the chemist's door latch, she thought of Michael screaming for his lost mam, and she wanted to run home and take him in her arms and tell him everything would be all right – in a while, when the ripples ceased – and to put a hot poultice on David's chest and tell him the same.

The chemist opened his door and at his polite "Excuse me" Mrs Hanlon moved out of the entranceway. Gwen whirled behind her and left the woman standing open-mouthed.

iv

A frantic Monday for every city official, with one hospital out of commission and several others badly damaged; in Webster Road mortuary over half the bodies nameless; water in short supply; wavering

193

sheets of flame still flaring upwards from burst gas mains; dangerous electric cables snaking over many a road and in and out of wrecked buildings; hordes of hungry and homeless people; and the centre of the city a mighty funeral pyre.

To those Liverpool housewives who still had a home, however, the main problem was that they could not do their washing. Monday was national washing day and on Tuesdays one did the ironing.

As Gwen hurried through her back yard, on her return from the chemist, she realised that even if the trickling kitchen tap provided enough water, she could not hang the washing out in the yard to dry. The air was filled with tiny bits of grit and burned paper – she had a piece in one eye and it was watering miserably. A sandlike film had formed on all her brightly polished window sills, and when she ran her finger along the clothes line as she passed, she found it thick with dust.

She paused for a second, her hand on the doorknob, to get her breath before entering the house, and looked down at the neat sealing-waxed parcel the chemist had made of a feeding-bottle and comforter. Then with shoulders bowed like an old woman, she opened the back door and went slowly in.

David lay on the sofa, asleep. His usually ruddy face was ashen and Gwen noticed with a pang that his two days' growth of beard was grey, not black. He was still in his overalls.

Michael snuffled gently on the hearthrug. He was awake, sucking his thumb as usual. He held the little, brass-handled hearth brush in his arms as if it were a teddy bear.

She ran upstairs to get a woollen shawl with which to

cover David and was immediately thrown into a towering rage when she discovered, in passing, that the drawers of the chest in Nora's and Brendy's room had been opened and the contents were scattered all over the floor, amid feathers from a burst pillow. "Blast them!" she cursed, nearly crying.

She had just tucked the shawl over David, who did not stir, when there was a polite knock at the front door. Expecting the doctor, she hastily took off her overall and smoothed down her skirt, before answering. She was still shaking with suppressed anger.

On the unwashed doorstep stood a nun. Gwen glared at the tiny elderly figure in a spotless white wimple and a shabby, but perfectly pressed, black dress. Little highly polished black boots peeped out from under the heavy skirt and a large rosary hung from her waist. Her hands were tucked into her big sleeves. The face in the stiffly starched frame was paper-white and lined like crumpled tissue. Two gentle grey eyes surveyed Gwen and showed faint amusement, as Gwen stepped hastily backwards as if to avoid contamination.

Assuming that the nun was begging, she asked rudely, "What do you want? We're Methodists. We don't give to Catholics." She started to close the door.

"I have come with regard to the Donnelly children. I am from their school." The voice was soft but authoritative and Gwen opened the door slightly again. "I wanted to inquire if you need help with them."

With a long sigh Gwen said, "Well, I'm managing." She bit her lower lip and, remembering her manners, asked, "Will you step in for a minute? The parlour is wrecked, but come in anyways."

The nun floated in after Gwen and surveyed the dying

aspidistra lying amid its earth and the broken shards of its pot in the middle of the red Belgian carpet, the linoleum nailed roughly across the windows, and the soot in the hearth.

Gwen hastily brushed broken plaster off a straight chair brought from her mother-in-law's house. "Sit down," she invited cautiously.

"Are *all* the children with you?" asked the visitor, seating herself.

"Yes." The word came in a little gasp, and suddenly Gwen was pouring out to another woman, a woman, not a nun, all her worries about Michael, her fears that she could not keep Patrick under control, about Ruby's little shoulders having to carry such a terrible load in the future, and about foul-mouthed Nora and Brendy. "Their gran's supposed to come today," she finished, pushing back her wild hair from the eye that was still watering. "And me husband come back this morning with a pain in his chest. He's asleep back there. We're waiting for the doctor now."

"I understand. I can quite understand your concern." Gwen had been standing in front of her, and now the sister caught her hand and patted it. "I'll have some additional clothing sent over to you – and a box of groceries – you could pass them on to their grandmother – if she arrives safely."

Afterwards, Gwen warmed some milk and put it into the new feeding-bottle. How strange it was. Under all that black cloth lay the kindest of human beings. She said to Michael, who was sitting on the rug, rubbing his eyes and whimpering, "I won't be a minute, luv. Auntie's coming with a nice bottle – and an old lady's goin' to send you some little pants – specially for you."

She picked the child up and held him in the crook of her arm, his drooping head against her flat chest, and put the teat into his mouth. After a moment's experimentation, he began to suck eagerly.

v

The shops which had survived were closed. The black-clad assistants were hurrying home, after a frantic Monday of dusting and sweeping and the resorting of stock blown off the shelves. The foreman of the rescue squad wriggled out of the zigzag tunnel he and his gang had moled into the ruins of the air raid shelter under the canteen. He took off his breathing apparatus.

"We're into it," he announced to the anxious little crowd hanging about outside. "But there don't seem to be nobody alive."

Mr Robinson's mouth tightened and Higgins threw away his cigarette end angrily. They climbed as close to the tunnel entrance as the foreman would allow them. There, they leaned on their shovels and waited. Both were covered with dust, their blackened shirts clinging to their backs with perspiration. Not by so much as a quiver did either show their agony of mind; yet Alec Robinson thought that if it were not for the support of the shovel, he would collapse. The tall, thin chauffeur took a cigarette packet out of his shirt pocket and offered a smoke to his companion. Without taking his eyes off the tunnel entry, Alec Robinson nodded refusal.

He was able to identify his wife of thirty years by the modest engagement ring on her crushed hand. The chauffeur, faced with the naked, torn body of his

197

beloved mistress, peered in the gathering gloom at her contorted face and then at the three magnificent rings on her hands, and muttered, "Yes, it's Her Ladyship," before quietly fainting. He had to be carried across to the other side of the street by two exhausted labourers and revived by the First Aid contingent. When the body of Her Ladyship was turned over to her family's undertaker, the rings were missing.

The police reported to the constable in Toxteth that no one answering to Emmie's description had been found.

vi

It was as if the whole population was swaying on its feet. One more blow and it would, if from nothing else, collapse from fatigue. By Monday evening Gwen had decided that the Sunday night raid must be the last one; the Germans had never before raided four nights in succession; she reckoned they would not come a fifth time. If it wasn't the last of the series, she felt she would drop dead; she could not take any more.

Conor Donnelly had not helped this feeling of despair. He had slapped the children's and his ration cards on the kitchen table, as if they had come to stay another week at least. Then the doctor had arrived, taken one look at David and hurried home to his telephone, to order an ambulance; Gwen had hardly had time to wash her husband's face and hands and help him out of his dirty overalls, before the vehicle arrived and whisked him off to Walton Hospital.

"They would choose the hospital furthest away," she

grumbled to Mari, Patrick and Ruby, at lunch-time. "How'm I goin' to get out there to visit him, I'd like to know. This mornin' I'd no one to leave Michael with, so as I could go with him, to see him settled in, like."

Mari ignored her mother's whining complaints. "He's not going to die, is he, Mam?"

"Of course not," snapped Gwen peevishly. "If they can't cure a heart attack we're in a proper bad way." Her panic regarding Dave must not be conveyed to Mari.

In the afternoon, she announced to Michael, who was having a great game on the heathrug with a collection of saucepans and lids, "Now we got to go and do the ration books – yours as well – 'cos Annie's corner shop's gone with the wind. Got to find a new grocer. And all that beastly red tape, to register again."

As she trudged back home up her own familiar street, carrying a very tired and fretful Michael, she passed the pile of rubble which had been Annie's shop and she stopped to sigh sadly in front of it. The pillar box still stood amid the rubble, and Mr Marsh, the neatly uniformed postman, was just unlocking it to collect the letters from it. "Nice day," he said mechanically, and she laughed almost hysterically, "Aye, I suppose it is."

A few yards further on, she met Bridget Mahoney, her neighbour from across the road. Bridget was looking red-faced and sullen, but she listened as Gwen told her about the Donnelly invasion of her home, something she knew about already. "And to crown all," Gwen finished up, "our Emma is missing down town somewhere, and I'm worried to death about her."

Bridget regarded her dully, as she nursed her bandaged arm, cut when she had removed the incendiary bomb from the gutter of her house. Her body trembled and she could not answer Gwen at first. Then she muttered, "So's me husband – in Greece. Got a telegram just now."

Gwen was aghast, stuck for words, knowing that she should say something optimistic and comforting.

Bridget swallowed. "I don't know how to tell me boys."

vii

Conor received with some anxiety the information that Emma had not been found in the canteen's air raid shelter. The constable on duty, who had given him the news, added heavily, "Either she were struck down on her way home – or she took shelter somewhere else and got buried there."

"We could try checking amongst the unidentified." Conor sighed. "Could start with the living. I'm off duty now – I'll see what I can do on the phone."

Four unidentified women between the ages of 25 and 35 lay in three different hospitals, their names unknown, though only one had been found in a street Emmie was likely to have traversed on her way home. The voice at the other end of the telephone added laconically, "Of course, there's several hundred unidentified bodies, a goodly number unidentifiable, at Webster Road mortuary."

Patiently, Conor hitched lifts to the various hospitals; looking at the women was the only way to be certain.

One woman had recovered consciousness and had identified herself. Another had been claimed by a frantic husband. The third one had just died and Conor was allowed to view the body before it was wheeled away to the mortuary.

To see the fourth one, he followed hopefully a young probationer through a packed women's ward, filled with lively chatter. Behind a screen, a person lay on her back, arms neatly arranged at her sides under tightly tucked-in bedding. Her breath fluttered uneasily from blanched lips. Her eyes and head were sheathed in bandages, as if a white turban had slipped half way over her face. Her head was supported on either side by what Conor supposed were sandbags. An angular, elderly nurse raised an eyebrow, as Conor intruded softly.

He whispered, "I've come to see if she's Emma Thomas." The nurse nodded and stepped back, while Conor peered down at the end of a nose, prettily curved white lips and a rounded chin with an unexpected dimple in it, totally unlike Emmie's long narrow face.

The nurse's face softened, as he nodded negatively. "Poor little lass," she murmured. "It's her eyes, you know."

With a dreary ache in his heart for Ellen, mixed with sorrow for the pretty young woman he had just seen, he decided that he would try the dead.

A delivery van driver gave him a lift to within a couple of streets of his destination. He had to wait, while a calm, slender woman in a white coat dealt with a sailor in a tight-fitting Royal Navy uniform, who could not have been more than nineteen. The sailor stood timidly at the counter, his round white cap clutched in both hands in front of his chest. The acne spots stood out on his face and neck against an unnaturally pale skin. Together, he and the woman went through a series of large brown envelopes holding the effects found on or near the bodies in the mortuary. Time and again he nodded affirmatively, as he recognised the pitiful possessions. Sometimes he hesitated uncertainly and the woman put those envelopes on one side.

Conor felt himself reeling at the strong smell of disinfectant mixed with the ghastly odour of disintegrating bodies. He lit a cigarette and drew on it heavily, as he watched the pile of envelopes in front of the hapless sailor grow and grow. Finally, the woman drew the shaking boy further into the building. Conor began to whistle softly to keep his courage up; he had seen enough at the shambles of The Dwellings to understand what the youngster was going through. Thanks be to the Holy Mother that his Ellen was decently wrapped in a winding sheet in a proper coffin, and tomorrow, when his mother had arrived, they would see her respectfully committed to her own grave.

The sailor suddenly bolted past him and out of the front door. When the woman turned inquiringly to Conor, tears were streaming down her face. "He's from Seaforth," she burst out, as if she must share her agony of mind with someone. "He had fourteen bodies to identify, and some of them were a mess."

She had no trace of anyone who could be Emmie; the only likely corpse, picked up in Whitechapel, which was the continuation of Paradise Street, had been identified.

She rubbed her damp eyes with the back of her hand. "I'm sorry, Mr Donnelly. Try the temporary mortuary near the scene." She paused and tapped the table with the end of her pencil. "If I were you, I would talk to the men on the spot."

Between the mortuary and Paradise Street lay

Emmie's home. He thought he should drop in *en route* and assure Gwen that the fact that he had no news of Emmie was probably good news.

He was surprised to find the front door open and, after a perfunctory knock, he walked in.

He was immediately engulfed by his children, their faces smeared with jam, as they rushed from the tea table. They were followed by Gwen holding a feeding-bottle. Behind her, a man half rose from his chair by the fire. Robert Owen had duly received the information through the police that his fiancée was missing, and, since not much more could be done regarding the still exploding cargo of the *Marakand*, he had been given a few hours' leave. He had come just as he was, blackened and reeking of fire, his eyebrows and hair singed. When, at last, he had found a tram blundering along in the right direction, he had endured with suppressed fury the stares, and occasional giggles, of the other passengers, at his outlandish appearance.

Gwen looked inquiringly at Conor above the children's heads. He nodded negatively and she sucked in her lips as her sense of guilt returned to her. She shouted suddenly, irritably, at the children, "Now, Patrick – you kids – get back to the table and finish your tea. Now, Mike, you come to Auntie and I'll put you on the sofa, and you can show your dad how you can hold your bottle."

When the child had been propped up on the sofa cushions, he put the teat in his mouth and looked triumphantly at his father out of the corner of his eye. His father had, however, other things on his mind.

"You must be Emmie Thomas's intended," he said to Robert. "I been lookin' for her just now."

203

The air raid siren interrupted Conor's and Robert's conversation with the police constable they found on duty at the corner of Paradise Street.

"Oh, blast 'em," rumbled the constable exasperatedly.

Robert's heart sank, as he looked out over the enormous, smoking pyre facing him. He thought he'd seen the worst in Seaforth, but here was just such another scene of devastation – and possibly his Emmie was under it. He wanted to run across the road and start tearing it aside single-handed, to find her, but instead he had to listen to the doubts expressed by the constable that there were any more bodies there; certainly nobody alive.

High in the sky anti-aircraft fire flashed white. There were few clouds. Despite the smoke haze, it was much too clear for comfort.

From the south, where Toxteth lay, the guns spat forth. Conor, so tired that he was becoming a little incoherent, prayed in the back of his mind that his children would be spared. With a quivering match he lit a cigarette handed to him by Robert; one more flash of light was not going to help the Germans; the fires still burning would guide them beautifully.

The constable glanced uneasily at the firemen, rescue teams and a demolition squad still at work amid the destruction, and the women of the WVS mobile canteen nearby. The blue flash of the men's lanterns made them look like ghosts. Nobody ran for cover as the gunfire increased. He began to herd the chattering crowd of sightseers into a nearby underground shelter. It beat him where all the onlookers came from. He'd have thought that every man and woman in the city had enough to do at present; and if they didn't, that they would be thankful to sleep. But here they were, come to gloat. Ruddy vultures, the whole bloody lot of 'em. He blew his whistle impatiently, to summon one or two stragglers, and to draw the attention of the solitary telephone engineer, still toiling in the nearby crater.

The engineer took no notice. The whole job was almost completed and he continued to check the lines which he and his colleague had been sedulously splicing together all day. In cooperation with the exchange operators, the reconnected phones were rung in nearby offices. Sometimes the line was still dead, the telephone shattered under the debris. Occasionally, a late-working clerk or a firewatcher or cleaning lady would lift the receiver and assure him that *everyone* had gone home, which never failed to make him smile. Now, with the increasing noise overhead, he was frightened and was glad of these nasal Liverpool voices responding to him. George, he told himself wearily, you're getting a bit old for this game. When a piece of flak whizzed down and buried itself in the clay side of the hole, he clapped his tin hat on to his bald head, clenched his teeth over his cold pipe and went on working.

The constable returned to Robert and Conor and they all stared skyward. Beneath the hissing of water from the firehoses and the rhythm of the pumps, they could hear the steady chug of engines from the east, and they moved to the shelter of the sandbags surrounding the entrance while they discussed what could have happened to Emmie. The sandbags had been pierced by flak and were slowly bleeding their contents on to the pavement. Conor absently poked a bigger hole with his finger, while the constable assured him, "They cleared the shelter, the rescue squad did – they were proper tired – and then they went home to get some sleep." He turned, to rebuke someone trying to leave the shelter, and then, in answer to an impatient query from Robert, he said, "Well, you could talk to the new incident officer – the other one was killed last night."

A series of thuds not very far away announced the arrival of the Luftwaffe, and George nervously collected his tools into his tool box and said to himself, "Me lad, this is where you beat it."

He hastily had the line he had been working on rung by the operator. It failed to ring, and he cursed his wasted effort. The exchange operator said sharply, "Mind your language, if you please," and transferred her plug to another call. He made a face and was just about to remove his instrument from his ear, when distantly down the line came a hoarse female voice singing falteringly *Men of Harlech*. He grinned. The receiver must be off the hook and some cleaning woman probably dusting round it. He listened for a second; the sky directly over-head was quiet, though more distant sounds of combat warned him not to linger. The song became a series of harsh sobs. It seemed to him that very faintly he heard also the rumble of a male voice, and then, a little more strongly, the tune again sung in Welsh. He gave a small laugh. Welsh miners sang it a lot better, probably because they were always singing; he had been told that they sang even when they were entombed in a mine accident.

Entombed! My God!

"Can you hear me?" he shouted, in incredulous apprehension. There was no reply, only the weak, cracked voice carrying the tune.

He called the telephone operator. Could she heard it? But the voice had stopped and the operator told him loftily not to be so daft. Lips pursed, he put a clamp to mark the line and scrambled out of the hole. Like a lumbering bear with a tin hat on its head, he ran down the newly cleared pavement, looking madly for the constable.

The WVS volunteer, a mug of tea in each hand, directed him to the entrance to the shelter.

"Get away," exclaimed the constable, when he poured out his suspicions to him.

"I'm not joking," spluttered George furiously. "I tell you I heard it. It's possible, I tell you. And buried miners always sing – and this woman was singing in Welsh. Me grandmother was Welsh – I know Welsh when I hear it. Damn it."

"It's her," Robert interjected with conviction. He caught at the constable's arm. "Come on. Who do we have to see to start 'em digging?"

The constable swallowed, while Conor said simply, "Emmie Thomas is Welsh."

George looked a little bewildered at this exchange and they hastened to explain to him about the missing woman. "And you think this is technically possible, that the telephone fell somewhere near her and still managed to remain connected?" the constable asked the engineer.

"You've just said the canteen was on the ground floor. It wouldn't have far to fall, if it wasn't blasted

207

out; if it were protected by a wall that didn't give, like. Anyways, I heard her."

"Let's try the line again," Conor suggested impetuously. He started to move out of the sheltered doorway, but the constable held him back and pointed to the bit of sky they could see above the sandbag wall. It was filled with flashing light, and a series of reverberating booms came from the direction of the docks. "You're chancing your own lives," warned the constable. "What number was it?"

"I've forgotten. I can find out. I marked the line."

"For God's sake, let's try it," Conor urged. "Come on," he called to George and Robert. He started to run across the road, George skittering unhappily behind him, followed closely by Robert. A shrill shriek overhead sent the three of them into the gutter, hands clasped over heads, noses in the dirt.

The missile passed over them, to fall into a fire slightly closer to the river. Its explosion sent a mass of burning debris flying into the air, to start fires in buildings hitherto untouched. Firemen dropped their hoses and ducked for cover wherever they could find it, only to regroup a few minutes later and continue their tasks. Conor, George and Robert stayed firmly in the gutter until the remainder of the stick of bombs had been deposited in a neat line across the city, and had sent to Kingdom Come one ambulance driver and her assistant, twenty-two homeless people in a rest centre, two pedestrians never identified, one firewatcher and one special constable; the thin red line was becoming frighteningly thinner.

A series of bombers sweeping the length of the fan-shaped city, now dived one after the other to loose their deadly loads, and sent up fountains of rubble as their bombs scored hits. The three men cowered in the gutter, hearts racing, as all kinds of lethal odds and ends pinged and plonked on the road and pavement round them. A group of soldiers and rescue men, their hooded lanterns bobbing, chanced running for the air raid shelter. Robert heard a muffled cry, as one was hit. He crammed himself further into the littered gutter.

During a moment of lessened hubbub, Robert cautiously turned his face to peep upward. The gun flashes were like an enormous storm of sheet lightning. Tracer bullets and flares added to the scarifying display. A further beat of heavy engines made him push his face tightly against the pavement's friendly curb. George, his head near Conor's feet, stretched out a careful hand to touch the warden's boots for comfort. He could feel panic rising in him, but he was haunted by the sound of the quavering voice and he tried to concentrate on the technical arguments why he should be right. He'd *prove* he was right, he would, even if he had to dig for her himself.

In Paradise Street, a big Victorian chimney, balanced by a piece of side wall from the building in which the canteen had been, shivered and fell, its stonework rattling over the wreckage at its foot. The usual cloud of dust spumed upwards. Through chattering teeth, Conor prayed for his life to his patron saint, who had not heard from him for some years. Conor had said bitterly that he was accursed; yet even so, life seemed unexpectedly precious when it looked like coming to an end.

The Defiants succeeded in disorganising the raiders and the bombing moved further north. Robert was so stunned with noise and fright that it was a moment or two before he could make himself scramble to his feet, to find the constable bending over George, as he got to his feet, and shouting through the noise, "Come on, get back in t' shelter."

Though terrified out of his wits, George was determined. "I'm goin' to try that line again. Won't take a mo'."

"You're clean out of your mind," the constable bellowed. But he ran with them to the cavity in the street.

They crouched together in the clay hollow. George found the wire with a clamp on it. He clipped on his headphones.

"No." He found also that he could no longer contact the telephone operator.

"It could've been one of the WVS women at the corner singing," suggested the constable.

George boiled with frustration. He checked his splicing again.

Conor leaned closer to him and shouted into his ear, "I believe you."

Robert thought he would lose his reason if one of them didn't do something constructive soon. "It must've been the chimney what fell just now – broke whatever connection there was." He turned to the constable and asked, "Who do we go to – to ask for rescue men?"

"The incident officer, like I said." The constable was feeling most unhappy and cursed his indecision. He was, in principle, the ultimate authority, but he did not want to pressure the incident officer into a wild-goose chase; yet the engineer presumably knew his business. As they crawled over the gummy clay and out of the hole, he said finally, "Let's talk to the incident officer."

A curious chug-chug-chug, like a train coming rapidly into a station, made them all slide back into their refuge and hug the side of it. Not too far away, something crashed into the wasteland. Tensely they waited for the explosion.

Nothing happened.

Cautiously they lifted their heads. Again the sound of a train. Again they pressed themselves into the clay. A tremendous detonation in the direction of Exchange Station drew a string of vivid swear-words from the constable. "Now I know what we got – a bloody land-mine – unexploded. Now isn't that nice?" His sarcasm was bitter. "Blow us all into next week, it could, while we're lookin' for this woman."

TUESDAY, 6 MAY 1941

"I've never heard of such a thing before." The hard-pressed incident officer sounded kind, but he was used to survivors clutching at all sorts of straws to assure themselves that a loved one was still alive. "I think you *must* have misheard," he added to George. "It's easy enough."

"We can trace the number," George informed him coldly. "Look in your telephone book and see what the canteen's number was, and I'll trace if the line is the same."

It took a little while and the close co-operation of the telephone exchange supervisor to establish fairly certainly that it was indeed the canteen telephone line. Then, with his nose in the air, George climbed into his van and went home to bed. Let the high-and-mighty incident officer work out *where* she was.

The incident officer wasted no time. He sent for a heavy-rescue foreman, recently off a train from London, and to his surprise the man said calmly, his Cockney accent sounding strange to the men around him, "There was a case like this in London."

The plans of the buildings in the Paradise Street area, carefully prepared at the beginning of the war, had been burned with the command post the previous night, but an off-duty warden, who might know the canteen, was traced with commendable speed, through the warden of his home district; and he tumbled out of the Anderson shelter in his garden and came down on his bicycle while the raid still raged.

He could not suggest where Emmie could be, but, when asked to draw a plan of the canteen, he included the cobbled back-yard.

"Where was the phone?" asked Robert.

"It were in the kitchen at the back."

"Exactly where?"

"On a little table by the window, as I remember – though I can't be sure." He stubbed out his cigarette. "T' window faced the yard."

"She must be in the yard, or in the wreckage of the kitchen," interjected Conor between a series of yawns. His legs felt like lead and he told himself that once they started to dig, he would go home and kip down for a while.

To Robert Owen, the dark small hours were a nightmare, while with infinite care the heavy-rescue foreman from London and a group of miners from nearby St Helen's, with other experienced people, plotted Emmie's possible position. They decided to explore whatever might remain of the light well.

Robert was sick with fatigue from the battle in No. 2 Huskisson; burns on his hands were a throbbing misery. Conor tried to persuade him to go home for a few hours, but he refused. Someone thrust a mug of coffee into his hand and he drank it gratefully. Then he insisted on going down to Paradise Street to help the rescue squad. Shoulder to shoulder with the miners, he helped to pass debris back to the road, as painstakingly slowly a new tunnel was made, to pass over the huge stone wall which had formed the back of the canteen shelter. Pieces of office equipment, beams, furniture and some precious pit-props were carefully eased into place, to hold the tunnel open. He worked like an automaton, the fear he had felt when he went to the Mercantile Marine office to obtain another ship long since forgotten, lost under greater and more immediate terrors. Nothing seemed to matter now, except that Emmie be found alive.

When the All Clear howled across slateless rooftops, to be followed shortly by the first rays of the rising sun, the pace of work increased. A rotund WVS woman, a flowered wrapover pinafore covering her uniform, brought mugs of tea and a basket of fresh scones with a scraping of margarine on them. "Made them myself before I set out," she told them proudly. "We've still got gas on our side of the water."

Her face showed the same weariness as that of the rescue team, but she was so fresh and clean that Robert felt as if his mother had come all the way from Hoylake to help. "Have you heard her yet?" the woman asked.

"Nay. T' foreman's goin' to go in a bit further, now he's got a block and tackle rigged. Then he's goin' to ask the fire engines and everything to be quiet, while he listens – afore the streets get busy, like. Couldn't do it while the raid was on – no point in it, with guns and all."

She touched his arm and said comfortingly, as the weary group munched and slurped thankfully. "Och, you'll find her if she's there. You're all great lads."

Robert lifted his mug to her, his eyes twinkling suddenly. "You're great ladies," he said.

It was only when the new police constable on duty managed to organise a short period of quiet that Robert realised what a shambles of noise they had been working in. In the stillness, he was surpised to hear a seagull squawk, as it came to rest on top of the

217

broken roof of the building behind him. Not very far away, burning wood crackled, and from the direction of the river a ferry boat hooted cheerily.

The squad waited, tense as Olympic runners, while a miner as small as a jockey eased his way along the tunnel they had made. Apart from his torch, he carried a piece of piping to use as a listening device.

To Robert, it seemed a lifetime before a soft rustle and a tumbling pebble heralded the man's careful emergence. Once clear, he stood up and removed his mask; he coughed helplessly to rid his lungs of dust. His watering eyes made little rivulets through the dust on his cheeks. He nodded negatively.

Robert's teeth began to chatter. He clutched the foreman's arm. "Let me go down," he pleaded.

"No, son. You're too big."

ii

During Tuesday morning, Gwen, with Michael on one arm, squeezed into the stuffy privacy of the nearest public telephone box. It was still functioning, so she telephoned Walton Hospital.

A tired, uninterested voice assured her that Mr Thomas was resting comfortably.

Gwen determined that on Wednesday morning, she would keep Ruby home from school to care for Michael while she attempted the journey across the town to visit the hospital. She fully expected, however, that keeping Ruby home would not be necessary. Grandma Donnelly would surely arrive in time for her daughter-in-law's funeral that very afternoon, and would remain to care for her grandchildren. After lunch she must see that Ruby and Patrick were clean and tidy, ready to accompany their father to the funeral.

She had had a sharp spat with Patrick that morning about the necessity of going to school. The broken nights had taken their toll and he wanted to remain in bed. It had ended with her slapping him hard across the head and threatening to complain to the headmaster, if he did not go. At first she had thought he would slap her back, but he had got up and gone sulkily to school with the other children.

At lunch-time, as she handed him a bowl of soup and a cob of bread, she said to him, "You're a bright lad, Patrick. If you learn to read and write as good as Mari, you'll never be hungry or out of work. And I would like that for you, scamp that you are."

He had nodded agreement and lost some of his sulky look. He dreaded the afternoon. He was afraid he would cry at the funeral.

Ruby sat silent, steadily drinking her soup. She knew *her* reading and writing days were over. She looked down at the soup bowl, spoon poised, and wondered what happened at funerals. Her thin lips quivered.

A box of groceries, some children's clothing and a parcel of nappies were delivered immediately after lunch by a cheeky youth on an errand boy's bicycle. Gwen smiled. The nun had not forgotten.

A worried Conor, looking incredibly neat in a clean blue overall, washed and ironed for him by Glynis Hughes, collected Patrick and Ruby. "Their gran and me brothers' wives haven't come from Walton yet," he told a very sober-looking Gwen. "Here's a slip of paper telling 'em which church. Will you give it to them, if they come late?"

"Where you goin'?" asked Nora, held back firmly by Gwen, while Brendy sucked his thumb and stared at the funeral-goers.

"Never you mind," Patrick told her savagely. "You and Brendy go to school." Ruby began to cry.

"You stay with me, and after school we'll go down the street and buy a sweetie ration." Gwen shepherded the youngsters back into the house, where Michael was trying to feed Mari's long discarded wooden bricks to a patient Sarge.

Grandma did not arrive that day, nor did any other relation, and an extremely hurt Conor went straight back to his post after returning Patrick and Ruby to Gwen's house. "I'll try to get through on t' telephone to the warden up there and ask him to send a message. They may've got t' lines restored by now."

Once more a resigned Gwen saw her charges scrubbed from head to foot and put into bed, Michael soothed with a bottle of milk and Brendy happily sucking his brother's dummy.

"What about me mam?" asked Nora, sitting up suddenly in her white bed. "A girl at school says she's dead. What's dead? Is it like when the cat was run over?"

Gwen gulped, while Ruby shivered by her in one of Gwen's own nightgowns. Ruby's eyes were huge and imploring. Gwen said coolly, "They're still mending your mam. You don't have to worry about her. And soon your gran'll come to take care of you."

"Well, what *is* dead?" Nora insisted, as she unhurriedly pulled the blanket over herself, and Gwen tucked the sheet round her chin.

"It's when you go to Heaven," replied Gwen, and added almost wistfully, "It's proper peaceful, like, and you're with God."

"Oh, aye," replied the child, just as if they were talking about lollipops, "Sister Theresa talks about it sometimes. Do you get lots to eat there?"

Gwen laughed, for the first time for a week. "To be sure," she replied promptly. "No shortages at all."

She waited for Ruby to climb into her bed beside Michael. The girl looked drained and as hagridden as Bridget Mahoney from across the road had looked that afternoon. Impulsively Gwen bent and kissed her on the cheek. "Now you cuddle down and sleep and don't worry about nothin'. You'll feel better in the morning."

When she went into her own bedroom to see Mari, the girl was sitting on the edge of her bed, pulling off her socks. She, too, looked older than her age, her eyes black-rimmed. "I wish we had news of Auntie Emmie," she greeted her mother.

Gwen sighed. "They'll find her. Don't worry. Now hurry up and get into bed and get some sleep."

She went slowly down the darkened staircase, automatically holding a corner of her apron under the candlestick, to catch any wax before it fell on to the stair carpet.

In the living room Patrick was sitting on the black, horsehair sofa. He had his head in his hands and was crying.

She put the candlestick down on the table and held him against her apron. "Now, don't take on so, luv. She's at peace now."

She took her handkerchief from her pocket and bent and wiped his tears. He took it from her and blew his nose hard.

Gwen felt as if she herself had hardly got into bed before the air raid siren went, followed almost immediately by a tremendous run of explosions. Once more, she gathered her frightened brood and hastened to the cellar steps, where, for four hours, she tried to cope with tears and quarrels, while outside a thundering tumult raged.

WEDNESDAY, 7 MAY 1941

As clerks and typists struggled over the debris to report for work in non-existent buildings, the incident officer offered to send a relief crew, to replace the men hunting for Emmie. The men refused to be relieved.

The incident officer did not argue with them. Amongst the motley gangs of workmen there was a stiff pride that they did not stop work until they had themselves carried the victims out.

An intact corner of the light well had been reached. The searchers tried listening there, but heard nothing. They did, however, find a woman's shoe and this gave them new incentive to continue.

Robert could hardly stand, but he continued mechanically to pile rubbish into skips and to lend a hand where he could. He could not identify the shoe as Emmie's.

Gathered as close as the police would allow was a large crowd of sightseers, clerks in well-pressed business suits, their female counterparts in neat black dresses with white collars and white summer hats, housewives in spring suits, with pretty baskets on their arms, and the male flotsam and jetsam of a port, who, despite two years of war, seemed to have nothing particular to do.

An untidy little office girl came out of a building still standing behind the crowd and pushed her way into the middle of the partially cleared street. She held a saucer of milk. "Kitty, kitty, kitty," she called, and, as a thin black cat sidled up to her, she put the saucer down, and explained to a young woman standing watching, "It's the offices' pussies. They got no home now." Another cat approached tentatively, and she renewed her call.

Young typists and clerks were searching the edges of the ruins for filing cabinets, account books, any records which would help to re-establish their companies, when it was agreed that a miner particularly experienced in mine rescues should go down the tunnel and decide how they should proceed further. In a moment he was gone, flicking himself along the tortuous zigzags and ups and downs, like an eel through rock-patterned water. Though the smell of this disaster was different from that of a mining accident, the dust was the same, and when he felt cobblestones under him, he paused to readjust his mask. It was surprisingly quiet, as he flashed his torch along the lines of what cracks he could see. It was clear from their angle that, further on, the yard had collapsed. This puzzled him. He turned the torch upward, to examine the fearsome mass above him. To move further in, he decided, could be dicey.

"'Allo," he called tentatively, not too loudly – it wouldn't take much to start a fall, he reckoned. "'Allo, there."

Dead silence, except for an uneasy movement overhead. Blast it. He drew his piece of piping from inside the front of his singlet and this time put it to the cobbles – afterwards he could give no real reason why he did so. He bent his ear to it and listened intently.

It seemed to him that he did hear something, a movement, other than the rustles in the wreckage bearing down round him. But it was from underneath him.

He laid his head, ear down, against the unfriendly

226

cobblestones and held his breath. Very carefully he tapped on the stones with the end of his torch.

The girl couldn't be under him? Or could she? He tapped and listened again. There was a small, strangled cry. And it *was* from underneath, but a good distance further to his right, he guessed. Taking a chance, he cupped his hands round his mouth and put his face to the stones. At the top of his voice, he shouted, "We're coming. Hold on there."

She heard him, a muffled echo. With overwhelming joy, she tried to shout back, but she had screamed so much, was so exhausted by fright, hunger and thirst that the noise was not enough for him to hear. Beside her, Dick muttered incoherently in a high fever, as if he had pneumonia.

Perplexed, the miner ran his torch again along any cracks he could find, to see their direction. He tapped the surface in several directions as far as space would allow, but there was no echo, and no further cry. He backed down the tunnel as fast as he dared, trying to imagine, as he retreated, how parts of the light well might have fallen, and into what kind of space. It had to be a cellar, he decided.

As he emerged, panting, scratched and mystified, Robert ran lightly up the debris to meet him, followed by a protesting foreman. "You shouldn't run over it like that, you fool," he bellowed. "Bring the whole mess down!" He forgot his complaints, however, when the miner said there was indeed someone there. "Under you?" he exclaimed in disbelief. "But it's a yard – a light well. Cobbled. Seen it meself when I went down a bit back."

"Well, get down there and get her out." Robert was

227

nearly beside himself.

"Hold on, lad." The foreman was aggrieved. "These buildings've bin blasted several times from different directions. It's not that simple." He turned to the miner again. "You're sure you heard her?"

The man smiled, his teeth flashing white in his filthy face. "I heard somebody, all right."

"Thank God!" exclaimed Robert in relief. But anguished dread then filled him. What horrifying hurt might Emmie have suffered? He fought down a wave of nausea.

The returned miner was talking again. "She must be lying in a hole under that yard. But most of the yard must be supported by solid earth – otherwise the cobbles would have caved in years ago. They'd be a dead weight."

"Some kind of arches might be supporting 'em," another man suggested. "Arches can hold up cathedrals."

"Aye, but we *could* be digging down through solid rock, if we go down through the cobbles."

"How far into the yard, measuring, like, from where you was lyin', do you think she was?" The foreman rubbed his heavy-muscled arms which ached intolerably. He was bent on pinpointing as accurately as possible where they must penetrate.

"A way," the miner said immediately. "I went over the stone foundation wall what you told me about – back o' where the canteen shelter must've been – and all me body was on cobbles. She must've been at least twenty feet from me, bearing half right; and I tell you, the voice came from below – not level with me."

Robert caught the foreman's arm. "I know!" he broke

in eagerly. "Me grandad told me often enough. Privateers – and smugglers – used to have hiding-places for contraband – and you said the cellar of the canteen was much older than the building above it. Could be there's some merchant's old cellar under that light well."

The foreman sighed and pursed his lips, and then said rather condescendingly, "It's an idea. But God knows how she fell into it."

"This fella here said it would be hard to go down through the light well itself. Could you still get into the shelter?" asked Robert, fatigue forgotten, and the plan of the building he had seen the warden draw clear in his mind.

"Oh, yes. It was all well nigh cleared out by the time we'd finished. Have to go down carefully, because of the of the big chimney collapsing over there, last night."

"Did you see any doors in the walls?"

"No, lad. We'd 've gone through 'em if we had – to make sure nobody was there." The tone was scornful now.

"Look again," Robert persisted. "If they had a secret cellar under the light well, then they had a place to get into it. Maybe it were bricked up when they built the offices. Round here they've bin building and rebuilding for centuries – even the offices were real old. There must be all kinds of little places built over – even small rivers have been."

The men stood round arguing amongst themselves, while the foreman thought this over. The ultimate responsibility was his and he was not going to put his men at risk unnecessarily.

Finally, when Robert had begun to think he could not bear another moment of suspense, he said, "OK. I'll go down meself and look." He turned to a young miner who was particularly small-made. "You, Evans, you can come with me."

They had been squeezing slowly round the shelter's walls for nearly five minutes, before Evans said triumphantly, "I've got it. See, this is brick, not stone."

The foreman flashed his torch along the wall. Once pointed out, it was possible to see a line under the whitewash where the texture of the wall changed. He crawled closer to the younger man and then carefully tapped on the brick and listened. No response.

ii

Some of the rescue crew, who could do nothing for the moment, went down to the WVS van to get some lunch, while, amid the smell of wet plaster mixed with that of a charnel house, the foreman dug out the first bricks with the care of a surgeon. The wall would be weaker at this point and the old brickwork could crumble suddenly under the weight of the wreckage above.

The wall proved to be four bricks thick, and when the fourth one suddenly gave and fell out on the other side, a poof of surprisingly cold, damp air blew out at them.

Evans broke into excited Welsh; then remembered his English. "The lad up there was right. There's space here." He put his face close to the hole they had made, and shouted, "Anybody there?"

In the light of the foreman's torch, his face fell. "Try again," the foreman urged.

"Anybody there?"

Very faintly came a croaking sound that could have been a human voice.

The wall was broken as fast as human hands could do it without causing a fall. As soon as the hole was big enough, young Evans wriggled through feet first. He felt around with the toes of his boots, to make sure he was not dangling over a hole. Cautiously, he stood upright.

"Lend us the torch." The foreman passed it to him and he flashed it round. "It's like a blinking castle dungeon," he reported. And then he called, "'Allo! 'Allo!"

From beyond a massive blockage facing him came a faint response, a distant sob.

"We're coming. Hold on. Are you by yourself?"

The reply was unintelligible.

Evans tried again. "Are you badly hurt?"

There was a pause and then Evans clearly heard an effort at a throat being cleared. "No," came the answer.

Meanwhile, in preparation, other men worked feverishly, pushing pit-props and tools down the tunnel and through the hole in the wall. They whistled when they saw, by the light of a powerful lantern, parts of hefty stone arches. There was room to stand against the wall through which Evans had clambered; but the rest seemed to be an almost solid mass of wreckage.

"She's on the other side of that," said Evans, his young face gloomy in the light of the lantern, as he gestured to his right.

The foreman, who had followed Evans through the hole in the wall, glanced quickly round. He said, with more optimism than he felt, "We'll find her. God, it must be five hundred years old, this place. They knew how to build in those days – and that's what's saved her, though there's more'n one fall here." He rubbed the end of his nose and then went on, "Reckon she's tucked up not far from the wall we've come through, but it's goin' to take a while afore we get through that lot."

The floor of the cellar was earthen, which at times was a help to them, in that they could loosen large pieces of debris by digging for a little way under them. Miners can almost sink into the earth when they dig, but a bucket brigade had to be formed, to move earth and debris out of the way as it was dug, and these men had difficulty in keeping up with the moling miners.

"At this rate, we'll be home in time for tea," one of them joked.

The moles themselves, though fast, moved with the greatest care, with the minimum of noise, with the least disturbance of the dense mass poised above them. A faint smell of burning made Evans shiver; occasionally small runnels of water would cascade down on them. "From the fire-hoses," the foreman told them firmly. "Water and gas is turned off. You're not goin' to drown."

Every so often the gasped curses would cease and the leading man would call to Emmie, partly to reassure her, but partly to keep them on course.

She would answer them with a faint croak. Every tired nerve alert, she had listened through an eternity of time to the muffled sounds indicating that help was coming. Sometimes the men had paused, to consider how to deal with an obstruction facing them; there was no sound, and at such times her spirits would sink. They had given up, deserted Dick and her. Dreadful, agonised fear went through her parched, starved body. She tried to shout but little noise came. She felt around the sick man beside her, to find her petticoat with which she had earlier wiped Dick's burning face. It was half under her, and she laboriously hauled it out, to suck it and dampen her mouth. Though they were lying on wet ground, it seemed impossible to do more than moisten their lips and tongues.

She found the stone with which she had tapped earlier and hit the wall unsteadily with it.

"That's good," said a voice surprisingly close to her. "Every time I call, you tap, eh?"

She tapped once in acknowledgment and prayed she would not pass out.

Outside, Robert Owen stood hunched in his Red Cross, brown jacket, nearly out of his mind with the frustration of the long wait. As he mechanically emptied buckets or handed in pieces of wood, his mind would hardly function, and suddenly he heeled over and fell face down on to a pile of debris. The watching crowd murmured and shuffled.

A First Aid man who had been checking his canisters of milk and water, and the tube which he could poke through a small hole in the obstruction between himself and a victim, and thus feed the sufferer until he was freed, dropped his satchel and ran to Robert. He went down on one knee and gently turned the exhausted man over. The doctor and driver from the ambulance also hastened across the street and together they lifted the limp figure and laid him down on the pavement, which had earlier been so sedulously cleared by Alec Robinson and Lady Mentmore's chauffeur. The lady doctor knelt to wipe gravel from his bruised face and half turned him on his side, so that he was less likely to choke if he vomited. She checked that he had no false teeth in his mouth and then lifted one of his eyelids. She smiled and took his pulse. Still amused, she got up slowly, dusted down her slacks and said laconically, "Gone to sleep on his feet."

She turned to the warden, who had come from helping the constable keep back the crowd. "Better find out who he is," she suggested, "and send him home."

"He'll be right mad if I do. It's his girl what's bein' dug out." He ran his tongue round broken teeth. "I'll get a couple of blankets and we'll lay 'im in the hallway of the office opposite."

The First Aid man returned to digging through his satchel. For the third time, he checked its contents: hypodermic syringe, pain-killers, sterilised pads, sticking plaster. A stretcher had already been carried as close to the tunnel entrance as possible. There was nothing he could do but wait. He envied Robert, sound asleep in the hallway. It was thirty-six hours since he had been to bed himself.

Far below the horrifying ruins, the miners burrowed like ferrets, thin sinewy arms flashing in the lantern light, flat-stomached bodies swinging in rhythm, as they passed buckets of earth back to a space near the broken entry to the old cellar.

Jimmy, the foreman, moved his helpers around as if he were playing a complicated game of chess, his seamed face a picture of intense concentration, as he improvised the steps of the rescue. No two rescues were ever the same; no two buildings ever fell in exactly the same way — their stresses and strains had each to be weighed up anew, and their constant tiny shifts watched with feline intensity. Not only had he to rescue those buried; he must at all costs ensure the safety of his team,

234

and as he sometimes remarked, "Me old woman would be proper put out if I buried meself and she was done out of a good funeral."

They came up within two feet of her, to a tight tangle of splintered wooden beams and what might have been part of an iron girder, the same obstruction Emmie had felt in her first search for the dripping water. Now she squeaked with shock when her foot was grasped by a warm hand slipped under it.

They were stalled.

"Sufferin' Christ!" The foreman's disappointment was as bitter as if his own daughter lay beyond the girder. "Get First Aid to bring some water and a shot for her, while we decide what to do."

The nervous young man crawled down the tunnel and fed both Emmie and Dick with water and then a little milk through the tube he thrust over the girder. She refused any sedation. Without a hint of his inward horror of the tight confinement of the suffocating tunnel, he whispered encouragement and told her that her fiancé was waiting outside.

"He's there?" Her voice was suddenly comparatively clear. "Thank God, thank God." She began to weep, soft, helpless crying in which was mingled a tremendous joy. He was there, he was safe.

When the miners were ready to start again, he backed down and told the surprised foreman that he had two living victims to get out.

Like dogs getting at a bone buried under a tree root, Evans hollowed out a space in the earthen floor under the girder. He then grasped her ankles firmly and told her he would help her wriggle down and under, on her back. When her knees were through, he grasped her bent legs and heaved her upwards. She cried out at the scratches she received, but she was through, her eyes dazzled excruciatingly by the blaze of the torch held by a second man behind Evans.

After calling Dick and getting no response, Evans turned himself on his back and squeezed himself into the space Emmie had occupied. He flashed his torch quickly round the tiny refuge, sickened by the stench. Near Dick's head, neatly wedged between a piece of stone and what looked like the remains of a table, was a telephone. So the engineer had been right. With a grin, he turned to the job of easing the barely conscious Dick out.

With difficulty, the warden managed to wake Robert. "They're bringin' her out," he said, a smug satisfaction in his expression, "and she's not badly hurt."

Without a word, Robert stumbled to his feet. Across the road he saw her being carefully carried down the slope of the debris. She was wrapped in a white sheet and strapped to a stretcher.

He pushed his way through the crowd of excited onlookers and ran across the road. Emmie was alive – and absolutely nothing else in the world mattered.

iii

On its way to Walton Hospital, the ambulance carrying Emmie, Dick and Robert, passed the bus in which a very subdued Gwen was travelling back home from her visit to David in the selfsame hospital.

Regardless of the thirty-odd other men in the ward, she had put her head down on the white coverlet of David's bed and cried. Too ill to do more than hold her hand, he had been staggered when she had laid her cheek on his work-scarred palm and told him he must get better, because she could not face life without him. She had paused to give a weepy sigh, and added, "Half the time I dunno what to do for the best."

"I'll be all right," he had whispered with an effort, and closed his eyes. It was nice to be wanted and not to be regarded as merely a walking pay-packet.

When she got home, Nora and Brendy were rolling round on the kitchen floor like a pair of angry young wolves. Patrick was kicking them none too gently in an effort to separate them, while Mari watched him from the living room, where she was seated at the table, trying to do her arithmetic homework. Ruby sat near her with Michael in her arms, feeding him from his new bottle. She was shouting, "Leave them be, Pat. They'll stop of themselves in a minute."

Gwen took one look at the fighting youngsters and total exasperation seized her. She strode through the crowded living room and squeezed quickly behind Mari's chair and into the kitchen. "Stop kicking 'em," she ordered Patrick, and he slunk back, muttering, "I were only tryin' to stop 'em."

Nora rolled triumphantly on top of a beleaguered Brendy, and Gwen bent down and administered the heaviest slap she could on the girl's small cotton-covered bottom. As quick as a cat, the child loosed Brendy and jumped to her feet. A stream of invective poured from her, as she rubbed her stinging bottom.

"Any more of that and you get no jam for tea," threatened Gwen, as she picked up the kettle to fill it from the kitchen tap. Nora made a face at her, and

Ruby hastily called the little girl to her. "You coom 'ere afore you get into more trouble, our Nora."

Brendy lay on his back and laughed, as he watched her go.

Patrick had a tin bowl of grain in his hand, some of which had spilled on to the kitchen floor in the mêlée. He squatted down and began to scoop the precious seeds together. "I were goin' to feed the micks," he told Gwen defensively.

"Aye, feed the pigeons – and you'd better do your dad's cocks, too."

After he had fed the cockerels, Patrick stood, empty bowl in hand, and looked round the familiar muddle of the Donnelly backyard. He burst into tears. Where *was* his mother? Where had she gone after death? Her body had been in the coffin the day before, but that wasn't her – not really her. Would he never again come through the back yard, to see her leaning against the doorpost, waiting for them all to come home from school? He did not know how to bear the pain within him.

An hour later, Gwen surveyed her troublesome brood across the littered tea table and prayed that their grandmother would turn up soon.

Patrick looked as if he had been crying. Deep compassion for him and for Ruby welled up in her; they must both be feeling terrible despair. Yet they were being very brave. Impulsively she leaned forward and pressed Patrick's grubby fist lying on the tablecloth. He looked up at her, startled, and saw the pity mirrored in her faded blue eyes. Quickly, he withdrew his hand and picked up his piece of bread and margarine. "Everything's going to turn out all right," she assured him, feeling a little shy herself.

He nodded.

She turned to Ruby. The girl looked crushed. She was staring vacantly at her empty plate. "Would you like another butties, luv? I can soon cut you one."

"No. I'm all right."

"Coom 'ere."

The girl rose and went to stand by Gwen's chair, like a schoolgirl called before the headmistress. Gwen put an arm round the thin body and gave her a hug and a smile. "Come on, now. Cheer up. Your gran's goin' to come soon – and I'm goin' to be next door all the time, and you can ask me." The girl smiled faintly, and unexpectedly put her arms round Gwen's neck, as she had so often done with her mother. She did not cry.

Mari watched in jealous shock. Her mother never hugged her. All she ever got was a peck on the cheek and an admonition to be a good girl. She had endured the invasion from next door, because of the strange magic of Patrick's presence. Now she wished crossly that they would all go back to their own house and that her father was home to give her a smacking kiss and call her his pretty young lady.

At midnight, she was sitting on the cellar steps, reading *Gone With the Wind* aloud to Patrick and Ruby, while one of the worst raids Liverpool had ever experienced raged outside.

On a mattress dragged down to the bottom of the steps lay Nora, Brendy and Michael, mercifully sleeping the sleep of the totally exhausted.

Gwen nodded over a cold cup of tea, while her mind went round and round in weary confusion. What if Emmie is injured – not killed? Do I have to nurse her as well as Dave? It would, she felt be a fit judgment on her,

239

for not helping Emmie with her parents; the pain-filled face of her acid-tongued mother-in-law haunted her for the duration of the raid.

THURSDAY, 8 MAY 1941

Constable Doyle consulted his notebook and then knocked on Gwen's front door. At least for this family he had good news – as far as it went.

He made himself smile as the door opened, to reveal Gwen in her dressing-gown, followed by five children in differing states of readiness for school.

"Me husband?" Gwen faltered, at the sight of the uniform.

"No, missus. Miss Emma Thomas live here?"

Relieved, Gwen replied that she did normally, but she was missing.

"Well, missus, you'll be pleased to know she's resting comfortable in Walton Hospital. Be out in a few days."

"Thank you kindly for stopping by to tell me," she began to close the door.

The constable cleared his throat. "I should tell you, missus, that we've heard as the hospital was bombed last night. We don't know the extent of the damage yet. I'll know in an hour or ..."

Through white lips, Gwen murmured, "Dave!" and fainted on her neglected doorstep.

Though the constable was resigned to carrying news that had this kind of result, Gwen's collapse was unexpected. He helped to carry her in and lay her on the living room sofa. She came round within a minute or two and, through chattering teeth, asked if he or Mr Donnelly would let her know when they had more news of the hospital. "Me husband's in there, as well as Emma. I'll go over meself as soon as I've got the children away to school."

"The north end's a shambles," Constable Doyle warned. "I doubt you'd get through. I'll come as soon as I've any news." He turned to Ruby and Mari – never had he seen two sisters so totally unalike – and told them to make a strong cup of tea for their mam. "Lots of sugar in it – and see she rests a while."

ii

On the previous Wednesday, the day before the raids began, Mrs Owen, Robert's mother, had said a thankful farewell to the evacuated mother and children who had occupied her spare room for some months. "I can't stand the quiet out here a day longer," the mother had told her. "I'm goin' home to Great Homer Street."

Now, on this perfect spring morning, she asked Mr Burnett, the chemist in Hoylake village, for something she might sprinkle round the newly scoured bedroom, to kill off any vermin that her unwelcome guests might have left there. "Me daughter-in-law elect is coming out to live with me. She's in Walton Hospital at present, recovering from being buried under the canteen she worked in. Poor girl. She's real nice. I'll be happy to have her."

Mr Burnett looked over his gold spectacles. He swallowed. "Do you know Walton was bombed last night?"

Mrs Owen's hand flew to her throat. "Oh, no! Poor lass, poor lass – and poor Robbie."

She had trouble waking Robert from the sleep of the absolutely worn out. He would have to go into

Liverpool, anyway, she told herself, to be signed off from the *Marakand* and then find himself another berth. She sighed at the thought.

When he heard the news, he was wide awake in a moment and jumped out of bed. He seized his trousers and struggled into them.

"The phone to the hospital's dead. I tried it – or rather, Mr Burnett did."

"I can go over."

"Well, you have some tea first. The kettle's boiling." Dear Lord, what a mess he was in, too. A black eye, hardly any eyebrows or eyelashes – all singed off – likewise his front hair. And both hands bandaged by the hospital, because of the burns on them.

iii

Conor had not been home since before his wife's funeral on Tuesday. Now, on Thursday morning, after what Glynis Hughes described as a lively night but not in the usual sense, he hesitantly opened his front door. He had snatched an occasional nap at the post, but now he knew he must really sleep; otherwise, he would collapse.

On the floor of the passage inside, lay his letter to his mother, returned through the dead-letter office. A wobbly hand had scrawled in pencil on it, "Address Unknown. Return to sender". Then in brackets the writer had added, "Whole street bombed. Tried to trace in Rest Centre without success."

He stood in the narrow hall, paralysed. He could not believe it. He had been so harassed himself that he had not thought about his parents' danger.

If they were hurt or killed, why hadn't his married sister, who lived in the same street, let him know?

A slow coldness crept through him. From bitter experience, he could visualise the scene so well. A dozen houses down, a whole series of families related to each other carried out dead or dying; no one surviving long enough to give names to the authorities. Those same authorities, hopelessly overloaded by the sheer magnitude of the raids, would in time name most of the victims – but not yet.

He leaned his head against his paintless front door, and cried aloud, "Holy Mother have pity on me!" He beat his fist against the unresponsive wood. "I'm damned! Accursed!"

Nearly demented, he fled back to his post – and the telephone.

With some difficulty, he got through, on the newly restored line, to the wardens' post nearest to his parents' house. Then he came slowly back to his own street. Instinctively, he sought the only people left to him, his children; he turned the rapidly tarnishing brass knob of Gwen's front door and walked in.

Michael was asleep on the sofa, an empty feeding-bottle lolling by his cheek. From the kitchen came the splash of dishes being washed.

"Are you there, Mrs Thomas?"

The splashing stopped immediately and Ruby came running in, wiping her hands on a dish towel. "Dad," she cried eagerly.

He held out his arms to her. She ran into them and with his head bowed over her he began to sob helplessly. She drew back. "Dad, what's up?" she

246

whispered, frightened by such a lament.

While she sat on his knee in the muddled room, he told her. He wept unrestrainedly, unable to hold in his despair and grief any more.

Half girl, half woman, she listened quietly, arm around his neck. Then she started to comfort. "Don't cry, Dadda. We'll manage," she said hoarsely. "Mrs Thomas'll help me – while I get started, like." She clung to him while he tried to control himself.

"I'm sorry, luv," he said, and wept on.

She was frightened to see her hot-tempered father cry, but it also put him on a level with Patrick, and she said, "Aye, everybody cries sometimes, Dadda," and gritted her teeth and hugged him closer.

When her father's weeping ceased, she said quite eagerly, "Let's go and buy a bit o' food, Dad, so as we can move back home."

That afternoon, Gwen and Mari sat and looked at each other over their teatime toast and dripping. The house was extraordinarily quiet and seemed to exude the misery of its damage and neglect. Gwen thought her heart had never been so heavy. By dint of taking three trams in a circular route and walking quite a distance, she had managed to reach Walton Hospital. The fright engendered by the bombs on the hospital had given David another heart attack. He had, however, survived, though he would need much nursing and would probably never be able to return to work. She had also briefly visited Emmie, who was heavily sedated and an alarming bundle of bandages and sticking plaster. There she had met Robert, sitting by her bed. He had told her that when Emmie was discharged from hospital, his mother would take care of her at his home in Hoylake, until they were married. It was the only good news of the day. Confound her – and her furniture – she could have the lot of it.

Mari broke into her gloomy contemplation by saying brightly, between sips of cocoa, "Tomorrow's your day for Blackler's."

Gwen nodded. "It's burned down. I'm out o' work – like plenty of others."

"They might start up again," Mari replied. "You could go and see. There's probably a notice set up in the ruins, to tell the staff what to do."

"Aye. I'd be glad of a full-time job, now your dad's so poorly." Her face brightened. "I'll go this evening. People's got to buy clothes and bedding from *somewhere*."

"I'll walk down with you, if you like."

"Would you, dear? I'd enjoy your company."

iv

One of the loneliest people in Liverpool lay unvisited, except by Robert Owen, in a huge, overcrowded men's ward at Walton Hospital. Identified by the pay slip in his wallet, still in his back pocket, Deckie Dick opened his eyes on Thursday evening, to the long glinting rays of a setting sun reflected on a shiny, white ceiling. He was in a bed and shivering; yet at the same time feeling dreadfully hot. He had been vaguely aware of being bundled about, of being sponged and feeling chilled.

A face loomed over him. It was topped by a little white cap above a wrinkled brow. A pair of sharp blue eyes, red-rimmed, peered at him. His wrist was clasped by cold, bony fingers.

A misty mouth said, "He'll be all right now."

Another blanket was tucked over him. He fell asleep, only to be awakened by more fumbling hands. The air raid warning was wailing its devil's notes, and two giggling young women were lifting him out of bed. They stuffed him underneath it. "Safest place," they assured him, and wrapped his blankets round him.

"Where am I?" he asked.

"Walton Hospital," they told him, and he breathed, "Thanks be," and slept contentedly on the floor through the rest of the night.

The entire population of Liverpool had been waiting tensely for the warning to go. Some of those who still had a bed had climbed into it, feeling that they *must* sleep, no matter what happened to them. Now they raised their heads to listen. But the raid was small, short and scattered; many of the townsfolk slept through it. London became the main target, though German squadrons were beginning to regroup in preparation for an attack on Russia. In the days following, mass funerals were held, and people who thought they could not cry another tear, wept some more.

One morning, a curiously shrunken and shaky Deckie Dick, dressed in clothing supplied by a charitable organisation, tottered out of Walton Hospital and went back to the room he rented in Pitt Street. The landlady had relet it. "Ah thought you must be dead," she told him. She had, however, stored his few belongings, in case he had a relative to claim them.

Weak and bewildered, he went into a tiny café, sat down at a greasy table and ordered a cup of coffee.

From his wallet he took out a small piece of paper with an address written on it and he smoothed it between thumb and finger. The granny of the young conscript he had met in the shelter also lived in Pitt Street. Robert Owen had told him that everyone in the shelter had been killed. She must be feeling bad, he ruminated, as he slowly stirred his tasteless coffee. It wouldn't hurt him to go up and see her; the old biddy might even know of a room to let.

Ten minutes later, he was climbing the bare, littered stairs of a lodging house similar to the one he had lived in, though this one seemed to smell even worse.

He did not have to knock at the door of the first-floor front room. The occupant had heard his footsteps and had opened it a crack.

"Mrs Pickles?" he inquired of the one grey eye peeping at him.

The crack widened. In the dim light he could make out only a female form draped in a black shawl. "What d'yer want?" The voice was full of suspicion.

"Ah come about your nephew, Wilf."

A sharp intake of breath. "Well, what about 'im?"

"Mrs Pickles, can I come in and sit down? I bin ill or I'd have come before. I met your lad in an air raid shelter and promised to look you up."

A pause. "Come in."

Inside the bare, clean room, he turned to the woman. She was very small, with a pinched, thin face out of which large steel-grey eyes regarded him with sudden compassion. Her skin looked pale from poor nourishment and lack of sunshine, and was a mass of fine lines. She had no teeth. About 55 years old, he reckoned.

250

She said, "Aye, you are ill, I can see that. Sit down on the sofa bed. I was just goin' to make a pot o' tea and a bite of toast." She picked up a kettle from off the small fire and poured boiling water into a teapot, much blackened from being kept hot too near the fire.

Dickie sank thankfully on to the edge of the sofa; the springs complained bitterly.

"What about Wilf?" she asked. "You know he were killed? He were all I got – a real nice lad."

As gently as he knew how, he told her about the scene in the air raid shelter and of his promise.

White cup and saucer in one hand, she looked down at him, her mouth quivering. He thought she was going to cry, but she did not. She simply sighed and sat down abruptly. She took the lid off the aluminium teapot and stirred the tea vigorously.

As she handed a cup to him, she asked, "What was you ill with?"

He told her about being buried with Emmie and his subsequent pneumonia, and as he talked some of the stress went out of him.

She listened patiently, and at the end she said, "I don't think any of us will ever be the same again after all this. It's as if all our lives was overturned in the course of a week, isn't it?"

"Aye." He smiled wryly, and stirred his tea. He wondered if he still had a job. Then he burst out suddenly, "Being buried like that – it taught me life was worth having. Funny, isn't it?"

She smiled and her eyes crinkled up with a promise of laughter, when she felt better. "Have another piece of toast," she invited.

Through two pots of tea and a pile of toast, they sat

knee to knee, two lonely people tossed together by a war they did not understand.

He stayed with her for the rest of his life.

SUNDAY, 29 JUNE 1941

"It feels proper queer – to be married at last," remarked Emmie. "I thought we'd never make it."

"You mean when you was buried?"

They were wandering along Hoylake Promenade, idly pausing from time to time to watch children digging in the sand, while their elders snoozed beneath copies of the Sunday newspapers, and dogs ran yapping after balls tossed by strolling owners. It was hard to believe that, not too far from them, out to sea, men stalked each other mercilessly and that, in Europe, the art of murder was reaching new heights, while in England itself cities burned.

"Not so much being buried," Emmie replied uneasily, "Though that were bad enough. But you havin' to go back to sea afore I were out of hospital – and bein' so long in the hospital, with me nerves, and lookin' like a piece of red raddle when they took the bandages off me face; I were fit to die when I saw meself in the mirror. I thought you wouldn't want me no more."

"Tush, luv. I'd always want you. There's more to a woman than a face. Anyways, there's nothin' that time and a spot o' warpaint won't cover." He bent and kissed the top of her newly permed hair. No need to tell her that he had been nearly shocked out of his kecks when he had first seen her. But the doctors had been right. She was healing and they'd done some neat stitching on her, which they swore would fade, and the bruises on her poor body were going, too. The doctors had said it was a pure miracle that she had no broken bones and she wasn't blinded.

He tightened his arm around her waist and he saw her

wince and immediately loosened it again. Bugger the Nazis. Just wait till he got a chance at one, he promised himself bitterly. He'd never felt such boiling hatred in his life before. It bubbled in him, awaiting only the opportunity to explode.

She turned her face towards him. "I love you so," she said unexpectedly, and he was diverted immediately by a fresh surge of longing.

"Look, duck. Let's nip 'ome. Me mam and dad allus goes over to see me brother on Sunday afternoon. Let's go 'ome and have a little matinee. What say?"

She bit her lip and then grinned quite cheerfully. Why say that so much of you still ached that you could hardly bear to be touched. He'd be gone on the eight o'clock train, back to his boat and the god-damned Atlantic. She'd have weeks of nothing before he returned – always supposing he got back safe. Time enough to get herself well again – and try for a job in munitions, so she could send a bit back to the Jerries with her best compliments.

Madame Barbara

This is a novel, its characters and settings products of my imagination, and, likewise, its situations, the egg hatchery and poulterers, and the Hôtel Michel. Whatever similarity there may be of name, no reference is intended to any person, living or dead, or to any business, past or present.

I am very obliged to Mr John Jammes, Cranfield University, UK, and Mrs Jeanne Pfannmuller of Edmonton, Alberta, who went out of their way to obtain for me information regarding Normandy, and to Mr Peter Stirton of Copy Plus, Victoria, BC, for technical help.

In addition I owe my editors, Mr Nick Sayers and Ms Jane Barringer, much gratitude for patient and thorough editorial advice. I have also received generous support throughout the writing of this book from my son, Robert.

I wish to thank all six of them for being so kind and helpful.

From generation to generation it shall lie waste;
none shall pass through it for ever and ever.

Isaiah 34:10

Chapter One
Spring 1948

'Permit me, Madame.' The taxi driver lifted out of Barbara Bishop's arms the ornate bunch of flowers she was carrying. He was careful not to crush the red, white and blue bow which held the stems together. 'I'll lay them beside you on the back seat.' He spoke in French, but his gestures made the meaning clear.

Tired by her long journey from Liverpool, the young widow said mechanically, '*Merci, Monsieur,*' and climbed into the cab.

She had been told by the English-speaking receptionist at the Bayeux hotel into which Messrs Thomas Cook had booked her that this precious vehicle was the only taxi remaining in Bayeux. He had gone on to say, with a sardonic grin, that the German Army had failed to find it when they had requisitioned every French vehicle to aid their retreat from Normandy.

'When the Allied Army invaded Normandy in 1944, Madame, and, after the Battle for Caen, Germany was defeated, the German soldiers became desperate. They took cars, lorries, every bicycle they could find to help them get away.' He threw up his hands. 'We're still very short of transport of any kind – even work horses.'

As Barbara Bishop climbed into the taxi, she noted with disdain that its interior still had a faint aroma of manure from the old racing stable in which the receptionist said it had been hidden since 1940. She wrinkled her nose;

1

in England it was widely believed that the French were dirty – but a taxi smelling of manure . . . ?

Its seats were upholstered in cracked black oilcloth, and the glass in one of its side windows had been replaced by a piece of roughly cut celluloid.

The taxi driver held Barbara's flowers with decent reverence – were they not destined to be laid on a grave? As he waited for her to get in, he observed with interest a pair of remarkably pretty legs, and a neat little bottom clad in a plum-coloured corduroy skirt.

She was wearing heavy, plum-coloured shoes which matched her skirt, and nylon stockings. He noted the nylons and wondered if she had an American lover; even in this quiet spring of 1948, nearly three years after the war had finished, he knew of no other way that a young woman could obtain nylon stockings.

Lover or not, the smart little rear end was enough to make him sigh wistfully at his bachelor state. And her light brown hair looked so bright as it glinted in the sunlight; it had been carefully set in a bunch of curls and clasped at the back of her neck by a fine old-fashioned tortoiseshell hairslide.

This thin slip of womanhood did not look like most of the English widows he had recently driven to the local military cemeteries. Despite her long stride and the determined lift of her chin, she looked poorer, and the taxi driver wondered how she had afforded to make the journey from England. Most of the others had been obviously well-to-do, with hair professionally dressed and, on their left hands, huge diamond engagement rings as well as wedding rings. They had asked to see the graves of officers, and had been condescendingly polite to him.

He knew that type of English woman. Long before the

2

war, he had sold eggs and fresh chickens from his father's poultry farm to an older generation of just such women. They had been part of a large number of English retirees who had settled near the coast of Calvados. They had, of course, expected their orders to be delivered; women like that did not come to the market. So he had done the deliveries on his bicycle. Some of them lived permanently in Normandy, some only for the winter months. Not quite rich enough to live in Deauville or Trouville, they were, however, very aware of their status, particularly, he recollected with amusement, when dealing with peasants like himself.

Driven by an ambition to improve himself, he had, from the age of ten, patiently learned a great deal of English from them. They rarely spoke good French. He could, he thought with conceit, discuss in detail in the best of English the merits of a dressed chicken, even if, before knocking on their back doors, he had had to look up in his pocket dictionary the new words he wanted to try out on them.

During the first year of the war, when nothing much militarily had happened in France, the ladies had, nevertheless, quietly retreated back to England, taking their retired husbands and their horrid little dogs with them.

This young woman – Madame Barbara Bishop, according to the slip of paper the receptionist had given him when booking the taxi – had greeted him with friendly politeness, which had been a pleasant relief. She was, Reservations had said, going to the grave of an ordinary private.

Her wedding ring was a plain band; she wore no engagement ring. He presumed that wartime marriages in Britain, as in France, did not allow for much show in

3

the shape of jewellery – unless one had suitable pieces already in the family.

Furthermore, unlike most of the other ladies, she was shorter than he; she could not literally look down on him. He was unable to place her exactly, but decided that she might be the daughter of a small shopkeeper.

Unaware of the fast analysis of her social standing, Barbara seated herself. She laid her black, heavily embroidered handbag on her lap.

He enquired, this time in English, 'Madame is comfortable?' He smiled at her. But if he hoped to encourage her to flirt with him, he was unsuccessful.

Barbara Bishop looked up at the lined nut-brown face of her driver with little interest.

He had a thin face, its outline, by English standards, a surprisingly aristocratic one. Norman forebears, she supposed idly, the same as some Englishmen had. His smile exposed uneven teeth heavily stained by nicotine. On his head was perched a black beret. His much-darned sweater was also black, as were his loose trousers. A very thin man, his heavy boots seemed too big for him. She noted absently that his left shoulder was slightly hunched, and, like his taxi, he smelled as if he could do with a wash.

'Madame is comfortable?' he repeated.

She nodded wearily and replied, '*Oui. Merci bien.*' She was dulled by grief, drained by a long night of useless weeping, while her whole body still ached from years of work too heavy for her small frame. Until last night she had not cried for months; life without George had become a dull ache which she lived with as best she could.

The driver closed the taxi door and went round to the door on the other side. He opened it and laid the flowers carefully beside his passenger on the seat, with the ends of

4

the stems nearest to her. In that position, she could easily grab them if they threatened to slip onto the floor when he started up the ancient vehicle.

During the three months he had been doing it, he had become quite experienced at driving young widows and weeping mothers to cemeteries, and he prided himself on knowing all the possible small snags that could occur, like expensive wreaths slipping off the seat as the taxi bumped its way over hastily repaired roads.

As he laid down the flowers, he glanced at this widow and smiled again. As with most of the women he drove, his passenger was interesting in her foreignness. She was, he noted, wearing a flowered scarf draped around her neck over a shabby pink tweed jacket. So unlike a perfidious French woman in black skirt and white blouse, he thought, his mouth tightening with long-suppressed rage.

As he climbed into the driver's seat, he asked in English if this were her first visit to Normandy.

'Yes,' she answered with a sigh.

He nodded as he started the taxi and put it in gear. It shuddered in protest and then, as he feared it would, when he pressed the gas pedal, it suddenly bolted forward like a startled horse.

She caught the flowers before they fell, but her handbag slid off her lap and onto the dusty floor.

'Oh dear!' she exclaimed. The black embroidered handbag was precious; she had fashioned this one herself from remnants of an old overcoat bought in a second-hand shop; the body of the coat had yielded a plain, black skirt, very useful in a tightly rationed country. She had spent several late evenings embroidering the bag with scraps of knitting wool and was proud of the design of roses on its sides.

5

As the taxi shot out into the main street of Bayeux, narrowly missing a heavily laden hay wain, she clutched an old-fashioned safety bar by the door rather than attempt to retrieve the handbag.

The hay wain's horse reared, and the beret-crowned wagoner shouted angrily at the taxi driver.

The taxi's bald tyres shrieked as the vehicle skidded round the back of the cart and into the outside lane.

The taxi driver muttered furiously to himself. Then, as he passed the cart, taking with him wisps of hay from its protruding load, he leaned out of the open window and shouted what was obviously an epithet at the wagoner.

In the cracked side mirror, his passenger caught a glimpse of the wagoner shaking a fist after them.

As the taxi driver sped down the almost empty street, he turned to reassure her. 'Pardon, Madame. These farmers think the road is for horses only. Germans steal all mechanical vehicles to facilitate their retreat, you understand?' He chuckled as he went on, 'The owner of this taxi hide it in an old racing stable – long time no horses – beautiful horses sent to America for safety, just before the Germans arrive. Lots of straw and horse shit left behind in the stable – Germans never look under it.'

She merely nodded at the driver's remark while, agitated by his poor driving, she continued to clutch the safety bar with one hand, and with the other held on to the bouquet. She had no desire to take the erratic driver's attention away from the street.

Despite the noise of the ancient engine, she had caught the gist of his remark about farmers – his English was surprisingly good, she thought. She herself had little French beyond the schoolgirl version taught her in her last year

6

at school and the contents of the phrase book which she had studied earnestly for some weeks before embarking on her journey. She was, however, far from stupid, and in the few days she had been travelling in France she had begun bravely to use the words she knew, though she pronounced them very badly. She had gratefully accepted correction by persons with whom she attempted to communicate, whether their remarks sounded good-natured or irate.

Barbara saw that the driver was watching her through his rear-view mirror, and she again nodded polite agreement with his remark regarding farmers and their horses. Though there were quite a number of carts, vans and even small carriages being pulled by horses through the streets of Bayeux, there were only a couple of cars and a small delivery van to be seen. Even bicycles were few and far between. She had, at first, assumed that an acute shortage of petrol was the cause of the unexpected return to horsepower in the streets, but it was apparently not the basic cause.

'The Germans took all the motor vehicles?' she asked in English, when the taxi seemed to be being safely driven in a straight line.

'Yes, Madame.' The driver cogitated for a moment, trying to collect for her benefit his knowledge of English. 'The Germans fight very hard to defend themselves here in Calvados; they were brave men, the Germans. Finally, they see that Caen and Lisieux are – what you say? – finish.' He let go of the wheel and threw up his hands in a gesture of hopelessness. 'They lose faith in Adolf Hitler. He does not send them enough ammunition. Their generals are confused. They fight well. They despair, retreat fast – in our lorries, our cars, our bicycles, when they find them.'

His English was imperfect, but he did not appear to be short of vocabulary.

She nodded. The explanation confirmed what Reservations had told her.

The taxi began to veer towards the ditch and the driver hastily grabbed the steering wheel again.

Despite her alarm at his driving, it was a relief to Barbara to reply in English, 'Didn't they believe that Hitler was invincible?'

'*Non, Madame*. That is big story. When Normandy is invaded by the Allies, he not agree with the plans of his generals. Support troops not come when needed. If he permit the German generals to fight as they plan, invasion very difficult for the Allies.'

'It must have been terrifying, anyway, for the French civilians?'

'Madame, it was most dreadful. After the Germans kill so many of us and they deport so many to Germany – 180,000 deportees die in Germany, 18,000 when the British bomb the railways and airports before they invade. Then, when invasion come, when we hope for freedom at last, so many more innocents die.' His uneven shoulders were shrugged. 'I do not know how many. I hear one-third of the people of Caen die. My fiancée's parents die somewhere on their farm. They are not yet found. In addition, how many injured, only the good God knows. The bombardment was terrible. It never stop. Hospitals round here are still full.'

'And yourself?'

'Myself? My family?' He swallowed. He was not used to being asked personal questions by strangers, and his experiences had been so traumatic that he found it difficult to talk about them. Then he said slowly, almost

8

reluctantly, 'We are three. Mama, my big brother, Anatole – he is very sick – and me, Michel Benion. We live now in Bayeux; my two married sisters in Rouen – Rouen is enormous ruin. Sisters and their husbands is alive.' His tone dropped, as he added sadly, 'One little nephew killed.

'Mama, Anatole and me, we wait for our poultry farm to be clear of anti-tank traps and mines. We cannot work the land – not walk on it – until it is clear. One neighbour go to his home and – boom-boom – he is dead.'

Barbara was interested. The sad story took her mind off her own misery. She murmured in English, 'It must have been terrifying. I'm so sorry about the little boy.'

Encouraged by her sympathy, Michel went on, 'Anatole, my brother, come home from Germany very sick. He was slave in Germany, Madame. Can you believe it, nowadays? A slave. No pay. Hardly any food.'

'I do believe you. I have heard about such things – and I saw a list outside the *hôtel de ville* – a long list of those transported who had died in Germany.' She sighed, and then enquired politely, 'I hope your brother is getting better? *Relever?*'

'*Merci, Madame.* He cough very bad.'

She quailed, as the driver again took one hand off the steering wheel to pat his chest.

'*La tuberculose,*' he explained. 'He is long time without help. *Incroyablement,* he try to walk back to Normandy. The Americans find him with civilian refugees from East Germany – they flee from the Russians.'

Barbara nodded sympathetically. 'Poor man. Tuberculosis, you say?'

'*Oui, Madame.*'

The driver swerved to avoid a stout woman in a black

9

skirt, who was riding a bicycle slowly towards him down the middle of the road.

'People still have bicycles,' Barbara remarked, as she resignedly settled down to a rough ride.

'Ah, yes, Madame. There are a few. A bicycle is easy to hide. Not like a bus or a lorry. But the Germans, they take lots of them. This taxi is hid inland. The stable has much bocage round it – how you say?' He saw her smile slightly.

'A thicket round it?' she suggested. Her voice faltered as she added, 'My husband wrote in his letters about bocage – thickets and hedges. He said there were a lot of them. And it was hard to get through them.'

'Yes, Madame. Very difficult for tanks and soldiers to fight through.'

She smiled wanly.

He was pleased to see the smile. He had forgotten his irritation at the traffic.

They were out of the city now, and bowling along a straight road which seemed to stretch to the horizon. It was lined on either side by Lombardy poplars. Between the tall trees, weathered stumps indicated haphazard cutting of some of them, and Barbara leaned forward and asked, 'Were the trees cut for firewood in the war?'

At first, the driver did not quite understand her, so she repeated the question slowly and pointed to some stumps as they passed them.

'*Mais non, Madame*. The Resistance cut the trees and lay them across the road. They block the roads to make the German retreat more difficult – Germans are caught and killed by invasion instead of safe retreat.'

He gestured with one hand, and added, 'No good. Tanks and big lorries go across the fields. *Naturellement,*

10

this winter we burn the trunks – firewood – a bad winter.' He sighed at the memory. 'Very, very bad winter, Madame.'

Barbara leaned back to rest her head. 'It was awfully bad in England as well.' Her voice sounded weary. 'The very worst winter I ever remember. No coal, no electricity, hardly any gas. Even bread was rationed this winter – and potatoes.'

'Yes, Madame. Also here. Bread ration. Sometimes no bread in bakeries.'

'My stars!' Barbara exclaimed, shocked by his remark. 'At least we get our ration.'

'English are lucky. Farms not fought over.'

'They don't feel very lucky.'

'Very difficult for everybody,' Michel responded diplomatically.

They were passing what seemed to have been a village. Only broken walls remained. Already weeds were growing between the stones. The driver gestured towards it and said laconically, 'Here they fight backwards and forwards. Nothing left.'

In the rear-view mirror, he saw the slight movement of her head in acknowledgment of his remark. He went on, 'Our farm like this village. It is within ten kilometres of the coast.' He slowed the taxi and turned his head towards her, old rage resurfacing as he said bitterly, 'So much is our farm fought over, and the one next to it, that there is nothing left – nothing. No house, no horse, no hens, no hen coops or brooders, no barn, no pigs, no cow – no people.

'Father die in 1941. Until the invasion, Mama and I work on the farm to keep it somehow until peace come. What peace, Madame?'

11

He had really caught Barbara's attention. This was information about the French side of the war that she had rarely seen reported in England, except for a line or two as back-page news.

He went on, 'When the invasion of the Allies begin, Mama and me – we hide in *la cave*. We are very afraid. House is destroy. *La cave* is very, very old storehouse – very strong, only little window. When the armies move away, we escape – walk to Bayeux.

'My uncle, Uncle Léon, sail out of Port-en-Bessin not too far away, you understand? We do not know, however, where the ships of the coast is gone. We hope news in Bayeux. Uncle will help us. You understand, Madame, the coast is in great disturbance. Where are our fishermen? Where are our little boats? Good question.'

She nodded to convey her understanding of the problem.

'As we walk, advancing Allied troops say Bayeux is not damage . . .' He took both hands off the wheel, to indicate with gestures a sense of turmoil.

Barbara held her breath until he hastily gripped the wheel again and continued to drive down the middle of the road.

'In Bayeux, very small damage. Much chaos because many refugee arrive suddenly. Help will be there – but maybe not for many days. I must find work – to eat. Monks give us clean clothes, and I work two weeks in hotel kitchen in Bayeux. I cook and clean – German Army cooks not very clean. Then the British Army requisition it. They not like French cooking.' He sighed and shrugged his shoulders. 'They bring their own cooks.

'What I do? Our neighbours caught in the battle – we have not found them. We cannot go on to our land. Too dangerous.' Yet again with his hands he expressed the enormousness of the damage, of the crowds of panic-stricken refugees swarming into the city.

Barbara swallowed as the taxi once more began to edge towards the ditch.

Michel quickly regrasped the wheel and did a theatrical turn towards the centre of the narrow road.

'Le Maire – hôtel de ville – is, how you say, overwhelm? Later, the Government – they promise money, 'elp for Normandy. But 'elp is for cities, Madame, not for poor peasant.' He sighed. 'It is always so. Government not care for peasants. They clear some roads OK. But now we wait and we wait.'

'I thought the Americans poured in help?'

'Americans give to Britain, to Germany. At first, they not trust the French or our General de Gaulle – we are forty per cent Communists.'

Aware of Communism in the back streets of Liverpool, Barbara said in surprise, 'But we have Communists too. The Americans are giving it to us.'

'Communists in France are – how you say? – a force political. Americans now fear revolution – perhaps a Communist one – may happen in France, if they do not give us help. So now it is that Marshall Aid comes – but first for the railways, the roads, the air fields, all destroyed by Allied bombing; and then for Le Havre, for Rouen, Cherbourg – the cities.'

'It must be very hard for your mother.'

'Hard for all,' he assured her gloomily.

Barbara changed the subject. She said slowly in English, 'It was very kind of the American soldiers – the under-takers at the hotel – to permit you to take me to the cemetery. The hotel says they booked this taxi for four

13

whole months. The reservations clerk said that you usually stay with the Americans at the cemeteries throughout the day while they work.'

The length of Barbara's remark made it a little difficult for Michel to understand. He replied cautiously, 'American Army very good, soldiers most kind, Madame. Lots of petrol! *Certainement*, they pay taxi four months – not like the Boches – he never pay for anything he can take, *les sales Boches.*'

Though he laughed, he sounded cynical, as he remembered how some German soldiers had demanded his best poultry breeding stock and had wrung their pretty necks in front of him. Then they had made his mother clean and pluck them ready for cooking. Cook some of the world's best breeding stock? It was murder. His poor Chanticleer and his pretty, fertile wives. *Hélas!* How would he ever find the money to replace them?

As he mourned his dead hens, Michel edged the vehicle round a pothole filled with water, and then continued, 'Taxi is the only transport to cemeteries, Madame. Now many people want to visit their dead. This is the only taxi in Bayeux. So I ask Americans, can I take civilians to the cemeteries, while they work? I promise to collect them from their American cemeteries exactly when they order. You understand taxi cannot be left for one moment unattended. Someone steal, dead cert.' Michel was rapidly extending his vocabulary while working for the Americans.

'They say OK. Take some lady to cemetery. Make a buck. So I drive American ladies, English ladies, one lady from Poland – widow of man who fight with British, *je crois.*'

He cleared his throat and spat out of the window. 'Two

German ladies come – they omit to tip me.' He half turned his head towards her. He sounded mystified, as he added, 'You know, they cry like everyone else.'

'I am sure they did,' Barbara agreed.

She felt fiercely that she did not care whether the Germans flooded the earth with their tears; they could never undo the ruination of her life by the taking of her George's life.

Let the German widows cry. Let them suffer. She hoped their cities remained shattered, their factories empty, looted by both Americans and Russians, their farms fought over and desolate. Let them pay.

After a while, to take her mind off her own troubles, she asked the taxi driver, 'What are the Americans doing here? Are they really undertakers? Aren't all the dead buried yet?'

'Ah, simple, Madame. They arrange for dead American soldiers to go home. Bury them in America.'

'What a lovely idea!'

'Very, very expensive, Madame.' Michel obviously did not believe in such a waste of money, even if it resulted in work for himself.

They swung round a corner into a narrow lane. At the end of it, an open ironwork gate faced them, and, beyond that, what at first looked like a sea of white and green.

As they drove through the gateway, the sea resolved into masses and masses of white crosses set in neat rows amid green lawns, stretching, it seemed to Barbara, into infinity.

She caught her breath. So many! Her mild amusement at the taxi driver's disapproval of American extravagance was forgotten in the shock of being suddenly surrounded by the evidence of so much death. Surely, it could not be?

But the evidence lay there, crying out in its silence.

She was appalled.

Just inside the gate, the taxi came to a halt. Michel opened Barbara's door and took her hand to help her alight. Her normal self-confidence left her. She was so shaken by the scene before her that she was grateful for the man's firm grip; though he smelled at least it was the smell of a man – a man such as she was used to, who worked hard.

'I get the flowers for Madame,' he said gently.

She looked at him a little helplessly, and then she pointed to her dropped handbag and asked him if he could reach in and rescue it for her.

'*Mais oui, Madame.*'

The cloth bag was covered with dust and not a few hayseeds, blown in when they had passed the hay wain. Michel carefully brushed it as clean as he could, before handing it to her.

He smiled. 'Very pretty bag, Madame.'

'Thank you,' she answered, and then, looking a little rueful, she muttered absently, 'I made it myself. It's still difficult to buy things.'

He made a wry face. He, too, knew about the shortages of everything. He leaned into the taxi to retrieve the flowers for her.

As he handed the bouquet to her, he saw that despite her casual remarks about her handbag she had gone as white as her lilies. Her dark blue eyes were wide with fright.

Pauvre petite! So little, so sweet, and, at this moment, looking so helpless. He wanted to take her in his arms to comfort her and tell her that all would be well, that she could be sure that Jules, the gardener, was very kind and that he looked after the graves with great care.

In the silence of the cemetery, his voice sounded harsh, as, instead, he cleared his throat and enquired hastily, 'Number of the grave, Madame?'

She told him.

He took her arm. 'I walk with you. Then wait by taxi.'

She was shaking, and simply nodded acceptance. Fearing she might faint, he held her arm firmly and guided her further along the little lane on which the taxi stood. 'Germans that side, Allies this side,' he explained.

She nodded again. They walked across the grass for a minute or two. From a little fenced enclosure at the back of the cemetery, a figure emerged.

'He is Jules – the gardener,' Michel told her.

She was pressing her arm against the driver's guiding hand, as if she never wanted him to let go, but she showed some sign of animation by saying, 'Oh, yes. I remember the name. I wrote to the Head Gardener of this cemetery. He replied that the cemetery was, at last, open for visitors. His letter was so kind. So I knitted a pullover – out of wool from old pullovers – and sent it to him as a thank you present for, for . . .' Her voice broke for a moment, then she went on more firmly, 'for looking after George.'

The taxi driver showed surprise. 'He like that. Nobody thank gardener before – *certainement.*'

As Jules approached, she smiled at him as bravely as she could. The driver repeated the number of the grave to him.

'Come, Madame.'

She unlinked her arm, and, hugging her flowers, her chin up, her face suddenly old and grim, she walked forward – like St Joan going into the fire, the driver told his brother, Anatole, sometime later.

Chapter Two

All the modest hopes of George and Barbara had come to naught. Without George, his young widow considered, life was not worth living. She wished passionately that she had a child to console her, but they had deferred having a family until the end of the war.

From the day the war began, Barbara and her mother, Phyllis Williams, had fought a stalwart battle to save their home and their means of livelihood until peace should be declared. It had been a hard, very long struggle, and, on top of that, to be bereaved was difficult to bear.

They owned a small bed-and-breakfast establishment abutting the seashore on the Wirral peninsula. It was about eight miles from Liverpool, on the other side of the River Mersey, and not far from the estuary of the River Dee. They had worked for years to build it up as a nice place for commercial travellers to stay overnight, and for people in search of a family holiday during the summer.

Their home was an old farmhouse, lovingly restored by its original owner. Barbara and her mother ran the business while her father went to sea. He had been torpedoed in 1941.

For the sake of her daughter, Phyllis wept for her husband in secret and dealt firmly with the other problems the war had brought her.

'We've got to eat, luvvie,' she had told twenty-two-year-old Barbara, who had been devastated by her father's death. And with considerable courage, like other Mersey-side bereaved women, mother and daughter continued to try to live as normal lives as possible. It was not easy.

As far as Barbara was concerned, the battle had seemed worth it once she had met George.

She had actually seen him once or twice in the village, a rather ponderous youth a couple of years older than herself.

She had met him again when he was on leave, handsome in his Army uniform, at a Red Cross dance held in the church hall. He had, he told her, not been much at home since leaving school; at first he had been learning his trade as an apprentice to a stone mason, working on repairs to Chester Cathedral. Then once he had his journeyman's papers, he had found a place working on the new Church of England Cathedral in Liverpool. He loved his work; he was devoted to his cathedral. But cathedral building can be put on hold until wars are finished, so George had been called up.

After Barbara and George's marriage in 1942, the newlyweds and Phyllis Williams had all three cherished hopes of living together in the bed-and-breakfast after the war was over. The women would continue to run it, and George looked forward to returning to his full-time work as stone mason on the unfinished cathedral.

Phyllis Williams had been very pleased to acquire such a well-placed, sensible young man as a son-in-law. Sud-denly, the need to keep the bed-and-breakfast going had acquired new meaning for her; it would be a great place for grandchildren, and the three of them would be quite comfortable financially.

Both women had been crushed and bewildered by George's death. But other people were dependent upon their business, and both women worked mechanically to keep the shabby farmhouse open.

'It's the small nightmares wot keeps driving you crazy,' Phyllis would lament. 'Some of them is the last straw.' And they would both blow their noses, and do their best.

Phyllis, however, became very worried about her widowed daughter as she watched her decline into a dull, disinterested woman, who rarely went out socially. It wasn't that Barbara did not do her share of the work of their little business; she did more than enough, and she knitted and sewed industriously to help eke out their sparse clothes-rationing coupons.

'You know, Ada, there's no life in her; and she's too young to give up like she is,' Phyllis had said anxiously to George's mother. Ada was herself a widow who did not have much life in her either, except when talking about her garden, when her face would occasionally light up.

'You know and I know, Ada, that you just have to put the war behind you and start again.'

Ada Bishop sighed deeply. Phyllis Williams was the bravest little soul she knew.

'Perhaps, in the back of her mind, she hopes he'll turn up again; it's been known to happen,' suggested Ada. 'You don't always think quite sensible when you're young, do you? I know he'll never come home. But she may still hope.'

'You don't always think sensible even when you're older,' replied Phyllis, with a wry smile. It had been hard for her to accept that her own husband had been torpedoed in Liverpool Bay in 1941, and would never return. But a lot of seamen never had a grave other than the sea. Then she said, with sudden inspiration at the thought of a grave, 'Perhaps she'd see different if she could look at George's grave! She'd really know then.'

The mothers agreed. They persuaded Barbara that she should take a break and go to Normandy.

So, after some argument, a listless Barbara had drawn on her wartime savings – it had been easy to save in wartime, because there was very little to buy – and had gone to see Thomas Cook.

Until catching the ferry at Dover and her subsequent arrival in Bayeux, she had felt fairly calm about the visit; in fact, she had regarded it as an unusual, but welcome break, taken to please Ada and Phyllis.

Now, thin and workworn, Barbara faced her loss as bravely as she could. She was physically exhausted, despairing in her own loneliness and that of her overworked half-fed mother, bedevilled by the continued strict rationing – and by the cold, the everlasting cold which Britain had endured in that hopeless winter of 1947–48, the lack of gas and electricity – and food. Would there ever be any let-up, she wondered. There seemed to be absolutely nothing to look forward to.

While travelling to France, she had dwelled on the miserable condition of her home. It had been, in 1939, such a pretty seaside bed-and-breakfast establishment, with an excellent reputation.

The declaration of war had put an end to that. The house and garden had been ruined a few days before the war actually began.

Children and their mothers were evacuated from Liverpool and billeted upon them. She and Phyllis, with three extra mothers in the kitchen, had been thrown into chaos. They had accepted, however, that these refugees from the heavy bombing that was daily anticipated had to be housed. They did their best to cope.

She shuddered when she remembered the day she had discovered that all their beds had bugs in them and the pillows had lice, brought in by evacuees from some of the worst slums in Britain.

Mercifully, the evacuees had decided they hated living in what they regarded as countryside, where there was not even a decent fish-and-chip shop, and had returned home to Liverpool, as yet unbombed.

Phyllis Williams and Barbara had had to burn the pillows, boil the bedding, and ask the Town Council to get the entire house stoved for them. It stank for days afterwards.

They painstakingly went through the bedrooms again, armed with a local store's last tins of Keating's powder. To their relief they found no more invaders. The kitchen and all the floors in the house were scrubbed and polished.

The front garden was a mess, tramped over by both children and adults.

Barbara wanted to weep. Originally, she had herself planted the garden and it had become her hobby. Looking back, she thought how stupid it was to weep over a small garden; she had wept many more bitter tears since then.

Her mother, made of sterner stuff, said, 'We'll get a lad to dig it over, and seed it with grass. And we'll put a couple of flowerpots on either side of the front door.'

Barbara acquiesced.

'The main problem is, Barbie, it looks as if we're not goin' to get our usual customers. The commercial travellers is all going into the Army, and, if this summer's

23

any example, the older couples what used to spend their holidays with us don't seem to be taking holidays any more. So what to do?'

'I don't know, Mam, but if we don't fill up this house quickly, it'll be requisitioned again for something.'

They sat in silence, staring at their kitchen, once more restored to order.

Then Barbara said, 'You're right, Mam, about the elderly couples not coming. But I wonder if they'd come if we pointed out that if France falls – and it looks as if it might – the South'll be in range for bombing. We could offer them permanent accommodation well away from it.'

Her mother slapped her knee. 'I think you're right, luv. There's one or two people as has come up from London, staying in the village already.'

They had sat down and written to some twenty elderly couples from the South-East of England, who had in times past spent holidays with them. They made Barbara's point about likely bombing, and the comparative safety of the North.

The nervous anticipation in the South of being bombed was sufficient. Within two weeks, they had all their eight bedrooms filled, housing a total of seventeen people. Their biggest bedroom held three quarrelsome, complaining old sisters, who proved to be the most trying of their hastily acquired visitors.

The overwhelmed local housing authority, themselves disorganised by the sudden weight of responsibility thrust upon them by the immediacies of war, decided that they could not very well dislodge such elderly refugees from the South without causing a scandal. They accepted the situation.

As grossly overworked Phyllis remarked, with resignation, 'At least this lot knows what being clean means, thanks be to Mary.'

Phyllis and Barbara agreed that it was advisable to keep the house more crowded than it had ever been, lest the authorities suddenly change their collective mind and try to thrust additional, unwanted guests upon them. And there was always the overriding fear that the Army or the Air Force might requisition the entire property, though this did not happen.

So, for nearly seven years, as a constant background to their personal grief at the loss of their menfolk, the harassed hostesses faced continuous complaints about the difficulty of climbing stairs; and, though each bedroom had a sink, that there was only one bathroom and three lavatories in the place.

Regardless of the fact that almost every home in Britain was cold from lack of fuel, running wars were fought between old gentlemen trying to hog the chairs nearest the meagre gas fire in the lounge. Ladies complained of lack of hot water for washing clothes and having baths – even of getting into the bathroom in the first place.

Accusations regarding the unfair distribution of rationed food, particularly the tiny amounts of sugar, butter, cheese, jam and marmalade, flew back and forth between the little round tables in the dining room. Sometimes, perfectly respectable couples would accuse each other of theft of jam from their private pots, which had been specially provided by Phyllis to ensure fairness.

Frequently, Phyllis had to intervene in the altercations and point out the minuscule amount of individual rations. It all seemed so stupid to her. There were men like her husband Hugh, victim of a U-boat attack, and George, who would give their lives for them – and they screamed with rage over marmalade!

Anybody would imagine that they had no one in their families serving in the Forces; yet Phyllis knew that they did.

When, in 1944, George was killed, Barbara thought the refugees would drive her insane. She was sorely tempted to scream, 'Shut up! Get out!' at them, and she wondered how her mother could endure them so patiently.

When the war ended, most of them lingered for a while. A number had wrecked or damaged homes, which had to be restored before they could move down south again. A few, perhaps because they had been protected for so long from the reality of existence in a drained country, seemed unable to make up their minds what to do, and, meanwhile, had stayed on.

Particularly in 1947, the worried hostesses had had a real problem finding enough food, rationed or unrationed, to provide three meagre meals a day for the old curmudgeons. They had thankfully said farewell to the last of them at Christmas.

That same year Barbara and her mother had been very relieved to see the return of some of their usual clientele, commercial travellers. The gentlemen had little to sell. Wholesalers were anxious, however, to keep their company name in front of their old clients, so that, as soon as adequate goods were available, their pre-war share of the market would not be lost.

Once or twice, thought Barbara, the old folk had been very nice to her. Back in June 1942, when she had married George, they had insisted that Phyllis use some of their points rations, which meant very limited amounts of tinned food, like Spam or golden syrup, to make a wedding breakfast for the young couple.

In addition, all the ladies had set to work to embroider or knit or crochet little wedding gifts. Even the gentlemen, whom Barbara swore were the laziest bunch of old so-and-sos she had ever met, bestirred themselves. The result was a number of beautifully hand-carved gifts. Though she could no longer bear to look at them because it made her want to cry, she still treasured in her dressing-table drawer three neatly carved wooden spoons made from driftwood found on the shore.

She went round the lot of them to kiss them in gratitude.

They had been equally kind when they heard about George's death; they had all expressed their sorrow at her loss, as those who knew about it had done earlier, when her father was killed. There had not been a single quarrel for at least two weeks.

During the weeks following the loss of George, two of the residents lost grandsons and at last, it seemed to Barbara, the reality of the war truly came home to them; not even a string of bombs dropped across the Wirral peninsula, nor the news some had received of their homes being damaged or requisitioned had been able to achieve that.

When the war began, Barbara herself had wanted to volunteer for military service and join the ATS, the Auxiliary Territorial Service. It sounded exciting.

Her mother would not hear of it. 'With your dad at sea, I need you. Who else can I turn to?'

So Barbara, who loved her mam, stayed home.

When France fell to the Germans, Barbara broached the subject again. But Phyllis still would not hear of it either. Nice girls stayed at home with their mams. 'And, anyway, wot am I going to do without you, and a house full of old folks to run?' When her father was torpedoed, her mother was certainly glad to have her there.

A domestic crisis had occurred when, in December 1942, all married women under the age of forty were called up for war work. Barbara was directed to a contractor who was busy repairing damaged docks in Birkenhead. She worked on shift as a labourer together with one other girl. Her hours were long and the work, with all its lifting and carrying, was very heavy.

'At least it's better than the ATS,' Phyllis said, as she rubbed Barbara's back with surgical spirit. 'You can sleep in your own bed.' She imagined that she was being comforting.

Barbara's bed was exceedingly cold, especially without George. She shrugged and looked down at her hands, which were rapidly being ruined by hard labour, and felt that the Army would probably have been easier. She had not, however, wanted to quarrel about it. She admitted to herself that, in comparison with pre-war earnings for women, her wages were very good. Since there was nothing much in the shops to buy, she saved as much as she could by opening a bank account and also purchasing war bonds. Between her work shifts she helped her mother, so her social life was negligible. They all prayed for a rapid end to the war.

George's fourteen-year-old sister had left school the previous summer. She had since been working as a shop assistant for a greengrocer. When Barbara was called up, she volunteered, for a slightly better wage, to come to work for Mrs Williams, to make beds and clean floors.

In addition, two elderly women from the village came in as part-time help.

As a result of these changes, the elderly residents found plenty more to complain about. None of them, however, moved out; the bombing of London was by then unremitting, and the heavy bombing of Liverpool earlier in the year was sufficient to keep them in the comparative safety of the village by the sea. Though, occasionally, their provoked hostesses wished them dead, not a single one of them died during the many years that they boarded with Phyllis.

'We looked after them too well – or it was the good sea air,' Phyllis replied acidly when Ada once pointed this out to her.

When travelling to France, Barbara had passed through Birkenhead and Liverpool on her way to catch a train to London. She had been forcibly reminded of the toll of war in Britain by the destruction she could still see there, and she remembered, with a pang, the long civilian casualty lists pinned up in the city, the pitiful treks each night that the inhabitants had made to the outer suburbs such as Huyton, in the hope of survival. How had George's few surviving comrades felt when they returned home to this?

She was shocked at the miles of ruins she had observed in London. How many homeless people must there be in London? How many dead? She realised, with genuine distress, that there must be returning ex-service men who had lost their entire families in the broken, once close-packed streets of the capital. They must wonder what they had fought for.

Wrapped in her own sorrow while she grappled with the day-to-day problems of existence, she had not thought of such a situation before.

Seated in the train as it rumbled slowly into Euston, Barbara had queried mentally how careful, phlegmatic George might have faced coming home to a ruin – there had been bombs dropped close enough to the bed-and-breakfast for this to have been a possibility. And, in her self-searching, it dawned on her that she did not know; she really had not known him well enough to understand how his mind might have worked. And worst of all, now she would never know him any better – because he was gone.

As she walked towards George's grave, she thought her heart would break. Because she did not want to cry in front of Jules, she held back the heaving sobs that rose within her. Instead, she clenched her teeth and walked blindly beside him.

Chapter Three

Michel Benion, temporary taxi driver, ex-poultry farmer, slowly rolled up the front of his old black jersey and took his precious packet of cigarettes from inside his undershirt. Abstractedly he watched the little widow as she went with Jules to find the grave.

As he lit a cigarette and then sat down to wait on the step of the antiquated taxi, he felt again the well of pain and humiliation under which he himself still laboured.

It was ridiculous, he fretted in complete frustration, that nearly three years after the end of the war, because the Government had not yet cleared it of land mines, his chicken farm was still unworkable. In fact, the authorities, those mighty gods in Paris, were talking of buying the land from his family and making it into a park. Nearly three years – and they had still not made up their collective minds about it.

Just now, American money is being poured into Rouen and Le Havre where there are lots of voters, he fumed for the hundredth time. Simply because we are only small farmers with no clout, we can wait for ever, exactly like the farmers on the Western Front after the First World War.

And even if we got the farm back, would they lend us money to start again, build barns, buy breeding stock, sustain us financially until our flocks were rebuilt? What about our draught horse? Our cow, our pigs and vegetable garden that fed us?

Save as he and his mother did, in a desperate effort to collect a modicum of capital – living on little more than vegetable soup, bread and cheese, and occasional cigarettes when they could get them – he was beginning to realise that, alone, the family themselves could never acquire enough money to start again.

Of course, like most land in Normandy, their farm was owned jointly by all the members of the family: Michel's sick brother, Anatole, their mother and their two married sisters in Rouen. It had been hard enough, even before the war, to scratch a living from two and a half hectares, when so many people held rights to it. It had meant intensive use of every inch of land.

Michel's father had succeeded in buying out his own sea-going brother's share, which feat had taken him most of his life to achieve; Michel doubted, however, that he would ever manage to buy out his own siblings' shares, even under the best of circumstances.

And he had begun to ask himself whether he truly wanted to recommit his life to boundless hard work, just to stay alive and pay the rest of the family their share of what he managed to make. Would Anatole, perhaps, recover and be able to help him?

When their father had been alive, Anatole and his two sisters had, in addition to helping on the farm, all worked at other outside jobs and, with the extra money earned, the family had collectively managed quite well.

The girls were gone now, Anatole was very ill, and their mother had aged immeasurably during the ruthless occupation by the German Army. Michel knew he could not carry the burden of work alone; he would have to employ at least one labourer, a great expense when first starting up again, while for a time no money would be coming in.

Even if the Government bought the land to make a park, the resultant money would, after paying their debts, have to be divided between all the family members. Michel himself would still not have capital enough from his share to start a little business of any kind.

For the moment, his mother received an old age pension, and Anatole received a regular allowance and medical care because he was a very sick returned deportee who was being nursed at home. Without these, they would undoubtedly have starved, thought Michel gloomily.

But the value of the franc fell daily, and the cost of everything on the black market was, in consequence, rising formidably – and without the black market, which dealt in everything from bread to boots, they would be in desperate straits.

His mother and Anatole had refused to move further away from their land than Bayeux until a decision was made by the Government. Madame Benion had a fixed belief that if they did not remain close, someone would say the Benions were all dead and would try to claim it. 'And what is a peasant without land?' she had asked. 'Just a body without a soul,' Michel had fretted. Land was supposed to be the foundation of life.

In the meantime, he had worked for his Uncle Léon as a deckhand on his little coaster, and then had applied for all kinds of jobs in Bayeux in order to keep a roof over the family's heads. But the only special skill he had was in raising hens – and cooking.

In refugee-filled, but undamaged Bayeux, there were very few jobs for the unskilled, so competition was keen for any work available.

If he could have persuaded his mother to move to the

wreckage of Rouen, he could have easily found construction work. He would, he told himself, have cheerfully endured the pain in his shoulder, damaged since childhood, that heavy labour would have given him. But she woodenly refused. So, here he was, a taxi driver for old Duval, who owned the vehicle.

Duval had rented both driver and vehicle to three huge American Army officers for four months. The Americans were really civilian undertakers and were happily engaged in enjoying France, while they arranged for the bodies of their dead compatriots to be dug up and shipped home to the United States. The American Army had not seen fit to provide these civilian employees, even if they wore uniform, with transport; hence their use of the taxi.

Michel grinned slightly. At least, as far as he himself was concerned, the US Army was the soul of generosity. He was doing nicely on the side, ferrying to the local cemeteries people like the sad young Englishwoman this afternoon – and the Americans had said quite blithely that it was OK for him to do so. He hoped old Duval would not wake up to this happy arrangement and demand a cut of whatever extra he earned.

Michel carefully blew a perfect smoke ring, and his thoughts reverted to the carnage on the chicken farm.

Four years earlier, when the hopes of liberation from the German occupation had run high, whispered about in every small café, the French had been filled with new hope. The reality of the cost of being set free had been unexpectedly brought home to the whole district with terrifying suddenness.

At the commencement of the Allies' preliminary bombardment, many of the Benions' neighbours fled inland.

Unable to believe that French lives or French property would be destroyed, a number remained, including Michel, his mother, and his fiancée's parents, whose plot abutted that of the Benions.

For a day or two, it seemed that the Benions' choice had been correct. The attacks appeared to be directed at railway junctions and airports, the coast itself, and towards the destruction of the German Army and its likely escape routes.

While planes of every description flew over and occasionally fought pitched battles with each other above her head, Madame Benion remained determinedly calm. She fed her few remaining hens and collected some eggs, while Michel tended the vegetable garden, their frightened cow, and the squealing sow, which was about to farrow and was terrified by the noise of the diving planes.

The small detachment of German soldiers, camped amid the apple trees at the end of the Benion land, fled one night, leaving their anti-aircraft gun to its fate.

Madame Benion thanked God she would not be further bullied by them and placidly harvested some salad greens. Michel cursed the Germans, because the stable which should have contained their solitary horse was empty.

'The Boches must have taken it in the night,' he told his mother.

'It's more important that they are gone too,' she said calmly. 'We shall manage, somehow.'

But the next afternoon, a hot and summery one, a shell whistled through the clear blue sky over their home and exploded very near the house, blowing out all the windows.

Madame Benion stood in her tiny living room, soup ladle poised over Michel's empty bowl, and looked bewilderedly down at tiny slivers of glass caught in the hem of her thick serge skirt. It was a miracle that she had not been cut.

The whistle was followed a few seconds later by another one and then a whole series. The sound of the explosions was deafening.

Madame Benion dropped her ladle, while Michel shoved back his chair. '*La cave, Maman!*' he cried. 'Quick.'

He herded his mother ahead of him, through the arch that divided the room from the kitchen itself. In the far wall was the door leading to the vegetable garden. He pushed his mother through it. He hastily followed her, after swinging shut behind them the heavy fifteenth-century wooden back door. He did not latch it, which proved to be a mistake.

Very few homes in Normandy have cellars. A couple of strides, however, took the Benions across a narrow garden path to a small outhouse much older than the farmhouse. It had walls two feet thick and, at the far end, it was half buried in the earth. Its tiled roof was held up by ancient, handcut beams. It had long since been chosen by Madame Benion as the safest place to take cover during air raids; the family had, at various times during the war, already spent a number of uncomfortable nights in it.

Michel's father, alive at the beginning of hostilities, had pointed out that the outhouse had the advantage of there being no second storey to collapse on it and bury those taking refuge.

Its door, like the rest of it, had been built with medieval thoroughness to withstand the attacks of armed men in earlier frays; it was braced by a succession of iron bolts to hold its several layers of wood together. Huge hinges extended an iron grip halfway across the woodwork.

To give some light in the *cave*, there was one small

window high in the far wall. It had a single bar across its centre, to deter anyone small enough from crawling through it. The aperture was further barricaded by an inside wooden shutter, closed by an iron bar across it. Now, through the cracks in the shutter, came narrow flashes from the explosions outside.

This small refuge was normally the storeroom for barrels of cider, a primitive cider press and a small apple grinder, a stock of root vegetables and of eating apples. It also held firewood and odds and ends of farm implements not in daily use. Most of the consumable contents had long since been drunk or eaten by the Germans manning the nearby gun emplacement. It did, however, contain a covered bucket full of water, which Madame Benion changed daily, and a tin of homemade biscuits.

This afternoon, she regretted that she had not had time to bring with her a couple of old feather duvets, which she kept in the kitchen cupboard so that they did not go mouldy in this rather damp outhouse. After the heat of the day, however, the place felt blessedly cool, and she hoped the attack would not last long.

She sat down on an old bench in a corner where in a hollow above a beam, she had, long ago, stored a small parcel of family papers, her personal savings of little silver coins in a tiny canvas bag, Michel's Post Office savings book, and, best of all, a candle and matches.

Now, she felt around in the half-dark for the candle, found it and lit it.

By the light of the candle, she began painstakingly to pick out of her thick serge skirt the small shards of glass which had caught in the hem. 'I was lucky not to get this in my face,' she said, and then winced as she cut her finger.

Michel had come to sit cross-legged beside her. He nodded in agreement with her remark about her face. He did not believe, however, that their luck was continuing. It seemed to him, with the racket outside growing, that they were caught in the midst of a real battle.

As the noise increased, Madame Benion asked Michel to get down the small packets hidden above her. He did so, and she stowed them in the capacious inner pockets of her skirt.

With their faces buried on their knees most of the time, their arms clasped over their heads, they remained in the cellar for thirty-six agonised hours, as the earthen floor shuddered and heavy dust was shaken down on them from the roof. Despite the water and biscuits, their hunger grew.

At first, they screamed with terror; then, nearly out of their senses, numbed by fear, they fell silent. But the noise nearly drove them mad: explosion after explosion, the roar of shells from the ships anchored on the coast, the whistle of bombs, the rattle of machine-gun fire, the terrified shrieks of the farrowing pig nearby, and, worst of all, the dreadful screams of wounded and dying men, as the battle raged backwards and forwards over their precious hectares of land.

The candle burned down and finally went out. Amid thick dust and total darkness, they clung to each other, petrified.

When they heard the unmistakable rumble and crash of heavy tanks, the screech of brakes and tyres of personnel carriers, they were sure their refuge would be crushed and that they would die beneath the outhouse's heavy beams; and half-forgotten prayers were mechanically mumbled by both of them.

Roaring like a furious elephant, a tank ground its way through the further end of the house and sent stones rattling on to the *cave*'s roof. Later, something heavy exploded on the other side of the house. The pain in her ears from the blast made poor Madame Benion scream again. Michel held his mother close.

The huge handcut beams held, the thick walls shuddered again and again, but did not give.

As the hard-fought battle finally moved relentlessly on towards the River Orne and the Allies' target, the city of Caen, the noise gradually lessened.

Limp with exhaustion, Michel and his mother, miraculously not seriously hurt, finally stood up in the darkness. Michel held his mother in his arms, while they both trembled helplessly.

They did not realise until they spoke that they were nearly deaf, that the reduced roar of the bombardment from the naval ships along the coast, and the shaking menace of heavy tanks and personnel carriers rumbling past, were still quite close. The screech of fighter planes and bombers diving over them, however, was sharp enough to make Madame Benion again scream with terror, and they crouched back into their corner.

At last, it seemed that the vibrations under them had eased. Still not realising how deaf they were, it appeared to them quieter outside. They ventured to rise again.

Michel went to the little window first and opened the shutter. Together with a rush of dust, the faint light of dawn filtered in; to him, the noise had become a confused rumbling. He turned to edge his way round the apple crusher to get to the door. He confidently turned the iron ring to open it, but the door did not budge. He turned the handle again and, at the same time, gave it a hearty shove with his good shoulder. It gave slightly.

Encouraged, he pushed as hard as he could. It scraped open a crack.

He turned to his watching mother. 'Something's wedged behind it,' he said.

Madame Benion could not completely hear what he said but she saw the need for help. When he tried again, she added her small weight to his and pushed.

It gave slightly more.

Michel pressed his mother's hand to indicate that she should keep pushing. Hoping that it would not slam shut again and smash his fingers, he braced himself against it and ran his hand along the opened space. Halfway down the outer side of the door, his fingers touched wood. Below that, there seemed no further impediment. Whatever was there had certainly wedged the door shut.

He withdrew his hand. Already nearly frantic from that which had gone before, panic rose in him.

He stood firm, however, while he tried to control himself. Beside him, his mother shifted slightly. She said something but he could not hear what it was.

Keep your head, he warned himself. You must; otherwise you may starve in this rathole.

Again, he braced himself as firmly as he could to keep the door open as far as it would go. Then he shouted into his mother's ear, 'Quickly, Maman, bring me some wood chips and a couple of small logs.'

Despite the loudness of his voice she had not heard him clearly. Uncertainly, she picked up some pieces of firewood.

'That's right,' he shouted at her.

She rapidly collected some more wood and held it

towards him in her arms. With one hand, he picked three or four chips to wedge the door as far open as it would go. Very slowly, he eased away from it. The wooden chips cracked with the door's pressure, but held.

With a sigh of relief, he stepped back.

Gesturing to his mother, he said, 'Put the wood down here, Maman, and bring me the big mallet we use for pounding in fenceposts.'

While she hesitantly complied, uncertain that she had heard properly, he gave the recalcitrant door another heavy shove. It refused to shift any further.

'I'm going to give the door several blows with the mallet to see if I can loosen it. Stand back, Maman,' he shouted.

He swung the heavy tool with all his might, hitting the door several times in quick succession. He wanted to scream with the resultant pain in his shoulder. Undeterred, he aimed several more blows.

It sounded to him as if something outside slid. He stopped and then, once more, he shoved as hard as he could. The door opened about three inches.

Full of hope, he let it swing shut again and then continued to whack it with the heavy mallet, but the best he could achieve was an opening of about three inches – no more. Finally breathless, he gave up.

Her hands hanging loosely at her side, his mother was weeping helplessly. 'Perhaps someone will come to help us,' she sobbed.

He doubted whether there would be anyone in the vicinity who had survived. He did not, however, tell her this. He simply grunted and ruefully rubbed his shoulder while he considered what to do next. He was, however, desperately hungry and thirsty, and his usually clear mind was refusing to think constructively.

He leaned his head against the cold stone wall, and then, when he felt steadier, he walked over to the little window with its prisonlike bar, to look out again at a June morning marred by a fearsome amount of dust. In the near distance there was the scarifying sound of continuing conflict, though it was definitely receding; even his troubled ears noted that.

Beside him, his mother sounded as if she were speaking from a vast distance away. 'What are you doing?' she asked, her voice cracking.

He had to shout to make her hear. 'I'm going to try the door once more.'

She followed him trustfully as he returned to the recalcitrant door.

He felt for the smallest log he had picked out. With this in hand, he shouted, 'Push.'

They gave a concerted shove, and the door opened as much as it had before. Michel quickly pushed the log into the gap to wedge it open. On this more sheltered side of the *cave* he could now see light a little more clearly than through the tiny window. 'It must be nearly mid-morning,' he decided.

He then picked up another log of uneven width. This he handed to his mother, and told her what to do. Making her stand back, he swung the mallet as hard as he could, in a blow to hit the door at the edge of the opening. Then he flung his weight against it. His mother swiftly dropped the second log into the slightly further opened aperture as a rattle of debris came from outside.

Michel paused for breath.

After a moment, he cautiously stretched himself across the door as far as he could reach and ran his fingers down the open edge of it. He could feel that the wooden obstruction now lay wedged against the bottom of the door.

Several more tries failed to shift the door further.

Furious with frustration, he turned from his mother so that she should not see the intensity of his despair and strode again to the window. His mouth tight as he boiled with anger, he seized the bar across the middle of the window and shook it.

In a split second, he found himself thrown back by his own impetus, flat against the apple grinder, the bar still in his hand. From the window a small slither of debris fell to the floor.

He stared in astonishment at the bar, and then he began to laugh hysterically.

Startled, his mother eased herself round the grinder.

Bewildered, she could not understand what had happened. Then her son shook the bar at her. 'It came out,' he shouted. 'But the window's still too small to get through! It's so absurd.' He continued his manic laugh.

When she understood, her own mind began to clear. She went to look up at the aperture. 'It's too small for me – in my clothes.'

She continued to stare at it, 'Anyway, it's too high for me to reach.'

The laughter behind her died away. She heard Michel drop the iron bar. He came to stand beside her and looked down at her. She was indeed small, like a young girl, a wisp of a woman, just bones from lack of adequate food.

She said, 'If I could reach, I could get through – without my skirts.'

He made her repeat the remark, not sure that he had heard correctly. 'Could you?'

'I believe so,' she said slowly. 'I should go face down

43

and feet first, because I don't want to drop on my head on the other side.'

He rubbed his ears in the hope of persuading them to clear, so that he could hear better. Then he said loudly, 'I don't think you would have much of a drop, Maman. The potato patch slopes slightly up towards the window – and it would be soft.'

She made a wry face. 'I would still need to be face down because my old body won't bend backwards much in order to ease myself down the wall. I don't think even a young girl could do it face up.'

Despite the dire need to get out of their prison, this cold assessment of what a lifetime of toil had done to her body distressed Michel beyond measure. Maman was like a little tree constantly exposed to an east wind – she was indeed permanently bent forward.

Though she said with determination that she was prepared to try to ease through the window naked, and go for help, she was shy at appearing unclothed even before her son, never mind any foreign soldiers who might be around.

'I could push your clothes through after you,' suggested Michel. Then loath to put her through such an ordeal, he said, 'We could first try shouting for help. There might be somebody out there after all.'

They shouted and yelled at the tops of their tired voices. To no purpose.

Michel then tried to move the windowsill. It had, after nearly a thousand years, crumbled partially under the constant vibration of the attack, and had thus loosened the bar. The sill was badly cracked, but little more of it could be moved out of its stony, foot-long depth. Michel cursed his forefathers for building so soundly.

Women can be so brave, thought Michel now as he smoked peacefully in the sunshine at the cemetery while he waited for Barbara Bishop.

He remembered suddenly a story of the first day of the British invasion. A young French girl had run down to the beach, through the heavy fire and the general carnage, and had waded out into the sea to drag wounded soldiers to the shore before they drowned. She had stayed there, a lone woman, doing her best to reduce the suffering. She must eventually have been killed, he decided, but nobody knew for certain. Without doubt, alive or dead, women rarely got any credit for their bravery.

He and his mother had lifted the bench, on which they had been sitting for most of their incarceration, to a spot under the window. While Michel looked the other way, Madame Benion shyly divested herself of everything except her black stockings and shoes and her shift.

Michel had never seen his mother naked, so it was with embarrassment that he made several efforts to lift her into the window aperture; it was difficult, while facing him, for her to slide in feet first, though she kept her legs straight and held her arms high over her head, like a diver preparing to plunge.

They did finally manage the manoeuvre; and with further agony of mind he watched her face mirror the pain of her naked flesh sliding through such a rough wall.

There was a moment, when she was far enough through to have her legs dangling out of the other side, that he feared she was wedged. She used her hands, however, to push herself onward; and she cried out as the skin on her stomach and on her bottom was badly scraped by the cruel stones of the long narrow aperture through which she had to force herself.

She finally flipped out of the space, and he heard her call that she had fallen without breaking anything and would rest for a little while. He anxiously pushed her clothes out to her.

It was surprisingly quiet outside, and Madame Benion, so brave as long as her son could see her, crouched at the foot of the wall and cried bitterly. She was bleeding from numerous scratches and grazings. Her stockings were torn and her knees, elbows and buttocks were bruised and raw.

As she finally drew on her petticoat and skirt and put on her black blouse, once more catching her hand on a piece of glass still embedded in the serge of her skirt, she wondered what she had done in her life to deserve such misery. As she dressed she looked anxiously around her.

Through smoke and dust driven by the wind, she could see that her house was a ruin, as were the barn, the hen houses and brooders and their runs. Where the apple trees had been was a series of stumps.

Then she became aware of the bodies in various uniforms – or rather, shreds and pieces of them – of a smoking tank not too far away, of something that looked like meat spread near it. She shuddered.

She wondered if there was anybody out there still alive.

'Are you all right, Maman?' came an anxious enquiry from the hole in the wall.

She took a large breath and made herself shout cheerfully, 'Yes.' Then she added, 'First, I'm going to look to see what's wedging the door.'

'Bless you, Maman.' Michel began to feel a little relieved.

Heaps of rubble and a teetering kitchen chimney above it made the door difficult to approach.

Very cautiously, Madame Benion mounted the pile of debris. It slipped and slithered under her. She froze.

Yet the problem was so simple. It looked as if the unlocked back door had been swung off its hinges by a blast. It lay across the garden path, one corner firmly pressed against the door of the outhouse, the other corner against the stone back doorstep. Though there was a scattering of debris on it, it was not deeply buried.

Very carefully Madame Benion turned her head. She was looking for something she could use as a walking stick to help to balance herself. Nothing offered.

While the sound of battle growled on in the distance and flashes in the sky told of continuing aerial combat, she stood contemplating the problem. Then she kneeled down and crawled slowly across the pile, testing every stone before she put down knee or hand to go forward. Her thick long skirt, though an impediment, was painstakingly heaved forward each time she moved a knee, and it saved her already lacerated skin from further serious cuts. She was, however, crying with pain by the time she found a steady footing on the door itself.

Michel heard her and tried again to push the *cave* door open. The fallen house door wobbled under her.

'Wait,' she said sharply, and then as he obviously did not hear her clearly enough, she shrieked almost hysterically, 'Wait, can't you?'

Subdued, he waited.

She swiftly began to clear the debris. Whatever was not heavy, she threw as far as she could, so as not to disturb the pile over which she had climbed. On the other side of her, a sliver of pathway was bare before the commencement of a further pile of treacherous stones and broken beams; it might just give sufficient room to push the door to that side, she decided.

Some of the stones from the house walls were heavy, and these she laid carefully onto the slithery piles, hoping that she would not set off a cascade of debris back onto the door.

Finally, she had cleared everything up to the outhouse door. She was so exhausted that she prayed to the dear Virgin that she would not die before she got her beloved Michel out.

Swaying on her feet, she now very carefully considered how to move the door. Finally, she staggered the length of it to the outhouse.

'Michel,' she shouted.

'Yes, Maman.'

'Be ready – when I shout – to push hard and squeeze right through. Use the mallet, if necessary.'

'Exactly what are you going to do?'

She explained how the unhinged house door was the wedge. Her voice was hoarse from dust, from exhaustion, from simply having to shout.

'Don't touch your door for a moment. Let it shut entirely to give me leeway. I'm going to try to lift the corner of the back door – it's pressed against the rise of the back doorstep – so that it will clear the step. Once I shout, you do everything you can to get your door ajar.'

The first time she tried, she could not lift the corner. The damp, muddy grass seemed to suck the heavy wood down. She paused for a moment, and then with every scrap of strength she had she gave a frantic heave.

It lifted.

'Push!' she shrieked.

48

The door of the outhouse moved, as Michel pushed it from the inside.

'Push!' she screamed again.

Suddenly her end of the door jumped in her hands and slid upwards onto the second step of the house. She instinctively released it, and it bumped heavily down onto the top of the second step.

'Push.'

The corner of the door slid unwillingly across the step, wedging again when it hit the sill of the gaping house doorway. It was sufficient, however, to give space for Michel to squeeze out of his prison.

As he emerged, his mother collapsed.

'Maman,' he gasped, as she fell against the house wall.

Weak with relief, he stood for a second leaning against the outside of the sturdy little outhouse; then he stumbled towards her.

At first, he thought the effort had killed her. He burst into tears, as he tenderly laid her on top of the fallen door, the only clear spot. 'Maman!'

It seemed an eternity before she opened her eyes, to observe her younger son on his knees before her, crying like a child.

It took a moment or two more to realise where she was and what had happened. She smiled weakly at him.

'We did it!' she whispered.

He smiled back at her.

Amid the total destruction of their home, he knew that nothing really counted except that they had each other.

'Clever, clever Maman,' he told her, as he pushed back the thin grey hair from her filthy, bleeding face.

They lay exhausted under the shadow of the teetering

chimney for some time. Then Michel said, 'I'll try to get into the kitchen to get some food.'

'*Mais non!*' she responded forcefully. 'You haven't yet looked at it. See, the roof is broken in.' She glanced above her. 'And this wall is threatening to come down. We must move – very carefully, very softly.'

He raised himself on his elbow, and glanced around him.

He understood the danger immediately.

As, very cautiously, he got up and helped his mother to her feet, he was dumbfounded by the destruction which surrounded them. Aghast, he stared at it in disbelief.

He finally whispered to his trembling mother, 'Maman, what are we going to do? What can we do?'

But she could not answer him. What had happened to victory, to liberation? she wondered in dazed amazement. Here was no victory: it was yet another defeat.

Chapter Four

As Michel and his mother stood shakily in what had been the vegetable patch, their ears eased slightly and they became more aware of the high-pitched shriek of shells directed over their heads at the near distance, where heavy gunfire made a steady roar. Occasionally, through the general cacophony, they caught the distant screams and shouts of troops in hand-to-hand combat, while high in the sky planes dived purposefully towards the sound of battle. The horizon was flushed with fires.

Both of them were so covered with dust – faces, hair, hands, clothing all blackened – that they resembled statues carved from coal. In addition, amid the grime, Madame Benion's face was marked by copious tears and drying blood from abrasions on her forehead and one cheek.

Barely able to stand upright, together they surveyed, aghast, the utter decimation of their farm. They imagined, from the flushed skyline, the further destruction still being wreaked on the hapless countryside.

Two dead Germans, one decapitated, lay nearby in a churned-up hen run. A burned-out tank stood, still smoking, amid the stark skeleton of the barn. Even the apple trees had been blasted practically out of existence. The stable, where their horse had lived, the pigsty and, worst of all, the hen coops, were piles of smoulder-ing wood; and from them, as from the tank, came the nauseating odour of cooked meat and burned feathers, mixed with the smell of death from human corpses. Michel sniffed and reckoned that there were other dead nearby.

Nauseated, the Benions swayed unsteadily on their feet, overwhelmed by sickening terror. While shells continued to whistle over their heads and the heavy gunfire persisted on the horizon, they were unable to move further themselves.

From low in the sky, through the dust, they saw that a few German fighter planes were rising to challenge a further wave of Allied bombers.

Michel pushed his mother to the ground, close to the protection of the wall of the storeroom.

'We could go back into the *cave*,' he shouted into her ear. But she feared being shut into it again, and yelled passionately back, '*Non! Non!*'

As they lay with eyes closed, Michel realised that the naval guns from the coast now seemed to have altered their range to a setting to the south-east of this little homestead. Frequently shrapnel hissed to the ground, but the Benions barely heard it. The dogfights above them had also shifted further away.

Michel's instinct was to flee, to get out of this frightful carnage. But where could they go?

Both of them were much too panic-stricken to consider that, amid the chaos, there might be wounded in need of help. Or if they did, they were past caring; the wounded were unlikely to be French.

As Madame Benion lay with her unscraped cheek close against the earth that had nourished her for most of her life, she found it unbelievable that she could be the innocent victim of this outrageous ferocity. She had never thought that the Allies would, perforce, destroy the French countryside as they tried to oust the German Army.

They were both dreadfully hungry and their thirst was acute. They simply lay paralysed, barely able to keep sane, as they shook with fear, fear of the conflict still being waged overhead, fear of being attacked by equally scared, furious German soldiers that might still be around.

As they tried to gather themselves together, a further scarifying realisation broke in upon them – that without home or land they might as well be dead. Unless their disorganised Government helped them, they had no future except starvation, even if they survived this terrible battle.

In the colossal racket of the night it had been impossible to communicate properly; they had simply clung together and prayed. Now, in the warm sunlight, their throats dry and dusty, they mouthed words at each other. Both turned instinctively to look towards where the well should be, but there remained only mud and a trace of its round wall. They glanced back at each other in despair.

As they became steadier, the depth of their loss was further borne in on them. Everything that, as a family they had worked to create through generations was gone, obliterated. The Germans had been unmerciful predators; but this complete loss, when freedom was so near, seemed to both to be the cruellest blow of all.

Michel's brave little mother again wept helplessly, the tears making more white streaks through the dust on her cheeks.

Michel thought his heart would break.

As they surveyed the ruin of their lives the terrifying naval guns suddenly ceased firing, though flights of Allied planes continued to sweep overhead.

Michel did not care whether the planes were bombers or fighters, German or Allied. Instead, he was certain that the price of freedom from the Germans was likely to be starvation.

Madame Benion refused to be left alone while he stumbled over nearby rubble to assess more carefully whether any small structure had survived. Without much hope he called his watchdog, but there was no response.

For the moment, Michel decided not to walk right round their little property to see more exactly if anything whatever could be salvaged. It was a decision, he later realised, that had saved his life; the authorities had subsequently told him that the whole place was sown with unexploded munitions, and mines planted by the Germans as they retreated.

He did climb a part of a wall, despite his mother's protestations that it would collapse under him. He wanted to look further down the hill towards the home of his fiancée's parents to see how it had fared. He was not quite certain that the family had stuck with their decision not to evacuate their home, though Monsieur Fortier had, a couple of days before, again discussed leaving.

The remains of the walls of their home were barely visible. It was clear that their holdings had been equally badly damaged. Michel had been thankful that his Suzanne was working in Caen; he had, as yet, no idea of the havoc about to be wreaked upon that ancient city.

His mother was tugging anxiously at his trouser leg, so he jumped down. The Fortiers would have to look after themselves.

Now, as he stood beside his taxi parked in the lane which crossed the cemetery, he silently finished his kick-boxing exercises, which he did daily; waiting in cemeteries was the only period of his busy day during which he was not otherwise occupied. As he did them, he cursed the Boches and his own erratic governments of France. He heaped maledictions upon the political manoeuvring of a United States Government fearfully obsessed with anything savouring of socialism, who used the Marshall Plan to their own advantage, so that it did not help humble French peasants, who might be communistically inclined.

He remembered how he and his mother had dragged themselves through the drying mud to what had been the lane, and had then picked their way down what had been a reasonable gravel road to the village, to seek water and temporary shelter.

On the way, stumbling over the churned-up road, they met small groups of soldiers in British uniform. Though the soldiers looked filthy and exhausted, Michel feared that he would be stopped and questioned. The Britons, however, ignored them; a small male civilian and a weeping old woman, who were obviously as dishevelled as they were, held no terrors for fighting men driven nearly insane by the appalling noise and chaos of battle.

Michel was certain that nearly all of the inhabitants had fled the tiny village a day or two before. Like the road leading to it, it was in ruins and now appeared deserted. Not a groan, not a whimper; not a twitter of a bird, not a dog's bark. Only the distant roar of battle.

A terrified dusty cat cringed in silence in the corner of a broken wall. Traumatised, it stared unblinkingly at Michel.

Michel pulled off his dirty beret and scratched his equally dirt-laden head. He shouted, and then tried to listen intently.

No response.

Though he still could not hear very well, he mouthed to his mother, 'Everyone must have left.' He barely stopped to wonder what had happened to the villagers' animals, which they must have left behind. He was sure that his own livestock, even his watchdog, tethered near the hen coops, was dead.

A teetering wall crashed suddenly. Madame Benion jumped with fright. She looked as if she would faint.

Michel hugged her closer. '*Courage, Maman.* It seems the Allies are advancing – those soldiers were British. We may find support troops of some kind, who will give us water.'

Though she did not believe him, she gradually steadied.

'Wait here,' he ordered. 'I'll see if I can find something to eat or drink. There may even be somebody hiding here.'

'Germans?'

'No. I mean Claude or Maurice or the Desrosiers.'

He looked along the tiny street for a house not too badly damaged. As he went towards one, his mother, memories of the First World War ever before her, shrieked, 'Be careful. It may be mined!'

He nodded acknowledgement of the warning, as he paused at the doorless front entrance. Then tentatively he stepped inside.

Five bodies lay in the tiny living room. He knew them. Though the one window had imploded, it was not clear in the half-light how they had died, but the smell of faeces and decay was already strong. They must have been dead for some time.

It could have been concussion, he decided. From the

dark stains around them, he adjudged that they had bled. Once more, he felt sick with primeval fear.

He took a large breath and then looked carefully round. Hesitantly, he stepped over the corpses of poor Madame Lefebvre, her father, who had been the village shoemaker, and the three grandchildren. Michel knew the house from many a visit and he went straight to a cupboard at the back of the room. In it, he found a very dry loaf, a jug of milk, which had soured, and some cheese. There was nothing else. He gazed in amazement at the milk, which had, in its heavy pottery jug, survived whatever explosion had killed the family.

He hesitated again. He was well acquainted with the family lying on the floor and would not, for the world, have stolen from them. Then he told himself not to be a fool; they would never have need of bread again. He picked up the loaf and blew the dust off it. The cheese had been in a covered dish and the milk had several layers of butter muslin draped over it; they were not so impregnated with the all-pervading dust.

Balancing the milk carefully, he took the food back to his mother. She was still standing in the middle of the street, a lost soul with nowhere to go.

Afraid of booby traps left by the Germans, they remained standing where they were. They gulped down the whey from the milk and ate the bread and cheese between them.

The food revived them. Desperate to find some safety, they had a hasty consultation, during which they had to continue to speak loudly to each other.

'We should walk down to Bayeux,' Michel said. 'The other day, the postman mentioned that it was taken at the beginning of the invasion – undamaged. I can't think of anywhere else to get help, can you? And we might find out where Uncle Léon and his boat are.'

Madame Benion agreed. Anything to get out of the hell so quickly created round them.

As they walked slowly along the road leading out of the village, they were greeted, with relief, by four other terrified survivors whom they knew by sight, all rather deaf, each with faltering tales of dead children, ruined homes and ruined farms.

As they proceeded, people emerged, by ones and twos, out of side lanes or from the trampled fields and devastated villages. They were few, most having fled earlier, and fewer still were children. All were bent on reaching Bayeux in an effort to get behind the Allied lines and not be caught again between the opposing armies.

Apart from personal safety, they sought medical help for wounded relations and friends, who were too badly hurt to be moved or who still lay amid the rubble. This made Michel feel guilty that he had not searched the village for wounded French before he left it. The silence had, however, convinced him that there was nobody there. He forgot his impaired hearing.

One demented man demanded that they all turn round and go to his village, in order to dig out his family from the ruins of their home. The frightened little group stopped to argue about this for a few minutes, and then agreed that it would be madness to tramp back through the battlefield again; perhaps be blown up by Allied fire if the Germans managed to mount a counteroffensive. It would be better to press on to Bayeux from whence medical help, ambulances and soldiers who understood land mines – *les démineurs* – might be sent into the countryside.

They met Allied infantry being moved up to the front

in personnel carriers. The procession was closely followed by tanks and Jeeps with a vanguard of motorcyclists, who tried, not always successfully, to push refugees off the roads to make way for the advancing military.

The weary civilians found it difficult to walk on the verge of the road. They struggled through the long wet grass and, occasionally, flung themselves to the ground at the menacing sound of diving aircraft. Though they were equally afraid of mines lying in the undergrowth of the great hedges which often marked the edge of a property, the greenery did give an illusion of cover, when, in the hope of impeding the Allies' advance, the few planes the Luftwaffe had available swept low overhead to machine-gun all and sundry.

The forlorn little group struggled grimly on, trying not to stumble into the roadside ditch, which had several inches of water in it.

They were twice hastily scattered, however, by a British tank pressing its way through the heavy, deep-rooted hedges and on to the road. They also met a foot patrol of English soldiers with red crosses on their sleeves, which eased its way through the hedgerows from a field behind them.

A little surprised to find civilians whom, they had imagined, would have earlier fled the area, the medics said briefly, in English, that they were checking for wounded. They enquired of the refugees if they had seen anyone, Allied or German, lying hurt; they did not mention French casualties.

Seeing the bewilderment of the refugees at being queried in English, Michel appointed himself interpreter.

Once the soldiers had managed to make themselves understood, they were told sadly in chorus that only the dead had been seen. There were, however, frantic interjections that there were French casualties in the villages, for whom the refugees hoped to find help.

The patrol leader, a lance corporal, obviously shaken by their stories, kindly promised to do his best to inform civilian authorities. 'They're probably out there somewhere already,' he said rather helplessly.

'This is the last call for lunch,' he added, with an attempt at humour. 'Most of the wounded has been took in – a few Jerries amongst them.' And on being asked, he replied cheerfully with all the optimism of a nineteen-year-old that yes, he thought it was true that Bayeux was still standing, undamaged. He turned to his fidgeting patrol and chivvied the men forward. As the group began to move, some of them looked back at the refugees and shouted, 'Good luck!'

The little group of villagers, trailing behind three people going slightly faster through a deserted hamlet, were horrified by a sudden explosion which blew up those ahead, spattering their remains on those following them. It was the first time that Michel had seen his tough, silent mother so distressed that she vomited.

They were further very shocked and frightened at the sight of small, loose groups of British commandos casually looting the remains of homes, and shooting out windows or booting open shut doors. One soldier came out of a wrecked church, brandishing joyfully a glittering cross from the altar. A stranded car formed a great entertainment to the invaders as they reduced it to wreckage. A terrified horse was used as a target. When the frightened owner protested, he was shoved roughly to one side.

Since there were no officers with any of these groups, Michel assumed that they were deserters. He felt that since they had nothing to lose, they were probably much more dangerous than the more orderly units they had seen.

The tiny band of refugees, unanimous in their fear of the plunderers, edged in and out of nearby lanes or scattered through the hedgerows to avoid such menaces, and when they had passed, whispered to each other that they had never expected this of the Allies. 'Worse than the godforsaken Boches,' one man said.

'Every army has some criminals in it,' replied an exhausted elderly man with almost saintly acceptance. 'Saw it in the Great War.'

That evening, filthy, blood-bespattered, foodless and footsore, they walked into Bayeux, which looked blessedly normal after what they had seen en route, though there were crowds of civilians as well as military personnel in the streets.

While shocked passers-by, both troops and civilians, stared at them, Madame Benion looked at her son and mourned, 'Whatever shall we do?'

Michel had been thinking about this, as they struggled through the ruined countryside, and he replied, 'Find a church. The priests will surely be helping refugees. There must be some kind of help for people like us. Or the *hôtel de ville*?'

His mother was reeling with exhaustion. 'Find a church,' she muttered. She had a real distrust of French officialdom in the shape of a town hall with which she was unacquainted.

And now, as he smoked his second Gauloise and waited for Barbara Bishop, Michel was again thankful for the monks into whose hands they had literally fallen, too weary and hungry to go another step.

His mother had been put to bed in a narrow cell, where she had remained for a week until her skin had begun to heal. Her grief at the loss of her home was beyond healing.

Chapter Five

When Barbara looked down at the neat white cross which indicated the last resting place of Private George Bishop, 6th Batt., East Lancashire Regiment, died 27 July 1944, aged 28 years, she felt the same stunned emptiness she had endured when she had first heard of his loss through the War Office.

The gardener watched her from a discreet distance. One never knew how these women, whether mothers or wives, might react. He had had some who had flung themselves onto the wet grass and had lain there, crying for hours. Others had had hysterics and screamed so hard you could have heard them in Tessel. Still others came and went without a word, their expressions frozen into grim endurance.

Fathers occasionally came alone, to stand uneasily before a cross, tears running silently down their cheeks. Frequently, they wore their own medals, won in the First World War, as if to identify themselves as sharing the suffering of their boy who lay beneath the sod.

Barbara made no noise, though tears ran down her face.

When she felt steadier, she kneeled down on the damp lawn and carefully laid the flowers in front of the cross, tucking them close round its base, as if tucking a baby up in bed.

She felt she should say a prayer, but if God tolerated the

horrors represented by this single white cross, He must be insane and would not understand her prayer or her dire need for comforting. There was no point in praying.

Given different times, she thought with a burst of anger at fools who made war, George could have been watching a football match with the Germans on the other side of this carefully groomed cemetery. What was it about men that allowed them to be led by the nose into ghastly cruelty against each other? It didn't make sense.

These days, nothing made sense. The war was over, but George would not return; at home on Merseyside, each cold and hungry day seemed worse than the previous one. And this French countryside of shattered, deserted villages and towns had shocked her beyond measure. In the glory of a successful invasion, and the Allies having at last beaten the Germans, she realised that few people in England had given a thought to the suffering French civilians who had been caught in the middle.

She looked again at the cross before her. Is this how her mother had felt when her seaman husband had drowned in the Atlantic in 1941, his freighter sent to perdition by Germans, may they rot in hell? Mam had looked like a ghost for over two years. Even now, she was not the same woman who had kissed him goodbye before his last voyage; she had aged immeasurably.

The hopeless tears increased, running down Barbara's face to drip onto her flowered scarf.

She had not felt so alone in her entire life.

From his seat on the step of the taxi, the driver observed her a little anxiously. Her face had blenched as if she might faint. Then he saw that Jules was watching her, ready to go to her if needed.

A solitary ray of sunshine lit up her shaking shoulders,

her white, set face bent over the flowers, her hands clasped in her lap, as she finally sat back on her heels and bowed her head in helpless submission to forces beyond her control.

Death is truly the end, thought the apprehensive driver. There is nothing you can do to reverse it. As he frequently did, he silently cursed the name of Adolf Hitler and all his German brood.

After about five minutes, Barbara crossed herself mechanically, and then stumbled to her feet. She stood looking down at the flower-bedecked grave for a moment, heaved a mighty sigh, and said to it in a tremulous voice, 'Goodbye, luvvie. Goodbye, my dearest.'

She raised her eyes and saw Jules staring at her as he stood diffidently by the gate at the edge of the lawn. He smiled gently. Like a priest, he saw daily so much sorrow.

She forced herself to gather her wits together. 'Thanks, Monsieur Jules,' she said heavily in faltering French. 'Thanks for keeping the grave so well.'

She turned slowly back to the taxi. Realising that many of George's friends must be buried around him, she picked her way carefully between the crosses, anxious not to step on anyone.

Before she reached the taxi, she paused and gave one last, long look back. Then she slowly turned away.

She took a handkerchief out of her sleeve and carefully wiped her face clean of tears. With dead eyes, she observed the patient driver hastily rise from his seat on the step of the taxi. She did not say anything as she approached him.

'Madame wish the hotel?' he enquired softly. He put his arm lightly round her to guide her to the taxi door.

'Yes, please.' Where else to go? What else to do?

She had allowed sixteen days for her visit to Normandy itself. She had planned that, after seeing George's grave, she would have a walking holiday, exploring Calvados. She had never in her life had a real holiday and she had a vague hope that fresh air and good food would help to restore something of her pre-war energy.

But she had not allowed for this abject sense of loneliness, of desolation; and now, as far as she could judge, it seemed that most of Normandy had been wrecked – wrecked by armies sent to free it. The suffering it must have caused; it did not bear thinking about. To have visitors like her stare at it all must make the Normans feel that they were being reduced to a tourist attraction.

Now all she wanted to do was to lie down and be very quiet until she gained the strength to face, if she could, the rest of her empty life.

As the taxi driver cautiously shifted gears, she leaned her head back against the upholstery. Helplessly, she began to cry in earnest, deep rending sobs torn from her very heart.

Michel glanced back at her. He was tremendously disturbed by her obvious grief; she was too little, too pretty to suffer like this.

'*Madame, chère Madame*, please don't cry,' he implored. He was weeping himself, for himself, for all the hurt people he carried in his taxi, and particularly for the nice young woman behind him.

She barely heard his plea, though she did try to muffle the noise she was making.

'Please, please don't cry, Madame.' He paused while he aimed the vehicle carefully through the cemetery gates and onto the lane leading from it. Then he tried again.

'Believe me, Madame, if I own this taxi, I marry you myself!' He sighed. '*Hélas*, Monsieur Duval own it.'

There was a sudden cessation of the sobs, as the humour of the practical remark struck Barbara; the hard common sense of a presumably penniless young man anxious to help. She laughed through her tears, but after a second or two, she leaned forward and laid her head on her knee and commenced more quietly to weep again.

The taxi was carefully slowed, as the penniless one found that, with eyes clouded by tears, he could not see the road properly. He felt he too had reason to weep. Was not his own life shattered?

'I stop,' he announced. 'We sit down on grass. We smoke, eh? We are better. Then nobody at the hotel stare at you.'

She did not answer.

He sniffed and wiped his nose on his sleeve. Then he drew in to the side of the road. A drainage ditch ran alongside the asphalt; beyond it was a grassy bank, shadowed by a huge hedge.

He jumped down and opened the door for Barbara. 'Come, Madame,' he urged persuasively. 'We rest. You become calm before we go to hotel, eh?'

Numbly, she allowed herself to be helped out. She looked uncertainly down at the ditch.

'Jump,' Michel instructed, gesturing towards the grass on the other side. He himself cleared the ditch as effortlessly as a circus performer, and held out his hand for her to grasp.

In her flat-heeled shoes, the ditch was no real problem. Barbara held his hand and jumped. As she landed, he put his arm quickly round her waist to steady her. It was instinctive on his part.

To her, it was an unexpected shock, not because he seemed presumptuous but it gave her a sense that somebody cared enough to do so, even if that person was a total stranger.

In and around the docks, where she had toiled through the war and even since peace had been declared, she had often hit out at men who, in her widowhood, felt she was fair game, and had importuned or otherwise harassed her with their coarse familiarity. Now, as she still shuddered with sobs for her husband, she felt the warmth of the slim, tired-looking stranger beside her, smelled the strong tobacco and male sweat of him, and she was honestly grateful for his sober, sensible presence.

He eased her round and sat her down on the grassy bank. Then he sat down cross-legged in front of her, so that he could look straight at her face. He fumbled under his jersey and brought out his precious packet of cigarettes and a box of matches.

'Smoke?'

There were only three cigarettes left in the packet, and she hesitated; cigarettes were hard to obtain, and like gold in her particular English village.

He smiled and thrust the package closer to her. She heaved a sob, and then helped herself. He struck a match and held the light to her cigarette.

The lines on his face deepened and his brown eyes twinkled as he endeavoured to cheer her. 'Cigarette good,' he said firmly, as she inhaled the strong acrid smoke of a Gauloise.

She coughed, and smiled tremulously.

She watched him stick a cigarette in the corner of his mouth and light it. His face shone wet in the light of the tiny flame, and she realised with astonishment that he had really been crying. She wondered, with a feeling of profound compassion, if, in addition to the loss of his farm, he had lost someone in the war. Perhaps his fiancée? He had mentioned a fiancée's parents on the way to the cemetery. He had not directly mentioned the lady herself.

Chapter Six

For a while they sat in silence. As she smoked, Barbara's sobs slowly decreased, became dryer and finally came to an end. Occasionally, she sighed shakily.

The persistent drizzle of the morning had stopped, though the sky was still overcast. Damp from the grassy bank on which they were sitting slowly seeped through their clothing. Neither of them, however, seemed inclined to move. A few trees, interspersed with huge hedges behind them, offered a protective canopy in the wrecked countryside.

Except for an occasional raindrop falling and the breeze rustling through the heavy foliage, it was very quiet. No traffic passed them. It was as if they were suspended in space, insulated for a few minutes from a world destroyed.

Barbara took out her handkerchief again and carefully dried her face, while Michel watched her through the tobacco smoke. She looked ruefully at her handkerchief, pink-stained with smudged makeup.

'I must look awful,' she said apologetically.

'But no,' he reassured her. He smiled slightly and continued to look at her gravely. His eyes, sad now, reminded her suddenly of her golden retriever at home, who, if anyone cried, would lay his head on the sufferer's knee and gaze up at her in similar compassionate communion. Throughout the war, Simba had had to do a lot of comforting of both her mother and herself. He had done his best with Ada, George's mam, too, when she came to sit in their kitchen and have a cup of tea and stare emptily into the fire.

Now, she had a stranger seated before her, trying to do the same thing, to comfort her and – she had a sudden flash of insight – to be himself comforted.

The persistence of his gaze compelled her to look back at him and smile a little. She wondered what else he had been through to cause the multitude of lines on his face, the patient resignation in his attitude, as if there were no reason to hurry back to the cold real world, plenty of time simply to sit and recover what one could of one's sanity. Apparently impatient American morticians could wait.

At the remembrance of the Americans waiting for their taxi in the American cemetery, Barbara felt compelled to move.

'Oh, dear me, I forgot. You have to collect your Americans.'

Michel leaned forward slightly and put his hand on her arm to restrain her. 'There is much time, *chère Madame*. Rest a little longer. The Americans work as long as there is light – perhaps two more hours. And they are not far distant.'

He drew on his cigarette. 'They stay in your hotel. I collect them en route. OK for Madame?'

'Me? I don't mind. They look like nice fellows. I saw them at breakfast this morning.'

She smiled at him, woebegone, her cigarette smouldering between her fingers, and he continued to sit quietly with her, to give her time to regain her equilibrium.

The Americans are generous, he thought. He had, however, grave doubts about how they might behave with an unescorted young woman; Americans seemed to have pockets full of nylons and piles of chocolate bars with which to seduce unwary females. It distressed him to think that his pretty passenger was herself wearing a pair of nylon stockings. That she might have bought them on the black market, which flourished as merrily in the port of Liverpool as it did in France, did not occur to him. Nevertheless, despite her obvious fall from grace, he would be in the taxi to protect her, and would see her safely into the hotel foyer.

He was not in the least afraid of three very tall, out-of-condition Yanks. Though he himself was so thin and had a hunched left shoulder, he had a long reach, which he found very useful when defending himself. Was he not a very effective kick-boxer, a master of old-fashioned savate, so quick on his feet as to be respected by all? The Americans did not seem to be aware of this particular art, and knowledge of it gave him considerable confidence when he met them in the streets of Bayeux, rather drunk – and where did they get enough to be drunk on, he'd like to know? The Boches had not left much worth drinking. Fortunately, Michel had never got into a real fight with them; sheer weight would very likely have overcome any skill he had.

While enduring the humiliation of the German occupation, it had been essential not to draw attention to oneself and to accept every obscenity without a word of response. It was a relief nowadays to feel that you did not have to salute or otherwise show respect to the Americans when some of them were drunk or abusive.

With regard to Barbara, such a respectable woman, he finally decided, could have come by her nylons legitimately; someone in the family might have brought them home as a gift. He hoped he was right.

He found her gentle, particularly now that she had lost her look of self-confidence and was crushed by grief. She appeared to have no pretensions and to treat him as an equal. The way she had given that choking, good-natured laugh at his remark about not being able to marry her suggested that a ready sense of humour might lie beneath her tear-soaked exterior; under other circumstances, he sensed she would be great fun.

He thought of her in her hotel bedroom, crying silently all night. He wanted to prevent this, if he could, by easing her into a better mood before he let her go. She was much too nice to be left to weep.

In the back of his mind he considered that probably the most comforting thing he could do for her would be to accompany her to bed. But he did not want to offend a foreign lady; and there was, of course, the practicality of the fury of Monsieur le Patron, if Michel were found in one of his hotel bedrooms.

Also, Englishwomen were notoriously faithful; she might feel she must be faithful to her dead husband.

He was astonished that he cared enough that he wanted to be careful what he said or did. What did it matter? She would be gone in a few days' time, and he would be driving other widows with the same polite indifference that he had driven previous ones. Except that this little lady was different.

He sensed that to a man like himself she could give real pleasure. He felt free to consider this point, since his own love life was, after all, absolutely nonexistent at present; so he could honestly let his thoughts stray.

Finally, as he regretfully stubbed out his cigarette, he had an inspiration about taking her mind off her sorrow. He asked her if she had seen any other parts of Normandy. 'Not all of it is damage,' he assured her.

She gave a shivery sigh. 'Yesterday I walked down to Arromanches, to see where some of the British troops landed. I saw the remains of the floating harbour we built.'

He was astonished. 'A long walk, Madame!'

'Not really. I found a little café there and had an omelette, and rested – and then walked back. It was late by the time I returned, of course.'

'Bravo!' He was impressed.

She gave a little shrug; she had hiked before the war, and the hard toil she had endured during the war had made her muscles strong. Even the steady physical work she did in her mother's bed-and-breakfast provided daily exercise.

'I've still eleven full days here,' she confided, 'if I want to use them.' She looked up at him suddenly, and said with more enthusiasm, 'You know, I would really like to see Caen, because George died on a bridge across the river during the battle for Caen. His friend told me.' She paused, and then said with bitterness, 'I want to know what kind of a city was worth his death – and thousands of other English lads.' Her face twisted in renewed pain.

He thought she was about to cry again, and did not answer her for a moment. Then he said reflectively, 'Caen is still ruin, Madame. Streets are clear. A few people try to make new life.'

She replied absently, her mind deflected as she pictured narrow bridges choked with dead soldiers, 'Is it very difficult for them to have to start again? Is it all destroyed?'

'Yes, Madame, practically all of it is. They are without much help. You understand, the Government give plenty attention to the big ports – lots of votes. Very little thought

74

to smaller cities like Caen – and nothing to small farmers like myself. Peasants' votes are not in one place – we are spread out. So not much power.'

He was back to his earlier complaints. He shrugged, and sighed. Then he added more fairly, 'Government must also repair all the roads, the railways, the airports of France – much bomb damage by Allies. But here we all wait – and hope. The railway train now come to us – that is something.'

Then, as a detail which might amuse her, he told her that the churches that William, King of England and Duke of Normandy, and his wife, Matilda, had built in Caen, in thanksgiving for the Norman conquest of Britain in 1066, were still there, practically undamaged. 'The Duke and Duchess thank God for victory and they build good. Those churches last nearly a thousand years – through many wars, many invasions.' He grinned suddenly at her, as if the churches' survival of the recent conflict was something of a joke.

He had recaptured her interest. 'Really? How strange.' She appreciated the irony of the survival of the churches after such a huge British bombardment during a reverse invasion.

He grinned. 'British miss good chance to revenge on William – bomb them!'

There was a slight movement on the other side of the empty road, and Michel glanced across. On the verge opposite sat a rabbit, its nose quivering. Suddenly it vanished into the hedge.

He was diverted. Wildlife is returning, he reflected with a gleam of hope.

He looked again at the young woman opposite him, and said impetuously, 'I take you to Caen tomorrow.

Americans go to Paris for the weekend. We go, yes? Take a little lunch? Look around.'

'How much would it cost? I owe you already for this trip. I had thought I would walk round the countryside. I'm a good walker and the distances are not very great. I can do twenty miles in a day – easy.'

She would be safe enough walking, he considered, but Caen was a bit too far to do in one day. Worst of all, he would probably never see her again and, even though her stay in Calvados was to be very brief, he longed to talk with her again.

He responded quickly. 'I take you. No charge. You pay me for this trip to the cemetery, and I do tomorrow free. OK?' While she considered his offer, he went on, 'I went there just after battle finish. And I take Americans once or twice. I believe most roads now clear.'

And when I went there the first time what a shock I had, he thought, fury surging through him once more.

Chapter Seven

From the moment he had first glimpsed the totality of the destruction which had hit his little poultry farm and that of the Fortiers, Michel had been worried to distraction about the fate of Suzanne.

He had had no direct news of her for nearly three months, though her parents had told him that they had had just a few letters from her before the invasion. He had promised himself then that he would, as soon as possible, go to see her, but his mother had not been able to manage the poultry farm alone, and he could not easily leave her. His first thought, once he was in Bayeux, was to try to get through to her employer, at the café where she worked, but he had no success. All lines were down.

He could not find her on any casualty list available to him in Bayeux, but he was told that, so soon after the Germans had retreated, the casualty lists were, sadly, far from complete. The Fortier family was listed as missing; Suzanne's name was not included. This added to Michel's fears that she might have been killed in Caen during the subsequent battle; it was said that one-third of the population had been killed and another third wounded.

Though the engagement had been arranged by their parents, Michel was fond of his lifelong friend who was to become his wife, and he racked his brains for further sources of enquiry.

Patiently, he had asked at the hospital in Bayeux, in

case she had been brought in there. She was not listed. However, he was invited to visit a woman so traumatised that she had not yet been able to identify herself, in the hope that he might recognise her. The woman was so hurt that he was thankful that she was a stranger to him.

Suzanne's parents would remain listed as missing, presumed dead, until such time as the Army could demine a path into their farm and confirm it. Michel argued that whoever put the Fortiers' names on that list – probably another neighbour – must have known that Suzanne was not at home on the day her father's farm was destroyed; otherwise her name would have been there along with those of her parents.

He reminded himself that Suzanne was an only child, so he could be the sole person from nearby who would immediately set in train a hunt for her. She had other relations, he knew, somewhere near Falaise, another place which had been devastated. If he had no luck in Caen, he would go there to ask the few survivors if they had news of her.

Meanwhile, he had to find at least temporary work, and a place in Bayeux where he and his mother could stay.

Once Maman had recovered a little, they had been billeted in a house with a small empty attic room to spare. There was no fireplace in it, and even in July the bare floor was cold to lie on. Their reluctant landlady, moved by their plight, had lent them a straw mattress, and an old duvet liable to spill feathers from every corner.

She allowed Madame Benion to use her kitchen occasionally, to make the thin fish soup which, together with bread – and cheese when they could get it – was all the food they could afford in a city where the price of everything was soaring.

Madame Benion applied to the hastily reorganised civilian authorities in Bayeux for the re-establishment of payment of her old age pension at her new address. Unfortunately, the steady fall in the value of the franc made it harder and harder for her to manage on it.

After much hasty hunting, Michel found a job in the kitchen of a hotel recently vacated by the retreating Germans. The desperate owner was trying to get it cleaned and in shape as fast as possible. So Michel scrubbed and disinfected with the same thoroughness that he had cleaned hen coops and brooders for his parents.

He was occasionally able to augment his and his mother's diet by hoarding table scraps from the dining room of the hotel; he was supposed to throw all food scraps into a pig bin, but some were still edible. He was also allowed a meagre midday meal with the hotel staff, part of which he often took home for his mother.

In their attic room, water was their greatest problem, since the only source in the house was a pump in the ground-floor kitchen.

With a few of the precious francs hoarded in Michel's Post Office savings book, which Madame Benion now carried stuffed inside the top of her corset, they bought a large bucket and a washbasin. Once or twice a day, Michel filled up the bucket in the house kitchen and carried it up to their eyrie under the eaves.

The whole telephone system appeared hopelessly damaged, but on the chance that at least some mail was getting through, Michel had, after moving into the attic room, written to Suzanne at her lodgings in Caen, to tell her his new address. The local post office had accepted the letter, but there had been no response to it or any subsequent ones.

On his enquiry for news of her from her parents at the beginning of April, they had told him that the few letters they had received since she left for Caen simply said that she was all right and was enjoying her work in the café. She had sent no message for him. Madame Fortier was very troubled. Had the young people quarrelled, she wondered.

They had not quarrelled, and Michel had been mystified by his fiancée's silence. Despite his uneasiness, he made every possible excuse for her neglect of him. He never doubted her integrity; she was going to be his wife. She would surely write soon.

In view of warning movements of German troops in the month prior to the invasion, it occurred to Michel that she might, at the last possible moment, have come home to be with her parents. So he went back to the *hôtel de ville* and checked the casualty lists yet again.

The official there said flatly that the list was still incomplete. What else did Michel expect, he asked helplessly; there were still pockets of fighting all too near to Bayeux. And on no account, said the harassed man, should Michel try to get back to either the Fortiers' or his own farm. There were already too many civilians killed or injured by exploding anti-personnel mines and live ammunition: three men dead – they had tried to collect the bodies of their families in order to bury them – and two who had had their feet blown off, a woman shockingly wounded in the face. And two young boys with no hands, poor kids.

Bearing in mind the hopeless state of his own little poultry farm and others nearby, all well-nigh reduced to a mud heap, Michel accepted the stricture without comment. He did not need to be reminded of the dangers of explosives; he had seen, on his way to Bayeux, a whole family blown up by a heavy explosion, triggered by their passing. Only the good God knew what they had accidentally trodden on.

He was fairly certain that Suzanne's parents were indeed dead, and both he and his mother grieved for them; they had been good friends.

Feeling that they might just possibly have escaped, however, he had again enquired assiduously amongst other refugees who had straggled into Bayeux, many of whom knew each other at least by sight. He invariably heard the same sad story that a great many of the population of that area were believed dead or wounded. He continued to pray that his wife-to-be had not been with them.

If she had returned to her home just before the attack, he comforted himself, the first thing she would have done would have been to run across to see him – and she had not.

For some days more, as he worked in the Bayeux hotel, he continued to watch the casualty lists, while the battle to take Caen continued.

He soon learned that peasants were regarded as of little account unless the authorities wanted to get food delivered to the stricken city.

One day, before Anatole's return, he had, in bitter terms, expressed his anger to his mother about the destruction of Calvados.

'We've suffered so much from the occupation. We risked our lives – including you, Maman. A good many died horribly for it – and now we are being killed or hurt or ruined in the name of peace. It's crazy,' he said in furious frustration.

Madame Benion had been resting on the mattress laid

on the floor of their attic. Her deep exhaustion since the destruction of her home was still apparent.

She said wearily, 'It's true and it grieves me – and I worry daily about Anatole. Where is he? What did the Germans do with him when they took him away? What's happening to him now?'

Michel replied slowly, doubt apparent in his tone, 'They said he would be put to work in Germany.'

'Well, why hasn't he ever written?'

To this Michel had no answer. He thought bitterly that it was probable that his brother was dead, but kept this to himself.

'I don't know why he doesn't write, Maman. Maybe German mail is disrupted by the bombing of their cities. I'm more worried about Suzanne – she doesn't write either. It's obvious that the Boches are defending Caen with everything they have. The bombardment's constant.'

Madame Benion agreed. 'It is. The noise is maddening. My head aches and my ears ring.' She turned restlessly on the mattress. 'I'm sure that some kind of build-up is going on. General Montgomery himself is here in Bayeux. I heard the news when I went out to try to buy some potatoes.'

It was as if Michel had not heard her. He said, 'Maybe Suzanne doesn't know where we are – never received any of my letters. I hope to God she's found some safe shelter.'

'All we can do is wait, Michel. And pray.'

'I don't care what happens; I'm going to try to get into Caen, Maman. Some people have done it.'

His mother shot up from her recumbent position.

'No,' she stormed. 'How can you think of such a thing? If you're killed and Anatole is missing, I have no one, no one except your sisters – and only the good God knows what is happening to them in Rouen. Suppose you are stuck there, in Caen, and can't get out? *Mon Dieu*, it's not even that safe here,' she glanced at the sloping ceiling, and added wryly, 'particularly in an attic. It'll be much worse in Caen.'

As if to confirm the latter, there was a roar of planes overhead, followed by explosions in the near distance.

She was right. He knew it. Her own survival depended largely on him, not on her two married daughters in Rouen, which was itself being pulverised by the Allies.

Poor Maman, she was still so shaky from what she had been through. She must rest a little longer, before even thinking of finding work herself. Meanwhile, he must earn for her; she would starve on her miserable pension. The fact that he was himself worn out, very distressed by all that was happening to them, he accepted as a burden which, somehow, must be borne.

In a city crowded with desperate refugees, she had, anyway, almost no hope of getting work herself; she had aged dreadfully in the last few weeks, due to grief over the loss of her home and, he considered with a tinge of jealousy, the constant worry about Anatole.

'It's all right, Maman. I'll wait till the Allies have rooted the Boches out of Caen – and then go. Don't cry, Maman. This won't last for ever.'

He had to wait for weeks. The Battle of Caen was long and bitter, and when he finally did walk into it, there was little left of the beautiful Norman city.

He went first in search of the café where Suzanne worked as a waitress. There were very few people about, and the whole street was a shambles; he could not even say for certain exactly where the café had stood; the road was simply a narrow lane dug through piles of rubble, along which a few people sidled on their way elsewhere.

In panic, Michel followed the remains of the railway line, where it had been partially cleared, and began to climb a slope where the damage was not quite so heavy. He toiled up towards the Abbaye aux Hommes, which was still standing.

He began to have hope. Suzanne had a room behind the Abbaye, away from the city centre.

He was right.

He found her sitting listlessly on the front doorstep of her house, as if waiting for him. The windows had been boarded up and part of the roof was broken open to the sky. Smoke from fire had painted feathers of soot up its walls. An older woman, her landlady with whom Michel was acquainted, was seated alongside her. The street was silent, without traffic or even a pedestrian. Most of the houses were obviously derelict.

When Michel shouted a cheerful greeting to them it echoed eerily.

Both turned, as if shocked. As he waved, and increased his pace towards them, Suzanne did not spring up to greet him.

He saw with a pang that she looked wan and tired, poor darling, and that she had had her hair cut very short. It was about an inch long and she had combed it close to her head, like that of a little boy.

As he reached them, he laughed with the sheer relief of finding her alive. He bent down and joyously flung his arms round his Suzanne.

Her companion gave a little snigger.

In his embrace, Suzanne rose slowly. She did not

respond to his greeting, and turned her face away as he tried to kiss her.

He leaned back, still holding her. 'It's me – Michel,' he said, and then his voice faded, as he realised the significance of the haircut and that the body in his arms was curiously clumsy and heavy; it did not have its usual willowy suppleness.

He slowly dropped his arms and stepped back.

'What happened?' he asked, though he knew already. 'Suzanne! Answer me.'

To cover the silence her companion spoke up. She sounded cold and cynical, a woman embittered by war, as she said, 'Can't you see?'

He looked at her, appalled. 'A goddamned Boche – and you got your head shaved for it?' He exploded with rage. Words of condemnation poured out.

She didn't say a word to him in her own defence, never pleaded that she had been misunderstood, that it had been indeed rape, nothing that might have excused her behaviour.

Her pregnancy was now obvious. Michel had seen her about four months before; she must have suspected it then. It could not have been rape – the locals would never have touched her if it had been that. To be set upon by a mob, have her head shaved, be stripped to her underwear, and then paraded through the streets, she must have been seen to be fraternising regularly with the enemy.

She now began to giggle at his stupefaction.

He lifted first one hand and then the other, and gave her the hardest slap of which he was capable, one on each cheek. Scarlet patches stained her face. She probably carried the bruises for weeks, he thought maliciously.

'You dirty bitch!' he screamed, and the empty walls around them echoed, 'Bitch! Bitch!' Then he hissed at her, 'So that's why you didn't write! Well, you can thank God your father and mother are dead – he'd have beaten you to death for this.'

She must have been suddenly afraid for her physical safety because, without a word, she turned and ran clumsily up the steps into the house, and slammed the door. He heard the bolts being shot. The other woman had risen, also suddenly nervous. He turned and spat in her face.

Now, over three years later, seated at the side of the road to the cemetery on a damp, cold April day, Michel looked at a girl whose heart had been broken because a foreign soldier had given his life for the freedom of Caen, and for a bitch who had betrayed them all.

He repeated to Barbara, a trifle depressedly, 'Caen is still a ruin, Madame.' He stopped, as if his thoughts had strayed elsewhere, and then said with forced cheerfulness, 'Nevertheless, when I took the Americans there recently, there was some life. People try to begin again.'

He sighed, and Barbara became aware of his deep fatigue. He suddenly ceased to be the rather quaint taxi diver, and became a fellow human being who looked as exhausted as she herself felt.

He went on, 'Everybody in Caen lose somebody. Much sorrow.' With her big eyes puffed from weeping, she herself looked like our Lady of Sorrows, he thought. He repeated tentatively, 'I take you tomorrow, yes? Americans go to Paris for the weekend. We go to Caen, yes?'

He could barely admit to himself that he was desperately lonely for friendly female company. Not normally communicative about his private affairs, he had, on their way to the cemetery, talked a little to her about his family's misadventures, and had felt a certain amount of relief.

Since his fiancée's desertion of him, he had made no effort to find himself another girl; he was acutely aware that he was no hero, that his shoulder was hunched, and that he had no assets to attract a matchmaking father.

Even his engagement to Suzanne had been arranged by their parents, a marriage of convenience which would eventually, with a little luck and much hard saving, make it possible for the young couple to buy out Michel's mother and his siblings.

Originally faced with this same nationwide problem of the subdivision of land in each generation, Suzanne's father had already bought out his own brother's share of the Fortier farm, and Suzanne was his only surviving child; because of the problems of land tenure, peasants tended to keep the number of their children small.

But there had been no romantic love between him and Suzanne, Michel admitted frankly to himself, just affection and an agreeable sexual contentment. It could have been a reasonable marriage.

Now, inside him lay an unhealed wound, as if she had stabbed him. She had deserted him for a German, an enemy, probably some great hulking brute of a Prussian. He felt that he also had thereby been publicly shamed, stripped of his self-respect.

Another Frenchman he might have accepted with better grace. But he had felt sick at the idea of a German, one of Hitler's cohorts, who had tortured and killed men, like his friend Henri, because they continued to fight them underground.

She had got off more lightly than if she had been

a man, Michel thought. Men known to be quislings, collaborators who betrayed the Freedom Fighters to the Germans, had been summarily shot, if they did not commit suicide first.

To a degree, justice had been done, admitted Michel, but it did not mean that he had come to terms with the betrayal.

If she had not had a good woman friend to help her, she would have starved to death, he was sure of that. She would have been an outcast.

The ultimate insult had, however, come only the previous month. He had heard, through one of his mother's friends, also a refugee in Bayeux, that Suzanne's German had recently sent for her and his child to join him on his farm, a farm which had apparently escaped the ravages of both the Russian and American advances. He was said to be now sowing his second year of crops. It was quite a story and the news spread fast in the back streets of Bayeux.

It seemed to an outraged Michel very wrong that his own land, and that of his fiancée's parents, should have been decimated, while one of the enemy's farms remained inviolate.

And who would ever have expected a German to do the honourable thing, and marry the girl? Enemy soldiers were not expected to do that, particularly a Boche.

Michel asked himself again and again why her father had, in the first place, allowed her to go to work in Caen as a waitress in such troubled times – miles away from parental supervision.

He supposed that the family must have had an urgent need for ready money during a time when farms were being stripped of their produce to be sent to Germany. It seemed the only explanation. He still felt, however, that her father had been most unwise – and so had his unfaithful trollop of a daughter. Though there did not seem much hope of it, Michel wished savagely that she would eventually starve amid the ruin which was Germany.

He had been truly happy and surprised when Anatole had eventually been sent home by train by the American Army in Germany; they had discovered him amongst a group of refugees from Eastern Germany fleeing the Russian Army; he was trying to walk back to France.

At least, Michel agreed with Maman, they could nurse Anatole, make him as comfortable as possible, until he died. And Michel was the first to say that, even confined to bed, his brother had given both their mother and Michel some moral support.

Anatole was allowed by the Government a small regular sum with which to maintain himself, because he was a returned deportee very ill with tuberculosis. He also had free medical care. Because there was nothing much that could be done to help him medically, he had elected to be brought home to his mother rather than be put into an overcrowded hospital.

Michel's small savings account was emptied in an effort to buy extra comforts for him, such as second-hand pillows to prop him up, and black market milk and eggs to augment his diet.

Madame Benion was almost beside herself as, in addition to losing her home and livelihood, she had to watch her elder, stronger son die. She and Michel tended him far better, however, than he would have been looked after in hospital, and while they did it she leaned, pitifully at times, on her younger boy for comfort.

The lifelong sibling jealousy between the two brothers

had melted amid the burning need to cope with disaster; and their mother, who had always had to work to the point of exhaustion and could not, therefore, give much attention to her children, had opened up to show her deep attachment to her sons. Misery, instead of separating them, seemed to fuse the remnants of the family together.

As Michel arranged to meet Barbara again, he told himself that he was being driven simply by need for a break from a ruthless routine. To break loose just for a few hours would do him good. If he took this unknown English widow to Caen, he had a hazy hunch that he would be setting out on a new path. What kind of a path he could not yet envisage, since, whatever she was, she was certainly not a peasant woman.

The widow was obviously quite startled at his offer of a trip to Caen and he could see that she instinctively hesitated.

He understood women well enough to read her mind. 'I take great care of you, Madame,' he promised. 'Have no fear.'

He lit his last cigarette after first offering it to Barbara, who politely refused it. He carefully compiled another sentence. Finally, he said grandly, 'I take you a little from your grief, Madame, and also you may see what happen to our cities.'

While she still hesitated, he added, 'The Americans produce petrol like a cow make water! Lots of it. They say to me "fill her up". And I do.'

She considered this and then unexpectedly chuckled, as she realised how apt his simile was. She decided that she might as well accept his offer. She really did, rather morbidly, want to see Caen.

'Thank you,' she said. 'I'll ask the hotel if they can provide a picnic lunch.'

And I hope I don't disgrace myself by crying in public again, she thought.

Chapter Eight

Barbara spent a sleepless, tear-sodden night. She was, like
almost everybody else, so deeply worn out with hard work,
poor food and generally doing without that she wondered
how she had ever managed to get up the energy to take this
trip to France; yet, haunted by the lines of crosses she had
seen that day, she could not sleep.

Why on earth had she come?

The answer was, she ruminated between sobs, because
her mother, Phyllis Williams, and her mother-in-law, Ada
Bishop, had been so persistent about it. She had given in
simply to please them.

Her mother had said, 'Don't be afraid, luv. Seein' the
grave'll settle you a bit. Your dad never had one, being
at sea, like. But your George has one. You go and look
at it. Then you'll know.'

Know what? More grief? She cried on.

When talking to Barbara, Phyllis had not added what she
was thinking: See the grave and then you'll know it's
finished. You got to march forward, not look back. She
wanted her girl to look at other decent men, like Graham
in the village, who had been in a reserved occupation
throughout the war. Barbara could marry again, have
kids, be normal. Not always a widow, as she herself was
likely to be.

Her Barbara had had nearly four years of mourning, on

top of the ruthless grind of the labouring job to which she had been directed during the war. It was enough plain misery for any girl, Phyllis considered.

Now the war was over and Barbara was free to work at home again. Since neither Phyllis nor Barbara had any but domestic skills, she believed that both of them must work to build up their bed-and-breakfast. No matter how unpromising the business seemed at present, it appeared to Phyllis to offer the best prospect of a decent living for herself and her daughter. Even if Barbara did remarry, it would still offer her and her husband a home as well as employment; the country was so short of housing that any man would be glad to live in such a place.

Despite Barbara's now being able to help her at home, the end of the war had not brought much rest to either of them. Added to their fatigue had been the continued daily monotonous struggle against rationing and shortages of everything; particularly hard for those like themselves, who had to be hospitable to an equally weary, irate clientele.

Further, many had to cope with the return of disoriented or wounded men, or, like Barbara and herself, the knowledge that their men would not return at all. Of the men who had come home, many had returned to homes and jobs that no longer existed, and to wives who were prematurely old – and so tired. They had also had to face children who had never seen their father and resented this strange man who took up so much of their mother's attention; several of Phyllis's neighbours had faced this problem, and had, in seeking comfort, wept helplessly on Phyllis's shoulder.

No matter which way you looked, the day-to-day struggle to revert to a normal life seemed unending. It was nearly as bad as when they had lived in a slum in the north of Liverpool.

Before the war, while her husband was at sea, Phyllis and her daughter had moved from Liverpool to run their little business. It was a fortuitous move, for during the war the little dockside street in which they had lived had been bombed out of existence.

In 1934, the Williamses had been desperate to get out of the city, as crime increased in their overcrowded, dockside district. Unemployment was rife and, even at that time, there was such an air of hopelessness that Phyllis was anxious to try to get her only daughter away from the area. Barbara's father was lucky to have a job which was likely to last for a while: 'But you could never be sure,' Phyllis would say darkly to Barbara. 'So many ships is laid up.'

One pleasant summer Sunday, as a treat, they took the train to Hoylake on the Wirral peninsula and went for a long walk along the seashore. At West Kirby, they turned inland to catch a return train from its station back to Liverpool.

One side of the road they took marked the end of West Kirby. On the other was a stone wall which ran down as far as the shore and then turned to continue along the sea frontage. They paused for a moment to lean on it and look out over the field which it shielded.

The field looked so neglected that Phyllis guessed that it had not been cultivated for several years.

'There's a house further up, Mam,' remarked Barbara idly.

Her mother turned to look. 'So there is,' she said, and peered at it. 'It's empty by the looks of it. What a big garden it must have had.'

They moved on and came to the garden gate. Unlike a farm gate, it was a slightly rusty, elegant ironwork gate. Grass had grown up round it, and suggested that it had not been used much for a long time.

'Let's have a look,' suggested Barbara. She lifted the latch and, with an effort, pushed the gate open.

'The place is empty,' said Phyllis, surveying the dusty, curtainless windows. 'I think it's an old farmhouse.'

Driven at first by curiosity, they walked round it. There must, originally, have been a huge garden, though no cultivated plan was now evident. The house itself, however, looked quite sound. Even the black enamel on the front door was unblistered by weather.

Phyllis looked slowly round. Gulls screamed overhead; the sea was close enough for the women to hear the incoming tide dashing against a breakwater. Distantly, there was the sound of a steam train approaching West Kirby station.

Spurred by sudden, almost absurd ambition, Phyllis said excitedly, 'You know, Barbie, this'd make a great place for a holiday. Looks as if it's got lots of bedrooms – and all this for kids to play in.' She made a sweeping gesture with one hand towards the enormous neglected garden. 'And there's sea and sand right here – and it's quiet, except for the train – and, as I remember, they stop round eleven at night.'

Barbara had laughed a little derisively. 'You mean a boarding house?'

'Yes, like your gran had in Blackpool. I had a good time in it, I did, when I were a kid.'

'It's so big! We couldn't even furnish it,' replied the practical fifteen-year-old, with a hint of scorn in her voice. 'And what's more, it'd be a lot of work – and wouldn't the rent be something awful? And who could manage a garden that big – it goes on for ever.' She kicked a stone along the asphalt path at the side of the house. Then she added, 'And what on earth would Dad say? He were born in our street. He's used to it.'

'He could get unused to it – and he likes fishin',' Phyllis replied quite savagely. Her husband was currently serving in a ship on the Australian run. She grinned, and then added, 'We'd need a farmer to do the garden, 'cos it's certain your dad wouldn't! He likes his rest when he's ashore.'

They plodded over to the back of a line of houses which abutted the garden at the far end, to look over a dilapidated wooden fence to enquire of a woman pegging out washing on her clothesline whether she knew if the house were to let.

'I don't know,' the woman replied. She shook out a nappy, took a peg out of her mouth and pinned the garment on the line. 'It's a real sad story, you know. It were bought by a Mr Travis, and made all ready for him and his new bride to move into a couple of years back. You'd nevaire believe it – it's got a washbasin with hot and cold in every bedroom!' She turned from the line of baby clothes, and folded her red arms across her chest while she contemplated the enquirers.

'Nice man, he were – businessman from Liverpool, quite old, he was. He's never lived in it, though. She were killed in a motor smash when they was on their honeymoon in Italy. They always say them Eyeties are mad drivers, don't they?'

The woman was highly interested. Why would such an ordinary woman want such a big house? She said she was not sure whether Mr Travis would rent.

'It were up for sale for ages. But who'd want seven bedrooms nowadays? You'd have to have a maid. And it's too close to the railway track to please them what could afford a servant. They say his wife were an artist, though, and loved painting round here.'

Phyllis and Barbara did not show any signs of walking on, so she said, 'You could have a look at it, no doubt. Mrs Jones what has the sweetshop in the village, she's got a key – looks over the place from time to time for him.'

The idea began to blossom between mother and daughter. A bed-and-breakfast by the sea, with a huge garden – and a beach for kids just down the road. And waking up every morning to clean air.

'Could I go bathing?' asked Barbara.

Phyllis laughed. 'Every day if you wanted to, when the tide's in.'

Barbara began to have visions of splashing amid the waves in a scarlet swimsuit and dazzling all the local lads with her glamour.

At first, Mrs Jones looked doubtfully at the working-class woman and her daughter who were interested in a house meant for gentry. She did, however, finally agree to show them round it, and afterwards gave them Mr Travis's address.

He proved to be a well-to-do businessman living with a manservant in a big flat near Sefton Park.

Phyllis plucked up courage and, accompanied by a silent, rather scared Barbara, went to see him.

It was clear to them that he did not care much what happened to the property; in truth, the very thought of it evoked memories he would rather forget.

At a time when the country was suffering a great depression, a large house with over four acres of unproductive semi-wilderness round it seemed to have little appeal to anyone. Even the council had refused to buy it for public housing, because the land lease was not long enough to suit them.

Like Mrs Jones, Mr Travis was surprised to be faced with such an eager woman and her daughter, whose accent betrayed that they came from the backstreets of Liverpool. What interest could she have in such a big house, far beyond her means?

When he understood what they wanted the house for, however, he lost his distant manner. It seemed to him a laudable ambition that they should want to improve their lives; they did, indeed, look very clean and respectable. He relaxed a little, and explained carefully to them that he did not own the land and would not renew the lease of it when it ran out.

'If you buy the house and the lease – which has about forty years to run – you'd be on your own when the lease ends, and your business would be at stake,' he warned. 'You'd have to persuade the landlord to renew the lease. Then you might have to pay a lot for the renewal.'

Their faces fell. 'We hoped you'd let it,' they chorused.

Anyway, forty years before they faced trouble seemed more like a century to two women who lived in a city where lives were often short and nasty.

'I could never buy it,' Phyllis owned up. 'But maybe you'd consider renting it?'

He smiled suddenly at their persistence. He liked this sturdy woman and her pretty daughter. Why not?

They cheerfully beat down the rent he then suggested, on promise of great care of the property. He was amused, and asked Phyllis if her husband was in agreement with their plans.

'Any debts you run up would be his responsibility,' he warned. 'What does he do for a living?'

Though young Barbara was a bit shocked that her father might be drawn into this wildcat scheme, Phyllis hushed her.

She said placidly, 'He's First Mate on a P&O boat. Takes immigrants to Australia. Nice new ship, it is.' She sighed. 'He's away most of the time. It'll be months before he docks. Can't complain, though. He's never been out of work.'

When asked, she unhesitantly named the ship. 'Been on it ever since it were launched,' she added.

'In the absence of your husband, who did you have in mind to be responsible, then?'

'Well, I'd be responsible. If it's the rent you're worried about, I reckon I can manage to pay it.'

'What with?'

'Well, me hubby and me – we got a bit saved, and I can cash it, if I have to. And me allotment from him is paid regular. And Barbara here is in service. Add to that, I wouldn't have to pay ten shillin' a week rent in Liverpool, like I do now.'

In those days, women on their own couldn't get bank loans or credit; even if they worked, it was always presumed that the employment was transitory or so badly paid that they could not afford to repay.

As Phyllis looked tensely at the elderly man in front of her, she thought: I'm mad. Why do I want this so badly? And putting up with being made to look so small, just to get it?

She answered herself: For clean countryside and sea air for Barbie. Maybe, just maybe, I could make enough money to send her back to school for a year longer – give her a better chance than I had – though her dad would think I were crazy if I did.

For his part, Geoffrey Travis wondered idly whether he cared a damn what happened to this house. He had other properties, and nobody to leave them to when he died. He had, legally, to pay the ground rent of this one until the lease ran out – but the amount was small. Other than that, he had kept the house watertight, and it would be sensible to continue to do so, whoever was in it.

If it were to be a bed-and-breakfast, it would be in the interests of these women that they keep the house decent.

He asked for references. After a little consideraton, Phyllis gave the name of the priest at her church, and her father. Mentally enlarging her father's corner store, she said, 'Me dad's a grocer. And he knows about bed-and-breakfasts, he does. He owned one in Blackpool till he saved enough to buy his grocery.' She paused, to consider what more she could add. Then, inspired, she said with great pride, 'He's got a telephone.'

About the best that can be hoped for, I suppose, Travis decided. He hoped that the priest also had a telephone, so that he could talk to him directly.

He took Phyllis's name and address, and promised to give her a decision in a few days' time.

Faced with the possible reality of her mad idea, Phyllis asked, 'Could you ask Mrs Jones to show us round it again, sir?'

This was the first indication Travis had had that Mrs Jones had already shown the house. He was a little annoyed. He would have been furious if he had known that most of the village had, at different times, been shown it, just to see the washbasins and the pretty wallpaper.

Considering the two women, the reclusive owner was left wondering at the extent of human optimism.

The greatest advantage of the house to Phyllis and Barbara was that, in addition to the washbasins in three of the bedrooms, it also had a complete, modern bathroom, and a washroom on the ground floor.

'Perfect for a B-and-B,' Phyllis breathed quietly to Barbara.

A servants' lavatory outside the back door made a total of three lavatories, which, both women agreed excitedly, was remarkable. 'Have to watch they don't all freeze up in the winter,' Barbara warned.

It took them two years to get every bedroom reasonably furnished, though it was surprising how well the modest pieces from their existing home looked when spread out. They went to bailiffs' sales, where one could pick up chairs and tables for sixpence or a shilling each; and an estate sale yielded a massive amount of bedding and bedlinen for a few pence apiece, simply because the heirs wanted to get rid of it. The women completed the bedrooms one at a time, and immediately advertised them in the windows of local newspaper shops, at twopence a week, as superior bed-and-breakfast accommodation.

They risked near bankruptcy by buying new single beds from the Times Furnishing Company in Liverpool on monthly payments.

Because of their excellent new beds, they found an unexpected market amongst travelling sales representatives, a much less destructive clientele than families were. Burdened by suitcases full of samples as they travelled from city to city, usually by train, these men were always looking for places with good beds and a well-cooked breakfast; they ached with years of sleeping on ancient, hammock-like mattresses. The word went round about the comfort of Phyllis's beds.

Phyllis also placed a modest advertisement in a holiday magazine. This attracted elderly couples from the London area, in search of easily accessible, inexpensive holidays, less noisy than those offered in Margate or Brighton, at a weekly rate which included midday dinner and tea. This meant a lot of extra work, but it paid quite well.

The nearby railway station, so useful to the representatives on their way to do business on Merseyside, also allowed holiday guests easy access to the entertainment of Liverpool and Birkenhead; it proved to be a great asset instead of a liability.

A few months after they obtained the house, Barbara had thankfully left her job as maid-of-all-work to a big family in Neston; keeping a bed-and-breakfast was much more interesting than going back to school, especially as some of the representatives were single young men.

Much to Barbara's chagrin, her mother kept a very close eye on her. 'This is a respectable house,' she would say, 'and you mind your Ps and Qs, me girl. And you're going to night school, milady, to get a bit more learnin'.'

And to night school she went, at first protesting, and then quite happily, because she realised that the commercial subjects she studied would be of use in the bed-and-breakfast; or, better still, might get her a post as a private secretary, preferably to somebody rich and famous who would marry her.

Not long after they moved to West Kirby, her mother had given Barbara the job of tidying up the front of the house, which had once been a little flower garden.

'Oh, Mam!' she wailed in protest.

'It won't hurt you, luv. It'll take you out in the fresh

air,' replied Phyllis firmly. The girl must help if they were to make a success of the place.

Not too sure where to start, Barbara weeded the cracked asphalt path between the gate and the front door. This attracted an elderly man pottering in the front garden of one of the houses across the road. He wandered across and admired her efforts to tidy up.

'It's a proper mess, miss, isn't it?'

She agreed mournfully that it was, and that she had no idea how to make it look nice.

He suggested she use a sickle to cut down the very long grass, and offered to lend her one. He brought it to her and showed her how to use it.

Much to Phyllis's amusement, he became her daughter's friend and mentor. She worked under his instruction much more cheerfully than if her mother had told her what to do, and it was he who suggested that she attend the upcoming church fête, where people would offer for sale, quite cheaply, surplus plants from their gardens.

Armed with a shilling, she bought peonies from a middle-aged lady, who said she was Mrs Ada Bishop and that she lived over by the Ring o' Bells, a pretty pub on the other side of the village. So she became acquainted with George's mother long before she met her son. Mrs Bishop was a keen gardener, and suggested some pansies and lilies of the valley.

Barbara and Phyllis had had no garden when they lived in a terraced house in Liverpool, so this world of gardening enthusiasts was quite new to the young girl.

'That place was beginning to be an eyesore,' Ada confided to Barbara, as she filled an old seeding box with plants at a ridiculously low price. 'I think it's wonderful that you're doing the garden for your mam. You'll find you'll love doing it after a bit. Just wait till them peonies come out. Now, all you have to do is make a little hole, put some water in it and cover the plants' roots. Pat 'em down gently – and don't forget to leave plenty of room for the peonies; they'll grow really big.'

As Barbara told George, years later, 'I never realised what would come out of it, I never did. She made me interested in flowers, and now I love the garden. I didn't even know she had a son, 'cos you was away so early to get to work, and you was in Chester for ages. It was real funny when I met you at the Red Cross dance and found I knew your mam.'

Since the end of the war, Barbara had done her best to rebuild the garden. Again, it was Ada who brought her plants to set it up, Ada who had her own grief to contend with. She never said much, but she had tried to help Barbara, and, in return, Barbara hoped she was a bit of a comfort to her mother-in-law.

A week after they had moved out to the new house, Phyllis's husband, Hugh Williams, had been informed of his change of address. In a letter posted from Sydney, he had approved Phyllis and Barbara's idea of living by the sea. The front garden was looking quite decent by the time he returned from a six months' voyage round the ports of Australia.

He nearly had a fit. He found he had a house far better than anything he could ever have hoped to live in, where strange men, whom he regarded with deep suspicion, came and went like some weird, briefcased merry-go-round. And his wife owed nearly thirty pounds to the Times Furnishing Company – just for single beds!

'How did you get credit?' he asked disbelievingly. 'You're only a woman.'

'Charm,' she replied, neglecting to tell him that her own father had chanced his savings and had co-signed with her for the purchase.

His little daughter, who suddenly seemed to have become a young woman, had produced a penny note-book, in which she had kept an account, something she said she had learned how to do in night school.

'See, Dad. It's not paying much yet, because we're still buying stuff for it and paying the Times, but it's broken even for the last three months.' She grinned at him happily. 'The word's going round about it. And whoopee! You know, we can now charge ten shillings and sixpence a night for the high-class chaps from the big firms!'

Hugh expostulated, raged, to no avail, said his prayers and went back to sea. He did, however, give them one good idea: he suggested that, to increase their income, they rent part of the land round the house to a farmer, either for grazing or haymaking – which they did.

Either because of his prayers or the unremitted hard work and business acumen of the two women, the enterprise began to pay off.

None of them gave credit to Phyllis's grocer father for the coaching he gave them. He made numerous helpful suggestions to limit theft, produce meals quickly, buy wholesale.

'Grandpa talks 'is head off,' Barbara remarked to her mother; nevertheless, she was learning from him without realising it.

She found herself with more pocket money than many of her own age in the village; it wasn't a wage, but it was generous spending money.

Grandpa counselled saving. 'No matter what you earn,

put ten per cent by, luv. When you want somethin' big, you'll have the money.'

Barbara wanted a bicycle, but Phyllis said it was an unnecessary expense; she must save up and buy it herself. Barbara wept in frustration. But she learned and eventually Grandpa gave her a whole ten shillings for her birthday to make up the sum required.

He had long been dead before Barbara realised how wise he had been – and how kind.

In the depression of the 1930s, young people were having real problems finding work, and when she saw the pittances which her girl friends in the village earned, and how they envied her, Barbara had enough sense to take a serious interest in a business which could, in time, be hers.

And, who knows, she thought as she dealt daily with very decent men, one day I might marry one of them.

As she lay, unable to sleep, on a decidedly old bed in a foreign country, Barbara remembered her parents, all her mother's hard work, and the happy days before the war. And now, all that work – her whole life, indeed – seemed to her to have come to naught.

Their clientele had been, on the whole, so pleasant. But then the war had come. Though it had not been bombed directly, her home had been in the path of German bombers on their way to Liverpool; a pile of earth like an outsized mole hill, at the back of the house, still bore witness to the explosion of a bomb jettisoned by a frightened pilot. Their home had, however, been very nearly destroyed by misuse.

The sales representatives had vanished into the Forces. The evacuees and their mothers billeted on them had been a disastrous intrusion.

After the evacuees decided to return to Liverpool, as yet unbombed, Barbara and Phyllis had recovered from the worst of that invasion; but, even, subsequently, as a refuge for the elderly from the bombing of London and the South of England, they had been unable to keep the house up. Civilians had to make do with what they had for the duration: no paint, no new bed linen or china dishes, no plumbing repairs, no flower garden – just a vegetable patch. And never enough coal for heating.

When peace came, practically everything they owned was worn out. There was not an unpatched sheet in the house, not a curtain left other than blackout ones.

The problems of repair and renovation, even now in 1948, seemed almost insurmountable, though damage to their property had been almost nothing in comparison with the havoc wreaked on Liverpool and its environs, or the almost total destruction of parts of Normandy. It had, however, the same overwhelming look of shabbiness and neglect which most of England had. And the faces of the people in the village shared with their French counterparts the same look of intense fatigue and of bad health.

Barbara spared a compassionate thought for the French people round her. Betrayed by their Governments, despised for their surrender to the Germans, their young men still being killed in the war in French Indo-China, and in Algeria, living in a province which was a heap of ruins, how must they feel each time they were called cowardly? Ready to collapse?

As she finally got up to wash and dress in preparation for going with Michel to Caen, she wondered if, in similar circumstances, without the Channel to protect them, the British would have done any better than the French had.

Chapter Nine

Michel found Barbara sitting waiting for him in the foyer of the hotel. She wore a pink woollen dress with the same jacket that she had worn the day before. Despite makeup, carefully applied, her eyes were black-rimmed from lack of sleep; her tears and ruminations of the night had not been conducive to sleep.

She was not particularly looking forward to the promised expedition; she had been stupid to have even mentioned Caen to the driver. She told herself crossly that she was bound to feel even more depressed after looking at such a place. Still less, however, did she wish to spend the day by herself, wandering round Bayeux. And George's mam had said, when kissing her goodbye, that she wanted all the information that Barbara could collect about what had happened to her son.

She felt numb, unable to think clearly. It was as if she were floating in space, afraid to put a foot down on the earth, lest she be roused and burst into tears again, in mourning not only for all that she personally had lost, but also for a sad, sad world.

As on the day before, she was hatless. Hats were another small thing that had vanished during the war – unless one was in the Services, where a hat was still part of a uniform. Her hair was elaborately swept up on either side of her face, to become curls on the top of her head. Similar curls were, as usual with her, confined at the nape of her neck by a precious tortoiseshell hair slide. This style tended to make her look taller than she was.

As Michel walked into the foyer, he noted her makeup, and found himself wondering exactly where she had obtained such powder and paint.

The paint reminded him how foolish he was to get involved with a foreign woman who had access to such luxuries as makeup. What chance had a poor French peasant against the irritatingly rich American soldiers still scattered around Europe – particularly the three who were staying in the same hotel? Then he pulled himself up. 'I'm not in competition with anybody,' he told himself firmly; 'I'm simply taking a woman, for whom I feel sorry, to Caen because her husband died there.'

In spite of her swollen eyelids and the shabbiness of her dress, however, she looked to him as exotic and interesting as if she had come from some faraway oriental country, instead of from just across the English Channel. It seemed to him a pity that all he could offer her was a taxi ride – no nylons, no chocolates, no makeup, no handsome uniform by her side.

When he had told his mother and Anatole that he would be busy this Saturday, neither of them had queried it. If Barbara was seen in his taxi, it would be assumed that he was carrying yet another war widow to yet another grave. The most important point, he felt, was that old Duval should not notice a lady in his taxi on a day when the Americans were out of town, and, therefore, not easily available to say that he had their permission to help war widows.

The old taxi had only one seat in front, for the driver. At his side was a platform on which heavy luggage could be carried. Today, of course, it was empty. Barbara managed to smile quite cheerfully at him as he opened the door for her and saw her comfortably ensconced in the back seat.

He drove her along a main road which, he said, was newly repaired. There was not much traffic, and, occasionally, he would slow down to show her damage done to villages and farms in the great battle. It amazed her that the famous, huge bocages, dense thickets of bushes and young trees, had, in many places, withstood the onslaught of tanks, artillery and bombing, whereas walls and stone cottages had been pushed down and crushed.

They passed a quaint, moated farmhouse. With pride, he told her that it had, occasionally, been a meeting place for the Partisans.

He laughed, and then went on, 'The owner pull up the drawbridge – difficult for the Boches to get in without noise.'

From that house, he told her he had, one night, taken a downed British airman and hidden him in one of his chicken coops. He laughed again, as he added, 'How he complain of the smell! He nice guy. Very grateful to us. His papa big guy in England. I learn much English from him. I write to him sometimes – old friend now.'

He eased the taxi a little to the side, to allow a van to pass him. He waved to the driver.

'Another old friend,' he told his passenger. 'He teach me to drive. He is engineer electrical – very clever fellow.' Then he went on with his story, 'Later, we keep the airman in the roof of our cottage for six weeks until my father take him to Port-en-Bessin.'

'What happened when he arrived there?' Barbara asked.

'Uncle Léon put him in his boat – he is Master of a tramp coastal, you understand. *Les Boches* watch the fishing fleet very closely – difficult to do anything but fish.

It is difficult to put someone on a fishing boat. Tramps not quite so much – Uncle Léon have regular route to Cherbourg and often carry cargo for the Germans. None of his cargo ever lost or stolen. He is very careful – so they trust him a little. However, he wait for the dark of the moon. Airman dress like me and use my seaman's book, looks like crew. In Cherbourg, he land like the rest of crew going ashore. There he go to safe house. From there the British have system to get him to Britain.'

'Did the British really work from Cherbourg?'

'They come and go in Normandy, sometimes, *je crois*, by air – parachute. Spies. Information. Guns for the civilian Partisans and for the maquis. Regular service!' His laugh was grim this time.

'Who were the maquis?'

'Many of them were very brave soldiers of our Army, Madame. They fight on throughout the war – civilians feed them; Germans kill many.'

'Humph. I never heard about them.' She reverted to his story of the airman. 'It must have been very dangerous for your uncle – and for you, if it was your seaman's book which he carried?'

'Certain. Big, big danger that someone betray us. Germans have spies, French ones.'

She felt it would be indiscreet to comment on his being betrayed by his own people. She had read in British newspapers of the deadly revenge taken on such people, the minute the war was over – and even during the war, where the opportunity arose. 'I was told the Partisans were in touch with Britain,' she said.

'Yes,' he agreed. 'When Germans first come to Normandy, they demand we give them our radios.' He half turned and grinned at her. 'Some families have more than one radio.

We say we are very poor, say we have no radio. We keep ours. Lots of hiding places for small radio on a chicken farm. We have electric – keep chicks warm. We plug in the radio.

'We listen to the BBC and tell news to our friends. Some Partisans very clever – build good radios themselves. Sometimes, Germans jam British broadcasts.' He was silent as he negotiated a woman pushing an ancient wheelbarrow full of logs down the road. Then he said very soberly, 'Sometimes the radio of the Freedom Fighter is traced – not all Germans are fools. Then the SS come – and always some are taken and tortured to say who help them. This cause – how you say? – a run of arrests and executions by the cursed SS. We not always know names of men helping us – difficult for Germans to squeeze names out of us. We are all very afraid – nearly all the time.'

Barbara shuddered. Hitler's SS had been dreaded throughout Europe. The very thought of their ever getting into England had, on more than one occasion, made her flesh crawl.

The taxi was entering Caen, and she was immediately staggered by the vast amount of damage. Like the cemetery, it was overwhelming.

The road on which they were travelling was clear, but their route was lined on either side by huge piles of rubble, or what had once been basements, now filled with rainwater. In one great pile of debris, three young boys were dodging, slipping and sliding amid the wreckage, shouting 'Bang-bang' at each other as if they were fighting an imaginary battle.

Barbara saw here again a picture she had already seen in Liverpool – a duck swam placidly across one of the pools of water, and, from hollows between the broken stones and concrete, long sprays of pink willow, yellow ragwort and coarse grass waved in the breeze.

At the side of one of the roads there was a series of little stalls. One, she could see, was selling children's clothing, another small trinkets, whether new or second-hand she could not judge. Two women pedestrians had stopped to examine the goods, and were being attended to by a woman in a black blouse and long black skirt. Other than this little group and the boys playing, the place looked deserted.

Michel turned the taxi into a side road and went up a slight slope, towards a series of buildings, either churches or monasteries, which appeared to have survived with little or no damage. For a moment, it was as if they had left the war behind them. However, the same uncanny stillness, the sense of lack of human occupation, pervaded the area as it had the ruins. Barbara wondered if these ancient monuments had been abandoned.

'L'Abbaye aux Hommes,' Michel announced, as he pulled the brake. 'I take you in the church – Eglise St Etienne. Build by William, the Conqueror of England.'

He got down and opened the door so that Barbara could descend. He held her hand to steady her, as she made the rather long step down onto a steeply sloping pavement. When she was level with him, he smiled and announced, 'Afterwards, we see L'Abbaye aux Dames, build by Queen Matilda, also undamaged.'

Barbara's Liverpool street sense of humour surfaced. 'One for Ladies and one for Gents?' she responded promptly, with a tiny mischievous grin.

Though he suspected that she was making a little joke, Michel failed to see it. He nodded his head, however, and laughed.

113

In the church, he took off his beret and genuflected towards the altar. Barbara stood politely by his side and looked around her – she saw no reason to bow to a God whom she had become convinced could not possibly exist.

The place was dimly lit, and a red light at the eastern end glowed like some malevolent eye. She wondered, for a second, if George had been in here. Then she remembered that he had died in the confusion of a huge army trying to cross the choked narrow bridges over the River Orne.

Bitterness overwhelmed her as she realised that he probably never even saw the inside of the city for which he had given his life. And it occurred to her that, when the taxi man had driven her over the bridge, now roughly repaired, he had not pointed it out. With a sigh, she gave him credit for not wanting to remind her of her loss.

'When Caen is shelled, people shelter under the church and the abbey,' Michel was explaining, and she nodded. It had obviously been a good choice. Except for part of a tower, the buildings did not appear to have been damaged.

Michel solemnly led her in a circle round the church to admire the choir stalls and the vaulted roof.

'It's surprisingly like some churches in England,' she remarked as they came out into the spring sunshine.

'No surprise, Madame. Normans build in England when they live there.'

He wondered why she had not kneeled in the church to pray for the soul of her dead husband. To give her an opportunity to do this, he had paused in their stroll round the building and had asked her if she would like to sit alone for a few minutes, but she had said simply, 'No, thank you.'

He had shrugged slightly and told himself that it was none of his business. She was from England and therefore Protestant; and he had no idea what Protestants did.

Once outside the building again, she looked idly around her. There were houses nearby which looked as if they had been on fire and then repaired. Some of their walls, particularly above the windows, were stained by soot. They boasted newly painted doors, however, and all the windows were glazed. She asked Michel if there had been much fire in the city as a result of the bombardment.

'Yes, Madame, great fires – especially in the centre of the city. From Bayeux, we see it burn.' And how sick with worry I was for Suzanne, living in that very house over there, he remembered.

He sighed heavily, as if he were reminded of something painful.

Barbara looked at him, a little surprised. The sight of this historical city largely reduced to rubble was enough to depress anyone, she considered. But it wasn't his home. Yet his face had the closed-off look of someone trying to control unbearable grief; she had seen that look on so many women's faces, particularly in Liverpool during the war.

He had spoken of the ruination of his family's chicken farm, so she had understood that he was a countryman, who, like so many in France, had lost everything in the invasion. But he had not mentioned a loss here in Caen.

He had made mention of a fiancée. Had he lost her? Barbara was too shy to ask if this were so, but was distressed that such a patient, pleasant man should suddenly look so stricken.

He had stood politely by her while she looked up at the twin towers of the church. He was overwhelmed by memories of the times he had come up this very road on his way to visit Suzanne, humming to himself as he pushed his bicycle up the hill. It was a long bicycle ride from the farm, and one never knew what fussy Boche would stop you, demand your papers and tell you that you had broken some stupid restriction recently imposed. The bicycle, like his horse, had vanished when the Germans had finally retreated.

He had always felt that Suzanne was worth any amount of trouble. Childhood playmate and devoted friend, she had accepted him as her future husband, despite his slightly hunched shoulder.

He jumped when a hand was slowly linked in his. 'Are you all right?' Barbara enquired.

She had been suddenly conscience-stricken that, perhaps, he had not had any breakfast, and now it was afternoon. With rationing and unemployment, one never knew what anyone might be quietly enduring. If one was hungry, one became depressed – having to survive on rations during years of heavy manual work had taught her that. And it was obvious to her that the French had a lot about which to be very depressed; and her gallant little taxi driver had, for a moment, looked absolutely distraught.

Surprise replaced his pain. He had not realised that, rather than admiring Norman towers, she was watching him. His mind still half on things past, he responded, 'Madame?'

If Henri had been alive, he thought, they might have made this Saturday trip, the two of them on Henri's bicycle – if the Germans had not stolen his bike also – just to see what progress had been made in repairing the city. Henri had also been turned down for recruitment by the French Army, because he was too short. But Henri was dead, murdered by the Gestapo for carrying messages to the Resistance. Michel himself, dutifully driving his little cart with its quota of eggs to a German depot for shipment to Germany, had several times passed unsuspected; in those days, he worried more about whether he would get any payment from the goddamned Boches than whether he could deliver the verbal messages he was carrying to Antoine, a carpenter.

Antoine had for months, Michel remembered, sheltered a Jewish child, passing the boy off as his own solitary offspring. They had finally managed to send the child to Cherbourg, to be smuggled eventually to Ireland, a neutral country. And there had been more than one downed British airman who owed his life to men like Michel Benion, Henri and Antoine, he thought with faint pride, and who had been safely returned to England.

It was strange how ordinary people had done such extraordinary things when a need presented itself. At times, he was not even very sure why he himself had done such things.

Now, suddenly, an Englishwoman was still holding his hand and looking at him uneasily, and was worrying that he might be ill. It struck him suddenly how much Henri would have laughed to see his embarrassment, as he felt his weather-beaten skin go pink because he did not know what to say.

She broke the silence by saying, 'It's dinnertime.' She squeezed his hand, and added quickly, 'I've brought a picnic from the hotel, since you have so kindly provided the taxi – and your company.'

Pride again made him stiffen, and she felt it. 'Since bread's rationed, I thought it might be difficult to buy anything,' she went on hastily.

As he slowly relaxed she let go of his hand and smiled at him. In a way he was thankful that the problem of a midday meal was settled. As a visitor, she could certainly buy a meal for herself – if she had enough money to pay for it. But a poor native might have a problem finding something cheap.

She is better today, he thought. Her eyes are still swollen, but she is trying hard. 'Thank you, Madame. A picnic on such a fine day – very good.'

He took her elbow and turned her round towards the parked taxi. He was thankful to see that it was still there. He knew he had been careless in leaving it while visiting the church.

She laughed softly, and suggested, 'And a bottle of wine? Could I buy that, do you think?'

He cheered up. '*Mais oui, Madame*,' he responded promptly, with a certain jauntiness. 'Perhaps Madame would like to try our excellent *cidre doux* – cider – rather than wine? It is sold by the glass. I know a decent place where Madame could enjoy it – if the building is still standing.'

She readily agreed. She imagined it to be something like lemonade. Being from the North of England, she had never tasted cider.

The sun warmed them as they sat on the broken wall of what must have once been a warehouse, the precious taxi safely parked in front of them. There was a pile of rubble at the back of the site, but the remains of the building's outer wall, alongside the pavement, had been evened out to a level sufficiently high that people would not stumble into the great hole which had been a cellar. It was at a convenient level on which to sit, though Barbara feared her pink dress would be made dirty by it. She did not want to break the more cheerful mood of her companion, however, so she did not mention it.

When they had seated themselves on the wall, she opened the long narrow package of lunch and revealed a baguette. She tore it into two, and Michel used his penknife to divide up a piece of soft cheese which smelled delicious. The hotel chef had also managed to find two small pieces of cold chicken, and Michel looked at them as if they were gold. The apples included in the package were a little wizened from long storage. Michel said he thought they were imported, and gave her a mouth-watering description of Normandy apples, which would come in September, if the trees were sufficiently recovered to produce them.

'Last year's crop small,' he told her. 'Many trees destroyed or much damage.'

She nodded sympathetically as she handed Michel half the baguette. She said, as she brushed a cascade of crumbs off her lap, 'We're lucky in England that our country-side wasn't fought over. In fact, the crops were greatly increased during the war – we used to import much of our food before the war.' She paused in astonishment as Michel pushed a big hunk of bread into his mouth and followed it almost immediately with another hunk. The poor soul must be starving.

She continued her conversation, as if she had not noticed. 'Our ships were being sunk by the U-boats in the Atlantic so often that we thought we would really starve, there was so little to go round.' She paused, and then added sadly, 'Dad was drowned at sea – went down with his ship.'

She had spoken too fast for him and she had to repeat it slowly, sentence by sentence.

He clicked his tongue. 'Condolences, Madame.'

She nodded in acknowledgment. She missed very much her father's sporadic appearances in his home. For what had she and her mother worked so assiduously, if it were not to provide a friendly, happy home to which he could return?

As he took the piece of chicken she offered him, Michel remarked on her mentioning the countryside being unspoiled. He said, with his mouth full, that he knew the English farms were on the whole OK, because he had seen them.

'You have?'

'Yes, Madame. Like I tell you before, I have seamen's papers – how you say? Ordinary seaman book? Before the war, to earn some money, I serve under my uncle a few voyages – he own a small freighter, like I tell you. He trade between England and France – and, sometimes Ireland, wherever he get cargo. In 1940 Germans come. Finish.' His gesture signified a cut throat, and he made a face. 'My brother, Anatole, taken by the Germans for work in factory, is sent down a coal mine. My father die naturally – not from Germans. I come home to help Maman. No more go to sea, except one voyage when I arrive in Bayeux. At that time, it was work I could do immediately.'

She smiled. 'So you saw England?'

'Yes, Madame. Have shore leave. I ride in bus. Look at farms and villages. Plymouth look like Caen – but the farms OK.' He bit into an apple.

'Why don't you go to sea again?'

The question was personal, and he was not sure that he wanted to answer it. He had, like many French, a dislike of personal questions.

Then he thought that it did not matter. She would soon be gone. 'A seaman's work is hard. I get much pain,' he replied ruefully, as he touched his malformed shoulder.

Her look was sympathetic. 'I see,' she said – and thought that cleaning up after hens must have been nearly as hard.

She offered him part of her bread. 'It's too big a piece for me,' she lied. He accepted it with a muttered, '*Merci*,' and ate it, this time more slowly.

He suggested that they go in search of cider, to which she readily agreed. She slid down from the wall and dusted the crumbs off her dress. He put two remaining apples back into their bag and handed them to her. She accepted them, and said, 'Perhaps we shall be glad of them later.'

He bowed slightly. How could he say that his mother would have been very glad of them?

He drove her into a part of the town which appeared to have more life in it. He parked the taxi near a tiny café with tables set out on the pavement in front of it, though its windows were still boarded up. They chose the table closest to the taxi.

'I watch taxi,' he explained to Barbara.

After the ruins they had seen, Barbara felt relieved to be in a small area where normal life seemed to have re-established itself. The café was not very busy, but there were young couples there gossiping over drinks, as well as an old gentleman enjoying a cup of coffee while he read a newspaper. She smiled slightly at the latter: every café seemed to have its old gentleman deep in a newspaper. A dog slumbered at the feet of one young man.

As Michel seated Barbara, there was a momentary pause in the conversations at the other tables. Everyone glanced at an obviously foreign lady, accompanied by a nonde-script fellow, who was apparently the driver of the taxi which had just been parked.

A waiter came forward and flicked a grubby cloth across their table, while he asked what Monsieur wished. Michel told him, and he brought two large glasses of cider. Michel took change out of his trouser pocket and paid the man.

He lifted his glass towards Barbara in a silent toast. She smiled and made the same gesture towards him. 'Cheers,' she said.

He grinned, and they drank slowly. They did not speak. In the company of interested observers, they were both shy.

Seated so very close to the other patrons, who were obviously townsfolk, Michel feared that, if he made a mistake in English, someone who knew the language better would snigger at him. Because he had travelled further and done different kinds of work, he was more aware than many peasants of his lack of education, though he had received as much as a peasant could aspire to in pre-war France, and his working knowledge of English was much better than he realised.

For the first time since the dreaded telegram had come to announce George's death, Barbara felt truly relaxed, content to sit in the sun and watch the passers-by. Most of them seemed to be women shopping in little temporary stalls across the square.

There were few children, mostly small, and they stayed close to their mothers. She noted two who were bow-legged, and she wondered if they had acquired this afflic-tion from a shortage of milk in their early years; during her whole life, she had seen only one English child with bow legs, though she had a vague recollection of her mother saying that the affliction had once been common because the poor could not afford milk.

Michel asked if she would like another glass of cider. She refused politely, feeling that she should not be an expense to him. She had also realised that the drink was quite potent. When he suggested a little walk round the square, and she rose from her chair, she felt dizzy and had a strong desire to giggle at nothing in particular.

Michel laughed at her, and then took her elbow to steady her. 'First time you drink cider?' he asked.

'Yes,' she admitted. 'It's made me a bit giddy.'

Though he did not know what giddy meant, it was obvious that she was not quite steady. Still laughing slightly, he put his arm round her waist and held her fairly close. Like this, they promenaded slowly over to the stalls, Michel glancing back occasionally to check on the precious taxi.

'Not much here,' he remarked when he saw the goods for sale. 'Shortages of everything.'

'It's the same at home,' she told him. 'You have to hunt for everything.' She described her search for paint – paint to put on walls, she had to explain, not paint for pictures.

'You paint walls?' he asked incredulously.

'Yes. Mum and I did them before the war – we run a bed-and-breakfast. It's very shabby and needs a lot of repairs. First job is to paint the bedrooms, make them look clean and cheerful, and then make new curtains and bedspreads. But you simply cannot obtain paint – and as for curtaining . . . ! I've tried everywhere.' She shrugged.

He stopped walking and looked down at her in shock.

He did not know what a bed-and-breakfast was, and assumed it was a colloquialism for a brothel. 'For prostitute?' he asked.

She looked at him blankly for a second, and then began to giggle again. '*Non, Monsieur*. No prostitutes.' She choked with laughter. 'A kind of hotel for travellers – we provide simply a room and breakfast.'

He began to chuckle too. His hold round her waist tightened, 'Chambres d'hôte?'

'Yes, I think that is what it is in French.'

'A few in Normandy long ago – before the war.' He corrected himself, 'I forget sometimes – war is still on – in Indo-China.' Then he burst out, 'Trouble also in Algeria. We still fight to save our Empire. Much goods go to soldiers – war take money, take munitions, take men. We have few young men left.'

They were both suddenly sober again. More deaths! thought Barbara. Suddenly she lost her gaiety, and wanted to cry.

By mutual consent, they turned back towards the taxi. A couple of slick-looking townsmen in business suits, briefcases in hand, were inspecting it.

As Michel and Barbara approached, still entwined, the men looked up. They saw an obvious peasant walking in an intimate way with a woman, who, from her dress, was a foreigner. They were puzzled by her. Looking back at them, she knew the type – they were too well dressed in a loud kind of way: in Liverpool, they would be purveying hash – spivs, shady types.

They ignored her, and asked Michel if he were the driver.

Barbara felt him tense as he let go of her, and replied, '*Oui, Monsieur*.'

'Who owns it?'

'Is that any business of yours, Monsieur?' Michel was offended.

'It may be stolen.'

'Certainly not, Monsieur. Are you calling me a thief?' He bristled. 'It is leased to the American Army, here to attend to the graves of American servicemen. I am their driver. Now, if Monsieur will kindly step back, I have to go to Bayeux to pick them up.' He gestured them away from the door of the vehicle, which he opened. 'Please come, Madame,' he said in English to an apprehensive Barbara.

She had sensed only that the men were not selling something but were bent on making some kind of trouble. Michel watched the men all the time as he held the taxi door open for her. She saw him suddenly shift his weight lightly onto his left foot, almost as if he were going to kick the nearest man.

Without taking his eyes off them, he said sharply in French to Barbara, 'If Madame will be seated. We must hurry. The colonel does not like to be kept waiting.'

With her nose in the air, Barbara frowned at the men, and got swiftly into the cab. Michel slammed the door after her. He swung into the driver's seat and immediately started the engine.

The men had read correctly the slight movement of Michel's feet. As neither wished to be laid low with an agonising kick, they had hastily moved back slightly. Their movement had enabled him to get into the cab. Now, as he swerved the vehicle backwards, the men hurriedly stepped further out of the way.

'*Au revoir, Messieurs*,' Michel said frigidly as he passed them. He was obviously very put out.

'Phew! What was all that about?' Barbara asked sharply.

There was no reply, but she could hear his angry, heavy breathing.

She shrugged, leaned back and awaited events.

Outside the city, back on the road to Bayeux, he drew into a tiny side lane, and stopped. He swivelled round in his seat in order to speak to her. He still looked upset.

'Excuse me, Madame, that I not go to the Abbaye aux Dames?'

'That's OK. Don't worry. Who were those men?'

'I don't know. I believe they try to make trouble for me. To make a disturbance, so that I have to leave the taxi. Then one of them steal it.' He rubbed his jaw with one hand, and glanced at her to see how she was taking this.

'Surely not?' she said, though she had sensed that they were spivs.

'I think so, Madame. You understand, Madame, I am a poor peasant – and they know it. They think me stupid, and they know the taxi is valuable; it cannot be mine. They are rude. They say perhaps I steal it. To them, I am nothing – and they are dressed like businessmen; how you say in English?'

'Smart alecks? Spivs?'

He shrugged. He did not know the words, but felt she had understood him. 'They say they call a gendarme. They say I steal. Who is the gendarme going to believe? Two men like that – or me? Gendarme ask for my papers. I show them and they see that Monsieur Duval of Bayeux own taxi. Gendarme decides to take me in – and you, too – who are you? He check by phone with Mr Duval. Duval is furious. What is taxi doing in Caen on Saturday? And he doesn't know who Madame is.' He paused a moment, to give her a sly grin. 'I cannot say to gendarme I make trip for Americans – they are in Paris. Duval think I am washing taxi and checking engine today. Get tank fill, ready for Monday – clean up garage and his stable. Weed two gardens, which I do for a market gardener and a rich man. So I am suddenly having big problem. Taxi outside vanish.' He shrugged. 'Eventually gendarme sort everything out. But dead cert lose my job, and only the good God know where taxi is.'

'Good heavens! Are you sure?'

'I believe so. If not, why they insult me? Lots of bad people, at present, Madame. Black marketeers, thieves, looters, many deserters from all the armies. Car or taxi or van worth a lot of money on the black market. Even a loaf made of wheat flour has good price.'

Barbara leaned back in her seat. 'Well, I'm dashed! I knew there was something wrong about them. But I thought these things only happened in England.' She smiled at him. 'Of course, it doesn't matter about the Abbaye aux Dames. You certainly got out of the situation quickly.'

He gave a little laugh. 'Madame, if I am not quick up here,' he tapped his forehead, 'I am dead years ago.'

She smiled. She could imagine a slightly disabled small boy learning to be very quick-witted about saving himself from bullies; and he had had four years of facing professional bullies, the Germans.

She nodded her head slightly as she thought this over. She was sure that he would be able to smell trouble a mile off, just as she could in the streets of Liverpool or Birkenhead. And those men had looked like trouble personified.

As he restarted the taxi and slowly backed into the main road, Barbara said, 'Wait just one moment. I have something for you.' She opened her handbag and drew out a packet of twenty Player's Navy Cut cigarettes.

Mystified, Michel resignedly turned off the engine, and glanced back at her. When he realised what she was holding, he looked incredulous.

'For me?' he asked.

'*Oui, Monsieur.* Thank you for taking me out today. It has done me a world of good.'

Slowly, he took the packet from her, and looked at it before stuffing it under his sweater.

He turned slightly to look back at her again. Despite his smile, his eyes looked sad. 'Thank you. Madame is most kind, and thank you for lunch,' he said. 'It was my pleasure to take you to see Caen.'

Though touched by his formal courtesy, exhibited despite his evident semi-starvation and his pathetic shabbiness, Barbara was also oddly disturbed by it. An immense pity nearly overwhelmed her that someone so obviously proud and capable should have to endure such deprivation.

Chapter Ten

As they continued their journey back to Bayeux, they were mostly silent.

Michel was angry with himself. He realised that, in using the taxi at the weekend, he had endangered his already precarious livelihood.

If Monsieur Duval had checked with the hotel, half the staff could have confirmed that the generous Colonel Thomas Buck and his two assistants had gone by train to Paris for the weekend, and that it was unlikely that the driver had permission to use the taxi while they were absent.

The agreement he had with the Americans was that while they were occupied in the cemeteries, he could do short trips to enable mourning relatives to visit graves. The colonel had said it was OK if he received a tip; Michel had, in fact, charged his passengers according to the mileage and, in addition, usually received a tip.

It was unlikely that the colonel cared what Michel did as long as he turned up at the hotel promptly at eight on Monday morning, ready to take him and his assistants to their latest cemetery. If Duval, the taxi owner, found out, however, he would raise a storm, largely because he was not receiving anything for the additional use of his taxi.

Imbecile, Michel almost shouted to himself.

Anatole and Madame Benion received small government allowances, and Michel received a weekly wage from the Americans, so Anatole and their mother would not starve if Michel could not make the extra trips to the cemeteries. Without the money from those trips, however, the three of them would never save enough to start up the farm again when they received their land back – or be able to pay for Anatole's funeral, when that dreaded time arrived.

All the extra money Michel earned, therefore, was stuffed into a black stocking kept under Anatole's mattress.

While Anatole lived at home, Michel ruminated, he needed practically all his mother's attention and a good deal of physical aid from Michel. Maman could not work, even if she could find something to do, and, at the same time, nurse him.

The harassed, overworked doctor in the crowded hospital had told them that nothing medical could be done for Anatole, other than to keep him as comfortable as possible; it was simply a matter of time. While he waited to die, he had drugs – and, thank the good God, the family did not have to pay for them. But they did feed him, comfort him and keep him clean to the best of their ability.

From the hoard saved for the farm, they had bought him a bed and bedding, and shirts. It was he who received any fruit or milk Madame Benion could buy, he who was always fed first.

So he lay by a dormer window, waiting for release from his misery in much the same way as his kind had done for centuries. And his mother tried not to weep in front of him.

As Michel manoeuvred the taxi round potholes, his thoughts wandered from contemplation of his own stupidity.

He decided that, although it would undoubtedly bring on another of his terrible coughing spells, Anatole would love a really good cigarette such as those now lying next to Michel's protruding ribs under his jersey. They would smoke together, he promised himself, share the luxury.

Maman herself was growing old. The long years of work during the German occupation – when they had had to produce a fixed schedule of eggs and chickens for export to Germany, leaving very little for themselves – had left her thin and very weary. And those years had been filled with frightening uncertainty, an uncertainty even more acute than that of the harsh life they normally endured.

Like other families, they had never known from day to day what next the German *Kommandantur* would impose on them.

In addition to the ruthless requisitioning of the Benions' produce, a small encampment of troops had been bivouacked on their little pasture, with a stinking latrine and constant, unofficial demands for eggs or vegetables, or to get their clothes washed. If one refused what was asked the soldiers would take it anyway. Better to give, and then hide every egg one could.

The soldiers had ruined this scrap of pasture land for a whole year. Consequently, Michel had had difficulty in producing sufficient feed for the horse that pulled the cart they used to carry the rapaciously extracted quota of eggs and chickens to the depot established for their collection and transhipment to Germany.

Remembering, Michel's smile was grim. He would have, long since, had the horse and cart taken from him by the occupying troops, except that he had argued with them that there was no way the farm could function without it; eggs had to be moved with care; otherwise they broke.

He had been told by the little runt who ran the *Kommandant*'s office, that it was Germany's intention that France should become a solely agricultural country to feed Germany after the Germans won the war. They wanted the farmers alive and functioning – just.

Michel had longed to spit in his face.

Now, as he drove through the outskirts of Bayeux, he was filled with pity for his mother. She had been widowed in the second year of the war; now she was about to lose her elder son, and the site of her home continued to be forbidden territory until some oaf in Paris had decided what should be done about it, or at least ordered it to be cleared of explosives.

And, today, he berated himself, he had put in jeopardy even the poorly paid job he had, because he wanted to take a young English widow to see Caen. He must be mad.

Perhaps it was as well that he had never heard of a nervous breakdown, because he had been through so much that he was getting dangerously close to one.

The young widow sat in the back of his taxi and quietly watched the countryside pass by. It was, she noticed, being farmed in patches, presumably where the worst of the fighting had bypassed it. Already, there were one or two fields green with young cabbages and other crops. Little orchards of still small apple trees had shed their blossoms, and in the ditches, flowering weeds were emerging in profusion. She caught a glimpse of a herd of brown and white cows grazing, and smiled to herself; they were presumably the source of the excellent cheese she had enjoyed in the hotel.

She thought of England, her own green and pleasant

land, and the melancholy which had overwhelmed her yesterday came creeping slowly back.

She was worried that the driver had perhaps risked his job by taking her to see the city for which George had given his life: dear simple George, whose modest desire in life had been to continue cutting and carving sandstone for Liverpool's Anglican Cathedral. He had said once that he hoped he would live long enough to see it completed.

Well, he hadn't, Barbara thought with a pang of pain. Instead, its fine stained-glass windows had been blown out and a lot of the interior stonework damaged, as if the Germans were bent on abolishing his life's work as well as its creator.

Today, she did not cry. After last night, she told herself she had finished weeping.

Liverpool women always said, in bad times, 'A good cry will set you up. You'll feel better.' They had, during the war, cried enough to make the Mersey overflow, as seamen in their thousands, sailing out of Liverpool, lost their lives in the Battle of the Atlantic. The dead like George had become treasured pictures, icons, on mothers' and wives' mantelpieces. George's image was on Barbara's bedside table, looking very solemn in his battledress.

No wonder we all look so old and tired, she thought. The French she had seen had the same drawn, exhausted look – like this man who was driving her. How old was he? In his forties? She suspected that he had lost more than just his farm. Had he perhaps lost a wife and children? Not the fiancée he had mentioned?

She sensed that he had, in a way, the same simplicity as George – though he had a more expressive face; it mirrored everything: compassion, rage, pleasure, cunning, pride. He's as proud as a peacock, she decided with quiet

133

amusement, though he says he's only a peasant. There's nothing cloddish about him, though. He was so quick this afternoon, when he saw trouble coming in Caen.

What she did not know was that behind him lay a thousand years' history of survival. His forebears had remained wedded to the land through other invasions; through famine and pestilence; through heedless, arrogant governments in Paris, and iron discipline from a Church determined to keep its power; through ruthless rebellions and revolutions. They had been exploited, looked down upon, regarded as infinitely expendable; yet he and his kind had survived.

Though she did not know the history of France from the French point of view, Barbara had begun to realise that men like the taxi driver probably had difficulty in visualising life without land. She had no inkling that French peasantry, at last weary of back-breaking work without much recompense, had, for sometime before the war, been voting with their feet for a better life; they were moving to industrial jobs in the cities. Michel's two brothers-in-law and his seaman uncle were good examples.

The taxi driver had, she knew, been dislodged by the war. She assumed that he would finally go back to his patch of land.

She would have been surprised to learn that only during the last twenty-four hours had Michel decided that his dislodgement was permanent. He had waited long enough, and now that his work with the Americans was coming to an end, he had to plan, long term, what he was going to do. He would not wait for the return of his land. Like his brothers-in-law, he would try for something better.

Though it was his own decision, he had not yet managed to resolve the problem of what kind of employment he should aim for.

In the ruined cities, as they were being rebuilt, there was plenty of work of a labouring kind or for skilled craftsmen. But labouring would mean for him further years of pain in his shoulder. He had had enough of that.

For the moment, he could not move elsewhere because of Anatole. Everybody would be afraid of coming into contact with tuberculosis; his current landlady had been unusually kind and tolerant in accepting Anatole's unexpected return.

Michael had given anxious thought to trying for work in Caen after his taxi job ended. If he had a bicycle he could cycle the distance from Bayeux each day. There were small signs there of money being invested in rebuilding hotels and restaurants; soon they would need staff. Such was the lack of public transport, however, that without a bike he was marooned in Bayeux.

He had recently found, in a ditch, the frame of an old bike and was hunting now for other parts. To buy new was impossible; to find used ones for sale or discarded almost as difficult; he had not seen a new bicycle for years.

He could not bring himself to admit that, without a bicycle, he must wait for Anatole to die before he could think constructively about his own and Maman's future . . .

The taxi stopping at the door of her hotel wakened Barbara from her reverie.

Michel opened the door for her and helped her down.

'Thank you, Mr . . .' she said to him in English, and then she said, 'I don't know your name, do I?'

He smiled. 'It does not matter, Madame. But I am Michel Benion. I tell you once before.'

'So you did.' Her eyes twinkled. She said again, 'Thank you, Mr Benion.'

'Thank you, Madame, for the cigarettes. I am sorry that the day is not so good as I hope.' He opened his lips, as if he hesitated but wanted to say something more. He still held her hand. Then, his English stumbling a little, he asked if she would like to see the Bayeux Tapestry. 'It is again shown here in Bayeux. There is a little fee to see it. I take you tomorrow afternoon? Yes?'

'We wouldn't need the taxi?'

'*Non*. It is near.'

She said slowly, as she saw a flicker of nervous doubt on his face, 'You know, I would like to see it. I had forgotten all about its being here.'

He had begun to close the taxi door. He did not want to linger outside the hotel. As he earnestly examined the taxi door handle, he thought: I am crazy to do this. I have no money to waste on women, no home except a lousy attic. I am a nobody. Then: Come on, he told himself. She's not going to shoot you.

He glanced at her out of the corner of his eye. She was waiting politely for him to speak. He said softly, as if the whole of Bayeux were listening, 'I not come here. I see you outside the flower shop in the side street over there, yes? Two o'clock?'

She nodded agreement, said goodbye and ran up the hotel steps.

It was only when she entered her room and flung her handbag onto the bed that she realised that she had, in fact, just accepted a date.

It's not a real one, she uneasily told the ghost of George

and her own conscience. He's just a taxi driver, trying to be kind.

Not really, she hedged. He's a chicken farmer, a skilled man – like George himself. He owns a little farm, even if it's infested with mines. And he's sweet.

She had not previously associated sweetness with men, and she smiled to herself, as if she were being a little absurd at such an idea.

Then, as if to beg forgiveness of her beloved ghost, she muttered, 'I'd never have gone to see it if he hadn't mentioned it. It was his idea – to make up for cutting short the trip to Caen. The tapestry is famous. In all my life, I may never get another chance to see it.'

Having put the blame for what seemed to be a dereliction of a grieving widow's duty firmly on to Michel, she felt better about it.

Chapter Eleven

Michel took the taxi back to the old stable which was its garage, drew a bucket of water from a pump and dutifully washed down its exterior. Then he wiped its battered upholstery. The interior still smelled slightly of some kind of perfume. He smiled. The sweet odour moved him sexually. Reluctantly, he left the doors open in order to air it.

Barbara had left the carefully wrapped apples on the seat, whether through forgetfulness or deliberately he did not know. He gratefully took them home.

The American morticians always teased him when their taxi had an odour of women's perfume in it; an odour of apples mixed with the faint perfume might confound them, thought Michel with a wry grin. He found their rough humour about sexually hungry widows offensive.

He was quite prim about sex. There was the kind you bought and the kind you expected when you married, and both were private, each sanctioned by long custom. The Americans' easy picking up of girls – any girls – reminded him of the Germans, and he did not want any such reminder. He'd suffered enough anguish over Suzanne.

He felt that he did not want anything salacious said about Madame Barbara Bishop. She was a very nice woman, nicer than any of the other foreign widows he had ferried to cemeteries. Few of them had been as polite to him as she. She had added a modest tip to his fare to her husband's grave, and then she had given him the cigarettes – a gift which one might, nowadays, give to a friend after a difficult search to find them. To him, it was much more dignified than a tip, though, God knew, he needed money.

Although he could not afford to spend money on her, he would try to give her a pleasant afternoon tomorrow. With regard to that, he would have to let her pay the fee to the caretaker of the tapestry if he were to stand her a coffee afterwards. It bothered him, but he hoped she would not be offended. He knew a little café, recently reopened, where he could take her afterwards – and he would, somehow, find money for that. He rarely spent anything on himself, except for a few Gauloises to smoke, when they were available.

He paused, dirty rag halfway across the step of the cab. Tomorrow would be a special treat, coffee with a woman with whom it was easy to talk – despite the problem of language being added to a certain amount of shyness. While driving her, he had not hesitated to give her an outline of his family's situation, because it illustrated only too well what had happened to many of his neighbours. And he felt that any interested foreigner should learn what Normandy had endured.

But tomorrow would be different. To her he would no longer be simply the taxi driver. He would be a new friend who had invited her out. And what they would find to talk about, where the invitation would lead him, he was not too sure. At least, he thought with pride, I can make her understand.

When he was a boy, he had become good friends with the English lady who had, from boredom, taught this bright little peasant lad her own language. He had confided to her that sometimes he dreamed of getting good work in a hotel, as a concierge or a receptionist, or even a manager, which was why he was so keen to learn. He had stated firmly, 'Not to leave the farm, you understand. Earn more money, buy out my brother's and my sisters' shares. Then farm it.'

Now, while he wrung out his cloth, a mad longing struck him. As he thought about Barbara she became so desirable to him that he ached with longing. And yet, he told himself, to think like that about an Englishwoman was stupid. Nothing could come of it. You couldn't casually bed a respectable woman like her. It would put him on a level with the Boches – or the Americans.

What about as a wife? For a moment, he imagined her lying, looking up at him from a linen-covered pillow in the cosiness of his bed in his old home on the farm, her hair loose about her shoulders; and he was drunk with desire.

He dropped the cloth into the bucket. The resulting splash soaked his trouser leg, and the illusion receded. He stood shaking as common sense took over. To aspire to marriage with her would cause innumerable difficulties. She wouldn't know anything about dowries, for example. She said she and her mother had a business in England; presumably, she would want to go back to it, even if he could offer her some hope and security in France.

If only he owned the taxi and could get enough petrol to run it, he would have a small, but firm basis on which to build a livelihood, and, with luck, maintain both his mother and Barbara.

Despite his effort to disillusion himself, he continued to dream as he sloshed water over the wheels of the old machine. They were dreams that had been put aside since the loss of Suzanne and the chaos to which his life had been reduced by the Allied invasion. He dreamed of a home and a wife like Barbara – and enough money to keep her in talcum powder and nylons.

He wondered if, perchance, a surgeon could fix his shoulder. No doctor had ever looked at it. When, in childhood, he had fallen out of an apple tree his mother had underestimated the injury. In her opinion, time was precious, not to be wasted by an unnecessary walk of several miles to see the local doctor. She assured Michel that the pain would ease in a little while, handed him an egg basket and told him to go to help Anatole.

He learned to live with the pain, which did lessen, except when he was doing heavy manual work; when he grew older, he did not consult even an ordinary physician about the injury for fear treatment might mean he could not work for a time. Latterly, he had always to remember that there was Maman and poor old Anatole; as the franc continued to fall in value, if he took time off work it meant less for them.

Up to now, the three of them had grudged every centime spent, as they tried, franc by franc, to put enough money together to buy, the minute their land was cleared, new breeding stock and laying hens, wood for hen coops, brooders, a barn, electric wiring and new fencing – their needs would be endless.

It was only very recently that Anatole himself had ceased to talk about what they would do on their return to their precious hectares, and Michel knew that it was the silence of resignation.

His face was suddenly grim. He slammed the door of the taxi angrily. Poor Anatole, he must be certain now in his own mind that he would never ever wash another egg.

Michel was filled with anguish. He could not imagine life without his stolid elder brother, nor yet a normal life while he still lived.

He unlocked the petrol pump. He was the only person who had a key to it, except the American petrol tanker driver who refilled the holding tank – Colonel Buck had seen to that. He slowly filled up the taxi.

He wiped down the bonnet of the vehicle with sudden furious energy. When its rusted exterior seemed as clean as possible, he paused to lean against it, tired. Then he roused himself and patted it as if it were a dog.

'If only I owned you, Monsieur le Taxi, I would at least have a start. I can manage you without my shoulder acting up. And if I owned you, let's be honest, I would never let little Madame Barbara slip away.'

'And, now, Monsieur,' he said to the taxi, as he closed the garage door and locked it, 'I must go to do some weeding or Monsieur Duval won't be the only employer liable to fire me.'

Chapter Twelve

Towards nine o'clock that evening, a very weary Michel climbed the stairs to his attic home. During his patient weeding of a large strawberry bed following the garaging of the taxi, his worries had continued to close in upon him. Most pressing was the departure of his American employers, together with their boundless supply of petrol.

Old Duval, blacksmith and motor mechanic, had repaired the antiquated vehicle and then leased it for four months to the morticians, with a driver who spoke English and knew the district, as Colonel Buck had stipulated. He had been thankful to find lessees who had petrol to run it. He had not worried too much about the amount of mileage they might run up.

Duval trusted Michel and had, for this reason, appointed him driver and caretaker of the taxi. As far as Michel was concerned, steady work for four months was too good to miss. He had lied when Duval had asked him if he could drive; he had never driven anything bigger than a small farm tractor.

Immediately after the rental had been agreed upon, to commence at the beginning of the following week, a scared, but excited Michel had hurried round to see an old friend, an electrician employed by the Government.

Paul drove a small van. Laughing heartily, he had, during that weekend, given Michel several quick driving lessons in his vehicle. It was, however, a fairly ignorant Michel who first took out the Americans.

They had been annoyed at the snail's pace which he had maintained. He assured them that he was nervous about mines buried under the roads; he must be careful.

This nervousness, however, became less apparent as he gained practice on the almost empty roads, and he began to enjoy driving.

Duval's, and his, greatest and most valid fear had been that if he left the taxi for a minute, it would be stolen.

'Jeeze! This isn't Chicago!' protested his clients.

'Problems everywhere,' responded Michel. 'You let me watch it for you.'

They had taken his advice. He remained glued to the vehicle.

As a result of the increase in their income, Maman had decided that it was advisable for Anatole to have a room of his own, but they had searched without success for two rooms in overcrowded Bayeux. When, after close questioning by prospective landlords, Michel had had to admit that one of the tenants would be an invalid, doors had been firmly closed.

Now, it was with deep depression that Michel opened the door at the top of the long staircase of the house in which he lived, to enter the single attic room.

Gnawing at him was the worry that their small savings might, once again, be totally dissipated, while he searched for further work.

At the same time, dancing at the back of his mind were thoughts of Barbara. Was she totally unobtainable? Could he be lucky and find work sufficiently lucrative that he could give her, at least, the same standard of living as his married sisters enjoyed? In theory, anything that his sisters' husbands, Bertrand and Guy, had done, he could too. In practice, however, it did not seem very likely; he had Maman and Anatole to care for.

He told himself sharply to stop thinking like an idiot.

As the door swung open, he forced himself to smile and say cheerfully, 'Hello, Maman – Anatole.'

Madame Benion was seated at the end of the second-hand bedstead they had recently purchased for Anatole. Under it was a chamber pot, also for Anatole's use, since he could no longer get up and down the long staircase in order to use the privy in the back yard of the house.

Despite the window's being open to the spring sunshine, the room smelled of sickness and of urine.

Wrapped in the duvet originally given them by their kindly landlady, and elevated by the bed, Anatole could now see out of the dormer window. It was a great pleasure to him, a real improvement after lying on a mattress on the floor.

The room was tidy. A washbasin was neatly tucked in a corner, beside a bucket of water, a saucepan and some dishes. Above these necessities hung a clothesline, which held one or two pieces of drying washing. Stacked against a wall were two straw palliasses, on which Michel and his mother slept. What little food they had in store was kept in a cupboard in the roof, where it sometimes fell prey to marauding mice. They had talked about getting a cat, but an attic with no easy access to outdoors made the idea impractical.

Like Barbara and her mother, the family had suffered terribly from the cold of the previous winter, the worst winter on record. It had caused great suffering to the victims of the invasion, many of whom, like the Benions, had lost all they possessed.

Fearing that his mother, as well as Anatole, would die because they had no heat in the room, Michel had gone in despair to Monsieur le Curé, Father Nicolas, for help and advice.

The poor priest, himself very cold, had lent Michel a paraffin stove, a great help – provided one could find paraffin to burn in it.

Fuel could be found, like everything else, if one had enough money. In this regard, Paul, Michel's electrician friend, had again been helpful. He regularly bought petrol for his personal use 'on the black', and he managed to get some paraffin for Michel. During that dreadful winter practically all that the Benions had hitherto managed to save was expended on this precious fuel.

The priest spoke to one of his parishioners, and this lady sent them a pair of blankets left behind by the retreating enemy. They were of excellent quality, though rather smelly. But beggars can't be choosers, and Michel thankfully wrapped one round his mother and the other one round Anatole. He himself slept in all the clothes he possessed, and covered himself with an old overcoat, which Anatole had worn during his long walk home across Europe.

Now, on his return from his visit to Caen with Barbara, Michel asked himself what she would think if he showed her his poverty-stricken attic.

She would recoil in disgust, he decided. He knew that both his sisters would; it was as well that they had never seen it. Now that the railway to Bayeux and Cherbourg had been restored, Michel felt that they really should visit, if only for an afternoon but though they wrote to their mother, they refused to come for fear of carrying the tuberculosis germ back to their children. This was very hard on Madame Benion, who badly needed their affection and support, and Michel smouldered with resentment at their unhelpful attitude. Anatole tried not even to think of them.

Neither Government nor family really cared a damn about the dispossessed, Michel thought bitterly.

He knew that he himself was running out of endurance. The fearful experience of the actual invasion was still very fresh in both his and his mother's minds; the loss of all certitudes in their hard lives, the loss of friends, family and, not the least, the daily suffering of Anatole, with his constant broken nights, all weighed heavily on both mother and younger son. In addition, Michel was still smarting from Suzanne's desertion of him and the public humiliation of her conduct, which had seared his soul. Even the death of her parents, old and trusted friends of his family, had left an emptiness impossible to fill.

He had increasingly feared lately that his mind would split, that he would go insane, and that one morning he would simply not be able to get up to go to work. Yet, he must. He must.

And on top of this was laid something he had never dreamed of: he simply could not get Barbara out of his mind. Just thinking about her brought on such a surge of desire that he did not know how to control himself. It was wonderful – and yet it was too much to bear.

Fool that he was, he upbraided himself, he had arranged to meet her again tomorrow. He knew he was behaving like a moth which courts the flames that will burn it to death, but he was certain that he would keep the tryst.

He approached Anatole's bed with a determination to show nothing of his inward apprehensions. He took off his beret and its removal revealed black, wavy hair in need of

147

a barber. As he unflinchingly bent to kiss Anatole on each cheek, his mother noticed, with a pang, the beginning of a bald patch on the top of his head.

As she rose to get him some soup, she thought sadly, our men age young.

'How are you feeling?' Michel asked his brother.

The bones that were Anatole's shoulders moved in a slight shrug. He realised that Michel's kiss was not necessarily meant as a greeting but rather as an affirmation that he was still a close part of the family, not to be feared as a disease carrier. As he did every evening, he struggled to raise himself to return the caress, and, as always, Michel told him, 'Don't disturb yourself,' and sat down on the edge of the bed very carefully, so as not to shake the invalid.

Anatole put out a long thin hand and laid it on his brother's.

He was twelve years older than Michel. To Michel, when he was a little boy, he had appeared to be a third parent, who ordered him around and smacked him when he was disobedient. Michel had naturally resented this and had regarded him as a bully. So they had never, in their younger days, been particularly close. Also, their experiences during the later years of the war had been sharply different. It had been some time before they had been able to talk to one another about these awful times. Anatole's helplessness had, however, changed the relationship markedly; the elder brother was now dependent upon the younger one, and during the last winter they had finally learned to communicate much better.

Despite their youthful disagreements, they had stood together as one when, after their father died, the Germans marched in. From the very beginning of the occupation, they had been united in protecting their small poultry farm and in aiding the Resistance whenever the chance arose.

It was a more worldly-wise Anatole who, at that time reminded Michel and his friend Henri that the Resistance was actually a motley crew. It included deserters from the French Army; some known criminals; men who had gone underground rather than be deported to Germany to work; well-organised Communist cells; and plain, ordinary citizens who helped out of conviction. Any of these groups, he warned, could have been infiltrated by the Germans – or bribed by them; 'So, for God's sake, you and Henri be careful what you do.'

None of them had felt very brave, but they shared what food they had, when rationless remnants of the French Army in need of refuge, slid silently up to their back door.

Moved by sudden compassion for a despised minority, they had hidden a panic-stricken Jewish woman trying to flee French authorities rounding up Jews on behalf of the Germans.

It was Henri who knew the escape route for Jewish persons. Much later, he paid for his compassionate help of them by being tortured and then buried alive by the SS. He died rather than pass to them his knowledge of the pipeline out of Occupied France. He also managed not to betray the Benions' succour of the Royal Air Force men.

Michel had been heart-broken at the loss of his friend, particularly in such an inhuman fashion. Even now, he cringed at the thought of Henri's terrible end.

Madame Benion had, with the aid of an old retired doctor, once nursed a badly wounded French soldier. She hid him in the *cave*, the old outhouse which had later sheltered her and her son during the invasion battle. The boy lived to fight again.

The common threat of the German occupation had definitely brought the terrified family closer together at that time. Suddenly, however, Anatole, a bachelor, had been whisked away to work in Germany. Because he was physically big and very fit, he had been chosen in preference to Michel.

Scared to death of what might happen to him, mother and younger son clung to each other, trusting neither friend nor neighbour. Without Anatole, the work of the farm was almost impossible to keep up. While they themselves went hungry, they worked harder than they had ever worked before, as the Germans enforced their demands for eggs, chickens and apples, to be sent to Germany.

Now, his health broken by the treatment he had received in Germany, Anatole was completely dependent upon them.

After Michel had drunk his tepid soup with bread soaked into it, the three of them discussed, rather fruitlessly, the need for Michel to find fresh employment, how nice it would be to have a room with a fireplace where they could burn anything they could find to keep them warm, and how their sisters in Rouen were getting on.

Anne-Marie was the worst placed, they agreed. She and Guy had lost their younger child, Philippe, in the raid that had destroyed not only their home, but also Guy's petrol station with its adjoining workshop. Though, as a motor mechanic, he had a marketable skill, without at least a new set of tools, he could not follow his old occupation, so he had thankfully taken a job as a lorry driver. The lorry was a ramshackle affair and he risked an accident every time he took it out but, without spare parts, his employer could not do much about its repair. At Michel's request, Guy had promised to look out for a lorry-driving job for him, though he had pointed out the acute shortage of trucks of any kind.

Guy, Anne-Marie and their little daughter all lived in one room in shattered Rouen. Whenever he had a load for Bayeux, Guy came to see Maman, though he never came into the attic. Despite their own problems, he sometimes brought small gifts for the invalid, such as a shirt or a clean sheet or, once, a very useful pile of rags for cleaning.

One day, he brought from Claudette, Madame Benion's other daughter, some black market loaves of bread, baked by her husband, Bertrand, in their bakery. Madame Benion had been immensely grateful, but she still longed to see her daughters.

Anatole's only visitor remained Monsieur le Curé, Father Nicolas. Michel wondered what Anatole would think if Barbara came to visit him. For her part, would she be, as he feared, shocked at the whole situation of his family?

As they gossiped, Michel mentioned Guy's promise to watch for a driver's job for him, and he said, 'Driving the taxi doesn't bother my shoulder and I don't think driving a lorry would either. Working on the farm was hell sometimes, and being a deckie in Uncle Léon's boat was sheer murder.' He squeezed Anatole's clawlike hand. 'It would be nice to have a job which wasn't painful.'

'Tush, you never complained during the war,' exclaimed his mother. 'After all, you only fell out of an apple tree when you were little – and the bruise healed well. Boys are always doing things like that.'

Michel refrained from telling her that he had cried about it enough until his father told him that other

151

boys put up with small hurts; he must stop being a namby-pamby and get on with his work unless he wanted a whipping.

So he had endured. He remembered other children jeering at him because he did not want to play games which involved throwing a ball. He was, at times, bullied unmercifully.

Then, Jacques, an elderly great-uncle, had seen the child's predicament and had taught him a few of the finer points of kick-boxing, real, old-fashioned savate, fighting while wearing heavy farm boots. Naturally quite agile and fast-moving, and with a long reach, Michel found he could endure an occasional sharp jolt as he kicked. It was a long-forgotten skill not familiar to the other boys, and he had had the supreme satisfaction of inflicting enough damage on his tormenters to deter further bullying. Anatole had been amused, on his return from Germany, to learn that Michel still did daily exercises to keep up his skill.

After Madame Benion's impatient remarks about his shoulder, the conversation lapsed.

In pain, facing death, Anatole had learned to appreciate the patience and endurance of this dumb little brother of his. That his brother's silent endurance was wearing very thin had not yet occurred either to him or to their harassed mother.

Chapter Thirteen

It felt to Barbara almost unseemly to be meeting a foreigner, a stranger, so soon after having wept her heart out for George. She had not yet managed to admit to herself her intense loneliness, her torment at unsatisfied sexual needs, her fear of a future which threatened to become increasingly lonely and unpredictable.

Even her wartime marriage had been lonely; when George had married her, he had been a serving soldier based in Yorkshire. But both she and George always hoped that the war would not last for long and, she had once said wistfully to Phyllis, there were lovely leaves to look forward to, even if they lasted only forty-eight hours.

To add to the loneliness of those days, the one or two girl friends Barbara had made when she had first come to West Kirby had been scattered by the call-up to military service or war work. When she went to a local dance, she met more strangers than local people.

Only one other woman had been employed by Barbara's wartime employer. Bound together by the need to maintain their dignity in a very rough male community, the two had got along quite well. But the friendship had not continued once the war ended; Mavis had gone thankfully back to her home in Glasgow.

Soon after the war, whole shiploads of young women, who had become the war brides of foreign soldiers based in nearby camps, had gone abroad to join their husbands. Barbara noticed the loss of familiar faces from her own village.

Now that peace had come, the bed-and-breakfast needed endless work and ingenuity to regain its prewar clientele. She had begun to wonder if it would ever flourish again. She had certainly not had much spare time since the war ended to go out and make new friends.

As she walked up the road to meet Michel, it was, however, with a fair amount of instinctive wariness that she observed him waiting for her.

In a quiet way, he's endearing, she decided. She had imagined that a peasant would be solidly built, clumsy in movement, but he was thin, and when he moved, it was with the swift economy of movement of a dancer, not the steady plod of a countryman who had spent his life in muddy fields.

A cigarette hanging from the corner of his mouth, he was loitering outside the flowerseller's tiny shop. He looked extremely neat and clean, though still shabby. Instead of blue jeans, today he wore black trousers with his black pullover. He had evidently done his utmost to achieve a good shave.

He greeted her shyly with a little salute. He did not doff his beret, and she had a whimsical thought that French baby boys were probably born with such caps on their heads, never to be removed.

She responded with a smile and a quick, 'Hello'. Then she could not think of anything else to say.

As Michel straightened and moved eagerly towards her, it was obvious that, though glad to see her, he, also, was tongue-tied. His smile was cheerful, however, the eyes narrowed as if he were enjoying a secret joke.

In fact, he was finding his own lunacy in meeting her an ironic joke.

While traversing the narrow, cobbled street, she had been surprised that the flower shop, by which he was waiting, had metal drums of cut flowers sitting outside its door and was, therefore, presumably open – on a Sunday? She now seized on this to provide a possible line of conversation.

As he took her elbow to steer her across the sunlit road, she remarked upon the shop's doing business on the sabbath. She told him that in England, the Lord's Day Act forbade Sunday opening, except for shops selling a few basic necessities.

He stopped, his eyes twinkling. 'How people buy, if shops are closed Sunday?' he asked in some surprise. 'Here, shops shut Monday – when everybody else go to work.'

Barbara thought of the short shopping hours imposed on British shopkeepers by a government bent on limiting demand for goods of any kind. 'It sounds a good idea to me,' she said approvingly. 'Provided they have anything to sell.'

'Lots of flowers, Madame. There is shortages, many shortages.' He sighed, and added, more honestly, 'Buy anything if I have much money. It is . . .' He paused, to gather a sentence together, and then went on, '. . . how you say in English? – they are under the counter.' He looked quite triumphant at having remembered the idiom.

Barbara smiled and looked up into his face, a twinkle in her eye. 'It's true in England too. Everything interesting is under the counter – because many factories were bombed flat and the others have not really got going again since the war, and a lot of whatever they manage to produce is exported.' She laughed. 'I bought my nylons off an advertising rep, who stays with us regularly. He got them from an American seaman he met in a pub.'

In his mind, Michel carefully translated.

So that accounted for her nylons. No Americans! He was secretly absurdly happy. Then he asked suspiciously, 'What is an ad – what you call him – rep? Useful friend?'

'Oh, he's not a friend, really. He's one of our regulars.'

Michel looked bemused. He said, 'Explain to me, *s'il vous plaît, Madame.*'

She laughed again, and said carefully, 'OK. My mum and I run a bed-and-breakfast – a little hotel for travellers. You remember, I mentioned it to you yesterday? People who want to stay only one night, you understand? Have breakfast and then go to work.'

He nodded, and she continued, 'Our regular customers are sales representatives – salesmen. They travel from city to city. They represent their companies – that's why they're called reps – a short name for them. They come to Liverpool to talk to businessmen and sell their companies' goods.' She glanced at him to check that he was following her successfully. Then she went on, 'They like to stay with us because our house is by the sea, and yet we are near a railway line to Liverpool and Birkenhead where they do business.'

He silently digested her remarks. 'Liverpool big port, like Le Havre? I have seen it once.'

She nodded. 'It's huge.'

'I go there with my uncle one time only – I not see much. We have also men in France like reps – before the occupation.'

'Did you? They often carry samples of what their companies make, to show to customers – and sometimes they'll sell one or two on the side, or exchange them for something they themselves want.'

She paused in her explanation, while they crossed the road. Then she added, 'Nowadays, they often have nothing to sell, but they call on their old customers to remind them that they'll soon be in business again.'

'Why don't they have anything to sell? The war's over for nearly three years.'

'I'm not quite sure. As I said, lots of factories were destroyed. Sometimes, they can't get raw materials – everything in the world seems to be in short supply. We export most of what we manufacture to America, to pay for the war. But, sometimes, there are not even enough freighters left to carry the stuff.' Her face was suddenly full of pain. 'We lost so many ships.'

He saw the pain when he glanced down at her, and it troubled him.

'For breakfast, you make big English breakfast?' he asked, to try to divert her to a more cheerful subject. After all, English breakfasts were famous, weren't they?

'Yes. It used to be bacon and eggs and tomatoes and sausages – and toast.' She sighed regretfully at the thought of plates heaped with breakfast. 'Even now, we're still tightly rationed.' She shrugged and lifted her hands in a gesture of hopelessness. 'Now it's usually pancakes with syrup or baked beans and fried potatoes. The reps eat other meals out – in cafés, thank goodness.'

'I understand bed-and-breakfast. Before the war, I remember there are some here – by the sea.'

She nodded.

'I remember you say you need paint to make house clean again.'

'Yes. It's like everything else, hard to find.'

'Same problem in Bayeux. No paint. Nothing much. No factories left in Rouen, *je crois*.'

They proceeded quietly together, he holding her arm to guide her.

There were not many people on the street, and Barbara asked out of curiosity, 'With all the shops open, do people go to church on Sundays?'

'Some do. Maman does. Not so many as before the war.'

'Do you?'

Although he was a little surprised at the question, he answered cautiously, 'Not often.' Then, feeling that he now had a right to ask a question, he enquired, 'Do you?'

'No. Since the war, even Catholics like me don't go very much in England, except for christenings or weddings – or funerals.'

'You're Catholic?'

'Yes. There are lots of Catholics in Liverpool.'

He smiled down at her with new benevolence. The desperate longing that he had felt since meeting her became more than a madness; it became a hope, admittedly a distant one, a tiny light flashing out of a darkened sea. Though religion was out of fashion, it was important where girlfriends were concerned. Mothers would be very anxious if you took out a Protestant – even just to see *la Tapisserie*.

Not that his mother knew where he was. He normally went out on Sunday mornings for an hour, after she returned from Mass, to hang around a bistro or café for a little while, to pick up news of work and, of course, to gossip endlessly about the indifference of governments. And then he would go to mow somebody's lawn, or weed, or even walk somebody's dog – he was not very fond of dogs, but it did bring in a few more francs, and it only took half an hour.

They turned a corner. 'The Bishop's Palace – and *la Tapisserie*,' he announced with unexpected briskness. 'This morning, I ask the concierge, "Are you open?" *Non*. No open. So I ask if she permit us to see. She say OK. You give her *un bon pourboire*, yes?' He rubbed his fingers together to indicate money.

When he said that the place was closed, Barbara's face had fallen with real disappointment. She brightened, however, when he mentioned that a tip would open the door; she doubted if, in similar circumstances, it would do so in Britain.

She immediately agreed to the tip.

As they walked through the silent Sunday streets, he watched her out of the corner of his eye. Today, her face was not swollen with crying, and he was relieved.

She is trying to be a good guest, he thought. She had been kind yesterday, when those two no-goods – spivs, she had called them – had tried to get at the taxi. She understood what they were. Suzanne, he felt, would not have understood what was going on. Madame Barbara was smart, he decided.

As he walked beside her, her skirt occasionally brushing him, he was filled with sheer physical hunger for this sweet-smelling young woman, who could laugh in between her tears.

He pulled himself up sharply. Where are you going, Michel, my lad? Seriously, you haven't a hope.

Then why are you taking her out, you idiot? He could not answer his own question. So forget it. Today, for better or for worse, was his day with Madame Barbara.

He had kept his hand on her elbow, and she felt him grip her quite hard. She glanced up at him. Despite her smartness, Madame Barbara was not quite sure where she was going either.

She saw that he was staring straight ahead, his mouth set in a fierce tight line, the thin face, set as if carved out of stone like the bust of some ancient Greek.

Though she did not know this man, she could not help but sense his need. If she were to be sensible, it was still too soon, she agonised, to think of even a casual love affair, never mind a new husband.

Though she had been a widow for nearly four years, only in the cemetery had she felt that she had actually buried her dead.

Her mother's advice to come to France and see George's grave had been correct. Graves were important. They told you Amen – so be it. And, though it had been terribly painful, the sight of that white cross with George's name on it had told her exactly that.

During her widowhood, she had continued to be absolutely faithful to him. Now, the suppressed sexuality of the empty years threatened to betray her. This man was handsome in his dark way – thin, but fairly muscular. Very different from anyone she had met before. She was not afraid that he would find an opportunity to force her; he seemed to her to have a practicality that would rule whatever he did. Common sense would prevail.

She longed to ask him more about himself, but she was afraid that if she asked many personal questions, she would be thought rude.

She had not been idle during her time in Bayeux, and had begun to understand a little about how, at least, to address other women.

On the morning of her arrival at her hotel in Bayeux, she had demanded immediately a taxi to take her to the cemetery. She was told by the receptionist that there was no transport except for Michel's taxi, and he was booked up for the next two days. When she enquired if the cemetery was within walking distance, she was told that it was fifteen miles away. She hesitated. She knew she could walk it, but she would be back very late in the evening.

Frustrated, she told the receptionist to make a reservation with Michel for the third day. Then, tapping her fingers irritably on the counter, she had asked how far it was to Arromanches, where, she knew, George had landed.

The receptionist shrugged. 'About ten kilometres, Madame.'

He was surprised when she calmly said she would walk down to see it the following morning. Such a distance!

During the two days which she had had to wait for Michel, she had wandered for hours, alone, round Bayeux and its environs. She wanted to be able to tell Ada as much as she could about the invasion, and to do that she had to speak, somehow, with the French themselves, because they had actually experienced it.

Rather than first looking at the old city, she had, therefore, watched its inhabitants. They were definitely different from the crowds in Church Street in Liverpool; she remembered how, at home, most of the men walked with a seaman's roll; even if a boy did not himself go to sea, he tended to imitate his father's walk and stance.

On the first morning, she had noticed a monk on a bicycle, a net bag of potatoes hanging from the handle-bars. She had stared at him in surprise; though she knew there were monks in Liverpool, she had never actually seen one before. On observing her, the monk had cast his eyes heavenward, as if to say, 'Keep me, Lord, from temptation.' It had made her laugh quietly to herself.

Elsewhere, two very old women, dressed in unrelieved black, had caught her eye. They were seated on each side of a tall, narrow window, the shutters thrown back and the lower half of the window open to the street. The sill was so low that she could have leaned in and touched them. Each woman had a small pillow on her knee. The pillows had bobbins attached to them by white thread.

She forgot her good manners and paused in front of the window. 'Lace!' she exclaimed with delight. It was a pretty commodity which had vanished completely from Britain during the war.

Two old heads shot up, and weary, bloodshot eyes stared at her.

In confusion, Barbara's face went pink. '*Pardonnez-moi, Mesdames.*'

Little lines of laughter wrinkled round the tired eyes. Barbara's dress told them that she was probably a visitor.

'*Bonjour, Madame,*' one woman greeted her. She gestured to her to come closer, to see more clearly what she was doing. Barbara shyly did so.

She looked regretfully at the delicate lace which hung down from the pillow; in the austerity of her life, she had almost forgotten that lace existed. 'Exquisite, Madame,' she said.

'You buy?' asked the other old lady.

'*Je n'ai pas d'argent,*' replied Barbara promptly. She sought for the word for widow, '*Une veuve,*' she added with a deprecating gesture, hoping they would understand.

162

The woman looked compassionately at her. '*Une Anglaise?*'

'*Oui, Madame.*' She bowed slightly to the lacemakers, and, in English, thanked them for showing her their work.

Though they obviously did not understand the words, it seemed they got the intent of them because they both nodded and smiled and bent again to the manipulation of their bobbins. Barbara was grateful to them for not pressing her to buy.

Using her few words of laboured French, she had not been afraid to try to talk with women, whether townspeople or peasants. Most of them had seemed older than herself and more self-assured than she herself was; and, in their movement and walk, much more aware of their sexuality than Englishwomen. On the whole, she could judge by dress which were peasants, and therefore likely to be refugees from the shattered countryside, and which were not.

In a bakery, she had found a woman baker wearing a big white apron over her tremendous bust, the only plump woman she had seen. She spoke a little English.

Barbara needed a snack and she asked for two rolls.

It was obvious from her dress and her awful efforts at French that Barbara was a visitor. The baker replied politely that bread was rationed. She had barely enough bread to fill the ration. She shrugged her shoulders. 'Very little bread today, Madame.' She added with a smile that if Madame were staying in a hotel, they would be pleased to serve her a lunch. Hotels had special rations for visitors.

The other customers nodded agreement with the baker, and then, as Barbara thanked her and turned to leave, one of them enquired, in French, if she were from England or America.

'From England. I'm visiting a cemetery,' Barbara responded slowly in English.

At the word 'cemetery', they immediately became less formal. Several women joined in the conversation in a babble of French. So while the baker handed out loaves and made change, she good-humouredly did her best to translate for her customers.

They told of men lost in the course of their Resistance efforts. One had lost a daughter, one a son in the French Army at the beginning of the war. One woman whispered in broken English that the lady baker was running the business for a lost husband, presumed dead. 'He never return,' she said sadly. 'My son – he serves in Algeria.'

Barbara discovered that shared grief was a wonderful door opener.

She went into a fairly close-packed café for a coffee, which was not very good, if indeed it were coffee at all. When paying for it, she laughed with the waitress over the muddle of mixed coinage in her change purse. A lady at the same table, who addressed her in English, offered to help her sort it out. This led to a polite enquiry as to whether she had come to France for a holiday, and Barbara, with tears rising, told her that she had come to see her husband's grave.

An elegant-looking older woman, who, although at the next table, was almost shoulder to shoulder with them, suddenly clapped her hand over her mouth and burst into tears.

Barbara whirled round in her chair and, in the tight space, found herself putting her arm round a perfect stranger and asking if she could do anything to help her.

In a few words of English, the woman told her that she could not help overhearing Barbara's conversation, and it had reminded her of her own loss, of the torture and death of her son. She apologised for her tears, and, when Barbara said it was better to cry and patted her gently on the back, she told her baldly what had been done to her boy.

Barbara, whose sole intention had been to gain some understanding of the Normans' experience, berated herself for impingeing on people whose grief was even more acute than her own. She wondered, with horror, who had been cruel enough to tell the mother the terrible details of her son's death.

Swallowing hard, the woman smiled at Barbara and rose to leave. She bent and kissed the English woman on each cheek, and then she said, '*Merci bien, Madame.*'

Handkerchief to mouth, she walked swiftly out.

As a chastened Barbara got up, she whispered her question to her table companion.

'Why, the *sales Boches*, the SS, of course, Madame,' she was told. 'They tell – frighten us. SS is terrible, Madame.' Her companion's face was suddenly pinched and old.

The SS, the most feared of all Hitler's forces! That makes two of us who hate, Barbara felt furiously, even if George died in battle, not under torture. I'll never forgive. Never let them forget.

When, yesterday, she had seen Caen it had been an appalling shock to her. Even Liverpool did not look as bad as that. Michel had told her that Rouen and Le Havre were in even worse states. And as for Lisieux and Falaise, both famous battlegrounds to Barbara, he had said simply in response to a question, 'Finish.'

As a result of this acquired knowledge, it was with a sense of great pity that Barbara was considering Michel, as they reached the rear of a fine eighteenth-century building, and he pulled a bell. She wondered, again, if he had lost someone.

The door guarding *la Tapisserie* was answered by a short, stout woman wearing a shapeless beige cardigan and a white apron. She surveyed the pair a little sullenly, as if she were being put to unreasonable trouble.

She obviously recognised Michel and gave a slight nod. Then she bade them enter.

They climbed hollowed steps, and then went along a stone passage dimly lit by tall narrow lancet windows set high in the wall. They were led into an empty room, which was almost completely dark.

The concierge hastily switched on lights, single bulbs hanging by wires from the ceiling. They lit the huge room dimly. Along three walls hung a narrow white strip of embroidered fabric. As Michel led Barbara to the beginning of it, small detailed figures began to emerge.

He grinned mischievously at her and began, 'See, here.' He pointed. 'King of England sit on his throne. He is sick. He have no children,' he explained, pointing to the little figure, complete with crown and sceptre. 'He tell Harold – this is Harold. "Go to France. Tell Duke William of Normandy he is King of England when I die."'

'Oh, yes. Edward the Confessor,' interjected Barbara, remembering her school days.

He smiled at Barbara. 'Problem. William is bastard. His *maman* not married to father. Harold is not bastard – could become King of England. Much trouble come.'

'And this is Harold setting out for the coast?'

'Yes. See he have hunter dogs and he carry a hawk.'

'Is that all his luggage?'

'I believe so. I do not see suitcase or trunk.'

Barbara giggled.

She also laughed at the next panel of the embroidery which showed Harold and his courtiers holding all their clothes up round their waists, as they waded out to the boats which would carry them to France. 'Why are they carrying their dogs and the hawk? Why not let the dogs swim?' she queried with a little chuckle.

Michel grinned. 'Good hunter dogs and hawks very valuable,' he told her. 'Worth more than cold, wet feet.'

While the concierge stood yawning by the door, he took her slowly through the whole tapestry, which was, to all intents and purposes, a linen scroll.

In the last panel, Harold and his Saxons were shown in full retreat, Harold with an arrow in his eye. 'Harold dead,' he announced.

'Yes, I remember how he died,' agreed Barbara.

At the end Michel spread his arms out in a large gesture, as if to encompass the whole tapestry. '*Voilà!* Duke William is King of England,' he exclaimed, and gave a little bow. 'He is also Duke of Normandy; that cause much trouble between English and French.'

Barbara smiled her agreement. '*Merci bien, Monsieur.* You are an excellent guide. And you are right about the – er – troubles between the English and the French.'

She opened her handbag as they slowly approached the concierge. 'How much?' she whispered to Michel. He told her. She hesitated for a moment – it did not seem very much. So she added five more francs, and pressed them into the open palm of the waiting attendant. The tip did not elicit a smile, only a dull '*Merci, Madame.*' Barbara assumed correctly that Michel must have advised a very small sum indeed.

She had little idea of the gulf between the income and

ideas of the value of money of a very small French farmer compared with that of a French townsman, but she knew that French peasants were thought to share the reputation of Scots when it came to spending money.

Before I go home, she thought, I'll ask the American undertakers about tips for the hotel staff.

The three military undertakers had been thankful to discover someone who spoke English, and had, on several occasions, stopped by her table in the hotel restaurant to chat with her. They had teasingly suggested that she spend the weekend in Paris with them. When she said she could not, that she was here to visit her husband's grave, they had sobered up immediately, and had been very courteous ever since.

Chapter Fourteen

When Michel and Barbara left the Bishop's Palace, they paused on the pavement to blink in the bright sunlight until their eyes adjusted.

'Why do they keep the place so dark?' Barbara asked.

'Electric bulbs hard to find.' He paused. 'Perhaps light cause *la Tapisserie* to – to . . .' He used a quick gesture to show something breaking up.

'Rot? Fade?'

'*Oui*. Also, light electric cost much.' He changed the subject by enquiring if Madame would like a cup of coffee.

Madame would.

He took her to a small, stone, cottage-like building, which had chairs and tables set out in an unkempt front garden. It was a little away from the centre of the town, and was quieter, he explained, than those cafés with tables on the pavement.

Since it was a time when many of the local inhabitants would still be taking their Sunday nap, there were only three other people in the garden, a young couple holding hands in a corner, and the inevitable elderly gentleman immersed in a newspaper.

Michel had decided that, at this time of day, it was also less likely that he would be seen in her company. Apart from those with whom he had done business in connection with the farm in those long ago days before the occupation, and who were also refugees in the city, he was acquainted with quite a number of people in Bayeux.

He had endured enough gossip over Suzanne. He did not want to add to it by having his name linked with a bourgeoise, an English one moreover; Barbara would have been surprised to learn that, because she could obviously afford to come to France and stay in a hotel, and her clothes, though shabby, were, in his eyes, quite elegant, Michel believed that she had a higher social standing than was the case.

He was sure that women with whom his mother had become acquainted would, if they saw him with Barbara as they walked to the Bishop's Palace, put the worst interpretation on it. Without the taxi, he lacked protection from their innuendos. Wars may come and go, lives, hopes, dreams come to an end, but gossips were never idle; and he was anxious that his harassed mother should not be upset by reports of his supposed misdoings; just imagine if they hinted that he had become, perhaps, a ladies' man – *un étalon?* He winced, and then he sighed. *Hélas*, what a joke that would be.

He wondered again how old Barbara was. It was difficult to tell nowadays because everyone was so careworn.

A painfully thin elderly woman in a white apron came out to them, and Michel ordered coffee. She asked whether Madame would like a little milk in hers.

Unaware of Michel's misgivings about their meeting, Madame said cheerfully, 'Yes, please.'

When the woman had gone away, Michel explained that milk was still in very short supply because the Germans had commandeered so many herds of cows; and many others had, like their owners, been killed in the invasion. He did not tell her that a few teaspoonsful in a cup of coffee would increase the price markedly.

While they waited for their coffee, he sat back in his chair and looked at her. Bees buzzed comfortably in the flowers of the hawthorne bush behind her; the perfume of the tiny flowers was sweet and heavy with the promise of summer.

Barbara asked him how he knew the story of the tapestry so well.

'I go to school, Madame,' he reproved her, a little hurt at the question. 'I read whenever I have time. Also, my grandfather take me to see the tapestry. He tell me the story; it is about a great Norman victory! He bring me here when I am small.' He paused, and then, his chin up, he added, 'I know much about Normandy. Grandpapa tell me 'istory, while we work together.' He sighed. 'Maman wish me to be educate and be a priest.' He looked impishly across the table at her. 'I am 'appy not to be a priest.'

She accepted the implied compliment with a faint smile, and suggested, 'You should be a tourist guide – *un guide.*'

His defensiveness melted at her attempt at a French word. 'Not enough English,' he replied flatly.

She laughed. 'You teach me French. I'll teach you more English. You have a huge vocabulary. You just need some grammar – and idioms. You could get along very well in England.'

Though they had to use her dictionary to decide what an idiom was, he was delighted by her praise.

He's got a good brain, she considered. He's quick mentally as well as physically.

Michel thought what fun it would be to be taught by her, if he himself could give her lessons of another kind.

Now more at ease with her, he leaned back in his chair. With renewed interest, he studied her face and wondered what kind of a background she had. A bed-and-breakfast was a little hotel business, so she must understand how to run it. She was, indeed, *une bourgeoise* – so different from Suzanne, who knew that, whatever her father might plan for her or however careful Michel was of her, she would probably end up working on a farm until her back was bent, and at forty she would be old. Since Barbara had made no mention of children, he presumed that she had none.

His fixed gaze began to disconcert her. Then her lips began to curl mischievously, and she shot at him, 'Why are you staring at me?'

He sat up straight, totally confused by the sharp question. '*Je . . . Madame . . .*' He swallowed and then said, 'Because Madame is so pretty.'

She laughed. '*Merci beaucoup, Monsieur Benion.* It's a long time since anyone said that to me.'

'Perhaps Englishman not look, Madame. And you are young – time will improve their sight, perhaps.'

Her lids half closed over her eyes, as if she did not want to give any of her thoughts away. She replied, however, 'I'm twenty-eight years old.' She sounded a little depressed as she said it. 'Now the war is over, I've got to really work to rebuild our B-and-B, make a living for Mam and me. My mam isn't getting any younger. I feel as if I missed my youth. Do you ever feel like that? As if it got lost in the war? There was no time to be young – so much time wasted. Being uprooted, whether you liked it or not, waiting for the air raids to stop, waiting for the war to end, so that something could be normal again. Do you feel like that?'

He did not know quite how to answer her. He was amazed at the age she said she was; it seemed to him much

172

older than she looked. He himself had never expected to enjoy his younger years – life was work from the time you could stand and carry an egg basket – but he did deplore the waste of time.

'*Oui, Madame, moi aussi*,' he responded doubtfully. 'I have twenty-nine years. Much time wasted while the Boches occupy us. And then the years I wait to get back the farm.'

She nodded, her expression sympathetic. Then she changed the subject, and asked, 'I think we are friends, aren't we?'

'Dead cert,' he responded promptly, remembering his American and knowing that this remark had previously made her eyes crinkle up as if with secret laughter.

This time, she burst into laughter. 'Then, Monsieur Michel Benion, will you please stop calling me Madame. I'm Barbara Bishop.'

'*Avec plaisir, Madame Barbara*.'

'Just Barbara will do.'

'Barbara.' He said the word slowly, giving it an intonation she had never heard before, as if it were a caress. It jolted her, and she thought of the empty years without George when the only male advances had been the usual crude ones frequently made to new widows. She felt she had suddenly been fed a taste of honey.

Embarrassed by her own thoughts, she was relieved when at that moment the coffee arrived.

As a gnarled hand carefully placed her cup in front of her, she looked up, and, forgetting that she should speak in French, said, with a smile to the old woman, 'Mm, it does smell nice. Thank you.'

The old lady smiled back and then glanced at the peasant with her. She said something to Michel. He translated

Barbara's remark for her and, as if joking, she responded to him as she turned away.

'What did she say?' Barbara asked, seeing a pleased expression on his face.

He hesitated, his face alight as he looked at her. Then he told her, 'She said I was a lucky man.'

'Are you? Was she telling your future?'

'*Non, Madame – Barbara.*' Again that soft silken accent on her name. He picked up his coffee cup, and took a small sip. Over the rim of the cup, his eyes danced. 'She meant I was lucky to have you with me.'

He was amused to see her face go pink. Not wishing to embarrass her further, he put down his cup slowly and looked down at it, anxious that she should not read what was in his mind.

She was disconcerted. She examined the dark, lined face before her, the truly Norman nose, the eyelids with their short black lashes, an expressive mouth with just an upward quirk at each corner, the ridiculous beret set straight across a high forehead, the neatly darned pullover across a well-proportioned chest, the slight curve upwards of one shoulder. A simple man who had been kicked about a lot, by the look of him; at this moment, she guessed, a very confused man.

Since she did not say anything, he looked up at her, his expression extremely sober. The eyes had lost their twinkle. Brown eyes searched blue ones.

He was quiet, his lips quivering as if he sought for words. Finally, he asked her, 'You remember in the taxi when we return from *le cimetière*?'

'Yes.' She was very serious now, not sure what was coming.

'You cry very much?'

'Yes.' She felt tension rising in her.

'And I say I marry you myself – but I don't own the taxi?'

'Yes. It was very sweet of you.'

'It is true. I mean it. If I have work, if I have a home to offer you, I never let you go. I hope you take a peasant. I marry you.' He smiled, his mouth curving up a little mischievously. 'I learn good English with you.'

Then the smile vanished. 'But I do not have a proper home – or regular work,' he went on, grimly. 'I must help Maman and my sick brother. Perhaps I get my share of the farm, only God knows. I have no hope.' He paused, and sighed. 'It is the wrong time – I have nothing to offer. Your father would refuse me.'

One of his hands gripped the table edge while with the other he held his teaspoon and gestured forcefully with it, as he acknowledged the mess his life was in and guessed what her father would say.

She was dumbfounded. Her face expressed her profound surprise, her eyes wide, her pretty mouth half open. She had never dreamed that he had meant what he'd said; she had taken it as a small compliment to comfort or amuse her.

At a moment of her own sense of absolute loneliness, when she had kneeled by George's grave, this man who had suffered such losses himself had thought like that about her?

As she stared at him and the full realisation of what he had said sank in, she was overwhelmed. It was as if his admission had blown away blackout curtains, allowing light to flood in.

And now he was humbling himself to admit the problems that made his hopes impossible.

She swallowed. She believed him; the man was being disarmingly honest. Had he meant to cheat her in some way, he could, to attract her, have spun some story that would have shown him in a much better light.

Primitive desires, so carefully kept under control since George's death, surged to the surface. She wondered what it would be like to lie in this man's arms – and then, looking at him, she knew.

She leaned forward and laid her hand over his on the table. She did not say anything until she felt sure he had finished what he had to say.

He slowly put down the spoon and closed his eyes as if to shut out an impossible, unfair world. He did not remove his hand from under hers.

She whispered softly, so that the man reading the newspaper was less likely to hear: 'We don't even know each other – but given a little time . . .' she faltered. Then as a glint of amusement surfaced, she went on, 'Nobody can tell me who to marry or anything else. I'm English and I'm free to do what I like.'

Very gently, she stroked the back of his rough brown hand. She shivered, trying to keep her own feelings at bay. 'How could you make up your mind so quickly?'

Idiotic question, she told herself, you know perfectly well – you've just done it. He's plenty to offer in himself.

He did not open his eyes. He did not reply. She could feel the tension in him, and her greatest desire was not to hurt him in any way, to respect his dignity.

She made a great effort to keep calm. 'You know, at the cemetery,' she reminded him, 'you were just the taxi driver. I was thinking only of George and saying goodbye to him.' She stopped, scared of the strange situation into which she had stumbled. Then she went on, her voice faltering, 'Another man, another husband, was simply not in my mind.'

He did not fully comprehend her. His eyes were still crunched tightly, as if he were waiting to be shot. He felt he had been a blundering ass.

After a moment, he simply turned his hand and clasped hers tightly. She continued with a little more self-assurance, 'In Caen, it was different. Then you were a very pleasant man, a most unusual one, who got out of a tight corner very smartly.'

He opened his eyes, but still did not look at her directly. He gently loosened his hand from under hers, and then turned hers palm up, grasped it firmly, and sat looking at the neat little hand now cradled in his own.

Very softly, with one finger, he stroked the inside of her wrist, noting the delicate blue vein that ran up under the plain black band of her watch. He wondered if she were that white all over. Suzanne had been quite dark.

Ciel! How he wanted her.

Both of them were mesmerised by the simple touch. Long-pent-up desire roared through them, primitive and strong; yet both were trying to hang on to shreds of common sense. Each was thinking that they were not that young. They did not have the excuse of youth for unwise behaviour. Despite their religious doubts, they had been strictly trained by Church and family in the kind of behaviour which was acceptable.

'I love you,' he said quietly and firmly. 'I've never felt like this in my life before.'

The arrival of the café owner to enquire if they would like more coffee reawakened them to the real world.

Barbara hastily withdrew her hand. She looked at Michel and said, '*Non, merci beaucoup.*'

They rose. Shakily, she picked up her handbag. He hastened to pay the bill. He took her hand and slowly they walked out and into the street.

'*Pardonnez-moi, Barbara,*' he begged. Although he now had control of himself, he had not let go of her hand, and he tucked it under his arm as if they were a courting couple.

Barbara was still caught in a tumult of feeling, her ideas of her future, of her inner self, blown apart by a few simple words. Even if she never saw Michel again, this was a moment of profound change in her life, much greater than her marriage to George had been.

In a few moments, it had opened up to her what the relationship might really be between man and woman. Suddenly, all the great romances of history were clear to her; the madness that drove a couple to disaster. It was terrible; it was wonderful. Her normal self was swept by this passionate realisation.

This was real; not just a sexual attraction – much more than that. Her mother had once said that a happy marriage was much more than sex, and Barbara's parents had been happy just between themselves; even as a little girl she had sensed it. No matter what hit them – unemployment, illness, the catastrophes of life – there had been this private closeness between her parents.

If her mother had loved her father like this, no wonder she was still grieving at the loss of him.

As far as George's military service had permitted it to be, her own marriage had been satisfying, hadn't it? she asked herself wildly.

It was her turn to be honest. It had not. She had had

no idea that a man could make her feel as she did now, this minute, standing shakily outside a makeshift café in a foreign city, her hand tucked underneath the arm of an almost unknown foreigner.

She sought for breath, for her lost common sense, and then looked up at him and said softly and warmly, 'There is nothing to forgive. I feel honoured that you have been so honest with me.'

She did not say what she was thinking deep beneath this gentle reply: I don't care a damn if you come to me with nothing. Just share my bed and love me truly; it's all I ask. We could work out everything else together; I know it; I just know.

Chapter Fifteen

She was honoured? Because he, a nobody, had confessed his feelings for her? Was it truly because he had been honest with her?

There were few shops in this corner of the city, and as they walked slowly through the narrow medieval streets, they were, despite the carnage in the countryside, bathed in the sleepy calm of a peacetime Sunday. Yet both of them were in turmoil.

He could not believe what he had heard, nor what he had been so mad as to set in motion. Did she really feel any affection for him?

She had not said so, Michel warned himself. But neither had she got up and left him in disgust. And he knew, without the slightest doubt, that he himself was besotted.

Not all the humiliations heaped on the nation as a whole as a result of their surrender to the Germans, nor those forced on him personally by the greedy occupying army, had ever succeeded in reducing his peacock pride to real humbleness of spirit; all those had been insults about which he could do nothing; one simply endured them and promised oneself revenge some day.

His sense of Barbara's sincerity did make him feel truly humble; she had put herself on an equal footing with him, made him a gift, at least, of trust, made him feel she valued him for what he really was.

Barbara could not, in her bewildered state, have said

exactly why she trusted him, a foreigner as poor as a street child; a man of a very different calibre from anyone she had ever met before and she had dealt with many men in her time.

'Just because the war's put money in civilian men's pockets, they seem to have lost their sense of decency, if they ever had it,' she had once fumed to her mother as they sat together by the kitchen fire, while the anti-aircraft guns round the ports of the Mersey roared like some great landslide, and an occasional bomb blast nearer at hand told them that they were not themselves immune from oblivion.

That evening Barbara had being doing the bed-and-breakfast accounts, while Phyllis peeled the next day's potatoes, for use in connection with the inventive breakfasts she made for her complaining elderly residents.

'Well, even the men who stayed with us before the war would try it on sometimes, luv, as you well know,' her mother had reminded her. 'But you could usually put them off with a joke. And if I got someone who was a real pest, I used to say we was full up – and they got the message eventually. Your dad used to worry about the pair of us sometimes, when he were at sea. But he didn't have to – you simply put 'em off.' She dropped a peeled potato into a bucket of water. 'At worst, you could land them a good old-fashioned slap in the face.'

Barbara had unwillingly agreed that such a sharp refusal usually worked, particularly if administered in public.

Because of the profound disturbance of the population during the war, when so many men and women were far from home, she had looked into dozens of hopeful, impudent faces – and felt sick because it was, sometimes, difficult to avoid them. Now, by a miracle, she seemed to have met someone honest enough to trust.

She had trusted George because he was a local lad – after all, she knew his mother. He had told her on their wedding night that the moment he had asked her for a dance he knew he would marry her. 'You always know,' he had said gravely.

She had laughed at the idea, but he had indeed married her; it had taken her rather longer to decide that she loved him enough to marry him.

Now, she knew that what George had said could happen. She yearned for this unknown quantity walking beside her more desperately than she had yearned for anything in her life. But it was absurd; though she had been widowed for nearly four years, only yesterday she had wept for George. What was she thinking of?

Michel swallowed. He knew nothing of Barbara's thoughts. He realised, however, that he was floundering in waters very deep for him; yet he was impelled by primeval instinct to continue.

At her remark that she felt honoured by his honesty with her, he squeezed the hand tucked under his arm in warm acknowledgement, and, after a small silence, he begged her, 'We talk some more, somewhere quiet?' He stopped walking to look directly at her, eyes pleading.

That an elderly woman in a café should, with a gentle joking remark, release this nonsense in him, against all that he had ever been taught – it was against custom; it was not remotely sensible. Marriage was largely a business contract.

But these were not normal times.

In ordinary circumstances, he would probably never have met her; and, if they had met, his first thought would have been, as usual, to wonder what dowry she had.

Yet now he suddenly had thoughts of marriage spinning dizzily in his head, though he had no idea how on earth he was going to achieve it. Not simply to lay her, but to spend the rest of his life with her. He had never felt like this about a woman before. He didn't care whether Barbara brought a dowry with her or not; all he cared about was the woman herself.

When he had watched Barbara kneeling by her husband's grave, torn with sorrow, though trying hard to control herself, he had felt at first an overwhelming desire to comfort her, to love her better until she smiled again, and they could laugh together.

How good it would be, he had meditated, to be loved by her as she had obviously loved her husband.

Now, as if by reciprocal consent, they walked slowly round the outside of the great cathedral. On the other side was a formal garden, not very well kept but green with new spring growth. It was a hushed, almost deserted close, bounded in part by the houses of the cathedral clergy and in part by the cathedral itself. Despite its shabbiness, it was a haven of peace, untouched by war.

Michel paused and surveyed it. He felt unexpectedly so overwhelmed by the hopelessness of his situation that he wanted to burst into tears. To cry to God, to anybody to help him out of his predicaments.

It was ridiculous, cowardly, to feel so helpless. He inhaled deeply to try to steady himself. Men faced their problems; they did not weep.

Barbara heard his inhalation and turned to him. She was distressed to see that his usually brown face had turned almost yellow. 'Are you OK?' she enquired uncertainly.

He shivered as if cold, and then forced himself to smile. 'Certain, I am OK.'

The garden was furnished with several benches already occupied. On the nearest one sat an old man accompanied by an equally aged dog.

Barbara and Michel sat down at the other end of his bench. Their tightly clasped hands lay on Michel's knee.

The old man turned to them and smiled. He remarked politely that it was a lovely day; it had been a great spring for tulips.

The man nodded absently. He looked ill. His white-faced, obviously foreign companion did not look much better. The old man noted her quivering lips; she looked as if she might be about to cry. He thought he understood the tension between them – almost certainly a dissension of some sort.

After a minute, he decided to be kind and leave them to it. He heaved himself up, gave the dog a light shove with his foot, bowed slightly, and slowly walked the animal down to the other end of the close to another seat. He wondered what had happened to them; nowadays, one never knew what horrors a person had endured.

He smiled to himself. Anyway, now they would be able to embrace.

He plodded over the grass to the other side of the close, and settled himself again. He glanced over to them. How lucky to be still young. The woman was certainly being comforted.

Barbara eventually struggled free. She laughed weakly up at Michel, and was thankful to see his normal colouring was returning. She reminded him that they had come here to talk.

In order to help her recover her own sanity, she asked,

'Tell me about yourself. I know about your work. But what do you do in your spare time?'

Calm down, you imbecile. She's right. He reluctantly withdrew his hand from under her jacket. He sensed that for all her pliability, he might lose her right then and there if he carried matters any further.

He gritted his teeth and tried to pay attention to her question. What an absurd one it was.

'We never have time, once the Germans take over and my father die. We work much and sleep little. If hens and chickens are to live and lay eggs, they must be very clean. Scrub. Scrub. Scrub! When I work I smell of hens, creosote and disinfectant.'

She giggled like a young girl.

'It's hard work,' he insisted. 'Move coops and brooders regularly to sit on fresh stones – big job – feed, water, hatch, keep warm. It last for ever. Milk cow, feed horse, clean stable, plough, sow forage, make vegetable garden, slaughter hens for market. Clean and pluck them. Wash eggs. Take them to the *sales Boches*. Nicest job – prune apple trees, pick apples, make Calvados out of them. Dig up potatoes.' He paused for breath, and sighed, as some equilibrium returned to him. 'In peacetime, late in the evening, go to café in the village for *un petit noir* and read the newspapers. In winter, read a book by the fire, perhaps. At Christmas, go to dance. Often little jobs take the evening time – mend harness, mend shoes, cut up logs.'

'Phew!' she exclaimed. He still had his arm round her, and she cuddled closer to him.

He turned to kiss her again. 'I decide yesterday that even if our family go on our land, I cannot work it alone – I can find a labourer, perhaps – but there is

185

much shortage of men, you understand? And labourer cost money. I decide, now, I never go back to the land. I never make my wife work like Maman and Bonnemaman. Maman work too much already. Anatole – my brother – is very sick. My sisters both married to men from Rouen. I start new – something else.'

'What would you like to do?'

He hummed under his breath, while he tried to concentrate on her questions. Then he said, 'All I know thoroughly is about hens and eggs – and make good use of a small piece of land. Now, I can also drive. Guy, my brother-in-law, is lorry driver. He look for job for me. But I want better – more safe job. His lorry is – how you say? – an ancient monument!'

She gurgled with laughter. 'I know just what you mean,' she said. 'That's about the level of all our lorries in England, too. So, what do you think you could do?'

'What I really like is work for a big, big egg company or hatchery. Not wash eggs or clean hen coops. I would like organise breeding, be in office – keep records, inspect brooders, learn management. I have big knowledge – I could use it to run a big flock.' She felt him shrug his shoulders. 'Big ideas. I need school to learn to manage men to do what I say.' He stopped. Then he laughed derisively at himself. 'Who am I to do things like that? I'm crazy. No hope.'

'Why not?'

'Nothing in Bayeux. Look in Rouen, Cherbourg, perhaps, once they are builded again. But there is another problem – we can't move there.'

He went on to explain the problem of moving Anatole; and, further, his mother's reluctance to go far from their land until the Government made a decision about it.

She accepted his explanations and admired him for his loyalty to his family; and then she said thoughtfully, 'Liverpool – and the rest of Merseyside – used to be full of big food companies, and I know of at least one which made cattle feed – I don't know about hen feed. A lot of them have been bombed flat, and I don't know which ones will rebuild.' It was her turn to shrug. 'It's too early to say. But I'm sure that somewhere on Merseyside there'll be a hatchery or an egg company.'

'Truly?'

'I could soon find out.'

Here was an idea to be explored. But Michel knew that, at least for the time being, he must stay in Normandy. She had, however, not crushed his idea of what he wanted to do next.

Had she truly meant to imply that his hopes could, perhaps, be fulfilled in Britain, if he were free to go there? It was too new an idea – in his shaky condition, he could not totally grasp all the inferences of what she had said; he would consider them carefully, when he felt more in control of himself.

She was watching him, awaiting an answer to a suggestion which she herself had made without much forethought.

The shadows on the grass were lengthening. He glanced at his watch, and stirred reluctantly. 'We talk about Liverpool another day. I must go. Weed and water the garden of Monsieur Dubois,' he told her, 'and then stay with Anatole. Maman go to visit her friends for a little while.'

'Of course.' She sighed wistfully, as she slowly rose and picked up her handbag.

He got up with his usual litheness and stood for a

moment facing her, so close that she could feel the rise and fall of his chest.

'I see you tomorrow? OK?' He smiled softly. 'We talk more. Reservations say you are in hotel nine more nights?'

Her eyes danced at this revelation of communication with cool impersonal Reservations. 'Yes,' she assured him. 'Shall we meet here?'

'I meet you by cathedral door – we pass it just now. Six o'clock. I expect we be at hotel by then. The colonel's work finish soon – they not work late now.'

'OK.' She smiled and leaned forward to kiss his lips. He caught her arms in a firm grip and kissed her in return. As he held her, he said, 'If I'm very late, go to hotel. If Americans not return – I am still with them. I give Reservations a message to send to your room when I return.'

She nodded and turned away quickly. She had discussed his hopes and desires quite calmly, but she felt anything but calm. He had certainly set off a riot of ideas within her.

Chapter Sixteen

That night, lying sleepless on his rustling straw mattress, thinking of his long day, Michel acknowledged to himself that this immense, insane desire for a particular woman was new to him. It was different from the ordinary desire which hit him not infrequently, a desire which any lively woman – like Suzanne – could quench. He would have dutifully protected Suzanne and died doing so; she would have been his working partner, the mother of his children. He was equally dutifully taking care of his mother and brother.

For Barbara, it would not be a duty. He would live for her, love her, use all his innate ingenuity to see that she was happy and comfortable.

In return, he dreamed that she would love him with the same uncritical passion, simply love him for being himself.

The thought crossed his mind that he was being tempted because they were both older than many people falling in love. They had experience, and were, therefore, likely to be more understanding of each other's human frailty and make a greater effort to adjust to each other.

Apart from all that, Barbara was so dainty that she roused in him a genuine desire to protect and cherish her, like a new apple tree at its first blooming.

She had aroused in him a level of sexual desire – plain lust, he rebuked himself – such as he had not known since he first went to a prostitute to learn how to make love.

Nothing doing, he had told himself, if he did not marry her. Despite her allowing his advances that day, he believed her to be a respectable woman who would undoubtedly repulse him if he tried anything more.

And I can't endure that she should marry anyone else but me, he thought mournfully. But, my God, I am so hard up.

During that restless night, he had considered again the neat slenderness of her beside his own build. He himself was not very tall in comparison with many of the towns-men of Bayeux – and he was at least twenty centimetres shorter than the Americans he drove every day.

In comparison with the latter, he was also dreadfully thin – he had none of their exuberant look of abounding health; but, he told himself defiantly, that was largely because he had been hungry for years. Other than my shoulder, I am strong and fit, he decided.

He stretched himself on his bed like a cat. Darling Madame, he muttered under his breath, I could make you so happy if you gave me the chance. He lay and thought about being married to her, and let himself dream. He had a difficult night.

He was more than usually tired and fretful the next morning.

While his mother went out to buy vegetables and get the bread ration, he helped Anatole to wash himself and put on a clean, dry shirt. His nightshirt was sodden from the sudden sweats caused by his illness.

While he smiled and chatted to the invalid, his mind was full of disjointed ideas of how to build a future with Barbara. Even as he washed down and shaved his brother, Michel knew Anatole was the main blockage to any ambitions he might have and he could have wept with frustration. Dear God, he prayed feverishly for the hundredth time, perform a miracle: let Anatole recover. Let him have the farm. All I want is to be free.

Driving the taxi for the Americans had been his first solid financial break since the night of the battle, and it was about to come to an end. I have been patient too long, he told himself savagely. I am twenty-nine years old and if I don't start now, I shall be a casual labourer for ever – or until I'm crippled.

I must have a little time; I can't do anything much in the few days before Barbara leaves. I must somehow keep in touch with her in a way that will not scare her – so that she, at least, remembers me.

As he washed and shaved in a litre of cold water, he argued irritably with himself that, though he could not even think of marrying anyone for the foreseeable future – he would not admit that he meant until Anatole died and he could find work further afield – there was nothing wrong in enjoying Barbara's company for the few days she was here.

He had never intended so much as to hint to her that, from the moment she had stepped into the taxi, he had found her so attractive. Now she knew – and his life was changed totally.

While he fed Anatole with bread and milk, made from a stale roll left from yesterday, his mind went round and round like a spitting Catherine wheel. His life was half done; yet still he could not, thanks to the *sales Boches* and the subsequent invasion, do more than dream of the comfort of marriage – or a family. Not that he wanted to bring children into this cruel world, simply to see them slaughtered or starved out by Germans; the *sales Boches* would, doubtless, spill over the border for the fourth time in a hundred years, as soon as they had bred themselves enough cannon fodder to achieve it.

He wondered if Barbara wanted children. Regardless of that, he felt she would be a great partner in life. It would be a joy to have someone to share everything with – his ideas, his modest ambitions, whatever money he managed to make. Someone he could look at with pride.

He did not want to condemn her to work outside her home all her life, as many married French women had always done. She would die, he felt sure, if she had anything like the weight of work that his mother had endured.

So, how, Michel Benion, do you propose to keep a wife as frail as that?

The first answer was negative, but firm. It confirmed his earlier decision: never return to the farm.

He seized the filled, smelly slops bucket and the empty water bucket and took them down to his landlady's kitchen. As he put down the water bucket in the kitchen, on his way to the outside latrine to relieve himself and to empty the slops, he muttered to her, '*Bonjour, Madame Blanc.*'

She looked up from her morning bowl of coffee, and smiled absently at him.

There was a rusty water tap on the outside wall of the house, and Michel rinsed the bucket and washed his hands under it before re-entering the kitchen.

Madame Blanc was a generous woman in her way and was fond of Michel. She watched him fill the water bucket from her kitchen pump. He seemed unusually taciturn this morning. Normally he would joke with her as the big bucket filled. Today he had an abstracted air; in fact, he looked sullen, which was most unlike him. She heaved herself up from the table, picked up a newspaper and tucked it under his arm.

'For Anatole to read,' she told him.

He replied morosely, '*Merci bien, Madame*.'

She wondered if Anatole had taken a turn for the worse, so she enquired about him.

'He is as usual, Madame. Thank you.' Michel swung the heavy bucket out of her sink, picked up the empty slops bucket, turned carefully and trudged back up the narrow staircase.

'Humph,' muttered the lady sarcastically. 'He must be in love.'

Chapter Seventeen

Upstairs, Anatole licked his dry lips, and said, 'I wish we could make coffee up here.'

'Patience, *mon frère*,' Michel responded as he handed his brother the newspaper. 'Maman will be back soon. She'll make it for all of us on Madame's fire as soon as she comes with the bread.' He did not need to tell Anatole that coffee was expensive even if you could get it, and not to be brewed lightly.

He plonked himself down on the end of his brother's bed, and grinned at him a little ruefully. Though Anatole was indubitably a burden to him, Michel dreaded his impending death, and, in consequence, his own intense loneliness.

Before the war, he had felt that together with Suzanne and her property, he and his brother would build up their smallholdings into a highly productive business again. They would improve their breeding strains and use more intensive methods of raising the birds, about which he had learned from young farming friends and from reading well-thumbed copies of agricultural magazines, one or two of which sometimes reached the café in the village that he frequented.

Anatole had attended only primary school, but he was, Michel knew from long discussions, much more open to new ideas than their father had been.

Now the farm was a mud heap – a highly dangerous

one – and Anatole would soon leave him. And into his life had come this beautiful woman, who had probably no idea of how a traditional French peasant lived out his bitterly hard existence. His mind went round and round in useless turmoil.

How could he give her a life which would not, at best, reduce her within ten years to the kind of bent old woman that his poor mother was? Even in the city, he knew from his sisters, life could be hard for women.

Anatole licked his dry lips again and asked for some water, which Michel immediately gave him. As he put his arm under his brother's shoulders to lift him a little so that he could sip the cup of water, he was again astonished that anyone as big and heavy as Anatole could shrink to a feather lightness, so that he could be lifted like a child.

Anatole sank back on his grubby pillow and watched Michel rinse the cup in a pannikin and throw the slops into the covered bucket.

When the younger man again sat down on his bed, Anatole, with all the clarity of vision granted to the dying, grinned knowingly and asked weakly, 'Who is she?'

Michel was startled. He looked sheepishly down at the back of his hands. He shrugged, and was mute.

'I won't tell Maman.' Anatole's voice had a rasping sound. Conversation was an effort. Though he was so ill, he felt sometimes that he was being bored to death, lying on a bed watching birds on the windowsill or rain clouds pass over. He welcomed anything that could divert him, anything that allowed him to have a share in the world revolving round him.

'Come on. Share,' he whispered. 'Why else are you so keen to find a different kind of work? Why else are you so restless at night? And where's your tongue? You didn't really speak much when you came in last night. Not like you at all.'

So Michel poured out his bewildered thoughts. He told him everything he could about Barbara; and, since Anatole did not laugh at him, he felt better.

Anatole was highly entertained. The confidence allowed him to re-enter a world from which he had felt himself cut off, a place in which he had no power or influence. Here, he might be able to bring influence to bear by giving what advice he could.

'This complete lunacy is love,' he announced quite cheerfully. 'You lucky devil.'

'I know that, imbecile! I don't know what to do about it, though. To be truthful, I don't think there is anything I *can* do about it. She is a most respectable young woman, and I can't play around – at least, I wouldn't harm her reputation in any way.'

Anatole nodded, and was quiet while he considered these admissions. 'Do you really want to marry her? It doesn't sound to me as if she could cope with farm work.'

'Of course I want to marry her – if I can. And, as for farm work, I don't feel I could ever cope with it myself any more.'

'But you want her badly?'

'*Mon Dieu*, yes!'

Anatole was again silent. He did not want his brother to see the sudden tears in his own eyes, so before he answered he glanced out of the window and watched the male swallow do a power dive after an insect. Then, with a dreadful sadness, as if he were half choked and every word were an effort, he rasped out, 'I used to feel like that for your friend, young Henri.'

'You did? *Vraiment?* You amaze me.' Michel was shocked. He said bewilderedly, 'I know you were always kind to him. He loved talking to you.' He made a wry face. 'And I know when Father tried to find you a wife you always put him off.'

'It's true. You see, I never cared for women.' He sighed. 'I never touched Henri; I truly loved him and he was much younger than me. I thought that, if I waited a few years, he might learn to love me. Once he was an adult, it would be different. And it was so.' His eyes closed as if he were in pain. 'I thought I'd die myself when the Boches got him.'

Michel suddenly saw his brother with new eyes, as a lot of small memories of him fell into place.

'*Bon Dieu!* You know, I never thought of that. I was so horrified myself – he was my best friend. I never thought of anyone else's grief, other than his family's, of course. How extraordinary. How could I have missed seeing it?'

'You were always pretty innocent, mon petit.'

Michel made a face. Then he saw, with horror, how he might feel if the Germans had done the same to Barbara as they had to Henri. He looked for a second down a tunnel of pure agony – and much that he had not understood about Anatole was immediately clear to him.

'God, I'm sorry,' he said to the pale ghost on the bed, and, with all his heart, he meant it.

'It's all over for me now, Michel. It doesn't matter any more.'

Michel did not deny the reality of Anatole's remark. Instead, in a desperate effort to comfort his brother, he suggested, 'Perhaps Henri is waiting for you?'

Anatole smiled a little grimly. 'Hardly, little one. Such love is against Church teaching.'

'Bah! Jesus loved St John.'

Anatole sighed. 'So it is said,' he agreed. Then he continued slowly, 'Perhaps you are right about Henri. These last few days I've felt that he's very close to me.' His voice trembled, and Michel thought Anatole would cry; he had cried helplessly a great deal when he had first come home from Germany; but Father Nicolas had spent quite a lot of time with him, and he had seemed to have drawn comfort from the old man; lately, he had appeared more at peace with himself.

'I'm sure Henri is there,' Michel affirmed with a determination intended to ease his brother's sorrow.

'He may be.'

Michel wondered fearfully if Anatole was so close to death that Monsieur le Curé, Father Nicolas, should be asked to visit him; the old man had continued to come occasionally to give Anatole Holy Communion, and his brother must not die without Extreme Unction. The Church's shattered parishes were more in need of its priests and of their comfort than they had been at any time since the First World War, though Michel felt certain that the number of true believers had shrunk considerably.

Perhaps he should not call the old priest yet, in case it was premature. He guessed that his mother would know when to call him; better not bother him unnecessarily.

They could hear their mother slowly labouring up the stairs, and Anatole whispered, 'We'll talk again. You, at least, have something to strive for.'

Chapter Eighteen

On this quiet Monday, while the Americans had been engaged in investigating a mass grave, Michel had taken a pair of tall English patricians to see where their son was buried.

The couple had not spoken to him, except to give him the address of the grave and mention that their son lay there. As he closed the door of the taxi on them, Michel had murmured his usual sympathy.

During the return journey to their hotel, both of them had simply stared silently out of the taxi windows. They seemed to their taxi driver to be the epitome of the famous British stiff upper lip. They had, however, tipped him well, for which he was most grateful.

Barbara would be waiting for him, he rejoiced, and later, as he drove the Americans back to the hotel, he caught a glimpse of her. She was standing in a niche of the cathedral wall, leaning against a huge buttress, while she smoked a cigarette.

Until she saw the cab sail by, she had begun to wonder if he would really come. He could easily have regretted his impulsiveness of yesterday. Now, she knew he was merely running behind schedule, and she smiled.

Ten minutes later, having quickly locked up the taxi in its stable, Michel hurried to her, his face aglow. She got no opportunity to straighten herself, as he pinned her against the wall. She hastily removed her cigarette, before he kissed her soundly on the lips. Enjoy while you can, he told himself.

She responded instinctively by putting one arm around him, while she held her cigarette well away from him.

With almost motherly instincts, she thought once again how very thin he was for his height, and feared, once more, that he might himself be carrying tuberculosis.

Dear God, she prayed, don't let me be cheated again.

He held her firmly enough, however, while he whispered endearments in her ear, and the same dreadful longing for him surged in her.

Reluctantly she pushed him back a little.

'Where can we go?' she asked desperately. 'We need more time to get to know each other – we really do.'

He nodded silently. To hold her should be pure happiness, he felt, and yet he was filled with intolerable sorrow. If he renounced his land, he was nobody. Without land and hens, Michel Benion, poultry farmer, did not exist any more, could not use his solid knowledge of the humble hen to earn even a basic living for a wife. Without his cheery American morticians, he could not even help his mother and Anatole, never mind keep an English widow, who smelled sweetly of talcum powder and probably spent a fortune on makeup.

He could feel Barbara trembling in his arms.

While he pondered for a moment about where to go, she swallowed. The tension in her was hard to control. Whatever happens, she told herself, you can't simply fly into bed with the man. He's foreign, a total stranger. He may be lying like a Liverpool street vendor, and you're a decent woman; you don't want a fatherless French child to cope with on top of everything else. Be sensible, woman. Calm down.

She pictured suddenly, the immense, fine parks of Liverpool, great stretches of lush green trees and gardens, the refuge of generations of lovers. Nobody minded your cuddling there.

With this remembrance in mind, she suggested, 'We could go into the garden of the close again.'

'*Non*. It is overlooked.' He grinned down at her wickedly.

As she felt him stir against her, she said, 'It might be as well if we were overlooked.'

He did not quite understand, so she went on, 'George and I sometimes used to sit and talk in the cathedral or in the yard, where he worked on the stones.'

An aching lump rose in her throat. I mustn't think of George, she scolded herself. He's gone for ever. Dear, stolid George, who would never have dreamed of pinning me against a wall in a public place.

Like frightened mice, her thoughts scrabbled round her tired mind, and came up against a sobering fact: you've had four lonely years, and you're going to have to live many more of them. Here is your chance to break the cycle.

The very thought of the dismal continuation of her years of widowhood made her want to cry for her dead husband; he had always seemed so safe.

She shivered quite violently, as she tried to swallow her tears and calm her mixed emotions, and Michel, in quick response, held her closer.

She buried her face in his shoulder. She did not look at him because she did not want to betray her distress.

As he kissed the shining, sweet-smelling curls on the top of her head, Michel knew that all was not well with her. He gently rubbed her back, and it was comforting to her, though, at the same time, definitely seductive.

'*Chérie?*'

Reluctantly she looked up at him. He was obviously concerned.

She tried to smile. This is a new life opening up, she told herself. He's a sweetheart of a man. Enjoy him, but be careful.

With the warm, delicate little body pressed between himself and the wall, poor Michel was nearly beside himself with pure desire. He was, however, not as foolish as he had seemed to himself earlier. He was no careless boy; he was a man who longed for a faithful wife.

He saw the hint of tears in her eyes, and he knew with certainty that, for the moment, he must comfort her.

When Barbara had mentioned the cathedral, he had decided that such a sacred place would help to keep him in line.

'The cathedral should be empty at present,' he said with a wry smile. 'No more Mass tonight. *Les curés* rest. Come.'

God must have felt kind today, considered Michel. His house was indeed almost empty, and in its venerable hush he began to relax. In the nave, a nun and, near the front, a single man, both kneeled in prayer. A verger, in his black robes, was leisurely tidying up prayer books and hymnals.

Michel had not been inside the place since he was a boy, visiting Bayeux with his grandfather. He stared at a glittering altar so breathtakingly beautiful that, for a second, he wondered why it had not been sacked by the Protestant Germans.

Bah! Priests were not fools; at the very mention of the invasion by the German Army, they must have stripped down and hidden everything of value: the paintings, the altar furnishings, the lamps, the priceless books.

He remembered suddenly the British commando flourishing the golden crucifix from a parish church en route to Bayeux. He wondered if he had yet discovered that it was probably only a fairly modern brass one, and of little value. The ancient silver of the altar would have been buried in the presbytery garden.

On first entering the nave of the cathedral, Michel automatically genuflected towards the lovely altar, while Barbara stood woodenly beside him. Then they had walked slowly round it. They finally moved quietly towards one of the side chapels, where they paused before a statue of the Madonna.

In despair, Michel breathed silently to her, 'Help me,' as thousands had done before him.

Barbara stared dumbly at her blank little face, absolutely certain that there was no hope there. Her single prayer for years had been for George's safety, and it had gone unheard. One of her school teachers, a nun, had once warned her impatient, energetic little pupil that sometimes God's answer was simply 'No'.

'And you must accept that He knows best, child,' she had admonished.

It had been a dreadfully hard lesson to learn.

In the cool, incense-perfumed air of a sacred building which had survived for centuries, with a medieval, stone Madonna looking calmly at them, they sat down in the shadow of a huge pillar.

Michel slipped his arm round Barbara's waist. He touched her chin and turned her face to his. She was so white that her makeup looked tawdry.

Did she fear him? he wondered. Or was she finding it shocking to be held by another man so soon after she had seen her husband's grave?

But we have so little time, he thought. She will go home, and I will be left with just a memory. He stroked her cheek.

'Don't be afraid,' he said.

She smiled again. 'Oh, I'm not afraid of you, exactly. It's strange, that's all.'

'I love you,' he said in French.

It was the avowal of a mature man, who until yesterday had almost forgotten that there were humble joys in life which did not altogether depend upon finding something to eat. Slowly and carefully, he kissed her.

The response was more than he had hoped for. She slipped her hand round his neck and pressed him to her. It seemed absurd that he should be surprised that she opened her mouth to him, but he was. This woman was not a virgin, he remembered, and the freedom with which she responded to him spoke of a growing passion. Her dark blue eyes twinkled suddenly at his consequent discomfiture.

When she reluctantly drew away from him, he laughed quite joyously, showing for once the light-hearted character which lay beneath his present misery.

The laugh echoed through the little chapel, and Barbara, afraid that they might draw unwelcome attention to themselves, hastily put her fingers over his mouth. 'Michel! Hush!'

He kissed her fingers and then straightened himself a little. In a city still packed with refugees, where he did not have even a bed, never mind a room of his own, where did a couple go to make love?

Even a secluded piece of grass outside the city itself was a potential death threat, and, anyway, who wanted a first encounter under dripping bocage? He knew that there were shops, such as dressmakers' tiny stores, where the rich could make a rendezvous and utilise a room behind the business – but he had no money for such a luxury.

'We talk, *chérie*.' He rubbed his lips with the back of his hand, and looked slyly at her.

Ruefully she assented. 'We're not being very wise, are we?' Her voice was unsteady; she was still a little shaky. She bit her lower lip and then glanced sideways at him, a hint of a smile creasing her thin cheeks. 'The truth is, you know, we're both suffering from night starvation!'

He did not fully appreciate her remark, because he did not know the old joke about Ovaltine, a popular British milk drink often taken at bedtime – to avoid night starvation, as the firm's advertisement stated. But her remark still struck him as funny, because it was, indeed, so true. He laughed and kissed her on the lips, lightly this time.

Was this real love? She did not know. It was certainly different; she was riding a rollercoaster of feelings. And, Jaysus, he was handsome in a dark saturnine way, the lines in his face deep, as if carved out of rock, the cheeks a little reddened by exposure – and a body the same – hard and weathered by work, judging by the feel of him. And yet so dreadfully thin.

It was she who began the serious conversation by enquiring gently if he had a wife or children. 'I seem to remember that you mentioned your fiancée.'

'*Mon Dieu! Non!* My fiancée is lost to me. You believe I sit with you now if I have wife or anybody? *Non!* I want to marry you, but I have nothing to offer except problems – big problems.' He blew out a great breath. 'Have you childs?'

'Children? No. Only a mother. We work together, as

I told you – though Mam would like to retire. She's in her fifties.'

'As I told you, I have Maman – and Anatole. And Uncle Léon who goes to sea; he sail out of Port-au-Bessin. And two married sisters in Rouen; they have childs – children – one each, little Colette and Annette.'

He stirred uneasily, and she cuddled in closer. He heaved a great sigh. 'Anatole die soon, I fear.' He dragged this admission out with difficulty, but he was anxious that she should know exactly how matters stood.

'Oh, I'm so sorry. It must be hard for all of you,' she responded with genuine concern. It was her turn to sigh. Then she added, 'TB is very common in Liverpool.' She understood the possible complexities of his life.

'Yes?' He was absently stroking her cheek again with one hand. Instinctively she caught it, opened it and planted a kiss on his palm. He closed it sharply. 'No,' he said a little desperately. 'We talk.'

Her spirits had risen a little, and she looked at him wickedly through half-closed eyes, 'Yes, sir.' She decided that she must be truly insane.

'I must help to provide for Maman and for Anatole – and, most important, help Maman to nurse Anatole. You understand? Maman cannot do it alone. So I am not free. I tell you how we cannot work on our land, nor can we sell it – it's thick with mines. Our home is ruin, our birds, animals dead.' He threw up his free hand in a passionate gesture, to indicate the totality of his ruination.

She had seen, after air raids, this same despair in the shattered streets of Liverpool, and she nodded.

He went on angrily, 'When he come to Bayeux, General de Gaulle make promises. Communist Party – they are big part of Resistance – they make promises. Everybody make promises. General de Gaulle is big man, so I believe him. I work at anything – immediate, fast – to feed us, while I wait for Government to clear the mines. But what Government? As always, a herd of imbeciles; they don't care about peasant. Now I know de Gaulle lie. He is like Hitler, but without real power. He makes Americans quiver like rabbits with nerves over our socialism.'

Once again, he surprised Barbara with his intensity. She understood exactly what he meant and reminded him cautiously that the Americans had just agreed to give Marshall Aid to France.

'True. Very late!' His face was set in grim straight lines, as he went on, 'Now, I think very much what I do for me – and you. But I cannot move Anatole – he is too sick. Otherwise, I go to Le Havre or Rouen. Look for work.' He was desperately anxious that Barbara should understand his situation clearly.

She nodded acceptance of his explanations.

He continued, 'Also, Maman want to stay close to our land. She fear someone take it – say we are dead and steal it once it is clear, you understand? I get chance with taxi. I learn to drive. I make a little saving, to buy things for Anatole.' He sighed. 'Try to buy a front wheel and tyres for a bike I build, so I can do work at a distance. No wheel, no tyres, up to now.'

He turned to her and caressed her neck lightly. 'I see you and I know immediately what I want.' His expression changed, he smiled down at her, and she felt weak and very vulnerable. She let him talk on, however.

'Now I have ambition. I cannot wait for Government. I can only try to prepare for better times. I cannot do everything.'

'What do you want to do?'

'Marry you,' he replied promptly.

She felt like a drunk, as she plunged. 'That's probably a very good idea.'

He laughed, and kissed her. Then he loosened his grip a little, and went on relentlessly, 'Another problem. I am peasant farmer. You're bourgeoise, a townswoman, I believe? Big difference in France.'

'Tush! I'm a working-class woman – my dad went to sea. What exactly do you mean by bourgeoise? I'm not rich. I work hard.'

'Much difference here. You do not know how hard is a peasant's life when he has so little land – a small piece owned jointly by family members.'

He paused and took in a deep breath. 'I want to work in a town with a decent house and a decent wage. I have problem with my shoulder – you must notice. There is much construction work in Rouen, but I cannot do very, very heavy labour every day. The pain is much.'

'I do understand about heavy work, indeed I do,' she replied with vehemence. 'How did you manage on your farm?'

His smile was suddenly grim. 'Much pain. I want to scream – like pig on killing day. *Mon père* say I'm lazy boy – a coward. Life is hard for a peasant. His earnings are so small that his children also, must work if they are to be fed.'

'Poor Michel.' She considered for a moment what he had told her, and then added, 'Poor Papa,' as she saw how a parent could be caught in such a situation.

She had once again surprised him. 'You understand?' he exclaimed. 'It is not simple, is it, when you must feed a family?'

'So what plans have you?'

He tightened his grip round her, and was silent. Then he said reluctantly, 'First, you must understand, we have to wait for Anatole.'

'Are you sure he is going to die?' The question was brutal, but she felt she must know.

'Certain, except a miracle happen. Doctor say nothing can help him. Anatole suffer very much in Germany – overwork, starvation. It is much sadness for Maman and me.' He sighed heavily. 'We love him, we take care of him. We say no to hospital – he stay with us. Even if I have good job, nobody want to rent house or rooms to a family with *la tuberculose*. Anyway, house to buy or rent very hard to find anywhere in Normandy – so much ruin. So we wait – until now.'

'You poor souls. Then after Anatole passes away, what next?'

'I think Maman live with my sister in Rouen. Claudette still have home over shop – Bertrand and Claudette is bakers. Maman be big help for them. My other sister, Anne-Marie, lose her home and her younger child, little Philippe – bomb – so she have problems. Most sad. Her husband very kind – he drive a big lorry. He bring things to help Anatole – sometimes milk.'

'What will Madame Benion live on?'

'You mean money?'

'Yes.'

'She have small pension from Government, though each day it is worth less. But I send her money. My sister feed her, give her bed. There is talk of regular, new pension for old people – if she get that, she enjoy life, help to care for little Colette. Claudette is much kind.'

As far as she could judge, he was trying to be absolutely truthful with her. Yet, she had heard that the French were very reticent! Perhaps he regarded her already as an instant addition to the family.

She smiled at the latter thought; you don't simply marry a man, she told herself. You must remember, old girl, that you also marry a family. And that could certainly complicate life.

Though she already knew George's widowed mother, she had not even considered the rest of George's family when she had said yes to him. But then, the war was on and one did not look ahead very much.

Now, who could say what would come out of a France that, she had been warned by the Thomas Cook's agent, did not yet have a stable government; or, come to that, out of a bankrupt, dreary Britain with a Labour government bent on changing everything in sight? How long would American bankers put up with the latter, she wondered.

'How did you learn so much English?' she asked inconsequentially.

He grinned. 'I speak terrible.'

'No. You know a lot of words.'

'I learn when I am a young boy,' he said, and explained about the old English retirees to whom he had delivered eggs and roasting chickens. 'I buy little book for traveller, and I ask them, "How you say this, how you say that?" They laugh – they tell me. I learn.'

The ladies, he told her with a chuckle, had certainly been tickled at his clumsy attempts at English. Then some of them had become interested in his struggle to learn and had been very helpful. One of them had been kind enough to give him a big French/English dictionary and, later on, a short lesson at her kitchen table each week when he came to her house. She had made him pronounce the strange English words again and again until, with the exception of the letter H which constantly eluded him, he had, he hoped, almost the same clarity of pronunciation that she had herself. He came to the conclusion, he declared with a grin, that he had become her hobby, a luxury limited to the English retirees; no one like himself had time for such things.

Confidences poured out of him, some of which he had previously alluded to more casually.

He reminded her of the English pilots they had hidden, and how he had talked with them every night. 'Also, German officer speak English, not French. I talk to them in English about food for Germany, which I must send them.'

'Why did you want to learn?'

'I think I get job in hotel – easy job, like Reservations – not like farm. Now I teach you French, eh?' He grinned mischievously.

She straightened herself in the hard wooden pew. Now she understood his predicament, and she smiled a little sadly, as she responded doubtfully, 'Perhaps, my Michel. Perhaps.'

In a world in such a mess as theirs was, she considered, you could not foretell the future; she, like other English people, had tended to assume that daily life would return eventually to what it had been before the war began. But it certainly showed little sign of doing so.

In her heart she had realised, on seeing George's grave, that all the safe, mundane assumptions of peacetime life – that your home would still be there in the morning, that governments knew what they were doing, that your men would probably come home, even if they were seamen – were by no means certain.

Worst of all and most terrifying, nobody knew when

or where the third atomic bomb would be dropped, but everybody was sure that it would be dropped; the authorities were, in anticipation, already digging deep shelters; and training school children, poor little lambs, to take refuge under their desks the moment the air-raid siren sounded.

All that was unequivocal to Barbara was the ardent man beside her, though she feared that even he might fail her because of the difficulty of getting out of the morass he was in.

She leaned forward to kiss her newly acquired Michel on the cheek as if saying a sad, gentle farewell.

Chapter Nineteen

They stayed in the cathedral until the sun's rays faded and the gorgeous colours of the glass of the western windows began to darken. They had not talked much more, simply sat, warm body to warm body, both drained by the continuous effort demanded of them by years of war and a bleak and empty peace.

It was as if the little candle of hope in each of them burned low. Occasionally, as if to reassure themselves, they would turn to kiss each other, long and softly, the torrent of passion, for the moment, held back.

Yet, even if neither of them had much hope of a future together, they drew consolation from each other's closeness and a deep sense of the shared experience of hardship and deprivation.

As they reluctantly left the cathedral and proceeded down a side street, Michel pointed out to Barbara a lovely front garden lit up by a streetlamp. It was full of rose bushes beginning to bud.

'I return you to the flower shop, and then I do an hour's weeding in there – a job of sharp prickles, especially when it's a bit dark!'

She laughed, and said, 'It must look magnificent when all the flowers are out.'

'It does,' replied Michel with a grin. 'I do not bleed for nothing! Madame Dubois love roses – very kind lady. Monsieur Dubois give her a front garden full.'

'Do you do a lot of gardening?'

'*Non*. I do tidying up, mowing, weeding – in the evening, when the Americans are finished early and the taxi is safe, locked up in the garage.'

Barbara was impressed. His day must be as long as mine is when I'm at home, she decided.

In front of the flower shop where they had met on Sunday, they parted rather formally, shyly, reluctant to unclasp their hands, both doubtful of what the future held for them.

Michel said with determined assurance, 'I take Colonel Buck to Caen tomorrow, and the other two to a new cemetery. Then I come for you about eleven in the morning, yes? Monsieur le Colonel return by train. His 'elpers I collect at four p.m.'

Barbara agreed.

'I'll bring some lunch,' she promised. She hoped that the hotel would have sufficient rations to provide her again with a packed lunch.

Though she was enchanted at the thought of spending time with Michel, she was vaguely disturbed that he took it for granted. Admittedly, she had said that it was a good idea that he should marry her, but she had meant it more as a sly teasing aside, a piece of Liverpool repartee.

He seemed to her a sensible man, a fine, straight-forward person; yet, he was in a most unpromising situation, and she continued to be afraid to let her hopes rise.

As she washed herself, in preparation for dinner in the hotel dining room, her despondency grew. How could she possibly hope for anything between them, except for a casual, holiday love affair? She felt foolish to look for anything more.

Grow up, woman, she ordered her image in the mirror quite angrily, as she applied fresh makeup.

I want him permanently, she insisted. Casual affairs? I could find them, two for a penny, in Liverpool.

'I wish to stay with you,' he had told her regretfully. Then he had shrugged. 'Maman is all day indoors with Anatole, and she visit her friend for a little while this evening. So I must stay at home. First, though, I go to Dubois's to weed and water his roses.'

'Of course. Could I meet your mother?'

To meet his mother would be a good way of opening things up, she had considered; of testing how serious he was in his intentions. In Liverpool, if a man were courting a girl seriously, he always took her home to meet his mam; it committed him. She smiled at the memory. She could, however, perhaps learn more of Michel from another woman, particularly his mother – if she were friendly – though Michel would have to translate for them. Just looking at the woman would tell her a little.

He was startled. He had not thought of such an encounter as an immediate possibility, and he had the instinctive reaction of a French person to any invasion of his private space, particularly his home – if his could be called a home.

He had been, up to then, unusually open with her, simply because he was totally bewitched by her. Also, he was dreadfully lonely; he had no close friend with whom he could discuss honestly the problems which beset him, except Anatole and, very occasionally, overworked Paul, the electrician who had taught him to drive.

Certainly, both Anatole and Maman had enough worries already without his adding to them.

He replied slowly, doubtfully, 'I wish it very much.

But not yet, *chère* Barbara.' He paused to think, and then went on, his voice earnest, 'She worry much about Anatole, about the farm, about my sisters – she does not see them. If she meet you, she know – dead cert – she lose me as well as Anatole. Too much grief, you understand. We wait. We plan first, yes?'

Barbara saw his point, and agreed with him. Nevertheless, on later consideration, it nagged at her. Bearing in mind the Liverpool custom of a young man taking a girl to meet his mother, meeting Madame Benion would have settled the matter for her; Michel would indeed be thinking of marriage.

Was the need to relieve his mother from her nursing duties merely an excuse? she asked herself uneasily.

She didn't really know him. Was he, perhaps, lying like a trooper?

Nonsense! His story of his problems made reasonable sense; the argument began to seethe within her.

Before turning to walk up to Dubois's garden, Michel looked after her regretfully. A sharp pang went through him; their attraction to each other had not yet put down the deep roots which he knew it needed to sustain it. For him, she represented all he had ever dreamed of, and, like some lovesick swain in a folk tale, he had told her that he had fallen in love with her – told her so precipitately, perhaps too precipitately, but without any doubt in his own mind.

She had not said that she felt the same. She had responded to his advances, but she had not truly committed herself. She had joked about the idea of marriage.

He wanted commitment.

She could, possibly, decide that she had become

embroiled in a hopeless situation. To escape it, she could easily cut short her visit to France. Trains for Paris, and thence to Calais, now ran every day. Once in Calais, she could take the British ferry and go home. He sighed. It was so easy to escape, if one had money and no responsibilities.

She was lucky to be free to escape from Normandy. He wished passionately that he, too, had been born upon an island. England had been heavily bombed, but its beautiful countryside had remained largely intact.

A wave of depression overwhelmed him, and he muttered suddenly to himself, 'To hell with Dubois's roses. I'll do them later – or maybe tomorrow.'

As he turned for home, a long-felt resentment at his hedged-in situation overwhelmed him, a sense of betrayal by his own people, hatred of the Germans, the ruination of his own little place in the world by armies bent on saving him. Even the fact that Dubois could afford to grow roses, while he himself was so hungry, made him boil with anger.

He turned a corner and nearly bumped into a pair of nuns. '*Pardonnez-moi*,' he muttered mechanically, as he dodged round them.

His memories seethed up within him, of how the French had been called cowards, by sanctimonious Britons, for submitting to the Germans, an insinuation that they still had to bear.

He had been loping along quite fast and became suddenly aware that he was very hungry, to the point of physical weakness, which was not improving his profoundly disturbed state of mind. He stopped to lean against a high wall and regain his breath.

He had not smoked while with Barbara. Now he

remembered the cigarettes she had given him. He drew out the precious packet of Player's Navy Cut; a smoke would assuage his hunger. He shakily opened the packet and took out a cigarette. His hands trembled as he lit it and drew on it. The previous night, he had forgotten about the cigarettes. Now, behind his frantic distress, he reminded himself to offer them to his brother when he got home.

Smoking would certainly make Anatole cough; but if he were to enjoy anything of his very short life, he had to take chances.

And so do you need to take chances, Michel, if you want to live a decent life, flashed through his scattered thoughts.

But he was tired beyond belief, and his mind refused to concentrate, so overwhelmed was he by anxieties.

Every week he feared that he would not make enough to pay the rent, buy candles and paraffin to give some light and heat for Anatole, keep his mother's and his own boots repaired, even enough to buy expensive bread on the black market, if the bakers failed to fill the bread ration. These were just the necessities of life.

Now looming over them like some impending thunderstorm was the fact that Anatole must be given a decent funeral – somehow.

The thought tore at Michel – how could he face the loss of him?

His feet dragged, as he hastened round a bend into an alley lined with very old houses, once the homes of small merchants.

His fatigue seemed permanent. Even when he longed to sleep, he had to relieve his mother in caring for Anatole and that often meant broken nights.

Despite being enormously excited at having met Barbara, the hours he was giving to her were those when he would normally work, either with the taxi or in the gardens he usually tended. The hours would have to be made up by working ever later.

And what would he get out of it all? An occasional packet of black market Gauloises – and minimal food and lodging. And probably he would lose Barbara as well.

As he pushed his way through the crowded alley, he weighed it all up and thought he would choke with sheer frustration.

On his arrival home, he found his mother alone in their landlady's kitchen. She was making soup for supper. As he went through to the privy in the backyard, he greeted her, and asked absently if there was anything he could carry upstairs for her. She promised to call him when the soup was ready, so that he could carry up the heavy iron cauldron. Then she remarked on his being home a little early.

'I'll do Dubois's garden after supper,' he muttered. 'I'm hungry.'

His mother shrugged. Hunger was a permanent condition.

Upstairs, Michel opened the door of their room quietly. Even though Madame Benion did her best to keep everything clean, the smell of sickness now rolled out over him. A great lack of soap, which had priced itself almost completely out of reach, or of disinfectant which was practically unavailable at any price, made cleanliness a luxury.

Anatole seemed to be dozing, their landlady's newspapers spread on his bed.

Michel looked round his home.

How could he ever show this to an Englishwoman?

Short of living in the street itself, it spoke of the greatest poverty.

It never occurred to him that Barbara had seen such places many times before, in a city famous for pollution and the acutest poverty; that she had once lived in a narrow street of tiny row houses, most of them holding more than one family, or at least a lodger or two in addition to a family. Her mother would have been glad to tell him of the frantic effort they had made in order to better themselves.

He made a wry mouth. What else was a peasant other than poor?

Insufficient land to support a decent level of existence, had meant his family had always been poor, a poverty endured for centuries. So what's new? as Colonel Buck occasionally asked. Michel wanted to weep.

Yet his old home had been comfortable in a rough way, and he felt heartsick when he remembered it. There had been in it the friendly, familiar accumulation of family possessions fashioned through the years by ingenious craftsmen. Feather quilts made by Maman and his sisters had kept them warm in winter; they never lacked feathers. The womenfolk's knitting had provided sweaters, undervests and socks. From their own apples they had made Calvados, Normandy's brandy, and had used fallen branches for fire wood. Their hens, a few rabbits and a pig had kept them in meat. Their intensely cultivated vegetable garden yielded both greenstuff and root vegetables, the latter carefully stored to help them through the winters. A single cow, mated with a bull belonging to Suzanne's father in return for butter, had, when she was in milk, provided dairy products for both families; the calves had been sold for veal. Nothing that could be produced at home was ever bought. All the ramshackle collection of chicken coops and the barn had, over many years, been built by the family itself. Even their little cart had been manufactured by Michel's grandfather; only the wheels provided by the local wheelwright. The buying of the small, underfed horse had been a great expense, but one that had repaid the investment; they were able to sell much more produce at a better price to the English community along the coast; and when the Germans moved in, Michel did not know how he would have managed to serve their heavy demands without it.

Through the generations the family had wrung a living by careful husbandry and the total use of their little patch of Normandy. And there had always been hope: the hope of adding to the size of their land holding either by purchase or by marriage, as in the case of Michel's arranged marriage to Suzanne.

As he gazed emptily at the garret and at Anatole sleeping by the window, he suddenly remembered his grandmother, sitting in the doorway to get not only the warmth of the sun, but also a good light in which to work. She had been teaching his sister, Claudette, to tat. Claudette had been bitterly resentful when her father had made her give him the money she earned from the resultant lace edging; after a few years of effort, it had, however, proved a nice addition to her small dowry when she married Bertrand and moved to Rouen.

Somehow, the family had saved precious little silver coins, or, in the case of Michel, kept a Post Office savings account. These little hoards were added to by work outside the farm itself, to help them if infection culled their hens or a bad winter destroyed their garden produce.

Apart from going to sea with his Uncle Léon, Michel had once worked as a labourer in a pottery.

His younger sister, Anne-Marie, had gone to be a maidservant to an English family on the coast. She had seen a standard of living there that had made her ambitious for more than her patient husband, Guy, had ever been able to supply. So she was known as the family whiner – though, in recent years, because of the loss of her home and of her little son, Philippe, in the invasion, she really had had something to whine about, poor girl. Philippe had been a fine little boy, and the whole family had mourned his passing.

As he stood in the doorway, staring at Anatole – at least Anatole was kept warm and fed, though he looked ghastly – Michel's sense of despair grew. They had all tried so hard and it had come to naught.

Like everybody else, in 1939 both brothers had hoped that the war would be averted – or that, at least, the effects would not be felt in Normandy. Thanks to the Benions and their ilk, Normandy was, until the German occupation, relatively rich in agriculture.

Even in 1944, when rumours of an imminent Allied invasion of Normandy had circulated behind the backs of the occupying Germans, and had become the main topic of subdued private conversation of the peasantry, a few of its inhabitants had laughed over their precious glasses of Calvados and had agreed that they might even make some welcome money immediately after such an invasion. They would, at last, get a fair price for their produce, something they could never extract from the Germans.

It would help to make up for the débâcle of a war lost, lost because the accursed government in Paris had not properly prepared for it. It was passionately agreed in the village cafés that They – the almighty They in Paris – should have realised that with a population heavily decreased by the Great War, France was sorely lacking in men of fighting age. At least, avowed the village worthies, they could have trained men better so that they were not simply offered up for slaughter as their fathers had been in 1914.

As Michel stood shakily leaning against the door jamb, his mind wandering in a black sea of misery, he recalled the building of the Maginot Line to thwart yet another German invasion; that had given some small, temporary, sense of safety. But even the poorest peasant could have told Them that they should have continued it along the Belgian border. Was not poor Belgium the cockpit of Europe, weakened by the usual ineptitudes of politicians and wars going back for centuries? How could it hold back a man like Adolf Hitler, who, to attack France, would not hesitate to march through such a tiny country yet again, and, in doing so, circumvent the Maginot Line?

And what use were the French guns drawn by horses against a highly mobile, mechanised German Army?

Looking at his pitiful home, these desperate, wild memories bedevilled Michel: the awful disgrace of Vichy; and the acute humiliation of the occupation of the rest of France, which had irrevocably split the country into warring political factions. The pride of the French, his own pride, had lain in the dust, something which personal insults from the Germans had failed to accomplish.

A totally distraught Michel remembered that their well-respected old leader, Field Marshal Pétain, had, like many Frenchmen, never believed that Britain could win the war. Because of this belief, he had refused to ally himself with them. He had truly believed that the best policy for the survival of France was to collaborate with the Germans. He had staked his excellent reputation upon it and that of his fellow Frenchmen – and he had lost. Michel remembered that the field marshal had said that to make union with England was fusion with a corpse. The corpse had been resurrected, and the result was, finally, the destruction of much of his beautiful department of Calvados. Pétain's mistaken estimate had been the root cause of the death of English troops there.

Finally, as the indirect result of the old field marshal's mistake, an English widow had come to Calvados to mourn a dead soldier – and had ended up in Bayeux's only surviving taxi. And in his own heart.

Michel was swamped by helpless rage. Underlying it was the insult of being regarded by the triumphant Allies as a collaborator of the enemy, no matter how much you had suffered, how brave you had been. What an irony!

Masked by her pretty manners, what did Madame Barbara really think he was? Just another French coward? A collaborator? Or, perhaps, just a dirty peasant to play with, like a cat playing for its amusement with a mouse?

Surely not? And yet, in his tortured state, he wondered.

The longer he stood staring at his miserable home and his dying brother, the worse he felt.

Barbara had made no profession of love. Had she responded to him simply from physical need?

Or was she perhaps really seeking a subtle revenge for her husband's death? Had she led him on as far as she could, prepared to drop him when she felt like it, tread on him as if he were a spider which had crawled out of the barn wall?

He told himself he was mad to think that Barbara would

ever be so mean. On the other hand, he had never dreamed that Suzanne would betray him; yet she had done so.

Suddenly, he began to laugh at the cruelty of circumstances, of being in the wrong place at the wrong time. What had he done to deserve it? There was Suzanne's German lover, with a farm with crops on it – and soon he would have Suzanne and her three-year-old son as well; while he, Michel, had nothing but a heap of mud on to which, because of land mines, he dared not even walk.

His mad laughter grew and grew until he could not stop. A huge pain rose in his chest.

Amid the chaos of his mind, he saw again his martyred friend, Henri, and his awful death. Had Henri died in vain?

The wild laughter became a great sob, and then he was crying, sobbing helplessly.

Anatole's eyes had shot open at the first explosion from his brother. He laboriously turned to look.

'Michel!'

Michel was leaning against the door jamb, his arms wrapped round his head. The dreadful noise of his frenzied weeping filled the room and echoed down the stairs.

Doors flew open.

Madame Benion heard him. She took the soup pot off the fire, and then ran to the foot of the stairs. It was indubitably Michel's voice.

Anatole – *in extremis*! She flew up the first flight of stairs, only to bump into her landlady coming out of her bedroom.

'Anatole?' queried Madame Blanc, as she immediately followed Madame Benion up the next flight, her flabby weight making her pant.

'I fear so,' replied Madame Benion through tight lips, as she swung round the banister and up the last flight.

Lit by the skylight in the roof of the hallway, Michel was still leaning against the door jamb. He continued to sob uncontrollably.

'*Mon Dieu*!' exclaimed both ladies between pants.

Madame Benion glanced first at Anatole.

He looked as he had done for weeks. He greeted her anxiously. 'Maman, what's the matter?'

She had turned to Michel, and put a hand on his shoulder.

'Are you hurt?' she asked him quite anxiously. He turned a grief-stricken face towards her.

'*Non.*' He continued to weep, tears pouring down his lined face.

'What are you crying for?'

'I don't know,' he sobbed.

She thought that it was some kind of hysteria, so she promptly slapped his face.

It had little effect, and she immediately regretted the blow.

'Come in, my son,' she said more gently, and put her arm round his shaking body. She looked back at her silent, worried landlady and then at the staircase where two of the other tenants stood staring at them.

Though frightened to death, she feared to call a doctor. Seeing Michel so distraught without apparent reason, he might well send him for attention to an insane asylum, something to be dreaded; yet she badly needed help.

She remembered how Anatole had wept similarly for days on his return home and how the local priest, a stranger to her then, had comforted him. The priest now visited her elder son regularly and she herself went to him for Confession.

'*Chère Madame,*' she whispered to the landlady, 'would you send for *Monsieur le Curé, notre Père Nicolas?* Ask him to come urgently. He was so understanding when Anatole first came home, you remember?'

Madame nodded. She turned to the first tenant standing at the door, a gawky youth, who was watching with great interest the drama before him. She asked him if he would go to the presbytery. He nodded, took one more glance at the scene before him, and ran down the stairs.

Chapter Twenty

'Anatole Benion?' asked Father Nicolas, as he snatched up a small case, in which lay everything needed for the administration of the Last Rites. He clapped his biretta onto his head, and turned to peer again at the panting messenger, through a pair of spectacles held together across his nose by a grubby binding of sticking plaster.

'*Non, mon Père*. It is for Michel, his brother. He's collapsed. He's crying like an infant!' The dull face lit up. 'It is very strange, *mon Père*. Madame Benion asks for you to come urgently.'

The priest paused, his shabby black cassock swinging loosely in the breeze from an open window. He said gravely, 'Such an event is not uncommon nowadays; I'm not very surprised that it has happened to young Benion. Come, my son.'

As they hurried along the street, bodies bent against a chilly wind, the priest asked, 'Madame did not send for a doctor?'

'*Mais non*. Doctors are for real sickness.'

The priest smiled slightly. Madame Benion may already know what ails her son, poor woman. Though I believe it's probably the result of great stress, it could, of course, be that he has discovered that he also has caught the dreaded *tuberculose*. And what good is a doctor then, except to comfort? An old friend or a priest can do that.

The staircase up which he climbed to the Benions'

room seemed even longer and darker than usual. I am growing old, Father Nicolas thought, and, like everyone else, I am tired.

The young man followed him slowly and respectfully.

Standing furtively in the upper hallway were two women and another man whom Father Nicolas recognised as tenants in the house. They moved back to make way for him. As he paused to pant before knocking on the door, he ignored them as ghoulish curiosity-seekers; he knew that they would not follow him into the room if they were aware that Anatole had tuberculosis.

From within came the muffled sounds of extreme grief.

The priest sighed. He knew those sounds. A number of his parishioners had exhibited similar breakdowns; Anatole had been one of them.

From his experience, he believed that it was the more sensitive ones, or those who had been badly hit by a particularly horrifying aspect of the war, who finally collapsed. He had met prisoners of war who, like Anatole, had borne with fortitude dreadful hardship and abuse, only to be stricken, at some point, once they had returned home.

Because of his visits to Anatole, Father Nicolas was well acquainted with Michel; he recalled him as a man who was superior in intellect to many of his parishioners, a good man who, in his opinion, should have been given by his family to the Church. Landless Michel Benion, *le pauvre*, caught in the Battle of Normandy, would be well aware of the broader, longer-lasting implications of the disastrous invasion which had ruined much of Calvados. He would, presumably, also understand some of the problems of the current political situation. On top of the loss of his home, these matters could weigh heavily upon him.

From the gossips of his parish, the priest had heard

the story of Suzanne. He could well imagine what that disgrace had done to Michel.

As he had almost run down the narrow alley in which the Benions lived, he had recalled details of others he knew who had suffered the kind of collapse he suspected Michel was enduring. He believed that his experience of them would help him with Michel.

They had, certainly, all behaved similarly. They faced bravely whatever had occurred – the torture, the deaths, the woundings, the destruction of their homes. Then, months, even years, later, as a result of another lesser misfortune while safe in Bayeux, their courage suddenly deserted them. They wept the tears they should have wept long before, began a mourning which should, for example, have begun at a graveside. Another reaction which occurred occasionally, tripped by a sudden memory, was a bout of helpless anger, carefully suppressed in front of the enemy. It could suddenly surge forth in violent rage or grief. He had seen it. He had seen it all.

The best that could be said about it was that once it had been well vented, the patient slowly recovered and was unlikely to be severely bothered by it again.

He took in a large breath of fetid air, composed his face to its normal expression of gentle enquiry, and knocked.

The door was answered by the landlady, whose sudden relief at seeing him would have amused him had the situation not been so grave.

'*Mon Père.*'

She opened the door just sufficiently to permit him to squeeze through, without again exposing the entire room to the interested onlookers outside.

As the door was quietly closed behind him, the priest hesitated.

Bathed in the light of the sunset from the window was a tableau reminiscent of a medieval painting. Lying on a mattress on the floor, his mother kneeling beside him, Michel was sobbing steadily; occasionally, the sound rose and fell in wails of pain. By the window itself, lay Anatole, looking even more exhausted than usual; he smiled weakly when he saw the priest.

While he considered exactly how to tackle the situation, Father Nicolas moved swiftly over to Anatole, took the man's hand lying on the coverlet and squeezed it gently. He then blessed him. 'All will be well, my son,' he whispered.

Anatole tried to cross himself, but did not quite manage it. He relaxed visibly, however, as the priest turned towards Michel.

Madame Benion had half turned on her knees to greet him with obvious relief. He smiled benignly down at her.

Michel lifted his head from the mattress, saw who had arrived, and struggled into a sitting position.

In between sobs, he said imploringly, 'I'm so sorry, *mon Père*. I don't know what's the matter . . .' He turned back to Madame Benion, put his arms round her, and said, 'Maman!' And cried all the harder.

The priest put his little bag down on the floor. Then, slowly and laboriously, he kneeled down by the stricken man.

Still weeping, though trying hard to control himself, Michel loosed his mother and turned again to the old man.

'Don't be afraid, my son. This spasm is the Good God helping you. There is nothing to be afraid of.' The priest eased his position to be more comfortable with the bare boards beneath his knees, and smiled at the distraught man seated awkwardly before him on a mattress.

'There, now. First, we are going to say the Ave Maria. The blessed Mother is a great comfort to us all, and she will help to calm you and clear your mind. Then we'll say the Paternoster.'

Still sobbing, Michel nodded his head.

'After that, I am going to ask Madame Blanc, your good landlady, to let us sit together in a room by ourselves so that we do not tire your brother.'

He glanced meaningfully up at the landlady, and she nodded. He did not look at Madame Benion. To get to the root of his woes, he had to have the young man to himself; not all a man's secrets could be shared with his mother.

Trustfully, like a child, Michel turned on to his knees. Breaking down here and there, he repeated mechanically after the priest the Ave Maria and then the Paternoster.

The priest knew what he was about. While a very distressed Madame Benion silently watched him, he went on carefully to talk the patient down to a level of coherence.

Then he rose to his feet and held out a hand. Michel grasped it, like a drowning sailor will grasp the body of a dead comrade, hoping dumbly to be kept afloat. He stumbled up, careful not to put too much weight on the older man.

Still holding on to him firmly, the priest turned to the landlady. 'Madame?'

She nodded, and moved towards the door. The priest looked down at Madame Benion. 'My daughter, be at peace. If God wills, all will be well. Stay with Anatole – he must be exhausted by it all. A hot drink for him – and for you?'

She nodded acquiescence.

That will give her something to occupy herself, he thought, as he led her younger son to the door.

The landlady was already outside the door, scolding the skulking onlookers. She sent them all downstairs and blocked the doorway until she heard their boots on the lowest flight.

'I'll take you to my sitting room,' she told the priest.

Still quietly crying, despite his best efforts to control himself, Michel clung to the older man's hand. The priest led him down the long staircase.

The landlady opened the door of her best room and ushered them in.

'Would you like a glass of Calvados, *mon Père*?' she asked the priest. 'I have a little.'

'Thank you, daughter. It would help us both.'

While she went to get the Calvados, Father Nicolas sat Michel and himself down on a dusty green velvet sofa. The room smelled damp and unaired. Heavy green curtains half blocked the window. Dark wooden pieces of furniture loomed in the poor light of a streetlamp below the window.

The priest produced a fairly white handkerchief from his cassock pocket. Michel took it gratefully and blew his nose. He then wiped his face, and the priest noticed, though the light was so poor, how very lined his face was. Peasants aged young, he knew that – he had been born a peasant himself. But Michel looked much too old for his years.

'How old are you, my son?'

Surprised by the question, Michel replied with a half-sob, 'I shall be thirty in June, *mon Père*.'

'A turning point in a man's life.'

'Indeed, *mon Père*.' He rubbed the handkerchief wearily over his forehead. 'At thirty, I had hoped for regular work, a little home . . .' He trailed off into another sob.

The old man nodded agreement. 'At present too many are also in the same situation, my son.' He sat for a minute silently contemplating the bewildered, beaten man. Then he went on gently, 'I know that, like many others in Calvados, you have borne unspeakable burdens. But I do not think you have ever given in. This distress may have been triggered by something more recent. Have you, perhaps, also lost someone recently?'

Michel's weeping was receding now, and he answered fairly clearly in a puzzled voice, 'No, *mon Père*.' He nearly added: But I fear to lose someone; yet, he felt too shy to mention Barbara, afraid that his sudden love for her would sound irrational to a priest.

He bit his lower lip, and it seemed to Father Nicolas that the dreadful crying was about to return, so the priest hastened to continue, 'Or perhaps, during the war, you lost someone you loved very much, yes? And dared not weep for them at the time? And something brought his memory back to you?'

Michel's face registered sudden despair. Already haggard, he now also looked yellow as his colour receded.

He was silent for a moment. The priest must have second sight!

'Yes, *mon Père*.'

'Would you like to tell me about it?'

The story of Henri's terrible end at the hands of the Germans poured out. The priest himself was shocked, though he had seen enough himself to know that what he was hearing was the truth. Sometimes it was very hard to accept the Will of God.

'We had to be quiet, not draw any attention to ourselves, you understand, *mon Père*, for fear our part in the escape of the Jewess was discovered. You know about these things, Father.'

'Yes, my son. Sometimes we have to accept such horrors and simply trust in God.' He was pensively silent as he considered the dumb bravery of the dead man. Then he added with a sigh, 'But your friend Henri was a very brave young man.' His voice lifted. 'I believe it is important that his sacrifice be remembered, don't you? Perhaps we can do something that would perpetuate the story of his bravery, to be an inspiration to future generations?'

As intended, the constructive suggestion diverted Michel a little. It was a comforting idea, and Michel nodded.

'We will talk further about it another day, Michel. I am sure something can be done. Perhaps a tiny garden for the public to rest in – or a plaque on the cathedral wall, eh?'

He squeezed the clinging hand, and said, 'Now, tell me what you were doing when this memory came back to you? Do you have work? I believe that, like many others, you cannot yet get back to work your farm.'

Michel let out a huge sigh. 'I've been driving the taxi for the American morticians who are here – you will know about them, Father?'

The priest ventured a small joke. 'Yes, I do. Who could avoid seeing three such huge men? Monsieur Duval's taxi, I presume?'

Michel nodded. He was still sobbing, but quietly now.

'Were the Americans obnoxious to you in some way?'

'Oh, no. They are most kind to me.' Despite the firm reply, French pride intervened, and he added, his lips quivering, 'Naturally, they think that they won the war.

And I don't disillusion them by saying that many others helped, including us – because they do mean well.'

'And, as well, I hear the taxi takes relations of the fallen to the cemeteries?'

Michel hesitated, and then admitted, 'Yes.' He paused again. 'Colonel Buck gave me permission,' he said defensively.

Michel's face suddenly had a stubborn closed look. There is more to this, considered the priest. He sighed again.

The landlady knocked and bustled in without waiting for permission. In each hand she held a tiny glass of Calvados. She carefully set one before the priest. As she handed the second glass to Michel, she was relieved to see that he appeared much calmer. She warned him with a smile that it was strong. 'Sip it slowly. It is really good – the Germans never found it!'

To give them some light, she took a box of matches out of her apron pocket, and turned to strike a match and light a candle in a tall wooden candlestick on a small side table.

Dead match in hand, she hesitated in front of them, perhaps hoping to be invited to join the party. But the priest said, 'We shall be here a little while longer, my daughter. Monsieur Benion needs to rest.'

She was dismissed. 'Of course.' She retreated, and then went upstairs to report to Madame Benion that Michel seemed more tranquil.

Chapter Twenty-one

Michel shyly sipped the Calvados. The priest did not. He let the glass lie on the side table, and turned thoughtfully to the man beside him.

On an empty stomach, the drink was warming, comforting to Michel, and he slowly relaxed. In between the careful sips which he took, he sometimes gave a dry sob.

'My son,' the old priest addressed him gently, 'I have seen, since you have been here, that you and Madame Benion have borne bravely the troubles besetting you. Your care of your brother is commendable, and, once or twice when I have spoken with her, your mother has been full of praise for the way you are supporting her in nursing him at home. The strain on both of you must be heavy. Yet, Michel, it is you who have suddenly succumbed. Not Madame Benion, who must be in great sorrow at the impending loss of her elder son. Did something special happen to you?'

I am being most insensitive, he thought, but I must get to the root of this, otherwise they will call a doctor, who will prescribe pills which will do nothing to heal the man.

Michel cleared his throat. 'Maman does grieve, as I do, no doubt about it. She holds up amazingly,' he said. He stopped for a moment, and the cleric gave his hand a little squeeze. Then Michel continued, 'We worry also that we cannot make our room more comfortable for Anatole.

The money he receives because he was taken by the Germans is enough to feed him and what medicines Monsieur le Docteur prescribes are free, of course, but nothing replaces the comforts of our lost home.'

He stopped to consider his mother's quiet stoicism, and then went on slowly, 'Since driving the taxi, I can pay a little higher rent, but nowhere can I find a decent place in the city to live; the town is still full of refugees from Caen.' He sighed. 'And with an invalid it is a real problem. Immediately a landlord hears that Anatole has tuberculosis, he might put us out.'

'Madame Blanc knows, I presume?'

'Indeed, yes. She has been a saint. Since Anatole cannot move about the house, she says he's unlikely to pass on the disease.'

Michel's voice was steady now, though he still sounded weary and uncertain, as if he had himself been ill.

In an effort to clarify what had actually triggered his collapse, the priest plunged into the subject of exactly what he had done that day, commencing with getting up in the morning.

A little surprised at the question, Michel began with helping his brother to wash and then listed his morning's work, until he reached his going to the cathedral.

There he stopped. He gave no indication as to why he went. He thought irritably that Monsieur le Curé was almost putting him through a Confession, without the guarantees of the sanctity of the Confessional.

'So you sat in the cathedral? I cannot quarrel with that,' the priest said with a gentle laugh. 'Do you do that often?'

'*Mais non, mon Père*,' Michel replied with disarming honesty. 'Normally, I have no free time. When I am not driving the taxi, I work in Carnot's market garden – his strawberry beds, at present. I weed. I pick peas, lettuces – whatever he wants. I also cut the grass and weed, and water the roses for a Monsieur Dubois.' He made a wry mouth. 'I should be at Monsieur Dubois's house now.'

Dubois was a notorious black marketeer and no friend of Mother Church, so the old man replied a little tartly, 'It is now dark. His flowers will not come to harm for a day or so.' Then he asked, 'Are you, perhaps, making a novena in the cathedral for your friend Henri?'

'*Non, mon Père.*' Michel sighed a great sobbing sigh.

'Would you like to tell me what you sought in our beautiful cathedral?'

There was silence.

'It is difficult to explain, *mon Père.*'

'Try. I want to help you, you know that. You can do it in the Confessional, if you would prefer.'

'Oh, I have done nothing wrong, Father.' The Calvados was loosening his tongue, and he was suddenly quite indignant. 'I just saw how pleasant life could be – given ordinary luck.' The hand which the priest still held tightened its grip. 'You see, *mon Père* . . .' He turned to face him, 'I am nearly thirty, halfway through my life. But I have no wife, no children. I have nothing. No way that I can see of getting out of my present situation, either, unless we can get back on the land. And even then, how does one build new flocks from nothing?'

The word wife gave the priest the clue for which he was looking. 'What did you see – a young lady at her prayers, perhaps?' His question was amiable, almost teasing.

Michel's mouth dropped open as he stared, shocked, at the gentle face before him. Unaware that he had so simply given himself away, his pain was mixed with astonishment at his questioner's perception.

'*Oui, mon Père*. A young English widow. She has come here to see her husband's grave. She was not at prayer, though,' he confessed. 'We talked to each other.'

'Humph.'

Michel withdrew his hand from that of the priest and covered his face. Dry sobs again shook him.

Slowly and with difficulty, because he did not believe that a celibate priest would understand, the story of Barbara came out, and his despair about her. 'I may even have frightened her, *mon Père*, with the rashness of my approach. She is still in grief.'

To his surprise, however, the priest nodded a gentle understanding. 'Since you were both in the cathedral, I assume that she is a Catholic?'

'*Oui, mon Père*. There are many Catholics where she lives.'

Michel had underestimated the wise old priest. Father Nicolas had heard many a dreadful tale and he was quite pleased to learn about something so innocent – and he had no doubt in his mind of its innocence. Thus does God heal, he thought; just as the grass grows again to cover the earth's agony, so do human survivors cover their wounds by finding joy in each other.

Chapter Twenty-two

At the hotel, Barbara came slowly down the stairs from her room. She was on her way to the dining room to have an early dinner. As she abstractedly descended the last flight of stairs to the lobby, she was turning over in her mind the details of her afternoon with Michel. She was filled with doubt. Meeting Michel was almost too good to be true, she told herself; yet internally she was in turmoil – and all because of him.

She hesitated on the bottom step, as if to recall where she was, and looked over the shabby hall towards the reception desk.

At that moment, Colonel Buck, the mortician, came through the swing door of the hotel. In his usual impatient way, he strode across to the desk clerk.

'Can you get a message to the cab driver for me?' he enquired, as he took a diary out of his top pocket and consulted it. 'I need to change the time he's to pick me up tomorrow.'

'Now, Monsieur le Colonel?'

'Yes, now.' The colonel snapped his little diary shut.

The clerk looked glumly at the American, and prayed to be delivered from all Americans, particularly this one, who was always in a hurry. 'It may be difficult, Monsieur. He will have gone home.'

Patience, patience, Colonel Buck told himself. He asked

241

painstakingly, 'In that case, where could I find the owner of the cab?'

'Monsieur Duval shuts his garage at five o'clock, Monsieur.' The clerk threw up his hands in a gesture of despair. 'There's not much petrol to sell, few vehicles to service – why stay open later? You understand his problem, Monsieur? We have many problems at present.'

'Jeeze!'

Reservations pursed his thin lips, and turned to consult a note on a board behind him. He swung back to the irate colonel. 'Benion will come in about seven thirty tomorrow morning, well before he expects to pick you up. He will check – er – for messages.' He was not sure how much the colonel knew about the illicit use of his taxi, so he did not mention that he already had a message from a huge, strangely dressed Canadian male, who had registered at the hotel only an hour before and who wanted to go to the Canadian cemetery.

The colonel did not care, he would have assured the clerk, what happened to the goddamned cab so long as it was where he wanted it, when he wanted it – and Benion was good at arranging that – he was a very helpful fellow. Knew the countryside like the back of his hand. Always knew where to get a drink or a decent meal. The colonel opened his mouth to respond when he observed Barbara coming towards him.

She had heard the enquiry about the taxi driver, and the American's show of impatience had refocused her troubled mind.

'Good evening, Colonel.' She greeted him with the polite, professional cheerfulness she normally used when coping with B-and-B guests.

The colonel's face cleared. He had already connected

Barbara with the taxi driver. His assistant, Wayne, had seen the kiss outside the cathedral, and told him about it only twenty minutes before. The budding romance had given the colonel something pleasant to think of, at a time when he had not much to laugh about.

Even though he had been an undertaker all his life, having inherited a thriving business from his father, the number of young lives lost in France had shaken his usual aplomb in the face of death. His being co-opted by the Military gave him high rank and many privileges while he helped them to sort out its cemeteries, not to speak of exploring what had been a wonderful country. The work had, however, been overwhelming to both mind and body. He would be thankful to go home to his wife and family in Richmond, Virginia, to sell elaborate coffins to the well-to-do, and be a much-respected professional comforter to the entire community.

His longing had made him more than usually irritable, but he turned thankfully to the young widow. 'Dear lady,' he said, all smiles. 'I need the address of our cab driver. Do you happen to know it?'

'No, Colonel, I don't.' Barbara paused. 'I know it's not far from here.' Then she brightened. 'I think I know where you can find him, though. Last time he drove me, he showed me a lovely rose garden in which he said he usually did an hour's work between five and six before going home – if you didn't need him.' She looked down at her wristwatch. 'It's not quite six. A Mr Dubois's garden, he said.'

Thankful for the information, Reservations interjected, '*Oui, Monsieur le Colonel.* Monsieur Dubois lives less than five minutes from here.'

'Where?'

The clerk embarked on a long description of the tortuous route through narrow streets laid out in the thirteenth century.

Barbara clicked her tongue; she knew that the colonel had a very short fuse, though he could be kindness personified. She said quickly, 'Let me take you. I know exactly where the garden is.'

The colonel hastily stuffed his diary into his top pocket and said, 'Great, if you don't mind.' That she might be in need of dinner did not, at that moment, occur to him.

The colonel held the swing door for her and they went out into the courtyard together. The evening air smelled pleasantly of flowers.

'This way,' ordered Barbara, as Colonel Buck let go of the door and zoomed ahead of her through the great iron gate, which was ajar. He stood poised on the pavement, ready, it seemed, to take off to the moon if necessary.

As they set out, he did, however, lessen his long stride to accommodate Barbara's shorter one.

'I just gave my boys the evening off,' he told her, as they walked down a street made shadowy in the half-light. 'They'd gone just before I got this call from the base. Otherwise, I could have given them the job of finding Benion.'

Barbara laughed. 'I'm sure they would appreciate the evening off much more.'

The colonel nodded agreement. 'I'm sorry to trouble you about Benion, but he's invaluable to us,' he said.

As they crossed a road, he stopped suddenly to avoid being run down by a woman pushing a wheelbarrow heaped with small household goods. Then he took Barbara's elbow and guided her forward.

'When I was in Caen this afternoon I was warned that

a senator would be landing there tomorrow,' he confided. 'But I didn't know until just now, from Wayne, that he would be arriving so early. He's coming via London. The party expect to be met at the airport at 7.30 a.m., and to spend the day touring the cemeteries. It's a real drag,' he confided. 'I'll hafta leave here early myself and drop the others en route at the next cemetery we have to check on.'

Knowing little of American politics, Barbara missed the inferences of the senatorial visit, and was surprised when the colonel added exasperatedly that senators could always find an excuse to travel at government expense.

'Are they very important? VIPs?'

'Senators? Humph. They think they are. I suspect he's here to gain headlines. To show veterans and their families – who have votes – his immense interest in the care of their dead – who don't have votes, of course,' he said, with heavy sarcasm. 'You can bet they won't promise any more money for the job we're doing. It's publicity they're after, looking to the next election.' He eased Barbara round two women pushing ancient prams with new babies in them. 'The loss of my time doesn't matter,' he fumed.

'Will they stay in Caen?'

'Yes, the whole party's going to stay at a private château – which is not much damaged. Thank God, I don't have to do anything about that. Frankly, I would have thought that the French Government would have provided transport for them.'

'Perhaps they didn't get enough notice,' suggested Barbara. 'With so few cars around, it can't be easy to arrange something decent for them at a moment's notice.'

'Maybe. Maybe.' He stopped in mid-stride. 'Where are we now?'

'That's Monsieur Dubois's house. Aren't his roses lovely?'

A housekeeper who answered the black marketeer's door was a little nonplussed at an obviously high-ranking American on her doorstep, enquiring for Monsieur Dubois. Accompanied by his wife, presumably, since the lady was certainly not French.

After looking them over uneasily, she told the couple that Monsieur and Madame were dining out this evening and had just departed.

The colonel controlled his sense of frustration as best he could, and then asked if Madame could tell him the address of Monsieur's wonderful gardener, Benion. Her roses were fabulous. He had never seen such a lovely front garden. He wanted to talk to the man.

The woman relaxed visibly and immediately gave them Michel's address. She also told him how to find it. 'It is a narrow alley, Monsieur – a poor part of the city – not dangerous, however.'

By this time it was dark, and the colonel offered to walk Barbara back to the hotel before he proceeded further. Barbara had, however, become curious to see where Michel lived so she said that, to save him that trouble, she would accompany him – if he did not mind.

That was OK by him, he assured her.

Five minutes later, they were walking cautiously down a narrow, shadowy lane, with houses that opened straight on to it. There was a strong smell of rotting garbage mixed with the odour of bad drains.

The arrival of a uniform, glistening with brass in the dim light from house windows, caused a ripple of interest. Made ghostly by the long shadows, people sitting on doorsteps stopped chatting, and stared. Two little boys playing catch hastily moved to one side. A man leaning against a wall eyed them doubtfully. Many French had reason to fear any uniform and they had no love for Americans.

Most of the houses did not seem to have numbers, so in bad French the colonel asked a very old man crouched on a doorstep where the Benion house was.

The man took his cigarette out of his mouth and gaped toothlessly, almost fearfully, up at the soldier.

He did not know. He drew on his cigarette again, exhaled, and then shouted across the alley to a woman holding a baby in her arms.

Neither the colonel nor Barbara understood the rapid reply. The old man, however, repeated to them, 'Five doors that way, the house of Madame Blanc.'

While this exchange was going on, Barbara glanced round.

So this was Michel's world. It was as bad as anything in the north end of Liverpool, she thought, though none of it had been ruined by bombing, as similar districts in Liverpool had been. Looking at it, smelling the odour of it, she began to understand the possible reason for his not wanting her to meet his mother. Since he regarded her as someone more prosperous than himself, he would be reluctant to show her this.

She smiled softly. She remembered how she and her mother had clutched at the chance to get out of their own primitive row house in Liverpool, which had not smelled much better. How lucky she herself had been to live so many years by the sea. Michel had been a farmer, used to country smells, admitted, but to good sea air as well – how awful it must be for him to live in a city as crowded as this – and care for an invalid in it.

A great understanding warmth filled Barbara as she trotted down the alley behind the colonel, who was already in hot pursuit of his driver.

Used to the freedom that the war had, in a way, brought her, it never struck her that her accompanying the colonel might be misunderstood.

If she had been challenged about it, she would have replied smartly that she would decide who were her friends – and that a friend did not necessarily mean lover, either present or future. She dealt with men every day of her life and she was quite capable of sound judgement.

They were lucky. Madame Blanc herself filled her doorway.

After reassuring Madame Benion about her son's feeling easier, she had come down, to catch Monsieur le Curé when he left, and, perhaps, learn a little bit of what the upset had been about. The priest was, however, certainly taking his time.

She welcomed the interesting diversion made by such a senior American officer and his wife.

'Monsieur?'

Once again, Colonel Buck gathered up his French, and asked for Michel Benion.

Madame was in an immediate quandary. She was uncertain how to reply. Finally, she said, 'Michel is not available at present, Monsieur. Would you like to give me a message for him?'

Colonel Buck swallowed hard. Nothing in this bloody country was simple or straightforward. Just what did 'not available' mean? And why did she not ask him in? He was not used to being kept waiting on people's doorsteps, even if the resident was poor.

While he hesitated, Madame Blanc's black eyes narrowed until they sank into her fat face. She sensed the colonel's irritation. Since she knew who he must be and that, indirectly, he represented Michel's rent, she tried another tack.

'Perhaps Monsieur would like to speak to Madame Benion?'

'Yes, please,' replied the colonel between gritted teeth. At the same time, a sharp little pain went through Barbara. Had Michel lied about not being married? But then she remembered Michel lived with his mother.

The two children who had been playing ball in the alley, gave up and came over to stare at them. Madame shouted to the elder one, 'Gaston, run up the stairs to the top floor and ask Madame Benion to come down. She has visitors.'

The child went up the stairs like a squirrel up a pine tree, visions of a piece of American gum dancing before him.

Madame Blanc smiled benignly on the representative of the United States Army standing on her step. She did not address him further. Americans were so ignorant of all things French. Digging up their corpses to take them home, the newspaper had reported. As if we do not know, after three invasions within a century, how to care for cemeteries, she considered irritably.

Madame Benion's light step was heard coming slowly down the stairs. Madame Blanc wondered what excuse she would give the officer.

Barbara caught her breath. She was swept by sudden shyness as Madame Blanc made space for her overtaxed, white-haired tenant.

So this was Michel's mother. She was so tiny! She must

be only about four feet nine; yet Michel had said that she had worked all her life on the poultry farm. She was dressed in unrelieved black, her snow-white hair drawn tightly back into a bun on the top of her head. Her eyes were red-rimmed, as if she had been weeping, her colourless face deeply lined as if with great age – the saddest face Barbara could remember, in a world full of sorrowing people. She realised that she could not, very well, introduce herself, and she began to regret that she had not gone back to the hotel.

Madame Benion nodded politely to her. Then she folded her hands neatly across her stomach and looked up at the immense soldier before her. 'Monsieur? Madame?' she enquired with quiet dignity.

'Colonel Buck, ma'am,' He bowed his head slightly.

Madame Benion smiled gently. 'Ah, yes. Michel's colonel?'

The colonel was not sure that he was exactly that, but let it pass. He explained his errand. He wanted Benion to take him to Caen airport tomorrow, starting out at six a.m. At that hour, thought the colonel, they would have a chance of getting there on time, despite any mishaps en route, even a change of tyre – if the wretched vehicle even had a spare tyre.

Not by a flicker of change of expression did Michel's *maman* allow the colonel to see the quandary into which he had plunged her. The boy was obviously very unwell and was still with Monsieur le Curé. Would he be fit to drive?

He has to be fit, she considered frantically. Somehow, he must do it.

Quite used to facing rank in the German Army, never mind their common soldiers, her polite smile remained fixed, as she replied, 'Of course, Monsieur le Colonel. It will be his pleasure.'

One never knew, she told herself. The *curé* had worked miracles with Anatole. *Dieu seul le sait*, he may do the same for Michel.

'Six o'clock at the hotel gate, Monsieur?'

The colonel relaxed. So far so good. 'Thank you, Madame.'

She bowed, and turned her toothless smile on Barbara, and bowed slightly, 'Madame.'

Quite charmed by her, Barbara smiled at her and bade her, '*Bonsoir, Madame*,' as the colonel stepped down into the alley, took her arm, turned her round and marched her briskly back towards the street.

There was a flutter of feet behind them. He turned.

Gaston trotted up beside him, his hand held out. 'Got any gum, chum?'

The colonel nearly burst with irritation, while Barbara tried to control her laughter. '*Non!*' roared the colonel.

'Oh, come on,' cried Barbara. 'I think I've got a pepper-mint.' She opened her handbag, and dug around. Thankfully, she handed the little rogue the wrapped sweet. 'No gum,' she told him.

He grabbed the sweet and ran back to the Blanc house.

The colonel said fretfully, 'You shouldn't bother with them. They're a permanent nuisance.'

'Tush. He's a beguiling little thing.' Because the alley was narrow and uneven, she slipped her hand under the colonel's arm, and then said soothingly, 'You must be sorely in need of your dinner after such a long day in Caen.'

He grinned suddenly. 'I am. Have you eaten yet?'

'No.'

'Well, let's eat together. I'm sure my boys won't be back until midnight, at least, and I dislike eating alone.'

Barbara hesitated for a moment. Both of them were staying *en pension* at the hotel – he was not asking her out. And in crowded Liverpool one frequently found a perfect stranger seated at one's café table, with only the merest, 'If you don't mind, madam . . .' on the part of the waitress. Added to that, with six years of war behind her, crowded into trains and buses, into air-raid shelters, into public dances, with troops from around the earth, Barbara was used to being on sociable terms with strangers; she had a shrewd idea of the likely treatment she would receive from anyone. Only Michel had surprised her; his reactions had been unexpected enough to make her feel she had trodden on a land mine, she considered with a rueful grin. In the colonel's case she was sure that she would get nothing but respect – and she would owe him nothing, because her meal was already included in her *en pension* arrangement with the hotel. She had nothing to fear. And she was proved right.

'That would be very nice. It is a bit dull by oneself,' she agreed with a smile.

As they walked back to the hotel through the ill-lit streets, her thoughts returned to Michel. She wondered idly if, after finishing the Dubois garden, he were, despite the near darkness, working at the market garden he had mentioned to her. She now knew, having seen where he lodged, how much he must need the money.

Chapter Twenty-three

Madame Benion passed her landlady's sitting-room door. She could hear the hum of voices, but could not discern what was being said. She longed to enter.

With a heavy heart, she stood for a moment and then reluctantly decided that it was better to leave the priest uninterrupted.

She continued slowly up the staircase and entered her own room, lit by a single candle stuck in a bottle. For once the room smelled pleasantly of real coffee. Dear, kind Madame Blanc had, from her own secret store of beans, insisted on making coffee for both Anatole and his mother.

'Who was it, Maman?' whispered Anatole, as she went to sit on the edge of his bed.

She explained the visit.

'He wants Michel to pick him up at six o'clock tomorrow morning!' She looked glumly at the invalid. 'I doubt he will be able to do it, do you?' Then she shrugged. 'I didn't know what to say. In the end I told him he would. What else could I do?'

'He may be able to, Maman. Michel's trying to do too much, that's all. He's exceptionally exhausted. And Father Nicolas is a great old man – he may be able to sort him out.'

He turned his head to smile at his worried mother, and then went on, 'After I'd talked to Father Nicolas a few times myself – you remember, when I returned home – I was relieved in my mind. I saw things clearly. He is able to divide the important from the unimportant. He gave me faith – and that helps me to endure what I have to endure – and things to rejoice about. He pointed out that I have a loving mother and brother to care for me!' He laughed weakly. 'He couldn't heal my lungs, however – though he's been a good friend to me ever since, hasn't he?'

His mother smiled back at him, and said more cheerfully, 'Yes. He's been a good friend. He has, I believe, great experience – and great faith himself.'

'That's something we all have to have, Maman. How else do we get through?'

She took his long bony hand and held it as if she never wanted to let it go. There was a break in her voice, as she agreed with him. What else was there?

The door was open, and they heard a murmur of voices. Footsteps went slowly down the staircase. Maman rose from her seat on the bed, and went to the door to listen. 'Michel is seeing Father Nicolas out,' she told Anatole.

She stood in the doorway, to wait until Michel came slowly up the stairs. In one hand he held carefully a glass of Calvados.

His first words were, 'He made me take his glass and told me to drink it before I go to bed. To make me sleep.'

He came slowly into the room, balancing the glass with care. He said cautiously, 'The glass I had has gone to my head – it was the best I've tasted in years.' He actually smiled at his mother. 'I should have waited until after supper to drink it.'

Maman felt a huge sense of relief. He might be a little drunk, but he sounded normal enough.

254

She actually laughed. 'Do you really feel better, my child?'

'Yes, Maman.' He gave a huge sobbing sigh. 'I am myself,' he assured her.

He turned and carefully put the glass on a shelf. Then he took her in his arms and kissed her. 'I'm so sorry, Maman – to make such a fuss. I should tell you that he warned me it could happen again. You are not to worry, though. He feels sure it will pass.'

'My dear, it doesn't matter. Simply let me know if you would like Father Nicolas to come again. I'm sure he would.'

She forced herself to comfort him. She knew very well that he had been stretched to the limit during the occupation. The years since the invasion had, in some ways, been even worse.

She sighed as she patted his back as if he were a little child. And then there had been Suzanne, she thought. How could such a nice girl do something so shocking?

That she herself had been equally stressed was something she felt she must forget. The loss of hope, as the months went by, had affected her more than she had ever acknowledged to her sons. She knew, however, that she must endure, keep a cheerful face, at least while Anatole was with them. When her big lad left her, then she would rest; then she could cry.

As she held Michel, he said, 'I'm so hungry, Maman. You were making soup?'

'Yes. I was.' She laughed as she let go of him. 'I'll go down and get it. Madame Blanc said she would watch it did not burn. You sit with Anatole for a few minutes. I'll just make sure it's hot and then I'll call you to bring the cauldron up for me.'

She went purposefully downstairs to the kitchen.

Michel gave a big sniff and wiped his nose on his sleeve. He had absent-mindedly put the priest's handkerchief in his back pocket. He sat carefully down on the bed.

'What a fool I am,' he said to Anatole. 'I don't know what came over me.'

A brief smile lit Anatole's face. 'Don't berate yourself. I understand,' he said. 'Every man has a breaking point.' He carefully eased himself round to look at his brother more directly. 'You know, when we talked the other night about your pretty English widow, I thought what a comfort she would be to you. What happened?'

Michel threw up his hands in a deprecating gesture. 'She's another frustration. She's the type you marry. There's no way I can do that, situated as we are.' He faltered, unwilling to hurt Anatole.

Then gaining courage, he blurted out, 'What actually triggered it off was the memory of Henri. It just hit me. Our helplessness, our stupidity in such a crisis.'

Anatole took in a big breath that made him flinch with pain. He waited for it to ease, before he said, 'You mustn't blame yourself. If something could have been done, I'm sure you and Monsieur le Docteur and Maman would have done it. It was a miracle that they didn't pick up all three of you as well. By refusing to talk, he saved you. After all, you were all three involved in caring for fugitives.' His voice expressed the resignation of those who know that, whatever happens, they are helpless to remedy it.

'I know, Anatole. But he paid a dreadful price – for our sake. That's what hit me. It suddenly put my own petty worries in perspective. Made me feel what a fool I was in comparison with him.'

'You'd have done the same for him,' responded Anatole

with assurance. He did not mention that the news of Henri's horrible death, broken to him when he had returned home, had been a dreadful blow to him in his already weakened state. Determined, however, to comfort his brother, he added, 'And I don't think your problems are petty. They are very real.'

He rested himself, and then he enquired, 'What did *mon Père* say?'

Michel chewed his lower lip. 'He is kind, you know that. And like you, he really understood. He took me through everything, even my thoughts about Madame Barbara.' He stopped and sighed. 'I understand better now how you must have felt about losing Henri. I cannot bear to lose Barbara – and, God forbid, that I ever lose her in such a terrible way. It must have been frightful for you to learn about that.'

'It's a walk through hell,' Anatole replied flatly. And it's ever present; only your own death, he thought, will ever relieve you of the pain.

'I'm so very sorry, Anatole.'

Anatole lay quietly. Only his laboured breath broke the silence. He knew he must not let his brother slip back into the kind of melancholy which must have preceded his sudden earlier distress; he, at least, had to go on living.

To Michel's surprise, he asked, 'Did Father Nicolas make any comment about Barbara? And her being English?'

Jolted back from his brother's mourning, Michel replied almost mechanically, 'He didn't say anything about her being English. But he seemed to approve of her, a good Catholic with a small business. He is a very practical man.' He smiled slightly at Anatole – the alcohol had lightened his spirits.

Diverted, Anatole also lost his sorrowful look, and

actually grinned, as if he were involved in some amusing secret conspiracy.

'Maman?'

'Exactly. If ever things go right for us, Maman can never object that Barbara is a penniless Protestant.'

'That's something, at least.'

'I suppose it is.' Michel was quiet. He was exhausted and so very hungry.

Then he remembered the priest's words about Henri, and he told Anatole of the old man's proposal that there should be a memorial in their parish church or, possibly in the cathedral, or perhaps a garden to perpetuate their friend's name and his bravery as a Resistance fighter.

'I know it won't bring him back, Anatole. But it will tell people in future that a lot of us didn't collaborate with the Germans. Many of us defied them in our own way, as best we could.'

Anatole was silent. A memorial for one man seemed distant and pointless to him. He had personally seen too many French die in Germany. Altogether, there had been 180,000 of them lost there, and 330,000 more, at the last count, killed during the invasion. Even now, with no one left alive to claim them, many lay under the ruins of their homes, on land still too dangerous to penetrate. It had certainly been a horrible Pyrrhic victory.

Yet he knew that he would have given his own life to save Henri if he had had the chance. He moved his shoulders restlessly. He said, nearly choking on the words, 'Try to arrange it, Michel. It would be something, at least.'

He hoped suddenly that their little parish church, which his mother had told him had been badly damaged, would be repaired and be there for centuries more. Perhaps a memorial in it would whisper down those centuries the story of a personal victory amid defeat. It might inspire someone yet unborn to be as brave as his beloved Henri.

Michel nodded. 'I will,' he promised.

He rose from the bed as he heard his mother coming slowly up the stairs. The soup pot was heavy cast iron, and he ran down to meet her and take it from her.

As she came in behind Michel, Maman recollected the American visitor, and told him about the early morning start to go to Caen airport.

Despite his long days as a poulterer when early hours were a necessity, the very thought of having to begin work at such an unearthly hour made Michel want to yawn. He was also anxious about meeting Barbara. Having thought he knew the Americans' schedule for the day, he had not expected to work for them in the morning and had promised to see her at eleven o'clock.

'Do you think you can drive him?' Maman asked.

'Oh yes, I'll be all right. I'm OK now, Maman,' he lied, in the forlorn hope that he would feel less shaken in the morning. He put the soup cauldron down on a piece of slate on the floor, which they used to prevent the hot pot from searing the wooden planking, and hoped that, indeed, he would be fit in the morning.

Maman took a loaf from the cupboard and tore it into pieces. She filled a bowl with soup for Anatole and then dropped small, soft pieces of bread into it. 'I'll feed him tonight,' she said to Michel.

'No, Maman. I can do it as usual.' He took the bowl from her. 'You eat.'

She accepted what he said, and filled a bowl for herself. She kept the remainder in the iron pot so that it would be warm for Michel.

Michel crushed up the bread into the vegetable soup and then slowly spooned the soft mass into his brother's mouth. As his mother sat down on the mattress on the floor to eat her own meal, she remarked that the colonel looked most formidable, in marked contrast to his wife.

Michel looked round, a spoonful of soup halfway to Anatole's mouth. 'His wife?'

The surprise in Michel's voice made her defensive. 'Well, I supposed it was his wife. She was definitely not French. Her jacket was pink – tweed.'

Michel was trembling, as he eased a spoonful of soup into Anatole. He wanted to cry out with passion, 'No! *Mon Dieu!* It can't be!'

Chapter Twenty-four

It was something that he had feared since the moment he had set eyes on Barbara. Three amiable, rich Americans far from home in the same hotel as a lonely pretty English widow – to a French peasant it seemed a potent mixture.

What chance had he against such competition? His hand shook as he put the spoon to his brother's lips. It rattled slightly, when it touched Anatole's lower teeth, and the patient gulped when the soup flowed into his mouth too fast for him.

Michel was recalled to what he was doing. He avoided Anatole's questioning eyes. 'Sorry,' he said, and steadied himself before giving the next spoonful.

Anatole had immediately understood the import of his mother's remark, and he muttered, 'Don't worry,' before he took in the proffered spoonful.

Unaware of Michel's discomfiture, his mother continued idly, 'She seemed a pleasant young woman. Not the kind to allow herself to be picked up by a soldier.'

Anatole gravely winked at his brother.

The sly wink helped. Some comment had to be made so with an effort Michel replied carefully, 'There are ladies staying at the hotel. They come from many countries to see their sons' or their husbands' graves. I told you that I even had a German *Hausfrau* one day.'

'Of course,' replied his mother placidly. 'You did tell me. She could be one of them – and also need the taxi when next you are free.'

'It may be so.' Barbara would not be walking to the Benion home with the colonel for that reason. He said dully, 'It looks possible that I may be in Caen all day tomorrow. The colonel must have something special coming up to be persuaded to start so early.'

After he had finally wiped Anatole's chin and had, thankfully, eaten his own soup and bread, he produced Barbara's Player's cigarettes, saying that they were a tip he had received.

His mother did not smoke, but Anatole was delighted; even though they were not as strong as French cigarettes, they were unadulterated and tasted pleasant.

The smoke dulled Michel's continuing hunger. He shook out the remainder of the cigarettes and put eight of them on the windowsill by Anatole.

'*Merci*,' responded Anatole fervently. He knew that it was madness to smoke, that it might well suddenly kill him if it caused him to cough; but the relief, the relaxation of being able to smoke good cigarettes, would be such a pleasure in a pleasureless world.

He hoped that Maman would agree to light the cigarettes for him – he was not sure that he could strike a match any more.

Michel then handed over to Madame Benion the tip given him by the English couple that day.

For once, she did not put it into the black stocking holding their savings tucked under Anatole's mattress. She looked at the amount in some astonishment; the money would buy several fertile eggs once they had a broody hen and some land to put them on.

Tush! What a hope! The boys shall have a treat, she decided.

She announced firmly, 'I'll try to buy a piece of chicken for tomorrow. It'll do us all good.' She smiled at her smoke-wreathed sons. 'Or, perhaps, a piece of pork.'

Worn out, Michel nodded agreeably and announced that he would drink the priest's glass of Calvados immediately before going to bed, and not share it. 'Because I must sleep, Maman.'

Anatole would have loved a sip or two, but he saw the sense of Michel's remark, and said nothing. Maman merely nodded her head; the day had not, after all, been so bad as she had anticipated. And she, too, would enjoy a little chicken.

Their ancient alarm clock was wound and set with care. When, at five in the morning, it went off, Michel pounced on it, in the hope that it would not wake the other two. To no purpose.

Maman struggled up and put on her blouse, skirt and shoes. 'You must have something before you go out,' she insisted, and went quickly down to the kitchen to concoct a bowl of coffee made, as usual, with a substitute ground-up mixture, exact origins unknown. She also gave him a piece of dry bread, which she had kept back specially from the previous night, for him to dip into it. It was too early to get fresh from the bakery.

Meanwhile, Michel shaved and washed himself as best he could in a small basin of cold water. His mind was clear enough, though he felt dreadfully weak physically. When he thought of Barbara, he wondered, with anguish, what on earth, if anything, he could say to her about the colonel.

He decided that at this early morning hour he would leave her a message, which would seem normal to Reception, to say that he could not drive her at eleven o'clock; he would try to contact her during the evening to arrange another time. It would give him a chance to think what further he could do. Though his hand shook as he took the mug from his mother, he was thankful for the hot drink, even if it did taste awful.

'*Bonne chance!*' Anatole wished him, as he crammed his beret on his head and fled to get the taxi.

He was standing smoking a Player's while he waited for his fare outside the iron gate of the hotel courtyard when one of the chambermaids came running towards him down the street. As she ran, she was struggling out of the black coat that covered her uniform.

'*Bonjour, Michel!*' she shouted as she ran towards him. '*Mon Dieu*, I'm late if you're here already.'

He grinned at her. 'Relax, I'm an hour and a half earlier than usual.'

'Oh, thank goodness,' she panted. 'I saw you from down the street. I thought my clock must be wrong.' She plonked her handbag on the bonnet of the taxi, and paused to chat. 'Where are you going today?'

'Caen. I'm taking Monsieur le Colonel to Caen airport.'

'Humph.' She looked roguishly at Michel. 'I hope he's enough strength left to cope this morning.'

'What do you mean?'

'Well, he's not a young man,' she giggled. 'He dined with an English woman who is staying here. I served them, because Jeanne was away sick. And two hours later, when I was going home, I saw them in the lounge having a drink.' She winked knowingly.

As the chambermaid gossiped on, Michel felt quite ill. The story linked all too neatly with his mother's remark about the colonel being accompanied by a foreign lady, whom she had presumed to be his wife.

It was one thing to complain to Anatole that Barbara was a frustration to him, quite another to feel he had lost her to a bloody American nearly old enough to be her father. To lose her would be unbearable.

The little tart in front of him must be mistaken. She had to be. He pushed the girl lightly towards the gate. 'You'd better go. The Americans will be coming any moment.'

She made a vulgar derogatory remark about them, and, because the remark reflected badly on Barbara, Michel wanted to slap her.

Incensed, he quickly turned and climbed into the driver's seat.

The three undertakers, clad in olive-drab and fine big working boots, emerged, yawning, to climb reluctantly into the cab.

He greeted them politely, but without his usual enthusiasm. He noted that the colonel did not look particularly haggard this morning.

'*Bonjour, Messieurs*. Where do you wish to go today?'

The colonel heaved himself into a more comfortable position, while Wayne pulled down a folding seat facing him and crouched on it. The other assistant, Elmer, sat beside the colonel.

'First, into Caen itself – to the office of the Mayor. I heard on the phone yesterday that a man brought two American dog tags into City Hall; he found a couple of skeletons in a ditch.' He turned to his underling sitting opposite him. 'Sort it out, Wayne. Then the pair of you

265

could walk over to the cemetery we were originally going to look at today. We've still to find the Goldberg boy's grave before we leave Bayeux.'

Wayne agreed, and Elmer maintained his usual silence.

The colonel turned back to Michel, and repeated, 'City Hall, first. Then Caen airport to meet a senator.'

'*Oui, Monsieur*.' The taxi's gears ground as Michel shifted them.

The thought that the Americans were nearing the completion of their work added to his depression. While agonising about Barbara, he had, in all honesty, to admit that his time with them had been pleasant, the best thing that had happened to him since the war had begun, long ago in 1939. It would be a miracle if he could find another job in Bayeux that would pay as much.

When the assistants had been put down outside the temporary City Hall, the colonel said more cheerfully, 'Michel, remember that nice restaurant you recommended to us last time we were here? It was great. Before we go to the airport, let's book the senator and ourselves into lunch there. We've got to make this guy happy.'

'I'm not sure that the restaurant will be open yet, Monsieur le Colonel, though you should certainly make reservations, if possible – you must have seen, last time, how busy it can become.' God, how he himself would like a meal at such a restaurant. To fill his stomach entirely with really good food.

As the colonel rapped peremptorily on the glass door of the restaurant, Michel wondered how such beautiful glass had been found to repair it. Caen had been so dreadfully bombarded that he doubted if a single pane of the city's original glass would have survived. Truly, however, you could get anything in France – if you had enough money

– lots and lots of beautiful hard currency, like American dollars or even British pounds.

Influenced by the sight of an American uniform on the other side of the precious glass, a cleaner was reluctantly persuaded to open up.

The colonel demanded a luncheon reservation.

The obsequious domestic scuttled round helplessly, looking for a pencil and something to write on. The fuming colonel provided both. He startled Michel by demanding a table for ten.

'I need you there to translate what the maître says about wines,' he explained to Michel with a wink. 'You might as well get a decent meal on the American Government, for once. Then the senator is likely to have with him at least one security guard and a secretary or similar busybody. And some kind of French official – perhaps his host for tonight – will be tagging along; someone will be there to translate for him. And, for sure, there'll be somebody from War Graves.'

The thought of eating a meal with an American senator made Michel quail. But then, was not America the place where all men were truly equal? It was an interesting thought.

Cheered up, he thanked his kindly employer for including him. He almost forgave him for dining with Barbara. That dirty-minded chambermaid could be wrong. Tonight, he would try to find out.

Chapter Twenty-five

Michel was surprised to see two limousines drawn up at the tiny airport. One of them sported a fluttering Stars and Stripes on the front of the bonnet. He eyed them enviously. Together with the chauffeurs standing near them, they looked as if they had been wrapped in tissue paper for the duration of the war. Where had the cars and the uniforms been hidden from the avaricious Germans?

He parked the battered taxi neatly behind them. The colonel got out stiffly and stared at the tidied up ruins of the airport buildings.

Michel leaned out of the cab and pointed to the shining curve of a Quonset hut. 'Over there, Monsieur.'

The colonel nodded, and with slow dignified tread, as if he were following a coffin, he went to find his guest. He had never in his life met a senator and looked forward to telling his wife in his next letter home about this present encounter.

As he walked, he comforted himself with the thought that, though the group he was about to cope with might be very élitist, he doubted if they knew as much as he did about corpses and, what was more important, the care of the mourners who usually accompanied them.

Michel watched him go. The colonel walked like an old man, he considered, not at all like a trained military man. It occurred to him correctly that as an undertaker, Colonel

Buck might be classed similarly to the priests who served armies, and not as a fighting man.

Except for the two chauffeurs chatting together and the distant sound of heavy machinery, the airport was very quiet. A windsock flipped in the breeze. A control tower, still standing, looked deserted. A small plane landed; another one took off. Michel lit one of his precious Player's, and awaited events.

A man in a dark suit hurried out of the shed-like office. He came up to the taxi and, in bad French with a strong American accent, asked Michel what he was doing there.

Offended, Michel flicked his cigarette ash at the man's feet, and asked in carefully pronounced English what business it was of his.

The stranger was obviously nonplussed by the quality of Michel's English accent. He stared at Michel – a mere peasant. Neither this driver nor his shabby vehicle fitted into the scene. He suspected there was something wrong about the taxi and its driver.

Michel watched the stranger's whole stance change to real hostility and felt it wise not to provoke the man further. He announced in his best English that he was waiting for Colonel Buck, who had gone into the office to meet an American visitor. Had the gentleman not seen him arrive? He was in American uniform.

'Humph.' The man looked again at the decrepit taxi and turned to hasten back to the temporary building into which the colonel had vanished.

Almost immediately, he returned with a gendarme, who followed him leisurely. The gendarme had been sent out that morning to add to the security of the visitor, or more accurately, to add to the visitor's sense of security. Nobody really liked the damned Yanks, but it was unlikely that, in the present circumstances, anyone would attack a senior member of the US Senate just as every newspaper was announcing that Marshall Aid was beginning to pour into the country – even if France was the last country to be granted this aid. And, anyway, thought the gendarme comfortably, it was probable that not many people even knew the visitor was coming.

So the gendarme did not hurry, particularly as he immediately recognised the taxi; it was often to be seen in Caen, creeping through the shattered streets carrying US soldiers. It was famous as the only surviving taxi in Bayeux.

Nevertheless, watched by the American security officer, he dutifully asked for Michel's driver's licence, which was equally dutifully produced by a laconic Michel.

The gendarme asked what he was doing at the airport, and Michel told him that he must have seen the American Army colonel in the airport office. He had brought him in to meet *un Américain – une huile!* Michel permitted himself a laugh. 'According to the colonel, he wants to look at cemeteries!'

The gendarme grinned, as he handed back Michel's licence. 'The senator hasn't arrived yet,' he said.

Michel allowed his eyes to shift slightly towards the impatient civilian standing behind the gendarme. 'Who's this type?' he asked in patois.

The gendarme shrugged. 'American security. Arrived last night from Paris.'

'Put him straight about me, will you?'

The gendarme nodded, and turned away. He spoke to the American, and they both went back to the airport office.

Michel took a last pull at the stub of his cigarette. How

good it would be, he considered, to be decently enough dressed and of the right nationality so that one was never at the receiving end of suspicion – or bullying. He threw his cigarette butt angrily out of the cab window. The world was mad – beyond doubt mad.

The sound of a plane circling the airport broke into his reverie. He correctly assumed that their visitor was arriving.

A few minutes later, the makeshift office decanted a whole group of civilians, with Michel's colonel and another American army officer bringing up the rear.

Together with three neatly suited civilians hunched closely round him, a small white-haired man was hustled into the car with the American flag on it.

The senator, decided Michel with a slight grin. Big politicians must get very morbid about safety to put up with such handling.

The Mayor and three other Frenchmen, gravely talking together, got into the second limousine. Michel scrambled out and opened the door of the taxi for the colonel and his fellow officer. Michel did not recognise the rank of the new man, but it was obvious from the deference with which the colonel addressed him that he was the senior rank. Michel presumed that he was the colonel's boss, a mysterious personage always referred to by the undertakers as 'the War Graves Commission'.

Michel swung back into his seat, and in his best English, asked where the gentlemen would like to go. He was given the names of two cemeteries. The first was the principal American cemetery between Colleville-sur-Mer and St Laurent.

Michel sighed. This visit would take them back past Bayeux, and westward along the coast. Obviously the senator and his handlers did not know anything of the geography of Normandy.

'Shall I lead the other cars to it?' he asked.

'No,' said the colonel. 'The car with the Mayor in it will lead off, then the senator's car, and then us. Behind us will be that blue car parked over there – that's part of his security.'

The limousines took off fast, and Michel realised that his taxi might be unable to keep up with them.

He concentrated his whole attention on keeping the taxi in the centre of the practically deserted narrow winding roads.

In his opinion, the visitors and the Mayor were unwise to allow themselves to be driven so fast on roads which had been heavily mined. Admittedly, they had been cleared and repaired, but every driver should remind himself that deeply buried mines could, even so, work their way to the surface exactly as could stones in a farmer's field. Or a stray one covered by the bocage near the verge of the roads could be shaken – and boom.

He did not care about the politicians in the limousines, but he did care about himself – and, oddly, about the colonel, whose modest status he had only really understood when he had suddenly seen him in comparison with a bunch of politicians who could command almost new limousines.

Being an honest citizen, Michel regarded politics as something unclean, which decent people did not touch. He had tolerated the Communists, because they had fought the occupying Germans, and he and Henri had sometimes worked in close collusion with them as with other maquisards; but not with politicians who travelled in limousines.

An American newsman, accompanied by a cameraman, and a local reporter wheeling a bicycle, met them at the cemetery. The cameraman took pictures of the senator putting a small wreath of flowers on a grave, and then shaking the hands of the French officials. The newsman asked a few questions of the senator and scribbled in a notebook, while the Frenchman laid his bike down on the grass and got his information from the Mayor.

They were left at the cemetery to find their own way back to wherever they had come from; Michel assumed the Americans must have American cars or motorbikes parked nearby. He wondered, with a quirk of amusement, whether their petrol would have been siphoned off before they got back to their vehicles.

In ten minutes, the little entourage was on its way to the second cemetery. War Graves was, this time, allowed to walk with the senator. Michel gathered, from his later conversation with the colonel in the taxi, that the senator wanted details of a planned memorial to be built in commemoration of American losses.

They then turned deeper into the countryside to see the battleground that had been St Lô. The senator was not allowed to walk into the devastated streets. Security felt that it was too dangerous, it having been such a frightful battle zone. Goodness only knew what awful, still undiscovered boobytrap the Germans might have set there, which nobody had bothered to remove. Foreigners were so lax, the security man explained to the senator.

A few pedestrians watched the operation. Their expressions were sullen, and, as the senator got into the car with the flag on it, a number of pithy French expletives followed him. That area of Normandy was still bleeding, the number of its French graves counted in thousands, and nobody, least of all the Americans, seemed to care.

The long drive back to Caen brought the party thankfully to lunchtime and the restaurant, outside which lounged a couple of gendarmes. They straightened up immediately they saw the approaching limousines.

At the sight of the cars, a prosperous-looking man scanning a newspaper folded it up. Watching a crowd of idlers carefully, he moved closer to the limousine with the flag on its bonnet.

He then nodded to the nervous security guard, who had swung out of the first car immediately it stopped. The door of the beflagged limousine was swiftly opened to disgorge the senator, and three other gentlemen who tightly surrounded him as he was hustled across the pavement and into the restaurant, to be met by a bowing *maître d'hôtel*.

Michel watched with interest because he had met the man with the newspaper during the war; the man had been a Partisan. Now it looked as if he were a plain-clothes policeman. Someone, he thought, must have telephoned from the airport to arrange additional security for the important visitor. It all seemed like theatre to him.

He wondered why, if they were so afraid for the senator's safety, they had not put him in the taxi or in the small blue car following after it. Then, as decoys, they could have put the uniformed men, with a civilian, in the limousine with the American flag, couldn't they?

Recollecting his duties, he quickly got down from the driver's seat, and opened the taxi door for the morticians.

Remembering his promise, the colonel said to Michel as he got out, 'Come on in. The cab will be OK with the gendarmes.'

Having been apprised by the police that it was no ordinary colonel with party whom he was expected to feed, the very experienced *maître d'hôtel* swooped down upon the group which swarmed in.

It was led by the man from the Paris Embassy. While at the airport, he had checked with the Mayor that the choice of this restaurant was suitable, and had then confirmed the reservation by telephone.

Poor Colonel Buck, who had so innocently planned an impressive lunch for the senator, found himself relegated to a secondary table with sundry unknown Frenchmen, while Michel shared a table in a corner near the kitchen with the two chauffeurs.

At first, the chauffeurs did not know what to make of Michel, a man who looked as if he should be driving a lorryload of manure, not two senior American officers in a taxi as old as the Ark.

After years of facing uniforms with terrifying power behind them, Michel was not impressed by mere chauffeurs' uniforms.

It became immediately obvious from his accent that one chauffeur was a Parisian. He tried hard to present himself as extremely sophisticated. The other proved to be a local man, privately employed by the wealthy, landed aristocrat who was to be the senator's host for the night. Michel decided that whoever had driven the blue car, which had, throughout the trip, followed the taxi in procession, must be with the bigwigs at the other table.

The three were at first stiffly polite to each other. Realising that he was at the bottom of the social heap, Michel was particularly careful about what he said. Though miserably in the background lay the problem of Barbara, his mind was largely concentrated on the coming meal.

While waiting to be served, the idea had also occurred to him that if these two could get regular jobs as uniformed chauffeurs, he might be able to do the same – once Anatole was gone. On top of his fears about Barbara, the latter thought was so painful that he could have wept; yet, some sort of plan he had to have for when the day came.

While so burdened it was difficult to think clearly, but he did decide that, before the colonel went back to the States, he would ask him for a written reference; it might help.

The three minions were not consulted about what they would like to order. A bottle of white wine, its cork loosened, was plonked on the table. Exquisitely arranged servings of three prawns, sitting on fronds of fresh dill and tiny sections of lemon, were placed carefully in front of each of them.

Was that all that an expensive lunch consisted of? Three prawns for a starving man! Lunch was surely more solid than that, wasn't it? Even for rich people who would eat well at every meal?

What's more, Michel did not know how he was supposed to eat prawns when in an expensive restaurant.

Unhesitatingly, however, each of the two chauffeurs picked one up, shucked it out of its shell and popped it in his mouth. Michel promptly followed suit and did his best not to bolt it down. A beatific smile went slowly across the faces of all three. The flavour was delicious.

Their united approval opened up the conversation. The local man confided that, when he had been a *Déporté du travail* in Germany, he had amused himself by dreaming of such luxuries.

Michel promptly told them that his brother, Anatole, had been similarly taken to Germany as slave labour and that he was now dying of tuberculosis. This led to enraged discussion of the number of French lost in Germany as a result of the mass deportation.

The Parisian elected himself host of the table, removed the loosened cork of the wine, poured half a glass for himself and a generous glass for each of the others. Then he delicately sniffed his glass and took a sip.

Having satisfied himself as to its quality, he proposed lugubriously, 'To our beloved dead.' They drank.

'And to the fifteen thousand who were shot for Resistance activities,' suggested the local man. They drank.

Michel began to feel much better. 'This will be a good meal,' promised the Parisian.

It was. Tiny dish followed tiny dish. The *pièce de résistance* was steaks big enough, the chef had ensured, to suit *les Américains* followed by a cheese board to rouse the envy of any ordinary Frenchman.

It was as well for Michel that the meal took two hours. If, on such an empty stomach, he had eaten it quickly, he might have thrown it up. And what appalling waste that would have been. He shuddered to think of it.

At the main table, the senator could be heard demanding to be taken to where the American Airborne Troops had landed on D-Day, the first day of the Normandy invasion. One of his nephews had been killed there.

Since they had, when going to the first cemetery, driven very close to the landing place, this caused some consternation amongst the French at the table. Such a visit had not been included in the hasty arrangements made from London. A sharp New York voice suggested smoothly that perhaps it could be arranged for tomorrow – it was rather a long trip to do this afternoon and still be back to address the City Council of Caen in the early evening. The Parisian cursed under his breath. 'I'm supposed to get my man back to Paris this evening,' he muttered.

The employer of the second chauffeur was heard to say in stilted English that his car and chauffeur were at the service of Monsieur if he wanted to make such a visit tomorrow morning.

'*Zut!*' muttered the affected chauffeur.

Michel sighed. He wondered if he too would have to drive up to Omaha Beach. He had warned his mother that he might be late because he had hoped somehow to see Barbara if they returned to the hotel at a reasonable hour. He would be really late if they had to go to Omaha Beach. He had, also, rather counted on having a more normal schedule the following day, so that his mother could, for a few hours, be relieved of nursing Anatole. If he failed to get hold of Barbara today and if the next day's schedule was to be upset, he must consider how to find another time and place in which to talk to her – if he could think how to broach the subject of the colonel without exploding with grief.

He wanted desperately to know exactly what had happened the previous evening. Soothed by a good meal and wine, and aware that the colonel would soon leave France, he found it difficult to believe that the amiable man had seduced her. But she could have changed her mind about himself – she could have done so for many reasons. An American would be a far better catch.

Michel admitted to himself with a grin that a full stomach and excellent wine had calmed him like nothing else could have done; his mind had begun to work in its usual careful way. In any case, common sense suggested that he had little to lose by asking her how she came to be dining with a distinctly plain, quite elderly man. But, despite any rationalisation he could think of, deep inside him sheer primitive jealousy gnawed remorselessly.

There was a shifting of chairs, while the argument continued against going so far as Omaha Beach. The drivers drained a second bottle of wine which had arrived during the meal, and hastily rose. They bade each other a friendly farewell and rolled a little unsteadily out to their vehicles.

There was still a small crowd outside, made up largely of women and white-haired men. They were interspersed with a few older youths jostling each other and making rude jokes; the jokes were being received by the other bystanders with silent, prissy disapproval. All the onlookers were being kept back in a good-natured way by the pair of gendarmes.

As the main party emerged, the senator was tightly sheltered by his security guards; the gendarmes relaxed, as he was safely packed into the back of his car.

Michel opened the taxi door, in preparation for the arrival of his two officers. They were the last to be seen out by the *maître d'hôtel*, and had paused to say something to him. Michel had his back to the main party. He idly smiled at a pretty girl in the front of the crowd. At her left stood three youths on the edge of the pavement.

The bored gendarmes turned to look at the uniformed colonel and his senior officer from the War Graves Commission, who, chatting to each other, began leisurely to move towards the taxi.

Out of the corner of his eye, Michel saw one of the youths swing his arm up.

Instantly, Michel hurled himself at him, half-twisting on his left foot, as he moved. With all his own weight behind it, he landed a deadly back heel blow at the youth's crotch.

The youth screamed, stumbled and fell backwards to the pavement. He dropped the piece of concrete which he had been about to throw at the colonel, and clutched his outraged private parts.

Unable to recover his balance, Michel staggered, tripped, and collapsed on top of him.

The other youths knocked aside the shrieking women and fled.

The gendarmes whirled round. The little crowd was scattering in all directions.

Pushed against the window of the restaurant, the pretty girl also shrieked with fright. Then, realising exactly what Michel had done, she yelled, 'Bravo! So brave!'

The struggling youth, held down by Michel, tried to bite him. Michel slapped his face hard, rolled off him and on to his feet.

The *maître d'hôtel* quickly shut the door of his restaurant and locked it. The two limousines took off like moon rockets.

The uniformed undertakers stood paralysed. Both had seen the reason for Michel's split-second move, and they were both very shaken at the unprovoked attack.

All thoughts of security had been concentrated on the wretched senator; they had not given a second's thought to their own safety.

As the startled gendarmes stared uncertainly at the cringing youth and at Michel rolling neatly to his feet, the youth tried to crawl away.

The colonel gathered his wits. Outraged, he pointed at the young man on the ground. 'Arrest him!' he ordered one of the gendarmes.

The gendarme looked nervously at him, as if he had not understood the English order. He turned to his fellow officer.

Michel raised one foot, as if he were about to kick the youth in the face. The lad lay still.

The colonel and War Graves joined the police conference, while Michel continued to guard the offender.

Finally, and, it seemed to Michel, reluctantly, the youth was manacled and made to limp round to the local police station, while the taxi carrying the two Americans was slowly driven behind them.

War Graves immediately demanded a telephone in order to call the American base. Again, this was reluctantly granted by the officer on duty; the Americans were not popular and, further, the police did not want it reported that they had failed in their duties. The Americans were, however, adamant. An incident involving the visit of an American senator had to be taken seriously.

Nobody had said a word to Michel, except to order him to follow the gendarmes to the police station. He was privately delighted to find that his daily savate practice had kept his skill intact.

I should have been able to maintain my balance, though, he upbraided himself. He forgot that a half-starved man can only do so much, and that he had probably drunk too deeply.

He was scared, however, when, at the police station, it was suggested that he had attacked a young man who had done nothing.

The colonel was immediately furious. The youth had threatened him with a piece of concrete. Did a man have to wait to be hit before the confounded, inefficient gendarmerie took action? All this in almost incoherent French.

French pride was hurt to the quick. The phone call was made. A Jeep arrived from the base. Three privates and a young officer, anxious to show off his legal knowledge, tumbled out.

The array of hated American uniforms was overwhelming. A charge of threatening behaviour was agreed upon.

By the end of the afternoon, an exhausted colonel, his two assistants, who had had a most restful afternoon doing nothing at the base, and a smug Michel, were on their way back to Bayeux, having delivered War Graves back to the comfort of his base office.

Neither the colonel nor Michel had any idea what had happened to the senator – and certainly in his present mood the colonel did not care very much. A senator who wanted to visit a foreign country, without giving time for proper arrangements to be made, could expect problems.

At the hotel, he thanked Michel heartily. 'If you hadn't spotted the man, I could have had my face smashed in.' He paused, and then grinned. 'And the lunch was great.'

'Monsieur is most welcome,' Michel responded warmly. With a full stomach and over half a bottle of wine in him, he felt he could take on the world.

The colonel hesitated before turning to enter the hotel. 'Why did the kid pick on me?' he asked curiously.

'The uniform, *je crois*, Monsieur. Only two uniforms in the party, and you are closer to him. A good target. He throw straight.'

'Is the American uniform so much disliked?'

'Not like?'

'Yes.'

Michel considered this before replying; he did not want to offend his employer. 'French in Caen lose much,' he explained finally. 'Lives, homes, work. You see how terrible is the city at present. Invasion make much damage, more than Germans. British take the city, while General Patton get to Paris. Now local people hate all uniform. Also, unfortunately, Americans are rich. Buy much food in expensive restaurant.' He shrugged. 'Maybe young man is hungry.' He smiled wryly and lifted his hands in a helpless gesture.

The colonel solemnly nodded his understanding.

Good old Michel. Colonel Buck felt that his gratitude to his driver had not been sufficiently expressed. Apart from the uncomfortable episode outside the restaurant, the man had been a godsend during the undertakers' work in Calvados because he knew the countryside so intimately. In addition, the colonel and his colleagues had never worried that he would rifle their jacket pockets or open their briefcases when left in the cab. Soon all three of them would be back in civvy street in a country largely untouched by war or shortages; and would probably never see him subsequently.

He said, 'What about garaging the taxi and then coming back here for a drink?'

Michel expressed himself delighted. 'Five minutes, Monsieur le Colonel,' he replied grandly.

Chapter Twenty-six

While heart-sick Michel had brooded dejectedly about Barbara as he drove to meet the senator, Barbara had not forgotten about Michel. How could she forget a man who had upset all her preconceived notions of what her future might be like?

She had received his message that he could not meet her at eleven o'clock, so she decided that, during the evening, she would stay within the hotel, so that he could communicate with her again, as he had promised. Meanwhile, she would explore Bayeux further.

On her way out, she paused to pass the time of day with Reservations, who, since the hotel was still trying to find a clientele again, was not particularly busy. In order to get some inkling of when Michel might return to the hotel, she asked if he knew whether the taxi would be busy for the entire day.

Reservations solemnly stated that he believed the Americans were gone for the day. There was, however, he said, already a gentleman in the hotel who wished to be taken to a Canadian grave as soon as Michel could do it, the first Canadian to come, he believed, and that Michel had already said that he would be busy for the Americans until tomorrow.

Satisfied, Barbara pulled on her black hand-knitted gloves, and, contentedly swinging her embroidered handbag, went for a long walk through the narrow, winding streets of the city.

There was, as usual, very little wheeled traffic, except for cyclists, a few horse-drawn drays and delivery vans; very occasionally, a car or a small van would slide past. Unlike in devastated Caen, pedestrians crowded the pavements, frequently spilling on to the street itself, which tended to disconcert the few drivers.

The crowd was neatly, though shabbily, dressed. Barbara noticed, with envy, that many women wearing only black, sometimes with a white blouse, had a simple elegance missing from British women. She became more aware of her own long, self-confident stride, so typically English, and of her pink clothes.

As in the Wirral peninsula, there were few young men around, and Barbara wondered if the male population was at work, or had been so seriously culled by the war that there were few of them.

Although she knew that the French Government was trying to encourage a higher birth rate, there were, compared with the baby boom only too apparent in Britain, not many toddlers either. The few that she saw clutched the hands of adults as they were dragged along the narrow pavements; they seemed to have to dodge swinging handbags or shopping baskets as best they could.

Though gaunt of face, few pedestrians looked as emaciated as Michel. But, like Britons, their faces and the way they moved suggested that they were uniformly tired and dispirited.

The black-and-white-timbered shops and houses were interspersed with even older medieval stone walls, broken by dark lancet windows and doorways. They had low doorsteps hollowed by generations of shuffling feet. As in England, there was a general lack of fresh paint. Over all, a grey sky threatened rain.

The city reminded her of Chester. Like Chester, it had not received much damage, but it had obviously become shabby from neglect while its inhabitants had dealt with more urgent matters of life – and death. And also like Chester, this city had Roman origins, she recollected. Only French signs and French chatter told her that she was in a foreign country. Again, she was impressed by the sense of a shared history.

She stopped occasionally, to peer into the windows of small shops. They rarely had much in them, but it was attractively displayed. In dress and jewellery shops no prices were exhibited. Barbara decided, with a quiet laugh, that this was probably a high-class part of town; as Liverpudlians said, if you had to ask the price of a garment, you knew it was too expensive.

She did not want to purchase anything beyond a small gift to take back to her mother; the limitations of the British laws regulating the taking of cash out of the country meant that she had to be careful of the money she spent. She had prepaid her hotel bill, including all meals, direct from England; some complicated method of international book-keeping, she had assumed, known only to travel agents; and she hoped her payment would cover the packed lunch she had shared with Michel.

She decided that she would ask Michel's advice about an inexpensive gift for her mother.

She found herself in a part of town where the streets were even narrower. They led her into a small square where lettuce, tomatoes and other spring vegetables were being offered for sale from barrows. Here, women in shawls and black skirts and blouses, hair screwed up in

286

buns on top of their heads, pinched tomatoes with worn hands and then haggled over a few sprigs of bright green parsley.

A fishmonger stood outside his little shop, fresh fish displayed in a window open to the street. He seemed to have an adequate stock, and Barbara remembered Michel saying that Bayeux was not far from Port-en-Bessin, a fishing port from which lost airmen and Jewish refugees were sometimes smuggled out of France during the war. Judging by the amount of fish displayed, some of the fishing fleet must have survived the havoc wrought by the invasion.

The fishmonger said something to her cheerfully, and though she did not understand, she laughed before passing on.

Une Anglaise, from her clothes, the fishmonger decided, and a pretty one.

She found herself on a narrow secondary road leading out of the city, and continued along it. On the verges straggled fresh growths of weeds; she did not know their names, but some were familiar to her from the land surrounding her bed-and-breakfast.

In places, the high hedges that lined her route had been broken down. Through the gaps she saw miles of flat farmland, often irregularly green. Except for one field where several brown and white cows lay chewing the cud, the landscape was empty of human beings and animals, though it looked verdant enough to sustain big herds. She noted the lack of the occasional sound of dogs barking in the distance, a sound so common in England, and that there was not much twittering of birds. Had they been casualties too?

Occasionally, she caught a glimpse of broken-down

walls; a church with a partially destroyed bell tower; a cottage set in from the road, roofless and gutted by fire.

In what must have been a hamlet, a row of tiny shops or dwellings, doorless and windowless, were sodden with rain. Ivy was already tentatively climbing one damaged wall, and round the front doorsteps rough grass was sprouting.

Further on, there was a gateway without a gate. It was cordoned off, and a sign said, '*TERRAIN INTERDIT*'. Mines, she presumed a little nervously.

She thought sadly, as she interpreted the notice, that there must be hundreds of miles of France which were off limits because of half-buried explosives. As a result, if they had survived the invasion, many countryfolk like Michel must be out of work. Michel had said that in the north there were thousands of hectares of land still full of mines and cordoned off from the days of the First World War.

How many broken lives did these untouchable lands represent, she wondered. How many of the peasant owners, together with their livestock, were dead in both wars, caught between two remorseless armies, bombed and shelled – infinitely expendable – in the violent struggles? And regarded as cowards in Britain? She began to understand the sullen faces she saw occasionally.

In her silent contemplation of it, she realised that the war had been much more complicated than she had been led to believe by the British popular press and by the newsreels in her local cinema. She remembered a remark that Michel had made – that France had been so unprepared for the war just over, that they had faced the highly mechanised German army with guns pulled by horses. And, he had said, they had been desperately short of men of call-up age.

It was beginning to rain, so she paused to button up her mackintosh. She wished she had an umbrella, but she had not been able to find one in Liverpool.

Standing in the middle of a Calvados lane, she considered herself lucky. Not only was her home still in one piece, albeit rather dilapidated, but the wind-swept seaside land on which it sat had not been mined. There was, however, a notable shortage of men of her own age in her village. It was a district of middle-class people who largely worked in Liverpool offices, and their occupations were not on the reserved list. So they had been called up. A good many of them, like George, whose cathedral could be finished after the war was won, would never come back.

Already shaken by the events of yesterday, Barbara wanted to cry helplessly, because she could not imagine how all the desolation of the war, both physical and spiritual, was going to be healed and some sort of normal life restored. Bayeux was, in her opinion, a fortunate exception; the minute you stepped outside it, the reality of the carnage hit you.

In England, there were still people around – villages with busy lanes; even badly bombed Liverpool had not been evacuated and was still quite crowded with people. Here, in Calvados, where were the country folk, the cows, the horses? Were they dead – or had they fled? If the latter, would they ever return?

Since leaving the little vegetable market, she had not met anybody; yet the vegetables she had seen must have been grown somewhere, presumably locally, by somebody.

To protect her hair from the rain, she took a scarf out of her pocket and deftly wound it round her head into a neat turban, while tears ran down her already wet face.

As she tucked in the ends of her scarf, she turned to look at the other side of the road.

On that side, there was a similar entry to a field – bocage had partially shielded her view of it as she approached along the road. Now, she was startled, because, in part, her questions were answered. She wiped her eyes with the back of her damp glove.

Standing quietly inside the gateway was an emaciated Percheron harnessed to a plough. Beside the huge horse stood a man, his beret held to his chest, his eyes closed. He was muttering something to himself. After a moment, he crossed himself and opened his eyes.

He briskly fitted his beret on to his head and said something cheerful to the horse, and turned to grasp the shafts. It was then he saw Barbara.

With a smile, he shouted something to her.

She did not understand, but thought it might be a joke, so she smiled weakly back at him. He waved, and then called to the horse. As the animal slowly began to move forward, the plough reluctantly bit into the soil.

The sight of this piece of normal life made her feel better. She wondered if French farmers always said a prayer before they commenced to plough a field. She must ask Michel.

The rain was light, but she decided to turn and walk back to town. She would try to find a café for lunch.

As she again passed the cordoned-off gate with its forbidding notice, it occurred to her that the ploughman had probably said a prayer asking for protection against any mines left in his field. Perhaps when he called to her, he had asked for her prayers, too; it could be. His stance, as he started the plough, had been that of someone bravely attacking a difficult problem. She duly sent a little prayer skyward both for the man and his horse, quite forgetting that she had decided that God did not exist. Habit dies hard.

The consideration of the ploughman's prayer led her to think about Michel. Was it that he was a farmer and she a townswoman which divided her world from his, and not necessarily his dependence on temporary employment or his need to help his family? He had brought up this fact, so it must be of some importance.

But farmers were the same the whole world over, weren't they? In England, town and country frequently mixed and intermarried.

She had little conception of the obdurate peasant roots of someone like her taxi driver, an attitude lost in northern England in the maelstrom of the Industrial Revolution. No matter what he did for a living, he would take the knowledge with him that he was a peasant, just as a Hindu knows his caste. With him, also, would be the stubborn endurance of his antecedents.

He had a quick mind, she decided.

What would he do? What could he do to get himself out of the poverty into which he had been plunged?

Barbara had seen only the outside of the house in which he dwelled, but, from her childhood experience of living in the north end of Liverpool, she could have described to the colonel what its interior was like – she could judge by the odour of it and the obvious poverty of the people in the alleyway.

His mother, thought Barbara, must be quite remarkable. But then so was Michel, for the brother must, after all, be a major stumbling block to Michel's mobility. If

Michel had been free to go elsewhere in France, she was fairly sure that he could have found himself a decent job. By no means all of France had been fought over, though its roads, railways and airports had been made a shambles by Allied bombing; the intensive bombing, at least, had been well reported in British newspapers.

She herself was an only child, a rarity in Catholic Liverpool. She thought wistfully that it must be good to have a sibling who cared about you when you were in trouble, as Michel cared about Anatole. She had little idea of the give-and-take of a family, the quarrels, the vendettas, the tears, the making up. With a father who went to sea, there had been only her mother and herself.

She had forgotten, for the moment, that the Benion brothers had, according to Michel, two married sisters, neither of whom seemed to be doing much for the invalid.

It occurred to her that it might be kind to send some flowers to Anatole, something to cheer up the beleaguered family. Flowers were not terribly expensive, she had discovered when buying a sheaf for George, particularly if you paid in English money. She would give them to Michel – he need not say who sent them. She wondered idly if Madame Dubois, the lover of roses, had, perhaps, thought of giving some roses to Michel.

Happy with this idea, she found a tiny café which offered her an omelette with fried potatoes. Except for two workmen drinking coffee in a corner, she was the only customer.

The omelette was made with fresh eggs, and she ate with gusto. Fresh eggs were rationed in England. There was, of course, a small quantity of dried egg, which she used in her bed-and-breakfast to make omelettes and puddings.

It was, however, a poor substitute, which, if it were old, could give one food poisoning.

Afterwards, she leisurely lit a cigarette and drank a cup of bitter coffee.

When the workmen had paid their bill and left, the proprietor, curious about her, came over to ask if Madame would like something more.

'*Non, merci.*' She smiled up at the woman.

'Madame is English?' the woman asked in French.

'*Oui, Madame. Je suis une visiteuse. Mon mari – un soldat anglais.*' Her voice broke suddenly, as she stumbled along in French. '*Il est mort – le cimetière.*' She hastily took her handkerchief out of her sleeve and pressed it against her trembling lips.

The owner clicked her tongue in sympathy. She said in slow French, 'My husband was also killed.'

Barbara sniffed, and said with feeling, 'I sympathise.' Then she said, her voice suddenly very weary. '*L'addition, Madame, s'il vous plaît.*'

Madame brought the bill. Barbara paid it. It was low in English money, dirt cheap.

Barbara then said in English, 'The omelette was delicious.'

Madame understood and beamed.

'Eggs – are they rationed?'

'*Non, Madame.*' She ran fingers and thumb together to indicate money.

'Expensive?' Barbara opened her hands and placed them together to indicate a handful of money.

'*Oui, Madame.*' She sounded regretful.

Barbara said goodbye and left. She cursed her small knowledge of French. She would have liked to ask where she could buy some eggs. It had occurred to her, as she

293

ate her omelette, that eggs or fruit might be a better gift for an invalid than flowers.

Ask Reservations where I might possibly get some, she thought suddenly.

She meandered back to the hotel, and went to bed for the afternoon.

As she drew the duvet over her, she thought what a relief it was simply to rest, to be able to do nothing for a little while.

As she cuddled down, she remembered with a smile a bumbling government collector of statistics visiting the shipyard in which she had worked during the war. The investigator had asked the two women labourers what they did in their spare time.

Barbara and her fellow labourer, Mavis, had laughed at her. Married working women were stretched to the limit.

Even to get to work was difficult; if they had any money, they were dependent upon erratically timed trams or buses, much reduced in number and usually packed.

To buy almost anything in the shops involved hours of queuing.

Overwhelming, also, was the constant fear within them that their men would be killed or terribly injured; it was like a nagging toothache.

All they longed for was the luxury of doing nothing. So they laughed in the face of an official representing a government which had not the slightest idea what married civilian women were quietly facing – which did not care, as long as they turned up for work.

Peace did not bring them much relief, but for these few precious days in France, Barbara felt herself privileged. She had time, time to weep for George, time to consider a glimmer of a new life, time to do nothing. Except sleep.

She knew now that her mother had been right in sending her off to see George's grave. Beyond confirming the certainty of his death, her trip was giving her the chance to get her breath again before plunging back into the problems of continuing to rebuild something of their pre-war life.

What on earth would her mother think of Michel's passionate outburst, she wondered. Would she ever understand the sudden fire of passion in her daughter which he had precipitated?

She hoped uneasily that Mam, left alone, was managing the old B-and-B all right; as soon as she returned home, she would try to persuade her to take a holiday herself – in the summertime in Blackpool. She loved Blackpool, did Mam.

Her thoughts reverted to Michel. Since he could not meet her that morning and had given her in his note no hint of how long he would be absent, she presumed that, if he could, he would try to see her in the evening, as promised.

With this hope in mind, a hope which made her feel dizzy, it was some time before she slept.

Chapter Twenty-seven

As Michel walked back from locking up the precious taxi in its garage, the euphoria engendered by his excellent lunch wore off.

It had been such an eventful day that he had, for the moment, on accepting the invitation from the colonel to have a drink, forgotten that he was supposed to contact Barbara.

Now, as he walked through the hotel's courtyard, he remembered. He hoped that Barbara would be in the hotel after he left the colonel, and that she would have a reasonable explanation for her conduct; he dare not even contemplate losing her. Yet, he knew that it was vital to keep the goodwill of Colonel Buck; he wanted a written reference from him; furthermore, in his heart, he could not help liking the man.

As he ran up the steps of the hotel, he was a little nervous about entering the lounge as a guest. He had never been in it before, except to empty ashtrays and collect dirty glasses or, latterly, to find whoever had ordered the taxi. He was acutely aware that a very shabby peasant, even a peasant wearing his Sunday best suit, might be unwelcome in a first-class hotel lounge.

With a nod to his old accomplice at the reservation desk, he asked, as if he were collecting his client, 'Monsieur le Colonel?'

'In the lounge.'

Head held high, Michel entered. He was immediately greeted by the colonel, who rose to meet him as if he were an honoured guest.

Warily, Michel took the chair offered to him. He noted that there was no sign of the colonel's two assistants, nor of the hotel manager, a prospective employer not to be offended at any cost.

'What would you like to drink?'

Michel's first instinct was to ask for an aperitif. But, if he suggested such a prelude to a meal, Monsieur le Colonel might think he expected to be asked to dinner. He settled for a glass of Calvados.

The colonel grinned, his greying moustache turning upwards at each end. 'I'll try one myself.'

So in the comfortable gloom of a wood-panelled room, they sipped Calvados together, and reviewed with amusement the quandary of the gendarmes in the police station, who at all costs did not want their superiors to know that an incident had occurred in their sector during the visit of an American senator.

'The Paris Americans – they complain?'

'I doubt it. The embassy people were gone the very second it happened; the chauffeur must have seen just a hint of trouble in his rear-view mirror.'

'*Le rétroviseur?*'

'Yes, that's the word. I doubt if anything will come of it.'

Michel gave a theatrical sigh of relief, and they both laughed. They each took a sip of Calvados.

'Tell me. Where did you learn a kick like that?'

In the best English he could muster, Michel explained the ancient art of savate, kick-boxing while wearing heavy farm boots. 'Very few men know it now – men who fight without gloves – pug . . . pug . . .' he said.

'Pugilists?' suggested the colonel.

'*Oui*. They use it long time ago,' Michel replied. Then, encouraged by the colonel, he told how, as a boy, he had been bullied at school.

'Much hurt in bad shoulder if I hit a boy who hit me,' he said ruefully. 'But my old great-uncle, who live with us when I am small, say, "I teach you. This hurt your shoulder but not so much."'

He allowed himself a small smile and another sip of Calvados. 'I learn well. In my farm boots, you understand, I kick big boy in the face – first time. Big damage. Nose bleed – lip bleed. He try to catch me. I kick again. Other boys very happy. They do not know this fighting.' His expression became grim. 'Nobody touch me again.'

He continued, 'Great-uncle teach me. Every day practise. I practise in cemetery while I wait for you – you might notice – think I dance? I am usually distant enough from the graves not to disturb anybody.'

The colonel said he had not noticed, but the cemeteries were very large, and often he and his men had to walk quite a distance from the entry road where Michel parked the taxi.

'In 1941, I win a little medal,' Michel told him shyly. 'I win a fight against another Frenchman. We do not tell the Germans about this little competition that we hold. I do a handstand kick – that hurt me. Hurt the other man more,' he finished with obvious satisfaction.

The colonel was fascinated. 'A handstand kick. How do you do that?'

'Step back from other man, face him. Do a handstand – your back is towards him – same time, swing your heels in his face. Very fast, you understand?'

'And does it hurt your shoulder to fight?'

'In a big fight, yes. One or two blows, *non*. Not like boxing or wrestling.' His voice suddenly rose with enthusiasm. 'The shoulder does not hurt so much as when I begin to learn; it is much improved. Daily exercise – it move more easily. But a handstand hurts.'

'You could be right about the exercise,' responded the colonel, as he lit a cigarette. 'I was amazed when I saw you move so fast. Maybe you could show my boys a bit of it.' He sighed. 'I'm too old. But they'd love it.'

Michel replied, with an exact Virginian twang, 'Sure, I would.'

Colonel Buck laughed. 'You sure have an ear for accent. How did you learn an English accent?'

Michel told him of the English retiree who had taught him English and how he practised at every opportunity.

'Kinda useful?'

'Dead cert,' responded Michel promptly, with a twinkle in his eye.

The colonel was amused by the colloquialism. He was enjoying Michel's company.

'Can you understand the English lady you have been ferrying around?' he enquired. 'I had dinner with her last night, and found her accent difficult.'

The colonel's casual mention of Barbara shook Michel. He did not know what to say, could only feel a resurgence of acute anguish.

He took a breath, while he told himself to stop being a fool; eating with her did not mean necessarily, that the colonel had taken her to bed as well.

Lucky man, to have a bed to take her to, he thought sardonically. Despite his misery, he wanted to laugh; he wanted to weep.

The threat to the colonel that afternoon had reminded

Michel how much he owed the fretful, older civilian, temporarily encased in a uniform; and his effort to save him from being hurt had been automatic.

That the colonel already knew of the connection between Michel and Barbara; that because he knew and was pleased about it, he would be particularly careful of her, never occurred to benighted Michel.

'Accent?' He tried to consider the question sensibly.

'Yeah. She tells me she comes from the North of England. I guess they talk different.'

Michel threw up his hands. 'All English still big problem to me. But I learn.'

'Can you write it?'

Thankful to avoid the subject of Barbara, Michel replied, 'Since the war, I not try much, but yes, I can. I write to an Englishman I know.' He added mournfully, 'Spelling *très difficile*!'

'If you know the word, you can always look it up in the dictionary,' replied the colonel, with a grin. He gestured to his top left pocket in which he himself kept a French dictionary.

'What kind of job will you look for, when we're gone?' he enquired. 'Will you still drive the taxi?'

'If Monsieur Duval wishes it. However, the taxi is old – it will not last. And there is no hope of buying a new one – or even getting parts for it. Duval is a blacksmith, and he himself makes some parts for it.' He gave his usual expressive small shrug. 'You understand it has not much future.'

The colonel laughed and sipped his Calvados. 'You're right. It must date back to the 1920s.'

'From 1928,' replied the Frenchman.

'What would you like to do?'

'If my land is not cleared soon, I try, first, to work for a poulterer who still has his land so I not forget my knowledge of hens, while I search for other work. I know much about hens and maybe I return to work in connection with them, though I long to do something else.' He cleared his throat. 'As you know, we have no public transport. I cannot do anything much, until at least I have a bicycle to ride to undamaged areas where there is work.'

He accepted a cigarette from the colonel and lit it. '*Merci, Monsieur.*' He then went on, 'The biggest problem is truly public transport, no bus – even the railway Paris/Cherbourg come only last year.

'I believe I can find work with hens. While I do this, I see what is happen in other towns – see if hotels are rebuilt, and so on. Maybe get job as truck driver or in hotel.'

As he became more animated – and the colonel, long used to listening quietly to the sorrows of the bereaved, listened attentively – Michel began to open up. 'My mother and I cannot move at present because of my brother's terminal illness,' he told the colonel. 'If I have a bicycle I could go to work, say, twelve miles away from Bayeux.'

'Bikes are hard to get?'

'Almost impossible. The Germans, in their retreat at the end, took every one they could find – buses and trucks, anything to get themselves out fast.'

The colonel thoughtfully ran his tongue round his teeth, as Michel continued, 'You know, some British troops landed with bicycles – and, later, you could find an abandoned, damaged one. Very quick they get found – and into the black!' He sighed. 'I myself have a frame. But to buy wheels with tyres and brakes on the black is not possible for me.'

'Humph, I see the problem OK,' grunted the colonel. 'Good luck to you, anyway.'

'Thank you, Monsieur.'

Colonel Buck stared emptily over Michel's shoulder towards the lobby, and wondered if he could get his hands on a bike. Then he said suddenly, 'Why, there she is. I'll ask her if she would like an aperitif.' He sprang up and went towards the lobby. 'Mrs Bishop,' he called.

She had overslept. Conscience-stricken, she had just discovered from Reservations that, yes, the taxi had returned.

If she wished to arrange a ride with the taxi driver, he had gone into the lounge to see Monsieur le Colonel, he told her. Madame would doubtless recollect, however, the Canadian in the hotel who had already arranged a trip with Reservations, about which he had yet to tell the driver.

Troubled, yet reluctant to intrude, she had decided to go in to dinner and leave Michel to contact her.

At the sound of the colonel's voice, she turned enquiringly towards him, and smiled. 'Mrs Bishop, come and have a drink before you go in to dinner. I've got Michel here.'

'That's very nice of you,' she said, a little surprised to see Michel drinking with him. He guided her to a chair between Michel and himself.

She looked at Michel and smiled.

Michel rose. He felt suddenly shy, out of his depth. He clutched his beret to his chest as he looked down at her. Simply to be so close to her jolted him.

'Sit down, sit down,' urged the colonel to him, as he flagged down the waiter, and then asked Barbara what she would like to drink. At the same time, he proffered a cigarette, which she took. He took out his lighter and lit it for her.

An aperitif was brought and they drank to each other's

good health. Michel accepted another Calvados. Then the colonel described to Barbara how Michel had saved him from being hit by a stone thrown by a young hooligan.

Barbara expressed admiration. Bewildered, Michel grinned, and said he had practised savate all his life. He was sorry that the colonel had been threatened.

'It could happen in Liverpool,' Barbara said. 'Young-sters ran loose during the war while their dads were away and there was no one to belt them into shape, and many of the dads – being seamen, like – never come home. Tearaways, those kids are. I don't know what they're going to be like when they grow up. There doesn't seem to be nobody left to tell them where they get off.'

This was all a little difficult for Michel to understand. He did, however, get the idea that France was not alone in having unruly youngsters capable of throwing rocks at Americans.

The colonel said with some curiosity, 'Last night, you said you lived in the country?'

'Oh, aye, I do. I used to live in Liverpool, but now I live in a village about ten miles out on the other side of the river.' She turned to Michel and smiled at him, gently, sweetly. She said slowly, 'Our bed-and-breakfast is a farmhouse, which's been built on to.' She gestured with her hands to explain its enlargement. Then she laughed. 'We've got nearly five acres of farmland instead of a real garden, more'n we know what to do with.' She spread out her right hand to show five fingers. 'Me mam – my mother – rents most of it out to a farmer for pasture or for hay.'

Michel was spellbound. Farmland? 'How big is five acres?' he asked.

Barbara pondered for a moment. 'I'm not sure,' she said, 'but I think it's about two hectares.'

'We own two hectares, and, before the war, we make good business on it,' Michel said impetuously. 'Eggs, boiling fowl, some roasting chickens. A cow, a little horse for the cart.' His face fell, and Barbara saw grim exhaustion mirrored in his expression. 'All gone,' he finished.

'I'm so sorry for you and your family,' she said sincerely. Then she told him about the farmer crossing himself before he ploughed.

'For land's sakes!' exclaimed the colonel. 'How strange.'

'I believe he pray not to plough a mine,' responded Michel, his tone matter-of-fact. He asked where the field was situated, and she told him as closely as she could.

He nodded. 'Ah, yes. *Les démineurs* work that side of the road for two years. Clear mines. Several farmers blow up. Always, there is one more mine!'

The colonel said flatly, 'It's too bad.'

'It's terrible,' murmured Barbara. She lifted wide blue eyes towards Michel. They were full of sympathy. 'I hope you'll not try to get to your farm before it's cleared.' She put out a hand to touch his knee, and then withdrew it shyly because the colonel was with them.

Michel noticed the half-gesture and nearly choked with desire. He caught his breath, and then replied with an effort, 'I promise, Madame. It is too dangerous. Thieves try sometimes – or a farmer. But often they are kill.'

He paused, as he remembered the fearful night of the battle, and then went on, 'Sometimes I say to my mother we walk safely away from it to Bayeux. We can walk back safe into it.' He shrugged. 'Relations of the family on the next farm try to reach the ruin house. They wish bury bodies. They walk over my land to get there. And poof – something big explode. Two man dead, one no feet.'

He clicked his tongue. 'They are stupid. Anybody want a body off land like that must ask for *les démineurs* to clear the path first.'

And Suzanne's parents may still be lying there, he thought, like so many French, with no survivor to claim them, skeletons waiting for the *démineurs*. He shivered slightly.

Barbara had listened, spellbound. She loved the French rhythm of his voice. She thought suddenly that with that voice he could sell anything.

As they looked at each other, the colonel, placidly sipping his drink, realised the real closeness between them. He remembered meeting his wife at a big dinner and the instant attraction there had been between them. Here it was, repeated before his eyes. He sighed. Happy days.

He decided with amusement that Mrs Bishop was just right for this lonely, beaten man, who had, he believed, good potential; he would do something with his life yet. She struck him as being sensible and self-assured, a woman with sound experience behind her. She would keep her head – in middleage, he guessed, she would be intensely motherly.

Despite the chaos of their countries, he hoped they would make it. He would tell his wife about them when he wrote to her later that night; she would enjoy hearing of such an unusual romance.

A very mixed-up Michel rose from his chair. 'I must go home, Monsieur. What time Monsieur wish taxi tomorrow?'

'About nine. It should be an ordinary day tomorrow.' He too got up.

'You will work in one cemetery?' This was important for Michel to know, so that while the undertakers were employed in one place, he could leave them to take a visitor to another cemetery.

'Yes. You're thinking of the Canadian who is staying here?'

'*Oui, Monsieur*. I not know he is *Canadien*. Reservations say there is message, as I pass him just now.'

'OK. You should be free from about ten. He's a big burly fellow. Very pleasant, though. Says he's from Yellowknife.'

'I take him OK.' Michel rose from his chair and hitched his trousers. 'And thank you, sir. Thank you for everything.' His voice was warm.

The colonel laughed. 'I owe you,' he said. He half-turned to Barbara. 'Mrs Bishop, come and join the boys and me at dinner. I see they've just gone in.'

Michel felt as if he had been shot. Would Barbara accept? 'Nine o'clock,' he repeated dully, looking not at the colonel but at Barbara.

As the colonel heaved himself out of his chair and helped Barbara out of hers, he repeated, 'Yeah. Nine.'

Barbara said, 'Thank you. It will be nice to have company.'

Then she stood there, smiling sweetly at a devastated Michel, as if nothing were wrong.

What was she thinking? He was desperate. In front of the colonel he did not know how to invite her for the following day. But he had to talk with her. He would be wise, he thought frantically, not to pursue her further, but almost intolerable longing told him otherwise. What was it, he cogitated, that he did not understand about her?

He bowed to her and then to the colonel, turned and clumped out, to arrange with Reservations about picking up the Canadian.

Chapter Twenty-eight

As Michel was walking through the courtyard of the hotel, he paused to pass the time of day with the gardener, whose neat bed of perennials seemed to continue to flower so well. The old man was fond of Michel, and had recommended him for the two part-time gardening jobs that Michel now did.

'You're working late, Gaston.'

'Weeds,' replied Gaston, sitting back on his heels. 'And what else can an ancient like me do to amuse himself?'

'Sit on a bench in the sun and drink Calvados. And thank the good God that you have nothing else to do,' responded Michel with a grin.

'*Zut!* You aren't married. Wait till you've got a wife to complain about prices going up and up.' He shook a muddy finger at the younger man. 'For the sake of peace, you would have to work longer – and buy less Calvados.' He laughed, and carefully hauled out some groundsel, which he put on one side as a gift to his canary.

'That's not likely. I'm not a good catch.'

'Come on, now. I complain, but marriage has much to recommend it. Who would care about an old so-and-so like me if I had no wife? Eh?' He nodded his head, and then pounced on another offending piece of groundsel. 'Tell your maman to look out for a likely girl for you with a nice little dowry – or do a little shopping yourself.'

Michel had to laugh. 'First I get a decent job. Then I think about it,' he promised.

Then he winced. How could he say that once Anatole died, he would be free to go anywhere a decent job was offered – and only after that could he think seriously of marriage?

He watched the gnarled fingers deftly moving in and out between the plants.

Do a little shopping yourself? But the only person he wanted was Madame Barbara, and he dreaded her being influenced by three very presentable and kindly Americans.

It was ridiculous. What if Barbara believed in him, wanted him, despite her inexplicable fraternisation with the Americans?

He stood uncertainly in the peaceful, darkened court-yard. Despite good food and wine, he felt spiritually drained; dreadfully aware of his own inadequacies when compared with a rich American.

He did not need to shop, he decided, as he stood watching Gaston. If he wanted Barbara, he had to fight for her, carefully and cunningly, not simply watch her being taken away from him.

Why not?

Father Nicolas had counselled acceptance of fate, and prayer for strength. But he had also, in his gentle under-standing way, been quite interested in Barbara. Once he knew she was a Catholic, he had not condemned Michel for looking at her, even though she was English. Was the *bon père* wiser than he?

Tush, what did a priest know about love? Or the need to defend the beloved?

'*Merde!* I forgot something,' he said to Gaston, his

mind made up. He turned on his heel and went back in to the reception desk.

'What time does the Canadian want to go out to the cemetery?' he enquired. 'And I need to leave a note for Madame Bishop. Give me a pencil and a piece of paper.'

The receptionist automatically put a pad of scrap paper and a pencil in front of him. 'Monsieur Cardinal said that you are to set the time. I told him that the Americans hold a lease on the taxi, and that you must attend to them first.'

'OK,' replied Michel automatically, as he pondered. Better meet her after I've brought the Americans back home at the end of the day, he decided, and then he wrote in French, 'Six p.m. courtyard entrance. Michel Benion, taxi driver.'

He felt that it sounded businesslike enough, if Reservations should read it.

He watched while the receptionist put the note in a pigeonhole behind him, and then he said, 'Tell Monsieur Cardinal 10.30 a.m.' He'd get him safely back before he had to fetch the Americans from their cemetery. This time Reservations wrote the note and put it in another pigeonhole.

Michel wished him good night, and then went to use the public washroom.

Back in the courtyard, he said *au revoir* to Gaston, who was slowly getting to his feet, having won his battle with groundsel.

The old man grinned a toothless grin. 'How's your brother?' he asked, as Michel went by.

'As usual,' replied Michel, 'thank you.' It had been a long day, and he felt he had drunk too much Calvados, but his mood lightened when he remembered that he would certainly have an interesting story to amuse Anatole.

He was late, and, as he loped down the streets to his home, he hoped Maman and Anatole had had a peaceful day.

His mother heard him as he ran lightly up the stairs. She smiled slightly. It sounded more like her lad. So often he plodded up, torn with weariness.

She was used to men who worked to absolute exhaustion. That was life. But, in her heart, she had hoped that Michel might escape from it by entering the Church. Though many families gave a child to the Church, as far as she could recollect, no Benions had done so in three generations.

Then her husband had shown her the benefit to the family of an alliance with the Fortiers next door. She had immediately agreed. The young couple had been friends and neighbours all their lives and Suzanne was a hard-working girl; she would not be too difficult to live with.

Now, as she heard his almost boyish run up the stairs, Madame Benion wondered if perhaps the lad still had the energy to study for the priesthood – though how she would run the poultry farm, if it was decided to restart it, without either Anatole or Michel to help, she did not know.

Though Michel had probably never considered who would inherit Anatole's share of the land, Anatole himself had. With the aid of Father Nicolas, he had made a simple will, leaving all he possessed to his brother. When Maman herself died, her own share of their land would automatically be divided between her remaining three children.

She glanced over at Anatole. He was sleeping peacefully. The doctor had called that day and had increased slightly the sedative he was free to take as needed.

Monsieur le Docteur had been most kind; in fact, he had sounded too kind – she was very apprehensive about it.

As she showed him out into the stairwell, he had taken Madame Benion's hand, and said, 'If he has difficulty in swallowing his pills, call me immediately and I'll come and give him a shot.'

She had wanted to cry, first at the merciful kindness of the busy physician, but also because it sounded as if the boy's time was near; if he expected that Anatole might not be able to swallow, it would be the end. And how I am going to face it, I don't know, she thought. There is no more strength in me.

Now, however, she rose to greet her baby with a cheerful smile on her worn face. Was there not a whole pot of chicken and vegetables with a full ration of bread awaiting him?

As usual, he opened the door quietly and glanced first at the bed by the window. Then he came to his mother, put his arms round her and kissed her on both cheeks.

'A good day?' she whispered.

He made a face. 'No tips. It was a good day, though. After supper, I'll tell you and Anatole all about it.'

'Yes, do.' Then she announced with pride, 'I promised chicken, and chicken it is. Do you want to wash first?'

'No. I washed in the hotel.' He did not mention that the hot water in the hotel lavatory had been a real luxury, even if there was no soap.

He paused uncertainly in the middle of the room. 'Would you like to wait for supper until Anatole wakes up?' he asked. 'Monsieur le Colonel stood me a good lunch, so it will be easy for me to wait.'

His mother looked doubtfully across at her elder son. 'I think that, if we're quiet, he'll sleep for a couple of hours yet. While he was here, the doctor gave him a slightly higher dose. Anatole was complaining of pain in his left side.'

Michel turned uneasy eyes upon his mother. 'It's usually his right side which bothers him. What are we to do if he wakes and he's still in pain?'

'As long as he can swallow it, he can have another pill.' Maman wrapped her hands tightly in her apron. 'I'm to send for the doctor immediately if he can't swallow.'

Michel wanted to ask if, in such circumstances, they should also send for Father Nicolas. He did not wish, however, to frighten his mother unnecessarily, so he nodded his head, and said, 'Then, I'll go down to the kitchen and get the soup pot for you.'

His mother agreed, and went to the little cupboard to get out bowls, spoons, and a loaf of bread. She had wrapped the bread in a damp cloth to keep it from drying out, and she now carefully unwound it and laid it, together with a knife, on a bread board. She then put everything down on the floor beside the mattress on which she slept.

Most of the inhabitants of the rooming house ate their main meal at midday, so, when Michel entered it, the stone-floored kitchen was empty and the fire was low. At the side of the stove, the soup cauldron seemed comfortably hot when he picked it up.

As he slowly climbed the stairs again, their landlady came out of her living room and peeped down at him over the banisters.

'Ah, Michel. How goes it? Are you feeling all right now?'

He stopped and looked up at her. 'Yes, Madame. I am sorry that I caused such a disturbance. Thank you for allowing Father and me to use your sitting room.'

'It was nothing.' She waited hopefully for a further explanation. Holding the soup pot carefully by its hooped handle, he told her frankly that he had lost his best friend in the war – tortured by the bloody Boches – and he had suddenly remembered it in all its detail at a time when he was very weary.

Her eyes were full of pity, as she replied, 'You poor man.' Her huge bosom heaved, as she added, 'We all have such memories, Monsieur, either of the Germans or the Allies and their invasion. It's a cross which we must bear for the rest of our lives.' She leaned more comfortably upon the banister, and then said, 'I'm relieved that Father Nicolas was able to comfort you.'

'He was very good, Madame. He understood – better than a doctor.' He did not tell her that Father Nicolas had warned him that a lesser outburst could occur again, and that he should let himself cry freely – and, perhaps, find a friend with whom to talk it out.

She smiled, heaved herself upright, and let him pass on up the stairs with his burden. Madame Benion was fortunate in having still one son who was fit and well. She sighed lustily again. Her own son was in gaol, doing time for looting – so stupid to get caught.

While his mother was dishing out the chicken stew, Michel went quietly to his brother's bedside. He was so thin that old friends would not have recognised him as the big silent man who could shift a henhouse to a new position without even taking an extra breath. Now each breath, though shallow, seemed an immense effort. A day's beard showed very black against a skin like ivory; even the lips lacked colour and the girlish rose on each cheek, which was a symptom of his disease, had vanished.

'Come and have your supper,' hissed Maman, careful not to raise her voice.

With a heavy heart, Michel sat down cross-legged on the mattress to eat.

The chicken was delicious. Although he had enjoyed one good meal that day, he was quite ready to eat again. 'Maman, you're a wonderful cook,' he told her. And for a few special moments she was happy.

As he wiped a last piece of bread round his dish, he asked, 'Maman, do you think it's time for Anne-Marie and Claudette to be told to come to see Anatole? They've been good about sending stuff for him, though they've never been near us since *la tuberculose* was diagnosed.'

His question cut like a tiny knife into his mother's heart. Ever since the doctor's visit that morning, she had been worrying over the same question.

She understood perfectly her daughters' fear of the deadly disease and of carrying it to their children. It had not stopped her, however, from occasionally feeling a dull resentment that they lacked the courage to come to see her.

After all, she was their mother, wasn't she – and it was Anatole, their own brother, who was dying? Did they never think how much both of them would have enjoyed a visit from them? And if Michel could, fearlessly, day in and day out, wash and shave his brother and could, as necessary, empty the bloody contents of his bowl for him, surely they could come and stand by his bedside for a few minutes, to ask him how he was.

Madame Benion admitted cautiously to Michel, 'Perhaps they should.' Then she burst out, 'I know it's been difficult to get here from Rouen, but now they could come by train – or perhaps Guy could give them a lift in his lorry.'

Though he agreed that Claudette and Anne-Marie had not made much effort, he did not wish to damn them any further in his mother's eyes.

He replied cautiously, 'We could ask Guy next time he comes – he could bring one at a time, perhaps.'

'I'll write to them tomorrow, and suggest it.' His mother dipped another piece of bread into her stew, and chewed it while she reflected. Her face was carefully expressionless, as she finally said, 'I think they should come soon.'

Suddenly the joy of eating two good meals in one day vanished. Michel said dully, 'Yes, Maman.' It was difficult to swallow his last piece of bread.

Since his return home, Anatole had been a heavy and frustrating load to carry. But he had been a steady moral support to his younger brother, someone to talk to, someone to crack a joke with; someone who had, for months, read the newspapers and had, in spite of his weakness, retained a lively interest in matters political where farmers were involved. Pressed by the need to earn every penny he could, Michel had little time to read the papers; he would have been sadly ignorant of what was going on if Anatole had not told him. His radio, which he had clung to all through the occupation, had been lost in his ruined home.

There was something deeper, too, between the brothers.

Nursing the dying is not a one-way street; at no other time does the communion of two persons become so intense. Michel's ideas of what was important in life had shifted completely, as he and Anatole faced the finality of death together.

Michel slowly put down his empty bowl.

'You must accept,' Father Nicolas had said. 'God does not give you a burden greater than you can bear; suffering brings understanding – and wisdom. Be patient, my son; this too will pass. And life has a way of bringing compensations, not necessarily in money, but in human regard and in understanding of God's Will.'

Good advice, no doubt. But hard to accept, when you wanted to scream to high heaven, because you are going to be so terribly alone.

His mother was putting the lid back onto her big black soup pot, as he said carefully, 'Do you think we should send for Father Nicolas – for Anatole?'

Chapter Twenty-nine

The next morning, his mind still engrossed by thoughts of his struggling brother, mixed incoherently with how he should deal with Barbara that evening, Michel filled up the taxi from Monsieur Duval's pump.

The Americans were dependent, to a degree, on the honesty of the Frenchman regarding the use of the fuel. The colonel was supposed to keep a note of his group's mileage in the vehicle; but he never did. Routinely, therefore, Michel entered against the Americans' account more petrol than he had put into the cab. This small swindle did not bother his conscience; he owed Duval something for getting him the job.

As to most Europeans at the time, the Americans seemed so immensely rich to him that he believed that they would never even notice such a small peccadillo. If they wanted to protect themselves, Michel would have argued, Elmer or Wayne could have come each morning and checked on him.

It was not as if they were using the taxi to help forward the repair of desperate, ruined Normandy, Michel always felt a little resentfully; they were simply taking their own dead home, a luxury that only the richest country in the world could afford. How much did they care about French dead packed into every churchyard in Calvados?

While fraught with great anxiety about what might be happening at home, he absently dusted the seats and wiped over the bonnet and windscreens. And then there was Barbara; it was only a few days since she, too, had wept her heart out for someone dead, he reminded himself. What was going on in her mind?

He himself was very sleepy. Anatole had woken in the small hours of the morning. Michel had managed to warm a few tablespoonsful of soup for him on the kitchen's banked-up fire. The invalid had drunk them sip by sip, but had refused little bits of bread dipped into the liquid. Then his mother had crushed a pill and mixed it with water. He took it eagerly. It made him cough when he swallowed it, but, with the aid of a little more water, most of it seemed to go down. Then, Michel held his hand until he eventually slept again.

He had been still asleep when Michel left for work.

Filled with silent dread, Michel had loathed leaving his mother. But what he earned from his taxi driving made all the difference in their lives; and Anatole had to have a decent burial when he finally left them. That hardly bearable thought would take every centime they had – and they would probably still be in debt. And what would he do if Barbara also left him? It was too painful to contemplate.

He greeted his Americans with his usual friendly grin, duly deposited them at the cemetery, and was back at the hotel in time to collect the Canadian visitor.

While he waited for the man to be called, he looked around for Barbara, but could not see her. He hoped she had received his note of the previous evening. Though he yearned intensely to take her to a quiet place and really talk with her, he did not feel inclined, for the moment, to spend much time away from home. Warned by instinct, he knew that it was paramount that he should go home as soon as he could.

The burly Canadian, his huge hooded jacket flapping open, wore boots of a quality even greater than those of the Americans, Michel noted enviously. Under his big jacket he sported a checked flannel shirt, unlike anything Michel had seen before. A camera was hung round his neck.

'Hi,' he said. 'Know where this place is, eh?' He thrust a card under Michel's nose.

'Sure,' replied Michel in English, and named his price.

The man nodded. 'OK.' Then, as he climbed into the taxi, he asked, 'You speak English?'

'Yes, Monsieur.'

'Jeeze! You come from Quebec, maybe?'

'No, Monsieur, I was born here in Calvados.'

'Humph, my grandfather spoke French, but I never learned it.'

Michel nodded politely, and then asked, 'Monsieur has, perhaps, a brother in the cemetery?'

The man grunted. 'No. My boy cheated on his age and joined the Army. Wanted to see Europe, I guess. Silly bugger. He was only seventeen.'

'My sympathy, Monsieur.'

To Michel, the Canadian was a curiosity, and when the man began to take an interest in the country through which they passed, he answered him at length, and pointed out where the Canadians had made their breakthrough towards Caen. Michel stopped the taxi, at this point, while Cardinal got out to take some photos.

'Were you in the Army?' he asked Michel, as he put his camera back in its case.

'No, Monsieur. I was exempt. One shoulder is damage.' Then he felt a little annoyed, and, in defence of his apparent lack of valour, he said, 'I help the Resistance.

Resistance blow up railways, bridges, roads, telegraph poles. Make life hard for the *sales Boches*. Hide British airmen and spies.'

Because the Canadian wanted to know everything: about the shortage of transport; the story of the antique taxi; life under the Germans; what might have happened to his son; what the invasion was like, Michel's troubles at home were relegated to the back of his mind. His English was stretched to its limit while he tried to cope with this inquisitive Canadian – so very unlike the Americans.

While a cemetery gardener led the Canadian to his son's grave, Michel, with time on his hands, discreetly did his kick-boxing exercises, poised on one leg, turning on his heel, particularly to practise to keep his balance perfect – he did not want to be in another fight where he stumbled as he had done on the previous day.

To the returning Canadian, he looked like a ballet dancer.

The Canadian paused by the cab, to take several views of the cemetery, and then took a picture of the taxi.

'Like to do that high kick again? I'd like a photo of it – you must be a dancer.' He sniggered; to his way of thinking, a male ballet dancer was almost certainly a homosexual and therefore to be despised.

Michel's lips tightened. He said primly, 'I'm a kick-boxer.'

'A what?'

'A kick-boxer. I fight. It hurt terrific.'

The Canadian became a little more circumspect. 'Never heard of it,' he said, and sighed.

His mind was really on his stupid imp of a son; if he had no kid to leave it to, what was the use of an excellent business as a hunting guide, with a fishing lodge, to boot, to which he had clung through the worst recession in history. He was an ass to have come on this trip. It had just made him feel bad.

Michel had sensed the slur in the man's earlier remarks, and would have dearly loved to kick him. The sigh, however, reminded him that this peculiar person, who at this moment looked like a ferocious bear on a bad day, was presumably mourning, just as his previous passengers had been. So he swallowed his anger and enquired if Monsieur wished to return to the hotel.

'Yeah, I suppose. You stop when I tell you. I wanna take some more photos.'

'Of course, Monsieur.'

Michel began to wonder if he would get back in time to collect his Americans.

'I want a picture of some ruins.'

'Yes, Monsieur. Ruins from the war?'

'Yeah, what else?'

'We have ruins that are very ancient, even Roman ones.'

'Humph.'

So they stopped at several villages that were little else but heaps of stone and slate.

Where the outer walls of a farmhouse still stood, the Canadian had to be restrained from plunging into it.

'Monsieur, it may be mined,' Michel yelled at him.

The man laughed. 'You're kidding? The war's bin over three years now.'

'No, Monsieur. I insist. You must not go in.'

'Gonna kick me, if I do?'

Michel wondered if he should. He said diffidently, 'If Monsieur insists on killing himself, who am I to stop him? Madame, your wife, however, lose a husband *and* a son.'

The man laughed as he absently lifted his camera and snapped a broken tree. 'Her? She left Gary and me years ago. Don't even know where she is.'

Michel was shocked. At least with Suzanne he knew where she was.

He said in conciliatory tones, 'Life is precious, Monsieur. You are not old yet. You live in a fine country. You have much to live for. The future – it still wait for you.'

The Canadian lost his sardonic expression. He was suddenly all attention. 'The future's still waiting for me?' He was quiet for a minute, and then he said in a puzzled way, 'Nobody ever said that to me before.'

Michel, anxious to get the man safely back into the taxi, simply changed the subject by suggesting briskly that he must be in need of lunch and that the hotel was the best place in Calvados to get it. And, incidentally, had he tried a glass of Calvados yet? 'It is an excellent drink.'

'No,' said his passenger, his bumptiousness drained from him. 'But I sure need a glass of something.'

Michel glanced at his watch, and decided that, for once, he would chance being late. This man needed to ease his misery. 'We can stop at a little bistro in the next village, if Monsieur wishes,' he said.

'I'd like that.'

So Michel took him into a tiny place, which had been, until the invasion, the front room of a private house, and after checking with him, ordered a Calvados. He regretfully refused one for himself on the grounds that he had to do the driving.

'Get me another,' ordered the visitor.

'You realise it is very strong, Monsieur?'

After downing a second glass, Cardinal obviously felt better. He leaned back in the taxi, closed his eyes and never said a word until they arrived in Bayeux. With a practised eye, Michel occasionally glanced at him through his rear-view mirror; even this bear of a man was mourning, no doubt about it. A nap would probably do him good.

At the hotel, Cardinal laboriously counted out the fare in French francs, and gave a tip that seemed small compared with some of the British and American ones Michel had received.

Chapter Thirty

Michel sat for a minute or two outside the hotel gate. Though the trip with Monsieur Cardinal had taken him longer than expected and he had not much time, he contemplated going home to see how Anatole was. He decided, however, that it would not be safe to park the taxi in front of his home while he ran up the stairs. Further, he doubted if he had the skill to turn it in such a narrow space, in order to get out of the alley – and to back it out would be equally hazardous.

Wiser to go to collect the morticians, he decided. Since their work was coming to an end, they might be glad to see him a fraction early.

Barbara was sitting peacefully in a corner of the hotel lounge window. It was very quiet; all the other visitors appeared to have gone out. She enjoyed looking at Gaston's efforts in the garden. Today, he was pegging a trailing plant up the twelve-foot garden wall, using a mallet to hammer in, with rapid taps, the hooks to hold it; she therefore had not heard the taxi arrive in the street outside, nor did she notice, rather later, a murmur of voices as the Americans went through the foyer.

She had received Michel's note, and had, to pass the time, brought some knitting downstairs with her. She was concentrating hard on a design of chains up the back of a cardigan intended for her mother. She had found the wool offered without clothing coupons in the market at Birkenhead; she had asked no questions and had thankfully bought it at a price much higher than if she had tendered coupons; her mam, she had determined, was going to get a decent birthday present.

A huge, ungainly man plonked himself into a basket chair near to her; it creaked threateningly.

The sunbeams pouring through the window lit up her bronze-coloured hair and her pleasant face. She glanced up at him and recognised the Canadian she had seen once or twice before in the hotel.

She smiled shyly, and then returned to counting her stitches carefully.

The new arrival shouted across the room to the barman in English, 'Hey, you, bring me a large Calvados.'

The barman caught the word Calvados and turned to fill the order.

The Canadian twisted himself back to examine Barbara in more detail.

Not bad.

He enquired fairly politely if she would like a glass of Calvados.

'Oh no, thank you,' she replied, with a little laugh. 'It would be too strong for me.'

He was surprised to receive a reply in English. 'You from England?' he asked.

'Yes, I am,' she replied, and picked up her third needle in order to turn a chain.

His drink came, he gave his room number and initialled the bill.

He picked up the drink and sniffed at it suspiciously to make sure that it was the same drink that he had had while with Michel. Satisfied that it was, he tossed about a third of it down in one swallow.

Watching him out of the corner of her eye, Barbara expected a sudden splutter. But he swallowed it as if it had been lemonade.

'Watcha doing in Bayeux?' he asked.

Caught off guard, Barbara dropped her knitting in her lap. Her lips trembled, as she replied, 'I came to visit my husband's grave.'

The man took another gulp of Calvados.

'I've been to see my boy's. Sold the hunting lodge a month back, and didn't know what to do. So before I settle down again, I came to take a look at this place.'

Barbara looked at him gravely. 'Me mam says you must see where a person is buried – to convince you that – that – a person is really dead. Otherwise, you might look for them for the rest of your life. This last week, I've begun to think she's right. She should know. Me dad was lost at sea.'

'Too bad.' The bear drained his glass and called for another. Then he leaned forward as if to impart a confidence.

He said, a little laboriously, because his thoughts seemed to be becoming muddled, 'You know, when I saw that cross over Gary, I was so lonely; I couldn't believe how lonely I was. The cab driver, he knew it, you know; and he told me not to give up. The future's still waiting for you, he said.' The man paused in an effort to clear his muddled thoughts. Then he remarked, 'He's a real oddball.' His last words were slurred.

He looked her over lasciviously, and went on, 'Mebbe you're my future waiting for me.'

His fresh glass of Calvados arrived. He drank it in one straight draught as if he were a Russian drinking vodka.

Barbara decided to retreat. She rolled up her knitting and said quickly, 'I must go.'

He caught her arm as she edged out round a coffee table. He said, 'You don't need to go. Stay'n be company.'

She pulled away, and dropped her knitting. He laughed, and held on to her.

She glanced hopefully at the barman. The barman had discreetly pressed a button that he had not had to use since the Germans left. It rang a warning at the desk of the concierge.

'Let me go,' snarled Barbara angrily; she'd seen this type before in Lime Street.

His gorilla-like grip tightened as he sprawled in his chair. She pulled hard, and carefully ground her high heel into his instep.

His boot protected him from the worst, but the jab through the tongue of the boot was still painful. 'Getting nasty, eh?' Still holding her, he rose unsteadily to his feet.

Scared, she pulled again as hard as she could, and he immediately let her go. Released, she stumbled and fell headlong over another small table, hitting her head on a wooden chair arm.

He had played an old trick on her, and he roared with laughter.

The barman urgently pressed his button again, and then came quickly round the bar to help her. Wakened from his afternoon snooze in his chair behind his high desk, the concierge, a heavy-set man, ran in, followed closely by tall, thin Reservations.

Barbara scrambled out of the way, and got to her feet.

'What's up?' asked the concierge. Then, viewing with shock the trickle of blood on Barbara's face, he asked in alarm, 'Madame? Are you all right?'

Swaying on his feet, the Canadian gazed round at the sudden muster of men. He was at least a head taller than any of them, and was used to bar-room brawls.

'Nothing's up,' he announced ponderously. 'Silly bitch tripped up.'

He underestimated the experience of the men facing him. The barman winked at his friends and bent to move the coffee table. The concierge stepped smartly behind the Canadian, and the man suddenly found himself in a hammerlock applied with the full force of a heavy man, and a right arm round his throat that threatened to throttle him.

Nevertheless, he ruined a couple of tables, sending ashtrays, a planter and numerous magazines flying, as they fought to get him out.

The noise brought the *maître d'hôtel* from the dining room, who snatched up the phone on the reservations desk and called the police.

The Canadian managed to shift himself sufficiently to bite the concierge's arm. Outraged, the concierge tightened his hold. The man collapsed suddenly from pressure on his windpipe, and the concierge let him drop to the floor.

Help seemed to be arriving from all sides, so Barbara picked up her knitting and fled to her room.

Sorely shaken, she went to the sink, and peered at her face. She had a small cut above her right eye, and a big purple bump was rapidly materialising around it.

She hastily wrung out her face flannel under the cold tap and applied it. Then, still holding the pad to her eye, she flopped down on the end of the bed, and began to cry, the helpless crying of someone defeated.

She cried because her hard-won peace had been shattered. Rested, diverted by her taxi driver, the change from home had done her a lot of good. She had begun to think more sensibly – and on her dressing table, wrapped in newspaper, lay six eggs, the result of a walk to the market that morning, a present for a sick man whom she did not know.

Sitting in the window after lunch, with time to knit while she waited for Michel, she had been quietly content.

Now, she felt weak and vulnerable, and wished George had been there to give the oaf a black eye.

Though an experienced businesswoman in her own country, it had taken considerable courage to organise this visit to France, her first trip abroad, and she felt she had done very well in managing alone. Now, the unexpectedness of the attack had shaken her confidence and she was not so sure.

She was still sniffing miserably while sitting on the end of her bed, trying with shaky fingers to get her knitting back onto its pins without dropping any more stitches, when there was a polite knock at her door.

She put down the knitting and rose. The knock came again, so she opened the door and peeped out.

There stood the dignified, English-speaking manager of the hotel, and behind him a housekeeper with a tray with a cup of coffee on it.

'Dear Madame, I hear you have an injury from a drunkard in the lounge. Indeed, I see that it is so. My sincere regrets, Madame. Thérèse, here, has brought some coffee and will help you. Would Madame like to see a doctor?'

The concern made Barbara want to weep again. She assured the anxious manager that the damage was not serious, and she would love the cup of coffee.

'When you have had time to collect yourself, Madame, the gendarmes in my office would like to ask you how it happened.'

He stepped back to allow Thérèse into the bedroom; she put the cup on the bedside table, and stood waiting for orders.

All the fear of police learned in the slum from which she originally came surfaced in poor Barbara. She muttered, 'Jesus Mary!' Then she added hastily to the manager, 'Thanks for the coffee. I'll be down in a couple of minutes.' She also thanked the maid, and said she could manage.

Management and maid retreated.

She thankfully gulped down the coffee, and then hastily rinsed her eyes, reapplied lipstick and powder, and replaced a couple of kirby grips in the curls piled on top of her head.

Feeling nervous of foreign police, even if they were, presumably, on her side, she went downstairs to the manager's office.

There was no sign of the Canadian; he had been removed to a police van outside the gate.

There were two policemen who both rose as she entered, and they noted immediately the cut and bruise over her eye, which was rapidly becoming black; no amount of face powder would disguise it.

They asked her what happened, and she explained. The manager translated.

'Madame does not know this man?'

'No, I saw him in the hotel restaurant last night, that's

330

all. Today, I think he became very drunk quite quickly. He drank two big glasses of Calvados as if it were lemonade.'

'Surely not?'

There was a rapid explanation from the manager.

'What was that all about?' Barbara enquired of the manager; the flow of language had been bewildering.

'I said that I had had Polish troops in here who could do that easily. If we had vodka, they would drink it steadily until they fell to the floor.'

'Does Madame wish to lay a charge?' enquired one gendarme. 'Perhaps Madame should consult a doctor to confirm that her injury has not seriously affected her eye?'

The hotel manager kindly translated for Barbara.

Barbara hesitated. She had no wish to face a court case; goodness only knew how long that would take.

She smiled sweetly at the elder gendarme, and said that she did not. The man had just come from seeing his son's grave; it was understandable that he would need a drink, and she did not think he had realised how potent good Calvados was.

She turned to face the manager. 'I think my eye's OK, except I won't look too good for a day or so.'

Rapid-fire conversation ensued between the manager and the police. She did not understand a word of it, so she said, 'Excuse me, may I go now?'

All the men rose and she thankfully went upstairs.

Someone, presumably Thérèse, had put a bowl of ice cubes on the dressing table, and a small towel.

She never saw the man again. She hoped he had not been charged for brawling, that he had paid the hotel, and that he had found his future waiting for him somewhere far distant from either France or Britain.

Chapter Thirty-one

Michel brought the morticians safely back to the hotel early, and there was still an hour before he was to meet Barbara. He garaged the taxi, and walked home as quickly as he could.

He was relieved to see Anatole lying quietly in his bed, his eyes open. Maman was napping on her mattress. She sat up quickly, and asked in a sleepy voice, 'You are home so early?'

He lied that he had still to report to Monsieur Duval, which he did about once a week, mostly to say how well the taxi was standing up to steady use, and, sometimes, to get a minor repair.

'I came to see how you both were,' he said brightly, relief obvious in his voice.

'We've had a quiet day, haven't we, Anatole?' Maman said.

Anatole smiled faintly.

'He doesn't feel like eating,' Maman remarked, as she recoiled the bun on the top of her head. Then she added pointedly to Michel, 'He drank some water – and swallowed his pills, like a good lad.'

So it's not quite yet, Michel considered with relief.

Though in his saner moments he would have said that he no longer believed in God, as he drove he prayed frequently to the medallion of St Christopher which hung from the rear-view mirror in the taxi. He begged that, despite the blatant evidence of his steady decline, Anatole would recover.

Now he went over to his brother, took his hand and held it gently, as he sat down beside him very carefully so as not to shake the bed.

Anatole did not say anything, but Michel felt the small pressure of a squeeze on his hand. He heaved a sigh. 'I must go back. I have also to find the colonel again. He left his cap in the taxi.'

He refused his mother's offer of a hot drink. 'Back about half-past seven, Maman.' He got up, and bent over Anatole, to kiss both cheeks. Then he turned to his mother, who was struggling to get up off the palliasse. 'Want a hand, Maman?' he asked mischievously; she hated to acknowledge that she was getting a little stiff.

'*Merci. Non.* I'm not that old yet.'

There was a faint gurgle of amusement from Anatole: nothing could have done more to cheer up Michel.

'She's with the manager?' exclaimed Michel, a little surprised. 'Is something wrong? I'm supposed to pick her up now.'

Reservations shrugged, and then grinned. 'Ask Monsieur le Patron.'

'Is Colonel Buck in?'

'*Non.* He went across the road to get a haircut. Incidentally, he's lost his cap.' Reservations' usually immobile face cracked into a small grin, as he added, 'He looked undressed without it.'

'He left it in the taxi. I'll walk across and give it to him. Then I'll come back here for Madame Bishop.'

Colonel Buck looked quite quaint draped in a barber's towel. He was, however, grateful for the return of his cap.

Michel spent a few minutes in courteous nothings with the colonel and the loquacious barber, and then strolled back to the hotel.

'Madame has just gone up to her room,' Reservations announced. 'I told her that you had come. She'll be down in a few minutes.'

Michel nodded, and was about to cross over to the concierge's little office, to pass the time of day with him, when the door of the manager's office opened and *le patron* ushered out two police officers. He had noticed a police vehicle parked to the side of the garden gate, as he came in. Another petty theft, he had supposed.

The concierge was not at his post, neither was his underling, who helped with luggage; he was in the kitchen, having a small wound in his arm bound up by a solicitous and excited chambermaid. Cardinal had succeeded in making a small nick sufficient to cause a trickle of blood. The tough keeper of the gate, adviser to guests and general factotum was rather enjoying being a hero in the kitchen.

When Barbara, still feeling rather shaky, descended the stairs, therefore, Michel was completely unprepared for a lady with a well-powdered, but extremely obvious black eye. Apart from her handbag and gloves, she had a small newspaper parcel in one hand.

Just in time, he remembered ever-nosy Reservations, and he did not cry out. His face was expressionless, as he asked gravely, 'Madame is ready?'

Madame nodded assent as she steadied her parcel against her chest. Michel opened the front door and she swept through it.

Outside the courtyard gate, all thought of her dinners with the Americans went out of his head. He turned to her, shocked, '*Chérie*, what happened?' He lifted his right hand and tenderly stroked her cheek below the bruise. 'Tell me. Shall I take you to a doctor? I know a good one.'

She smiled, and replied, 'No, no, it's not that serious. Let's go and sit in the cathedral garden, and I'll tell you.'

He was profoundly upset. He thought of the clock ticking mercilessly towards 7.30, but did not care. His darling little English lady so hurt!

He turned her quickly and almost ran her towards the garden, regardless of the fact that she might be unsteady after such an obvious blow. He placed her on the only unoccupied seat and sat down close beside her.

'Tell me,' he ordered. 'Here, let me take that.' He lifted the parcel out of her hand and laid it beside him on the garden seat. Then impulsively he put his arm around her back and cuddled her to him. '*Ma pauvre petite!*'

So she told him, her voice trembling because she still felt weepy.

He understood, and his grip tightened. 'I'll kill him,' he bristled in immediate outrage. 'I'll get him.'

She laughed. 'No, no. He was so drunk he won't remember anything; he won't be sober till tomorrow. He drank the Calvados as if it were lemonade – but it didn't have the same result!' Though she did not believe it, she hastened to add, in order to save further bloodshed, 'He'd no intention of really hurting me. I just fell over the coffee table. My bad luck.'

Michel did not completely comprehend, but he understood most of the tale correctly. 'He'd no right to touch you,' he snarled furiously. 'He'd already had a couple of Calvados when he was with me. He should have known better. Wasn't René there?'

'*Le serveur?*'

'Yes.'

'Indeed, he was; he came to help when he saw the man was getting out of hand.'

'Is that why the police were there?'

'Yes, they arrested him. He did some damage in the hotel. It's a very good hotel, Michel. They wouldn't expect that kind of trouble.'

With his free hand, he turned her face towards him. 'My love,' he whispered in English. 'I am in grief that you are hurt.' He kissed her tenderly.

The quaint turn of phrase made her smile, and she kissed him back, and such a surge of passion hit her that she had trouble controlling herself.

I don't care, she thought, as his tongue searched her mouth and she was weak with longing. I'm not going to let this man go.

With the B-and-B, we could make it together. He'd be a help. Mam and me've got at least a living, and he can earn something from the garden.

They clung together.

They were wakened to the fact that they were in a very public place when some children shouted to each other, and then ran past them. Their dog paused to sniff around the couple's knees. A frustrated Michel kicked it away.

When the children had scattered on the grass lawn in front of them and began to play catch, they turned back to each other.

She smiled very sweetly at him, and asked, almost coquettishly, 'Would you consider living in England – at least for a little while?'

He came to earth with a thud, feeling dizzy. 'You mean with you – marry you?' He gazed at her in amazement.

'Sure.' She was convinced that Michel was a very practical man, and she pushed on almost urgently, 'Mam and I've got four or more acres of land, crying out to be farmed. It's still listed as farmland and our lease must have about thirty years to go on it. I don't know whether we could get a permit to build anything like hen coops, though.' She paused for breath.

That she should calmly ask him to marry her, and almost in the same breath list her assets, shocked him as much as his own declaration of love had shocked her. Despite what she had told him about her being free, he still thought parents – or at least the man – should do the business negotiations. And yet it seemed that she had thought about it; she understood about land. Or was she just seeking cheap farm labour, he considered uneasily.

He leaned back from her, gazed at her shrewdly. Then he laughed at himself, and threw caution to the winds. 'Nobody propose marry to me before – but I like it very much!'

She chuckled in sheer glee. 'I've never done it before,' she admitted. 'Michel, you're a sweetheart – how could I resist?'

He liked the idea of being a sweetheart, too, and kissed her again.

Reluctantly, he drew back from her. He took a big breath and warned her, 'We must talk sensible. You know, for the present, I cannot leave Maman and Anatole. You remember about Anatole?'

'Yes, I do,' she said soberly, 'and the parcel beside you is a little present of some eggs for him.'

'*Un cadeau* – for Anatole?'

'Yes. I was going to buy some flowers – and then I

thought eggs might tempt him to eat – and I understand they are hard to get.'

She omitted to say that they are soon found if you are prepared to part with almost your last pound note for them.

He was touched, though he did not know how he was going to explain them to his mother.

'*Merci bien*. It is very amiable of you.' Then he sighed heavily, as doubt overwhelmed him. 'Are you serious? Certain?'

'Of course, I'm serious,' she replied determinedly. 'I know a good man when I see one.'

'*Merci*.' He grinned, and ran his free hand down her thigh.

'Holy Mary!' she exclaimed. 'Don't.'

He laughed at her discomfort. Then he sobered. '*Chérie*, there are many problems, apart from Anatole. How I stay in England? I need a permit, dead cert.'

He held her close again. Then he predicted, 'Marry me and you are French, not English – French law is different. Hard for women. Maybe you not like it?'

She was already aware of this fact, and she tried to think about it while he surreptitiously caressed her. She took his hand and held it firmly. 'You know, I don't lose my British citizenship if I marry a foreigner. The French may consider me French, but I would still be English to the English.'

'I am surprise.'

'It's a newish law. Sometime, I'll tell you how it came about.' She bit her lower lip, and then added, rather hesitantly, 'Before we plunge in, I'll ask a solicitor what problems there are likely to be.'

'So . . . sol . . . ?'

'*Un notaire*, I think it is in French.'

'You are not only a very lovely woman, *chérie*; you have much sense – I love you for it. But there will be problems – certain.'

Her discomfort over the Canadian forgotten, Barbara gave one of her wicked little chuckles. She said carefully in English, 'Liverpool women are born with common sense, Michel; they have to be – our men are away at sea most of the time. We have to bring up our children alone – and we often have to snatch our opportunities for happiness between voyages.'

She stopped to think and to survey his troubled face, and then went on, 'I think you should come as a visitor, first, if you can manage to. See if you would like to be there.' She wagged a warning finger at him. 'You may love me but my country.'

He sighed. Faced with a definite offer, he did not know the immediate answer. And there was Anatole. He glanced at his watch.

'It is necessary I go home, *ma petite*. I am very worry. Anatole does not eat. We are much afraid,' he gestured helplessly. 'I do not wish to leave him or Maman long unattended, you understand?' His arm tightened round her. 'We talk tomorrow again about your propose, yes? Meantime, we both think hard about it?'

She nodded and rose reluctantly. 'I'll walk a way with you.'

'Not all the way,' he replied immediately. 'Maman worry if she see you that she lose her other son to a most beautiful English lady.' He got up from the bench, and sighed again.

She did not laugh. 'I do understand, Michel. I can wait. Except I must go home in a few days.' She picked up her handbag and put on her gloves. 'Don't forget the eggs.'

He stood still, looking at her, and then he said solemnly, 'You make me very happy. You understand that we can do nothing for a little while? We wait.'

She nodded agreement. 'I don't know how we're going to fix it all, luvvie. But we will.'

'I have to consider how to get permit to live in England, what Maman want to do, what to do about our farm. Many things.'

'I know,' she said, suddenly very sober.

He put his arm round her, as for a few minutes they paced a magnificent cloister walked by monks and clerics for almost a thousand years.

As they strolled, he reminded her, 'We lose everything on the farm. All our clothing. We do not have much. Before I come, I must get a suit and other things. Present myself to your maman – look good.'

She stopped in surprise, and then laughed out loud. 'You look all right to me. Mam and me are used to men in working clothes, who work hard – and smell as if they do.'

He looked down at himself in a puzzled way. Even Suzanne, when she went out with him, expected him to look properly dressed.

Continuing her line of thought, she said, 'You should have seen me when I worked in the docks – in grubby overalls – and boots and a turban.'

'You would look beautiful in anything – or nothing,' he told her with a grin.

'Get away with you!' she teased.

'First, and most important, I need permit to stay in England?'

'You will.'

'You enquire about it?'

'As soon as I get home,' she promised.

'We write to each other, yes? I give you my address.'

'And I'll give you mine.'

As they traversed the busy street to the hotel gate, he said, 'We do it tomorrow.'

It was very hard to part. They stood looking at each other hesitantly.

Michel said, 'I expect to come about four o'clock tomorrow.' Then, as if he had a premonition, he added uneasily, 'It is not certain.'

'Anatole?' she asked.

'Yes. I fear much.'

'I am so sorry, my dear.'

The lines on his thin face deepened, as he said, 'I ask a neighbour to bring a message if I cannot come.'

He glanced hastily round him. The street was momentarily quiet. He leaned forward and kissed her, touching her neck softly with his free hand.

'I love you,' he said simply. 'I love you from the first time you step in the taxi. I will marry you – somehow. And I earn money for you. I promise.'

Holding the newspaper parcel in the palm of one hand, Michel turned and almost ran down the street, dodging irate pedestrians as he went. He was dazed; he had promised almost the impossible, he told himself. Nothing in his life could move while Anatole lived – and he dreaded losing him. Then, whether he worked the farm or not, sooner or later, there would have to be a settlement about it, and with so many owners, such things demanded endless negotiations. And there was Maman, who would be desolate.

Just to rehabilitate himself would take time and immense effort. And then, looming on the horizon, was the problem of getting himself to England and obtaining a permit to live and work there.

Barbara watched him out of sight. Then she went into the hotel, smiled politely at Reception, and dreamily began to climb the stairs to her room. About halfway up, she burst into silent laughter.

Now I know I'm crazy, she thought. I've just proposed to a man I've only known for a couple of days. I don't even know his postal address either!

Chapter Thirty-two

On the morning of the third day after Anatole's death, the slow clip-clop of the hoofs of the horse pulling the cart which carried him to the cemetery sounded to his mother, as she walked slowly behind it, like the halting beats of a tired heart. All she could feel in the depth of her grief was an incredible weariness.

She didn't want to be here in this small hushed procession, watching the men on the pavement snatch off their headgear in respect for the dead, as the humble cortège passed by. She wanted to lie down on her mattress and sleep and, if possible, never wake up.

Instead, she turned her eyes to the back of the cart, from which fluttered the heavy black ribbons which Anne-Marie had tied on to it. She hoped that the little bunches of flowers laid around and on the coffin would not blow off. It was a very modest funeral for her elder boy – he would always be a boy to her – but she felt that the ribbons and the flowers were enough to show that he had been well loved by his family.

She clung to Michel's arm. As so often during the German occupation, he had performed a miracle of organisation. In one day he had dealt with the local church, found a carter, a coffin of incredible cheapness, seen that the death was registered and that their doctor gave them a copy of the death certificate. He had then phoned Claudette from the local pharmacy and got her to tell Anne-Marie. He had also written to Uncle Léon in Port-en-Bessin.

Heaven only knew how much all of it must have cost, despite his desperate efforts at economy.

Then, her women friends, like Madame Bazaine and Madame Blanc, had come, with small gifts of food, to take their turn in sitting by the corpse. Those of their sons and husbands who happened to be free that day were attending the funeral, and were, with their womenfolk, walking behind her now. She realised how lucky she was to have such support; but she was so tired, so very, very tired.

The women were wearing their best black skirts, blouses, hats and jackets, very little different from their everyday dress; their sons and husbands were in their best suits, usually worn on Sundays, and each wore a black armband and a black tie. She herself was wearing a decent black jacket and hat lent her by Madame Blanc.

Behind her walked Anne-Marie and Claudette, both in unrelieved black, both sniffing into their handkerchiefs. Guy was driving his truck on a long-distance trip to Nantes and was, as yet, unaware of his brother-in-law's decease, while Bertrand, Claudette's husband, had to attend to their bakery in Rouen, and cope with his little daughter, Colette. Neither sister had brought her small daughter for the hasty one-day visit for the funeral, feeling that the children were too young to endure such a long day.

As Michel walked behind his brother's coffin, he was numbed by grief; he was also beset by guilt. He and his mother had spent most of two nights sitting by the corpse; they sometimes took a nap when a woman friend came to relieve them of this duty.

He had had plenty to think about in those long cold hours.

The need to care for Anatole had knitted together the three of them to the exclusion of all other considerations except for their belief, for a long time, that they were waiting for their little plot of land to be cleared of mines and other dangerous debris. Then they could all go home, they had assured each other bravely – and perhaps Anatole would regain his health on fresh country food.

For sometime, Michel had realised that the likelihood of a return, if ever, to the poultry farm was remote; it was not practical, and he had come to a personal decision about it.

In any event, no matter how much he prayed, it had been certain that Anatole would never live long enough to enjoy a proper home again. The house was hopelessly damaged, the barns were a heap of debris, likewise the chicken coops. The only place in which they could themselves take temporary shelter would be in the *cave*, and, if Anatole had not died before they returned, he would surely have died in that damp shelter long before they could rebuild the house.

Recently, there had even been talk in the town of making a memorial park of the area in which their land lay. In view of Barbara's proposal, Michel now hoped that this would be the case. It could settle a lot of acrimonious argument with his mother and sisters, his co-owners, as to what exactly they should do.

As matters stood, by the time they had paid for Anatole's funeral, Michel would not have a centime, and neither would Maman, beyond her pension.

Father Nicolas had recently suggested that the hospital was not quite so crowded as it had been, and a bed could be found for Anatole. But Maman and Michel had been united in refusing to condemn their invalid to the indifference of an overcrowded facility with a grossly overworked staff.

Before Michel could hope for any real future, Anatole had had to die, but the dreadful dilemma was now settled. Behind his grief, however, lay the hope of his marriage to Barbara, and all the problems that such an alliance entailed, not the least of which was his French distrust of the English as a race. There was also the almost insoluble problem of the family land holding.

Anatole had slipped quietly out of this life, as quietly and unobtrusively as he had lived it. In three days' time Barbara would leave, and, in the meantime, Michel had arranged to meet her daily in the cathedral. As he walked behind his brother's coffin, the thought of parting from her, almost immediately after losing Anatole, filled him with a sense of being deserted by those he loved best. Maman would be supported by daughters and grandchildren. He himself would be alone.

Although so long expected, Anatole's demise had seemed sudden, and had hit Madame Benion and Michel as hard as if it had been unexpected.

While Michel, as usual, had taken the Americans to the cemetery, Madame Benion had sat on the end of her son's bed, doing her mending. She occasionally glanced away from the stocking she was darning, to look at her boy, who was dozing.

She turned the stocking right side out and glanced yet again. Then she put down her work. Anatole had opened his eyes, and looked at her as if he did not see her.

What a fine face he has, she thought as she smiled at him.

The beauty of death! Some people died in such a state of composure that the face looked almost saintly. She had seen that look before, when helping other women with their sick.

Though Anatole's eyes did slowly focus and he smiled faintly, she shot up from the end of the bed, and, panic-stricken, ran out onto the landing. Faintly from the next room came the sound of the violin of the unemployed musician who lived there. She hammered on his door.

The music stopped, and the musician, unshaven and with no shoes on, answered the door.

'Monsieur – Monsieur – I think my son is dying,' she whispered urgently, hoping that Anatole would not hear her. 'Would you run for Father Nicolas at the corner church – or any priest?'

The man looked quite bewildered for a moment. Then he nodded and shuffled over to the bed and dragged his shoes out from under it.

'Please hurry, Monsieur – hurry,' hissed the frantic mother.

And, without a single word, he ran.

Father Nicolas was out, said his slatternly housekeeper.

'Well, any priest. A man is dying,' pleaded the panting messenger.

So a young, newly ordained priest, fleeter than the messenger, grabbed the case containing the beautiful enamelled box which held the holy oil, a little bottle of holy water, a tiny pochette of wafers, and a small bottle of wine, kept ready for such emergencies, and ran down the narrow alley, and up the flights of stairs. At the top, he paused for a moment.

Framed in the open doorway, he saw a woman on her knees beside a bed where a man lay very still.

He thought he was too late.

The panting musician caught up with him, and said, 'In there, *mon Père*. Madame Benion and her son.'

The youngster wanted to cry himself. He had seen much carnage in the years of his studies for the priesthood; yet he still found it difficult to look on death as the Will of God, and therefore to be accepted.

Nevertheless, he went swiftly over to Madame Benion and spoke her name. She rose quickly to her feet. She was haggard but dry-eyed.

She was startled at being faced with a stranger. But she said urgently, 'He's alive, *mon Père*. Be quick.'

As he snapped open his little case, the priest was already saying carefully the blessed words, and he immediately performed his duties, his movements gentle and compassionate.

Comforted and protected by Extreme Unction, a French peasant, after much suffering patiently borne, went to his Lord with a smile on his face, to join the thousands and thousands of his brethren who had died as a result of the war.

The priest did not catch his last word, but his mother, bending to kiss him, heard it and was surprised.

He said, 'Henri!' as if greeting someone in delighted surprise.

The priest covered the dead man's face with the grubby sheet, and eased the mother away from him. When she began to cry with deep agonised moans, he thought that Mary, the mother of Jesus, our Lady of Sorrows, must have wept exactly like that.

He turned to sit her in a chair but there was no chair.

He spotted the mattress on the floor, and asked if she would like to lie down. Obediently, she had fallen on her knees and then curled up in a foetal position. He gently covered her with a blanket. He then turned to the musician, who had stood silently in the doorway.

The man's eyes were closed, as he muttered a prayer. He crossed himself, and then opened his eyes.

The priest asked if there were another woman in the house, and if so, would he go to fetch her?

'*Oui, mon Père.*' He patiently trotted down the stairs to the kitchen to find Madame Blanc.

She was in the midst of washing the kitchen floor. She immediately left her bucket and floorcloth and ran upstairs. On the way, she stopped at her living room, to snatch up a bottle and a glass. Then she continued upwards.

The young priest was standing nervously by the mattress, fiddling with his beads. Madame paused, and then went quietly to kneel down by her distraught friend. She quickly poured out a thimbleful of brandy and put the glass down on the floor.

The bereaved woman was beating the mattress with one fist as she lay and wept.

Once again, Madame set out to comfort a tenant who had, long since, become her friend.

The young priest was thankful to have her there. He asked if there were any other members of the family – perhaps he could inform them?

'Her other son will be at the American cemetery. He's working with some Americans – American Army.' She paused, to lift up Madame Benion's head and put her arm under her. 'It's too far to send a messenger. He'll be home in the afternoon.'

She bent over to say softly to Maman, 'Hush, hush, dear friend. He has no more pain now. He's with God. There, there. Sip a little cognac – it will soothe you.'

The priest fidgeted, and she said to him, 'In a little while, I'll take her downstairs, if she'll come. I won't leave her until Michel returns.'

'Has she any other friends nearby?'

'Indeed, she has. I'll send a boy to ask Madame Bazaine. Then the word will go all round the neighbourhood.

Together we'll help her to wash the body and make it decent.'

She looked up at the priest. So young, so helpless, she thought.

'Don't worry, *mon Père*. She'll be all right with me.'

'I have Mass in half an hour.' He moved thankfully towards the door. 'I'll tell Father Nicolas when he returns.'

By the time Michel loped down the street, there was a small gathering of elderly women, wrapped tightly in shawls, gossiping on the step of the lodging house.

He slowed, as he came up to them. 'It's Anatole, isn't it?' he enquired, his face grim.

They nodded solemnly like some Greek chorus, and made way for him to run up the stairs.

He flew up to the top floor, and flung open the door, 'Maman?'

Madame Bazaine, seated on a chair kindly lent by the musician, turned towards him. Behind her lay Anatole, stiff and straight, arms crossed upon his breast. A lit candle glowed on a small shelf above his head.

She said, 'Madame Benion is downstairs, dear boy. Father Nicolas came half an hour ago to see her. He has just left.' She rose so that Michel could come close to his brother.

Michel stood silent for a moment. He felt overwhelmed by loss, like a child deserted by its parents. Dear Anatole! He bent over and put his hand over one of his brother's cool ones.

'Goodbye, my brother,' he said huskily. Then, after staring down at him while he tried to control the raw pain of separation, he turned, stony-faced, to Madame Bazaine. 'I must go down to Maman.'

'Of course. I will sit all night, if necessary.'

'Thank you, Madame.'

And, now here he was, wallowing in self-condemnation, as he walked behind the coffin and held his mother firmly; he hoped she could bear the interment without collapsing.

In his mind he was talking to his brother, begging him to forgive him for his sense of relief that he could now try to put his own life to rights: could, perhaps, by some miracle yet to be performed, marry his lovely Barbara and begin a life in England by tilling her two hectares for her, no matter how much it hurt his shoulder, while he perfected his English and looked for better work.

She had said that it would make a good little market garden; it could provide vegetables and some fruit for themselves and their clients, and they could sell the balance locally. And she knew he could raise twenty laying hens without a special permit. It wasn't a great deal, but if he could get a resident's permit, it was a start. Just a few miracles will be needed, he thought ironically.

Maman had told him of Anatole's last word. 'It was strange,' she had said, 'that at the end he remembered young Henri.'

Michel eyebrows rose in surprise, but he replied carefully to her, 'Well, you and I owe our lives to Henri. It was a tremendous sacrifice on Henri's part – probably Anatole was thinking of the past – it would be natural – we were all three good friends.'

'Indeed, yes. I suppose it's quite possible.'

Although he was no longer sure that there was a God, Michel hoped, for Anatole's sake, that his brother was happily swinging on a cloud with Henri, under the benevolent care of an almighty understanding Being.

Except for the grief she had to bear, he was not worried about his mother. Both her daughters would comfort her;

and they had both assured him that they would be glad to have her to live with them, a patient pleasant woman to help them with their children. Her small government pension would give her a sense of independence, and he himself could probably add to it, once he got on his feet.

As the coffin was slowly lowered into the ready-dug grave, he prayed to Anatole for forgiveness. 'I love you, Anatole,' he muttered to himself, as he dropped a symbolic handful of earth on the coffin. Then he turned to his whey-faced mother, and to his sisters, who were holding her.

'Let's take Maman home,' he said.

But at home Madame Benion had to sit in Madame's gloomy sitting room and receive formal condolences from the little group of mourners. Some of the menfolk had never actually seen Anatole, because it was their wives and mothers who were Madame Benion's friends; Madame Benion was a part of their women's world. Pressed by their womenfolk to attend the funeral, to provide bigger male support, the men had kindly done so.

Now they came back to the house, to eat a little of the donated food and drink a glass of wine. Finally, after chatting awkwardly to each other, they took their leave. How could one make the usual little jokes or recite the usual funny anecdotes about a man you'd never seen? It was difficult, wasn't it?

Chapter Thirty-three

About ten o'clock on the night of Anatole's death, while Madame Bazaine sat by his bed, his mother was persuaded to come downstairs again to drink coffee with Madame Blanc and another neighbour. Round the landlady's dying kitchen fire, they discussed at length the virtues of the deceased, and Maman was a little comforted.

A haggard Michel, who feared he might collapse again, said he would go for a little walk to clear his head, and think about what must be arranged the next day. He would not be long.

The ladies gently agreed; a death was a particularly heavy burden for the young to face, they told each other tearfully.

Michel fled to the hotel. The concierge was sitting in for Reservations, who was off duty.

The concierge was a little surprised at the taxi driver's request that he ask Madame Bishop to step down to speak to him at such a late hour, and he hesitated.

On his way over, Michel had tried to think of a reason to do this. He had finally decided that he could say that he had arranged to take her, once more, to her husband's grave the following day. He could not, however, do this, because of his brother's death that afternoon. But he could make some other arrangements for her, if she would like him to.

'I must give tomorrow to arranging my brother's funeral,' he explained. 'I won't have time to come over and tell her then. And I must leave a note for Colonel Buck to say that

I can't drive him for a couple of days. I'll leave the keys of the taxi and the garage with you to give to him. Probably Monsieur Wayne will drive.'

The concierge, of course, knew Michel well, and he said, 'I've just heard about your brother from one of the chambermaids. I'm sorry; it's too bad.' He uncertainly tapped the desk with his fingertips, and then said in warning, 'Well, if Madame complains because you're here so late, be it on your own head – not on mine. She may be in bed.' He left the silent lobby to plod upstairs to tell Barbara that the taxi driver wished to speak with her.

She guessed immediately what had happened, and when the concierge stepped on one side to give her precedence, she ran down the stairs. Michel seized her arm, and before the surprised concierge was halfway down the staircase, the pair of them were on their way out of the front door.

'Your brother?'

'Yes. I'm sorry I couldn't let you know earlier.'

'Don't worry about that. I'm so sorry for you – and your poor mother,' she replied with compassion. She looked around the dark courtyard. 'Will the cathedral be open?'

He nodded.

'Let's go there.'

And it was in the silent, dark cathedral, that Michel finally gave way and wept. She held him, his head on her shoulder, and let him cry, while she soothed him as if he were a child.

'It's goin' to be all right, luvvie. You'll feel better tomorrow. There now. I'm sure you and your mam did everything you could for him.'

A vague figure in a long robe emerged from the gloom, and asked in whispered French, if she were all right.

She guessed what the question was, and answered first

in English. 'He's just been bereaved,' she said quietly in English. Then added, '*Son frère est mort.*'

She was a little surprised that the figure, whom she supposed was a verger, evidently understood her French, nodded his head and went away.

A couple of hours later, they emerged, arms still around each other. In a niche made by a great buttress against the wall of the huge cathedral, in the silent darkness, they made love for the first time.

It was not the most comfortable union, but it brought some sense of peace to Michel, a confirmation that Barbara meant what she had said, that life truly did still hold something for him.

With Barbara's arm around him, he walked with her back to the hotel. He even managed a rueful laugh, as he checked, before she entered the hotel courtyard, that her clothes looked undisturbed

He promised to be with her in the cathedral at ten o'clock the next night, if he could possibly get away. 'You'll be safe in there, if I can't come,' he said, and then he went on, 'I'm sorry to be a cry – what you say? – crybaby.'

'Tush,' she retorted, with a little grin, 'troubles shared are troubles halved.' She wiped his face with her handkerchief as if he were a child, kissed him, and said warmly, 'I love you, Michel. I'm so thankful you've come into my life.'

'I love you, too – and I work for you all my life,' he promised her earnestly.

He watched her, as she went into the courtyard and shut the gate behind her.

Determined not to be embarrassed about the lateness of the hour, she walked smartly into the hotel, passed the concierge with a polite 'Good night', and went upstairs, followed by his questioning stare.

Chapter Thirty-four

The day following the funeral, of necessity, Michel went back to work. In his absence, Wayne, the colonel's assistant, had driven the taxi, with a solid flow of bad language at its awkward gears and its marked tendency to veer suddenly into the wrong lane on the potholed roads. The three morticians had, on one occasion, also managed to get lost in the wandering, bocage-lined lanes of the battered country; the colonel's limited French had been misunderstood by a villager of whom they asked the way, so that they were misdirected and were hours late for dinner. They were very thankful to see Michel again.

They were jubilant at the thought of going back to the States the following day. So, in order that they could buy gifts to take home, Michel spent the day taking them to see various craftsmen, who were trying to restart their businesses. To the joy of their creators, the Americans bought yards of fine lace, locally woven tapestry cushion covers, recorders for their children, old-fashioned, copper weighing scales, brass candlesticks, and bottles of Calvados.

As he watched them, Michel clicked his tongue irritably. Why had he not thought of encouraging some of his cemetery visitors to take a little memento home? There was now a whole row of small stalls in Caen and one or two places in Bayeux where the struggling owners would have been thankful for the trade – and Michel himself would have been glad of a small commission from the stallholders. It would have helped to balance out the small gift he gave each week to Reservations for his co-operation.

At the end of the day, Colonel Buck, with a grin as wide as his moustache, presented Michel with a folding bicycle.

Jolted out of his grief, Michel stared at it with amazed delight. He recognised it as similar to the ones parachutists had carried on their backs when being dropped into Normandy. Some of the British Army had also carried bikes ashore with them on D-Day, whether folding or ordinary ones, he was not sure. This bike, so kindly found for him, was obviously not a new one, and, he decided, it must be a renovated British one. Someone had put considerable work into it because it had new tyres and chain, and a fresh coat of paint.

The colonel wrung Michel's hand. 'Wayne and Elmer and me wanna thank you for making our time here so interesting. We had a lousy job to do, but you always seemed to have somethin' interestin' to show us or to joke about – and we sure appreciated it.'

Michel grinned. 'I enjoy I work for you,' he assured them sincerely. 'And the bike . . .' He was overwhelmed. He looked a little shyly at the colonel. 'It is a big gift for me.'

The colonel laughed. 'I'm just sorry I couldn't find a new one, but this'll get you around until you can get a car.'

One day, he would have a car? What a wild American idea! With luck, a horse and cart, perhaps, to carry to market the eggs and vegetables which he would raise for Barbara, if he could obtain no better employment. But a car? *Ce n'est pas possible.*

To the Americans' amusement, he rode the bike carefully round the hotel courtyard to try it, and found that the brakes worked perfectly. Colonel Buck was happy to see a face that had been woebegone, almost sullen all day, light up as his driver laughed like a young boy.

As he dismounted, Elmer, the younger of the two assistants, produced a brown paper parcel and announced laconically, 'Wayne and me got you a lock for it. I guess you'll need one.'

Michel was dumbfounded. He had thought he might get a small tip from them, but the bike was worth its weight in gold; and a decent lock would have been hard to find, and yet was so necessary to prevent immediate theft.

The bike was carefully folded up again and secured with a piece of rope to the luggage platform of the taxi beside the driver. They parted with hearty handshakes and back slaps all round, and promises to write – and then forgot to exchange addresses.

Michel drove the old taxi into the stable behind Monsieur Duval's workshop, and wrote up his last report on the Americans for his employer. He would drive them and their luggage to their base the following morning, and then return to lock up the taxi and hand the key to Duval.

Duval sighed at the ending of a very lucrative contract. He would now advertise that the taxi was generally available. He offered Michel part-time employment as driver; they would arrange the hours when he saw the result of his advertisement.

Michel thankfully agreed to this. Meanwhile, he promised himself that, depressed as he was, he would hunt for a decent position. More than ever, he needed immediate money. It was the key to being permanently in Barbara's arms.

Michel undid the bike and lifted it down from the taxi's luggage platform. Duval examined it. He laughed, and said he had always wondered where the bikes brought ashore during the invasion and those carried by parachutists eventually went. He had never thought of their being picked up by Americans. He could sell a thousand if he could lay hands on them.

'You never see this particular kind in the street,' he went on thoughtfully, as he ran his hands along the handlebars and tried the brakes. 'I believe this one actually came from parachute troops – I know they had a special folding bike to carry on their backs.' He straightened up, and added, 'You're lucky.' And Michel had to admit that, yes, he was.

He rode it home and caused a sensation as he turned neatly down the narrow alley.

He carefully carried it up to his room and propped it against the wall. Being able to fold it meant he could usually take it indoors, he congratulated himself; and, consequently, he would be much less likely to lose it.

This cold attic room, in which they had suffered so much, was his room now. But without Anatole and Maman, he hated it; it made him feel almost physically nauseated.

On the evening of the funeral, after collecting her sparse belongings and tying them in her shawl, Maman had said a fond farewell to her son and Madame Blanc, and had accompanied Claudette back to Rouen, to begin, after she had rested a little, a new life as resident grandma to a wide-eyed three-year-old Colette.

Michel had no desire to remain in the room for any

length of time; he could not even persuade himself to sleep in Anatole's now vacant bed; it was where he had expired, and it was customary to clean thoroughly a bed and room where someone had died. This had not been done. So he still slept on his narrow mattress on the floor. Madame Blanc had agreed that he could take an evening meal with her each day, for which he would pay her. Unless the taxi proved to be very popular, he was not sure whether he could continue to do this.

He had put out feelers already, looking harder for a job locally. Now he had the bicycle, he could get work on a farm, he knew, but he wanted, if possible, to avoid hard, physical labour. For that he would need to go elsewhere.

He lay on his mattress and smoked his last cigarette as he considered the implications of having the bicycle.

With patience, he could range all over Normandy. For temporary work, he could probably find another poulterer desperately short of labour, a place where he could use his considerable expertise. But they would not pay much, he decided.

What he most needed was to save enough money to buy some decent clothes, and to maintain himself in France – and in England for at least a little while. He wanted, also, to take Uncle Léon into his confidence, tell him about Barbara, and his idea of living in England; ask his advice as to how best to go about it all. Uncle Léon knew some of the English ports really well, and would, he felt, be able to advise him about costs and any problems.

Then he remembered the breeder from which his father had sometimes bought eggs to improve his own small number of breeding stock. The man had had a big business; before the war he had even employed a book-keeper/clerk who kept the careful records of the hens skilfully selected and mated to produce the best breeds: that was where Chanticleer had come from – poor Chanticleer, who had ended up as dinner for three *sales Boches*.

He decided that, with his last week's pay from the Americans and his gardening money, he would buy himself a respectable-looking second-hand mackintosh and a trilby hat, and get a haircut. His mother had always cut his hair while they had been in Bayeux, using Madame Blanc's scissors. In the second-hand stalls in the market, he might also find some trousers, which Madame Blanc might be kind enough to press for him. And, thus disguised as someone a little better than a dreadfully deprived peasant, he would try for a clerical job in the egg and poultry business of his father's supplier.

He rolled on his straw mattress and smiled grimly, as he thought how much fun Anatole would have got out of this dress-up effort at self-aggrandisement.

To give himself some idea of what else might be on offer, he had spent an hour in the corner coffee shop consulting the 'Help Wanted' advertisements in the various newspapers available to its patrons. And in order to gain some insight into what was happening in England, he read, with far more attention than he would normally have given them, any small snippets of English news which the papers happened to carry. His survey did not turn up much that was useful.

He had, in his pocket, written references, one from Duval, resigned to losing his driver eventually, and an absolutely glowing one from the colonel, testifying to his integrity, his driving ability, his knowledge of Normandy, his excellent English and his reputed years of experience as a farmer.

After some thought, Michel decided he could also take

a look at the holiday resorts along the coast, and see what hotel work he could find. Not all the coast was a total ruin. Trouville and Deauville, pre-war English playgrounds, might not have been so wrecked as other places; he could try the hotels there if he had no success in his application to the poultry farm.

First, however, he would use a precious day to go to Port-en-Bessin to find his uncle and see if he could get his seaman's papers replaced; like everything else, they had been lost on the farm.

Once he had some decent clothes, some sort of a suitcase in which to put them, and money in his pocket, together with a replacement of his seaman's book, perhaps Uncle Léon would himself take him on, let him work his passage to Portsmouth or Plymouth, his usual ports of call.

Shortly after coming to Bayeux, when both the South of England and Normandy were in a very chaotic state, Michel had done one voyage with his uncle without his identifying book. Now, however, with order restored, he would not get far without it.

In England, he could cycle up to Liverpool on his bike; he reckoned he could do two hundred miles or so in three days. He could sleep rough en route, find a haystack or a barn to curl up in – except for the last night, when he would have to find a place where he could wash and make himself respectable before arriving on the doorstep of Maman Bishop; he must never forget that the B-and-B was primarily her enterprise, not Barbara's. A good first impression on Maman would be vital.

Michel sighed. It was nice to have relations, but nobody knew better than a French peasant how families could feud over property. He must be careful with Maman Bishop.

It was a pity that Uncle had not been able to attend Anatole's funeral; his housekeeper, Hortense, had written that he was en route home from Cherbourg, and that Michel's letter about Anatole was awaiting his return to Port-en-Bessin. He knew Hortense so well that he was not surprised that she had opened a letter addressed to his uncle – she ran Uncle Léon as well as his home. Only this morning Michel had finally received a response from the man himself.

After his condolences, he had asked about Maman's and his plans.

Well, Maman seemed quite happy about staying with Claudette. She had whispered to Michel that she did not want to go to Anne-Marie. The poor child still did not have a proper home – the destruction of Rouen had been so extensive that only the good God knew when she and Guy would be rehoused. And though bereft of her little boy, Anne-Marie was so self-centred that she had never even seemed to realise that the loss of her son was also Guy's loss. She might be careless of Maman's needs and feelings.

So stout, placid Claudette promised Maman a warm little room of her own, right above the ovens, and had happily taken her home.

Michel was very content that this should be so. His elder sister and her husband, Bertrand, would, he knew, protect her mother; she would never be exploited. The couple had even opened their door to Michel himself, though the best they could offer was a truckle bed at the back of the shop.

He thanked her effusively, but refused the offer.

With an understanding smile that he might have his own plans already made, she immediately agreed, though

Maman protested wearily that she would be losing her second son.

He assured her that he would visit her as soon as he was settled. Meanwhile, she must rest and enjoy the company of little Colette.

Though Michel had wanted to tell Claudette about Barbara, he refrained. He was not sure how antagonistic his sisters would be to an English sister-in-law. Take one problem at a time, he decided, and what he needed now was a little ready money.

The brothers-in-law and his uncle had all offered to pay part of the funeral expenses, so, to Michel's relief, he was not in debt for that. He had his final week's wages from Duval, and small amounts to collect from his two gardening jobs.

Where should he start?

As he waved the family off on the train to Rouen, he suddenly found the absence of Anatole unbearable. Tears ran slowly unchecked down his face. Once again, he beat himself for feeling such relief at Anatole's death, at being free at last. He wished he had been able to discuss, hammer out, a sensible plan with him, the last really close friend left to him in an almost devastated existence.

Not quite the last friend. There was Barbara.

Chapter Thirty-five

When, that evening, he had to face the empty attic, Michel was thankful to go down to the kitchen and eat the supper Madame Blanc had provided for him. As soon as he could decently take leave of her, he would walk over to the cathedral to meet his darling Barbara.

The thought of having to say farewell to Barbara, on top of losing Anatole, tore at him, and he was rather silent as he ate.

On the other hand, Madame Blanc, in an effort to comfort him, was quite loquacious. She praised Madame Benion and his efforts to keep Anatole comfortable, until Michel felt he could not stand any more, but he was aware what a friend she had been to the family, and assured her that none of it would have been possible if she had not been kind enough to rent the attic to them.

He glanced up at the clock on her mantelpiece. In half an hour, he expected to meet Barbara to say goodbye. He nibbled a last piece of cheese and drank his coffee. Madame put down his heavy sigh to the loss of Anatole. She herself was going to miss the dear friend she had made in Madame Benion, so she ventured a small sigh too.

Michel told Madame Blanc about the gift from the Americans and that he had left it secured with a bicycle lock, in the attic. Since the attic door had no key, he hoped that it would be safe up there.

This made her a little uneasy, because other tenants

might consider the room empty and wander in; one woman had already asked her, on behalf of a friend of hers, if it was now available for letting. She suggested that he put the machine in the cupboard in the roof, if it would go in.

He did not want to have to leave it outside the cathedral, so he agreed to try this.

He took his leave, and went upstairs to see what could be done. It was awkward, but he did finally slide the bike into the roof, and shut the cupboard door on it.

Barbara was not standing at the cathedral door as they had arranged, and Michel's heart missed a beat.

He paused uncertainly on the other side of the road, and then almost ran across it.

He found her in the porch, with one toe propping open the door into the cathedral itself. She was listening to the choir practising.

Immediately, she heard his step, she let the door slam and turned to fling herself into his arms. He caught her and held her. Then he eased his grip in order to kiss her. He was astonished to see that there were tears in her eyes.

He had assumed that she would grieve at their parting just as he was grieving, but somehow he had not expected her to cry; on the previous evening, she had, on sitting with him in the shadows of the great nave, discussed with him extremely practically what action they should take. Today, however, passion held sway.

'Don't cry,' he said gently, as he touched her blackened eye, which was beginning to turn an even uglier yellow under her face powder. 'It won't be long, I promise you.'

She half choked as she answered him. 'I'm trying not

to.' She sniffed, and then said in a strained whisper, as someone passed by on the pavement, 'Let's go in and sit somewhere away from the choir and the organ.'

He held her tightly round the waist as they crept up a side aisle where a pillar stood between them and the organ; the music was glorious, but not particularly appreciated by a couple trying to communicate with each other.

Unnoticed, except by the vigilant verger, they sat down. By this time, the verger had become used to the little couple who talked in whispers to each other in any dark corner they could find. Remembering how he had found them earlier, the man weeping in muffled, hoarse sobs, he had identified Michel as the man who had lost his brother, a tragic experience. Moreover, the woman was a foreigner – which was interesting. So since they did not disturb those at prayer, he left them to themselves. Where else could an obviously poor man in grief go outside his home? To a tavern to get drunk?

As the sung Mass soared to the roof, the poor man held his beloved and wondered how he could let her go.

And Barbara feared losing him as much as if he were going off to fight. It was an eerie, haunting feeling sitting in her subconscious mind, which she had tried unsuccessfully to shake off in the few precious days they had enjoyed together. Imprinted on her brain was her last farewell to George. He had never returned. Women friends in her village had been given great send-off parties before they left to join husbands in a dozen different countries. They never seriously expected to return. They left a frightening gap in her daily life.

In fact, there were dozens of gaps. Who would have believed that you cared about who delivered your milk? But young Freddie had died in Tunisia, and his old, broken-hearted father was continuing the deliveries he had done on his son's behalf throughout the war. She missed Freddie and she missed her neighbour, Mr Baines', girl and boy. And other familiar faces – they had simply vanished.

Now she had this dear sweet man in her arms, a gift from God. And she whimpered with fear that, despite his protestations, she would lose him too. After all he had been through, he might find the problems they faced too much and simply give up.

As they hugged and kissed and swore eternal love, at the back of both their minds loomed also the spectres of their mothers. They were old enough to defy their elders with impunity, but Barbara's – and probably his own – future livelihood would depend on her mother's goodwill; and Michel knew that he was going to hurt his own maman irredeemably if he went to live in England. There was also a smaller problem that Barbara and Maman could not even converse fluently with one another.

They had no keepsakes to exchange to remind each other of their very existence during their separation. Barbara wished desperately that she had been able to get film for her old camera so that she could at least have a snap of him. Michel wished that he could have bought a ring for her.

The best news he had for her was about the bicycle, and she immediately saw its possibilities. She agreed that it would really help in his hunt for immediate work.

'I earn. I come,' he promised yet again.

She cuddled closer and tried to forget her ghosts.

The choir master finally called a halt to the practice session, the organ shut down and the chattering singers streamed out. Finally, the lights were dimmed and Michel and Barbara were left undisturbed.

Michel managed to say at one point, 'I order the taxi to take you to the station the day after tomorrow.' He grimaced. 'I have to charge you for it – but tomorrow I take Americans to the airport. Duval has to know about your trip to station.'

'I realise that. Don't worry. I can pay.' She smiled up at him. 'I shall see you yet one more time.'

'Yes – but I am then again the taxi driver. All I can do for my Madame Barbara is find her a porter.'

She smiled again. 'My most beloved taxi driver.'

In the greater darkness, they caressed each other to the point of recklessness, and, as if by mutual consent, they rose hastily and left the cathedral.

The streets were almost deserted, except for a patrolling gendarme. A frantic Michel whipped Barbara into the darkness of a recessed shop doorway, and there they made love for the last time.

Chapter Thirty-six

'You never!' exclaimed Phyllis Williams, completely dumb-founded when her daughter told her that she was engaged to a Frenchman. Her mouth opened and closed with amazement, as she sought for words. 'But you was only gone eighteen days! How could you?'

She stopped running her sewing machine, while she regarded Barbara with horror. 'A Frog? He'd have a bad time of it here, he would. Remember the French sailors, when they was here. Lost all their red pompoms off their caps, they did.'

Barbara laughed. 'Mam, that was in Liverpool – and you know well enough, down in the docks, a British Army officer could be jeered at just because he's posh. Or an American, just 'cos he looks fat. Michel's real quiet, a real sweetie. Don't you worry, Mam. He's not a young fool who'll go lookin' for a fight.'

She paused, remembering again his soft seductive voice. She was replacing a missing curtain ring on a white curtain, and she sighed longingly, needle poised, and asked with an effort, 'Do you think these curtains will ever hold together with all the bleach you used on them?'

'Hope they last long enough till we can find some new material to make curtains out of, but no luck so far. Not nothing worth having,' replied Phyllis lugubriously. 'Blackout curtains look so miserable now the war's over, so I thought I'd try bleach – and they come out OK.'

So that it did not slip onto the floor, she eased onto her knee the curtain she had been rehemming. Then she demanded, 'Stop trying to hide things, and tell me about this lad. What's he like and how did you come by him?'

Barbara patiently told her the tale of the taxi. Her voice trembled a little as she told how they had sat by the roadside, and he had been so gentle – and had not tried to take advantage of her.

'On a roadside? I should hope not! But then you never know with them Frenchies.'

'The roads are nearly deserted, Mam. There's hardly any cars or trucks. The Jerries took them. You can't even buy a bike.'

In regard to the latter remark, Phyllis said gloomily, 'You can't buy nothin' much here, neither,' and she looked down in disgust at her bleached blackout curtains.

'What's he look like? Got a picture?'

'No. I tried to get some film for our old camera before I went, remember? Nobody seemed to have any – or if they had it was under the counter.'

She dutifully described her lanky sweetheart, with his fine Norman features, deeply lined. 'He's twenty-nine years old and he's gone through hell with the Jerries, Mam.

'And to crown all, after they hoped to be rid of the Germans, the Allies fought all over his land, flattened his apple trees, killed his birds in their coops, and ruined his home.' She looked up from her sewing, and exclaimed, 'Do you know, Mam, his farm's full of land mines and shells and unexploded bombs? He's still waiting for them to be cleared. Nobody can even walk into the place till it's cleared.'

'What birds?' Phyllis asked suspiciously.

'He and his family is poulterers, Mam. They raised hens and sold eggs and chickens. Before the war, with their neighbours, they was planning to send eggs to Britain. They made cider from the apples they grew. It's sometimes very strong.'

'Humph. And how much did you drink, young lady, to swallow his line? It could be a pack of lies.'

'I don't think so, Mam. He was driving the taxi for some American soldiers who were staying in the same hotel as me; and they thought very highly of him. One night, I had dinner with their officer, Colonel Buck, and he told me a lot about him.'

'Humph.' An American might've been a better buy, considered her irate mother.

While Phyllis slowly turned the sewing machine handle, Barbara described Anatole's tuberculosis and his terrible years in Germany, 'like a slave.' She stood up to fold a curtain. 'He died a few days before I was due to come home. And I held Michel in a dark corner of the cathedral while he wept it out,' she told her mother baldly. 'He said he hadn't a friend left alive, and I said, "Oh, yes, you have. You've got me, my love." And he has,' she concluded defiantly.

She turned her back on her mother, as she laboriously completed the folding of the heavy material. She wanted to cry out to God to keep him safe and send him to her – and give her mother some compassion for him. Only God wasn't there any more.

As she turned back to ask which pile of curtains needed more rings, Phyllis was saying philosophically, 'Oh, aye, Joyce Talbot's girl got TB in the ATS and she died. Can't do much about it.' Then she looked up at her daughter, tossed another curtain to her, and asked, 'He's not got it, has he, for God's sake?'

'I don't think so, Mam. He's half-starved by the look of him, but he's quite spry. He does kick-boxing and he still exercises.'

'And just how's he going to work here, speakin' like a Frog? And how am I supposed to talk to him?'

'That's rude, Mam.' Barbara was suddenly annoyed. 'How do you think he talked to me?'

Phyllis accepted the thrust. 'Right,' she grunted irritably. 'But, look here, girl. He'll never fit in. Can you imagine him in this village – in the pub?'

'I don't know, Mam. Get him some English clothes and an English haircut, he won't be that obvious. Actually, I can't imagine him in a pub – more likely he'd be in a café drinking coffee.'

Phyllis exploded. 'In a café, drinking coffee? That'd be a sight to see. Him amongst all the ladies!'

'They'd love him,' shot back Barbara, seeing him in her mind's eye turning his undoubted charm on all the elderly local matrons sipping their morning coffees. Then she said, pleading, 'Don't be cross, Mam. We both know that it's going to be a long job getting him here, getting settled, finding a job, hopefully, in the poultry line – though he could probably go to sea if he had to; they're so short of men.'

Phyllis's lower lip trembled. 'They are,' she agreed, her voice a little hoarse.

Barbara glanced at her mother and was immediately contrite. She dropped the curtain she was folding, and went to kneel by Phyllis's chair. 'I'm sorry, Mam. Try not to grieve.' She put her arm round her mother's bowed shoulders. 'It could be nice for you to have a man about the place. He'd take some of the headaches off you.'

Phyllis stiffened up. She sniffed, 'I'm OK. It's just sometimes, I do miss your dad, even now. And I was looking forward to your Georgie coming to help, like.'

'I know, Mam. But he can't come, and we both have to face that fact.' She sighed heavily. She couldn't say that she was convinced that Michel would be better for her than ever stolid George could have been; it would be unfair to say anything about a decent man who was dead; because George had had an innate goodness in him, and she was aware of it.

Instead, she said, 'Michel could be a big help here, you know. He and his dad only had about five acres of land; yet they made a living. And we've got about that much here – and it's farmland, not just a garden.

'And that reminds me, how long has Joe got on his agreement with us for taking hay?'

'Renews it every October. He's started grazing a few of his cows on it this spring, as you know. Are you saying your Michel could farm it?'

'Sure he could. Whether he can get permits to build barns and hen coops, we have to find out.'

'Look here, girl, this lease is mine, not yours,' Phyllis snapped in exasperation.

'Oh, Mam, I know that, but you wouldn't mind, would you? We'd get veggies and fruit, eggs, chickens, maybe milk from a cow. Even if it's not a big moneymaker, it would be a boost for the B-and-B with everything fresh.'

Phyllis meditated while she held some pins between her lips, preparatory to turning up yet another frayed hem. It's my livelihood, she repeated to herself, and very nice it was before the war. She took a pin and stabbed it into the curtain hem. What would I do with a Frog around the place?

But, then, Barbie's put in a tremendous lot of work, even with that awful job in the war. She's not being unreasonable, if the man's liveable with. If I were real unhappy with them, I could put 'em out, anytime. It's my house.

Then she smiled at herself – as if I could ever put our Barbie out. And the garden's a proper mess, she reflected. Neither Barbie nor me'll ever get it to look anything – we haven't the time. And not a single neighbour has complained about Joe's cows being here this month – or them being smelly.

She temporised. 'I wouldn't want anything smelly near the house. Our gentlemen reps wouldn't like it, for sure.' She glanced at the pile of folded, fairly white curtains on a chair. 'And you can take that pile up to the front hall room and stick 'em on the bed. I want to scrub the walls down afore I hang them.'

'I'll do that, Mam, and the scrubbing, first thing tomorrow morning.' She sighed again. 'It'd be nice to be able to get some paint, wouldn't it?' She picked up the pile of curtains.

As she passed her mother, she bent and kissed the top of her head. Then she paused, hugging the curtains to her, and said, 'You know, Mam, this place is too much work now. Having a man about the place could help a lot. And we could have an agreement with him about how much share he gets, so everybody knows what we're doing.

'And you could keep the books, so you'd know everything's shipshape – no cheating. Not that he'll cheat us.' Her voice warmed, as she went on, 'You'll love him,

Mam. He says English words real nice; he's got a voice like Fluffy's purr. And you've been saying for ages that you wanted to take things easier. With a man to take some of the load, now's your chance.'

'Tah!' spluttered her mother, and pulled another curtain towards her. 'I want to see him first – and I won't drink any cider before I take a dekko at him! Have you fixed for him to come yet?'

Barbara shifted the pile of curtains in her arms. 'Well, he's going to get a passport so he can come for a holiday, first – give you a real chance to get to know him.' And, she admitted honestly to herself, for me to know him too.

'Well, I suppose that'd be all right. It means one of our bedrooms doesn't earn anything for the time he's here, though.'

Barbara hadn't considered this point. 'I suppose you're right, Mam.' She stood silent for a minute. Then she said, 'I could put a bit from me savings into the pot, 'cos it's true you might be short.'

In Phyllis's view this reflected on her own naturally hospitable nature. 'No, I wouldn't take it, I wouldn't.' She pursed her lips primly. Then she added, 'If he's your friend, you can have him to stay and give him a nice holiday. And then we'll see.'

Barbara dropped the curtains, and turned to hug her. She wanted to cry with relief. The first battle had been won. 'Thanks, Mam.'

Phyllis unwound herself from her daughter's arms, and said unsmilingly, 'Never let it be said I denied you having a friend to stay. And just you pick up them curtains. What are you doing, girl? White curtains on the floor!'

Chapter Thirty-seven

Five days after Barbara and Michel's final, quiet public farewell at Bayeux station, when she left for Paris, a letter arrived for Michel. It lay waiting for him on Madame Blanc's well-scrubbed kitchen table.

'I knew you'd be coming down to dinner so I kept it here,' Madame told Michel.

It smelled as if Madame was preparing tripe; she had seemed determined to feed him properly, and he hoped that this would give him the energy he badly needed to get through the next few months.

Madame was nearly beside herself with curiosity that he should get a letter from England, the address of which was written by hand. The other occasional letters he had received from there had been typewritten; she had understood that they were from the airman he had rescued. As she examined the new letter awaiting him, she had been disappointed that it carried no return address on it. Young Michel could be quite secretive.

Michel had had a busy day. He had decided that he would first look for work in Calvados, simply because it was his birthplace. Wrecked as it was, some of it had been cleared and there were signs of life. Today, he had tried one or two small places within a twelve-mile radius, where he knew there had been hotels, but without success. He had realised that he really was too shabby for the work he wanted. He would have to begin by working on a farm or something similar.

Out of the corner of her eye, Madame watched Michel open the letter. There was such a satisfied smile on his face that she was further intrigued.

After loving greetings, Barbara went on to advise that, to begin with, he should indeed come to England as a visitor. During that time they could be married from her home by special licence. He could then look round for work.

From the point of view of English officialdom, marriage would be a good reason for his desire to stay, she said. Then, they would try to extend his time with her – one way would be to obtain a student's permit and enrol at a college for a few months to study the English language, or even an agricultural college, if it were not too expensive; she had, she wrote, a little money saved which might help with fees. As a student, he could certainly stay for a while, and, in his spare time, he could see what could be raised in her huge garden. Then, perhaps, with his knowledge of the poultry trade, he might get a work permit. She was making further enquiries about work permits.

She was also checking on what her own legal position would be if she married him.

She reminded him that the B-and-B had a telephone, which made enquiries blessedly quick. She had given him the number before she left.

His faith in her was justified, any haunting doubts swept away. She had not been idle since her return home. She had even found a university student in West Kirby willing to give her French lessons, she told him.

Though he longed to telephone her, to hear her voice, it seemed an enormous, unnecessary expense, which he could not possibly manage.

Open letter in hand, he contemplated her with unrestrained adoration. His spirits rose to dizzy heights, over-riding both grief and fatigue. What joy it would give him to make her two hectares fruitful. And how very sensible in her enquiries in England she was proving to be.

One day, perhaps she would be able to speak to him fluently in his own language. In return, he promised himself, he would try to perfect his English.

In front of Madame Blanc, he had to control his desire to laugh aloud. Meeting Barbara had been little short of a miracle. If he ever told anyone how short their acquaintance had been, he would be castigated as totally without common sense.

Anatole, he remembered with a pang, had said that he longed to meet such an interesting lady, who had made such an impression on his kid brother.

And wise old Father Nicolas had not condemned him for his desire – once he knew she was a Roman Catholic, of course; and that would be his best argument when trying to sell to Maman the idea of his unusual marriage.

He had not yet told Maman about her. He wanted Maman to get used to being with Claudette and without him, before he went to Rouen to tell her. In addition he had not been quite sure what he and Barbara would be able to plan together; he wanted to present his family with firm arrangements in view.

He winced at the thought of telling his mother. He knew it would hurt her; no one but himself would quite understand the traumas she had endured. No one else had shared the memories which knitted mother and son together.

Despite my darling Barbara, despite my high hopes, the separation is going to hurt me too, he thought with sudden unhappiness.

Because he wanted to break the news to Maman as gently as possible, he did not want to give Madame Blanc any inkling of what he had in mind; she might, after all, write to Maman.

He returned to reading the letter.

To get permanent residence, Barbara went on, could be a slow matter, fraught with red tape. He had to get his worn pocket dictionary out of his back pocket, to look up red tape.

He surprised Madame Blanc by unexpectedly laughing out loud. Red tape? So what else was new?

'Joke?' enquired Madame hopefully.

He looked up at her. 'Yes,' he agreed, but much to her chagrin, did not enlarge on it.

And talking of red tape, *Ciel!* He would need a passport – and he must find out the cost and how to apply for one.

He turned over the page of the letter. She reminded him of the airmen he and Maman had sheltered, and how he had told her that the father of one of them was very eminent – a lawyer or a judge or something. Could he let her have their addresses? What about her asking them if they could advise him about permanent residence – and, eventually, citizenship, if he wanted it?

An excellent idea.

Michel scanned the last two paragraphs, and then hastily folded the letter, in case Madame, who had some English, could read upside down over the dish of steaming tripe she was bringing to the table. He would savour the end of the letter in the privacy of his room.

Meanwhile, he examined with some awe the plate of tripe she put before him. Had she really made tripe *à la mode de Caen*? He was being spoiled indeed. He had not seen the dish since before the war.

Chapter Thirty-eight

The following day, Michel rode over to Port-en-Bessin, in the hope that his Uncle Léon might still be in port. Though it was a pouring wet day, he did not want to waste time, so he had set out regardless of the weather. He could not admit to himself that he was desperately lonely. And there might be some kind of work he could do in the little port, he considered.

He was soaked to the skin by the time he arrived at the ancient cottage in which Léon Benion lived with the rather formidable middle-aged woman Hortense, who was accepted by his family as his housekeeper.

Léon was indeed in port, she told Michel. He had been held up by the storm that had brought the rain with it, she said, as she bustled behind him into the stuffy old-fashioned, stone kitchen with its blazing coal fire.

Arms akimbo, she then surveyed his dripping state.

'Come into the bedroom. I'll get you something of Léon's to put on while your clothes dry. You should buy an oilskin, you silly boy.'

'Hortense, I can't afford one,' he replied good-humouredly, as he followed her into a back room.

When Léon arrived home, his oilskins dripping, he found his nephew ensconced in his chair in his clothes, while a bedraggled outfit steamed on a rope strung across the mantelpiece.

As Léon greeted him, and handed his own raincoat and beret to Hortense, Michel sprang up from the chair.

There was a good deal of laughter, while Hortense dealt with a second sopping wet male. Hortense was not as grim as she looked, decided Michel; he had met her before, of course, but it had been Léon alone who usually came over to visit his brother's family.

'You came on a bike?' his uncle asked, gesturing towards a corner by the door, where the precious bicycle, neatly folded, was propped against the wall.

Michel said he had, and told him of the Americans' generosity. 'That job's finished,' he added.

'How is Maman – and the girls?'

'Anne-Marie and Claudette are as usual. Maman is exhausted. She's had too much to bear.' Michel lifted his hands in a gesture of hopelessness. 'She's borne up bravely all through the war, as you know, and then looking after Anatole. Now, it's caught up with her. She misses her home. Claudette's doing her best to comfort her; she's taken her back to Rouen.

'Claudette says she'll keep her in bed as long as she'll stay there, while she gathers strength. Despite the rationing, Bertrand's bakery is doing quite well; Maman will be well fed, thank God. Both Claudette and Bertrand want her to live with them. They really need an extra woman in the house, just to watch little Colette.'

He stirred uneasily. 'Things have been very tight with us, since the invasion. Maman insisted on saving everything she could – first, for Anatole's funeral, which she knew would come – though she never admitted it. Then for eggs to restock the farm. She didn't eat much, and it worried me. I gave her all I earned, but she wouldn't always spend it.'

'She always was a great manager,' Léon replied with a grin. 'Naturally, I'll be sending her something towards the funeral.' He pulled up another chair, and surveyed his nephew. 'Sit down, sit down,' he ordered.

The lad looked far too thin, the lines in his haggard face showing like deep seams, and his borrowed clothes hanging loosely on him. 'I'm relieved about your mother; Claudette will take care of her. And Rouen's normally a nice place to live in. It's recovering slowly, though it'll take years.'

Michel nodded agreement. 'There's lots of work there in the building trade.' He hesitated, feeling that his uncle might despise him for what he was about to say. Then he burst out, 'I'm looking for a job – better than labouring, which I could easily get in Rouen – because my shoulder objects strongly.' He grimaced ruefully. 'That's why I didn't go with Maman, though Claudette offered me a bed until I got started.'

'Well, what are you going to do?' enquired Léon. 'I doubt if we'll ever see the farm again.' He dug a packet of cigarettes out of his trouser pocket and offered one to Michel, who took it. 'I'm pretty sure the Government will make a huge coastal park – and our little patch will just about be enclosed in it. People are saying that it'll be a great tourist attraction – provided they can get rid of the mines.' In the light of the match he struck for their cigarettes, his face looked grim. Though he no longer had a financial interest in the property, he did not very much like such a valuable asset being lost to the family.

'I hope they pay for it, Uncle Léon – not simply appropriate it.'

'They will. Normandy has gone through so much,

particularly Calvados; there would be an insurrection if they didn't.'

Michel nodded, and replied firmly, 'I mustn't depend too much on compensation, because first, it has to be shared in the family, and second, we still have some debts to clear. The Boches were, sometimes, so tough on us that we actually had to borrow money in order to eat!'

'I know. So what're you going to do?'

Michel did not answer, while Hortense handed Léon and himself a mug of coffee each.

'I want to get a decent post, preferably in something connected with poultry. I want to sit at a desk – tell others how to do the heavy work. I know enough to be able to do it.' He gave a sideways glance at his uncle to see how he was taking this.

Léon considered this soberly as he sipped his coffee. Michel certainly had enough experience of raising hens – it was amazing what he had got off such a limited space, to satisfy the Boches.

Michel went on slowly, 'I can only do it by steps. After losing the farm, I've no decent clothes.' He laughed ruefully up at the garments hanging on the clothesline above the fireplace. 'I must earn enough to buy clothes that look right for an office job – or even for some sort of an outdoor supervisor.

'You know, I wouldn't mind working in a hotel, but as Reservations or Maintenance.' He stopped, and then added unwillingly, 'I may even be forced to do labouring, at first, to raise a bit of ready cash simply to get some decent clothes.'

His uncle gave one of his sly grins. 'You'll become a true bourgeois,' he mocked lightly.

'Why not?' demanded Michel promptly. 'It's much

more comfortable – thousands did it just before the war. They went to the cities. You went to sea, Bertrand's father did it – and now you've got your own boat and Bertie has his own bakery.'

'We voted with our feet.' Léon's grin broadened, as if amused that he had personally outwitted an oppressive hierarchy by simply laying down his spade.

'Right. Fed up with being despised and downtrodden good-for-nothings,' responded Michel with deliberate melodrama, which made his uncle chuckle, because it was so true. 'And, you know, I can speak English well enough for hotel work. I know some German, too, thanks to the *sales Boches*. And I can read and write and do arithmetic.'

'Well, why not, indeed? I did it. And, as you say, now I have the *Marie-Reine*.' He did not add that he had no one to whom he could leave his little freighter, which grieved him. He and his wife had remained childless from choice, while they both worked to improve their existence. She had died of cancer in 1938. Now, he had only Hortense.

Michel interrupted his wandering thoughts. 'I knew you'd understand, Uncle; that's why I came to discuss things with you – before I tackle Maman. She naturally hopes I'll go to Rouen.'

'Don't you want to go there? It's a huge place, with factories, and so on. There must be other work there. If there aren't jobs now, other than construction, there soon will be – now that France is finally getting Marshall Aid from the Yanks. It should facilitate other businesses in both Rouen and Cherbourg as they reopen.'

Michel nodded agreement, and then objected, 'It won't be us who'll make anything out of that immediately, Uncle Léon, and I need to get started now.'

'I see that. But it's essential for goods – and people – to move about. Look how difficult it's been for you. I don't suppose you could have looked for a job outside Bayeux?'

'Right. There are still no buses in Bayeux – and only one taxi. I couldn't move much, anyway, while Anatole was with us. Now I can live anywhere – and go anywhere – on the bike.'

Léon stabbed out the last of his cigarette and lit another one. He felt there must be an urgent reason for Michel's visit, and he asked abruptly, 'Well, what do you want me to do?'

'My seaman's book was lost in the house. Can I get it renewed?'

'Certainly. I'll give you the address.'

'And how do I get a passport?'

'Well, that's not too difficult, as long as you've got identification and the money for it. But why on earth do you want a passport?'

'I don't want it immediately. First, I have to get a job that pays more than subsistence, and find a room in which to live somewhere near it.'

'And what sort of job will you look for, first?'

'As I said, I'll work as a labourer; maybe on a big poultry farm. There are some that were not smashed up in the invasion. Then I'll try to get work in the office there.'

'And once you've got a little money?'

Michel hummed under his breath, and then said reluctantly, 'Well – well, if you promise not to say anything to Maman until you are sure I've told her, I want to work a passage to England.'

'*Mon Dieu*! Why? I'll take you on as ordinary seaman, of course. Not that you'll earn much.'

'All I want is to be discharged at a British port. I'll have

386

a visa – if I need one for a holiday – and a passport, and I want to go and see a friend of mine.'

'One of the airmen you sheltered?'

'Yes, I want to see him – I'll need his help.'

'There's more to this than meets the eye. Open up, boy, and tell me what it's really all about.' Léon took a sip of coffee. 'I hope it's got nothing to do with the black market or smuggling. I can't afford to lose my reputation, if you're involved in something illegal.' Over the rim of his coffee cup, Léon's eyes were suddenly steely.

Michel exploded with laughter, and assured him that it was nothing illegal. 'All I want to do is marry an English-woman,' he announced quietly, hoping that Hortense, busy at the kitchen sink, would not hear him.

'An Englishwoman?' Léon sat bolt upright in surprise. 'You're crazy. What on earth for? You must be out of your mind. Marry some stiff-necked, cold foreigner?'

Michel sighed. 'I don't think I'm quite dotty. I want to marry her for lots of reasons. She's a wonderful little woman. She and her mother own a bed-and-breakfast, a kind of small hotel, near Liverpool.' His voice rose with enthusiasm. 'They've two hectares of unused farmland round it – good possibilities there.' Cigarette between his fingers, he made a wide gesture to show how good the possibilities were.

Léon was still regarding him as if he had suddenly gone mad.

Undeterred, Michel continued, 'She tells me that Liver-pool's a great centre for importing food – and processing it. And we both know that that's likely true – you've taken cargoes up there. So there's a chance that I could get a decent job to do with poultry. They must need eggs in a city that big, and I could work her land in my spare time.'

He threw his cigarette end into the fire and then said wryly, 'They must be short of men, the same as we are.'

There was dead silence as Uncle Léon tried to grasp the implications of this most unexpected announcement. Michel smiled knowingly at his uncle, and then added one more bombshell, 'What's more, I'm truly in love with her!'

'*Ciel!* No wonder you don't want to tell your mother. It sounds absolutely crazy to me. Are you sure you want to do this?' He flicked his cigarette ash into the hearth. 'What about a nice French girl?' he suggested. 'I could look for one for you – with a dowry, possibly.'

'After Suzanne? *Mais non!* And you know and I know that Englishwomen are famous for their faithfulness.'

Léon made a wry mouth. 'I suppose,' he answered doubtfully. 'It's a nice story. But the war's changed England as well as France – I feel it every time I dock there.'

He called to Hortense for another cup of coffee. Then, his voice sombre, he said, 'What Suzanne did was hard on you. Against that, not all French girls are the same.'

'I know. Maman is going to say that, too. But once bitten, twice shy. And Maman can't complain that Barbara isn't suitable. She's Catholic. Nor can anyone complain much about a dowry – she's plenty to offer.' His eyelids half closed, as if from a sudden pain, and it was obvious to Léon that the lad was still very bitter at his betrayal.

Léon allowed Hortense to bring him his coffee, and waited until she had returned to the kitchen sink and her chopping of vegetables. Then he said, 'It's true, when I think about it, you've nothing much to lose here. However, Englishmen make any self-respecting Frenchman creep, you know that – ignorant boors. They aren't liked here; and you won't be liked there, I can tell you from experience.'

'I know. But you haven't seen Barbara.'

'I can't say I want to,' retorted his uncle irritably. 'She'll never understand you. It's a different outlook – and a different life.'

'She's got common sense, Uncle. She wouldn't have committed herself, unless she thought we'd make a go of it,' Michel replied patiently.

'Look here, Michel. You'd have to face Englishmen to get a job; every time you walked in the street, you'd be a target for any hooligan that may be around; and you'd have no friends to help to protect you. I know it.' Uncle Léon's knowledge of England was limited to dock areas, and he spoke from that experience.

Michel's heart sank while he inwardly cried for his *chérie* Barbara.

Determinedly, he tried another tack. 'She's suggested that I go first for a holiday, to her home. I can look around, get the feel of it all. It won't cost much, if you'll let me work my passage. I can use the bike to get me up to Liverpool from, say, Portsmouth.' He leaned across the fireplace towards his uncle, and went on, 'I can always return, if I don't think I can face it. She can come here, if she wants to, though it'll be years before Normandy is on its feet again.'

Hortense called that the evening meal was ready.

Without a further word, the two men clumped to the table, where, perforce, the conversation was taken up by Hortense, who wanted to know about the funeral and each member of the family; she had no family herself, and clung to the hope of belonging to her lover's family. They tolerated her, she knew, though they regarded her as an unnecessary expense in which Uncle Léon indulged himself.

After dinner and a glass or two of cheap wine, Uncle Léon was in a more tolerant mood. A holiday in England might be sufficient to put Michel off his mad idea. He had a real affection for the younger man, and a genuine desire for his happiness – and he could not imagine any self-respecting Norman ever being happy in such a benighted northern island full of traditional Protestant enemies of France. But a holiday? There was a compromise. He would have been surprised to learn that Phyllis had come to a similar conclusion.

After Hortense had done the dishes and gone to bed, Léon tried once more to deter his nephew from his mad idea, but to no purpose. He decided that the man must be absolutely besotted by this widow, that time in England was probably the only way to disenchant him.

'You don't only marry a woman,' he warned. 'You marry a family – and in this case, you'll be marrying into a strange society as well.' He made a wry face. 'I'll take you there, if you still want to go in a few months' time. If you can get a decent job here, you may change your mind.'

'I doubt I will,' replied Michel woodenly, though his uncle's description of his likely reception was the popular view of England and the English.

'Well, we'll leave it open. And I'll certainly bring you back if you do go and don't like what you find.'

'Thanks, Uncle. What you've said is sensible, I know,' Michel admitted aloud. Silently, he promised himself that, for Barbara, he would sacrifice his life.

Uncle Léon was saying, 'You can always return to Calvados, you know that. And I can give you a roof, if you need one,' he added kindly. Michel watched him lean back in his chair, and examine the smoke-blackened ceiling. 'Try it. Let me know ahead of time when you need a berth – though I can carry you as a passenger instead of crew provided you've got your passport and a visa.'

Michel felt that his uncle had been more reasonable

than many would have been, more reasonable than his mother would probably be. He said humbly, 'Thank you, Uncle. You're very good.' Then to change the subject, he suggested, 'Next time you dock in Rouen, I know Maman and Claudette would love you to visit them.'

'Naturally, I will.'

'There is one favour I want to ask you, if you would. Could you watch what happens to our land, and deal with whatever comes up? Consult Maman, of course. There's no one else I can trust.'

Léon shrugged. 'Of course, I will. But I hope you'll return to us.'

It was taken for granted that Michel would stay overnight, and while they sat over the last of the wine, Uncle Léon got out of his determined nephew, step by step, more details of how he had met Barbara and exactly how he intended to proceed.

'Why do you want to farm her land? It won't be easier than doing it here.'

For a man in love, the answer was unexpectedly practical.

'Because a bed-and-breakfast there might be built into a hotel eventually, if there is enough land. If I can't get into a poultry company or similar, alternatively, I would like office work in a hotel, if I could get it – get experience to help to run the place with her,' replied Michel, blithely unaware of the stultifying effect of British red tape where new construction or anything else to promote business was concerned.

'Well, there's nothing like ambition,' said Léon, determined to handle the boy with diplomacy.

Let the lad fly. Soon enough, he'd be thankful to return to Calvados.

Chapter Thirty-nine

The last instruction that Uncle Léon shouted after him, as, in Portsmouth, Michel carried his bicycle down the gangway of the *Marie-Reine*, was to ride on the left-hand side of the road.

Though he had been in England before, Michel had not remembered this simple fact. It was as well that he had been reminded, otherwise he would probably have been mown down by impatient, lumbering lorries before he had ever managed to get out of the dock area.

He was armed with a map of England, on which he had marked the general north-westerly route he intended to take, and the smaller towns through which he proposed to travel in order to avoid heavy city traffic. He had not, unfortunately, been able to obtain maps of the towns through which he would pass. His uncle had, with many further admonitions regarding the ferocity of some Britons, shown him a map of Portsmouth, and the road which would take him in the direction of Winchester.

Michel found, to his frustration, that the road suggested by his uncle was temporarily closed off by a barricade, while a bomb site was being cleared to make way for rebuilding.

As he dismounted and stood uncertainly on the edge of a pavement, his bike tucked into the gutter, he realised how badly the city had been damaged. It was nothing like the damage to Caen, but he could see from where he stood a number of gaunt shattered walls.

Warnings from his Uncle Léon still fresh in his mind, and predictions from his despairing mother, his family and one or two friends like Reservations and old Duval, about the traditional unfriendliness of the British to Frenchmen, made him hesitant. He stood there, amid hurrying shoppers, feeling very lonely.

'If you're lost, always ask a policeman,' Barbara had advised. So, with some reluctance, he finally crossed the road, to where a white-clad constable, his back to the barricade, was redirecting the traffic.

As the constable waved traffic across the front of him, Michel nervously asked for the road to Winchester.

At the sound of the foreign accent, the constable nodded, but continued to wave vehicles in various directions, as he waited for a break in the traffic. Misunderstanding this silence, Michel began to think that he was not bothering to attend to him because he was French.

Then the constable thankfully dropped his aching arms, wiped the perspiration off his cheeks with a hasty dash of a white glove, and glanced up and down at the clerk-like person in front of him, mackintoshed and trilby-hatted. He asked the stranger quite civilly, 'Winchester, you say?'

'Yes, sir,' replied Michel, not certain how one addressed the police in England.

The constable duly instructed him, and then he asked, in a friendly manner. 'You visiting?'

'I'm – er – holiday by bicycle.'

With his big boots, he looks like a Spanish onion man, considered the constable, except for his trilby hat and old mackintosh. And this man doesn't have any onions.

The Basque purveyors of onions came over from Spain regularly to sell their produce to English housewives, but they wore berets.

There was an uneasy moment, when the constable asked, 'How far are you thinking of going?'

Michel looked at the large red face before him. The expression seemed reasonable. 'I go to West Kirby near Liverpool, visit a friend's house.'

The constable did not reply as he weighed him up. Instead, he waved on some panting lorries bound for the dock road. Then he turned back to Michel. 'A friend?'

Very nervous, Michel played his best card. He said, 'I am from Bayeux. I work with Resistance. I save an RAF pilot from the Germans. Now he invite me to visit him. Very nice man.'

It was an acceptable explanation for a small, neat foreigner's presence, thought Michel defensively; and he had, praise God, in his inner pocket a letter which, if the constable required proof, said exactly that.

The constable considered it very acceptable too, and grinned amiably, as he impatiently held his hand up to stop an elderly lady in an equally old car, edging past him into turning traffic. 'It's a long ride,' he warned. Then he repeated the directions to Winchester.

'*Merci bien*,' responded Michel, as he mounted his bike and rode out of the intersection.

Thankful to have survived his first encounter with British police, he plucked up courage sometime later to ask the way to Wickham, the first place on his route, of a woman carrying a shopping basket, while she waited to cross a road.

The woman actually smiled at him as she described the route to him.

As he progressed from village to village, he found two big problems. One was that Britain did not seem to have any straight roads such as France was blessed with; between high hedges they wound their way through tiny, anonymous settlements. And, secondly, there were, inexplicably, absolutely no directional signs of any kind. He did not know that all signposts had been carefully removed at the beginning of the war so that a German invasion force would, it had been anticipated, get hopelessly lost.

As he progressed further and further into the countryside, however, the natives appeared friendly, though, when he paused to ask directions, they almost invariably asked what he was doing in England.

Britain was awash with ne'er-do-wells, many of them home-grown. But an uncomfortable number were deserters from various armies, refugees from overrun countries, riffraff of every kind, even German ex-prisoners of war who had, by one means or another, escaped being sent home to their devastated country. The stories of this floating population's running of the black market, dealing in drugs, smuggling anything they could sell, could be found in the back pages of most newspapers; and these reports made the long-suffering, tired-out British very nervous and resentful. Though people were polite to him, Michel sensed this underlying fear. It worried him. The road to Liverpool began to seem impossibly long.

He had brought with him, in the shabby suitcase tied to the back of his bike, two bottles of water. He had not considered that it might be difficult to get the bottles refilled. To save money, he intended to sleep rough while on his way north; a haystack or a barn would provide a warm and dry sleeping place, but it would not supply him with water; for that he would have to ask.

Thirst became a major preoccupation. He was nervous of knocking on a door to beg for something as ordinary as water; he could easily visualise what kind of belligerent hater of the French might answer – and plunge him into unimaginable trouble. Yet in the warm, dry harvest weather, riding steadily, he needed to drink as much water as he could.

Sometime after leaving Wickham, he came to a small humped-back bridge over a stream. He parked the bike at the beginning of the bridge. Old wine bottles in hand, he eased through a thin hedge into an apparently empty, uncultivated field and slid down to the stream. The water appeared clear, so he topped up both bottles and recorked them. Then he took off his hat and splashed his face, thankful for the coolness of the water.

He had just wiped the water out of his eyes and smoothed back his splashed hair, when a voice roared from the bridge, 'What're you doing down there? You're trespassing.'

Startled, Michel looked up.

By his bicycle, stood a heavily built elderly man. He was roughly clad in a faded tweed jacket, breeches and leather gaiters. Pulled down over his forehead was a battered tweed hat and tucked into the band of it were several fishing flies. As he shook a walking stick at Michel, he shouted again, 'You're trespassing!' A huge white moustache moved menacingly up and down as the man angrily sought for words.

'*Monsieur?*'

'Don't you Monsoor me! Come out of there.'

Scared because he could not remember precisely what the word 'trespass' meant, Michel hastily picked up his trilby and clapped it back onto his head. Then he picked up his bottles, and, tucking one under his arm, scrambled up the slippery slope and emerged to face the stranger.

The man was tapping the ground angrily with his stick, and, as Michel straightened up, the man lifted the walking stick and, none too gently, poked the Frenchman in the stomach.

'Can't you read?' he shouted, as if Michel were deaf. He again swung his stick upwards, this time to point to a notice board, almost obscured by heavy foliage. 'No trespassing!'

Michel instinctively ducked as the man swung the heavy stick back to point to the stream. 'That river and the fish in it belong to me – not to European trash. I'm sick and tired of tramps on my land – particularly foreigners. They shouldn't even be here.'

He paused for breath and glared at the intruder, and Michel hastened to interject, 'I am most sorry, Monsieur. I wish only water to drink.' He lifted up a bottle in each hand.

'Water? You dirty French wino. You were tickling trout, I'll be bound.'

'*Mais non, Monsieur*. I visit England for holiday.'

'Ha!' He scanned scornfully Michel's loose black trousers, his woollen sweater and his big farm boots; and Michel wished he had not, because of the heat, taken off his raincoat and strapped it on the top of his suitcase on the carrier. He believed that the raincoat gave him an air of middle-class respectability. He had a new suit folded carefully into his suitcase, but he wanted to maintain its pristine look until he reached West Kirby. He was, however, acutely aware of how shabby he must look to the beefy, furious man before him.

'Holiday? That's a likely tale. You're here to steal what

397

you can get.' The man was rapidly going purple in his rage. 'There're too many like you here. I know your kind.'

Michel had had enough. He edged towards his bike. Tight-lipped, he leaned in front of the furious landowner and put the bottles carefully in a small shopping basket strapped to the handlebars.

'Monsieur is much mistaken,' he said through gritted teeth. 'Now, if Monsieur kindly move himself, I continue my journey.'

The older man was a trifle nonplussed by the clarity of Michel's English. He blustered on, however, 'Get back to France, you scum.' He lifted his stick again and shook it at the hapless Frenchman. 'If I ever set eyes on you again, I'll call the police!'

Very angry, Michel moved swiftly round the back of the old man, then leaned in front of him and seized his bike by its handlebars. He pulled it forward sharply into the road; the pedals scraped the gaiters of his abuser.

He jumped into the saddle, sailed down the sharp slope of the bridge and rode off, followed by a stream of curses.

Though very shaken by the encounter, Michel made the best speed he could through a tiny hamlet, and then slowed as he began to move into hilly country. He did not stop, however, until he had put a number of miles between himself and the irascible landowner.

A couple of hours later, at a silent juncture of two lanes, where an elm tree offered shade, he dismounted and sat down on the rough ground. He put his head on his knees. He was breathless, offended, hurt – judged by his clothes, by his foreign accent. It seemed that Uncle Léon had been right: the British boors still hated the French as much as the French despised them.

Was it going to be like this all the way? Then, puzzled, he asked himself how *chère* Barbara could be so different?

He sat there until he steadied. Then he told himself philosophically that one man did not necessarily represent a nation. He must be calm, and get himself to his dearest Barbara.

He got up, opened one of his bottles, took a big slurp of warmish water and then unstrapped his suitcase. He took out a two-pound loaf of bread, one of two he was carrying, baked by the seaman who acted as cook on his uncle's ship. He tore off about a quarter of the loaf. As he slowly ate the already rather dry bread, he walked up and down in front of his bike lying on the ground in order to loosen his muscles.

When a young boy, dressed in working overalls, came whistling down the road, he asked him for the route to Winchester. The boy looked at him with interest. He was, however, civil and put him on his way, with the advice to ask again when he reached a certain point.

As Michel thanked him and mounted his bicycle, he called after him, 'You'll know Winchester when you see it – it's got a big cathedral and a real statue of King Alfred!'

Feeling reassured after this encounter, he sailed onwards through meandering country lanes. Occasionally, he would stop and consult his compass – he knew he must, generally, keep going north-west. Once or twice, he spread his map on grass at the side of the narrow roads he was traversing to try to check his whereabouts. As he examined the detail of the map, he tutted to himself. When compared with France, Britain really had a rotten road system.

He unexpectedly found a surviving signpost, which

helped him on his way to Winchester, and he crossed the River Itchen, while the sun was still high, and rode up the hill of what appeared to be the city's main street, and out into the country again.

He wanted to reach Andover before looking for a place to eat an evening meal. Though hungry, he pressed on through low hills, only to realise that he was lost. He slowed down.

The only living things Michel could see were sheep, until he was suddenly faced by an army Jeep carrying four soldiers.

The lane was narrow, so he drew into the side to let them pass. They slowed to pass him, and he was suddenly terrified. The driver, however, grinned cheerfully and, as he went by, gestured thumbs up in appreciation of the space made for him.

This encouraged him, so that when he met two infantry-men strolling towards him, cigarettes in hand, as if off duty, he stopped to ask if he were on the right road to Andover.

They looked him over cautiously. Instead of answering him, one asked, 'You're French?'

'*Oui, Monsieur.*'

'What are you doing here?'

It was a question he was getting used to, and he replied, as he had to others, 'I have holiday. I bicycle through your beautiful country to see it.'

'Lucky for you,' sneered the talkative one, as he took a cigarette out of his mouth. 'I was in the invasion and I saw men like you sitting on your arses, while we fought the Jerries. Cowardly swine.'

Michel took a big breath to control his outrage; they were far too big and fit for him to tackle alone. One man

400

dropped his cigarette and ground it under his army boot; then he grinned knowingly at his companion.

Michel had seen that look on the faces of Germans. He was sitting astride his bike, legs straddled on either side, and he now nonchalantly eased his right foot onto the pedal, as if to steady himself.

He glanced quickly down the lane behind them, and then grinned, and shouted, as if to greet an old friend, 'Hello, Joe!'

They turned to see who was there, and he shot away from them with all the force he could muster, and kept on pedalling.

There must be a military camp somewhere near, he considered, as soon as he could make himself concentrate again after such an insult; and he doggedly pedalled downhill for several miles of curving lanes, in the hope of escaping any other soldiery who might be lurking in the undergrowth.

In a desperate need to know where he was, he finally stopped outside an isolated little Norman church, similar to his own parish church, except that a notice board said that it was Church of England.

Next to it, was an equally small house. A presbytery? A priest would surely be civil to him, Michel decided.

He opened a wrought-iron gate and wheeled his bicycle up to the front doorstep. Tentatively, he pressed a bell. A dog yapped on the other side of the door.

To his relief, a woman's voice called, 'Down, Scampy, down!'

He heard a bolt being shot back, and a thin, middle-aged woman, holding a small terrier firmly by its collar, opened the door.

'Yes?' she enquired.

'Madame, I cycle to Andover, and I have lost my way.' Tired, black-rimmed brown eyes looked expectantly at her.

She smiled and opened the door a little wider. 'You're within a mile of it.' She picked up the straining dog, and stepped out to point the way. 'If you continue down this road, you'll see it in the distance. Just turn half left at the pub. That road will take you straight in.'

He thanked her in English.

Remembering her tattered back garden, which her priestly husband had rather neglected that year, she asked hopefully, 'Are you looking for work?'

'No, Madame. I have holiday on bicycle.'

Her face fell. 'Oh. I see. Never mind.' Then she laughed self-consciously. 'I was going to offer you a meal, if you would dig up our potatoes. I think they're ready.'

He jumped at the idea of a free meal. 'I do it,' he said promptly. 'No trouble.'

Two sacks of potatoes later, he was presented with a big plate of assorted boiled vegetables and a minuscule amount of stewed meat, followed by a large slice of tasteless steamed pudding with, to him, an unidentifiable, weird yellow sauce over it.

As he sat on a discarded kitchen chair in the garden, and thankfully ate the food, the vicar himself emerged to take a look at him. The minister was tall, bent and greying, his black suit shiny with wear.

Gazing gently at Michel over glasses on the tip of his nose, the vicar addressed him. 'Good afternoon,' he said. 'I hear you are taking a holiday amongst us.'

As Michel rose politely, empty pudding dish and spoon in one hand, he summoned up his best English, and replied that he was.

'Thank you for getting in the potatoes. It's difficult at present to get a jobbing gardener.' He cleared his throat, 'You are French, I take it?'

'Yes, sir. From Calvados.'

'You have friends here?'

'Yes, sir. I go first to a place call West Kirby – near Liverpool, and then to another friend in Manchester.'

The vicar was puzzled. The man looked like a tramp; yet he spoke credible English with a good accent.

'I believe my wife is making a pot of tea,' he said. 'Would you like to come into the kitchen and drink it there?' He smiled. 'We usually have a cup after dinner.'

Poor Michel could have wept on his shoulder with sheer relief at his graciousness. 'Thank you, sir. Where shall I put the potatoes?'

When the modest harvest had been safely stored in an outhouse, Michel was ushered into an untidy kitchen and seated at a table strewn with the remains of a meal.

It took the vicar about five minutes to get out of Michel the story of the RAF men his family had succoured and that he was also to visit an English lady he had met in Normandy.

Tea was not Michel's favourite drink, but the three of them emptied two extremely weak pots of it, and the sun was sinking before Michel reluctantly rose to leave his kindly hosts. They accepted his remark that he would find somewhere in Andover to stay the night.

Much comforted, Michel rode through Andover, after first asking the way to Swindon of a patrolling constable. The constable first directed him, and then warned him that it was about sixty miles away.

'I start now. Find bed-and-breakfast to sleep en route. Arrive in Swingdong tomorrow,' replied Michel.

'OK, mate.' The constable was amused at his pronunciation, but he made a wry face. 'Better get a lamp for your bike if you're going to cycle late,' he advised. 'I could give you a ticket for not having one.'

'Very hard to buy,' guessed Michel.

'For sure. That's why I'm not ticketing you now.'

With the well-meant advice of the constable still ringing in his ears, Michel faced a few more miles of hilly country, some of it well-treed, before he gave up and began to look out for a place to sleep.

He was dreadfully tired, and nervous too. Until he had met the vicar and his wife, he had begun to think that he was mad to continue his journey through such an alien country.

Better, perhaps, to turn back and forget his insane idea of marrying an English woman – and yet his longing for her was there and not to be denied, and it kept him pedalling until his legs ached.

He continued doggedly on until darkness began to close in; then the multitude of curves in the narrow road, which tended to bifurcate unexpectedly, confused him again. He passed through several dimly lit villages, however, until the strong smell of manure suggested a farm close behind the hedges which lined the road.

He dismounted, and furtively walked to a gate. A hump outlined against the darkening sky indicated a house. It showed no light. He hesitated and then decided that to open the gate would make too much noise. He pushed the bike further down the lane. Another gate led directly into a field.

He eased the gate open and slipped his bicycle through. He looked up at a starlit sky. Rain seemed unlikely. The field had a crop in it of some kind; he could smell its dusty, nearly ready-for-harvest odour.

It would do. Beneath the hedge he caught a gleam of water, probably a drainage ditch, he thought. So he laid his bike, unlocked, on the rough grass between it and the gently waving wheat. Then he unpacked, ate some more stale bread and drank the last of his water.

After a little thought, he laid down his mackintosh close against the first stalks of the crop to give himself the maximum of warmth and shelter if it rained in the night. It was not a comfortable bed, but he was so exhausted that he fell asleep immediately.

His weariness had been so great that the sun was high when he awoke to the noise of a tractor in the near distance.

Harvesters, he guessed. He sat up very quietly, only to moan with cramp in his back and legs. He jumped when a pair of frightened rats ran out of the wheat and splashed into the ditch.

Better get out before a dog found him, he decided. Reluctant to show himself to the harvesters, who seemed to have started their work on the far side of the field, he kneeled as he folded his mac and restrapped it to his bike, and put the empty bottles into the basket. Rumpled, unshaven, bits of straw all over his black trousers and pullover, he lifted the bike onto its wheels. Hunched over it to be as invisible as possible, he pushed the gate open and slid out into the lane.

He looked up and down the road. Nobody. Holding the bike upright with one hand, he hastily brushed at the loose straws on his clothes, but without much success.

He was dreadfully hungry and thirsty.

After cogitating wearily as to what he should do, he decided that the farm itself was most likely to yield some water and put him on his way.

The house door was ajar. To one side of it was a dog kennel with an empty enamel dish set on the ground in front of it. As Michel approached it, a large dog shot out to the length of the rope that held it. Barking ferociously, it leaped at him, straining to reach him.

Pushing his bicycle, he edged round it. A voice from within the house shouted, 'See who it is, Annie.'

With an apprehensive glance at the dog, Michel turned to face the door.

It was opened by a thin young girl in a grubby summer frock. She was so fair that she was almost colourless, and she stared disinterestedly at him. Then she half-turned and shouted back into the house, 'It's a tramp, Mum.'

'Well, tell him to go away.'

The girl woodenly repeated the message and moved to shut the door.

'Mademoiselle, I want only some water from your pump over there.' He pointed across the yard to a pump with a trough in front of it. 'I'm very thirsty,' he pleaded.

The girl paused, and then the door was whipped wide. He was faced with a hugely fat woman in a black apron. She flourished a rolling pin, and shouted into his face, 'Get out afore I brain you. You're the second I've had this morning. Lazy good-for-nothings, that's what you are. Go and get yourself a job.'

Forgetting that a day's beard had added considerably to his tramplike appearance, Michel turned without a word and, carefully avoiding the growling dog, wheeled his bike back to the lane. When safely outside, he stood trembling against his bicycle.

He had not been afraid of the woman; he could have whipped her rolling pin out of her hand in a second; it was the unthinking reception that had filled him with despair.

Despite memory of the kindly priest and his wife, this latest insult was too much.

Barbara, *chère* Barbara, I don't think I can face this, he cried inwardly. This everlasting doubt of me because I'm French. How can I work for you here if I am to be treated like this?

He stood debating whether to give up and turn back the way he had come.

Or would it be better to continue on to Barbara's village to tell her that he could not stay? Then, to avoid the hazards of another bicycle ride through this difficult country, he could find a berth in a ship out of Liverpool and work his way home to France.

He swallowed, unsure what to do in his isolation. No small problem was his lack of knowledge of where he was on the map.

'She's a real bitch, ain't she?' a hoarse voice said.

The unexpected interruption of his anxious cogitation made Michel jump. He glanced round.

On the other side of the road, squatting on the narrow band of grass in front of the hedge, was a very small man. With at least two days' beard on his chin and clothes so ragged that they barely covered him, he looked like a pixie who had wandered out of a storybook. The soles of his boots had holes in them and one sole hung loose at the toe. He wore a grubby flat cap which shaded a nut-brown face and beady, knowing eyes. Beside him on the ground lay a stick with a small bundle tied to one end.

Chapter Forty

Wrapped in his own misery, Michel regarded the tramp with suspicion.

'Where you bound?' asked the stranger.

'Swingdong,' replied Michel.

'You mean Swindon? You're foreign, ain't you?'

Enough starch remained in Michel to make him answer with pride, 'I'm French.'

'Well, I'll be buggered. Deserter, eh? Seen one or two of 'em.' The man blew his nose through his fingers, and then looked Michel up and down, and asked, 'How long you bin on the road? Not long?'

'No, I'm no deserter, you rat.' Such helpless rage enveloped Michel that he felt he could easily have dropped his bicycle and killed the man with a hearty kick in the neck.

With complete aplomb, however, the pixie proffered an immediate apology.

'Sorry, pal. No offence intended,' he said. 'I bin nearly twenty years on the road. Demobbed in 1919. Was in hospital with shell shock for a long while. Come out. No work. No family. No nothin'. Got used to it. Sally Army helps me out every now and then. Spend the winter in a workhouse somewhere.' He smiled ingratiatingly. 'Gotta fag?'

Until the storm of rage within him evaporated, Michel listened with gritted teeth to this potted history.

The tramp repeated impatiently, 'A cigarette?'

Michel stared at him. What a wreck of humanity! He must be the tramp who had begged at the farmhouse – and be as hungry as he was himself.

Michel could not totally forgive the assumption that he was a deserter, but he could feel a condescending pity for such human garbage.

He shifted his bike so that it leaned against him, and felt up his jersey. Careful not to expose a second packet tucked inside his undervest, he produced a battered package with two cigarettes in it, and moved closer to the tramp. He bent down and proffered the carton.

'Ta, pal,' said the tramp gratefully, as he took one with a hand so dirty that it was black. Michel put the other cigarette in his own mouth, found his matches in his back pocket, and lit both.

Both of them inhaled. Michel looked again at the tramp. No matter what he finally decided to do, he had to find a place where he could buy some bread.

He asked, 'How I go to Swingdong?'

The tramp laughed. 'You do say it funny! You mean Swindon. Give me a ride on your carrier, and I'll take you – guaranteed,' he replied.

Michel hesitated, and then decided that it would be helpful not to be lost yet again. The man was so small, he was no menace.

The suitcase and mac were clumsily packed on top of the basket on the front of the bike; the pixie arranged himself on the carrier rack. He placed his feet neatly on the long screws which clamped the rack to the bike. Then, holding his staff and its bundle on one shoulder, he put his other arm round Michel's waist and clung on to him.

Pedalling was considerably more difficult with a passenger to balance and an unsteady load on the front basket. They wobbled along, however, and each time they came to a hill to climb, Michel insisted that they walk up it and then remount, to coast down the other side.

During the afternoon, the Salvation Army at Swindon, finding them both sober, did not query them further but sat them down amongst a motley crew looking very much like themselves and fed them plentifully on slightly stale cheese sandwiches and very weak tea.

Michel then went to consult a uniformed man at the counter by the door, in whose charge he had left his folded-up bike and his suitcase. Laying his map open in front of the man, he asked directions for Worcester.

The officer showed him. He was used to drifters of all kinds who wandered up and down the country, but this foreigner seemed to have more purpose. Simply to see if he had guessed correctly, he asked, 'Is that your final destination?'

Michel stared dumbly at him. Doubt of him again? It was impossible to bear. Then he shrugged. What did it matter? He could endure this journey, see Barbara and beg her to return to France with him. Regardless of what she said, he would go home to France – by sea, if possible. She could follow him, if she wished. As he sought to reply to the Salvation Army officer, some of the hysteria which had once exploded when he was at home threatened to overwhelm him again.

'No, Monsieur,' he finally replied. 'I go to a village called West Kirby at the River Dee? I visit a friend.'

'Oh, yes. I know West Kirby. In that case, you could go from Worcester to here.' He jabbed a finger at the map. 'Bridgenorth. Then, if you make for Wrexham, there is a road from there which will take you into Chester. From there, anyone will direct you to West Kirby.' With a kindly smile, he folded up the map and returned it to Michel.

Michel asked if he would write down the names of the places he had mentioned, which he did.

'Thank you, Monsieur.' He collected his bicycle and made his escape, unnoticed by the pixie who was deep in conversation with a group as ragged as himself. Two people aboard one bike was too heavy going, Michel had decided. And, furthermore, the pixie stank.

With mixed receptions wherever he stopped, he fought his way north to Chester. He gave up trying to shave in streams, in cold water without soap, afraid always of irate landlords. His beard looked more fearsome every day.

At one point, in a tiny town square, he stopped at a public lavatory to take off his trousers and stitch up a hole in their seat with needle and thread thoughtfully provided by Claudette.

He was alone in the place and scared of being found trouserless. He had, however, just put them on again, when a heavily built labourer in grubby overalls, a man about his own age, came in to relieve himself. Michel was washing his hands and face at a tiny, filthy sink, his folded bicycle and suitcase close behind him.

On his way out, the labourer paused to glance down at the bike. 'Where'd you get a bike like that, mate?' he asked suspiciously. 'It's an Army bike.'

'In France,' Michel replied, his heart sinking. Now what?

There was no towel, so he hastily wiped his hands down the back of his trousers, hitched the folded bike up onto

411

his right shoulder and picked up his suitcase. Fearful of being cornered in a limited space, he deliberately crowded the Englishman from behind, and the man automatically moved up the steps to street level.

'Aye,' the labourer agreed quite innocently at the top of the steps. 'A lot of us had 'em for the invasion. Was you in it?'

He's going to accuse me of stealing it in a moment, thought a scared Michel. Why can't the damned British mind their own business? While he unfolded the bike and set it upright, he did not reply. Then he said heavily, 'Yes, I was.'

He began to buckle his suitcase and mac back onto the carrier, as the labourer responded, 'You couldn't have bin. You're not English, are you? You're French?'

Totally exasperated, Michel quickly closed the buckle on the strap and swung himself onto the machine, as he said with bitterness, 'We French were there, dead cert.'

He pedalled off into traffic at such a speed that there were frightened honks from car drivers. He was so angry that he didn't care where he went, and was soon lost, while a bewildered English labourer stared after him, and wondered what he had said wrong.

Early one evening Michel arrived at a railway station, which he knew should be Chester. He had endured five days of these mixed receptions, and they had doused any enthusiasm he had had about settling in England.

Pushing his bike, he wandered onto the platform and saw, from a huge notice board, that it was indeed that city. That most railway stations had newly painted notice boards facing the railway line itself, which showed the name of the place, was something he had realised rather late in his ride; it had, latterly, been very useful information.

Aware of being watched by a man in railway uniform, he hastened out.

Disillusioned, weary beyond words, his hopes in ashes, he knew now that he was within a few hours' ride of Barbara. How would she take his refusal to stay in her impossible country – so like his own and yet so horribly unlike?

Kindnesses he had received, he freely admitted; but the blatant suspicion of a foreigner, the not infrequent indirect references alleging cowardice of the French during the war, had wounded him immeasurably. Would the British never understand what had happened to his beloved Calvados – and the ruination of the rest of France?

Today, he must find a bed-and-breakfast, get a bath, make himself respectable. He did not like her country, but he would not let his darling Barbara down in front of her mother or her village.

The first housewife advertising in her window, 'Bed-and-Breakfast – Vacancy', took one look at his dishevelled appearance, announced that her rooms were full and slammed the door in his face. The second one, used to untidy English hikers, was more amenable, and agreed to provide bed and breakfast for ten shillings. He brought out his small supply of English money, acquired with difficulty in Bayeux; it had been secured by a safety pin in his back pocket. She gave him change for the pound note he proffered.

'I want a bath,' he told her.

'That would be another shillin'. I'll have to put the water heater on,' she replied. 'It takes about an hour to heat.'

413

He paid the extra shilling and received a confusing amount of coinage in change. 'I get a meal while I wait, yes? A café nearby?'

She directed him to a shabby café further down the road, and he asked if he could leave his bike and case with her. She smiled and said, 'Of course. Bring the bike round the back. I'll put your case in your room.'

I have to trust her, he thought. This town is busy – and I could lose the bike and the case if I left them outside a café.

Sick-tired, without hope, extremely hungry, he went to eat where she had instructed.

They had only one hot dish still available on the menu, the waitress told him cheerfully. He wondered why they bothered to write a menu if they were so short of food. He ordered her, however, to bring whatever she had.

He ate, without comment, a fried egg, a pile of baked beans, one sausage, and some fried-up boiled potatoes.

'Like some tea, luv?'

'Yes, please. May I have a glass of water as well?'

She raised her eyebrows in surprise, but said, yes, he could. He thought longingly of glasses of Calvados, lots of them, so that he could get drunk and drown his awful disappointment. Being afraid to enter a pub after Barbara's warnings about drunks, he had consumed no alcohol throughout his journey.

Now, he longed for drunken oblivion. His dreams of being with Barbara and running a snug bed-and-breakfast, raising hens for her, building a new life, were gone. It was not possible. He could not stand being quizzed, the dubiety, the insults, the awful tea!

He had nothing to be ashamed of, yet by subtle and not so subtle means, he felt he was regarded as untrustworthy, contemptible. English people could be so damned polite, yet put you down. He had not missed the raised eyebrows of the slut who was serving him in the café – just because he had asked for a glass of water. Didn't the English drink water?

Michel's landlady kept her word, however. The bath water was hot. When he mentioned towel and soap, she said that you had to bring them yourself. But seeing as he was obviously a Frenchie, he wouldn't know, would he? A very worn towel and a sliver of kitchen soap were provided.

Michel retired to the privacy of a tiny bathroom under the roof, where he bumped his head when he stood up straight. In five inches of hot water, he scrubbed himself clean. With his cut-throat razor, he cut off as much of his beard as he could. Then he shaved the rest at the little sink, being careful to husband a small piece of soap for a second shave in the morning; at least, he would meet Barbara looking decent.

'He looks quite respectable now he's shaved,' the land-lady told her husband in surprise; she had taken Michel in despite his uncouth appearance simply because she was in dire need of money.

Michel spent the late evening in their neglected back garden mending a slow puncture in the long-suffering bike's back tyre; the new wheels and tyres which Colonel Buck had found for it had stood up very well to a tremendous strain; this was his first puncture, mended today by courtesy of a small repair kit put together by old Duval himself. Duval, Michel remembered ruefully, had warned him about the English, as had his tearful mother, and two sisters and their husbands. He could never say, he thought, that he had not been warned.

Chapter Forty-one

The following afternoon, a solitary cyclist pedalled slowly down the long hill into West Kirby. He wore a trilby hat and a raincoat, and working trousers that looked as if they badly needed cleaning and pressing. New shoes, brightly polished, looked rather out of place.

Michel had refrained from changing into his new suit on that day, in case it got spoiled by unexpected rain or dust during the last part of his long journey. He would change immediately upon arrival, he had decided.

After finishing mending the puncture the night before, he had, however, spent some time picking bits of hay and other debris out of his pullover and trousers, so that he would look tidier on his arrival. On the rack at the back of his bicycle was strapped his battered suitcase.

At the foot of the hill, he dismounted by a railway station where a young woman was walking her dog. He took off his hat and politely asked the way to Mrs Bishop's bed-and-breakfast. Despite a reasonable night's sleep and a boiled egg with toast for breakfast, he was trembling with nervous apprehension, with fatigue and with hunger.

Standing before her, with the slanting rays of the sun behind him, the woman's first thought was that he looked handsome. Definitely a foreigner, though. She shaded her eyes to take a better look at him, while the dog snuffed suspiciously, and Michel suppressed a desire to kick it. He refrained, however; the British were so fussy about their animals.

Then she said slowly, 'You mean the Seashore bed-and-breakfast?'

'Yes. Mrs Barbara Bishop.'

'I think it belongs to a Mrs Williams,' responded the dog-walker doubtfully. Who was this foreigner who did not appear to have any luggage other than a rather dilapidated suitcase on his carrier? You never knew nowadays; there was a surprising number of no-goods in the country – been here since the war.

The suspicious-looking no-good bowed, and said, 'Thank you, Madame.' He replaced his trilby and remounted. He smiled at the lady, as he skidded slightly to avoid the ugly little dog, and went on his way.

At the end of a long road, he found the bed-and-breakfast, its sign prominently displayed on the gate. It stood alone within a very large patch of rough land on which grazed several black and white cows.

It seemed a big house to Michel. It had a fairly neat front garden, shaded by a tree which had been bent nearly double by the force of the wind from the sea. Under it was a children's swing on a rusty metal stand. A barbed-wire fence defended the garden from the cows.

The road itself appeared to end at an iron railing. Though tired, Michel was curious. So, before he entered Barbara's gate, he wheeled his bike down the road to the railing.

Leaning on the bike, he stood looking out at a great stretch of wet sand, on which lay a number of small sailing boats, their masts aslant, as they waited for the tide to come in and float them. To his right, a stone sea wall apparently marked the end of the bed-and-breakfast's land, and the beginning of the public shore. He turned to look back up the road. Facing Barbara's house, on the other side, was a line of small red-brick houses, presumably the end of the village.

It was just as Barbara had described it. Near a railway station, and a perfect place for family holidays or for men who had business in Liverpool and wanted a quiet night's sleep.

Full of trepidation, however, Michel turned back up the road, opened the gate and wheeled his bicycle in. He had written a letter to Barbara from Portsmouth, which Uncle Léon had promised to post for him, to say he expected to be with her in three days' time. But because he had been lost so often, and had encountered more hills than he could have ever imagined, the trip had taken a week.

Despite his unhappiness, he had been reminded again and again of his beloved Calvados before it had been so torn by the invasion; even the buildings, the churches and the houses in some of the villages looked similar. He wished the people had been similar, too.

Now he must tell Barbara that he could not face living amongst them. Acutely aware that he had not seen her for three months, he pushed his bike through the open gateway and propped it against a railing. How should he greet her?

After some hesitation, he rang the doorbell, and, immediately, somewhere at the back of the house, a dog barked.

Suppose her mother answered.

He heard a rush of feet downstairs, the door was flung open, and there she was, prettier than he had remembered, a small, vigorous woman in a faded flowered apron.

He shyly took off his hat. How was he going to tell her?

They stared at each other for a long moment, and then he opened his arms and she flung herself into them.

'Michel, luvvie,' she whispered huskily. 'I've been worried to death. I was afraid you'd never come.'

As often during his ride, he feared he might burst into tears, collapse as he had done in Bayeux; yet the chemistry between them was immediate and he instinctively responded to her embrace. He said nothing.

'Who's there, Barbie? Shut the door, there's a draught.'

Barbara giggled, and drew away from him. 'Come in, my love.' She gestured towards the inner part of the house, as she whispered, 'It's Mam. She's scared stiff of what you'll be like!'

'Me?' he shrugged, and smiled slightly. 'I am me. I am not, how you say, a fright,' he tried to tease. He was deathly tired, and he did not know how to behave towards her or what to say.

She closed the front door, and said, 'I'll get your case off the bike in a minute. Here, let me take your coat.' As she hung up his coat and hat in the hall cupboard, she raised her voice, and shouted, 'It's Michel, Mam.' Then she added to Michel, 'There's a washroom here. Would you like to use it?'

'*Merci, Madame Barbara*,' he said, and she laughed at the title.

He blessed her thoughtfulness, and thankfully went into the toilet. He washed the dust off his hands and face. Then he carefully combed his hair, which, he noted from his reflection in the mirror, was sorely in need of a cut.

After that, he braced himself to go out and face the dragon in the kitchen. He supposed he would have to talk to her too. But he could not simply blurt out, at the moment of arrival, that he had no intention of staying.

Barbara was hanging around in the hall, waiting for him. She said, 'I've taken your case upstairs.' She took his arm and urged hospitably, 'Come in and meet Mother.'

With oven gloves covering her hands, a stout woman with carefully curled black hair was lifting a cake out of the oven. She slowly put it down on a kitchen counter, and turned to meet the man who had mesmerised her daughter.

They stared at each other, she obviously a little resentful. Feeling that he would have to talk seriously to them both later on and really hurt his darling Barbara, he thought it best to establish at least a friendly atmosphere immediately. He went forward shyly, embraced her and kissed her on both cheeks, in French style. 'So you are Maman,' he said simply.

As he released her, he smiled at her and went on quickly to pay a compliment. He turned to Barbara. 'You tease me. She is too young to be your mama? Your sister?'

For such a compliment, Phyllis felt it had been worthwhile having her hair done that morning. And he was a lovely-looking man, though, in a shabby world, he was quite the shabbiest person she had seen for some time. But she could certainly see the attraction of him. Jaysus! No wonder Barbie had fallen for him.

She laughed and exposed a perfect set of excellent false teeth, and Michel remembered suddenly and sadly his mother's toothless mouth and thin white hair; yet she must be of the same generation.

She said cryptically to her daughter, 'Now I know just what you was talkin' about when you come 'ome.'

She was professionally hospitable, and this came out as she made Michel welcome, and tried to gain time to weigh him up more fully.

Nodding wisely to herself, she told him to sit down and she'd make a lovely cuppa tea and cut the cake specially for him.

He sat down on the nearest wooden chair, and Barbara brought another chair close to him, and sat down too. As yet unaware of the bombshell he was about to unload on her, in the shadow of the table she put a hand on his thigh. Though he was tired beyond endurance and very hungry, his senses swam.

Would she, perhaps, come to Calvados? He knew he could earn enough to keep her from starvation if he returned to the big poultryman who had engaged him as foreman since Barbara's return to England. His land had not been destroyed, and he was glad to employ Michel while he rebuilt his flocks.

He thought it unlikely that she would be willing to move; she knew what a mess the country was in and, moreover, she did not speak French. Meanwhile, with passion surging, he fought, in view of her mother's presence, to keep his face straight.

After Michel had eaten two pieces of hot cake and bravely drunk two cups of tea – he would never get used to tea, he decided – Phyllis suggested that Barbara should show him round while she prepared high tea.

When Barbara saw Michel's bewildered expression at this announcement, she laughed and explained, 'It's a real solid meal – usually cold meat, if you can get it, and stewed fruit, bread and butter and cake. Tonight we've got sausages and tomatoes.'

Her mother smiled. 'I got six guests tonight,' she told Michel. 'It's the school holidays, so I got two mums and dads and two kids, and then I got you, of course. Hope you can eat our food.'

Michel assured her gracefully that the meal sounded wonderful; in his state of hunger, anything would have seemed good.

Barbara swept him up a narrow oak staircase. The stair carpet was worn and faded, but, with its highly polished brass stair rods and with a big plant cascading out of a brass pot at the turn in the stairs, it looked incredibly rich to him. On the landing, she opened a white door with an old-fashioned, shiny brass knob and ushered him in. His suitcase was waiting for him.

The room was sparsely furnished with a big double bed, a white-enamelled dressing table and two matching bedside tables, all showing signs of wear. In one corner was a sink with two taps; towels hung at the side of it. Flowered linoleum covered the floor, its pattern of pink flowers nearly obliterated. Rag rugs were laid on either side of the bed. Though everything was spotlessly clean, Michel was reminded of Barbara's remark, when in France, that she badly needed to find paint for her rooms. The whole house looked uncannily like the house of the English lady in Normandy who had taught him English.

He glanced at the windows. They were hung with white curtains and framed a wonderful view of the incoming tide.

'For me?' he asked.

'Of course. I bagged a double room – being the week-end, we've no reps coming in. They'll turn up on Monday, I expect, and, anyway, they prefer singles.' She swung the door closed. Then she turned to him.

'Michel, luvvie, I thought you'd never come.'

He could not help himself. He opened his arms wide, and said ruefully, 'It was a long wait for me, *chère Madame Barbara*,' and closed his arms round her.

'Not Madame,' she said, as he bent to kiss her.

He was silent as he held her. Filled with an almost unbearable pain at impending loss, he was still swept by desire. He explored her with his tongue, licking, kissing round her neck, lifting her breasts.

Finally Barbara said desperately, 'Luvvie! Remember Mam. She expects us to explore the place – not each other. Hold on till tonight, aye?' Her eyes were full of promise.

Despite his fears, his fervour was genuine. I mustn't lead her on like this, he thought with consuming sorrow, as he let her go.

To gain time, he said, 'Go and help Mama. I can walk round alone.'

Mama would be the main objection to Barbara's coming to him in France, he thought. This is too big a house for one woman to run alone.

Barbara began to detect his reserve, and was hurt. She put it down to fatigue, however, and agreed.

'Just make yourself at home and go wherever you feel like. But don't go into the rooms directly below – they're full.' Then she turned to the washbasin, and said very practically, 'Hotels and places like this don't provide soap and towels these days. I've put you a bar from our ration, though. And Mam's put family towels in. There's a lavatory down the hall.'

Soap had been a luxury ever since the Germans had marched into Normandy; the Benions had reserved any that they could find for Anatole. And to have a proper indoor lavatory was something only richer peasants could hope for.

When she had gone, it seemed incredibly quiet. Michel wandered round the room. Then he switched the electric

423

light on and off; there was a light in the centre of the ceiling and another on the bedside table; he opened and shut the dressing-table drawers, and glanced into a big wall cupboard, which had a rail in it with one or two hangers, waiting for him to unpack. One wall boasted a fireplace with an electrical outlet, but no electric fire; the space was filled by a bowl of artificial flowers, looking very faded.

Over the mantelpiece was a print of the Liverpool waterfront, which he had once seen when sailing up the Mersey river with his uncle; its frame was screwed firmly to the wall. On the mantelpiece was a china ashtray. He idly picked it up. It had a picture of a tower on it, and said on its rim, 'A Present from Blackpool'.

He lit his last cigarette and then opened the dormer window and looked out. The sound of waves from a fast tide rushing in towards the shore was wonderfully peaceful, and in the further distance, he heard a train entering the station.

He thought of Barbara with longing. His welcome told him that he had not been wrong about her. And yet he couldn't face her country, he knew it.

These first minutes in her home told him clearly that she and her calm, young-looking mama knew what they were about; everything was as trim as the interior of a battleship.

For the first time in several days, Michel thought about Bill Spellersby, waiting to welcome him to Manchester. Should he even go to see him? Then, almost immediately, he decided that he must, which meant automatically that he was going to be some days more in West Kirby.

The Wing Commander, who was simply Bill to Michel,

had promised that he and his father would find an immigration lawyer for him. He himself would sponsor his old friend.

What was Michel going to say to such a friend? 'No, thank you very much'?

As he thought about Bill, he realised that the man had, of course, seen his tiny Normandy farm before the invasion ruined it, and so understood something of Michel's capabilities as a poulterer; one night, he had even been introduced to Chanticleer and his harem, just before they became dinner for the Germans encamped on his land. Bill had seen also, in the barn, his new experiment – an attempt at raising more eggs for the Germans in less space. Each hen was confined in her own small nest, where all they did was to sit on wire-netting and eat, sleep – and lay eggs. When they laid an egg it rolled gently down a small incline to a tilted shelf, where it awaited collection. The birds' ordure fell through the netting to an empty shelf below them.

He had inadvertently stumbled on the battery system, soon to be accepted as the usual way of keeping laying hens.

At seeing them, Bill had winced. 'Isn't it cruel?' he had asked.

The severely practical peasant with him had replied, 'How to produce more eggs? Big problem.' His query was dismissed. 'Biggest problem is to keep them very clean, so they not die of disease.'

If he stayed in Britain, Bill would not be sponsoring him blindly for immigration, Michel considered. And he was aware of what his family had gone through under German occupation. In spite of his despair, it was a comforting thought that Bill was very different from some of the people he had met during his long bicycle ride.

He must see him before he returned to France; it might be the only chance of a meeting that he would have in his life.

His holiday visa to Britain allowed him six weeks, a week of which he had already used up in getting to West Kirby. Barbara had insisted in one of her letters to France that, during that period, they must hustle – to use her own expression – to get married by special licence; and, equally important, she had joked, also persuade her mother that having a hard-working French son-in-law would be a great asset. The reality now burst upon Michel that if he undertook to farm her land and was unable to get other work in addition, he would be totally dependent upon his mother-in-law; working with members of his French family was different. This financial fact was new to him and it shocked him. It confirmed his decision to return to Calvados.

He felt sickened. Very soon, now, he would have to tell both of them that it was impossible for him to stay this side of the English Channel.

In a way, Barbara had prepared him for rejection by English people. She had, in one letter, advised him not to wear a beret. 'There's louts as used to collect the red pompoms off the caps of French sailors,' she had written. 'Of course, it always caused a fight – and a beret might give them ideas.'

Michel had laughed. He'd kick the hell out of them, he had thought cheerfully. But he was not so young, and he had understood, after dealing with the Germans for years, that it was wise to be discreet. With that fact in view, he had bought the trilby hat, now lying on the bed. His beret was still stuffed in his suitcase.

During his long cycle ride, though much tempted, he had also avoided public houses.

She must have known the problems he would be confronted with, he thought disconsolately, how deeply suspicious English people were of foreigners?

With elbows on the windowsill, he smoked, as he looked out at the stretch of rough land between him and the seawall. It needed some protection from the wind, he thought idly, as a breeze made the bleached curtains billow. But there was plenty of space to raise a lot of hens if one could get a permit.

Barbara had also emphasised the endless difficulty of getting any permit to increase a business; she had stated baldly that, with a Socialist government – they called it Labour here – you got free health care under a new scheme that had just come in; but, according to her, it was about the only thing which was freely given. Wanting to start a business or extend one was something else, she had assured him.

His bad shoulder ached abominably. All he wanted to do, at present, was to rest for a while to ease his physical exhaustion, and then think how he was to get himself out of the tangle he was in, without offending Bill or breaking dearest Barbara's heart.

Disconsolately, he sat down on the bed and unlaced the new shoes that he was wearing for the first time. He placed them neatly under the side table.

When Barbara came to call him for high tea, he was sound asleep on the bed, still dressed in his old pullover, and a pair of old black trousers. His socks, she noted, badly needed darning. His shoes lay discarded by the bed. On the end of the bed hung a decent dark suit, sorely in need of pressing. Beside it was a white shirt and

427

a nondescript tie. On one bed knob hung a very battered beret; on another sat a neat trilby hat.

The suitcase, empty except for a pair of old boots, two empty bottles and what looked like a pile of crumbs, lay open on the floor.

Barbara stared at the case for a moment, and understood the poverty its emptiness inferred. Poor darling. Her minefield – waiting to be cautiously explored.

Like her Liverpool Irish forebears, she was generous to a fault, and it did not occur to her that he might feel ashamed at being dependent, even temporarily, upon her and Phyllis, that he had taken more insults from her fellow countrymen than he could stomach, and that he bitterly regretted that he had ever set out for England.

Unaware that her minefield might well explode any minute in an unexpected way, she smiled, went over to the bed and gently kissed him awake.

Chapter Forty-two

His fatigue was still so great that, upon being awakened, Michel could not for a moment remember where he was or recognise the smiling face bent over him.

He gulped, as the white ceiling swam above him and a cheerful voice urged him, 'Wakey, wakey! It's teatime.'

Mon Dieu! Madame Barbara! He came to earth with a jolt and struggled to sit up. Flustered, he allowed himself to be given a hug, and to be urged, 'Hurry up, sweetheart. Mam's waiting on us.'

She stepped back to allow him to swing his feet to the floor.

'Oh, yes. I regret . . . I am not washed or changed.' He dithered as he sat on the edge of the bed.

'Don't worry. We've fed the visitors. We'll be eating, comfortable like, in the kitchen. Work clothes'll be OK.'

'I wash my face.' He pointed to the little sink, as he pushed his feet into his shoes. 'I come – two minutes?'

She gazed down at him, plain adoration in her eyes. Then she bent to kiss the top of his head.

'Aye, it's lovely to have you here,' she sighed. Then she agreed, 'I'll go down and tell Mam.'

Before he could answer, she had whisked away through the door, and he heard her swift feet running down the stairs.

Numbly, he splashed his face, and again combed his

untidy thinning hair. As his mind began to work again, he controlled a desire to fling himself back onto the bed and scream at an unfair world. What in the name of God was he doing?

He bared his stained teeth in the mirror, and then rinsed his mouth and spat into the sink. He looked old and haggard, and knew that for his own self-respect, he must, before facing Bill Spellersby, get a haircut, make himself neat.

He bent down to do up his shoes. As he pulled at the laces, he tried to think sensibly how to deal with these two nice women awaiting him below without hurting either of them.

He gave a final, hard tug at the laces, and then ordered himself, as if preparing for some great campaign, 'Eat, you fool. You're hungry – and your mind won't work.'

As he tucked his shirt into his trousers, he reminded himself of Napoleon's famous saying that an army marched on its stomach. Teeth clenched, he walked firmly down the corridor to the lavatory. Then, before descending the stairs, he stood holding the banister at the top, while the carpeted flight seemed to waver before him. When it again looked straight, he walked slowly down it. He was so hungry that his legs would barely carry him.

In the hall, a happy clatter of dishes and the smell of fried food greeted him. His mouth filled with saliva.

At the back of the hall was a built-in desk. On it lay a telephone and a large open account book. Behind it was the kitchen door.

As he opened it, he was not only filled with apprehension but also with a natural shyness at entering a world which was strange to him.

Phyllis was standing at the gas stove and had her back

to him. As she quickly slid some sausages out of a frying pan and onto a plate, she turned her head to greet him She then added to the plate fried tomatoes served on toast. The toast was so that they would go further, she would have explained, if asked.

She chuckled when she saw him. 'Barbie says you was so asleep, she didn't think you recognised her,' she teased him.

He laughed uncertainly. 'I sleep much,' he replied cautiously.

'Aye, you come a long way, lad. You must be beat.'

Though he had not heard the idiom before, its meaning was fairly clear, so he smiled politely in agreement. On a counter near the sink was a big pile of dishes, more dishes, he thought, than Maman had ever owned in her life. He presumed that they were waiting to be washed up.

Barbara, already seated at the table, smiled up at him, and told him where to sit.

He made himself eat the unusual meal slowly. It tasted much better than he had hoped, though apples and custard, he decided, were not his favourite dessert. There was plenty of bread, however, some butter, and homemade jam, and, finally, another slice of the big cake he had earlier sampled – it seemed more digestible cold than it had done when hot. The tea, hot and weak, at least made a drink, though he longed for a decent cup of coffee.

As he sat back, while Phyllis poured her third cup of tea and Barbara ate her piece of cake, he felt better, less agitated, more in command of himself. He answered their questions about his journey, praised the vicar and his wife who had given him a meal, made them laugh about the tramp he had picked up, and then he dried up. He did not know how to express, without giving offence, his inward storm of rage at many of his other encounters.

It was Phyllis who sensed his reticence; dreaming of the possibilities of the night to come, Barbara was a helpless bundle of pure desire.

I should give them time to themselves, she decided, give them something to do. He's a nice lad, nice manners. He'll open up a bit in time, no doubt.

And, though Barbie is a sweetie, I always did want a boy, too, around the house. I was so looking forward to George coming.

She contemplated her empty plate and hoped that, with this thin, handsome stranger, they could come to some sort of arrangement whereby he fitted into the business. He looked at present as if he didn't have a cent to bless himself with. She gave a tiny sigh. We've got a lot of honest talking to do with each other, she considered. And we've got to do it – because it's our Barbie's happiness what is at stake. She's so set on him – I've never known anything like it.

As she gazed at the weary face of her guest, she counselled herself. Be careful, Phyllis, me girl; this lad may not have much, but you can see easy enough that he's the proud type. Always got to watch where you tread with men like that. Phyllis dealt with men at her reservations counter almost every day of her life; and she often said to her friend Ada that she knew a good man when she saw one – and this lad looked likely, very likely, she had to agree with Barbie on that.

She said with determined cheerfulness, as she pushed back her chair and got up, 'Now, the system is that I take time off in the evening, and Barbie takes over. I'm goin' to put me feet up in a deck chair out in the garden, while the sun's still shining, and read for a bit – a lovely Ethel M. Dell, I've got.'

Michel nodded courteously, wondering what an Ethel M. Dell was, and what was to come.

Barbara woke up to reality, and hastened to say, 'You see, Mam gets up early,' she explained, 'and she makes the breakfasts and sees people out. It's my job to wash the evening dishes, tidy the kitchen, carpet-sweep the dining room and lay the tables for breakfast.' She rose from the table. 'And, in the evening, I look after the front desk in the hall there, and book anybody in who comes. And I do the book-keeping.'

'Please do what you usually do.' He wondered if she expected him to help her. How could you tell a girl washing dishes that, however much you love her, you can't stand her country and you want to go back to France where at least people are civil; after such a statement she might throw every dish within reach at him, he considered grimly.

Unaware of her beloved's predicament, Barbara answered him.

'Well, it all has to be done,' she said philosophically, 'Though I'm sure Mam would listen for the front doorbell tonight, if you'd like to come for a walk along the beach afterwards. The tide'll be going out, but it's pretty nice.'

Her mam smiled, ''Course, I will, luv. It'd give you and Michel time to talk to each other.'

And I hope they take the hint, she thought, glancing at her guest's tight, set expression. There's somethin' wrong here. Seems to me they need a bit of walkin' in the moonlight to set the scene.

When Phyllis got up to fetch her book and retire to her deck chair, Michel rose from his chair – and Phyllis gave him full marks for the small polite gesture. She stopped, as she was about to pass him, and laid her hand on his arm. She glanced up at him, and said, 'I'm real glad you arrived safe. We was both so worried about you.'

She saw the sensitive mouth soften and quiver, before he said, 'You are most kind, Madame.'

She smiled, and punched him gently in the ribs. 'You don't have to be that formal, luv. After all, I'm goin' to be your mam, too, aren't I, come next week?'

He was paralysed for a moment, his eyes full of sudden fear. She saw it.

'Don't be nervous, lad. Everything'll be all right.'

Nearly ready to choke, he managed, 'Thank you – Mama.'

'That's better. Now you give our Barbie a hand with the dishes, and there'll be lots of time for a nice walk.' Though not prone to putting her guests to work, Phyllis had decided that the more the young people were thrown together the more they would talk and that would be good for them. Dishwashing was a nice ordinary job tending to engender friendly conversation.

He nodded assent to her suggestion, and managed a faint smile. He began to collect the chinaware on the table and pile it together.

Barbara had watched the exchange with relief. Mam was obviously making up her mind affirmatively, and showing Michel that, no matter what, the work of the B-and-B must come first. She smiled at both of them, and took a pile of plates off Michel. 'We'd better tackle the lot on the draining board first,' she told him. 'I'll wash and you can dry.'

Relieved, Phyllis drifted away to find Ethel M. Dell, while Barbara learned that Michel was quite experienced at dishwashing. He had, he reminded her, worked in the kitchen of a hotel in Bayeux.

'We're awfully short of china,' she confided. 'I've bin watching for ages for an estate sale, so as to buy some more. There's almost none in the shops.'

The need to explain an estate sale to him helped to fill time which had threatened to be devastatingly empty. After her mother had gone, she had been surprised not to be grabbed and kissed immediately. He had, however, stood woodenly beside her, holding a tea towel she had thrust at him, as if his thoughts were miles away, though he quickly followed her instructions as to the disposal of the dishes.

He must still be dreadfully tired, she decided correctly, and proceeded with the kitchen chores. She would see that they did not walk too far after they had finished.

Chapter Forty-three

When they set out along the shore, Barbara's Labrador, Simba, bounding ahead of them, the sun was setting in the middle of miles of wet sand. The long, golden rays reflected on the puddles left by the tide made a glittering pathway towards them. The pathway was partly obstructed by the lumpy outline of a small island. Overhead, seabirds screamed. Closer to the couple, other people were walking their dogs, which barked and yapped round each other, happy to be free for a little while.

The air was invigorating, and Michel was reminded of Port-en-Bessin. He breathed in gratefully.

Barbara took his hand and turned him to look at the scene. 'That's Hilbre,' she said pointing to the island. 'We still can't get out to it, because it's got Government installations on it – from the war.'

He made an effort, and asked, 'Why would you want to go out there?'

She laughed. 'Whitebait – and shellfish,' she replied. 'The tidal pools round it have shrimps, and there's mussels on the rocks. And you can find cockles anywhere here, once the tide goes out. And, sometimes, there are seals out there – really funny they are to watch.'

He nodded. It sounded like a fisherman's paradise.

After a pause, since he did not say anything, she continued animatedly, 'Before the war, there was a fishing fleet out of Hoylake, just down the coast. But it doesn't seem to have got started up again.' She was silent for a minute, and then said reluctantly, 'No one to man the boats. Too many fishermen died in the war.'

Michel nodded again rather absently, as he sought for an opening to tell her his decision. As she mentioned the fishermen, she clutched his hand hard. The coast was haunted by deaths of sea-going men, she had told him, one day in Bayeux; Liverpool Bay was full of the bones of ships, and of seamen.

He remembered the loss of her father, and he turned to look at her. She seemed, unexpectedly, a forlorn little figure in the light of the dying sun, and his heart thumped. Full of compassion, he instinctively put his arm round her to comfort her. What right had he to hurt her more, he wondered despairingly. She was, after all, sticking firmly to her side of the bargain.

She looked up at him. Held suddenly close to him, she thought that this was more like her Michel, and she rejoiced.

He licked his lips. 'I have to talk to you – seriously,' he blurted out. 'We sit down, where it is quiet?'

His body trembled beside her. She sighed, and said, 'I suppose we must. We haven't much time, have we?'

He did not answer her, but continued to hold her firmly.

They were approaching Hilbre Point, and she suggested they sit up on the sandstone rocks. 'People won't walk up here now it's getting dark. It's too easy to trip up on the rocks. There'll just be the frogs and us,' she teased, and, sure enough, a series of small croaks announced the presence of the little amphibians.

He ignored her little joke and, with a heavy heart, he agreed that it did seem quiet. She led him to a huge flat stone from which they could watch the sky turn to emerald green, and then, as the moon rose, to silvery darkness peppered with stars.

She cuddled close to him, and asked light-heartedly, 'Where shall we start?'

He replied immediately and with bluntness. 'I can't stay in England.'

She recoiled as if he had hit her, and pulled herself away from him.

'Why not?' she whispered in shock. 'Mam seems to have taken to you like anything.'

'She is much kind,' he acknowledged immediately. 'But I not tell you yet everything what happen as I cycle here. It is very bad. I endure rudeness like I never expect.' His voice gained strength as his indignation came to the surface, and she, as if turned to stone, gazed at him appalled. 'The racial words so cruel – because I am French. It is intolerable.' His tone was biting. 'How will I get work from such people?'

He turned to her and put one hand on her shoulder. His voice changed. 'I love you, *ma chérie*,' he said with passion. 'Like I never love anybody. I want us to go back to France together.' His anger and his desire gave way to a more persuasive tone, as after a momentary silence, he went on, 'I know now that there is work there which I can do – not very good, perhaps, but we would not starve.'

As he spoke, all Barbara's plans crashed around her.

'I don't understand,' she stuttered. 'Have we been rude?'

'No, no, *chérie*. You and your mama are very good. It is the people I meet, while I bicycle here, never you.'

'I thought they had been very nice to you.'

'I tell you only about nice people. Now I tell you about others.'

He poured out every insult, large or small, suspected or obvious, which he had received during his long journey.

She listened in disapproving silence.

'English people aren't like that,' she finally interjected defensively. Then it began to dawn on her that, perhaps, they were sometimes. But only with Blacks or Jews, weren't they?

'Many are,' he assured her hopelessly. 'You warn me not to wear a beret, not to go in drinking places. Why?'

He waited.

She let the pain of loss go through her. It was not the loss of his affection which hurt; she was sure she still had that; it was a loss of innocent belief in the innate goodness and rightness of her own people.

When the silence between them became more than he could bear, he almost cried out, 'I do love you, *ma chérie*. You know I do.' He allowed his hand to steal from her shoulder, so that he again held her closely. She did not yield to him. 'I simply want us to live in Normandy.'

Finally, she awoke from her stupor. 'Normandy's wrecked,' she said dully. 'It'll be donkey's years before it's fit to live in again.' She turned her face to him and he saw that there were tears in her eyes. 'Trying to find a place to live would be real hard, I'm sure it would. Here, I've got a decent home – and you're welcome in it.' She stopped and turned her face away again.

'You and your mama are much kind,' Michel repeated. Then he added fuel to her unhappiness, by saying, 'Also, I do not wish to depend on you. I must find work myself – and where will I find it in England when the English people hate a Frenchman so much?'

She began to fight back. 'I don't believe that they care about foreigners that much. Liverpool's always been full of them – and since the war there's been more jobs than men. There's hardly a man out of work in the village.'

'You do not know what foreigners may have to endure – you are not foreign,' he responded tartly.

'No, I don't,' she retorted angrily. 'Except, at times, it didn't feel very cosy bein' Irish in posh parts of Liverpool. Out here, we don't feel it.'

She got up suddenly from the cold rock on which they had been sitting. She was crying now, as she irritably brushed down her skirt. 'You're not playing fair,' she upbraided him. 'You've let me arrange everything – I've even got a special marriage licence for us to be married next week – and now you're backing out. How could you? How could you?'

'I'm not backing out,' he snapped back. 'I want to marry you – and take you back to France instead.'

'That's all very well. Just give up a good home and go back to a ruin!' she sobbed. Simba heard her and snuggled close.

He swallowed his outraged pride and began to plead. 'Please, please, my love, consider. Think about it. Marry? We can, *certainement*! It is my joy to think about it.'

'Not till we've got this cleared up,' snarled a furious Barbara. 'In case you've forgotten, there's Mam to be considered. She's bein' that generous to you.' She was shouting now, her voice echoing amid the rocks and along the empty beach. 'And what do you do? You back out. Don't you realise that she can't manage without me? What would she do? And what would I do, anyway? The B-and-B will be mine, some day.'

He pushed the dog away. Simba snarled softly.

'French women work out of the home,' he reminded her quietly, determined to keep calm. 'Here, your mama could, perhaps, find help to work the house.'

'Not that she could trust,' replied Barbara, as determined as an angry terrier to defend her livelihood. 'You've got to watch all the time visitors and staff, 'cos of theft, 'cos of no-goods. There has to be at least two of you, and three would be even better.'

Driven into a corner, Michel felt again the overwhelming weakness of exhaustion. 'Hush, listen to me,' he begged.

'Listen? What good will it do me? And us both got to face Commander Spellersby tomorrow – remember my letter? Exactly what are you going to say to him, I'd like to know. Has he sneered at you?'

Michel had, of course, remembered Bill, and he had decided before he arrived at West Kirby that the appointment should be kept.

He answered her immediately, his voice calmer. 'Bill never sneer at me. You and I go to Manchester together. I talk with him. Tomorrow is the day, as you say.'

'It is. And we'd better get home. Mam'll want to go to bed.'

When Michel got up, he swayed a little on his feet, and he slipped, as they descended the rocks. He winced as his ankle gave.

She was still sobbing quietly, but she turned automatically to aid him. 'Be careful,' she warned quite kindly and took his hand to lead him down, and then added rather resentfully, 'We got enough on our hands without you breakin' an ankle.'

The ankle hurt sharply as he hobbled back to her home.

They did not speak again until they entered the kitchen.

In a faded blue terry dressing gown, Phyllis was seated at the kitchen table, drinking a cup of cocoa. After glancing at their sullen faces, she asked them if they had had a good walk, and received mumbled replies from both.

Trouble, she decided immediately.

Uncertain what to do, she took another sip of cocoa, and then warned herself. Mind your own business, Phyllis. Let them fight it out. She did, however, note Michel's limp and immediately enquired about it.

'It's nothing,' Michel assured her heavily, and, indeed, it was nothing in comparison with his worries regarding Barbara. 'I rest now. Tomorrow it is all right.'

She drained her cup and got up. 'Oh, aye,' she agreed briskly. 'Soak it in cold water if it bothers you – there's a bowl under the bathroom sink – and rest up.' She turned to her daughter, who was hanging up her cardigan on a hook on the back door, and said, 'Barbie, luvvie, I made some cocoa for both of you. It's in the saucepan there.' Then she half smiled at a haggard Michel. 'It's only dried milk in it,' she apologised to him. 'But I were that lucky to get a tin of cocoa I thought I'd try it.'

'It will be nice – *certainement*,' replied Michel bravely; it could not be worse than weak tea.

Phyllis turned back to Barbara. 'Mr Willis – you remember him, Walsingham Jam Company – is booked into number 4 – two nights.'

'OK, Mam. You go to bed now. You must be tired.'

After her departure, Michel sat down suddenly. I must rest, he thought frantically. I can't argue any more. I'm so tired, I don't think I could even make love.

Still in a towering rage, augmented by a sense of panic,

Barbara ignored him and turned on the gas under the pan of cocoa. It was already fairly hot, and in a moment or two it began to boil. She took two mugs off their hooks and filled them. 'Want to take yours upstairs?' she asked him without an iota of expression in her voice.

Thankful to escape, he nodded, picked up his mug and went slowly and cautiously towards the door, his ankle whingeing unhappily at every step.

He paused, as she turned to tell him formally that the three o'clock train from West Kirby would be about the right time to set out for Manchester. 'It's a dinner invite,' she informed him. Then she asked if he would like to get a haircut in the morning.

Although he had already decided that he needed a haircut, the remark implied criticism and, in his highly emotional state, it hurt him.

'Yes. I go to barber,' he replied dully, and went through the doorway to the hall. He wanted to slam the door in pure temper. But it would not do in a house full of visitors, so he closed it softly, and held onto the door knob until he felt strong enough to climb the stairs.

Chapter Forty-four

He undressed and slipped, naked, into the chilly bed. He desperately longed to be back in Normandy in a decently warm feather bed, a luxury he had almost forgotten until this moment.

How could Madame Barbara be so angry? He trembled with resentment as well as cold as he tucked the bedclothes round himself in an effort to get warm. He had dreamed that tonight they might for the first time lie together in a proper bed, and really enjoy each other. And here he was, with no desire in him, shivering alone as if he were still lying on the floor of the attic in Bayeux, or in the straw in the loft of the stable in which he had slept when he had found work at the poultry farm of his father's acquaintance.

During the last three months, he had worked long, hard hours and had saved every sou he could. He had eaten little and drunk less, had even smoked only to assuage his permanent hunger. For what?

Since he was Barbara's guest, he certainly had enough money to carry him through the visit; the only uncertainties he had were the costs of a wedding ring and of a suitable thank you gift for her mother.

To be insulted again and again was, however, unbearable – and now to be scolded by his beloved Barbara, as if he had done something terribly wrong. Would he even need a ring?

And he had yet to tell her of an incredible humiliation, quite a different one, which still rankled in his mind. As he recollected it, he wondered furiously if she would understand or even care about what had accidentally happened to his farm.

The French Government had decided that they would not buy his land or that of the Fortiers next door. They would make only a small, narrow park directly along the coast, which would not include the Benions' tiny holding.

Quite soon after that decision had been made public, there had come another offer, per hectare, from a private company, working through Paris lawyers, who sought small acreages that could be united into decent-sized holdings. They offered for several little farms in the neighbourhood, with the provision that the names of all the present owners could be clearly established and their joint agreement quickly obtained. The company would themselves provide *démineurs* to clear the land mines.

Their financial stability seemed excellent. It had been too good an offer to refuse, and most of the owners agreed to it. Even Michel's sister, Anne-Marie, the most awkward member of the family, had been coerced by Uncle Léon to agree. Though Michel understood that the whole scheme was not yet complete, the Benion family had already cashed their cheque. It enabled them to pay the debts incurred during the war, and leave a little over for each one of them. Michel's share and the share that Anatole had left him, though small, were, on Uncle Léon's orders, snugly tucked away in his French Post Office savings account. It would cover his first expenses if he had to return to Normandy, as his uncle had gloomily foretold he would; the money he had with him was from his earnings.

Fine. What better could one hope for?

Then had come the denouement. The *démineurs* turned out to be a group of uncommunicative, efficient Germans! The innocuous-sounding little company proved to be a subsidiary of a powerful German syndicate, which was buying farmland, not only in France, but, it was rumoured, also in England.

The family was thunderstruck. After all the long battle they had quietly waged against the occupation, they had sold out to the enemy. Uncle Léon and Michel were particularly outraged, but Uncle Léon, after talking to a *notaire*, counselled silence; the transfer was legal; the family had done well out of the sale. Don't stir up political dust, he urged.

Politics? They were suddenly nervous, though they felt cheated out of any small victory that they could have claimed.

Madame Benion had been more accepting. Who else, she asked resignedly, would have bought such a little farm? Most of the likely buyers, farmers whose land immediately abutted theirs, were dead. Only people with money could afford to buy so much available land.

Léon and Michel had seen the sense of her remarks. But, added to his loss of Suzanne to a German, the indignity of the sale still rankled in Michel's mind, and added to his depression. Would he now lose Barbara?

In her bedroom above him, an angry Barbara washed herself and prepared for bed. As she put on her old flannel nightie and climbed into her single bed, she sobbed unrestrainedly. How could they possibly get a decent life together in Normandy? England was suffering hard times, but at least she herself had a roof to offer him and a means of earning a living here. And Mam had been wonderful.

Mam also lay in her bed, sleepless and unhappy, and wondered what was up, and wished passionately that her husband was there to comfort her. Not that he would have been a particularly good conciliator – Hugh would probably have resented very much young Michel becoming part of the family; another man in his bailiwick would not have pleased our Hughie, she decided with unexpected humour. He would, however, have talked the matter over with her and have got out of young Barbara what the trouble was with her new boyfriend. He'd loved his little Barbie, he had. Suddenly, Phyllis began to cry with sheer loneliness.

Of the three of them, she got the least sleep that night. By the morning, however, she had thought out a modest plan to integrate Michel more formally into the B-and-B.

Give him his pride, she thought determinedly. I'll talk to him tomorrow night, when it's quiet.

Chapter Forty-five

The following morning, by the time Michel had got up and washed and shaved, Phyllis had had her own breakfast and fed her visitors. As Michel hobbled down the stairs, his swollen ankle objecting strongly to every step, she was bustling around the hall, dealing with the two young families about to go home. Through the open dining-room door, he glimpsed the solitary representative, the redoubtable Mr Willis, who had come in the previous night. He was finishing his breakfast, while he studied a notebook, presumably listing his calls for the day in Liverpool.

Michel mechanically said '*Bonjour*' to Phyllis, as he edged round the departing crowd and their luggage in the hall. Not knowing what was expected of him, or how Barbara would greet him, it was with foreboding that he entered the kitchen.

Barbara had just come through a door leading directly from the dining room and was carrying a heavy tray of dirty dishes.

The kitchen was bathed in sunlight. The sharpness of the light showed up Barbara's unmade-up face in great clarity. Her eyes were puffy and black-rimmed, her hair untidy. To Michel, she looked ill. He greeted her with a polite '*Bonjour*'.

She ignored it, and dumped the tray onto the counter.

'Sit down,' she ordered without preamble, 'and I'll give you some breakfast.'

He sat down, feeling thoroughly miserable, though much stronger than he had felt the previous day. Reasonable food and a night's sleep had lessened his sense of physical weakness.

She slid a cup and saucer, spoons and a knife in front of him. Then she went to the stove and, from a heavy iron pot, filled a bowl with porridge. This she laid in front of him. She then gathered from the other end of the table and put conveniently close to him a tin of golden syrup, a jug of milk and a salt cellar.

'Help yourself – you may like some salt on it,' she said. 'I'll make toast.'

He replied quietly, '*Merci*,' as she provided each piece of his breakfast. He was not certain how one took porridge in England, but her gestures helped him and he put syrup and milk on it, and ate it gratefully. She put a jar of homemade marmalade by him for his toast. 'Sorry. No butter. No more rations until Monday,' she told him, as she brought him a freshly made pot of tea.

He thought resentfully that Mr Willis in the dining room had probably been served with more kindliness.

As he finished his toast and drank the cup of tea he had poured for himself, he leaned back in his chair and watched her stacking dishes on the counter.

I'm fed up with this treatment, he thought crossly, and then he wondered if she had eaten breakfast before he came down. Possibly, she had not.

He knew only too well what hunger could do to one's state of mind and, knowing it, he held his tongue.

Finally, he could not stand the silence any more. He got up from his chair, went to her, took the little marmalade

449

pot she was wiping out of her hands and laid it down by
the sink. Then he took her in his arms.

She stood rigid and turned her face away.

'*Chérie*,' he whispered. 'Come. I love you so much.
Stop your anger.' He kissed the cheek nearest to him. 'We
make peace, yes? We talk. We love each other?' Today,
I feel strong enough to do that, he thought with some
relief as her closeness aroused him.

She crumpled in his arms. A great sob burst out of
her.

'Oh, Michel! I'm sorry, Michel. I'm so sorry I shouted
at you. But you frightened me so much, and I just don't
know what to do, I don't,' she wailed, as she poured
out her misery to him. 'I thought we'd got everything
settled.'

'We have yet some weeks, *chérie*, to think,' he said, as
he ran his hands down her back. 'First, we see Bill – he
is my good friend still. We enjoy seeing him. Then you
tell me how we marry – I do not know, exactly, the law
of England. You say you have special permit? We fix that.
Slowly, slowly, we decide what to do.'

She was crying steadily now against his shoulder. He
beguiled her, stroking her softly through her skirt and
then under it. She wriggled in mild protest.

'Remember, we buy a ring. Important, is it not?' he
suggested.

He dropped her skirt and lifted her left hand. She had
removed George's ring. He kissed her fingertips. The sobs
lessened and a woebegone face was turned towards him.
He kissed her with passion, and suddenly she responded.

Her mother called from the hall. 'I'm goin' to start
changing the beds, Barbie. Come up and help me when
you've had your brekkie.'

Reluctantly, Barbara withdrew in order to answer the summons. She gave a little quivering sob, and then shouted back, 'OK, Mam.' To Michel, she whispered almost tenderly, 'You're a proper rogue. I don't know what to do with you.'

He grinned down at her triumphantly. 'Have you breakfast?'

She sniffed. 'No. I didn't want any.'

'You eat breakfast. I wash dishes.'

'OK.' She withdrew herself reluctantly.

'We are now – how you say? – good friends again?'

She stood in front of him while she took a handkerchief out of her apron pocket to wipe her eyes. Then, as he waited, she sighed and then said with a wan smile, 'More than that – but I still don't know what to do.'

'I know, *chérie*. But we have time. We talk about everything – no anger – and we decide. Breakfast first,' he ordered her, feeling that he was now in command.

This brought another shy smile. 'You had the last of the porridge. I'll make some toast.'

He threw up his hands, and laughed. 'I'm sorry.'

His laughter was infectious, and she grinned. 'Don't be. I don't really like porridge. As soon as we've done the beds, I'll press your suit and shirt,' she promised practically, as she pushed two slices of bread into the toaster.

'*Merci bien, Madame,*' he replied, stifling a desire to say, 'Forget everything. Come up to bed.'

'And you'd better go to the barber.' Her voice was relentlessy firm.

'*Oui, Madame Barbara,*' he teased. 'Where he is? And how much money?'

'In the village. I don't know what it costs, but not much. Do you want me to come with you?'

'*Non, merci.*' He sighed and applied his mind to the immediately possible. He thought, with acidity, that it would be interesting to see what attitude the barber took, if his new customer appeared to be a foreigner.

He turned on the hot tap to fill the sink. Despite the complaining ankle, he felt much better.

Chapter Forty-six

Word that Barbara Bishop, George Bishop's widow, was considering getting married again had seeped out via his mother, Ada. Barbara had actually gone to see her, to break the news as gently as she could to her old friend.

Ada had been very kind and encouraging, grateful to her daughter-in-law for coming specially to tell her. She had, however, spread the news to others, who regarded it as yet another of their number becoming a war bride, who would go away to live in a foreign country, nothing very special. In due course it had reached the barber, who had cut George's hair since he was a small boy.

Like most barbers, he had a wonderful knowledge of the affairs of the locals and a great flow of friendly conversation. Michel not only got a neat head of hair, but found himself telling the old man all about the maquis and the Resistance, from the view of an insider.

At the end, when his shabby trousers and pullover had been brushed down, he counted out the price asked, and, on leaving, bid the barber a polite, '*Au revoir.*'

By the following day the whole village knew that Barbara Bishop's new boyfriend was not bad-looking, once he had had a decent haircut. He was a poultry farmer, who had fought with the Resistance. If Michel had heard this he would have corrected it, because most peasants were disarmed, so he had, more accurately, harassed the Germans in any way possible to aid those who were armed.

The villagers, however, if they thought about it at all, accepted the barber's version. Stories of French Air Force men who had been encamped nearby during the war were revived, and the fact that a couple of girls from Moreton had already gone to France to marry Frenchmen was sighed over by the ladies. 'We're losing all our youngsters,' they said sadly. But, on the whole, the news was received without animosity.

Unaware of the gossip, Barbara and Michel struggled in crowded, dirty trains to get to Manchester. As always, the trains were late, and it took time to find the right bus for Bill's suburb; then to find the road in which he lived. Barbara was glad that she had allowed lots of time for the inadequacies of transport.

It was a very tired and dishevelled couple who rang the bell of a large semi-detached brick house in a beautifully treed neighbourhood.

They were welcomed in by a tall, slender lady with fair hair done in pageboy fashion. She was dressed in a two-piece cardigan set, pearls round her neck, the uniform of the middle-class female. Though she rather unnerved Barbara, she was very charming, as was Bill.

A shy Barbara took one glance at Bill and decided he was a lovely man, Liverpool's highest accolade for a male. She smiled up at him and held out her hand to shake his. Bill saw a typical Irish face, the kind which peeped out from behind many a black shawl, yet was now made new with a modern hairstyle, a hint of merriment in the eyes, and a fairly self-confident manner.

He turned to his old friend, standing diffidently behind her, holding his trilby in one hand. Though thin to the point of illness, Michel none the less looked a little more prosperous than he had when Bill had been hidden in his henhouse and then in his attic, and Bill was relieved to see it.

Barbara was taken away upstairs by her hostess, 'call me Daphne', to a bedroom to tidy up and to wash her hands, and thence to a large drawing room on the same floor, to sit by the fire, where a tea tray lay ready on a low table and a kettle simmered on the hearth. They were joined a moment later by Bill and Michel, who seemed to have picked up their friendship as if they had lived next door to each other for years.

The room stretched the width of the house and was filled with Victorian furniture and boundless knick-knacks. On the walls hung a number of oil paintings, including one, over the marble mantelpiece, of a young girl in the full evening dress of early Victorian times.

Barbara stared about her with frank interest. Like most British people, she was always aware of class distinction, and she sensed that though they were definitely middle class, the house did not match the young couple living in it. It proved not to be a matter of class, however, but of generation.

As Daphne stirred the pot, to get the best out of a miserably small tea ration, a big, portly man entered.

What little hair he had was grey, and, in repose, the heavy-jowled face looked formidable. Barbara immediately had a sense of being out of her depth and that, perhaps, she should rise respectfully in his presence. Since Daphne stayed firmly in her seat, an empty teacup in one hand, she wriggled back into her chair.

Bill and Michel did get up, however, and remained standing until the older man sank thankfully into an empty easy chair. Barbara and Michel were then introduced to the elder Mr Spellersby, who greeted them politely and hoped that they had not had too much trouble getting to Manchester. 'Train service is impossible,' he rumbled.

Barbara and Michel lied in unison that they had had no trouble at all.

Then Bill, who was studying medicine at Manchester University, and was interested in its connections with murder, enquired if his father was getting any particularly interesting cases this session. As the older man answered, Barbara began to realise that he was an assizes judge, that he travelled to the assizes courts in various places and that it was his house that they were in. She remembered clearly being taken by her grandfather to see the arrival of the assizes judges in Liverpool.

No wonder he looked so formidable, even without his scarlet robes and huge white wig and the traditional bunch of herbs in his hands. On the social standing of this man, she thought apprehensively, Michel's permanent residence in England might depend. She guessed wildly that a judge would know all the right people to ease Michel in. The idea made her feel extremely nervous of making a social blunder of some kind.

Michel recognised only a man who exuded power, some kind of a judge, and he was, for no real reason, also suddenly nervous. What was he, a poor peasant, doing in the house of a man like that?

The judge, as he drank the tea provided by his daughter-in-law was, however, extremely amiable. This nondescript little Frenchie was the reason that he still had a son. He had not forgotten that fact. As he emptied his teacup, he smiled on him and said, 'I am most grateful, sir, for what you did to help Bill when he was shot down in France. Must have been very difficult for you, with a German gun site on your property.'

Michel shrugged. 'I do what most of us do then. We do what is possible to 'elp the Allies.' He did not know what more to say, but then added impetuously, 'We have big problems with *les Boches*.'

'I'm sure you did,' replied the judge. 'However, I am most grateful to you.'

Michel looked over at his friend and grinned, as he said, 'I am most 'appy he return home.'

Mr Spellersby turned to look at Barbara. The shy young woman, sitting by Daphne, was, he understood, the man's future wife. Kept a bed-and-breakfast, Bill had said once. She looked quite capable of doing that. Neat little woman, Irish probably. Quite pretty.

He glanced again at Michel. The family owed a big debt to this nut-brown Frenchman, who looked as if he had not had a decent meal for months. They would talk about it after dinner. He hoped that Daphne had found something decent to eat for their dinner. Rationing was a curse.

He asked Bill to get him a whisky, and enquired if anyone else would like one. Daphne said she would. The others elected sherry.

Thankful to have escaped whisky, Michel mumbled '*Bon appétit*' and sipped cautiously at a sherry; it was excellent.

The room fell silent.

Daphne did her work as hostess, and began to get a little conversation going with her visitors, by asking about the situation regarding rebuilding Normandy. This successfully deflected attention from the distant sounds of arrivals in the hall below. Daphne said hastily that she must go to the kitchen to see how dinner was progressing, and excused herself.

The judge got slowly to his feet and remarked that he

457

had one or two things to look at before dinner, and also departed.

Michel stood up with Bill until he had left the room, and then Bill said casually, 'I noticed that you're limping?'

'I slip on a rock last night.'

'Like me to look at it?'

Barbara blessed the fact that she had found a pair of socks of her own to lend to Michel, in replacement for the ragged pair he had been wearing. She knew she had been unkindly neglectful of the injury, and she hastened to say to Michel, 'Let Bill look at it, Michel. I thought it would be almost all right by now.'

Diffidently, Michel removed his shoe and sock, and the leg of his new suit was rolled up to the knee.

Bill bit his lip when he saw that, though the leg muscles were hard as iron and the ankle swollen, the leg, generally, looked like a stick.

As he rolled the foot gently to test the extent of the sprain, he asked if Michel had been ill.

'No.'

'You are too thin, old man.'

Michel replied ruefully, 'I work hard.'

'Is food very short in France?'

'We not die. Food is short.' How could he tell Bill of the hardships, the hunger of the last twelve months – and particularly of the last three months, when he had eaten minimally in order to save money?

Bill got up from his knees, and then gently leaned down to tip Michel's face upwards and pull down the lower lid of one eye. Definitely run down, he decided.

'Hm. You said in your last letter that you would be staying in England at least six weeks?'

'Yes,' replied a puzzled Michel.

The medical student glanced up at a suddenly anxious and mystified Barbara, and smiled at her. 'He's very run down,' he said to her. 'Feed him everything you can get hold of before he picks up flu or something serious. And make him rest for a week or two, at least.' He returned to the ankle, and said, 'I think we've got an elastic bandage. I'll bind this for you. Put cold compresses on it and it should ease in about a week. If it doesn't, show it to your local doctor. Excuse me for a minute while I go to look for the bandage.'

The minute he was out of the room, Barbara, acutely aware that, in her rage and disappointment, she had been totally neglectful of the sprain, turned to Michel. 'You should have told me the ankle still hurt,' she upbraided him.

He pulled a face. 'You angry with me. I am quiet.'

'Idiot!' she exclaimed forcefully. 'And why are you so thin? I was shocked when I saw your leg.'

'I not eat too well. I am anxious to come to you.'

'Well, if I have to go out and catch rabbits for you, you are going to be fed. I want to marry a man, not a skeleton.'

'Ha! You marry me, eh?' He looked impishly at her.

'Of course, I will, you chump. It's where we're going to live that I'm arguing about.'

He stumbled to his feet and kissed her clumsily. Then, he hastily sat down again as he heard Bill approaching the door.

The ankle was neatly bandaged. It felt much more comfortable, and Michel thanked him effusively.

Bill once more got to his feet. 'Daphne says that dinner is ready. Do you think you can walk down the stairs now?'

'Dead cert,' Michel replied quite gaily.

Chapter Forty-seven

Bill opened the door of the dining room, and stood on one side to let Barbara and Michel enter first.

They took one step into the room and stopped dead.

The room was in darkness except for two huge candelabra gleaming on a large table. Their light glinted on silver and lit up dimly the faces of a number of people seated quietly round it.

With a mischievous grin, Bill leaned over Barbara's shoulder and turned a light switch. A fine chandelier flooded the room with light, dazzling the new arrivals.

There was a scuffling of chairs being pulled back.

'Michel Benion!' shouted both male and female voices. 'Welcome to England!' Glasses were raised, his health was drunk.

As his eyes became accustomed to the light, Michel swallowed. At the head of the table stood the judge beaming at him. The standing guests, glasses in hand, were laughing at his confusion, as they drank his health. Other than Daphne and the judge, there were six men in Royal Air Force uniform, one lady in Army uniform accompanied by her husband in civilian clothes, and five nicely dressed wives of the servicemen.

Bill pushed the couple gently into the room. 'Ladies and gentlemen, Mr Michel Benion and his fiancée, Mrs Barbara Bishop.'

He turned to Barbara and Michel. 'All our uniformed

guests owe grateful thanks for their lives to people like you; they were all rescued at different times from France.' He proceeded to name them, one by one. When he got to the lady in khaki, he said, 'Mary is an accomplished archer; she picked off sentries with bow and arrow, a wonderful silent killer, until she had to run for her life. I believe the Germans were more scared of her than of any of the rest of us, weren't they, Mary?'

As Mary shyly denied this, the judge called for everyone to be seated.

Michel was alarmed to find himself next to the judge, but Bill opposite him smiled in a friendly way, and the judge rumbled comfortably about amazing men and women, and gradually Michel's panic subsided.

Barbara was seated at the other end of the table, beside Daphne and opposite a young airman with a badly scarred face.

She did not blink at his dreadful appearance, but smiled a little flirtatiously at him, and asked whether he had been a pilot. Relaxed at her refusal to see him as anything other than normal, he replied that, no, he'd been a rear gunner.

It was general knowledge how dangerous a position in a plane that of rear gunner was, so, while Daphne directed her serving woman, Barbara soon got him talking about how his machine had been shot down. He had been the only survivor, he told her, and been found bleeding on a pile of tarpaulins in the yard of a French brickworks. He had been taken in and hidden by the workmen, who had got a doctor to him.

The uniformed men began to talk, each wanting to tell Michel and Barbara of the miracles of rescue performed by the French. Occasionally, their wives also managed to get in a word of gratitude to him between their husbands' stories.

461

The elderly servant brought bowls of soup to them, while Bill undertook to serve the wine.

By his second glass of wine, with soup and a generous salad already inside him, Michel began to bloom. By the time he had consumed large portions of pheasant and vegetables and a huge bowl of fruit with mountains of thoroughly illicit cream on top of it, he was quite at home, and telling the judge of the awful smell his son had had to endure in a chicken coop.

In Barbara's heart, hope began to grow.

At the end of the meal, other toasts followed, including one to Absent Friends. The party was suddenly very sober, and Bill rose to say that they had traced the second man the Benions had sheltered, only to find that he had, later, died in the fall of Singapore.

Michel had not known this. He had, after the war, written to the airman, at an address given to him before he had handed him over to others to be smuggled out through Cherbourg. There had been no reply, and this had saddened him. Now, at least, he knew what had occurred, though it was bad news.

He was pressed to say a few words to the company, which he did, stumbling sometimes, as he told them that the British had many friends in France – and friends had simply helped friends in danger. As he had said to Barbara once, he now repeated that the French were only ordinary people doing extraordinary things in terrible times.

In the drawing room afterwards, the other ladies came to talk to Barbara. Two were obvious aristocrats who had served in the Wrens. Though they were very pleasant, she found it difficult to relate to them. The rest, however, were modest housewives, who, like her, had struggled, unsung, through the major problems of being civilians and therefore of little account in a war. One had been a land girl and had some hilarious stories to tell of life on a Welsh farm.

As the guests began to rise and say their goodbyes, Bill pressed Michel to stay for a little while, because his father wanted to talk to him. He himself would be in touch again quite soon, because he and Daphne would, of course, come over for his wedding. This latter remark surprised Michel, because it had not occurred to him that Barbara would have invited guests to the ceremony. There was no hope of any of his own family attending, and he had not thought of himself as having friends in England who could be invited. He hastily said that he hoped that both of them would be present.

After the last of the other guests had gone, Daphne invited Barbara to look over the house with her, and eased her out of the drawing room.

The interview was not nearly as bad as Michel expected. The judge merely wanted to get a better idea of the man for whom his son so badly wanted a work permit and, later on, citizenship. He knew he could not do anything directly – the man had to apply for himself. He could, however, support an application if he wished.

Michel dreaded having to tell him that he would not stay in England, but it did not arise. The judge simply learned from Michel what skills he had, what hopes of using them. And Michel said that he had, since Barbara had left France, worked as a supervisor on a poultry farm, and thought he could get such work anywhere, especially as he knew quite a lot about breeding flocks and how to keep them healthy. He grinned disarmingly at the judge, as he said, 'Hens are like children: keep very clean or they get disease – feed them well or they not grow big.'

This was a world very alien to Judge Spellersby, but he

was used to listening and watching his court hour after hour. He realised the self-confidence of the man before him as he spoke warmly of the work he was interested in. He judged him as being reasonably honest, though, he decided with inward amusement, a landowner might lose a pheasant or some grouse to such a practical man.

Eventually, he departed to his study, and Bill insisted on using some of his father's petrol ration to run their guests to the station.

On their way back to Liverpool, Michel and Barbara were sleepy from the drinks they had consumed, and, anyway, the noise of the crowded train was not conducive to conversation. At Liverpool, they changed stations.

The West Kirby train was, for part of the way, quite full of dock labourers coming off a late shift, and these exhausted men were of interest to Michel. 'Like Rouen,' he informed Barbara, eyeing them comfortably.

Since Phyllis was likely still to be up, they paused to kiss on the doorstep of her home, and took a long time about it.

It was a very thoughtful Michel who eventually followed Barbara indoors. It had been a bewildering evening, as well as a very pleasant one, particularly to have been surrounded by extremely friendly English people. It left him, however, with grave doubts in the back of his mind, not the least of which was whether he could possibly live with two obviously strong-willed, capable women, who even asked people to his wedding without consulting him – and to be financially dependent upon them would shackle him. At least in France he would have only Barbara, who was completely adorable – when she was not in a rage. And, most important, he would be the provider.

Chapter Forty-eight

In the kitchen, they found Phyllis surrounded by bed linen. She was ironing. The deal table had a sheet folded in half as she swept the big gas iron across it, and, on a rack hanging from the ceiling, several neatly folded ones were airing before they were taken upstairs and replaced on the beds. During the morning, Barbara had put them through their antiquated washing machine and had then pegged them out to dry on a line behind the house.

Now, iron still hissing in her hand, she paused to greet Barbara and Michel. She decided that they certainly looked less miserable than when they had left.

'Had a good time?' she asked, smiling brightly.

As they took off their outer clothes and said they certainly had, Barbara noted her mother's professional smile, and that she looked tired. Mam was troubled and trying to hide it.

She looked at the sheets still awaiting the iron's caress, and said, 'Leave them, Mam. I'll finish them in the morning. Look, I'll make a cup of tea, and you come and sit down, and Michel will tell you all about the party. Is there anybody in the lounge? We could sit in there for a change.'

'That's a kind girl. I'm a bit tired. There's nobody in the lounge, luv. The two chaps from the Government, as we was expecting, has checked in. They went out to get something to eat, and they haven't come back. They're probably having a drink somewhere.'

'Good.' Barbara seized a kettle and filled it. After she had lit the gas under it, she turned to Michel, and tossed the box of matches over to him, which he caught. 'Would you go and light the gas fire in the lounge, luv?'

Michel froze. He did not know how a gas fire worked.

Phyllis sensed his predicament, turned off her iron and put it down. 'Maybe you don't use gas in France,' she suggested. 'Barbie'll make the tea, so I'll show you.' She laughed good-naturedly as she preceded him through the hall to a big front room.

As he followed close behind her, he answered apologetically, 'In my village we have only electricity for the hens – and coal or wood for cooking.'

The lounge was very large, and crowded with easy chairs and a scattering of little tables. On either side of the gas fire were shelves holding a tattered collection of paperback books, and what looked like boxes of board games. In the centre of the mantelpiece stood a large black marble clock ornamented on its top by a bronze of a mounted Roman soldier. The clock was flanked on either side by bronze statues of Roman foot soldiers. It was a set picked up by Phyllis at a jumble sale, and she was quite proud of it.

She now knelt down on the faded red Belgian hearth rug and showed Michel where to turn on the gas, while at the same time holding a lighted match to the fire itself.

The gas fire gave an unnerving pop and blazed merrily.

'It's a proper help, havin' gas in here,' Phyllis remarked, as she heaved herself to her feet. 'Saves forever havin' to make a coal fire and watch it don't go out – and coal's rationed.'

She turned to Michel, and pointed to a chair close by. 'Sit down, lad, and get yourself warm. I bin wantin' to talk to you by yourself, like, for a while, and now's me chance for a few minutes.'

Michel sat down warily. Now what?

'While Barbie's bin planning your marriage – and we'll talk about that later – I bin thinkin' what'd make you feel most comfortable with us.'

Michel replied cautiously, 'You are very kind, Madame.'

She ignored the Madame, and went straight on. 'This B-and-B is a family thing, as you'll know. Barbie and I share the work, and what I do, these days, is pay her a small amount for her pocket money and clothes. At the end of the year, we add up what we've made and I try to put a bit by for things we'll need in the house and to save a bit, if possible. What's left, I share with her – and since the war, frankly, that's not been much.'

Though her accent was not easy for him, Michel understood her explanation. He nodded, and waited for her to continue.

'Now, you come along. And you haven't got a job, but we can use help.' She swallowed. 'What to do? The best at present is to do for you what I do for Barbie: give you a bit of cigarette money – pocket money – and help you out with clothes. And, of course, you'd have food and bed same as us.' She fidgeted uneasily for a minute, and then said, 'You'll understand that I'll have to think some more about what we do at the end of the year. If you was happy here and the B-and-B was doing all right, we could ask Mr Jones, the solicitor in the village, about making an agreement between us?'

She left the question open. From her point of view the offer was a generous one.

Michel did not answer immediately. He had honestly not considered any monetary reward for work he would, as Barbara's husband, contribute to their business; until the doubts aroused in him as a result of his long and hard bicycle ride, he had assumed that he would get an outside job and be financially independent; that he would, as a matter of course, maintain Barbara, and do anything he could to develop their large garden.

Barbara had told him of their adventures during the war and how, during the last three years, they had struggled to re-establish their business connections. To take on the maintenance of a third person must mean considerable sacrifice on their part.

He did not want to say to her that he did not wish to settle in England; that was an affair between Barbara and himself that had yet to be fought out.

'You give me work to do?' he enquired.

'What I need is what Barbie and me has talked about, and that is someone to do the garden, if you'd do it. To begin with, dig a good vegetable patch to help out our rations. Barbie says you know how to raise hens – there's piles of space for hens here, eggs and hens'd be real food – and rabbits, if you know about them. It could make a big difference . . .' She trailed off.

He saw the wisdom of her idea. In a tightly rationed world, a personal source of food – in a garden protected by high stone walls – had a lot to commend it. He began to be interested. Even if he were to return to Normandy at the end of his six weeks' holiday visa, he could, in the meantime, repay her hospitality by digging and preparing a bed for vegetables, which they could sow after he had gone. He ignored the pain this would cause his shoulder; he genuinely wanted to repay her kindness to him.

'Have you tools?' he asked.

'We got some – and neighbours'd lend us.' She looked at him hopefully. 'For one, Mr Baines, across the road, has got a cultivator.' She looked at him a little wistfully. For the moment, this was all she could do for her Barbie.

'OK. I do that. Bill is doctor. He tell me to rest my ankle for some days. After that, I start on big dig.' He grinned and leaned back in his chair, as if relieved. He hoped his shoulder would not fail him before he had completed this act of friendship.

She smiled as a little of her worry was assuaged.

Further conversation was precluded, as Barbara came hurrying in with a tray of tea things and some homemade scones with jam on them.

'The fire feels nice, doesn't it?' she said as she put down the tray. 'The wind's chilly tonight. The days are drawin' in.' She wrapped her cardigan round herself as she sat down by Michel. 'Will you pour, Mam?'

Mam poured.

Worried about a more immediate matter, which rested upon Barbara's coming to a decision to return with him to Normandy, Michel tentatively enquired, 'Barbara, who have you asked to the wedding, besides Bill and Daphne?'

She had not expected him to speak out as if anything in their future, even their wedding, could at present be certain.

In some alarm she wondered if, tugged by a desire which equalled his, she married him, and he still insisted on going back to Normandy, what she could do. Let him go by himself?

Not likely, she determined. If she married him she

469

would stay with him, not let him run loose to be picked up by some French widow or other. She heaved a sigh. First, she desperately wanted him to decide to stay.

'We haven't asked nobody, have we, Mam. It's like a wartime weddin'. Quick, like. There's bin lots of them in the last years.'

Mam said, more to Michel than to Barbara, 'I've asked friends of ours, Mr and Mrs Baines, from across the road, if they'd like to be witnesses for you and then come home here for a little wedding breakfast. Since they lost their boy in Malaya and then their Miranda married that Texan and went to America, they've bin proper lonely.'

'We need witness,' Michel agreed, not knowing what else to say.

She looked across at her daughter. 'Are you sure you don't want to ask any of your friends in the village?'

'Quite sure, Mam. If I ask one I got to ask the lot and the same with me cousins in Liverpool – and we don't have the money,' she replied flatly. She didn't know how to say that many of them had come to her first marriage, and she didn't want to be reminded of it. It would bring back memories of George, and, though he had been a great lad, she wanted a fresh start with the man sitting beside her, a man who made her ache with longing – which George never had.

'OK, dear. Ada, bless her heart, says she'll stay here in the house and answer the phone. Or deal with anyone wanting a bed, while we're at the church.'

'Who is Madame Ada?' asked Michel.

There was a pause, while the women looked at each other. Then Phyllis said reluctantly, 'She's Barbie's mother-in-law, and, because it would be too painful to her, she wouldn't come to the wedding, though she's an old friend of both of us.'

'I understand,' said Michel. He must remember that, if he stayed in England, he would be in her first husband's territory; it was a strange, slightly threatening idea. *Mon Dieu!* Life was so complicated.

Phyllis was continuing, 'So to help me out, she's said she'll come to the house. You'd be surprised, though. She's proper happy that Barbie's going to have you to comfort her.'

Michel glanced at Barbara. He hoped he had already comforted her – and he longed to continue doing so. He said, 'Madame Ada is most generous spirit.'

Barbara smiled at him. 'She's a lovely woman.' Then she asked, 'Will your mother come? She'd be very welcome.'

He grinned back at her. 'Thank you. *Mais non.* It is too expensive. She cannot bicycle far like me. The distance is very far.'

'Maybe she'll come and stay later on,' suggested Phyllis hospitably.

'Possibly.' Although his evening at Bill's had been splendid, Michel felt lost, very alone. He appreciated Phyllis's offer, but he was nervous of being dependent upon her. Further, although he was much in love with Barbara, the insults he had received from English people during his journey still rankled.

As he gazed at Phyllis over his teacup, her kind suggestion about his mother reminded him sharply of her. Poor Maman. She had wept at his departure, but had, like Uncle Léon, foretold his rapid return.

Nevertheless, as he glanced away to stare at the hot blue flames of the gas fire flickering like little blue butterflies, he began to weigh up which country would give him the most personal freedom, because, he was also reminded, Uncle Léon and Maman could be formidably domineering, despite spates of tears and kindly meant warnings.

He tested himself. If he could find work here, work amongst people who regarded him as one of themselves, as the members of the dinner party had obviously done, how would he feel then?

Could he live with these two fairly strong-minded women, now warming themselves before the fire in their easy chairs and talking about how they could provide a decent meal for the wedding, without denuding the rations allowed for their B-and-B?

And if, after marrying Barbara, she still refused to return to Normandy, and he could not bear the domestic situation, what could he do to alleviate it? Barbara could be a problem – her mother could be another. Together they could make his life a misery.

The obvious answer struck him in the cold dawn of the following day.

Chapter Forty-nine

About eleven o'clock, as the little party in the lounge finished their tea, the two civil servants, feeling quite merry, returned from the Ring o' Bells pub.

Phyllis locked up for the night and went soberly to bed, followed immediately by Michel and Barbara.

Phyllis was sure she had done her best to help the youngsters; though they were far from youthful, they both seemed very young to her. When absently saying her prayers, she remembered to add a few urgent words for their happiness, their safety.

When the house had settled down and the only sound was the wuthering of the sea wind in the chimneys, Barbara put on her dressing gown and crept carefully downstairs to Michel.

She was so quiet that he did not hear her coming. Curled up in his cold bed, he was concentrating on ways and means to have Barbara and, at the same time, live a peaceful life, preferably in Normandy.

He jumped in surprise, as she pulled back his bedclothes and slid, naked, in beside him. He had taken it for granted that the division between them, as to where they would live, would cause her to hold back until, at least, she was married to him and had some hold over him.

She was warm and urgent, her soft skin smooth as silk against him, and he was aroused immediately. Sanity was abandoned, until exhausted, they slept.

He was awakened by the sound of the first train of the morning leaving the nearby station. Barbara was inured to the noise and slept on. Very gently, he lifted the bed-clothes to look at her in the morning light. *Mon Dieu*, she was pretty, plumper and more curvaceous than she had been when in Normandy. And – *Ciel!* – she was witty. He remembered how she had made him laugh, as they had rolled happily in a bed grown suddenly more friendly.

He knew that his first observations in the cemetery had been right. He wanted to love her, protect her from sorrow or harm, to be a safe wall for her against the world's horrors. And, as the fresh sea breeze blew through the open window and made him shiver, he vowed, like some long-ago knight in armour, that he would do it. He carefully covered her again, and she stirred and turned towards him, but slept on.

He lay quietly by her and cogitated over steps by which he could solve the conundrum of managing two tough, little businesswomen, who undoubtedly knew their own minds.

The practical mind of a Frenchman planning a marriage began to take over, as if it were an arranged one.

First, he must be financially independent of his mother-in-law. He needed decently paid work, say, within a bicycle ride, somewhere in the countryside which he had observed the previous day between here and Liverpool.

Then, if the domestic arrangements did not work out, Barbara and he could have a home of their own in the village. Why not? The place had not been bombed; there must be living space somewhere. Barbara could come over daily to help her mother, and he would garden for her in his spare time. That would take some of the pressure off him.

Divide and rule. In his own home with his own income, he would have more say. All he needed was work.

And if he could not endure the racial prejudice which he believed existed, with the American help which the cities were getting, Normandy would be rebuilt within a few years. He might be able to persuade them to sell this B-and-B at that time and buy a similar house on the coast of Calvados. Why should not Phyllis run a B-and-B there? She could specialise in British cooking, British guests. It had a warmer climate, and lots of English women had lived there before the war. Or she might be glad to retire.

It was all possible.

Armed with ideas of compromise or of escape, Michel agreed to stay and he joyfully married Barbara on the following Thursday.

After phoning every egg company and poulterer in the telephone books of the area, Bill got Michel an introduction to a big poulterer, further inland, on the following Saturday. The poulterer wanted to institute a way of raising laying hens by the new battery system and needed a reliable and experienced foreman, who had no objection to keeping hens permanently in their nests. The idea was similar to the one Michel had, in despair, instituted amongst his own poultry in order to meet German demands for eggs. Unlike many Englishmen, he had no objection to confining the birds.

His reserve defences in place, and, after a long telephone conversation with Bill, Michel decided that the Wirral peninsula might be as good a place as any in which to live.

He went for the interview and got the job at a reasonable salary, with the promise of an improvement in pay if the new venture proved to be a success. The employer, thankful to have found a man who understood what he wanted, promised every help to get a work permit.

After the interview, he sped home on his bicycle, intent on breaking the good news to Barbara. He was overwhelmed by the civility with which he had been treated by his new employer; it had been two experts, equals, discussing the same interest – poultry. No hint of condescension, no rudeness of any kind – simply a long talk about new techniques in raising hens. And, finally, he had actually got the kind of position he had always dreamed of.

He could barely believe his luck. For the first time in his life he was going to do what he wanted to do, instead of what fate had imposed upon him.

'*Chère* Barbara, here I come,' he almost shouted as, macintosh flapping in the wind, he flew down the hill and into West Kirby.

Chapter Fifty
Summer 1997

'You know, Colette, every time I sit on this balcony and watch the tide come in, I marvel at what your Uncle Michel's done,' Barbara remarked in credible French to her favourite niece.

'When he first came to me, he didn't even have a toothbrush! And no undies, not even a vest!'

'It took me nearly a week to persuade him that, round here, people wouldn't eat him and he should keep his promise to marry me – and live here.'

Colette chuckled. A pretty, plump fifty-two-year-old, she reminded Barbara of her mother, Claudette, Michel's sister.

Barbara continued, this time in English. 'Nevertheless, I've never seen anybody, English or French, who worked like he has. He used his brains to make so much out of very little; it always astonished me how handy he was – he can still surprise me sometimes, bless his darlin' heart.'

She glanced down at the large walled flower garden below, at a more distant huge kitchen garden, the rabbit hutches and hen coops with a number of thoroughbred hens stalking round them, and then went on, 'And he still works. You can see him down there, by the side wall; he's trimming the rambler roses himself. Makes me feel sick every time I see him climb a ladder – and Dr Maxwell tellin' him he should take things easy.'

This amused Colette and she laughed again, as she

responded, 'You might as well try to stop a steam engine, once he gets started – he was always like that.' She spoke French, though she could manage English reasonably well. She sighed. 'My young Louis has the same perseverance – he'll be a real addition to this place, once he's graduated.'

'Oh, aye, he's a loovely lad,' Barbara agreed. 'Michel thinks the world of him.' Then she added, in defence of her husband, 'Michel may be quite tough at times, but, if you've got a sound reason for something, he'll always come round. My mam and I tried never to lose our tempers with him – then we knew we'd win!'

Colette laughed out loud. 'You and Auntie Phyllis were incorrigible,' she said. 'I can remember when my mother and I used to come to visit you. We noticed how you both got round him.'

As a smiling Barbara rose stiffly from her chair, Colette thought that Barbara still had the same dignified look and carried herself as well as she had when first she had come with Uncle Michel to Rouen to visit Grand-mère Benion, when Colette was still a girl.

'You've done so well, helpin' us, like,' Barbara said. 'It would've bin so disappointing simply to sell up and get out, now we're wanting to retire. We always wanted you to have it when we're gone.'

Colette replied with enthusiasm. 'Auntie Barbie, I simply love working here. It's what I needed – after all, I'm a trained nurse. And you've been so kind.'

She made a wry mouth. 'I was very lonely in Rouen after I was widowed and the two boys went away to university.' She paused, to look out at the sea, and then said, 'In my wildest dreams I never thought of inheriting a business like this – and in England, too!'

'Certainly, my dear, you'll never be lonely here in Hôtel Michel, full of dear old souls to look after. Meanwhile, though, we'll leave you to get on with the job, and there'll be me and your uncle in the little bungalow at the back, for you to come to if you're in trouble.'

Barbara gestured toward the rear of the property, where, beyond the hen run, a bungalow was in process of being built; a permit to build it had been hard to obtain, but it was going up at last.

'You'd never believe it to look at the place now,' she said reflectively, 'but, you know, we thought we were finished when the hotel began to fail. In the 1960s and onwards, people went abroad for holidays – and the reps who used to stay with us – they all got cars and drove straight into Liverpool. They didn't stop here. Phew! It was grim, Colette. We'd had a right royal battle getting a permit to build the extension to make it into a real hotel; we'd put in the lift and another eight rooms – and bathrooms everywhere – and we were in debt like you'd never believe. I've never been so scared in me life. And it was about that time that Mother began to fail too, poor dear.

'What saved us, Colette, was Michel doing so well in the Pure White Poultry Company.'

Her niece asked curiously, 'Did he care about being insulted because he was French?' Uncle Léon had once talked about this to her mother.

'Not much. He knew he understood hens better than any of his colleagues, and once he'd made one or two good English friends at work, he knew better than to take notice of the odd slight; and there was always Bill Spellersby to encourage him and take him out to meet his friends. They all knew the story of him and Bill, and they were proper nice to him; they thought he was a hero. And, Colette, he was.'

She stopped, and then said, with a little laughter in her voice, 'We've had a good life.'

'He couldn't have done it without the bed-and-breakfast to start with,' Colette pointed out.

'I suppose not, but he put a lot of work into the place from Day One.'

'You didn't have any children, Auntie Barbie?'

'No.' Barbara sighed. 'We'd seen too much of war.'

They were not alone; neither Bill Spellersby nor his brother had any children.

On the whole, Barbara did not regret their decision. All her innate motherliness had been expended on Michel himself, and he had thrived on it.

Barbara's reply about war had sent a cold shudder down Colette's back. She sometimes feared for her own boys; she could just remember the gaunt ruins that had been Rouen, and pictures of her little cousin, Philippe, on Auntie Anne-Marie's bedside table.

Colette sat silent for a while, listening to the placid shush-shush of the sea on the beach and the distant click of Michel's shears.

Barbara tied her new pale blue headscarf more closely under her chin – the wind was getting up. Then she turned back to her niece.

'You know, Colette, when it was obvious that the hotel was in the wrong place at the wrong time, it was then that we got the idea of advertising it as a high-class retirement home for couples, particularly for the slightly infirm.' She smiled at the memory. 'We promised first-class meals, diets if needed, a nurse in attendance, and a doctor nearby. And it worked, because there are a lot of well-to-do old people in England. Now, we're recommended right and left. It's so healthy here – they get a new lease on life. I've known a few who even started to drive again.'

After a moment's pause, she brought up another issue. 'Getting the land lease renewed cost us a heap, it did; I'll not forget that in a hurry.'

'*Certainement*!' agreed Colette, who had heard the story before.

'And after we'd won that, Michel built the walled garden,' continued Barbara, 'so that the residents could go outside without being buffeted by the wind – and all of them love that, and those in wheelchairs can get round all the little paths. As you know, sometimes the male residents enjoy doing a bit of work in it themselves. And you know how Michel takes them shopping – or wherever else they want to go – in his big Toyota – he's that proud of it. Or they can even go fishing, or play golf at Hoylake, if they feel strong enough.'

She was quiet for a moment, and then warned, 'Never forget, Colette, to keep the service first class.'

Something of the strength and energy of Grand-père and Grand-mère Benion was in Colette and in her sons, and she responded quickly, 'Of course, Auntie.'

She was thankful that her cousin, Annette, when asked if she would like to share the inheritance by working with Colette, had shuddered with horror at the idea of going to live in England.

Michel and Barbara had rewritten their wills. Let the one prepared to do the work get the long-term benefit.

'And watch the kind of staff you employ. Keep them in line, like your uncle does,' Barbara continued absently, her mind on the toiler in the garden.

'Of course,' Colette smiled. 'I think I do already.' Most

of the staff were healthily nervous of Himself, as they called Michel. He had an acid tongue, when he cared to use it. She added, 'When he's cross, he sounds exactly like Grand-mère Benion, when she used to scold about mice in the bakery – which she did quite often when I was a little girl.'

It was in Barbara's view, good that there had been mice to fight; Maman had been too quiet, too accepting, as if, having lost her world in the invasion, she was simply waiting to die. Every time she saw her, Barbara cursed the Germans anew. Maman had refused to visit them in England on the grounds that she was too old to travel; getting through each day, thought Barbara, had been challenge enough for her. So Michel – and sometimes Barbara – had gone to her.

When she died, Michel had grieved for a long time. 'Nobody else can ever understand what we went through together,' he explained heavily to his patient wife.

As she had done long ago in Bayeux Cathedral, she had held him in her arms and comforted him as he wept out his sorrow. As she did so, she had felt a pang of jealousy; there was a part of Michel which she could never quite reach. Sometimes, she also felt guilty about stealing Maman's remaining son from her. But Phyllis, who had lived rather longer, had told her sharply that marriage of children had to be faced.

'And I never grudged you to Michel, did I, luv?' Phyllis asked, ignoring the tears she had quietly shed in the first years of her daughter's marriage, tears of dreadful inner loneliness.

'No, I don't think you ever did, Mam.'

Barbara felt that, all things considering, Michel and her mother had got along fairly well; Michel had been unfailingly kind and polite to her, and she had become quite fond of him. Barbara looked back with amusement at the one or two disagreements they had had, usually about spending money.

To Phyllis's surprise, Michel had always argued against spending a cent that they did not have to; she had expected that he would be a spendthrift, like seamen often were. Weren't most men like that? 'Except for your dad, of course – at least, he always wanted to spend on you and me,' she had added loyally.

Men were not all the same. It took a while to persuade Michel that a commercial dishwasher was a necessity, that flowers in abundance were a good idea in a place like L'Hôtel Michel, that, as he gained promotion, he really must have another suit to wear at the office, and that managers did not smoke Woodbines.

Now, she leaned over the balcony, and shouted to the toiler in the garden, 'Come in and have a cup of coffee, luvvie.'

He half turned to look up at her, and grinned. She looked lovely up there in the sunshine; the scarf he had bought her as an unexpected present certainly suited her.

He carefully descended the ladder. It was teatime, sacred to the British.

One of the iron rules of L'Hôtel Michel was that Himself never drank tea, even at teatime; he drank only coffee – and it had to be properly brewed from freshly ground beans, or else the cook would hear about it.

Dead cert.

Select Bibliography

Arnold, Gladys, *One Woman's War* (James Lorimer & Co., Toronto, 1987).

Braudel, Fernand, *The Identity of France*, Vols. 1 and 2 (HarperCollins, London, 1988, 1992).

Davidson, Marshall B., *France* (American Heritage Publishing Co., Inc., New York, 1971).

Floyd, Maita, *Stolen Years* (Eskualdun Publishers, Phoenix, 1996).

Harrison, *Principles of Internal Medicine* (McGraw-Hill, New York, 1994).

Hastings, Max, *Overlord, D-Day and the Battle for Normandy, 1944* (Michael Joseph, London, 1984).

Hawes, Stephen, and White, Ralph (editors), *Resistance in Europe: 1939–45* (Allen Lane, London, 1975).

Marwick, Arthur, *British Society since 1945* (Penguin Books, Harmondsworth, Middlesex, 1982).

Newman, George L. (translator), *The Normandy Diary of Marie-Louise Osmont* (Random House, New York, 1994).

Webster, Donovan, *The Remnants of War* (Pantheon, New York, 1997).

Werth, Alexander, *De Gaulle* (Simon & Schuster, New York, 1967).

Wright, Gordon, *France in Modern Times* (W.W. Norton & Co., New York, 1987).

Young, Brigadier Peter (editor), *World War II* (Prentice

Hall Inc., Englewood Cliffs, N. J., 1981).

Zeldin, Theodore, *A History of French Passions*, Vols. 1 and 2 (Clarendon Press, Oxford, 1973).

For my darling Kayla, the new light in my life. My wishes for you are too many to count, so I'll just wish you love. Everything magic and everything real, everything that matters springs from that.